THEIR LIVES WERE HOSTAGE TO THE TIDES OF CHANGE... A NATION'S FUTURE WOULD BE SHAPED BY THE ACTS THEIR PASSIONS DICTATED

DORIAN TROZEN—He broke the chains of slavery—but as the rebel yells rang out across the South, he found himself bound to a past that could cost him his life.

IPHIGENIA TRÖZENE WALLACE—A Mediterranean beauty who would love her husband's bastard son as her own, she would embrace Dorian in a world of luxury, education, and dignity—a world he could never fully enter.

LUCAS WALLACE—A hard man for a hard land. His wealth had bought him a place among the gentry—but it couldn't erase his shameful past. Would it now go to pay for his own son's murder?

WYATT CRAIG—The pro-slavery son of a factory tyrant, he lived a despised alliance of pure conscience and stifling convention. His black powder could fuel the flash fire of rebellion. Would he live to become Dorian's enemy—or his most trusted ally?

GRACE RUHL—White trash hardened by hatred and schooled by necessity. She knew how to conceal her past as well as Dorian did. She also knew how to fight for freedom—even if it meant destruction to all around her... and to the one man who would dare to touch her heart.

BOOK ONE

— ★ —

DISTANT DRUMS

D. L. CAREY

— ★ —

BANTAM BOOKS
NEW YORK · TORONTO · LONDON · SYDNEY · AUCKLAND

DISTANT DRUMS
A Bantam Domain Book / July 1991

*Grateful acknowledgement is made for permission to reprint the following:
Excerpt from* Du Pont Dynasty *by Gerald Colby. Copyright © 1984, 1974 by
Gerald Colby Zilg. Published by arrangement with Carol Publishing Group. A Lyle
Stuart Book.*

DOMAIN *and the portrayal of a boxed ''d'' are trademarks of Bantam Books,
a division of Bantam Doubleday Dell Publishing Group, Inc.*

ISBN 0-553-28620-X

Published simultaneously in the United States and Canada

*Bantam Books are published by Bantam Books, a division of Bantam Doubleday
Dell Publishing Group, Inc. Its trademark, consisting of the words ''Bantam
Books'' and the portrayal of a rooster, is Registered in U.S. Patent and Trademark
Office and in other countries. Marca Registrada. Bantam Books, 666 Fifth Avenue,
New York, New York 10103.*

PRINTED IN THE UNITED STATES OF AMERICA

RAD   0 9 8 7 6 5 4 3 2 1

——— ★ ———

DISTANT DRUMS

————————— ★ ★ ★ —————————

THE BURNING FUSE

JANUARY 1820

Maine comes into the United States as a "free" state. Now there are twelve free and eleven slave states. Southerners who inherited huge investments in and dependence upon chattel slavery see their economy at risk. A balance is achieved when Missouri is admitted as a slave state, but an amendment to this bill bans slavery north of 36° 30' latitude. It's called the Missouri Compromise.

Eight years later the South feels slighted by protective tariff laws that favor Northern manufacturing at the expense of Southern raw-materials production. South Carolina condemns the tariffs and argues that state conventions should overrule federal law on every point, including the generations-old economic question of slavery, into which the South's agrarian way of life is inextricably woven.

States' sovereignty versus federal power becomes a major point of contention. This ignites a fuse that has been smoldering since the Jamestown settlers purchased twenty African slaves from a Dutch frigate in 1619. South Carolina proves its states'-rights point by raising an independent military.

It is now 1832, and the president is about to speak.

————————— ★ —————————

PROLOGUE

———— ★ ————

KING JACKSON

DECEMBER 12, 1832
TWENTY-NINE YEARS BEFORE THE AMERICAN CIVIL WAR

Ice floes clogged the Potomac. President Andrew Jackson coughed two or three times, trying to warm his throat. Today he was the most powerful man in an up-and-coming young nation, a nation watched by the eyes of the world. Today he realized better than any day before that the batch of states was held together by their single government and a thread of sheer tenacity. Today he was nervous.

Around him, blocking his way to the podium, his advisers argued back and forth. Should this speech be made? Should it be stalled? Should the president hold his silence?

The tension was palpable. The air held a tang of trouble. Jackson cupped his hands around his mouth and blew on his icy fingers. His advisers continued to quarrel, their beards thickets of frost, all hoping the nearby cluster of reporters couldn't hear. They looked like a band of Saint Nicholases arguing over who was the real one.

The president touched a folded handkerchief to his beardless mouth. Despite the cold he was perspiring.

He waved to silence the bickering. A few lingering barks of anger snapped around him; then all quieted but the crackling ice on the river.

3

"Ladies and gentlemen...the president of the United States."

Jackson approached the lectern. His hands were cold on the paper he held. His own orders drummed in his ears—reinforce the federal forts off Charleston.

Reinforcement. A heartless word echoing his nation's war for independence. He knew that memory would rise in the minds of the people. None had forgotten that war, except the very young.

Today he would issue a speech that would be tantamount to open threat to the people of South Carolina. They had dared the undarable. They had set up their own legislature as supersedent to the federal government. They had nullified the tariff acts of 1828 and 1832. They had mounted their own military.

Jackson made his speech, barely aware of the words. He could hardly hear his own voice over the battling of his conscience. Only the astonishment in the audience's faces proved he was getting his message across.

"Henceforth...no state may secede from this Union. It shall henceforth be unlawful for any single state or group of states previously consecrated as part of the Union to secede...to declare independence...to strike laws contrary to the laws of the nation...to gather an infantry...mount a cavalry, or launch a navy independent of the Union military...because secession destroys the unity which makes us a nation."

His voice hammered through the chilly air. It was done.

President Jackson stepped away from the lectern, conscious of the hush. Perhaps he had healed the wound.

Or perhaps he had pushed a blade into the flesh of the United States, which would ache long into the nation's night.

★

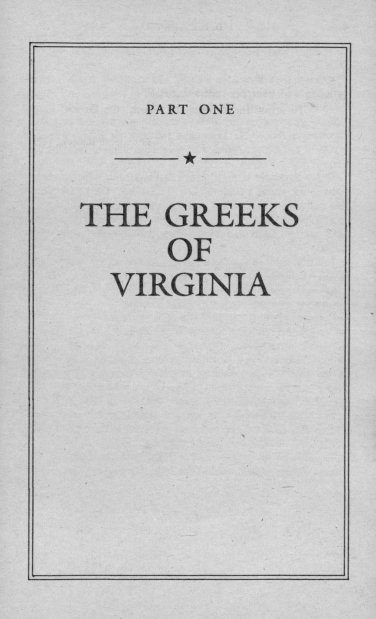

PART ONE

---★---

THE GREEKS
OF
VIRGINIA

He woke—to hear his sentries shriek,
  "To arms! they come! the Greek! the Greek!"

—Fitz-Greene Halleck, 1823

CHAPTER ONE

———— ★ ————

Simple as a dime. The rawboned slave girl's bare feet clattered down the boardwalk between the brewery and the forge. Her name was simple too, even plainer than the osnaburg dress she wore. Yula. Four letters. She could even write it out.

With her jaw jutted out in anger and her brow furrowed beneath the red turban, she rammed her heels hard into the boardwalk so everyone would hear her coming. To her right, field hands squinted from the thick yellow green rows of tobacco leaves. She ignored them. They weren't the guilty ones.

She had reasoned it out. It had to be Rowzee.

Of the three single cuffee women who lived with her in the cabin on the end, it had to be Rowzee. Yula clenched her fists. Her knees kicked up the grain sack skirt. She knew it couldn't be Palma, because Palma was too old. It couldn't be Hetty, because Hetty was lackwit from having been sold away from her children years ago. She was only good for sewing up holes in loading sacks and mumbling to herself. So it had to be Rowzee.

Yula jumped from the boardwalk and crossed the shoeing yard, her heels digging into the moist dirt like hatchet blows. She'd worked three plantations since she was ten, and this

7

one wasn't rough enough to shunt her to the back of the pecking order. She wouldn't be the runt pig sucking at the hind tit, even if she was new and even if she'd been cheap.

She gripped the shed door and threw it open. The heat of the forge struck her face. Her brown skin lit up, eyes ringed in white, set in a tribal war mask.

"Where Rowzee?" she demanded.

The *tang-tang* of the hammer against iron rang to a halt. Jonah and Alroy looked up from the red-hot forge, their muscular black shoulders sparkling with sweat. Overhead, smoke gushed out the open rooftop as the bellows sighed. The girl stood in the doorway like a gunslinger. She was only that much thicker than their wrists, but the two big slaves blinked stupidly for a moment. Then Jonah shrugged and said, "How we know, girl? We jus' workin'."

The door slammed shut. A wave of scorching air pushed back at the men.

Yula's bony cheeks flushed as she stomped through a flock of farm geese. She charged past the sickhouse without a glance, because Rowzee wasn't sick. Not yet.

She went right through the slave gardens, through rows of peas, beans, turnips, and pumpkins, her sharp feet throwing up clods of dirt, and past the cow shed and the tied-up mules and the cisterns. And past the chapel, because Rowzee was going straight to hell. She skimmed over the ground like a bat catching its prey's heartbeat on the wind. Her brown arms bent double and pumped the air.

Rowzee heard her coming, but all she had time to do was turn and catch a glimpse of that white-eyed war mask. Then, *smack*.

Rowzee's thick body slammed into the wall of the bleached gray barn. She saw the streak of blood on the wood before she realized it came from her own nose. By then she was fighting back.

Other slaves abandoned their chores around the farmyard and ran to watch. Whistles and hoots of encouragement skittered over the yellow acres of tobacco, wheat, oats, and flax under the late-day sun. Field hands straightened their backs and paused to listen, then called bets back and forth over the crops.

In the yard no one made a move to separate Yula and Rowzee. The two women's limbs interlocked and twisted against each other, dark skin glistening and streaked with ruby blood. Yula was smaller and thinner, but quicker in form and in wit. Winning would mean a boost in status around the yard. Men in linsey suits and women in bright calicoes and woolens and children in cotton shifts watched from all around. Fights between men were common enough, but a fight between two women was worth skidding up to.

In his office the overseer looked up. At first he'd thought the noise was just scattered geese. He took off his spectacles and stepped out his office door. His hip-high boots sank to the ankles in yard mud. The blond hank of hair in front of his eyes looked pink in the lowering sun.

Yula sensed the overseer coming. A lifelong victim of white men's whim, she instinctively knew when she was being watched by a superior. It seldom affected her once she'd made a decision, but no slave ignored such mental alarms completely. She'd have to win the fight now or never.

Her quick ears picked up the sound of the overseer's boots sucking their way across the yard. It was a different sound from the bare feet or rosin-and-lard-soled boots of the slaves. Just then Rowzee made the mistake of looking toward the overseer. That gave Yula the chance to swing. A skinny brown hand smacked flush across Rowzee's face.

"Keep it fair!" the overseer barked. He waved the crowd of slaves back a few paces.

Yula was glad she'd gotten that blow in.

The overseer crossed his arms, cocked his hip, and settled in to watch. He was the first to hear the clink of wheels and a harness, but he didn't turn around. He continued to watch Yula and Rowzee haul each other across the barnyard. Even so, he knew the master's open carriage was rolling up the rain-rutted driveway. A moment later he even smelled the fresh aroma of hay and soap that clung to the horse.

The fight went on, though the hooting of the slaves had dropped off. They all lowered their eyes. The carriage of the king had arrived.

The master turned in his carriage seat and looked past the overseer's blond head at the tornado of osnaburg and calico.

The smaller girl was winning. Rowzee's big bulk was already on the ground, puffing.

"Mr. McCrocklin," Lucas Wallace began, "don't you find something odd about all this?"

The overseer turned, his mustache glittering in the setting sun. "They started it, Boss. I figure a little wraslin's good for the soul of a bondsman."

"You don't notice anything strange?"

"Well, like what, Boss?"

"Like they're women, that's what."

McCrocklin smirked and shrugged.

Yula took that moment to sidestep a wide swing from Rowzee, and Rowzee went spinning.

Wallace didn't like to see a valuable yard hand like Rowzee being hammered, but he found himself captivated by the morsel who was doing the hammering. He remembered the girl, though vaguely. She'd been the last choice at the slave auction about two months ago. A hot, dusty day, if memory served. She hadn't looked like much of a buy, her skin covered by a film of sweat and crusted with dust, her spindle-thin body clothed in a hank of rags as she stood on the auction block. He could tell she'd stood there before.

Maybe he'd gotten a steal and didn't even know it. The cheap buy was beating the investment right out of Rowzee.

"Pull them apart, Mr. McCrocklin."

McCrocklin looked up at him. Wallace's stocky figure was silhouetted against sunset. His liver-colored hair looked like steel.

"Why, Boss?"

"Because if you don't, I'll have to. And I'm dressed to go into town."

"Something bothering you, Boss?" McCrocklin asked.

Wallace inhaled impatiently. "Why should I be bothered by a fifteen-hundred-dollar investment bleeding on the ground? Don't you know better than to let two breedable culluds go after one another like that?"

He swung down from the carriage. The tails of his new blue dress jacket swayed against his thighs, and his polished boots sank five inches into the muck. He clomped across the yard, grabbed Yula's arm, and hauled her back.

"Hold off! That'll do! What's this all about?"

The two panting women glared at each other.

Wallace looked from one to the other. "Well?"

Yula yanked her arm back with such force that Wallace had to let go. She fixed her eyes on Rowzee and stepped toward her, betting that Rowzee wouldn't have the nerve to hit in front of Boss.

Rowzee's flat nose grew wider with disdain, but she didn't move. Yula hooked her fingers into Rowzee's bodice and tore the calico. Out spilled a satin sash, bright pink, with tassels. Yula pulled the sash as she backed up, and it followed her like a long snake.

"This?" Wallace took a swipe for the sash, but Yula yanked it to her breast and gathered it into a wad. "This is all? This rag?"

"It mine," Yula squeaked. "It store-bought and it mine."

"For this there's blood on the ground? Don't I divvy out fresh new frocks to you culluds every spring without fail? And now you're fighting over a fancy sash you've no use for?" Boss's blue eyes appeared silver in the sunset, his gunmetal hair and trimmed beard nearly opal as he shook his head. "I'm ashamed."

Yula's resolve didn't fade. As plantations went, this one was civilized enough for her to test the water by sticking in one defiant toe. She knew Boss had a temper and might chop off that toe, but he wasn't like the gentlemen farmers who were never seen in the fields. She'd seen him knee-deep in sown fields, using his own two hands to help the slaves lift a loaded wagon out of stress, and she'd seen him so dirty he could've been mistaken for one of her kind. Maybe he knew what it was like to have toes.

She stood her ground.

One of the elder bondsmen, an ebony-skinned man called Moses, stepped between McCrocklin and Wallace. "Boss, she dumb. She don't know no better."

Wallace shook his head. "The penalty for fighting is five lashes," he said, looking at Yula. Then he gave Rowzee the same look. "And the penalty for stealing is ten."

Rowzee's wide face crumpled. She started whining with fear and misery.

But Yula glared back at Boss with a message in her eyes. *Lash me, then.*

"Mmm," Boss muttered. "But since I'm in a good mood, I'll be lenient. Any more trouble and I'll sell you both down into the Carolinas. McCrocklin, if I hear of these two women fighting again, I'll deduct a dollar from your pay for every drop of blood spilled. Moses, you got plans for tonight?"

Moses toddled forward another pace or two, leaning on a walking stick. "Boss, after pickin's, I'm gwin to the crick. Trout's nigh onto two foot and bitin'. I means to git us some for the cabins."

Wallace pressed his wide mouth into a line and shifted his weight. "Well...okay. But when you get back, it's up to you to watch these two women and make sure they don't do no more fighting. I mean, any more. That clear?"

"Yeah, Boss. Sho' it is."

"All right! You people break it up. Back to work. Got another half hour before sunset, so let's go."

McCrocklin stood behind Moses in mute indignation. Wallace stepped past his overseer and went back through the mud to the carriage, where he grasped the lantern hook and started scraping mud off his boots with his forefinger. McCrocklin watched as the bondsmen dispersed and went back to their work, and Yula and Rowzee were hauled off in two different directions.

"Boss," McCrocklin began, "Moses goes fishing?"

"Sometimes."

"Ain't that a mite slack? Can't keep control that way. At the Circles we'd whip the mossheads for going off fishing and hunting."

Wallace straightened. "First of all," he said, "don't call 'em that. We call 'em culluds or cuffees here on Plentiful. I don't tolerate them other words. I hired you away from a big plantation that's over seventy years old, run by cotton snobs who never saw the middle of their own fields. What I got here is a medium-sized tobacco plantation that's nine years old, and I'm about to turn my fourth profit in a row. Know why?" He flipped another fingerful of mud to the ground with a splat. "Because money talks to me. Money tells me what it needs and what it wants. It tells me how to take dung and make fertilizer. You got to apply scientific methods to running a plantation, not just the whip and the chain. You got to work with yourself, not against yourself. These are modern times.''

McCrocklin suppressed an urge to roll his eyes. "I think with all the abolitionist talk, best to keep a short leash."

Wallace straightened. "Oh, sheepwash. I got no generations behind me piling up dowries and bequeathals. You come recommended, and I'll take your advice, but don't be whackin' me in my assets."

He paused again, waiting to see if anything dawned in McCrocklin's expressionless eyes. Nothing did.

"Suffering Christ!" Wallace blurted. "You don't see it?"

McCrocklin's brow creased, but that was the only change.

Wallace huffed in exasperation. "Every trout Moses catches," he said, "is a meal at the cabins that don't come out of my pocket!" He nodded in agreement with himself, then hopped up onto the footboard of the carriage. Halfway up he turned. "I mean, doesn't."

With a slap of the reins across the pony's back, the carriage lurched forward. It wobbled down the driveway past the smokehouses, then turned out onto the main road.

McCrocklin shook his head.

As the road into Norfolk smoothed out beneath his carriage wheels, Lucas Wallace squared his shoulders, practicing. This was a gloomy autumn day, not the kind of day he would have preferred, but it was the day he'd chosen. Not even the clouds hiding Virginia's sun could dissuade him or provide an excuse to stay home. He'd come through on every one of a list of promises to himself when he'd started this plantation nine years ago. Fourteen hundred acres, more than 160 slaves, four successful harvests in a row, the big house finally completed and furnished.

He involuntarily reviewed the house in his mind, going over every inch of the three-story brick, the circular carriage drive in front that surrounded a garden of pear trees and hedges, the rows of dwarf boxwoods that were finally large enough to be proud of. Sure had taken long enough for them to quit looking like silly sticks. He turned back wistfully, but the house was already out of sight.

Smiling, he settled back in the carriage seat and listened to the pony's hooves against the soft road.

The plantation he called Plentiful was now a community unto itself, with brick cabins to replace the wooden shacks his bondsmen had lived in until this year. The small brewery was in full operation, and the ten new slaves he'd bought last month included a blacksmith and a leather worker. The females were learning spinning and weaving and had begun making their own clothing. Within a year he might begin rolling and boxing his own brand of cigars and marketing them, cutting out the middlemen. Soon he and his Plentiful would bask in self-sufficiency.

He was ready. The building of Plentiful had cost fourteen years of his life—nine years in building and five years before that to earn capital just to buy acreage and bond a handful of workers to start out. He'd endured discouragement and detraction, he'd done without loans and investors who had no faith in a former dockworker's potential as a Tidewater planter. He'd put his own blood and sweat into each crushed oyster shell that supplied the lime mortar that bonded every brick. Now he was forty-four years old. His hair was changing color. His last promise rang out at him from the streaks at his temples and the creases around his eyes. Tonight he would make good on that promise.

The low hills of Virginia's Tidewater Region drew away behind him and still he thought of the lush brown brick main house of Plentiful, gleaming red under thin shafts of sunlight. It was a proper baronial estate designed in the colonial style, to be accepted among the long-established plantations of Virginia and take her place there. The slave dormitories spilled out like little red chicks, watched over by the big house. Brick was good. It kept out pestilence, pleurisy, and febrile miasma with solid walls that could be washed down and didn't need painting, that prevented any breeze from blowing on the sleeping negroes, but also allowed free circulation of air. Inside there were plank floors and pins for hanging up clothes, to keep a sense of order and self-worth. The bedsteads had mattresses of shucks and cotton and homespun comforters, because the better the sleep, the better the work. It would be improvident to assume otherwise, just to save a nickel. Wallace had long ago learned that it paid to keep the slaves healthy and content. Sick ones didn't work and took the attention of others, and discontented ones often struck back. Other masters, he'd heard, had learned that hard lesson. Unless a man had an army of drivers or a fireproof house, he'd better have contentment between himself and his property.

Night had fallen by the time Wallace steered his carriage into the lanes of Norfolk, where street lamps cast yellow cones onto the small dogwoods lining the sidewalks.

The cocked-hat gentry were out, strolling in the gentle Virginia evening. Gentlemen with their ladies, men in groups laughing together, workmen on their way home. He listened to the jangle of carriage harnesses, the sound of a piano in a loud saloon. Couples on the street nodded to Wallace as he steered his carriage along, and he returned their greeting with his own little nod of pride. He knew he looked good tonight. He knew, and so did they, that tonight was special. *Tonight I have a real place among them.*

His price flagged only a moment when a recognizable voice hailed him, and a carriage rattled up behind his.

"Luke Wallace, hold up, sir."

Wallace turned partly around and waved a dismissive greeting but didn't stop. With a little luck he'd—

"Wallace, pull up, I say!"

So much for luck.

He drew his pony to a stop, slowly though, and the other carriage pulled up beside his. A negro footman hauled back on the reins when the thickset man in back was abreast of Wallace. The man's broad aristocratic face was set in disapproval, and he wasted no time.

"Mr. Wallace, I must speak with you," he said.

"Mightn't it be later, Mr. Van Meer?" Wallace returned, lifting his reins.

"One moment," Van Meer barked, leaning forward. "This needs working out if you and I are to have successful plantations so near each other, sir."

That was enough to make Wallace lower his hands, let the reins rest on his thighs. His throat knotted.

"My quashies have been talking to yours," Van Meer went on. The thick accent of his Georgia upbringing added an edge of pomposity. "It's said you're a soft slaveholder, that you go too easy on your bondsmen. I hear tell they live in fine houses now, near as fine as yours. Is that true?"

Wallace wished he could clear his throat, but that wouldn't look strong. All he could manage was a quick swallow. "Well, I did build brick cabins. . . ."

"And that you give new clothing twice a year rather than once."

"Well . . ."

"And I heard you communicated with an escaped quashie who was hiding in your woods to find out what was his dissatisfaction, and that you negotiated for his return."

Color flushed Wallace's cheeks. He'd heard of other planters communicating with escapees, but suddenly he had no acceptable excuse for it. Practicality wasn't acceptable, not socially, and not from a man with his background or lack thereof.

Timidly he said, "It was that or let him die out there last winter. . . . Where would he have gone to?"

"At the Oaks I'd have had him hunted down like the animal he was."

No doubt. Wallace pressed his lips tight. He knew Van Meer's reputation. Strict, even sadistic. Brutalities so awful they sounded like exaggerations. He'd heard of Van Meer underfeeding slaves to encourage their stealing from other plantations to lower his costs. That whipping was commonplace at the Oaks, that his drivers were hated by their own kind, that he daily threatened his slaves with being sold to Mississippi, the folklore being the deeper South, the more savage the conditions. Van Meer had been known to punish a slave or two by driving them to a city and dropping them off in the middle of the street, saying, "Go. Be free if it's what you want." He fully understood that a free slave was a lost slave, a thing to quiver in the night, to starve, to have no ties, to have no one to look after him, to be rejected by other planters because no one wanted to be accused of harboring an escapee or stealing another man's property. Even worse than the terror of the whip was the terror of being freed. More than once Van Meer's freed slaves, having no other opportunity for employment and no money to travel north, had found their way through desperation back to the Oaks, to be allowed back on the plantation by their master, never to complain again. With them they conveniently brought their story of the misery of freedom.

"I also hear," Van Meer continued, "that you've been searching among the plantations of Virginia and North Carolina for the children of one of your women who went mad crying for them. This is astonishing to me! Soft masters will lead the South to ruin, Mr. Wallace. Now my quashies are daring to demand better treatment, and I'm having to deal with that. This free thought of yours, it festers, sir. I suggest you take your true place as a master and learn the title's responsibilities. That, or keep your leniency to yourself. I would be ashamed."

Wallace said nothing. He had no excuses. The rumors were true. He had seen no harm in these things. Until now.

In the other carriage the big man leaned back, pressing his shoulders against the puckered velvet seat. "You know, the gentlefolk are talking about you, Lucas. They say it's indicative. That you're not really part of the aristocracy."

Wallace flinched visibly. Suddenly he felt like an underling being scolded, a feeling that crushed his heart into a hard ball. He should spit back to Van Meer that he'd made good profits in these times of depression. That he knew the Oaks hadn't had as good a year as Plentiful. That his methods of management paid off. That it was sensible to allow the bondsmen things that didn't hurt. These words pushed his tongue up against his teeth, trying to get out.

"I advise you," Van Meer said, "not to rattle the ladder as you try to climb it. You'll find those at the top to be your betters. And we are unlikely to tolerate changes. Charlemaine, drive on."

The carriage yanked forward, leaving Wallace astride his own carriage, speechless.

He took a deep breath, then shook his head. Van Meer puffed like an old chimney. There were as many ways to run a

plantation, as many ways to own slaves, as there were men to
own them, he reassured himself. He had found a way that
seemed to work for him. Why was he suddenly insecure about
it?

By the time he turned onto Tulaine Street, his hands were
so tight on the reins that his knuckles showed. He pulled up in
front of a stately narrow white house nestled in a row of other
similar residences.

He climbed down, cursed the wind for mussing his hair,
cursed Van Meer for drilling his confidence, and after
straightening his collar he started up the painted steps to the
door.

The butler showed Wallace into the library. There a familiar
but intimidating red-bearded gentleman waited. Wallace forced
himself not to appear intimidated by someone so close to his
own age, but it wasn't easy. The sting of Van Meer's
dressing-down still lingered, and the man he was visiting
tonight was just the kind of peerage Wallace had been flogged
with.

"Mr. Wallace, good evening," the man said, and wobbled
a carafe of brandy between them. "I've been expecting you,
sir."

Wallace nodded at the brandy and responded, "Colonel
Brookville."

The colonel poured two glasses of brandy while Wallace
drew a steadying breath. He tried to fill his head with a
picture of his future bride. Nell Brookville was attracted to
him, there was no doubt. A very proper Southern girl, she
had given many hints about how she would add her own little
touches to Plentiful. Wallace knew she would say yes and
there would be a wedding, and Plentiful would take its place
among the Tidewater's stately homes. Excitement shivered
through him. He was a schoolboy again. No matter how he
washed or dressed, he always felt like an old saddle compared
to Nellie Brookville. She would be a sparkling lady on the
veranda. The lady of his house. That was how it should be.
Man like a nail, lady like lace.

He basked in the rightness. It gave him courage.

"Colonel, sir," he began formally, "I've finally come
to—"

Still facing the other direction, Brookville held up a hand sharply, and Wallace was silenced. "I know. I know why you've come tonight. I've been anticipating it since you met my Nellie at the Haythorns' Christmas barbecue last year." Brookville's wide shoulders moved tensely. "But I'm sorry, sir. . . . I cannot offer you my daughter's hand."

The room shrank. Wallace felt his stomach drop to his knees and his eyes tighten. His face was suddenly icy. He was a corpse beginning to stiffen. A thousand things had crossed his mind in the days and hours past, but not this.

His mouth fell open, dry lips white against the pink of his tongue.

Watching the terrible change, Colonel Brookville fortified himself. "Nellie is now accepting the company of one of the Mount Hope boys from Emporia. She won't be . . . requiring any other suitors."

Impaled on despair, Wallace stared as the colonel stepped past him.

Brookville prowled past a sumptuous collection of books behind a wide carved desk. He plucked one of the books from its shelf and caressed it, searching for distraction. Hesitating then, he chose another book from a different shelf.

In the meantime, Lucas Wallace found his voice.

"But I've been paying her company for almost a year!"

"Do you know what this is, sir?" Colonel Brookville asked suddenly, turning and holding up one of the leather-bound books. "It's the autobiography of Davy Crockett. It's very popular. Have you read it?"

Wallace blinked, immobilized by shock. A moment later he shuddered visibly, then lurched forward, his fists cramping. "We had an understanding!"

The book clapped against the other one in Brookville's palm. He sighed. "You're over twenty years her senior, Mr. Wallace. You're forty-some years old, and you've had no wife at all yet. A man passes his prime, sir. A man loses the ability to father strong children."

"Is that the whole of it?" Wallace shot back, trembling now.

"No . . . I confess it is not. Mr. Wallace . . . try to picture what I will say now. The Brookville family, my ancestors, have been a Tidewater keystone since 1742. My wife's family can trace itself back to the *Mayflower*. We have lineage, sir. Substance. We don't feel—''

Wallace blurted, ''It's true I'm an orphan, I got no family, but I've built a farm that will stand the stress of time!''

Brookville's eyes flashed.

''You are new money, sir,'' the colonel said sharply. ''Your plantation is less than ten years old. I ride a horse older than your plantation, and that horse's dam still grazes in my field. There's talk of secession. Should that occur, only the solid establishment of the Southern society will allow us to survive as a separate nation. That lack of establishment will haunt you, sir, and I prefer it not haunt my daughter and her children. It's on her behalf that I wish you the best, but she'll not be accepting your favors any longer.''

Mortification creased Wallace's face and ironed his mouth into a line. He was caught fast between the fresh insult and the hard-won desire to show that even a contaminant could control himself in the face of disappointment. This could easily turn out to be a test of the dignity he insisted he had, if only in the long run, and the struggle nearly split his chest.

''I want to talk to Nell,'' he choked.

''Nell has nothing to say about it,'' the colonel announced.

Wallace clamped his mouth shut. His arms shuddered beneath the stiff fabric of his jacket, his thighs hard and knees locked inside their ivory breeches. For a while he looked like a mannequin, there only to display the decent clothing, a fake that would soon shed the trappings of sophisticated company and give them to someone who deserved to wear them.

Colonel Brookville waited for Lucas Wallace to accept the inevitable. There would be no wedding, no aristocratic mistress for Plentiful.

Knee-deep in humiliation, Wallace stared at the elaborate carpet beneath his feet. He combed his mind for a smooth way to get out of this room, this house, the city.

Colonel Brookville finally circled the desk behind which he'd been hiding and held the book out under Wallace's twitching eyes.

''Do you know what this is?'' he asked.

Wallace forced himself to focus on the brown leather and gold embossing. Slowly the scrolled letters made sense.

Brookville didn't force the stricken man to speak. "Alexandre Dumas," he said. "*Les Trois Mousquetaires. The Three Musketeers*." Have you read it?"

Wallace said nothing, turning his head a fraction for an answer.

"Have you ever read a book, Mr. Wallace?" Brookville asked. He lowered his tone then and added, "Do you even own a book?"

Wallace begged himself to lie, but by the time he thought of one, the truth already showed clearly on his face, and he knew it.

"A man's library is his mirror," Brookville said. He looked squarely at the man before him and offered a final gift of honesty, no matter how cruel. "I'm uneasy with a man who never looks in a mirror."

Lucas Wallace's efforts to become a man of distinction suddenly puddled before him. Somehow he had missed something. He had built and worked, schemed and collected, only to fall short of some mark of quality he never even perceived. It hovered all around him, on every shelf in this room, bound in leather.

"Take heart, Mr. Wallace," Brookville said, putting the book down on the desk. "Perhaps . . . you've just been casting your line too high."

This final blow almost knocked Wallace to the floor. He would have preferred lies. His eyes snapped up at Colonel Brookville.

Gathering his sharded pride, he stalked from the room, silent, his fists like tumors.

The butler held the front door open for him and politely averted his eyes.

Wallace marched down the front walk toward his carriage, but at the last minute he turned and headed down the lamplit street, paying no attention at all to the plush vehicle he left behind or the bewildered pony who stood twitching within her harness. He was a fierce, bitter scrap of a man who would never have a wife. He kept walking, his eyes riveted straight ahead, focused on nothing.

After a moment of confusion, the pony shook her mane to see if anyone would notice her. When no one did, she pressed her shoulders forward against the harness. Her hooves clopped on the hard-packed street.

Tugging the carriage placidly along, she followed the man who had paid for the reins.

★

CHAPTER TWO

———— ★ ————

"Tuggle, you are the largest boil of arrogance in all of Virginia."

"Oh? Does that mean you're abdicating the title?"

A heavy wooden door clapped shut in punctuation. Fresh night air gushed into the tavern.

The sunken bar dated back to 1794 and was saturated with a decades' old aroma of liquor and tobacco. Being a gentlemen's establishment, it was allowed, even expected, to smell.

From the corner by the old brick wall, dark alien eyes fixed on the four arguing men who had just entered. The stranger had learned early that this was a good place to watch people, to scan the personalities of the Tidewater Region. His drink was bottoming out, and he had been ready to leave, but as the four men came in, he decided a few extra minutes of watching might pay off in the long run.

He knew who they were. The first was a tobacco planter, the second owned the factory that processed most of the vicinity's tobacco, the third ran a wool mill, and the fourth a brickworks. Blue bloods.

And they also took note of him, though with careful brevity. He'd been appearing on and off in the tavern for a month now, and all he did, all he ever did, was hold a mug, put his back to the wall, and watch. He was always alone, and he never spoke. His swarthy Mediterranean complexion was always obscured by shadow, for he never sat under one of the lanterns along the polished wooden booths. No one ever saw him come in, no one saw him leave. He just materialized there. The barkeep would eventually notice and supply him a mug and beer. He always wore a dark sweater, blue or green, dimness making the color nearly black except for an occasional kiss of lamplight to trick the eye. Over it lay a black jacket almost defiant in its plainness.

Heavy black hair and black brows, hard nugget eyes, upper lashes thick, black, lower ones much thinner, making his face like an unfinished sketch that concentrated only on the eyes. Beneath the cheekbones his skin was rutted—always a sign of the devil.

Rumors had started almost immediately. He couldn't speak English yet, having just arrived on a foreign boat from Budapest or one of those darkish places, and was hunting work in the New World. He didn't like Norfolk and would soon be gone. That decided, the regulars had gone back to skillfully ignoring the coarse black eyes that watched, because it didn't matter; he couldn't comprehend what they were saying anyway.

By the third week, the dusky stranger had learned English but was mute. It didn't matter what he overheard, because he was incapable of spreading it. Deaf folk were brain slow. Another week made him an abolitionist spy, sent to observe Tidewater attitudes and report them north.

And he was here again tonight, ready to take on any persona they assigned, as Messrs. Tuggle, Plunkett, Barnes, and Van Meer entered the tavern.

"Keep talking, John," invited Howard Tuggle, a husky gentleman whom the others towered over except in stature of their personalities. He was the only one who paused to nod a greeting into the dim corner.

Van Meer adjusted his waistcoat around a broad chest and motioned to the barkeep for his usual drink. Then his foot went up on the bar rail. "Howard, it's 1833."

Tuggle gazed skyward and proclaimed, "Brilliant!"

Barnes and Plunkett accepted their own bourbons from the barkeep and grinned beneath their mustaches.

"It's 1833," Van Meer continued more loudly, "and the Greeks have maintained independence. It's an example for us."

Barnes wiped bourbon from his mustache. "How so, John?"

"Because it's an independence that they wrenched from the Ottoman Empire a full four years ago." Van Meer tilted his head up, giving extra room to his three chins. "The British fleet came in and assisted the Greeks in overthrowing the Turks. We can expect the same assistance from Britain in overthrowing the Northern yoke."

Frank Plunkett and Howard Tuggle exchanged glances.

"And we Southrons are much closer in kind to the British than the Greeks are," Van Meer continued. "A kinship among superiors. If the British would help barbarians such as the Greeks, surely they would rise to assist the South in a secession!"

From the corner the dark stranger continued watching these men, but this was the first time he noticeably moved, leaning forward slightly.

"I agree," Barnes was saying. "The European aristocracy is old and weak. They've lost their blood."

"They certainly have," Van Meer responded, almost swallowing Barnes's comment whole. "They need the vigor of the Southern states at their side. The South's time is coming, gentlemen. Ten years from now you remember that John Van Meer told you this that night in Norfolk. You all know about the president's little *faux pas* last winter. It had the opposite reaction to what was intended, did it not?"

Barnes nodded dubiously. "I should say. South Carolina lurched into rather... angry defiance."

"They raised an *army*," Van Meer clarified. His eyes widened to make sure this point didn't flop around like the previous had. "An army to repel any invasion by King Jackson. And rightfully so! These Yankee industrialists, people who grub in the dirt, are trying to dictate our way of life. Trying to take it away from us. Say we can't keep it. Our very heritage as Southerners!"

Uneasiness descended upon those at the bar. No one was quite able to accept what Van Meer was suggesting. Howard Tuggle stepped forward, his stout frame juxtaposed against Van Meer's, friction almost visible between them.

"Now just one moment, John," Tuggle began sternly. "My grandparents fought in the War for Independence, all four of them. I wouldn't care for a return to the excesses of monarchy. We are all still Americans here.''

"Yes, of course we are," Van Meer quickly said, "but we're the intelligent stratum. Virginia could band with South Carolina, then court an ally overseas. We can accept British help without accepting British habits. Yes?'' He paused, to see if he was having any effect. "The Greeks have done so. If the British would help *those* people . . . you see, according to the best evidence, these dark races linger on the scale of creation somewhere between white folk and the nigra. They're tribal cultures. Sponge divers and the like. Sheepherders. Yet the British came to their aid, and they are now independent.''

Plunkett removed his bowler, lowered his voice, and raised one eyebrow. "I would guard my words in a public place, sir."

In the back corner of the tavern, a grim smile twisted the spectator's mouth. After weeks of trying to ignore his presence, they were now performing for him, and he knew it.

He looked at these ivory individuals fanning their two-hundred-year-old heritage and was amazed. They genuinely didn't perceive what lay spread at their very back doors.

He had traveled around lately and had seen for himself. Everything here was new, moving, productive. The sheer wealth could stir the most sluggish heart. West of here there were tracts of land that no one even claimed yet. To a European the very idea was inconceivable. Places where no one had been, where it took months to ride to. Months, and all still in one country. Land that no one owned!

Dimitrios, you were right. These people are in search of roots, aching for something on which to anchor themselves.

In his mind he went back to his homeland, past the furrowed valleys and sun-gilded limestone islands, to places with history in their names, back to the house of his uncle. There he once again heard the postmillennial voice of Dimitrios ranting his own brand of wisdom. *"This new land is the defiant titan! Prometheus breaking the chains!"*

Dimitrios was one of those men whose thoughts had a certain cadence, his mind a certain crispness. He also had a regretful sense of the theatrical, but his nephew forgave that.

"I have an idea," Van Meer said then. "Let's ask Lucas."

The other men visibly stiffened.

They'd been aware of the sodden presence in the blue jacket who sat at the end of the bar, but this wasn't just a foreigner who hovered for a time in their county. This new target was a man who aspired to their peerage.

Luke Wallace was Van Meer's favorite pincushion. Had they truly paid attention to Wallace's condition tonight, they might have left him alone. Tonight the smoky man who watched from the brick wall wasn't the only ghost in the bar. There was this sodden silver ghost also.

Luck Wallace, the specter. He'd been pouring glass after glass of kill-grief on his broken spirit. His eyes were bitter holes. He stared into his drink, letting himself fester and liking it. And now Van Meer was going to pick at him.

Van Meer approached the bar and fingered one cuff of Wallace's jacket. He glanced back at the others. "Luke knows just what I'm referring to, gentlemen. Here's a man who built a plantation brick by brick, putting on airs so he could have heirs."

An unkind chuckle rippled through a few men, but most were silent.

Luke Wallace's eyes barely changed. He knew he dwelt in society's rural region, never knew it more crisply than tonight. So he sat there and took Van Meer's needling. Perhaps this was his place. Brookville had made it clear that Wallace was merely an aberration of success, missing the substance that would make him solid. He was a martyr to his own efforts, an unobliging upstart at best. People live in their own little cocoons where they're king, and it was wretched to discover the cocoon was ripped. Deep in his heart he knew Van Meer wasn't really any better, pound for pound, than he. But he was no good at verbal parley with men who had been raised being told they were better. All he could do was sit there and let Van Meer molest his hopes.

"That done," Van Meer continued, "he goes out courting only to find that he's been courting over his class."

At that Wallace looked up, his eyes ringed and wretched. From deep within his drunkenness, a burning humiliation reared its ugly head. Was he the only one who *hadn't* known Nell Brookville could never marry him?

In the brick corner the dusky foreign stranger watched without a hint of restlessness. Suddenly he had a chance to measure these men. If there was a difference, the dark man couldn't see it. Yet Van Meer was implying to the blue-coated man that they respected him, might even like him in a roughish, forgivable way, but that he'd never be one of them. *Dimitrios, these titans of yours . . . they make me curious.* He saw the raw humiliation that gripped Luke Wallace, the one thing that could break a strong man like a twig.

Van Meer leaned forward. "Now, Luke, you'll get the grippe if you worry yourself over this. Some things require time as well as money. Perhaps your grandchildren will be able to marry on the Brookville scale."

Suddenly Wallace exploded. His fists came together under Van Meer's chin, insult galvanizing him into action—but Tuggle plunged forward and wrenched Wallace's arms back, dragging him away with Barnes's help.

"Good work, John," Tuggle grunted. "Why don't you just supply him with a sword and expect him to do the honorable thing?"

"Lucas," Plunkett said, moving between Wallace and Van Meer, "you have to understand. No one holds it against *you*," he explained in his clipped Virginia way. He still held his bowler and now fingered the hat nervously. "When a man has a daughter, it's his obligation to see that she marry higher on the social ladder . . . or at least as high. . . . Do you see my point?"

Tuggle poked his face up from behind Wallace's shoulder. "I think he sees it fine, Frank."

"I simply want him to understand that—"

"A blind man could see it, Frank."

"Yes, I suppose it's obvious that—"

"Frank, put a boot over it."

Tuggle grunted again as Wallace broke away from him and wobbled in the middle of the room.

Wallace fixed his eyes on Van Meer. His boots clacked on the wooden floor several times. He straightened and tried to square his shoulders, to prove that even the unwashed among them could stand up straight.

Van Meer leaned on the bar. He would have liked to be socked in the jaw again. He'd have liked to see Wallace perpetuate his own commonness.

Perhaps that desire showed too clearly in Van Meer's eyes, in the quirk of his lips, for Wallace felt his fists clenching convulsively, but he somehow kept from lashing out. Maybe they were right. Maybe he'd never be anything but an obscenity, and his plantation would be unhallowed.

The dark man in the corner didn't miss Wallace's self-restraint. He knew what drunkenness could do to a man, and certainly what humiliation could do, and he looked at Wallace's face carefully. This was a destroyed human being, but behind the drunken glaze lurked a spark that was worth watching.

Luke Wallace shuddered like a tree being sawed down. Then, somehow, through all the rage and mortification, in spite of the effort they could plainly see, he managed to control himself. The shuddering subsided, muscle by muscle. To watch it was to be seduced by his courage. Lacking the splendid distinction of breeding, he shot one last glower at Van Meer and stumbled out the door in a waft of alcohol.

The door boomed shut.

Although he hadn't gotten quite what he wanted, Van Meer sighed and said, "Not unexpected from a man of lesser upbringing."

Tuggle yanked his jacket back into place and frowned at his peer. All that remained for him was the taste of Luke Wallace's mortification, and he found no pleasure there. "You've the touch of Solomon, John, really. You should be ashamed."

Plunkett frowned. "That was completely unnecessary, John."

"He'll be a better man for it," Van Meer said. "He'll someday be grateful for the truth. I believe it's crueler to delude a man."

Not one among them could speak up. None of them might have had the temerity. Cruelty, even necessary cruelty to keep a bloodline strong, was a heavy and demanding whip to hold. It gave a man sleepless nights.

Tuggle was the only one who spoke now.

"John," he began, "you were in cahoots with Brookville tonight, weren't you?"

Van Meer said nothing, but he didn't look away from Tuggle's accusation. Finally he nodded.

"I'm disgusted with you," Tuggle said. "Or at least with your methods. You should go cap in hand to Wallace and say you're sorry."

"All right, all right, Howard. Wallace will recover, and very likely he'll be tougher for it." Van Meer leaned back against the bar, both elbows propped up on it, his great barrel chest straining his waistcoat. "Where were we? Ah, yes . . . Greece."

"Let's leave Greece alone, John," Barnes grumbled, looking for the mug of brew that had disappeared since he put it on the bar a few minutes ago.

"John, you're an unchivalrous bastard," Tuggle thundered. "I'm tired of your self-appointed representation of Southern gentlefolk. You think everything breaks down to bread and water."

Barnes agreed. "I believe I've had it with this subject. This sesesh talk plain scares me."

"Then you're scared by destiny itself," Van Meer told him. "I shall prove my points. You, sir. Excuse me, you, in the corner."

One more time he did the unthinkable. He turned to the sequestered corner. For weeks this sable stranger had fielded the discomfited glances that ricocheted back at him, and tonight, for the first time, Van Meer addressed full front.

"Are you from Europe, sir?" he asked, the entire crowd falling dead silent.

The dark man never flinched as the moments dragged by.

"*Southern* Europe," he finally said in heavily accented English.

His rich voice quiet but full of confidence, was a shock in the silence.

Tuggle muttered, "Well done."

Van Meer threw him a glance, then paced toward the back corner. "Perhaps you can settle this debate then."

"I doubt it," the stranger said softly.

Coming slowly to his feet, the man straightened his coat.

He stepped out into the lantern light and strode across the stone floor to pause briefly before Van Meer.

He gazed into Van Meer's wide face as though memorizing him for a murder that would happen later on some abandoned side street.

"My tribe invented goat cheese," the accented man said with great ballast. "That is . . . *after* we began civilization as you know it."

He placed a simple cap on his black curls, nodded once at Van Meer, and invited himself out into the night. At the door he turned, touched the brim of his cap, and pulled the door closed.

Van Meer stared at the door as though bitten.

Howard Tuggle threw back his head and roared with laughter.

Good thing the pony knew her way home. Twice Wallace had tried to steer her down the wrong road, but an insistent tug on her bit brought him back to his senses long enough to realize she was right, and he was drunk.

The ride from Norfolk was a blur. Cool night air, dark sky above, the crank of carriage wheels beneath. The reins rubbing in his loose hands. Chalky moonlight. Nothing more.

But now there was something. Now there was the warm scent of the smokehouse, and underlying that, the pungent aroma of roasting bacon. The slave cabins.

It was a heavy aroma, mixed with the day's sweat, carried on the quick rhythm of "Walk-Jaw-Bone." The lively song whipped between the new brick cabins. Since completion of the cabins, Wallace hadn't visited them. The slaves were left pretty much to themselves as long as they did their day's work. But Wallace wasn't beyond opening his back windows occasionally and listening to the heavy songs the blacks liked to sing. A little African, a little Creole, a little hickory, a little this, a little that. The blacks weren't Africans anymore, not really. There hadn't been a legally imported African slave since 1808. They were all American now, and their heritage was a clutter.

In truth . . . he had less heritage than they did. He was an American mutt.

The thought made him spit. He gripped the reins with sudden acrimony, yanked on them hard. The sharp strips of new leather cut into his hands. He steered the pony off the circular drive and down toward the hot scent of roast pig and coal fire.

Their song fell off as the slaves picked up on the sound of the approaching carriage. The only light came from a big pit, in which a pork flank was roasting, and the nearby torches. It was a hot golden light.

The carriage came right across the property without regard to the grass and jerked to a stop between the fire pit and the nearest brick cabin. There it sat.

A form rose in silhouette upon the carriage seat. He scanned the dark faces staring up at him. Each face, one by one. Male, female, young, old, pudgy faces, some docile, some not so docile. They had minds of their own, his slaves. Was that an asset or a mistake? He no longer knew. His own weaknesses drummed in his head.

He'd been held in contempt by people he thought were his peers; he'd been told he was fooling himself. He wanted high for his grandchildren, yes, but he wanted high for himself even more. And he wanted it now. Fourteen years of his life had been the price, nearly a year of paying company to one girl, and tonight was supposed to be payment, but he'd gotten only dust. And he didn't know where to start over. He needed a young woman to keep himself young. But tonight his plan had collapsed. Now even his slaves were humiliating him. They should turn their faces downward in respect and fear, they should cower and beg—for these were the people he owned.

He reached back into the carriage. When his hand came up, a long, thin riding crop slashed the night sky.

Moving like a cougar, Wallace stalked his slaves. Once among them the big whip rang. It struck two men and a woman with the first blow and drove them to the ground.

He pivoted, and the whip sang again. Two more slaves went down, and a dozen backed away. Wallace's foul mood washed over them. With his eyes he dared them to stop him, so he could prove who was in charge.

He circled through them as they stood around the roasting pit. Twice more the whip made its irrational strike. But that wasn't enough.

Wallace stopped walking. He squared off in front of Alroy. The new blacksmith was a head taller and again as broad as the master, and he stood unmoving before Wallace.

Wallace glared into the man's widened eyes.

Through his teeth he whispered, "Fight me."

Alroy refused to move or even to respond. Even if he won, he wouldn't win.

Wallace's lips peeled back from gritted teeth. "Damn you, fight me!"

The short whip cracked across the wide black chest. Alroy went down.

Leaving Alroy crumpled near the pit, Wallace spun through the negroes.

"Any other time you'd fight me! Damn you, fight! Ill show you who's in charge! Goddamn your black hearts to hell! I own you! There's nothing you can do about it. Your name is Wallace, by God!"

Desperate to reestablish his manhood, he whacked and spat his way through the crowd of dark faces, and they didn't really know what to do about him. He was making himself madder with each swipe of his riding crop. Thoughts of calling for Mr. McCrocklin entered every mind, but was there time?

Old Moses shook his head once when he caught that very question in Esther's eyes from the other side of the roasting pit. Unfortunately Wallace caught the movement.

He plunged toward Moses, driven by demonic rage.

"What? What are you signaling about?"

"Nothin', Boss," Moses said.

"Fight me."

Moses looked up, and slowly he shook his head. "Ain't gonna waste fight on you right now, Boss," he said candidly. "Ain't no point. Dat's de ole prairie dew yellin' right now. Ain't really you."

"Ain't it?" Wallace roared. He drew the whip down hard

on Moses' head. The old man barely had time to save his eyes. "This ain't me either! And *this* ain't me. And *this* ain't me! And *this* ain't me!"

The slaves winced with each crack of the whip, but none of them had the nerve to step between Wallace and the old man.

Moses rolled helplessly against Wallace's legs.

The slaves were staring at the worst side of Lucas Wallace. They barely recognized the man as he appeared now before them. His eyes blistered across their faces again.

Then his gaze landed on one particular face and didn't venture farther.

He remembered the firm young flesh covered with sweat and droplets of blood, the determination in a high-boned brown face, and he wondered what the hair beneath the red turban would feel like. His last shreds of ego clung now to his power here, in these quarters.

No one said or did anything as he stalked Yula. With his whip he poked at her shirt. He circled her. The whip went between her legs, pushing the skirt up into a triangle in front of her.

Wallace grimaced and yanked the turban off Yula's head. Her hair tumbled out, long coils, like ropes, of uncombed hair. He pushed his fingers into the ropes.

Yula didn't move. Her lower lip pursed, but that was her only reaction.

Then Wallace's hand closed around the girl's corded wrist. He spun her around and dragged her toward the nearest cabin. She was yanked along behind him like a rag doll. As he mounted the porch steps, he pulled his shirttail out and yanked his trousers open in front, pausing only to push the girl into the cabin. He didn't bother to shut the door.

Outside, the slaves looked back and forth at each other, each wondering if any of them had the nerve to stand up for the new girl, but none of them cared enough about her yet to put her before himself. Rowzee made a little curl with her tongue and rolled her eyes toward Jonah, who scratched himself and looked in the other direction. Alroy helped Moses sit up. No one else even moved. The children among them watched the dark doorway unashamedly and craned their necks to listen.

There was no sound. None but the crackle of the fire and the crinkle of pigskin curling in the flames. That and crickets, and the sound of the bed scraping against the wood floor of the cabin.

Jonah filled his cheeks with air and pursed his lips, looking like one of the fish he'd caught a while earlier. It was a nervous habit. The children no longer laughed at it, except for the little ones. He didn't turn away, but he didn't dare look right at that doorway.

They all flinched visibly, every last one, when the bed sounded a final *thud*. A moment later Wallace staggered out. His face was a mean crumple.

He stuffed his shirt back into his breeches, but it didn't stay. Exasperated that the cuffees were all standing exactly where they had been when he went in, Wallace bullied his way through them, shoving any aside who were in his way, and threw the whip onto the floor of the carriage. After two tries he got back into the carriage seat and didn't fall off. He didn't pick up the reins but only plunged forward and whacked the pony's hind end with the flat of his hand. She jolted at the strange sensation, then pushed forward through the mud. The carriage wheels once again cut ruts into Plentiful's moist grass.

From the shadow beneath the cabin porch, Yula reappeared.

Sheathed in firelight, she watched him leave. She pushed her apron back down over her skirt. In her other hand she held her turban, now just a twist of red cotton.

By the time he climbed the wide front steps of the big house, Wallace's head was starting to clear. He vaguely remembered the cabins, but carved indelibly there were Van Meer's words and the pity he'd seen in his fellow planters' faces. He could have dealt with Van Meer with a fist and some spit, but the pity in those other faces . . . it couldn't be erased, not even in blood. He was a man burdened with a shame that wasn't his fault.

He wobbled into the wide foyer and went to a small secretary beside the archway to his private study. In one drawer he found paper and envelopes, pen and ink. In a moment he was scrawling the last couple of letters and bawling, "Samson! Samson!"

A thin butler with a pitch black face shot out of the dining room and wiggled toward him. "Boss! I din hear yawl come up. Boss, a man—"

"Take this." Wallace stuffed the paper into the butler's long, skinny hand. "Go into Norfolk first sight of dawn. I want you to order this for me."

Samson looked at the paper and pretended he could read it. "At the dockyard, Boss?"

"No, you mule-eared idiot. It's a book. See? A book. *The Three Muckteers.*"

"Oh! I see," Samson said, then paused again. "Boss, where we git books?"

Wallace waved his arms. "Hell, I don't know! Ask around. Get it from . . . wherever books are got from."

"Yessa. Boss, a man been waitin' t'see yawl."

Wallace caught himself on the edge of the secretary and forced himself to focus on Samson's long face. "Who is it?"

"I dunno him, sir. He a dangerous-lookin' man too, Boss. I want to go in with the gun behind yawl while you talk to him."

"You do? Why?"

"I think he got a knife, sir. He look like the kind of man who keep a knife."

Wallace pushed back a fallen lock of his silver-shot hair and shook his head. "Samson, I figure anybody who puts a knife in me tonight would just be doing me a kindness."

He tried again and this time succeeded in getting his shirttail back inside his breeches. It didn't help his appearance much, but at least it was in. He pushed away from the secretary and walked the straightest line possible to the closed office door. He went in.

For a moment he didn't see anyone. Only one feeble lamp was lit in the room, and there was a deceptive dimness everywhere. Just before he turned to accuse Samson of lying, he spotted a figure near the big dark curtains.

Taller than Lucas, and thinner, the figure was black on

black. Only when the man turned did his swarthy face show him to be anything other than myth.

It was a devil's face. Handsome, classically structured, yet damaged by pockmarks under each cheekbone. Hair like pitch beneath a flat cap, heavy black brows angled sharply over eyes even blacker because they were absorbing the lamp's weak light. The light sank into them and was swallowed. There was something familiar about him.

The man stepped out of the shadow. When he was close enough to read the expression in Wallace's face, he nodded a terse greeting.

"You are Lucas Wallace."

Wallace also nodded, once, confused for a moment by the heavy accent.

The man pulled the cap from his head as though removing a disguise.

"My name is Nick Varvaresos," he said. The black eyes tightened. "I think you would like to speak to me."

★

CHAPTER THREE

———— ★ ————

Plentiful buzzed with hopeful anticipation tinged by the rigors of running a plantation during lean times. Christmas would be spare this year.

Luke Wallace sighed as he stood on the veranda. The wide structure reached out from the eastern wing of the mansion, so that the colonial integrity of the facade was maintained. Right now the veranda was crowded hip-deep with stacks of blankets, folded dresses, shirts, pants, boxes of shoes, and woolen stockings, and in Wallace's hand was an itemized list of these and more. He was painfully aware of the large cluster of patient slaves who hovered around him.

He frowned over the list. Money had to be watched this year, lest it shrink till it pinched. But if the slaves didn't get at least a fair holiday celebration, their output would fall. Christmas was an important chance to raise spirits, and he had to consider that.

Unfortunately there were other considerations also. The price of cotton was down, which depressed the prices of everything else in the South, including, of course, tobacco. The industries up North were suffering too. The demand for manufactured goods was down, and until it rose, folk in the North would have more trouble than anyone who ran a plantation. Until the cycle hit an upturn, any plantation could live off itself for a while. Food could be homegrown, clothing homespun, animals fed from corn and grain on the premises. There were few salaries to be paid, and slaves would simply do without their allowances or the cash they normally got from trading their own harvests or crafts with the master. Folk in the South who had no plantation life, and certainly those in the North who hadn't even a concept of it, had nothing to fall back upon in hard times. Theirs would be a worse lot than his.

Wallace scanned his list and made another check mark beside a number. "Six blankets, three pair shoes, one box candles for you, Walker," he ticked off. "Go ahead, take 'em. Jonah, you got eight children now? How many under five years old?"

"Three, Boss."

"Take three extra blankets on top of your regular ten. And where the devil is that firewood I'm hauling to the cabins? Does it take the whole blasted day?"

He looked toward the road, seeking a glimpse of the wagon load of wood and supplies, but something else caught his eye, something that pleased him deeply.

Before him workmen chipped and strained, mixed, measured, and hauled, and great white columns took form on the corners of the veranda. Greek columns. The colonial face of Plentiful was getting a cosmetic change. The columns took the place of ordinary wooden struts that had been just fine for ten years. They were Ionic columns, not Doric. These had curled volutes at the tops and platforms at the bottoms. Wallace drew in a breath of joy that he even knew the difference. A couple of months ago, columns were columns.

He blinked his attention back to business. Slaves came and went away, carrying stacks of blankets and boxes for their cabins, the head of each household making an appearance to claim his stock and to say which sizes of clothing his household needed this winter. Children were fast to outgrow the white cotton shifts, and every year a new batch of pants and dresses had to be distributed. Since there was no lady of the house to donate her used frocks to the colored women, Wallace was always obliged to buy new ones. However plainer than a lady's fancy dresses, the clothes on his coloreds were always in good shape and generally clean. Appearances mattered.

He was so busy that the approach of the huge wagon

carrying three cords of firewood and supplies barely caught
his attention as it drew into the circular drive. As wide as the
road and fully the length of a railroad car, the wagon itself
was a wonder, never mind the high load of supplies and wood
making it twice impressive.

And the eight gigantic horses—big beasts with hooves wide
as dinner plates. The immense farm chunks were mixed
breeds, mostly sired by Howard Tuggle's dependable breeding Clydesdale, Big Dane. Some of these were the bright bay
of the Dane himself, with his white blaze and flopping white
fetlocks, others the drabber grays and bisque browns of their
dams, but all were docile and strong. Their thick necks
rippled, twitching against the heavy-duty harnesses, and their
thick bodies carried the aroma of sweaty horsehair and clinging hay. Wallace rather liked to see the chunks all hitched up
together in two great rows, as they were today. This was a far
more powerful aspect than seeing the horses teamed in twos
to till the fields.

The wagon pulled abreast of the veranda. Wallace imagined the swath they had cut as they hauled their vast load
through town and down the long winding road past other
plantations, past people who looked and knew this fine team
and this wagon and this load of provisions were on their way
back to Plentiful. He practically shuddered with self-satisfaction—
the wagons, the chunks, the Christmas plans, the columns . . .

As big hooves impatiently cut patterns in the driveway
below him, Wallace called to the black driver.

"Jeff, what took so long? Waiting for snow to soak that
wood before it gets in the shed or what?"

"Naw, Boss," the big slave called back affably, his own
body only a little less huge than the horses'. "Mist' Tredway,
he made me wait outside the mercantile. Got this here parcel
for yawl." He maneuvered his tree-trunk form off the wagon
and hiked the package to the veranda.

Wallace thrust his list and pencil at the nearest slave and
snapped, "Get Mr. McCrocklin to take over for me."

Wading through the provisions, suddenly eager, he swung a
leg over the rail and dropped to the ground. "Let's have it."

The parcel wasn't very big, wrapped in plain paper and tied
with a string. Anxious, Wallace almost tore the string with his

teeth before Jeff produced a knife and sliced it for him. The paper fell away. Sunlight glinted on buffed leather.

Wallace held the universe in his hands.

Mahogany cowhide and gold lettering flashed in the sun. *The Three Musketeers*.

Wallace scooted into the mansion's front door before letting loose with a titter of excitement. He burst into his office—his library—and went right to the shelf directly behind the desk. A swipe of one hand, and all the papers and ledgers flopped and rattled to the carpet. Then he centered the single volume carefully on the shelf, exactly at eye level. He retreated to the middle of the room and surveyed the book there on its throne. It looked bare, but promising.

He turned his back on it. Then he swung around and took it by surprise. It looked a little better, a little more used to itself. Still undressed, though.

He prowled the office—*library*—surveying the book from different angles. He sat in each chair and on the sofa, all three places on the sofa, looking at the book from each position. After careful consideration he collected a bourbon bottle, a box of cigars, a clock, and his spectacles and arranged them near the book. Two minutes later he removed the bourbon bottle.

"Boss?"

Wallace spun. Jeff filled the doorway. Beyond him, in the wide hallway, Wallace caught sight of a pregnant slave girl dusting—light work, because of her condition. Her thin body, in comparison with Jeff's, was like a twig that had swallowed a grapefruit. Wallace got a little rush of satisfaction that his slave village was growing.

Jeff pulled his hat off. "Anything else, Boss? 'Fore I take the load on down?"

"No," Wallace said, waving him out. "Yes! Jeff? C'mon back in here. Come right over here. Look at this chronicle." He snatched up a newspaper from his desk and flipped through it.

"I can't read, Boss," Jeff said.

Wallace shook the newspaper open. "I know that, man. Look here. I heard about these books. *The Young Duke* by

Benjamin Disrilly. And here's a review of *The Conquest of Granada*, by Washington Irwin.''

"Irving,'' the immense negro corrected, "and Disraeli.''

"What?''

"Irving. Washington Irving. Benjamin Disraeli . . . sir.''

Wallace's face tightened. "How'd you know that?''

His question was edged with suspicion, but the commanding element was that of a man upstaged. He glared up, up, up, into Jeff's face.

Jeff twitched. "Just heard about it in town, sir. Folk talking on this and that.'' He motioned at the newspaper.

Only then, for the first time in the six years this man had been driving for Plentiful, did Wallace notice how well-spoken Jeff was.

He straightened, and the newspaper slipped to his side. "Where'd I buy you from?''

Jeff shifted uneasily. "Up Alexandria way, Boss. The Yancy farm when Daddy Yancy died and they sold off all their stock.''

"Did they school you culluds up there?''

"Not regular, sir. But I was a house nigger for the Yancys. Daddy Yancy made us all talk better, so's he'd be proud. You know. . . pro-nounce.''

Wallace paced around the big man. Not a short trip, either. "Really,'' he murmured.

Jeff's collar stuck to the sweat on his neck. He didn't move as Boss circled him. "You want I should get a move on, Boss?''

"Mmm . . . yes . . . and get these books into my library by midmonth.''

"Right, Boss!'' Jess escaped from the library like a pebble from a slingshot.

Wallace eyed the empty doorway. His mind worked on the notion of well-spoken darkies. In the hallway the pregnant girl continued to dust. He wondered if she was smart enough to pro-nounce.

Doubts picked at Wallace as he leaned one thigh against his new oak desk. He touched the wooden desktop with two fingers. A man should have a desk. Now he had a book and a desk.

And columns. He had columns.

A movement at the doorway disturbed his musing. At first he thought Jeff had for some reason returned. But this movement, flickering in the corner of his eye, was far more deliberate and self-assured than that of a bondsman, even a big bondsman. So much so that it took his attention entirely.

His new ideas, the day's work, the arrival of his book, all were forgotten when he saw who stood there.

His vision sharpened even as his mind went to mush.

Black eyes gazed back at him from the vestibule. The features were strict, sheathed like weapons in the mystery that always followed them. Nick Varvaresos.

In his hand there was a letter.

Wallace stared at Varvaresos. At the letter.

He faltered forward a step or two, a question rising hot on his face.

Varvaresos antagonized him with a long, tempting silence.

Then he stepped fully into the library and squared off with the master of Plentiful. He drew the letter upward, toward his chest, and moved it slightly back and forth.

"Mr. Wallace," he announced quietly, "we agree."

The front door burst open.

Luke Wallace exploded onto the veranda, his boots ringing on the wood. In one hand he held a huge dueling pistol. In the other he had Nick Varvaresos. The pistol cracked and boomed. The bullet scored the air.

Workers, slaves, drivers—everyone flinched, then looked.

"Listen!" Wallace roared. "Samson! Jeff! Moses! All y'all listen here! Fire up the ovens! Get ten bags of flour out and bring the women up for bakin'! Slaughter the hogs and light the roasting pits! Break out the molasses and the brandy!" He coiled an arm around Nick Varvaresos and shouted, "Plentiful's gonna have a Christmas jubilee the likes of which'll make you *blind*!"

Cheers rose across Plentiful, riding on the crisp, sunny December morning air. And more cheers as the news spread to the forge, the fields, the brewery, the stacking yard, the barn.

At the open door of the mansion, a pregnant slave girl stood watching as her master and the mysterious dark-haired man shook hands on the veranda. Around her thin neck, since it no longer fit around her waist, hung a glossy pink sash. With one hand she touched the satin. Her other hand closed on a dirty dust cloth, and her quick little brain went to work.

★

CHAPTER FOUR

──────── ★ ────────

Earth breathed, and it was spring. Virginia's harbors teemed once again. Merchant ships spindled the sky with their masts and patterned it with sails. Incoming, outgoing, they were the blood of trade running on blue arteries, linking civilization to civilization. No longer stiff with winter, the ships stretched their sails like wings under a benevolent sun.

As noon approached, so approached a barkentine, fully loaded. She carried foreign sailors who spoke only barroom English. The *Clytaemnestra* was beautiful among ships. Her sails were not white, but rather they were made of tanbark sailcloth, and this cut an exotic picture as she came in against all the other ships with their ordinary white sails. Her great main and mizzen carried the red sails fore and aft rigged with gaffs that speared the sky in her wake. Her foremast, though, was rigged with square sails that argued with the schooner sails behind, and she seemed to move only by virtue of her own defiance. Only when her sails were furled and she was tugged up to dock did she look like the other ships harbored here.

The *Clytaemnestra* was a familiar enough sight in the harbor at Newport News, where Norfolk's businessmen collected their imported goods and loaded their exports. The ports she sailed from, and back to, needed the business. In her hold would be broad bolts of fabric for the Southern ladies to make their big dresses, silk pillows for their parlors, linens, blankets, spices, teas to serve in those parlors, veils,

45

brass and bronze, books and crafts, and an entire hold full of
boastable stuff. "It came from Athens," the proud murmurs
would go. "It came from Crete . . . the Black Sea . . . Con-
stantinople . . . the Aegean . . . the Sea of Candia . . ."

But this time something was different. The attention of
people on the wharf was drawn to the *Clytaemnestra*. Something was happening that had never happened before. This
time these were *people* coming off the ship. Foreigners.

First came men. They were sober figures in voluminous
shirts and mulberry fezzes, many with big black mustaches,
but few with beards. Each carried a crate marked with
triangles and squares. They filed from the ship to a string of
big wagons and coaches. Not buggies. Big polished coaches.
With tops *and* curtains.

Howard Tuggle's wife Tabby pulled on her husband's arm
and asked, "Mr. Tuggle, are those not the wagons and horses
of Plentiful's Lucas Wallace?"

Tuggle blinked into the bright May sunlight. Beside him a
second man also glared down the dock.

"You're quite right, ma'am," John Van Meer said, "though
I have never seen Mr. Wallace's wagons beside an import
clipper."

Tuggle murmured, "What the devil is all this?"

A bizarre merry-go-round had begun. The foreign men
deposited their crates in the first wagon and filed back onto
the barkentine.

Down the sagging gangplank the men came again. Some
led live goats and lambs. Others hauled carpets slung over
their shoulders in big red rolls. They carried vases, urns, and
jugs, all apparently full. Not the plain clay vases of primitive
lands, these were glazed, intricately decorated with geometric
designs and detailed drawings. Borders of meanders and
zigzags, rows of artwork—chariots and charioteers driving
across the fired-clay receptacles that smelled of spices. . . . Jugs
with friezes of sphinxes, gazelles, and bulls. Helmeted warriors turned their flat, painted faces to each other and crossed
lances. Male figures were rendered in henna or black, females
in white. The colors—the brightness of Barbaria. Red, yellow, henna, brown, black, azure.

The crowd nosed up like children to a toy shop window.

Now the foreign men were coming back not singly, but in pairs and in threes, carrying huge amphorae loaded with who knew what. The amphorae had frightening animal heads for spouts and were the color of wet Georgia clay. Behind them came more men, these wrestling potted dwarf trees from which whole oranges hung.

"It's an invasion of dirty-bloods," John Van Meer commented, his voice leveled by astonishment. "What could Wallace be up to? Are these Arabs? Or Turks?"

"The *Clytaemnestrà* is out of Athens, John," Tuggle drawled.

"Whatever could be inside those vases?" Tabby Tuggle wondered, secretly hoping her husband would stomp right down there and slay the dragon and look in its mouth.

"Even more," Tuggle added, "what could be inside *that*?"

Out of the hold, drawn by the heavy lines and block and tackle of the ship's winch came a huge black caldron, obviously full. Around its broad rim was a bright, active border of artwork, an entire army of warriors in crested helmets charging across its rim. Then came another caldron, with a fleet of ships painted on its rim, rowed by clay-faced sailors who'd probably been rowing for centuries.

The winch swung around, and the men in fezzes guided the caldron onto one of Plentiful's wagons. The tripod legs plunked to the wagon's bed, and with that jolt a slosh of green water broke over the rim of the caldron and cascaded to the dock.

"Look!" Tabby Tuggle squeaked. "Why, it's got animals for handles!"

"Griffins," Tuggle said.

The winch once again went down into the hold and again came up with another caldron, this with an elaborate marriage processional around its rim, rendered in great flat detail. The caldron wallowed at the end of the winch, so full that water crashed over its rim and splattered the onlookers. Men and women shied away.

And here came a third, also filled with water. This one had chariots drawn by horses with wings.

Van Meer squinted until his eyes hurt. "Why is Luke Wallace importing water, do you suppose?"

"Dear God in his heaven!" Tabby Tuggle gasped, clutching her own throat. "Whatever is that?"

The winch now swung again, but this time it held what looked like a small cistern painted with murals. The stone thing swung past the Tuggles and Van Meer close enough for them to see that the murals weren't painted but were actual mosaics set in limestone.

Howard Tuggle pointed at it. "Shells!" he murmured. "Pictures made of broken seashells. By heaven, look at the detail of them!"

Van Meer shrugged. "Yes, I see it, Howard."

The crowd whispered back and forth. Who were these people? Why did they bring these things?

This went on for almost an hour, and not a spectator could manage to walk away. The Plentiful wagons were soon brimming. The horses had their work cut out for them. Every load seemed bigger than the one before. When the urns and caldrons were loaded, other things started to emerge from the *Clytaemnestra*'s hold. But these would remain a mystery, for they were undefined shapes, some as big as a man, all rolled in heavy fabric. The crowd squinted and murmured. Had this not been broad daylight, some whispered, at the height of the business day, these men might have been smuggling out the corpses of murdered passengers.

One by one more than a dozen of the rolled parcels were loaded onto the wagons, then covered by sheets of canvas.

"Lucas Wallace has taken on some strange heathen religion," Van Meer decided.

"Stay here," Tuggle whispered suddenly to Van Meer and Tabby. The dock creaked under his stout body. He padded along the blind side of one of the wagons. The giant horses twitched as he passed, but only eyed him the same way he was eyeing the wagon. Behind him he heard Tabby doing her womanly duty: worrying.

"Ohhhh . . . ohhh!" she whined. Good old Tabby. He knew she was clinging to John's lapels; he didn't have to look back.

The wagon's rim was at eye level as Tuggle approached it. He took hold of the wood, got a toehold on the wheel spoke, and heaved himself upward, clinging like a bird on a cliff wall. He glanced around, satisfied that he'd gone unnoticed as the foreigners went about their business.

Tuggle peeked up over the sideboard, his nose hooking the wood for a moment.

There it was. The caldron with the griffins.

He straightened up and leaned over the sideboard. He put one finger in the caldron and drew it out again. Touching this to his tongue, he nodded quickly back at Van Meer and Tabby—it was water. *Salt* water.

In went his hand again, this time all the way. He flinched at the coldness of the water in the caldron. A coating of slime swallowed his hand up to the wrist. After several weeks in a ship's hold, the water wasn't exactly fresh. It wasn't, though, as stagnant as it should have been. Perhaps they had been replacing it with seawater from time to time during the voyage. But why?

Indeed, why carry salt water at all?

This was all part of some wild scheme to—

"Ahhhhh!" Tuggle bellowed. His heart went crazy in his chest. He tried to pull his hand out of the pot, writhing at the sensation in his fingers. "Something's got me! Something's got meeee!"

"Howard!" Van Meer shouted. He came crashing though the crowd and grabbed Tuggle's coat.

"Mr. Tuggle! Mr. Tuggle! Oh!" Tabby Tuggle bobbed down the dock, her rounded breasts wobbling like jelly over the stays of her corset. "Oh, Mr. Tuggle!"

"It's got meeeeee!" Tuggle's eyes were big as oranges. Water sloshed up his sleeve.

The crowd gasped, but no one quite knew what to do, and no one was quite ready to stick his hand in there to save Mr. Tuggle from dire unknowns.

"Howard!" Van Meer drew his pocket pistol and hoisted himself up beside Tuggle's wrenching body. He took aim at the water in the caldron.

The crowd trumpeted its shock. Women pushed their faces into the nearest gentleman's lapels. The men craned their necks in amazement.

Van Meer was about to pull the trigger when a hand grabbed his wrist, and he too was suddenly struggling—but this was no undersea creature who held him. This was one of those foreign men.

The man stood above them in the wagon, his big black moustache cloaking a definite disapproval. *"Stamata!"* he shouted. He pulled Van Meer's hand aside, then reached down into the water, up to the elbow. He casually felt around, pulled here and there, and rolled his eyes at Tuggle's desperation.

Suddenly Tuggle flopped backward. His hand came flying out of the caldron. He dropped off the axle, clutching his hand, and stumbled to the dock. His face was bright red, his suit soaked now, and smelling.

The foreign man worked inside the caldron for another few seconds, then drew his own hand out. He glowered down at Tuggle and Van Meer with a scolding look. He leaned on his elbows over the sideboard and crossed his wrists casually. Water dripped from his fingers to the dock below.

"Khehromeh poosahss ghnoreezo. . . . Ahmareekhanoss," he said, pronouncing each syllable as though speaking to a dog he was training. He shook the water off his hand, making sure some of it spritzed the two astonished men below him. Then he laughed broadly at their expense and went back to the loading.

"You all right, Howard?" Van Meer asked, examining Tuggle's soaked arm.

Howard Tuggle gaped back at the wagon, half expecting to see some prehistoric leviathan crawling up over the sideboard after him. "I . . . I . . ."

"Oh, Mr. Tuggle—" Tabby gasped, her pouchy cheeks stark white, her brows crooked in sympathy as she dabbed her lace handkerchief on his wet hand.

Van Meer lowered his voice. "What was it, Howard?"

Tuggle drew in a breath to assuage his panting. "I don't know," he choked. "I only know that it had hold of me. By God, I'm soaked through. You saw, didn't you, John? Why, I was under attack from within!"

John Van Meer glared through the bright daylight. "Who *are* these people?"

Once again the gangplank moaned. This time, though, there were no men carrying heavy crates or jugs.

This time there were women.

Exotic women. Four, six, nine, they filed from the ship. Women from some other world. Older ones guided younger ones as though to protect them from the New World's contaminations.

While the men carried an air of private business, as though they had expected to be watched but didn't care if they were, these feminine creatures were quite obviously on parade. They *wanted* to be watched.

Virginia's ladies and gents could scarcely ignore the processional of women in black clothing so unlike the dome-shaped gowns of the South's belles, offset with bright embroidered zigzags and pyramids, floral designs, stripes. Quilted aprons, all heavily embroidered, layered the stiff clothing. Some of the women wore coins across their foreheads on thin chains. Stiff muslin headdresses covered everything but their faces. What business could Lucas Wallace have with such elemental beings?

Virginia seaport society stared as the queue of otherworldly creatures filed off the barkentine. The women went to the coaches and climbed inside. The men drew great tarpaulins up and over the contents of every wagon and tied the covers tightly down. That done, they carefully boarded the wagons, and Plentiful's drivers snapped the long reins. Big horses yanked forward. Harnesses rattled. Wheels bit into the dirt.

As the confused crowd looked on, the coaches and covered wagons groaned forward. The mystery, it seemed, was in Lucas Wallace's hands, to keep or to divulge as he saw fit, no matter the curiosity he had connived so well to inflict.

"I wanted *red* roses! Why can't a man get what he wants!"

The veranda shook beneath Luke Wallace's stomping boots. He spun from one rail to the other, shouting. Samson followed him around.

"Great Christ in hell, are your feet made of molasses? This porch hasn't even been swept yet!"

"Sweep dat porch!" Samson snapped at the nearest slave woman.

"Get the serving table out here! Have you cuffees no concept of time?''

"Dat table oughta be out a here!''

"And where are the gifts? Great Christ, you can't get motivation into the heart of a cullud!''

"Get dem gifts and quick about it.''

"Samson, shut your mouth!''

House slaves scurried around them. Samson moved away, ready to supervise in a different capacity than just being Boss's private echo. Two servants dressed in black linsey suits came through the double doors from the dining room, carrying a table that was already set. Damask tablecloths waved in a slight breeze. Silver cutlery reflected the daylight, Wedgwood china and a melon-shaped tureen added some color. Inside the tureen was fruit punch. A crystal decanter held fine brandy, and a large oval serving plate held tiny lemon finger cakes and shortbreads. Sprinkled on the table were bits of dried potpourri. All vibrated with the master's boom.

"You'd think this started yesterday, for all the preparation I see! Samson!''

Nick Varvaresos uncrossed his legs and brought his brandy glass down from his lips.

"Relax yourself, Lucas,'' he said, just loud enough to be heard. He gazed thoughtfully at Wallace.

In a smoking jacket of heavy Damascus brocade over blood red velvet, Wallace looked more like a drapery or a piece of furniture than a man whose fingernails had been dirty yesterday. The luxurious smoking jacket was Nick's idea. Even the fanciest day suit couldn't match it for flamboyance. With his gunmetal hair combed back so that its waves showed, his face cleanly shaven, and his sideburns touched with glistening olive oil, Wallace's quite ordinary form took on an acceptable command. Now, more than just being in charge, he *looked* in charge.

Except for being paper white with anticipation.

All morning he had paced and blustered. First in the office, then in the parlor, by noon hammering the vestibule carpet, and finally out onto the veranda to prowl back and forth in the daylight.

"Lucas," Nick repeated, strictly this time.

Wallace paused where he stood, directly in front of a huge potted rosebush on the veranda, one of two that flanked the steps down to the lawn. A sudden calm came over him. Like giving up.

He pushed his fingers into a cluster of pink blooms. His eyes lost their focus.

He whispered, "I wanted red roses. . . ."

This brought Nick up out of the porch swing. Striding casually down the veranda, he paused beside Wallace. He leaned on the veranda rail with one elbow and looked up into Wallace's face.

"You're not going to embarrass me," he asked, "are you, Lucas?"

Perhaps he said it a bit too seriously.

Wallace's eyes suddenly focused sharply, and his face blanched. Really went white. He stared now at the rail beside Nick and choked, "Oh . . . my God . . ."

Nick let his spine roll back against the rail, and his laughter rang down the veranda. He clasped Wallace's arm sympathetically and shook it. Any man with such panic in his face at least had a good-enough set of intentions for their plan, Nick realized.

He'd harbored plenty of doubts, to be sure, since last autumn. Much had changed since then, not the least of which was his own accent, which had diminished over the months as he spent more and more time with Wallace, educating the other man about what to expect. He had worked at his own accent, consciously pronouncing the English words all the way across, the ends of every word particularly, which he noticed the black slaves usually left off. That was an effort, but once the cadence of English was in his mind, the effort became its own reward.

Today was supposed to be Lucas's reward. And there was Lucas, looking like a man about to hang. He was an erratic man, this American. Yet he had his worths. Nick's vacillations about their agreement had dissipated along with his accent. For all Wallace's flaws Nick had never seen a man try so hard.

"Boss!"

Moses hobbled toward them on the lawn. Among the house slaves who skittered about in their black dress suits and white shirts, he looked like a cast-off rag.

Wallace snapped straight. "Moses! Damn you! I told you field cuffees to stay in the yard!"

The old man slowed his hobbling and leaned on his hickory stick. "Boss, I think yawl oughta come to the yard. Sump' you oughtta see."

"Are you out of your mind?" Wallace roared. He clawed for his pocket watch and held it out in front of him for Moses to see. "Do you realize what the time is, man?"

Moses nodded, though the watch was nothing but a circle with little sticks drawn inside it. Boss knew he couldn't tell time, but this wasn't the moment to remind him. "I reeleye', Boss. But I reckon yawl betta come down anyhow. Yawl oughts be de firs' to see. Jus' case yawl wanna do innythang."

"Do? About what?"

"You jus' come see, Boss. I ain' gon' say right out loud."

"Snakes and piss!" Wallace shrieked like a wild man. He spun around. "Samson! Come with me! Buckie! You keep your fat eye on that road! Anything shows itself, you put your tail up and hike right down to the yard! Clear?"

His upstairs porter nodded. "Clear, Boss, das' clear."

Wallace went right over the veranda rail and dropped to the grass. His stride lengthened as he snapped his fingers at Moses. "Hop to it!"

Moses hobbled after him as fast as his old body would go, Samson's bowed legs twirling along behind.

On the veranda Nick Varvaresos grinned and shook his head.

The negroes around the cabins flinched at the sight of Boss striding toward them in that fancy red jacket, with his boots glossy and his hair looking like a silvered mane. With Samson and Moses wiggling and twirling behind him, trying to keep up, he made quite a sight. At the last minute he drew up short, barked a quick demand, and let Moses wiggle into the lead. The old man went straight to where everybody knew he was going—the cabin on the end.

The cabin was dark and warm. A fire crackled in the stone hearth. It was the only light in the room. Over the smoky aroma of firewood, there was the strong smell of blood, of sweat.

Wallace filled the entire doorway.

The women inside looked up.

"Over here, Boss," Moses said, squeezing past Wallace. He hobbled across the wood floor to a dark corner, and there he paused.

There, in the shadows, stood a cradle.

Made of leftover wood and brimming with flannel, the cradle was a little symbol of nothing. Moses leaned over it and drew back a drab flannel quilt.

Luke Wallace stepped over to the cradle, still perplexed.

He blinked, then squinted.

"Light a lamp," he snapped.

One of the women, an elderly cuffee who had worked for him since the beginning, swiftly obeyed the order and brought him a candle with a glass globe. He took it without looking at her and lowered it. Its soft, buttery light washed over the cradle.

"Lawsy...," Samson murmured as he too leaned over. "Dat ain' no mulat' baby," he said. "Dat baby white!"

Wallace's stomach twisted up with exasperation. There, lying asleep as though it meant no harm, was indeed a white child.

But white in a parenthetical way, for its hair was thick, silky, made of obsidian curls rather than the soft wool of negro hair. Obsidian curls, skin like watered sepia...not exactly white—but clearly his.

Until this moment he never asked of his memory any details of such indiscretions, because they were rare. There were only dulled images that told him of a little poontang one drunken night. He felt as though he'd left the stove burning and scorched his dinner, and he didn't like being made the ass in front of his slaves. A brown baby wouldn't have brought up such feelings. This child, though, would forever cling.

He paced in a circle, twice all the way around, then stopped and looked back into the cradle.

"Boy or girl?"

"It a boy, Boss," Moses said.

"Who's the mother?"

The old cuffee made a gesture with his stick. "Yonder, Boss."

In a dim corner there were three more women. A foggy memory budged in the back of Wallace's mind. He couldn't pin it down, but there was enough tingle to make him believe he wasn't wrong when he singled out the bony girl who'd been dusting the lower floors for a while. She was already getting dressed. Rowzee and Dinah were wiping blood from the floor and from the insides of the girl's knees and thighs, piling the soaked rags in a basket beside one of the beds. The girl was pulling a stiff shirt over her head. Somehow she managed to keep her eyes on him the whole time.

Wallace frowned and shifted his weight.

He looked back into the cradle, folded his arms, and covered his mouth. He tried to imagine taking the child for cuffee and couldn't. The little nose already had a strong line. The infant's jawline was a gentle curve, not the jutting feature he would have expected, and the rose-petal lips nothing at all like a slave's. Even as the hedge-born boy lay with miniature fists curled beside his tiny scrunched-up face, Wallace recognized the bone structure of his own family. This was a vest-pocket version of himself.

Even more—it was a *perfect* version of himself. Except for the coloring. Never had he possessed such gold dust in his cheeks, never such richness in his hair.

But neither had any negro.

"I can't have this here," he grumbled, more to himself than anyone, "not now. . . ."

As the slaves watched, he changed his mind two or three times, shifting from this foot to that each time.

"Boss! Boss! Where is you?"

They all looked toward the door at the sound of Buckie's voice.

Wallace's hand dropped away from his mouth, and he stepped back from the cradle. "Here," he called out the window.

"Boss!" Buckie sounded close. "Wagons comin' up dat road! Missa Nick, he tell me t'tell you."

"I'm coming! Samson, get back to the house. Moses, you all do like I say and stay in the yard. I can't have you showing yourselves about the mansion to people ain't never seen a field nigger before. I mean, haven't never.'' He dodged toward the door, his mind once again working on his own business. Only as he was leaving did he cast a hand back toward the cradle.

"Keep that baby hidden. As soon as it can be weaned,'' he said firmly, "it'll have to be sold off.''

His boots hammered the narrow porch as he struck off for the mansion, and he was gone.

The air settled.

No one looked at Yula.

The coaches turned into the circular drive like a royal procession. The wagons came after, all covered with the wide brown tarps, laden with such pageantry as Virginia had never before seen.

Nick Varvaresos watched with burgeoning pride as the black coaches drew up to the veranda steps and rolled to a stop. He repressed a grin, for the coaches and the wagons looked quite plain right now, closed and covered as they were. He glanced at Lucas.

Beside him Luke Wallace tensed up, feeling like the American mutt he was.

Nick stepped down from the porch. Before him the lead coach snapped open, the door pushed from within. A stout gentleman with a black beard, wearing a gray business suit, squeezed from the narrow opening, blinked in the bright sunlight, and threw his arms wide.

"Nicolas!''

Nick threw his arms around the large man, and himself was crushed in an embrace. *"Efkaristoss,* Uncle! *Poss ista?''*

"Poli kahla!'' The man wrenched Nick out at arm's length and surveyed him, then babbled something else and swatted Nick's growing waistline. He shook his finger and laughed.

Nick took the man's elbow and turned him immediately to the veranda, to Wallace. Instantly the man's eyes landed on Wallace and did not look away.

"Uncle,'' Nick said, *"boronassas gnoreeso* Mr. Lucas Wallace. Lucas, at long last I'm proud for you to meet Dimitrios Trözene.''

Wallace held out his hand, cold as a dead chicken. Somehow he choked his voice up out of his socks.

"Ti kaneteh, o kirios Trözene. . . . Ti qnomih ekehteh yiatin khorrah?"

Trözene laughed warmly and said, *"Khalah! Efkaristo, efkaristo poli."* Then he laughed again.

Wallace started to sweat under his velvet. His hand was cold in Trözene's grip, but he couldn't get it back. Trözene was patting it.

"Poor man!" Trözene suddenly said in English, chuckling. "The effort has killed you!"

Wallace sucked in a grateful gulp of air and, without thinking, blurted, "Thank God, you speak English!"

Nick muttered, "I *told* you he did. . . ."

Trözene laughed even harder, his dark eyes wedging with delight. The sound rolled across the bristling green lawn. He took a sprig of mint from his own lapel and searched for a buttonhole on Wallace's smoking jacket. When he couldn't find one, he laughed again, shrugged, and tucked the mint into Wallace's tied belt.

Nick covered his mouth and stifled a chuckle. He'd had no idea how this meeting would go and watched every nuance with great curiosity—and not without some nervousness of his own. After all, he'd negotiated all this at a great distance. Who could tell how things would spell out in person?

Dimitrios took Lucas's arm and led him toward the second coach.

"We have waited long for this, Mr. Wallace," he said as they walked. "Soon there will be many changes for us all."

"Please, call me Lucas," Wallace told him.

"Yes. Of course." Trözene motioned at one of the men who was stepping down from the wagons and waved him to open the second coach. "Lucas, may I present to you my wife . . . Ariadne."

From the second coach a woman emerged. She was possibly fifty years old—a fact that made Luke Wallace more than a little uneasy. Although her heavy layered black clothing and its tassels, bangles, and jewelry hid most of her shape, she wasn't portly at all. In fact she was nothing like his image of a Middle Eastern mother. Her face was narrow, her eyes shaped like rose leaves, and she had obviously once been stunning.

She made a little bow of greeting and murmured, "Mr. Wallace, I am an honored woman."

Her accent was so thick, the words were almost unintelligible.

The sunlight had favored her. Now that she was closer to them, the lines in her face and the texture of her skin showed more age than a moment ago. She took her place behind her husband without waiting for Wallace to return the greeting.

Wallace gave her a quick welcoming wave. "Glad to have you, ma'am. . . ."

Dimitrios's eyes glimmered. "We save the best for last. But for now, Lucas," he said, spreading his arms, "I give you Macedon!"

He clapped his hands sharply, and the men in fezzes jumped to life. They untied the half-dozen knots holding the tarp down on each wagon, and in a unison that might as well have been choreographed, they drew back the great brown covers with a collective *swoosh*.

With it came a gust of scents—spices, seawater, animal fur.

Sunlight rang across a symphony of bright surfaces—brass, leather, wood, fire-glaze, brushed fibers, tapestries, glittered in great pots of water and the eyes of live animals. On glazed urns and vases, the sun brought painted gazelles, sphinxes, soldiers, and winged horses to life. Mosaics shimmered. Goats and lambs stamped their protest in the wagon beds like a drumbeat. Antiquity bared itself to the view of the unschooled.

All the other coach doors opened. A dozen women stepped out onto the lawn, glorious women in black, red, and white, their layered aprons adazzle with embroidery of every color and dangling coins, jewelry whose intricate filigree resembled spiderwebs dipped in liquid gold. Their headpieces gleamed around faces stroked with the dark brows and full lips of some Byzantine painting. All the stuff that had caused a hush on the wharf at Newport News now caused the same hush here.

Nick felt Wallace stop breathing beside him. He had been communicating with Dimitrios over all these months, and still he hadn't been quite sure until this moment if Dimitrios clearly understood the situation. Nick had told him, on paper, what kind of man Wallace was, that he had raised a fortune out of nothing, that he had integrity, but that he lacked refinement. The refinement was what he wanted, for his greatest desire was the esteem of his financial and social peers.

He was the perfect clay for their molding, and Dimitrios had come prepared to give Wallace everything he wanted. It was a good bargain. His wealth and the fresh, raw nation, for their time, their blood, their background. Wallace had the abundant new money the Greek aristocracy had lost to the war with the Ottomans. The Trözenes had an ancient lineage that Lucas wanted to bring into his household.

"Ariadne," Dimitrios beckoned at his wife.

The woman bowed and went immediately to the first coach.

Dimitrios led Wallace toward the coach, and Nick followed not too far behind. He intended to gauge all the reactions very carefully.

Dimitrios waited as Ariadne's hand disappeared into the coach door. A grin tightened his lips within the black whiskers, and he also reached inside. "Lucas, I present to you my daughter... Iphigenia Varvaresos Trözene."

The name rolled like silk. A name it had taken Lucas two months to learn to pronounce.

The mother and father drew out two slim hands from inside, and out stepped a girl.

Nick Varvaresos forgot about Wallace and everything else. It had been three years since he'd seen her. Now he could only stare.

Iphigenia Trözene was the flower of antiquity. Her face was cupped by a gentle white kerchief. On her forehead was a filigree diadem that almost hid brows that were like black ink strokes. Her eyes were black and shaped like her mother's, her lips pink and full. Hers was a face barely out of childhood, but it had lost the childish puffiness. She wasn't the child Nick had left behind. She had poise. She had a Hellenic loveliness he would never again forget. She was all the *symmetria* of Grecian portraiture Nick had ever looked upon in his life—and he was relieved to see that she was.

One did not like to promise what one could not deliver.

Dimitrios held his daughter's hand as she curtseyed before

them. She made no move to speak or make her mark. She showed neither regret nor joy, only that she had a purpose to fulfill, and that she would fulfill it. She was duty bound.

Nick beamed openly, and he mused on what Lucas must have expected to see coming out of that coach. Did he think they would give him a fat girl with thin lips? Until now even Nick hadn't quite expected the little Venus who emerged from the coach.

The girl said nothing.

Nick looked at Wallace.

White again. Pale as dust, staring at the girl. He managed a choppy nod, but otherwise he simply stared at the girl, and she at the ground.

Taking a step, Nick began, "Lucas?"

Wallace blinked.

"Yes...," he uttered, his throat clogged. "Samson...where are you? See these women to their rooms... summon the field hands to unload these wagons... serve up the refreshments and... yes... fine... thank you..."

He backed away from the girl with an uncomfortable nod. "Glad to have you here...uh... miss." The girl didn't respond.

Immediately Ariadne Trözene took her daughter by the shoulders and steered her for the house. The other women, their strange Macedonian aprons rustling, fell into a line as if drilled, and filed in after them.

While Dimitrios Trözene watched the women troop inside, Wallace stole a moment to slip between the coaches. For a moment there was nothing around him but the coach and the horses of the next coach. Hiding there, he let out a great breath. His eyes closed. His face went numb.

He whispered, "What have I done..."

A rasping sound. The voice of a man who had acted upon desperation and now would have to ride it.

"Lucas?"

Wallace straightened as Nick approached his hiding place.

"Something's wrong?" Nick asked.

"No," he shot back. "No...no."

He gripped Nick's arm as he stepped past him, and with that touch begged him not to mention this. The whole county would be walking these grounds in only two little days. The invitations had been sent out over a month ago.

And there was nothing to be done about it.

"Lookit dem clothes! What kinda people is dey?"

Brown faces crowded out the windows of each cabin. In the cabin on the end, Yula poked her scrawny frame, now scrawny once again, over the windowsill and squinted hard. In her arms she held a tiny bundle against the open side of her shift.

"Git back to bed, girl!" Dinah snapped at her. "An' gimme dat baby." She tried to disconnect the shapely infant mouth from Yula's nipple while pushing the girl back into the room. "Ain't no use yawl gittin' in love wid dat baby. Yawl gon' do light work till he weaned, and dat gon' be dat."

Yula tightened her arms around her baby and actually snapped her teeth at Dinah's hand. The message was clear enough. Today the hand, tomorrow her head. She squirmed until Dinah no longer tried to take the newborn boy away. His tiny lips clamped to Yula's teacup breast as though to give Dinah the same message. Against her brown skin his soft black hair and creamy skin shone in the dim cabin.

"I wan' know who dem people be," Yula said. She set her shoulders in a way that told Dinah to keep back, to keep away from her baby.

Dinah shook her wide head. "Boss got comp'ny, dass all, you dumb niggawoman. Ain't you see dat?"

Yula moved again to the window.

She leaned against the frame and gazed out across the lawn, past the hogsheads and the smokehouses. Tiny figures moved on the landscape near the mansion house. Figures like none she'd ever seen before, carrying more luggage than made sense for visitors.

"Huh-uh. Ain't no company Boss got," she said slowly.

Dinah looked out the window, across the grounds to the activity that preoccupied the young girl, activity that had in fact gotten Yula up out of that bed faster than corn popping.

Yula's mind went up to the mansion, and she haunted it

like a ghost. She hugged the bundle in her arms and clung to the pulling sensation on her breast.

When she spoke again, she changed the future. She nodded in agreement with herself as the words wandered out.

"Boss got hissef a bride."

★

CHAPTER FIVE

---- ★ ----

House slaves served refreshments on the veranda. Dimitrios held his goblet of punch and watched while the Macedonian men and some of Wallace's black slaves carried trunks of clothing and personal possessions into the mansion. Astonishing, this house! These grounds! Wallace had built this estate in only ten years. To Dimitrios's Old World mind, so accustomed to wealth passed along generation to generation, constantly chipped away by time and trial, this estate around him was a dizzying feat of enterprise and initiative.

It proved he was right. He was completely right about this modern world of which Greece was a troubled mother.

Intimidating . . . but certainly it showed him what he must do. The task remained for him to drive home the last bolts of their project, to convince Wallace they had done the right thing, so he wouldn't change his mind.

Tragedy, if that happened.

Wallace was being so good about the token dowry that it was critical for Dimitrios to give him what he really wanted—recognition. A culture. Foundation. The real dowry was the adoption of Wallace into their culture, in letting him become the father of the New Greece.

Dimitrios had seen the simmering conflict between North and South in this new land and spied it as an opportunity. The United States was looking for cultural foundation, but they didn't yet know what they believed as a group. Dimitrios saw no reason that foundation shouldn't be a Greek one. The

Americans had no past. He could give them one. He could give them a culture that went back a thousand years.

Dimitrios looked down and across the driveway at Lucas Wallace, who in turn was watching the slow unloading of the wagons. Not a bad-looking man. A fairly robust figure, in fact, even standing beside the huge wagon. He wore good clothing. Still had his hair. Tall enough. Good shoulders. A bit pale, perhaps. At least he wasn't downright pug-ugly and Dimitrios didn't have to worry about having goblins for grandchildren.

He sipped his punch as his nephew Nick herded Wallace up the veranda steps toward the refreshment table. He thought of the things Nick had said in his letters about Americans, things that Dimitrios now saw were very true. Americans defied typification almost as though by design. There simply were no ten or two alike.

And that was why this situation remained unpredictable.

"Ah, Mr. Wallace," Dimitrios greeted. Crumbs caught in his beard. He brushed them away and handed Lucas one of the goblets from the table. "Soon we will be family."

Lucas only nodded and glanced at Nick. It was a quick glance; he couldn't look for long at the man who'd gotten him into this.

"You have a dazzling home," Dimitrios said.

"Oh, thank you . . . uh, *efkanisto poli.*"

Dimitrios laughed and nodded. "And I have yet to see the inside. Can it be as remarkable as the outside, I wonder?"

"Oh, it's fine," Lucas said, "fine. You'll have a look at my library. . . . I have many books. I have . . . I have *The Autobiography of Davy Crockett,* and I have *Eugene Aram* by Bulwer-Lytton, and I have Disrilly's new autobiographical—"

"Lucas," Dimitrios interrupted, "do you like my Iphigenia?"

"Pardon?" Lucas stammered.

"Do you like her? Do you think she's pretty?"

"Oh! Yes . . . yes, I like her. She's—"

Foreign.

"She's fine. Lovely." His voice echoed inside the goblet as he took a deep swallow. "Just fine."

Leaning his buttocks against the veranda rail, Nick shook

his head at this behavior. He clasped his hands tight on the rail to keep from throwing them in the air.

"Will you require a doctor's examination?" Dimitrios asked.

Lucas's eyes narrowed in question. "Pardon?"

The bearded man motioned toward the mansion's front door. "For Iphigenia."

"Uh . . . is she sick?"

Dimitrios chuckled. The sound rolled in his big chest. "No, not sick."

A flush blasted across Lucas's face.

Nick leaned toward him. "It's a formality. Simply decline."

"Uh . . ."

"Say no."

"No!"

Dimitrios raised his goblet. "Then let us drink to her." He handed a goblet to Nick with an insistent gesture. "To the Greek civilization that bred her. It will exist always. We shall see to that. To your bride, Lucas."

They drank—Dimitrios first, Lucas somehow last.

A sudden scream tore across the wide lawn. All three men choked and spun around. Like some wailing creature having the life squeezed out of it, the sound continued. Lucas and Nick went right over the veranda rail, with Dimitrios close behind down the steps.

It was Rowzee, at the back of one of the wagons. She clawed at her face, shrieking with every breath. Her eyes were saucers, fixed on the contents of the wagon in front of her. Several other slaves also cowered near her, the same looks in their faces.

Lucas and Nick ran toward them and looked into the wagon.

There, lying in twists of blankets, stone eyes gazed up at a sky. White shoulders and bared chests gleamed in the sun as though lit from within.

A man and a woman, life-sized, carved from marble.

Rowzee continued to let loose her shrill screams, gasping out of control. She was as close to heart failure as Lucas had ever seen anyone.

"Salt people!" she choked, writhing in horror. Spit foamed

at the corners of her mouth and dribbled onto her arms. "Dey gon' turn us salt! *Dey gon' turn us salt!*"

Those were the last coherent words before everything else turned to babble. She yammered irrational syllables until lather sprayed from her mouth, all the time twisting against the other terrified negroes.

Lucas grabbed her by the throat and shook her. "Woman, shut your mouth! Hear? Shut it! Get her out of here!"

Rowzee's panic was addictive and spread through the gathering crowd of slaves. They stared at the petrified naked bodies in the wagon. Caught by Rowzee's words, two other women started whimpering, clamping their knuckles to their mouths, and even some of the men shook like saplings at the sight. Stone people lying in state as a warning.

"Get out of here! All of you!" Wallace bellowed at them, swiping his hand before them to break their trance. He grabbed the nearest negro and shoved him away, then the next, and the next. "Go, damn you!"

The negroes climbed over each other to obey him—and to escape. The stampede left several of them trampled on the ground.

Lucas kicked them. "Get up! Get out of here!"

As the last crawled away and Rowzee's convulsive shrieking faded around the back of the mansion, Lucas was left standing there alone.

He looked up and saw Dimitrios.

"I'm so sorry," he gasped. "They're superstitious . . . ignorant. They never saw anything like this before."

Dimitrios pursed his lips and widened his eyes. "Have you?"

Color once again patterned Lucas's face. Dimitrios placidly covered the marble statues again, then motioned his own men to come and unload them.

"Perhaps this is a good time for me to freshen up," he said then. "These men will continue the work. If you will leave them to it," he added as he turned, "they will begin assembling my wedding gift to you."

Lucas could only nod and try to clear his head.

Nick glanced at him, his dark eyes ringed in shadows even

in the bright light of day. With a sermoning frown he followed his uncle into the house.

Luke Wallace was left there alone, the future staring him in the face.

Over the next two days, he saw little of Iphigenia Trözene.

However, he saw plenty of her father. Especially the very next morning.

When he awakened, he was stiff. Probably from having his muscles tense as rocks all yesterday. He ached like an old man.

"Buckie!" he called. His head pounded.

Half a second was all that passed before his valet Buckie ducked in the door of the master suite, his shoulders hunched and his face gray. He immediately doubled back and peeked through the keyhole into the hallway.

"Fetch my robe. What's the matter with you?" Lucas demanded. "Why you squirreling about?"

"Boss, kin I go work in the yard agin?" Buckie asked.

"Why?"

"Dem peoples, dey doin' odd about dis house. Dey bin up sneakin' 'bout de front lawn since befo' dawn. Sneakin' wit torches and lamps, lookin' jes like spooks in dem black duds. An' de things dey was carryin' . . . Lawd save us." He shook his head and ducked to look under the bed for Boss's shoes.

"What are they doing on the front lawn?" Lucas complained. "I didn't arrange anything for out there . . . did I?"

"Not dat I heard, Boss. I done took a peek out, but I ain't gon' look no mo'. I don' never want see dat sight agin."

"What sight?" Lucas pulled the belt of his night robe tight around his churning stomach and stepped out into the hallway. The front lawn?

He had to steady himself to keep from falling down the curved stairway. After a few steps he resigned himself to hanging onto the handrail till his legs decided they were awake too. Dawn . . . it wasn't much later than that even now. What was happening to his home?

With an effort he heaved the great front door open and walked out into the crisp morning air—

To find his front lawn utterly transformed.

Morning mist and dew burned in the first rays of sunlight before him. He moved outward and down from the veranda, not even aware of the steps he was taking. In a moment he was on the driveway. Now on the lawn itself, his mouth gaping.

"Ah! Lucas."

Emerging from the white mist, Dimitrios spread his arms like a dark Santa Claus and strode toward his soon-to-be son.

"Come! See my gift to you." He grasped Lucas by the shoulders and kissed both cheeks. "I bring you Mount Olympus!"

What had yesterday been only a disk of plain green lawn wreathed by the circular driveway was now a place of myth. Where yesterday there had been only space, now there was an entire Greek garden. Dwarf orange trees stood basking in the morning light, planted in carefully shaped mounds. The huge glazed amphorae and caldrons, which yesterday had held spices, rice, and dried vegetables, today served as decoration and color. The big caldrons with their complex designs and drawings were here now, still full of green water. Three stone tables with stone benches provided places to sit. But those were only the frills.

The true eye catcher was neither topiary nor amphorae— but the presence of Mount Olympus's very royalty and the animals that guarded them. Statues. A dozen of them.

All around, frozen in casual gestures, elegant in their repose, with a classical calm on every face, stood the gods themselves.

"This is the Greek pantheon," Dimitrios said, almost a whisper. "Let me introduce you."

Morning mist writhed lazily, caressing the figures of men and women on pedestals, in heroic nudity, or clothed only in carved garments so thin they were nearly transparent. The swirled drapery was the true provocateur of the feminine body beneath. Sculpted hips, breasts, and calves showed through the carved fabric like melons under wet silk. Most of the males were nude, and explicit.

Dimitrios pointed past the garden, to two animal figures that crouched on blocks of stone at the entrance to the estate. "Those are the Naxian lions. Pure limestone. Now you have lions to guard your place."

Lucas squinted in the misty dawn light. Yes, those looked something like lions, all right. Anyone driving into the plantation would pass between those lions.

"Look here." Dimitrios drew him to a statue of a large-muscled man cast in bronze. His green gold body was stippled with patina as he sat on some undefined rock, one massive thigh hiding his genitalia. His hair and beard were green metallic curls, his brow creased, and one arm was coiled up near his ear. He gazed off at nothing with eyes so real that Lucas actually shuddered.

"Poseidon," Dimitrios said. "God of the great sea. Where his hand is, he once held his trident. See how his eyes are limestone with amber pupils? And his nipples are inlaid with copper." He held up one finger and wagged it. "Very authentic."

Lucas stared up into the bigger-than-life face and wondered what it was like to be a god of the sea.

"Look at this one," Dimitrios continued, pulling him along. "A warrior from the Temple of Aphaea, 500 B.C. Well, a copy of him, at least. I commissioned most of these for you. Pretty good, eh? Take a look."

"My God, look at them!" Lucas whispered. "Why, they could step down and walk away!"

Cold morning air made him shiver as he empathized with the statues' nakedness.

Dimitrios hesitated a moment and simply watched Lucas.

To a plantation owner who came out of the pilot boat docks, these statues were only beginning to dawn. But to Dimitrios, whose culture had clung for a while only to the threads of its own past, they were blood and sinew. Dimitrios knew the significance of this pageant of life. He knew the statues' history. He was aware of their age. He knew how amazing it was for men with only chisels to capture the imperishable beauty of the body. It had taken Greeks to do it, to give life and balance to sculpture.

"This is the Greek garden, my son," Dimitrios said. "My

gift to you. Now, Lucas . . . you are one of us. You are the new Greek among us. The Greek of Virginia.''

"I bin tellin' you he hexified. Yawl don' never listen. Ever sin' dat crazy Christmas I bin sayin' it an' sayin' it an' jes sayin' it.''

Moses stuck a cob pipe into his mouth as though to cork it before he said more than he wanted to. He sat on a big log, the cookfire making patterns on his face. Around him other slaves milled in the late-evening darkness. Most of the heads of the households were here, and several of the women, most of those quietly mending something. There were some faces he missed, a few who had been transferred up to work in the big house, and lately he had come to fear for their well-being.

The only movement among the slaves who sat around the fire was a monotonous rocking of the bony girl across from him, her two knobby knees poking up inside her skirt and going back and forth, back and forth.

Yula cradled her baby with her thighs, because her hands were busy sewing. The open night was warm around her. This was her child's first day and first night in the world, and she was determined he should feel the large night around him. The community decided right after Boss left that the child should be brought out only at night, where few could see his peach gold skin and soft hair. By bringing him out on the very first night, Yula was establishing that she would set at least part of the pace, that she would not be intimidated, even if everybody including the baby was bigger around than she was.

Any other night like this, the bondspeople would be enjoying the pleasant weather and the restful feeling of having had an unexpected day off. All work had been suspended—quite unusual for the month of May. This was transplanting time, when the young tobacco stalks were being pulled out of the mold beds and planted in furrowed fields. The rains had come, and that was the work to be done.

Today the work had been stopped at noon. *Noon.*

It would have otherwise been an evening for dancing the

Buck 'n' Wing, cooking up puddings, putting extra time into tending their own gardens, but today the slaves paced in an uneasy hush. Conversation had come in gusts, bracketed by fits of silence.

"Yawl see dem pots?" Jonah asked. "What painted on dem?"

Moses shook his head. "I never seen no critters like dem befo'. Never seen no hoss wid wings, no cougar wid snake tail. Is dey waitin' in de woods? Lawsy, dis worl' so big . . . too big fo' Moses . . . too big fo' dis ol' boy. I never leave dis farm if'n dem critters be waitin' me out."

"What 'bout dem salt people!" Dinah demanded. "Yawl seen how dey struck down Rowzee, din yawl? Jes like de preacher say. Next time dey turn her to piller salt jes like in de Bible, and gon' do de same to us." She paced around the fire, her thick hands wringing. "Jesus done made me a field nigger, and I so glad . . . my heart so glad f'dat . . . I don' gotta go in dat front hall, look on dem salt people and git turn to salt too. . . ."

"Shet up," Moses snapped when Dinah's voice took on a whine. "We gots to decide what we gon' do 'bout dis. Dem butterskins done come in de house, done took root and put up dem salt people so's we keep away. Done took Boss mind. Took it right over. What we gon' do about it?"

"Gotta take him to de preacher someway," Jonah said as he sat on the ground beside Moses' log. "Take him and git it blessed out of him."

A murmur of approval moved across the tense gathering. Some of the men began pacing too, crossing past each other, or poking absently at the fire as though to make it burn better. Anything to diminish the oppressive conclusions.

"One of us gots to go to that mansion house. Ask Boss if he okay," Jonah suggested. He looked to Alroy, Jeff, and Moses first, to see if they approved.

"I scared t'go up dere," Alroy said, looking downward at the burning logs. Then he abruptly looked up again and sought the big body of Jeff leaning against the nearest cabin. "Yawl de biggest, Jeff. You bin up to de house. What you think?"

A long blade of grass wobbled between Jeff's lips as he

paced toward them into the firelight. "I don't rightly know," he said. " 'Pears like the butterskins done took over, I hand you that. Can't say why, though."

"What Samson say, den?"

"You know we don't talk to them house slaves, and they don't hardly talk to us," Jeff said. "All I know is Mr. Nick been living at the house. Sometimes him an' Boss goes into the office and shuts the door. We hear'm talking, but nobody sure what they say. Then Mr. Nick go 'way for a couple days. Maybe he come back, maybe he don't come back for a while. When he come back, them two go back in the office and talk some more."

"He hexifyin' Boss," Moses said, pounding his hickory stick into the dirt.

"Evil eye," Dinah agreed.

"Puttin' hoo-doo on him," Moses went on. "Makin' him witched so's he let dem butterskins come an' hide in his house. I sees him walkin' jes like a spook. Window to window, jes walkin' back'n fo'."

Alroy shook visibly and jolted to his feet. "You dumb dawky, you ain't see nothin' like dat!"

"I did," the old man said.

"You ain't never up to dat house! Quit makin' up thangs."

"Yawl don' know where I be all de time."

Alroy spun on a heel and stalked around to the other side of the cookfire.

Yula looked up from the glowing salmon-colored satin she was embroidering. She said nothing but let the knowing strike of her eyes work on Dinah.

Finally it was Dinah who blurted, "Yula say Boss git a wife!"

Beside Moses a field-worker named Claude changed the position of his legs and blurted, "Aw, what do dat girl know?"

"Maybe she do know!"

"Dat girl don' never talk," Alroy said. "Why she talk now?"

Yula's own voice was small in the night. "Maybe got somethin' to say."

Dinah strode toward her, swinging her body ominously,

large hands digging into her hips. "He right. You don't hardly talk till now. How come?"

" 'Cuz I knows," Yula said. "I knows a bride when I sees one."

Closing the already-tight distance between them, Dinah made a grab for the baby cradled between Yula's legs. "Gimme dat chile, anyway. Yawl ain't gon' git to—"

She yowled and pulled back her hand, complete with the needle Yula had stuck in it. With a yank on the thread, Yula got the needle back before her sash ended up on the ground. She collected it and the baby into her twig-thick arms and glared at Dinah.

Dinah stared at the drop of blood forming on her knuckle. "Strike me dead, she done picked me!"

Moses took the pipe out of his mouth. "You oughta be picked, woman, pullin' on dat chile." He peered across the fire at the bundle on Yula's lap. His face took on a quizzical expression. "What you call dat baby, girl?"

Yula looked down and trailed one thin finger around the gurgling infant's face. He was looking back up at her, enthralled by the firelight on her face, and when she spoke, his dark eyes sought the sound.

"He my lil marshmallow," Yula said. Since his birth only hours ago, she hadn't let anyone else tend him, afraid someone might have secret orders to spirit him away from her because of Boss's order. Her mandate included even the elderly women whose job it was to take care of the toddlers. No one would tend her marshmallow. She looked down into his coally eyes, and he looked back at the firelight playing on her face.

"Dat ain't no name," Jonah complained, striking at the fire with his toe, his mind on other matters.

Yula looked up. "Ain't gonna be me names him."

"Dass right," Dinah snapped. "You jes keep thinkin' dat. Be easier fo' you when de time come."

"Maybe de time come fo' all of us," Moses said "if'n we don' change thangs . . . thangs gon' be diff'nt. Real diff'nt."

The mood fell again, until only the cooing and gurgling of Yula's baby and the fire's crackling was heard against the night. They wanted to save their life-style. Each glanced at the others, trying to apply their hamstrung logic to an outside world that was little more than vapor. Theirs was the collective experience of children, but they were in fact adults and not really children at all. They were orphans, a gaggle of unenlightened minds trying to perceive the world with their bread-and-butter application. To them anything beyond the next few plantations was a sealed book. Where had these strange new invaders come from? Which county?

Yula watched the fear play in the minds of the other negroes. In her short life she had been more places than anyone here. Most of these people had spent the past eight or more years on Plentiful, and before that on a nearby plantation from which Boss had bought them. None of these had stood at auction as she had, at least not since they were too small to remember.

"I seen thangs," she told them quietly, drawing her voice lower and lower in the night, pulling their curiosity. "I been in de big world. Done worked at cotton fields, done been on auction block, done been on a real boat, done been all de way south. Seen thangs, did thangs yawl ain't never see. Dey *is* snaketail cougar in de woods, ten time bigger den Jeff. Dey *do* be folk what can turn you salt, can work other folks' heads, make 'em do thangs. Paint picture dat look at you and follow you wid its eyes, den carry tale 'bout you when you gone. Dey be critters can tell de boss if you whip too hard, or if you sleep when you spose be workin'. Such thangs in de big world yawl ain't never believe." She paused a moment, and looked one by one at each face around her. "I knows," she added, nearly whispering, "and I seen."

She made one little nod and didn't blink.

Silence crawled like the critters she warned about. Eyes ringed with white stared back at her, and shivers rolled down every spine.

The pacing resumed, and those who moved were like disturbed wraiths walking the night, restless and uncomforted, cursed.

Yula watched them, measuring her success. She knew that this plantation would have to get a lot worse before it was bad. She'd been to bad, and this wasn't it. She would say what she had to say to keep her baby in this not-bad cradle.

As Alroy paced behind her and several others shifted uneasily nearby, hunching their shoulders against the unknowns lurking just out of the firelight, Yula watched the fuse she'd lit start to burn.

"Maybe Mist' McCrocklin know what to do," Jonah finally suggested.

"He gone to town," Claude said.

Alroy whirled around. "Maybe we all oughtta run off!"

Moses twisted his old body and craned up at him. "What good dat do?" he bellowed.

"When de other white folk find out, dey take care of it. Dey come an' fix it."

The sound logic moved through them. They had always let the white folk do the worrying. When to sow, when to break, when to lay in the furrows, when and how much to top the stalks, when to cut and cure. When to build, when to tear down.

"Maybe de white folk take care of it," Jonah agreed. "Maybe we go to Oaks."

"Massa Van Meer, he know what to do," Claude added.

With a nod Alroy plotted the idea. "Can go right through the field and cut pas' de house and out."

Dinah shook her finger at him. "We tries to leave, dem salt people gon' see us an' tell on us!"

"Then we go through the woods," Jeff suggested.

Moses leaned forward, then waited until he had everyone's attention. He had a way of doing that, of looking as though he were about to make some documentable prophecy, and his timing was always right. The slaves looked to Jeff for strength and worldliness, but to Moses for decisions.

Sure enough, they were all looking at him by the time he spoke.

"Which of yawl," he pointed out, "gon' go through dem woods?"

They stared back at him, suddenly blank.

Beasts moved in the night.

Yula's baby squirmed then and let out a thready complaint. She put down her sewing and watched in fascination as his tiny lower lip squared off and actually made a little *w* so that he could say "wehhh . . . wehhh."

She gathered her fists against her chest for a moment and simply enjoyed looking at him while he made his little complaint.

Dinah stomped the ground. "Pick him up, girl! Yawl so dumb, cain't even tend dat chile!"

"Shet up!" Moses smacked his stick into the fire. Yellow flame licked the hickory, and red embers sprayed all over. "Fo'get dat chile! We gots to decide! Gots to git our Boss back! If'n Boss go over de broom wid a butterskin, ain't nothin' we can do. Gots to do somethin' befo'."

"Dat mean now," Claude said.

Moses got that prophetic posture again, slowly looking at each of them in turn.

"So how we gon' do it?"

"We goes in," Claude told him, "make a dist'action. Flush dem butterskins out the house. Jeff go in a diff'nt door, go to Boss bedroom, carry him out."

Jeff shook his head. "I ain't."

"You gots to. Boss ain't big as you."

"Lawsy," Moses said, "dem farm chunks ain't big as Jeff."

Dinah interrupted. "We gots to get de spell off Boss someways. Like de preacher tole us. In de Bible. We gots to spread lamb's blood on him so de hoo-doo pass him by."

"Ain't got no lambs dis year," Moses said.

"Got sheeps. We kin use sheep blood. Same thang, ain't it? Moses, you can do it."

The old man rolled back on his log and screeched, "Me? Why I gotta do it?"

"Boss trust you best, dat's why! You can git close to him."

Moses glared at her, shifted, then scowled openly. "Well, dat's true. It ugly, but it true."

Jeff hung his head and hunched his big shoulders. "This the craziest thing I ever heard tell of."

Dinah wiped her sweaty hands on her apron. "Plennifu' our home. We gots to perteck it."

Another fit of silence came in, but this silence was far from empty.

Finally Jeff got to his feet. He towered over them against the yellow flames. With one swoop of his great body, he picked up one of the smoldering split rails by its cool end and stood straight again. The log and its thread of gray smoke was an extension of his arm, and he was suddenly one of those mythical beasts prowling the night.

"Proteck," he said, gazing at his weapon. Responsibility and regret nested in his face. "If we gon' do it, yawl ought at least say it right."

★

CHAPTER SIX

———— ★ ————

Torches bobbed against the darkness, coils of rolling blue heat with yellow tongues. No one spoke.

They carried Alroy's blacksmithing irons and hammers, some of Jonah's brick-making tools, a few hunting knives, split rails, sewing shears, and good hard apples. In the darkness their black faces and hands disappeared, and they looked like a closetful of empty work clothes out for a walk. Clinging to their small torches and their weapons, they made their way toward the mansion, each trying not to be the one in front.

None was entirely convinced this was the way, but to their simple mentalities there seemed no other. They had known only control all their lives, dependent upon others to decide for them. Forever they had trod the fine bridge between the told and the telling. Beyond the routine of sowing and hoeing, cutting and curing, then starting all over again, they had no experience in a maze of imponderables. Yula's "big world" had never been theirs to grapple, until this night.

They had gathered the other men and whichever of the women wanted to help, and tonight they were going where they did not belong. Fresh in their minds were Jeff's warning words about how to tell one of these butterskins from a real white. Couldn't have anybody accidentally hacking Boss in half, after all.

Other than one whimper from Dinah, no one uttered a thought about turning back.

In the reluctant lead Jeff carried a torch and a coil of rope. Beside him Moses hobbled with a bladder of blood and the knife he would use to cut it. He struggled over dark ground without benefit of his hickory stick, thus obliging the cluster to move at his pace and no faster.

The torches provided poor light, poorer than lanterns would have, and this was a clouded night, dark as the inside of a coffin. Both Jeff and Moses felt the gaggle of doubts moving behind them, just as they felt their own. No one felt particularly brave. This was an enterprise more desperate than daring.

Undulating through the tobacco fields toward the mansion, the slaves tried to anticipate what it would be like to grapple an immeasurable enemy. Did the butterskins know how to fight? Or would they conjure and let the haints do their fighting for them? The negroes could tolerate blows, but haints were something quite else. Worse than blows was this empty anticipation, this not knowing what lay in the next half minute or the one after that.

They came out of the fields and moved to the edge of the lawn. Jeff's voice rumbled in the night. "Smother them torches out."

Fires guttered under wet rags.

The mansion house was a portend before them. Big, dark, a fortress. They moved toward it.

Without signal or word Jeff split off and went around to the left wing, to the climbing ivy that would provide a way up toward the master bedroom. Once up on the house, he would have to use his rope somehow to go the rest of the way.

This was their last chance to turn back. They were committed.

Moses hobbled to the veranda, the others pressing close against him. From where they huddled against the house, they could see the rim of the garden and one of the salt people, looking blue in the darkness.

"Well, we here," Moses muttered. "Who gon' go first?"

Everybody got a little shorter and a little rounder and very interested in the ground.

Dinah spoke up then, shuddering down her fears.

"I knows de steps. I go first."

In an act of unrenounced chivalry, they let her.

All might have gone well, all might have worked out—

Had Dinah not rounded the corner and run smack into a wall of drying octopuses, hanging from a clothesline.

When the wet tentacles hit her face, she hit a treble that peeled skin. She clawed at her face, tangling in the line, wormy dead things wrapping around her head as she tried to rend herself away. Pulling backward, she piled bloody murder into the other slaves, and the line snapped. Octopuses fell everywhere, a dozen of them dumping onto the heads of those unfortunate enough to be right behind Dinah.

Apples, hammers, and irons rained to the ground, forgotten. The negroes tumbled over each other, snagged in the clothesline.

Moses staggered back a few paces, kept his head clear, and rasped, "Get on, yawl!"

Healthy young men plowed past him, stumbling over the panicked heap in front of them.

The mansion burst into bedlam. Screams and shouts came from upstairs as the slaves plunged in, drumming their torch sticks and apples and irons on the walls and furniture. Hollers rang like war whoops, and that's exactly what they sounded like to the Greeks.

Greeks . . . who had just come out of a war.

The halls filled with people in night robes, tripping over each other in the dark, slaves going up the stairs crashing against Greeks going down.

Only when gunshots blasted through the house did the tide turn.

Upstairs the master bedroom door banged open. Greek women piled out, shrieking, and right behind them came the world's biggest negro. His eyes were ringed with white, his face demonic. How come Boss wasn't in that room, and how come these butterwomen were?

He stomped down the corridor. Rooms popped open around him, spilling people. Somewhere among them there had to be Boss.

Wraiths stumbled this way and that on the curved stairway. The great front door crashed open when one of the slaves ran into a pedestal topped by a statue and, fearing herself attacked by a salt person, went plunging through the nearest doorway—the front.

Once that door was open, providing a view of the Greek garden, the slaves went wild with terror. Greek women were flapping down the stairs in white nightdresses, looked like haints to the slaves who scampered among them.

The Greek men shouted and waved pistols, then fired into the air—CRACK-*BOOM*—CRACK—CRACK—

Now Jeff fled through the front door onto the veranda, lumbering under the weight of Boss, who was slung over one big shoulder, bellowing, "What is this! Jeff! Put me the blazes down!"

"That's okay, Boss," Jeff gasped, "I take care of you. Yawl just take this little ride—"

"Bedamned! Put me on the ground. On the *ground*!"

While he struggled, discharging guns pounded the night as though Plentiful were under siege. He tried to break the iron band of Jeff's arm around his legs and finally succeeded. He slid across the massive chest, landed upright, stumbled backward, and waved his arms. Slaves ran past him, screaming. Greek men rushed this way and that, waving pistols.

"What *is* this? Stop all this! For God's sake, hold your fire! These people are gonna take us for uncivilized!" Wallace cried over the shouts. "McCrocklin! Where are you!"

"Mr. McCrocklin gone to town, Boss," Jeff told him. "It his night off."

"By Christ, have you all got rabies?"

The slaves had never been violent in their lives. They hadn't been soldiers, or even brawlers. Most were timid about actually landing blows, and this gave the Greeks an advantage.

Wallace waved his hands, trying to draw attention to himself. He succeeded—Moses' attention.

The old black man hobbled forward toward Boss, holding his hands high. His right arm was covered with blood from the leaky sheep's bladder dangling from his hand. In the other hand a big knife reflected the torchlight.

Wallace saw him first and scolded, "Moses! You know better than this!"

In the corner of his eye, he caught a flash of motion—it

drew his attention. At the last second he shouted, "No, Nick!"

Night over Plentiful erupted with a rifle's big sound. *Boom*. Panicking people dropped to the ground and hid their heads.

Wallace fell backward as a body struck him. He hit the ground. The smell of blood filled his nostrils. The gunshot echoed in the hills.

Everything stopped. Sixty paces back Nick Varvaresos stood, holding his smoking rifle.

Wallace squeezed out from under the moist, smelly weight of Moses. Around him his negroes hugged each other and sobbed. Over there the Greeks were huddling, staring. The bladder, broken open now, spilled blood into the grass. It mingled with blood from Moses' chest. The old negro's eyes blinked once, twice, then froze open.

As everyone watched, the life fled out of Moses.

The slaves stumbled back to the cabins, shrouded by defeat, still not able to understand.

At the mansion Wallace stood to one side as Jeff and Jonah wrapped Moses' body in a sheet. The negroes were unwilling to let any Greeks touch the body.

There was no getting away from the blood. Sheep's blood and a man's blood were enough to soak everything. The ground, Moses' clothing, the sheet. Jeff and Jonah would take him away in the night. He would be washed clean and laid out on a plank while the others built him a casket.

Greek men and women stood in a guilty silence, not quite sure how this had come about or what it meant—or if it would even be safe to leave Dimitrios's daughter here.

Wallace spoke to none of them but stood with his face grim and stiff.

Dimitrios herded his family and servants back into the house. Their foreign mutterings were a steady grind on Wallace's bones. Even when the corpse was taken away and the lawn was empty, he remained out there.

He stayed until the crickets chirped again. The fit of melancholy gave him no quarter, no reason to move.

Even upon hearing a footfall behind him, he still did not turn.

"Lucas?"

Nick came into his periphery. Came, and stood there, and waited a moment.

"Lucas, I'm sorry," he said. He held his hands out in a limp gesture. "He had a knife."

"I know what he had," Wallace bit back.

Nick moved a step closer. His dark eyes carried their own shadows, needing no help from the night. "I misunderstood. You know what I mean, what I'm talking about. . . . I thought it was a slave uprising. A revolt. I've heard . . . stories."

"Yes, that's the trouble with this world," Wallace told him tonelessly. "Too many stories."

He faced Nick with a provocative final glare. His eyes were desolate.

"And too many people ready to believe what they hear."

He turned on his stockinged feet, soaked both with Moses' guts and with the blood of the sheep that was meant to protect him from the devil in his house.

★

CHAPTER SEVEN

————— ★ —————

It was the second day since the arrival of the Greeks. The grisly results of the slaves' night out had to be swiftly set aside at the mansion house. Preparations were overcast by knowledge of the activity down in the yard, in that small separate world of the darkies. At eventide the dinner bell from the cabins tolled slowly. *Dong... dong... dong... dong.* And on and on. Its hollow song was relentless.

dong... dong... dong... dong...

Ten. Twenty. And on and on. Fifty.

Seventy-two times. An unthinkable age for a man to live when most men died at sixty.

Seventy-two times for the life of Moses.

dong... dong...

No one, in the yard or at the mansion, would ever quite forget the bell of this day.

Moses was laid out with silver coins on his eyes. His eyes had forced themselves open four times, and it took two nickels each to keep them closed. While the cotton-padded casket was being made, the slaves walked by the corpse on its pine plank. The men wore black voile bands on their arms. The women wore little veils and would wear them for two months or more. All the children wore white. They sang mournful songs about promised lands, lyrics just as confused as the superstitions that had led to this.

His next-door neighbors dug the grave, a task reserved for the closest friends. All were quite affected when, in spite of the bedlamizing of Plentiful and all he had to think about, Boss had found a half hour to go down to the cabins and stand for Moses' burial.

Then it was all over. Except for the hickory stick leaning unused against Moses' cabin door, the whole incident might never have happened.

Attention at Plentiful turned quite abruptly to something else—celebration beneath this unerasable pall. The slaves were left alone in the yard, not invited to be part of what was happening at the main house, for their work was being done by others. After what had happened, this insult sat on them and sizzled. No one, though, was willing to go up and complain, and thus the two communities of Plentiful were divided.

As dawn glowed in the western foothills on the third day, the Greek garden was once again at peace. No one was here. Any daybreak activity was going on inside the mansion, if at all. Here, there was only the pink glow of early morning on one horizon, the smoky darkness fading on the other, and the early sunshine come to lay upon shoulders of stone.

On the other side of the circular driveway, wildflowers and uncut grass curtained a drainage ditch that led all the way back to a field in which tall seedlings of orinoko were now growing in their mold beds. Some of the Greek statues looked in that direction, formed in a circle as they were, any incongruity forgiven by the serenity of their stone faces.

Suddenly, in the grass, one skinny dark arm stretched forward, fingers wiggling. The grass rippled, and the ripples moved closer to the edge of the driveway as Yula crawled closer to the house. Stealthily she made her way to the Greek garden, between the caldrons and the big vases, skulking along the ground until she reached the statue of the lady with the hunting bow, which was nearest to the driveway. Yula's red turban appeared between the statue's folds, and a little black face came up with it.

Standing up slowly, Yula kept her spine bent over just in case she had to run away on short notice. She crept around the pedestal, then straightened enough to look at the salt woman's bare leg.

Cautious to the last, she peered across the garden to the veranda, but there were no signs of life yet. Tables were set up everywhere, including a very long buffet trestle on the grass overlooked by the veranda. That was the croquet lawn, but today it was decorated with a rose-covered trellis and dozens upon dozens of small metal and wooden chairs, all painted white.

But there were no people yet, no one to question her presence here or her intentions.

She turned back to the salt lady and raised herself up on her toes. Leaning inward, she pressed her tongue against the lady's foot.

Settling back, she glared upward at the woman's yellowed face.

"Ain't no salt," she muttered.

Her long skinny hand went up and she drew her finger down the leg. Her eyes narrowed slightly. Didn't feel like salt anymore than it tasted like salt. Felt like rock. Rock from the bottom of a running stream. She'd held those rocks before and had never been bit.

Rock and nothing but.

It wasn't flesh turned to salt. It was rock. No rock could hurt her. Only the living could hurt her. She was reasonably sure they hadn't turned themselves into rock, so someone else must have done it. If they got turned into rock, they were probably bad people and deserved it. Now they had to do their penance by standing here for all to see. If they were bad people, Yula was glad they were rock. As long as they couldn't turn themselves back, she wouldn't fret over them.

Certain of her logic, she scooted back across the driveway and disappeared for a moment in the tall grass. When she reappeared, she held her tiny son, wrapped in a fresh sheet of cotton. Until now she hadn't been willing to expose the infant to the rock people. Now there was no more crawling. She strode in confidence between the rock people, never giving them another glance.

★

"He's incompetent white trash in every other matter, but he gets good results from the bondsmen. I don't approve of the cruelty, and so I'm at an impasse. While I hesitate to dismiss him, neither can I watch him all the time. I charge my slaves to report his cruelties to me, but he punishes them for reporting, so what's to be done?"

"You leave him alone, Howard, that's what," John Van Meer instructed, leaning back in the open buggy. "A good overseer is too valuable to question. Keep your nose out of his business, and yours will profit."

With Tabby at his side, Howard Tuggle couldn't very well give Van Meer his true opinion. Tabby remained silent but gazed at him rather soulfully and hoped the two gentlemen would avoid such conversation during the afternoon's festivities. A wedding didn't come along every day, and certainly not one the whole county was invited to.

"Don't be so lofty, John," Tuggle said. "I don't run a plantation. I run a processing factory. Unlike you, I have to deal with my bondsmen on a more personal basis." The buggy jostled beneath them as the wheel hit a hole in the road, as though to discourage their argument from getting out of hand, as it usually did. The negro driver looked back and muttered an apology. Tuggle waved at him to just keep going. "I begin to think slavery doesn't fit the factory as well as it does the farm," he said with a sigh.

"You'll find it fits your pocketbook if you ever decide to take on white workers instead," Van Meer told him. "Like those Irishmen, Germans, and Dutchmen they hired up at the . . . where was it? Midlothian?"

"Yes," Tuggle said. "And Tredegar Ironworks right there in Richmond, practically next door. I've been hearing about these immigrants. Our nation will find itself burdened to feed so many, I'm afraid."

"As long as they don't work for free," Van Meer said, "they'll never take the place of chattel slavery. Virginia is still the largest producer of tobacco in the world, and tobacco cannot be raised on a northern rail yard, no matter how cheap the labor. Stand your ground, Howard. Men like you start going to white laborers, what kind of a message will that be to send north? Think of your roots when you talk like this.''

Tuggle grunted, dissatisfied. "You hardly care about my roots as long as I keep processing your yield."

"You listen to me," Van Meer said, tipping his big body forward. "Slavery was abolished in France in 1794. And now the British have done it throughout their empire. It bodes an ill fashion for us."

Tuggle shook his head. "I thought you were the one who wanted to follow an English example, John."

"I never said that. You weren't listening then, either. Did you know that in Boston there's now something called the Anti-Slavery Society of New England? How long do you think we can stay the tide without consolidating and making it known that we will not allow this wave to overtake the South? How long?"

"You're obsessive," Tuggle told him. "You planters think you're the whole South. You tobacco growers are near bad as the cotton people. Where would you be without my mill to process your yield?"

"Same as you'd be without my yield. Caulking a hull in some shipyard, next to a negro hireling, like Lucas used to."

Tuggle leaned forward. "Maybe, but mind this. For every plug and smoke leaf you grow, there better be a slave sitting in a factory ready to press it, and a tobacconist like me who's willing to ford the investment *and* the risk. You growers! You're isolated from the epidemics and the machinery trouble that hits a factory. That cholera wave is on its way here from Richmond; I can just smell it coming."

Van Meer screwed up his brows. "How bad is it now?"

"It's a nightmare. Of the fifty tobaccories up there, twenty are trying to wheedle out of their hiring contracts and move their slaves to smaller cities. Several have contacted me to buy them out."

"And bring their cholera to Norfolk? Don't you do it!"

"I'm not going to. But I've got forty-six negroes and twelve skilled whites living in filthy shanties behind the press building, tight as mice. Industrial slaves can't just go sit under a tree until the epidemic fades. You remember my friend Albright, who runs a sugar refinery?"

"I remember I didn't like him."

"He lost four cane cutters and two boiling-house hands in one week alone."

"Proves my point," Van Meer said, wagging a finger. "We planters should process our own yield right on the grounds of our own plantations. Some do it already. A plantation should be a contained enterprise, divorceable from the world if necessary."

"You go try it then."

"Maybe I will."

"Maybe you should."

"Mr. Tuggle," Tabby warned.

Tuggle glanced at her and leaned back. "Isolation is easy talk for you, John," he sighed. "Your slaves breathe fresh air. You can resell them. I tried to lease some of mine to a saltworks last month, and they turned me down flat. Try selling a poisoned slave. Have you ever tried reselling a drudge who's been breathing the effluvia in a tobacco factory half his life?"

"No, and I never will. I'm a planter."

"You're a snob."

"Mr. Tuggle!" Tabby admonished, spanking his wrist with her tone of voice. "This is a wedding day. We do not discuss business at other folks' weddings."

Tuggle bottled a response to Van Meer's last comment. "Yes, dear," he sighed, but both men continued the conversation in their minds.

The buggy fell into an uncomfortable silence for the last few yards before turning into Plentiful's driveway. The sight that greeted them there was enough to clear their heads of their own troubles.

Tuggle gasped, "Saints in Heaven!"

Tabby pressed her gloved hand against her mouth. Van Meer twisted around in the seat for a good long look. Almost as he did so, a sudden breeze around the tall hedges brought with it a blast of aromas so spicy that Van Meer almost sneezed. Hot scents, those of exotic food, very strong and unfamiliar. With the smells came music—a thumping Mediterranean beat from hand-struck drums, winding clarinet melody, and the mandolin's jangle.

On the front lawn of Plentiful, Southern women in immense pastel ball gowns turned like dogwood petals on a green river. They clung to the arms of gentlemen in ascots and tails. Over two hundred guests from all over Tidewater were milling between pedestals on which stood towering statues of stone and metal. They gazed hesitantly into the sightless marble eyes and at bodies of Lysippan proportion, bodies that were naked or might as well be, and they whispered among themselves. Their murmur was almost a constant hum behind the music.

There were Greek men where ordinarily there would be black slaves, serving resinated white wine and canapés. Greek men in strange, stiff white skirts cut well above the knee, and shirts with massive white pleated sleeves. On their heads were mulberry fezzes with black tassels, and they wore black vests with too much gold embroidery.

But those *skirts* . . . some kind of linen kilt. The men looked like proud flowers on white stalks, for their leggings also were white with black garters, and on their feet were black shoes with big yarn balls. They might have looked silly except for the curved, gleaming scimitars bobbing against their thighs.

When the Tuggles and Van Meer stumbled out of their buggy, confused by the spellbinding Greek music and the sights around them, they were immediately offered shallow glass goblets of water with a spoonful of mastic jam floating in each one and were given a thimbleful of something the servants called *raki* to throw on top.

There was a decided difference about this wedding. An undertone. Women spoke in subdued voices, not the usual gay babble, and they clung to their husbands. The men kept their eyes open, keyed to the swarthy faces and strange costumes mixing with the ivory Virginia crowd. Word had spread of Luke Wallace's strange and desperate decision. Perhaps he was punishing them. Perhaps this was his retribution for not finding an eligible lady among the crust.

More people showed up to this wedding than to any other in the past decade. Wallace had issued an open invitation to all plantation owners and businessfolk, and nobody wanted to miss it. There were even newspaper reporters here from as far as Richmond, having caught the gossip that something was up on one of the plantations. Word of the arrival of the Greeks had spread fast, and today was the culmination. The reporters too glanced around uneasily, the difference being that they gave written expression to their unease.

It was this undertone that Luke Wallace noticed.

He wandered the crowd, sweating on the outside, freezing within.

He was dressed impeccably, a perfect Southern bridegroom on his wedding day. His tailed jacket was royal blue, and he wore an elaborate lace jabot in the style of the French. Everyone who shook his hand was secretly relieved that Wallace wasn't wearing one of those linen skirts. He fulfilled his obligations, greeted all who approached him because he was their host, but his face was tense, and his eyes were hopeless. He made everyone nervous, because all could see his effort to keep the warmth in his hands and some semblance of courtesy going in spite of his despair.

Nick Varvaresos stood aside, observing Lucas, completely bewildered.

Nick had expected many reactions, but not disappointment. If anyone had opened a carriage door and handed him a girl like Iphigenia and said to him, "You can marry this," he certainly wouldn't be wearing *that* face right now. Lucas had made no sounds about calling the deal off, not even after the slaves' actions and Moses' death, yet there was this chapfallen behavior. Lucas had somehow become disenchanted at the moment he should have become enchanted. For three days Nick's family and their servants had been bustling about Plentiful, cooking, sewing, washing, preparing, setting up, and all they hadn't brought with them was Athens's violet sunset. Nick could not make himself understand.

Promptly at noon the music stopped. When it started up again, after the silence had gotten everyone's attention, the sound was somehow different, heavier, more substantial. Another melody, yes, but this one was executed just differently enough to ring some primordial chord in every spine. Something was about to happen.

Wallace looked at Nick. Nick gave him a nod. *The* nod.

The music grew louder, stronger.

From the side of the mansion house, a black coach appeared, drawn by two of Wallace's bay chunks, then a second coach. Jeff drove the first, Samson the second, and never had there been two prouder cuffees in Tidewater. Samson looked positively haughty as he sat up there with his chin pointed.

While Virginia's elite watched, the coaches moved slowly to the circular driveway, turned and headed away from the mansion on the curved path as though toward the road. But they didn't go out onto the road. They went the whole perimeter of the driveway, then turned back once again toward the house. The crowd realized they were watching some kind of ritual—a bridal exodus.

Now the coaches drew to a halt beside the Greek garden, the horses twitching.

Two Greek guards escorted Dimitrios Trözene to the coaches. He wore a black suit and red cummerbund, and this brought out the color in his face and black beard. He worked very hard not to grin.

The bride's mother exited the first coach, followed by her two sisters and two bridesmaids. A hum ran through the Tidewater gentry.

These foreign women were barbarians! Who but tribal heathens would wear straight black skirts? And why would they wear aprons to a wedding? Layers of heavily embroidered aprons? On the aprons were bold zigzags, stripes, and triangles, much unlike the bell-shaped gowns of the Virginia ladies. Their skirts were pleated, and inside each pleat was a strip of white, creating a geometric effect. Their vests and tulip sleeves were blue, with dizzying gold and silver embroidery, and they wore coins on chains all over their chests. *Coins!* On their *chests*!

"Amazons!" John Van Meer whispered.

"Good God," Tuggle wheezed, wishing he hadn't come.

"Their hats...," Tabby Tuggle gurgled, gaping at the ostrich plume curved in a semicircle on each woman's head. It was familiar somehow. Turning slightly, she looked back at the collection of statues behind her. She sought through them until she found the one with the crested helmet. A woman, but with a helmet. And these women were trying to imitate that helmet. Anyone with a mind to fashion would see that, and Tabby did.

Dimitrios was escorted to the second coach and opened it himself.

There was a flash of bright white silk, a glint of gold, a rustle of crinoline, and a jingle of coins, and Iphigenia Trözene bloomed onto the lawn.

But her gown was not straight or black. She wore no helmet.

The crowd's eyes were blistered by gleaming ivory silk, brighter than the marble statues towering around them. A gigantic fountain of tiered white flounces bloomed from her nipped waist, a ball gown as proper as any Southern belle's. Her shoulders were bare, the ivory bodice of her dress in the shape of a shawl, with gold silk tassels winking in the Virginia sun. From each flounce on the big skirt dangled more gold tassels, which rolled against the silk as she moved. Greek tradition had been maintained in a series of lightweight linen aprons with bright, heavy braidwork and embroidery, mostly in red, black, and gold. Her symbolic dowry was draped on chains at her waist—coins, jewel-encrusted bangles, tangled filigree. On her head was a polite white crest and veil, and her face was framed by rosettes of red and white flowers. A diadem with small gold coins winked on her forehead.

As she stepped out of the coach's shadow, the sun ignited on her gown as if to dawn again.

The guests collectively gasped, "Ohhh!"

Luke Wallace just plain stopped breathing.

This was no European misfit! This was no foreigner dressed for some gaudy funeral. This was grace itself, moving on his own lawn!

Iphigenia handled the vast ball gown as though she'd worn one all her life. She nodded at her father, then took a few moments to straighten the silk tiers of her skirt. Her pale skin was only a few shades darker than the ivory of her gown, but her black hair and coal-pitch eyes were a constant reminder that she was not exactly from next door.

"Stay on your feet," a voice muttered into Wallace's ear, but the words barely registered.

The crowd began to murmur, their eyes wide.

"Lucas, stay up. Don't fall over."

It was Nick. That was why it sounded familiar. It wasn't God. It was Nick.

Lucas managed to lock his knees.

Satisfied with her gown, Iphigenia raised her head. The veil and rosettes rustled faintly. Her black hair rested in a roll on her shoulders. She looked at Wallace before looking at anyone else. For the first time she smiled at him. A bolt went through him. He suddenly straightened and seemed to fill up with whatever had been missing a moment ago.

Iphigenia took her father's arm and moved across the grass toward the center of the Greek garden. Her immense ivory ball gown waved in gentle rhythm with the bridal march.

Lucas felt a push from Nick and moved forward toward Dimitrios and the bride. Each step seemed to invigorate him. He wasn't marrying a barbarian at all!

He shook hands with Dimitrios, then turned to Iphigenia. She took his proffered arm, gave him that warm smile once again, and a gush of unexpected applause washed through the crowd. Wallace looked up.

The applause grew louder, happier.

Somehow the Greeks had done it. Somehow they had taken their vastly different cultures and blended them like fruit and cream. The elaborate ornamentation of the Greeks made American fashion sensibilities pale and seem somehow bastardized. Iphigenia didn't look Greek, and yet . . . she did. But more than the secular Macedonian female with her eyes turned downward, this was a cosmopolitan society bride. She was the dream of every girl on every plantation, everywhere.

Luke Wallace felt the sweat dry up under his coat and the warmth return to his face and hands. Slowly the realization filled him that his life was about to become everything he'd ever dreamed. He himself, Lucas himself, would gladden the county and finally make his mark. If he couldn't do it by being proper, he'd do it by being improper better than anybody else.

He and his bride moved toward the white trellis with its drench of roses. The only inconsistency was an ostrich egg hanging from the arch, on which the minister kept bumping his head.

Wallace was bubbling with pure joy, and he nodded at anyone who caught his eye. Of course, he wasn't gloating when he got the chance to bob his brows at Colonel and Mrs. Brookville as he passed them.

As the couple reached the trellis, followed first by the *koumbaros*—the best man, Nick—then by the parents and the sisters and bridesmaids, a loud racket from the driveway made everyone flinch and turn to look.

The Greek men were taking sledgehammers to the second coach. The crowd stepped back from the driveway. The barbarians had reverted. Madness had taken over. While two Greeks unharnessed the horses, the others started demolishing the rear wheels of the coach. They heaved upward on the box and removed the axle pins, dismantling the entire undercarriage. Then the box dropped to the ground at a horrid angle.

As the astonished crowd watched, the Greek men carried the disconnected axle to the middle of the driveway and poured kerosene all over it. Finally, one of the men retreated to a smoking pit where several lamb carcasses were being turned on spits, and when he straightened, he was carrying a flaming torch.

The Greek whipped the torch through the air. The flame hit the axle. It exploded into a ribbon of fire. A bit tribal, but clear enough. The bride would never return to her father's house. This was her home now. She was now a Southern woman.

After the crowd stopped squirming, the ceremony began. To the relief and secret disappointment of the guests, it turned out to be a normal American service with normal American vows and a normal American prayer afterward. Fairly simple too, all considered. The only foreign flavor came when Nick Varvaresos, doing his duty as *koumbaros*, tied the bride's and groom's hands with a symbolic white ribbon and led them three times around the trellis. While unfamiliar, the act was enthralling in its way, a subtle reminder that there were other ways in the world to do things, even to get married.

The minister made no speeches, no sermons. He did what he was supposed to do in the simplest fashion and finally announced to the crowd, "Ladies and gentlemen, may I present Lucas and Iphigenia... Mr. and Mrs. Lucas Wallace."

Applause rang once again, this time with a flavor of the sincere. It was the first time anyone had heard her name. The bride and groom did look grand up there, turning to face their guests, standing together on the last page of their storybook. They looked wonderful. Why, they looked acceptable!

Suddenly every woman present was scheming to get Greekitude into her next soiree, and the gentlemen were wondering if they should speak to Lucas about foreign affairs.

Iphigenia smiled at the guests with perfect Olympian serenity, as if to tell them they would never see the like of this again and they should look carefully.

The drum thumped, the mandolin chimed, a few opening strains of the clarinet trailed across the grass. Suddenly the notes fell together, and there was music.

Such eating, such learning. After the initial hesitations, the guests began tentatively tasting. If at first they ate only because it would have been rude not to, they soon discovered most of the fare to be edible, if tangy, if unusual. The food began gradually to disappear, course after course, and soon a lively overture of happy chatter took the place of uneasy murmurs. The only pauses came when someone took a taste of octopus and had to chew. And chew. And try to swallow, then chew some more.

"So, Lucas," Dimitrios Trözene said between big bites of *dolmata*, "you're feeling all right about everything?"

Lucas glanced at the vision of a bride beside him, then nodded at the bride's father. "Sir, I am speechless."

Dimitrios laughed and nodded at Nick, with a conspiratorial wink. Then he turned back to Lucas and said, "I am impressed with you. Did I tell you? Well, I am. In ten years you've made all this from nothing. Nothing! From dirt and gristle you built a community that contributes to civilization. In Europe men are used to getting wealth from fathers and grandfathers. But you touched a coin and turned it into an empire. This is a talent, Lucas.''

"Thank you," the groom muttered, looking across the table for a supportive glance from Nick, who obliged.

The women and groomsmen continued to eat. No one spoke but Dimitrios, and Dimitrios seemed to think that was fine. "Lucas, what town were you born in?''

"Lynchburg.''

"And who was the wealthiest man in town?''

Another look at Nick told him he should simply answer, so he did. "I've no idea.''

Dimitrios shook his fork. "And who was the wealthiest man in Socrates' time?''

"Uh . . . sir, I don't know that either.''

"But you know of Socrates? Yes?''

"Uh . . . yes," Lucas said, relieved because he really did.

The fork wobbled again. "There's a reason for that," Dimitrios said. "The wealthy who have no culture only die rich and let their children squander the wealth. It's men of thought, Lucas, men of thought who outlast the ages. Now that you are married to Iphigenia, the most revered philosophers of antiquity are your ancestors." He shrugged. "No one ever remembers who managed to grub the most gold or father the most children. History remembers only the ones who shape a nation's thoughts. You can be one of those now, Lucas. Your children will be a part of the new renaissance.''

He paused, put his fork down, put his drink down, and took Lucas's hand in both of his.

"Keep my daughter well," he said. "Raise your children Greek, and you will always be one of the remembered.''

The bride basked in her own loveliness, for she enjoyed the sensation of the huge ivory silk gown and the approving glances she received from her husband's countrymen. She knew she was pretty today. Other days perhaps not so striking, but for today she was a goddess. A goddess must be gracious, so halfway through the banquet she rose from her chair, excused herself from her husband, her mother, her father, her cousin Nick, and attendants, and slowly made her way through the throng of party gowns and ascots. She greeted everyone, putting her schoolroom English to the test, and found these Southern people to be far more cosmopolitan than even they gave themselves credit for. While propriety urged them to scowl and hide behind their fans at today's sights, she could tell they were trying hard to accept the new experience. Most of them did understand her accented greetings and sincerely tried to converse with her, to welcome her into their strict society by making their society a bit less strict. Her father had warned her that such would not be the case. He was wrong, she soon decided, so very wrong.

She smiled. Every time Dimitrios was proved wrong, he would clap his hands and insist he enjoyed it. Being wrong was something to learn by, he contended, and so he was the smartest man in the world. The smart part she had believed all through her childhood and most of her teenage years. The part about enjoying being wrong . . . well.

Swirling her way through the scattered guests, she reveled in the feeling of her gown brushing the grass as she slipped around the veranda for a moment alone in a shadow. Once by herself she closed her eyes and let her cheeks relax from all the smiling, rolled her shoulders, and stretched her arms. The dancing would begin soon, and she should be supple for it. She shifted her rib cage, but the whalebone corset cut unkindly into the undersides of her breasts. She'd tried to get used to the undergarment—had been trying for over a year—but unlike these nip-waisted Southern women, she hadn't been wearing one since girlhood, and her rib cage wasn't properly molded to the hourglass shape. Only her own slimness and the blooming skirt of her gown gave the illusion that her body was trained to a fully laced corset. It was not. After a child or two, the secret might be out.

But that was for the future to worry about.

She adjusted her veil and made sure her aprons lay evenly. The broad silk tiers of her skirt rippled and puckered like frosting, catching sunlight and shadows in their crisp folds. Iphigenia inhaled deeply and sighed. Wonderful to feel so—

A movement caught her eye.

Two large rose topiaries graced the side of the house in the shade behind the veranda. Iphigenia moved toward them, positive she'd seen something.

And sure enough, crouched between the pots was a young negro girl. She and the child looked at each other. No, not a child—a teenager. A bundle of rags with a smooth chocolate face and small sharp features.

"Good morning," Iphigenia said, as clearly as possible.

Yula gazed up at the bride, stunned by her luck. Whether it was good luck or bad remained to be seen. She'd been here all day, wondering how she was going to sneak into the house, and now she didn't have to take that risk. Her quarry had presented herself by pure chance, and now they had a moment alone.

Assimilating the luck and the chance, Yula summoned her cramped legs and tingling buttocks and got to her feet. She nodded, wondering what the woman had just said to her.

Iphigenia glanced back at the wedding reception. No one was looking. At such a big affair, even the bride could slip away for a few minutes. Oh, they would notice that she was gone, but it wasn't polite to go searching.

She held out her hand to beckon the girl out of the shadows. The girl shook her head and pressed back against the brick. They both knew she wasn't supposed to be here.

Swallowing first, Yula said, "I gots a weddin' present fo' yawl."

Iphigenia's dark brows drew tight. What she heard was, "Ahgahswenpessenfo'yaw."

Was it English? A new dialect she had failed to study. So she nodded, hesitantly.

The girl hunted through the hanging rags on her body and drew out a folded piece of embroidered salmon satin. It glowed against the rags.

Yula held the sash tightly. She almost changed her mind, but only for an instant. The sparkling satin was puckered where she had stitched a picture of the big house. Luckily the house was brown brick, for brown was the only color of thread she had ample of. She'd undone the top of one of her wool stockings to get the charcoal gray of the shutters, and for the chimneys she had sewn on four bits of bark.

She turned partly away from the bride for a moment, peeking over her shoulder at the elaborate embroidery that shimmered on the bride's aprons, and she hesitated again, but for a different reason.

Then she stuck her long arm out and pushed the sash toward the bride, holding it so the picture showed.

Iphigenia's soft hands took the satin, and she ran her thumb over the coarse picture of the mansion. It was recognizable, though barely. The sash was low-quality French satin, but real satin nonetheless, and obviously valuable to the sorry-looking girl, whose eyes had welled briefly as she handed it over.

For a moment Iphigenia thought of not taking the possession, but to refuse a gift, even so precious a sacrifice, would be glaringly unkind.

"Oh," she murmured. "Oh . . ."

For a thank-you she cupped the girl's face and kissed her cheeks, touching for the first time an American negro.

To show her appreciation even further, she shook the sash out of its folds. Carefully she wrapped it around her waist and tied it so that the picture of Plentiful hung over the chains and coins that already graced her gown. The sash was garish and off-color for her wedding ensemble, detracting from the shimmering embroidery, but she smoothed it down over the aprons and turned so that the sun caught the color.

Yula's eyes beaded up with tears. Maybe her plan would work.

"What is your name?" Iphigenia asked.

The negro girl tilted her head like a puzzled puppy, barely able to understand the heavily accented English.

Iphigenia tried again, miming along with her verbal attempt. "N-hame?"

Understanding dawned on the girl's pointy features. "Name!" she squeaked. She thumped herself on the shoulder. "Yoo-lah. I Yoo-lah."

"Yoolah," the bride laughed. She gestured to herself and said, "Iphigenia. If-i-jen-ee-ah."

Yula blanked for a moment. Her lips twisted this way and

that. She considered the sounds, then cocked her hip and said, "Missy."

They both laughed.

Iphigenia squeezed the girl's hand and came within a step of going back to her guests.

But she paused. There was something behind the girl's eyes. An extra depth in the dark pools told her there was something more, something the girl had no words for.

With her own eyes she asked her own question.

The girl took one more guilty look toward the front grounds, then said, "Ahwanshoyaw'sump."

The bride blinked vaguely and let her helplessness show in her expression.

Yula pulled Iphigenia back toward the shadows and through the topiaries. Yula drew apart the rags she'd used to cover herself, and thus doing she revealed the real treasure.

Iphigenia's lips parted, and she gasped.

A tiny baby wiggled at the slave girl's breast. Not the girl's baby, certainly, for his two-day-old skin was like eggnog, and his hair was soft ebony curls. He turned his head as daylight struck him and looked for the light. His eyes were lumps of coal, so dark that the pupils were invisible within them. His mouth, no bigger than a coin, puckered in search of a suckle.

Iphigenia let out a womanly squeal and automatically reached for the child. If only she could hold him, just for a moment—

Yula handed the baby over like a ball of yarn. His soft, tiny head rested against the bride's neck and nuzzled there.

"Oooohh," Iphigenia cooed, holding the round butt in the cup of her hand. "Ooooh, beautiful baby. . . is boy?"

"Boy," Yula said.

"Your boy? Yours?" the bride asked, lowering her voice.

The skinny girl nodded, knowing what the woman was thinking. This was her mandate—to make sure someone else loved that baby besides herself. Someone important.

Iphigenia adjusted the awkward ball of baby. Her two hands almost covered him entirely, and it was tricky to get a grip. But he was lying against her neck as though ordained to fit there. She was captured by a sensation beyond instinct, utterly caught by primal memories and the beauty of something so pure, something that needed to be held and comforted more than it needed anything else. During the war with Turkey, she had seen displaced children whose parents were gone or killed. They were being clothed and fed by others who took pity on them, but the clothing and the food were not enough. There was an emptiness in their eyes even though their bellies were full. They needed holding. They needed to cling to an adult's body and to be guarded in an adult's arms. Children, babies, needed that.

Her own empathy squeezed her as instincts crashed in and she cuddled the baby deeper against her throat. Only as the infant's mother reached to correct the position of his little leg did Iphigenia once again see the difference between Yula's skin and that of her baby.

She looked at Yula, knowingly this time.

Turning slightly, she gazed past the shaded veranda to the banquet grounds, through the milling guests to the bridal table, past her parents, finally to her husband.

Then she looked at Yula. The girl had followed her gaze through the guests, to the face of her master.

Yula felt the bride's eyes on her, then looked away. Dark color stained her cheeks. She stared at the brown brick and waited.

Iphigenia nodded to herself. Her hands folded over the baby's curled body.

She rocked back and forth, catching the rhythm of the mother's waltz as though born to it. The baby wiggled briefly, then rested his tiny face like a cameo against her warm throat and enjoyed the moment with his whole tiny being, as only the innocent can. The bride closed her eyes, and her lovely face took on a special serenity. She began to hum softly to the baby.

Yula waited in the shadow of the veranda.

Iphigenia stopped and opened her eyes. "Name for baby?"

The infant's mother waved a scrawny hand. "You name."

"Oh, no," the bride said. "You mother. You name."

"Yoo de missus," the girl responded. She pointed one of those javelin fingers at the baby. "Name."

Was this another gift? Was it plantation tradition or rule?

Iphigenia felt the warmth of the infant beneath her chin, and she was in love. So helpless, so dependent . . . a baby. A baby.

She felt tears rise in her own eyes. Was there a special rule about the illegitimate child of the plantation master? If not, she would make one.

Somewhat sobered, she nodded and accepted the reality as quickly as that.

Looking at Yula, she suggested, "Dionysus."

Yula's eyes opened wide, then even wider. She blinked a couple of times.

"Deee-u-sus."

Iphigenia smiled. "Dee-ohn-ee-soos."

Squinting, the slave girl forced herself to think about what she had heard. If this was what it took, this was what she would do. She clenched her fists at her sides, took a deep breath, and tried again.

"Deeeee-soos."

The bride shook her head and laughed sadly. "Mmm," she murmured, thinking. After a moment she tried again. "Dorian."

Yula lipped the name a few times, then dared put sound to it. "Dohreen. Doreen."

"Dorian," the bride said.

Yula licked her lips, put her chin to her chest, and blurted, "Dohrian."

Iphigenia laughed. "Yes!"

"Dohrian!"

"Yes! Is good!" She rocked the baby and smiled. "Good."

"Dohrian," Yula belted again. "I likes dat! Dohrian."

They basked in their success, Iphigenia cuddling the baby and Yula picking thoughtfully at the rags she'd dressed him in, and a relationship began to set. Yula never once attempted to get the baby back. With luck she might never get him back.

The master's wife tilted her cheek against the baby's curly head.

"Dorian," she whispered.

The dancing caught on like a fever—Greek line dancing. A few Virginia ladies and gentlemen dared link themselves to the line, and still more behind them. The music grew more intense. The Greeks swayed and scooped, their embroidered costumes flickering, and behind them came the bobbing, uncertain Virginians, laughing at their own awkwardness. When the bride returned, she took her husband's hand and joined the dance. The Greeks cut a trail through the crowd, curving in a great circle. They swooped and kicked and slapped their shoes. The bride's new sash became part of the complex flash of her gown as it turned in the sunlight.

In the midst of it all, Luke Wallace basked in the glitter of his own future. He was being accepted. He could *feel* it! As the line dance passed Van Meer, Lucas took an opportunity that only days ago he would have passed up.

"Hello, John," he called, using Van Meer's first name for the first time. "Care to join the dance?"

"No, thank you, Lucas," Van Meer called back without missing a beat. "My congratulations! This is the best joke Tidewater has ever seen!"

He said it good and loud. Everyone heard, in spite of the music and the elegant shifting line of people.

But there would be no echo of times past, for here stood a new Luke Wallace who looked squarely at his prime detractor. He raised his voice even louder than Van Meer's, louder than the music. "Glad you're enjoying yourself, John," he said. "You should be. After all, my wife's ancestors were mapping the stars when yours were howling at the moon!"

A round of applause and supportive laughter bubbled about them. Lucas put his chin up, rejoined the dance line, and off he went.

Lost in the dance, Dimitrios Trözene nearly burst with pride and delight. Beside him Nick Varvaresos let loose a whoop of success and slapped his shoes. It was as though the musicians knew the exact moment to quicken the beat. The stars above would have sparkled if only they could get through the brightness of this day.

All during the dance Iphigenia felt the emptiness against her throat where the warm baby had been minutes ago, and she clung to the hands of her husband and her mother in the dance line. Her husband's victory would be her victory. She smiled an intuitive smile.

Sunlight crackled across the wedding gown, and suddenly everyone could see the Hellenic tendency to strive toward perfection and the heroic. It rang around them, and it moved through their bodies like a forgotten theme.

Music ran through the plantation. On the third day Greece rose again from the dead.

★

CHAPTER EIGHT

———— ★ ————

"Yassu!"

Beneath the morning sun pewter mugs sparkled and clacked rims. Luke, Dimitrios, and Nick downed their buttered rum toddies as if slogging beer. Somehow the three men managed to laugh while they were swallowing.

Luke and his new in-laws weren't even dressed yet. Still in their robes they had just said good-bye to their third visitor of the morning, who, like the others, had found some thin reason to drop by. Two had come armed with invitations for Lucas Wallace, Esq., and Mrs. Wallace to dine at their plantations. In ten years there had never before been such an instance at Plentiful's front door. None of this was lost on the three satisfied men, for the marriage was exceeding all dreams. Plentiful would chime with social grace, Greece would gain a foothold in America, and the groom had survived the wedding night.

Wallace's face was showing strain from grinning so much. What it had been for the woman, he could neither tell nor would he ever know. Genuine virginal discovery or gilded performance, he had no way to interpret, no meter against which to judge her responses. But it was morning, and he had lived, which was all he'd dared hope. He didn't feel like dock chowder after the steamers boiled open, the clap of thunder had never come, and when the sun rose, Plentiful was still standing under it—and he still had his chance to become an upper-cruster.

"Thank you, thank you," he murmured to Dimitrios and Nick's shout of toast to him on this bright morning. After swigging his toddy he swallowed hard and addressed his father-in-law. "It'd do me an honor if you and the missus'd stay on for a spell, sir."

Dimitrios's fuzzy round face took on a particular glow. "We shall, we shall, for a couple of weeks. You are gracious, my son. Hah, my son!" He struck Lucas's chest with the back of his hand and laughed, because that age thing had surfaced again.

Wallace blushed, both amused and sensitive to the years, but he only tipped his head and nodded.

Nick waited for the laughter to die down. "Iphigenia's sister and my other sister will stay on and live here, Lucas. We've already discussed that."

"To marry American men," Wallace agreed.

"We hope so," Nick said. "And you'll have Greek servants to tend and teach your children properly."

"Children," Dimitrios mumbled. There was a silly mystical expression on his face, and his cheeks got rounder and rounder. "Hah!"

He hit Wallace again.

"Ah, Lucas," he rumbled. Settling back in his wicker chair, he looked long and hard at this volatile man he'd brought into his family line. "At last the titan comes out of the chains! My grandchildren will know the taste of sweet *visina* and mumble Mediterranean lyrics in their sleep. *Koulouria* will bake in their ovens. They'll know about the theater of Herodes Atticus as though they had performed on its stones. They'll know the Golden Ratio and how mathematics apply to music and architecture. Athens's violet sunset will come to them in dreams, and they'll imagine what it is to stand on the vestibule of the Acropolis as I have myself!"

"They'll be American also, Dimi," Nick pointed out, turning his mug with two fingers as it sat on the table before him.

Dimitrios shot him a glare and pounded the tabletop.

"Of course American! My American grandchildren." He slapped his chest. "Americans! They'll have the land to spread out in such as nobody has ever had before, and they'll know what to do with it." Dimitrios sighed deeply. "I like this big America! The unstoppable Americans. There is nothing in this world," he added solemnly, "like you."

Bad enough to have to be a foreign aristocrat, but now Wallace was supposed to be a whole country. In spite of the success of everything, he had been realizing lately that he'd taken the ride-hard approach to heaven.

He glanced at Nick for support, then said to Dimitrios, "Well, sir, I sure intend to make good on your expectations. I want you to know that I plan to care whole-hog for that daughter of yours. We Southrons take our word to heart, and you got mine on this. I hope to provide for her in high style like she deserves and then die before she does."

Dimitrios spread his hands. "Who could ask for more?"

He raised his mug, and the other two men raised theirs, but they didn't get time to drink. The veranda creaked, interrupting their toast with a substantive wooden groan, yet something under the skin said these weren't the servants approaching. Distracted, the men turned at the same time.

There, at the point where the veranda took a sharp turn toward the side of the mansion, stood the new mistress of the plantation. She wore a lacy, flake white dressing gown that offset her dark hair almost to a defiance, and she would have been welcomed in her perfection were it not for her company. At her side stood the scrawny slave girl who'd been summarily banished to the cabins, if Wallace's memory served, and in Iphigenia's arms was the brat who could wreck everything.

The two women stood together, all defiance. The baby gurgled.

Wallace vaulted to his feet.

Thighs pressed up against the table, fists in balls, he glared first upon the child, then at the negro mother, but only at the last did he catch the eyes of his wife.

She held the hedge-born boy with a surprising dare in her eyes. Yula stood beside her champion, also without apology, willing to risk the displeasure of her master rather than put the risk on her marshmallow.

At the table beside Wallace, Dimitrios's pleasant expression dropped, a detail that Wallace noticed even in periphery. In Iphigenia's arms the baby with skin like eggnog and eyes like coal chunks wiggled as though innocent and thus drew the pure, blind hatred of his father.

Nick held his breath, and his nervous swallow was audible.

A thousand first lines crashed through Wallace's mind, from "What is the meaning of this?" to "Back to the house with you," but none of them would get him out of this without complicating things to the worse. For a fleeting instant he even considered shouting for McCrocklin to get charge of this, but how would that look? He was abruptly snowbound.

In moments he would be jestingstock, an obscenity, once again contaminating Tidewater. Disgrace cooed in his wife's arms.

He saw by her face that she knew the whole story already and there would be no escape in lies, in claiming the ulceration was McCrocklin's or anyone else's. If he could reach it, he would kill it right here on the porch.

And that impure cuffee bitch! Staring at him like she had an up on him! Wallace smelled punishment spreading on his body like a stench, humiliating him.

Iphigenia remained unmoved throughout the shifting expressions of the men. She knew they all had what they wanted—all because of her. She had asked for nothing. That would change now.

Dimitrios came slowly to his feet, glancing uncomfortably between the women and the man. All his talk of grandchildren was embarrassing now, and he would do anything to crush that embarrassment.

"Excuse me, Lucas," he said. "Nick and I will leave you to your business."

He stepped away from the table.

Nick didn't get up.

Dimitrios snapped his fingers at him.

Seconds crawled by. Nick watched the changes in Wallace's face.

Finally—because the marriage had to start sometime—Nick relented. The chair scraped beneath him. He followed Dimitrios into the mansion, leaving Wallace grinding his teeth.

Iphigenia shifted the baby to her other arm and nodded firmly at Yula. The slave girl lowered her eyes in sham complacence, turned, and disappeared around the side of the house.

The woman and her husband stood alone, alone except for the succulent morsel in her arms whose presence was meaningful in all the wrong ways.

Wallace tried to get control over the moment. He crushed his palm against his mouth for a few seconds, breathed a couple of shallow sucks, then stammered, "It doesn't . . . mean anything. I was drunk. I was crazy."

Iphigenia moved to the chair her father had just vacated and sat down. She said nothing.

Wallace spread his arms helplessly. "It was before I knew about you. Before I met Nick, don't you understand? Look . . . if it bothers you, I'll get it off the plantation. Tomorrow. And its mother too. Right away. Tomorrow."

"I want the baby."

"All right, today then."

She looked up at him, and in her shapely face was the whole story of his life to come. "I want him."

As he drank in her words, Wallace saw all his efforts crumble before his eyes. A roundeye bastard being raised right there in the big house. His neighbors would find out he'd laid pipe in the wrong chimney, and all his efforts would go up in smoke.

Desperately he paced around her, chafing his hands. How to explain, how to make it clear—

"That's not possible," he said, suddenly firm, because it wasn't. "This is Virginia, not Greece. He can't blend in here. Everyone will know!"

"I want the baby," she repeated. "I want him to be my baby."

"It's that cuffee woman's baby!" he hissed, pointing at the corner of the veranda and fighting for control. He paced again, and he tried another tack. "By the law he's a slave. Legally. No matter what I decide. . . . You see, the matter is out of my hands. He's fully one-half negro, and that makes him a bonded slave by the very law of the state. . . ."

He paused to see if this had any effect on her.

It didn't.

"It's the law," he repeated. "This proves to me that he's

got to be sold off, for his own good. He'll be better off on a bigger plantation where he can be lost among his own kind. I'm sorry . . . but he can't be our son.''

Stunned by the impact that this was his first real conversation with his wife, Wallace stood in his own sweat and awaited her response.

He had accomplished so much in the past twenty-odd hours, and she knew it—what would happen if he refused? The elegant, educated symbol of his success was standing there caressing the only crack in his foundation, knowing perfectly well that he didn't yet have the security to stand his ground against her. Mulatto children were common, but even a drop of negro blood meant a negro heritage and a negro's lot. Easy, for mulatto children might be fair of skin, yet most had at least one gawdy negro feature, Wallace thought, be it flat nose, jutting jaw, or wire hair. This newborn had no such flags that would place him irrevocably in the fields, and his wife knew it. The baby was clearly Wallace's son.

In fact, there was nothing so shocking as to see Iphigenia holding this baby, for he might indeed have burst from her own womb, he was so like her and her new husband. He had the same perfectly shaped eyes with those black marbles set in them, the same peach gold skin with a glow from within. No negro had that.

And yet, he wasn't *exactly* white.

Iphigenia collected her fosterling against her breasts, framing the infant in lace, and stood up slowly, for effect.

"He *is* your son," she told him. "Thus he is mine too."

He might have found a way around keeping the bastard if she had only deigned to discuss the issue with him, but she wouldn't. No matter his ranting, she simply said the same thing over and over again.

"I want the baby."

No matter how he explained the law and cajoled that she wouldn't like what folk thought of her, she would let him go on and on, then quietly repeat those four horrible words. A couple of times she even added a perfunctory "Lucas" to it just to show him where he stood.

"I want the baby, Lucas."

Round about dinnertime, just when he was faced with the nightmare of sitting down to supper with his in-laws under the pall of his indiscretion, he found himself squaring off with his wife for the fifth time since morning.

In fact, this was the first time all day that she wasn't cuddling the little outsider.

Wallace peered out the window of his library, where he had managed to get her alone one more time. Darkness swathed the grasses of Plentiful. Of course. It was evening. The real mother had taken that side-wipe and gone back to the cabins. Somewhat easier—discussing the problem when the child wasn't in Iphigenia's arms.

Wallace could manage a business deal, if nothing better.

"This is how it will be," he began, not looking into her eyes. He paced back and forth, ticking details off on his fingers. "You may have the baby here during the days, while his mother works. You may do as you please with him, I do not care one whit. You keep him away from me, is all. It's still my house, and he's not got one single entitlement to it. He is not and never will be a legal heir to my estate."

"I understand."

"His mother will stay in the fields without hope of promotion. He'll spend nights with his mother at the cabins, and he will work in the fields when he's old enough, so he knows who and what he is. In the house he will be subservient to the children you legally bear me."

She nodded her lovely head. "Yes. I want promise also."

He stopped pacing. "What promise?"

"Baby never be sold."

Sweat tickled Wallace's underarms as he looked down at her.

Hoarsely he grunted, "All right."

"Mother never be sold."

"All right."

Silence guttered around them like a candle going out.

"One more thing," he rasped.

Iphigenia met his eyes without balking. She knew his final

condition would be the guide for Dorian's life at Plentiful, and she steeled herself to hear it.

Wallace knotted his hands behind his back. "He will never leave the boundaries of Plentiful. He'll not be allowed off the grounds. And he will never—*never*—be seen by any visitor to this plantation. Is that clear to you? I want that clear. Never."

"It is clear."

He paused, trying to read her calm face. Did she really understand the implications? There would be no trips to town to fit the boy with new clothes, no hunting, no fishing, no going over the fence with the other children. He would, in fact, be far less free than any slave.

"And you're agreeable to these . . . absolutely absurd conditions?"

"Yes. I agree."

"Then I guess I'll see you at supper, madam."

"Thank you, Lucas."

"Just one moment."

"Yes?"

"I want you to understand clearly what I mean. Just this. The first time he is seen by anyone, anyone at all not residing on this plantation, the bargain is busted, and I will have him sold with the first wagon going south. You'll never see him again."

"But he is mine if this is done?"

"Yes, yes, b'God, and I'll regret it. I can see in your face we're going around in a figure of eight here, and you don't construe what kind of life the boy'll get under these conditions."

"Thank you. Excuse me, Lucas."

"Yep, fine, fine."

"Boss? Oh, 'scuse me, ma'am. Evening, ma'am. Boss?"

"Don't you Boss me, McCrocklin! Close that door! Where the bloody bedamned have you been all day!"

"I bin downcounty. I talked to Mr. Zeb Lumm's foreman, and he said they'd be happy to take that new baby boy off you. Offered a full—"

"I ain't selling him."

"Pardon?"

"I ain't selling! Are you deaf? I'm head of this plantation, and if I say the yeller fuckin' little runt stays, then he stays!"

★

There he sat. Not a half hour had passed since the bargain was sealed. There he was already, perched on the couch, drowning in brocade, tassels, pleats, and embroidery, a Greek outfit they'd taken off a doll.

There was his little scrunchy newborn face, lost inside a frilly hat with a tassel, his black eyes slightly confused. After supper the Greeks threw a party for themselves. Dressed in a crisp white kilt, red shoes, and pom-poms, the baby sat high in the air on Nick's big hand while Pilos and the others banged out music on their mandolins and drums. A line dance twisted through the house, the baby leading. The baby was ambivalent, however, and fell asleep in Nick's grasp.

Dimitrios was filled with happiness—a wedding and a grandchild all in one weekend! As for his wife, Ariadne Trözene was slower to accept the child, not sure how such an arrangement would affect her daughter's reputation. Lucas's child by a woman he wasn't married to... but a woman he legally owned... it had a certain ancient propriety to it, and this was America where things were different. But *that* different?

Her coolness lasted until Dimitrios had enough. He shoved the newborn into her arms, and she couldn't turn away from the little face. Seconds later it was clear to everyone that Ariadne wouldn't let anybody else hold the baby that evening.

The future began that night. Shielded by the love of his Greek mother and his colored mother, the boy would scarcely notice his father's cold hatred for years to come.

★

PART TWO

★

WHITE TRASH

———— ★ ★ ★ ————

THE BURNING FUSE

DECEMBER 1835

American settlers in the Mexican Territory of Texas threaten to secede from Mexico rather than give up their right to hold slaves.

MARCH 1836

Mexican President Santa Anna's troops besiege the Alamo. Over 180 Texans die. Enraged American settlers declare the Lone Star Republic of Texas independent of Mexico and draft their own constitution, which includes slavery. In April they elect Sam Houston president and demand annexation to the United States. Congress divides along North/South lines over the proposal.

———— ★ ————

CHAPTER NINE

———————— ★ ————————

Deep in the wild backside of the plains state of Missouri, on the side of the steep riverbank, squeezed between pines and scrub bushes, was a shack made of just about everything but real boards. At the door of the shack, which was actually just a discarded backboard from a covered wagon, the chalky glow of lamplight fell upon a woman. Shouting. In German.

"*Wit sind geschiedene Leute*! *Machen Sie fortkommen*! Hear me? Hear me, down there? *Mir langt's*! Stick out your face, you filthy goat!"

Her breasts wobbled within the dirty cotton dress as she hurled a tin pot down the hill. It clattered against rocks and splashed in pockets of mud, then finally dived into a bush, caught in the branches, and hung there, bobbing up and down in midair.

A broad, paunchy man dashed from behind that very bush to the protection of the nearest tree, a little higher up on the hill. Not bad. He'd started out at the riverbank, and progress was progress. Behind him his little rowboat was awash with rainwater. His heavy mustache, straight as a whisk broom, dripped rain from both corners now, his red undershirt also completely soaked, and his grayish hair dragged in his eyes. Another pot crashed into the tree.

But neither of them cared about the tree.

119

"*So können Sie mir nicht kommen!*" he shouted back. Being a generation removed, his pronunciation wasn't as good as hers, but he refused to be out-Germaned.

He picked up a rock, pounced out of hiding, heaved the rock up the hill, then ducked back behind the tree. She made a good target up there, silhouetted against the poor lantern light, her hair falling out of its knot, her legs going down like clubs into her dead mother's heavy wooden clogs. Like the small three-legged chairs, the huge worn-out dough trough, the rosemaled hatboxes with who knew what living inside, the lard press, and the pine-splint lamp, those clogs had made it all the way from Germany only to end up here. Life among the wretched.

"*Ach was! So sehen Sie au—*" His wife disappeared for just a moment when the rock hit the *bousillage* mortar of straw, sand, pebbles, and lime that held the shack together. Bits of *bousillage* spat back at him, but the woman was gone long enough for the husband to gain another quarter-way up the hill. Then he was hidden again, just in time.

Two more pots smashed into his tree. Her aim was getting better.

"That's it!" the man shouted. The rain spat from his mustache. "Where's a stick? Where's a stick?"

He began foraging for a stick heavy enough to crack her skull.

In the cabin the woman also began foraging. She dug through the clutter of wooden utensils and half-built furniture, dumping the tools and utensils because he had made or stolen most of them, grousing as she went.

"*Her fult er sich . . . es ist zum Kotzen . . . er soll mich kennenlernen!* I'll just show him. I'll show him, that's what."

She tore through her husband's belongings until she reached his favorite chair. Grumbling, "Bad fruit. That's what he is, *und dabei bleibt's.* That's what you are. You'll get the shock of your life. Just wait. *Sie werden Ihr blaues Wunder erleben,* son of a bitch."

She put her five-foot-nine German frame to work tipping the fat chair up on its rounded side and rolled it through the mess to the door.

From partway down the hill, her husband shouted, "Don't you do it! *Tu es ja nicht!*"

She pushed, panting. *"Her fult er sich. . . . Das haben Sie davon!"*

With a massive heave she sent the round chair cascading down the hill toward her husband. It caromed between the trees, then finally struck one with a *bonk* that echoed along the valley.

Even in the dark she could see the red of his face.

He shook his fist up the hill. *"Das had gerade noch gefehlt! Mir langt's!* What kind of woman puts furniture out in the rain!"

His wife's tall frame shook in the lantern light behind her.

"It ain't furniture!" she crowed. "It's a beer barrel!"

"Beer barrel? Beer barrel? *Jetzt reicht's mir aber!* I turned it into a fine chair! Look at it! With my own two hands I took a nothing and turned it into a something! So I'm something! You don't like it 'cuz you're still a nothing!"

"If you're such a something, how come you can't make a roof quit leaking? If I'm nothing, you're less than nothing!"

"You're loud for a nothing."

"Nothing? My spit is more than you are!"

"Fix the roof with your spit if it's so much something!"

"If you'd fix the roof yourself, it wouldn't drip on your beer-barrel chair!"

"I can't!"

"Why not?"

"I used up the nails to make the chair!"

"So you could be sittin' all the time!"

"So I could sit down to eat a plate of your pig puke and snake ass!"

"Ach, gehen Sie weg. And you're a ungrateful mutt too! Them are mock oysters and *Okserulader* as good as anybody ever cooked!"

"Snake ass. Pig puke."

"Then don't eat it! Maybe it'll plug the roof!"

"I never shoulda took that ten dollars to marry you."

"That was a dowry! And it came from my papa, who

brought it from Frankenmuth just so you could squander it. Good thing he died.''

''That's what I say.''

''Papa wanted you to be his apprentice, but no. You were too proud. You were going to California. Gonna start a plantation on that cheap Mexican land. Pull up gold like daisies in the dirt. Looks to me like all you got was the dirt! Where's them daisies?''

''I *did* apprentice to your stupid papa,'' her husband muttered. Then he bellowed, ''How many men you know can fix that clock in there?''

''It's the *only* clock west of Independence! Who cares if it works?''

He squared off between two trees, trying to make himself big. His arms went out at his sides like stovepipes, and his fist knotted. ''*Ach nein!* That's all I need from you! By damn! I'm gonna kill you!''

Bending his thick body into the climb, he dug his toes into the mud. His head went down, and his shoulders curved with determination. As he climbed, he fortified himself with his own voice.

''Nobody'll hang me for this. It's time to kill you. Bedamned bitch! *Ich bin ihe ewiges Gerede leid* . . . shoulda killed her last year. I shoulda killed you last year, hear me? I'm coming. *Zeigen!* I'm coming to kill you!''

The river churned lazily past a small trading post down the mountain, wobbling the canoes tied up to trees at the shoreline. Then it flowed between the ridges where it had carved its own path for ages. Silence fell on the porch of the trading post, but only for a moment. During that moment a companionable peace settled among the neighbors gathered there, as it had every Saturday night for quite a while now. The regular visitors knew they would soon merge into quiet, pointless conversation that made them each feel part of humanity even out here on the edge of nothing. None had a clue tonight would be any different.

And then the screams began.

Every spine went rigid at the chilling sounds. Never, not on any Saturday night before this, had they heard such a noise from up on the ridge.

They all looked into the moist night, looked through the rain pattering softly now, toward the ridge. The screams threaded down to them, gaspy now.

With a terrible bump the trading-post door opened. Oleg Reiner and Buck Johnson crowded outside, their mouths hanging open as they too stared up the ridge. Unearthly shrieks peeled the skin from their ears.

Sagging, the old porch complained about the weight of the eight people staring up the ridge.

Oleg Reiner, the owner of the trading post, was the only one to speak.

"Dear God in holy heaven above . . . what's he doing to her?"

Wolf and otter skins, heads and all, lined the walls for warmth, but only because they were too ratty to be sold for money or traded for anything better. "Who would buy holes with fur around them?" Moselle would say.

Among the skins, between the doorless cupboard and the rope bed where the woman had retreated to defend herself, Helmut Ruhl had his wife right where he wanted her. On her back, by the throat.

"I'm here to kill you!" he screamed down at her. "I'll teach you this time! That was all I needed! I told you so! You knew I would kill you some day, didn't you? Didn't you?"

He continued roaring down into her face as it turned redder and his knuckles turned whiter. He pressed her down against the side of the bed with such force that the rotted ropes under the mattress snapped, and most of the bed crashed to the floor. Only one leg under the far corner bore the strain.

"Bad fruit? That's what I am? The bad fruit is killing you. How does it feel? You ask for it and now you got it, you shrew bitch hound cat witch! Are you listening? Do you hear yourself dying? *Sperr doch deine Löffel auf!*"

His vulgar words pounded into her face. He reveled in her

pointy features turning orange beneath him, and she started to look like a pumpkin about to explode. Spikes of filthy blond hair spread out from her face, and her eyes screwed tight. Bubbles appeared at the corners of her mouth—joy! Her lease was up. Up, up, up.

Nobody would ever find him. The cabin was stuck on a ridge in the middle of the big nowhere, on the edge of a bigger nowhere. He could go out there. Go into the unorganized territory just as he promised her when they were married. Go to the plains. Go by himself, stake claims, get rich, alone, happy, gloriously by himself, without her, alone, free.

All alone!

Just before his glory was sealed, his wife managed to get her hand around a discarded wooden ladle and aimed for the side of his head and *crack*—victory for Moselle Ruhl. Or at least a chance to stave off murder for another moment.

She bounced across the crooked bed, taking most of the crazy quilt with her and tripping up Helmut in the process. The quilt was made of worn out clothes and coarse sacks and it had a life of its own. Like a loyal dog, it confounded Helmut when he tried to recover and go after her. Mats made of corn shucks skidded under his feet, and he screamed obscenities down at them.

When he recovered his balance and his bearings, he barreled toward Moselle, fingers clawing for her throat again.

She grabbed the pot of cornmeal and collards from the stove top, turned, and hurled. Helmut ducked but deflected the pot with one arm. The dinner crashed over him, splattering the wall, the bed, and both their heads. He got up.

He went for her throat.

This time she had nothing with which to defend herself. Helmut knew that when he reached out for her. There was nothing in his way. Before him his wife's filthy blond hair hung over her face and fanned in her hot breath. He could barely find her eyes within that jungle, like the eyes of a lioness during the hunt. He crushed her to the wall with his thick body, giving her no place to go, no way to move. Staggering pangs ran through him as his flesh crushed against hers. She wrenched her head loose for an instant and sank her teeth into his arm, sending bolts of reaction through them both.

Helmut ripped the dress from her shoulder and bit into her flesh like an attacking animal. Sweat rose beneath the rain-soaked shirt on his chest, making the smell of his body pungent, firing Moselle's struggles as coal stokes fire. Then Helmut went for her neck again.

In their passion they turned together like a weather vane in a storm.

The people from the trading post needed nearly twenty minutes to slog up that mountain. If they were going to witness a murder, they'd better make it in fifteen. By the time they crowded in on the Germans' shack, all were gasping.

Yet it was the silence from inside that stole their breaths and choked their throats. Had he killed her?

Inside the cabin a peculiar silence had taken over. There was a small scraping sound, but that was all.

Eight faces touched light at the same time, creeping up over the sills and around the doorjamb.

Two faces peered back.

The Ruhls frowned at their audience and pulled the crazy quilt up around their naked chests. They sat in their bed, side by side, their legs tangled, their hair matted with cornmeal, and gazed in moony innocence at the eight sets of widening eyes watching them from the windows and the door.

There they sat, two flowers of poverty for whom poverty was a way of life, who wouldn't know improvement if it chewed on their furniture like the rats did. They were lowbred folk who like to fight, who mistook sloth for self-reliance and thought apathy was the same as strength of spirit. And who didn't want any help, live or die. They were seamy, they were base, and apparently they were happy. It didn't figure. Yes, there they sat, in their broken bed, sweaty and satisfied, wondering what the fuss was about.

Oleg looked crosswise through the shack at Buck.

Buck shrugged. The others just blinked.

The unwanted audience sank back from the windows and the door and disappeared into the dark Missouri night.

In the bed, leaning against her husband's muddy shoulder, Moselle sighed.

"*Na also*," she complained. "They always listening t'us. Them down on that trading-post porch."

Helmut hung his big stocky arm around her greasy neck and murmured, "Aw, now, they're just jealous. Ain't everybody can have a woman like you. Lookit me . . . *allerliebst*." He plucked some cornmeal from a mat in her hair and popped it into his mouth.

She pouted. "Nobody got no respect for privacy."

"Poor thing," he cooed. As a gesture he scanned the wall, found a choice piece of stuck cornmeal to pull off, and offered it to his wife.

"Ooooh," she murmured appreciatively. After the morsel went down, she licked Helmut's fingers, then returned the favor with a bit of collard that had smashed onto his forehead. Altogether it wasn't turning out to be a bad meal at all. She hated to waste food. She'd gotten that from her mother.

They twisted to face each other at close quarters in the collapsed bed and happily mooed and cooed at each other through the rest of supper.

Then Moselle made the mistake of suggesting Helmut get a job.

★

CHAPTER TEN

──────── ★ ────────

APRIL 1839
TWENTY-TWO YEARS BEFORE THE CIVIL WAR

Helmut charged up the ridge, driven by good news and the
ideas it gave him, thinking about what they would take with
them and what they would simply chuck down the hill to rot
in the river. It was time for things to get different. He liked
that. Different always sounded good. Besides, he was getting
tired of having to "bark" squirrels for food.

Food struck his mind at about the same moment a new
aroma struck his nostrils. He grated to a halt on the hill and
sniffed.

Sweet-potato pone!

But that was crazy. Where had Moselle gotten sweet
potatoes from? She could barely walk anymore. Sure as spit,
that smell was sweet-potato pone. Crazy.

His toes dug into the hill, and he charged toward the shack,
ramming the backboard door open with one shoulder.

"Mose! Mose! I got me a—"

*"Na dann prost Mahlzeit! Jetzt können Sie nicht kneifen,
sau! Sie können mich gern haben! Da haben wir die
Bescherung!"*

Twisted with strain, Moselle's voice hit him right in the
face. The whole room was awash with her fury, and he got a
terrible vision of her face screwing up before him. He

recoiled, smacking his shoulder blades against the door. Another smell rocked his nostrils, overlaying the pone's aroma with something even more pungent.

Another face roared before him, shiny with perspiration and topped by a bright white turban. Brown fingers fanned under his nose.

"Man, you get out of here! This is no place for the likes of you!"

But it was too late for him to leave before seeing everything. The maw of Hades parted before him. His wife made one last great heave, then collapsed backward on the bed.

"Das war ein dolle Arbeit!" she gasped, blinking and rolling her eyes. Her arms sprawled out beside her, quivering, and her legs were spread in a wide *V*, puddled in soaked blankets.

The colored midwife wrestled with a trembling squawling wad of flesh, going about her business without casting another glance at the stunned man over there. If he was too stupid to turn around and leave, then he deserved to see whatever came out.

"Well?" Moselle griped from the bed. "Where is it? Give it over here! I earned it!"

"You just hold your tongue," the midwife snapped. Working swiftly, her long hands maneuvered a slippery, fleshy handful. She squeezed and rubbed and massaged until a little cough rewarded her. Her voice changed completely. She began twittering like a sweet bird. "There we go. Suck it in, baby. Suck in the good Lord's air. Lord knows, it'll be the last clean thing ever touches your tongue. Come on, little baby, breathe your first. Breathe!"

"I want to hold it," the mother insisted.

The voice changed back. "Clamp your mouth!"

There was a gurgle, a wheeze, and the little creature suddenly breathed. Air rushed through tiny lips, and a thin cry came back out.

The cry was not a shriek, but a gentle, thready bell, and almost immediately the baby's gray flesh began to turn pink.

"What I got?" Helmut demanded.

"You got a baby to feed, that's what," the midwife barked. "You better clean up this floor too. If I come back here and see this floor all bloody tomorrow, you gonna answer to me.''

Helmut puffed up and pointed at her. "Don't be telling me what to do in my own house!''

"You call this a house? I'd be ashamed to think this was a house.'' The midwife continued to work, massaging in the creamy lubricant the baby was born with. Within moments the cream had been soaked in thoroughly, as nature intended, and she put the little thing down on its mother's collapsing stomach.

The baby lay on its side in the cradle of hot flesh, quivering and gurgling.

"Can I hold it?'' Helmut asked. "Give it here.''

"It's still attached, you stupid man,'' the midwife said. "I ain't cut it free yet.''

"Well, cut it.''

"When it's good and ready, I'll cut it. The job ain't done, the cord's still throbbing, and there's more to come out. Get your fat face out of here.''

Helmut pranced to the bedside and said, "I'm tired of being snubbed by you nigger slaves with your cotton clothes and your tie shoes! Think you're so good. Think you're so fine. And I don't want your pone either!''

He whirled for the stove and the large pot stewing on top, but the midwife headed him off.

"Don't you touch that pone! My missy, she sent that up here for the mama to eat and give the baby sweet milk, and that's just what it gonna do. Can't get good breast milk from oatmeal hardtack and spoon bread. Hands back at your sides, man. Back! I'll cut 'em off! Back! Look at that baby. Look over there. Well, look! That baby counting on you to give her good food, and you go and toss the food out the window. It would *take* a man to do such a thing. Get away from this pone and let it bubble. Go on. Go on.''

She tried not to actually touch him as she maneuvered between him and the stove. She had been trying all evening to avoid touching anything in this shack. She hated visiting these itinerant white trash, but something else, something stronger, always drew her to the needs of a newborn. These people were as lazy as cows, but at least cows could do their own births. But there was always the baby, who deserved five minutes of clean and smart before beginning a lifetime of filthy and stupid.

Helmut Ruhl was looking at the baby. It was the only way to get away from the pone while still keeping what he loosely perceived as dignity.

"Look at that girl!" he blurted, pointing. "What a girl! What a fine girl!"

The midwife's words snapped like celery. "You keep your hands off that sparkling baby. God made her shine, and I ain't having you smudge her all up before she even got her first meal. Woman," she snapped at Moselle, "get your titty out for that baby. Can't you see her little head rolling and looking for it? How stupid are you? And wipe it off first. Ain't even got a cradle for this little thing to sleep in."

"I got a cradle!" he cried. He whirled into a corner and snatched up an oblong piece of worn, curved wood.

The negro woman glowered at him. "That," she said, "is no cradle, you lump of a man. That is a dough trough."

"Big enough to be a cradle, isn't it?" He plunked the dough trough down on the bed between his wife's sprawled feet.

"And you'll need a goat."

"A goat? Why a goat?"

"For milk for the baby."

"She's got milk for the baby right there! Where'm I supposed to get a goat? If I get a goat, right away I'll have to feed it."

"Helmut!" the wife cackled, squirming to get a look at her husband past the midwife. She ignored the other woman, who was working at pulling down the chemise so the baby could suckle. "We got things to do. Got to get a *Taufschein, ja*?"

"What?" The midwife came to attention. "What you gonna do to this baby? What?"

Moselle blinked. "Baptism."

"Oh . . . oh. Well." She continued introducing the baby to the nipple, working the soft little mouth with her finger. This horrible couple was strange. They were filthy and careless, yet they clung desperately to a few strands of being civilized. Among the trash in this shack were a few things that cried of a heritage. The clock over there, the *fraktur*-painted boxes over here, the rosemaled decorations that sure as heaven didn't come from anywhere in Missouri. They were baffling. She couldn't live this way.

"*Ja*, what do you take me for?" the husband grumbled. Then he suddenly puffed up and announced, "Besides, I . . . got a job."

"A job?" his wife blurted.

"A job?" the midwife echoed.

"A job," he said.

"Where?"

"Where?"

"Over the border. Over in Kansas Territory."

Moselle flinched at the sensation of the baby's mouth on the tip of her breast. "What job's out in that emptiness?"

"I heard tell of it down the ridge. Got word out that a man named Craig is hiring men to work a tannery at the edge of the territory. A tanning factory. Tanning and tooling leather goods to sell to folk heading west."

"Craig? Never heard of him. You don't know nothing about tanning."

" 'No experience required,' " he quoted.

She raised her eyebrows. "Kansas . . . ain't I proud of you? A man with a job. A fine figure of a man!"

He inhaled deeply, and his belly moved up under his rib cage for a few seconds.

Moselle pressed back her matted hair. "And we need an outhouse."

Helmut's eyes flamed. The stomach flumped down. *"What?"*

She nodded decisively. "Gotta have it. Got a baby now."

"What do we need a uppity thing like that for. *Ich danke!*" he raved. "God made trees to pee under! You gonna stick your nose up in God's face and say his trees ain't good enough to pee under?"

"A man with a job should have a outhouse."

"The outhouse'll be here, and we'll be in Kansas with the job!" He leveled a finger at the midwife. "This is your doing, ain't it? You put that idea in her head, didn't you?"

The midwife put her chin up and refused to answer. The horrible couple continued arguing past her. She let them rave but was poised to snatch the baby away in case they went for each other.

Helmut threw his hands in the air and spun to scream at his wife. "First you want a cradle! Now you want a outhouse!"

Moselle's expression suddenly changed, and she yelped, "*Ach!* Ow!" She yanked the baby away from her breast. "She bit me!"

Giving her an awful scowl, the midwife obliged the possibility by hunting around inside the baby's mouth with her forefinger. Her own expression shifted several times. Then she gasped, "A tooth! Why, she's got a little tooth in there! Sweet grace, she's got a tooth!"

Moselle laughed with pride and held the baby up in the air. "That's her name! Grace. Sweet Grace Ruhl. *Ja!*"

Helmut leaned his big smelly self over the bed. "And the devil himself'll be afraid of this one!"

★

PART THREE

★

THE
LAST GASP
OF
INNOCENCE

BY THE PRESIDENT OF THE UNITED STATES OF AMERICA.
A PROCLAMATION.

Whereas the Congress of the United States, by virtue of the constitutional authority vested in them, have declared by their act, bearing date this day, that, "by the act of the Republic of Mexico, a state of war exists between that Government and the United States:"

Now, therefore, I, JAMES K. POLK, President of the United States of America, do hereby proclaim the same to all whom it may concern; and I do specially enjoin on all persons holding offices, civil or military, under the authority of the United States, that they be vigilant and zealous in discharging the duties respectively incident thereto: and I do moreover exhort all the good people of the United States, as they love their country, as they feel the wrongs which have forced them on the last resort of injured nations, and as they consult the best means, under the blessing of Divine Providence, of abridging its calamities, that they exert themselves in preserving order, in promoting concord, in maintaining the authority and the efficacy of the laws, and in supporting and invigorating all the measures which may be adopted by the constituted authorities for obtaining a speedy, a just, and an honorable peace.

In testimony whereof, I have hereunto set my hand, and caused the seal of the United States to be affixed to these presents. Done at the City of Washington the thirteenth day [L.s.] of May, one thousand eight hundred and forty-six, and of the independence of the United States the seventieth.

JAMES K. POLK.

By the President:
JAMES BUCHANAN,
Secretary of State.

THE BURNING FUSE

1845

Texas is still a Mexican territory according to international law. President Polk sends General Zachary Taylor to occupy the territory against "invasion." In March and April of 1846, Polk sends Taylor across the Rio Grande, looking for an excuse for war. Southerners want the war, dreaming of a vast territorial acquisition with slave holding allowed. The North . . . doesn't.

There are things of which I may not speak;
　　　There are dreams that cannot die;
There are thoughts that make the strong heart weak,
And bring a pallor to the cheek,
　　　And a mist before the eye,
　　　　　And the words of that fatal song
　　　　　Come o'er me like a chill:
　　　　　"A boy's will is the wind's will,
And the thoughts of youth are long, long thoughts."

—Henry Wadsworth Longfellow,
My Lost Youth

CHAPTER ELEVEN

————— ★ —————

May 1846
War with Mexico
Plentiful, 1847
Fourteen years before the Civil War

"Why we gotta learn dis?"

"Jus' to learn. Yawl jus' say what I say. It easy."

If not daily, the school behind the fattening coops was in session at least twice a week. The darkie children liked the lessons, but mostly because they learned so much faster than the grown-up slaves, who sat around here too.

"Yawl see this piece of bark? This Plentiful. This piece here the Oaks. This whole coop yard be Virginia. This northwise, this southwise. Can tell by the sun what north, what south, like Jess said. If the coop yard be Virginia, den the whole sweet-tobacco field be the United States of America. That far-off ridge be California. Now look here. Be fifteen miles from the Oaks to Plentiful. How far you figger it be to California?"

"Hundred mile!" somebody shouted.

"*Hundred* mile. Yawl think! More like thirty hundred mile. Thirty hundred be call three thousand. Say 'three thousand.'"

"Shiiit, boy... ain't no three thousand mile in de whole worl'."

"Three thousand mile of plain empty be in just your head

137

by itself, Homer. Shut up and listen here. If coop yard be Virginia, then the curing house be Maryland way up yonder, and way down yonder, Jeff be South Carolina.''

Jeff showed his broad, shiny teeth in a proud smile and tried to puff up even bigger than he naturally was. There was something good about being part of Dorian's lesson. He couldn't figure it, but there was something proud about it.

Something about catching the elusive approval of the fourteen-year-old boy before them.

In all those years the boy's impact on Plentiful hadn't faded. With his magic he had stolen the Greek wife's heart, and she had protected him just as if he had a patron goddess.

Even now, when he spoke, his black brows arched like sickles. His overall appearance would both surprise and confuse. Even for those who had known him since the day he spilled from Yula's womb, to glance at him meant to glance twice. Even after all the years of labor beneath sun and bullwhip, his skin was still light and carried that tint of saffron. He still had the shock of soft black hair and brows, his eyes still ink drops on manila. Those eyes were set deep, like an elf or a demon's, and he could play both roles. He was forever a chameleon, blending for a time into the sandstone, only to draw attention to himself the instant he moved. Some were afraid of him. Whispers of haints and possessions still moved beneath the soil on Plentiful, and he had been born that night, after all. The night dark Mr. Nick first appeared on Plentiful.

This was part of the reason some came to hear his lessons. Plain, prudent fear of that which was right here as opposed to that which was all the way up at the mansion.

He was a boy conceived by the devil as done by Shelley, or a pearl by Poe.

Around him, beneath an autumn noonday sky, some three dozen bonded negroes listened for their own various reasons. Out of the roughly two hundred slaves on Plentiful, Dorian could usually round up thirty or so who would listen to him. He always tried to drag over the children, but some of the parents refused to let their young ones anywhere near him. He was stirring up trouble. He was dangerous. He was a waste of time. He'd bring wrath of the white folk down upon them if they knew Dorian scratched maps in the sand and made them count beans and drew ABCs on the barn wall with coal chunks.

"Watch," he said. His sickle brows shot high. He knelt to the ground. "This where we are in Virginia. Call Tidewater Region. Yawl say loud. Tidewater."

"Tidewater," the group mumbled at their usual timid pitch. Only about half of them spoke up.

"Why we gotta learn dis stuff?" Homer demanded again. When he spoke, the space between his big square front teeth showed plainly. "Dis be Sunday. I wants t'rest, like Boss say Sunday fo'."

The boy stood straight, his black eyes hard. "Yawl learn," he insisted. "There a big world out there. Big world with lots of talk. Someday won't be slaves anymore."

As he spoke, his tone different now from the lesson a moment ago, he prowled through their hunched postures toward the man who challenged him. Despite the difference in size, the boy was utterly dominant.

Some said he could hold a victim with his eyes while he sucked blood to get the saffron in his cheeks. Hoo-doo born, they said.

"Someday," he said, "yawl be out in the big world, no boss to protect you, no field to feed you. Gonna have to read. Gonna have to work a trade. Be boss' for yourself. Gonna have to add and subtract. What good your stonecuttin' be if you can't write a bill? Can't figure your wage? What you do then, Homer?" He glared down into the sitting negro's face. He leaned over the man and waited until hardly anyone dared breathe. Then he simply said, "You starve. And somebody smarter take your place."

"Yawl stir up trouble fo' us, boy!" one of the women said. Her name was Stepney, and for several weeks Dorian had seen her fear grow, ever since he'd started trying to teach geography.

He knew she was listening to the rumors and the stories. Until now there had been nothing more than an evil curiosity that brought her to his lessons, for certainly she didn't have to come, as many did not. She had been afraid not to know, and today she realized why she was afraid to know.

What good was geography to a slave?

Yes, there was an implied stain of rebellion on the whole idea.

Unsurprised, he straightened slowly and turned to face her. Before he could speak, a loud *snap* drew their attention.

Behind the bunched negroes, Yula was on her feet. The stick she held still trembled in her hands where she had cracked it.

She slivered her eyes at Stepney and barked, "He know. Yawl listen, 'cuz he know what comin' for us. Stupid niggawoman, gon' go on bein' stupid and scared, jump at a candle in de dark and run away 'stead of follow de light? Yawl listen to Dohrian. Yawl learn."

A silence dropped over them. They'd never been quite sure what to make of Yula for all these years. Because of Dorian's favor with the missus, Yula had manipulated herself to the top of the pecking order, no matter the resentment it caused her among the slave women and even some of the men. She had few friends among her own kind as a result, but her marshmallow was still with her.

"Nuff lesson for today!" she snapped, brushing the crowd away like flies with a flick of her hand.

The slaves crawled to their feet and scattered. She and her son came together in the center of the coop yard.

Then she hit him.

"What yawl think yawl do?" her high voice nipped. "Go too fast fo' dem, boy! Yawl scare 'em off from lesson, den what?"

"They gotta learn add and subtract, mile and ten mile, Mama," Dorain said sullenly. "Always be slaves if they don't. Even if they free some day, still be slaves."

He moved like a ghost to the edge of the coop yard, touched the wire fence, and gazed out over the tobacco fields. Sunlight played over the dirty folds of his drab calico shirt.

"Things change real soon, Mama. Change all the time. Mr. Polk be president now. Be 'lectro telegraph lines now. Lay lines all 'cross the country. Pretty soon to Europe. Folk know news same day it happen. Michigan a state now, Iowa a state, Texas, Florida . . . now we got war with Mexico. Maybe New Mexico be next. Be talk about secession again. Every time new state come, there be new talk about free soil or slave soil . . . someday it all gonna blow up. Blow right up."

Yula approached behind him, slipped her arms about him, and lay her head between his shoulder blades. The sweaty calico

formed to the shape of her cheek. For the first time she noticed
he had grown taller than she was. The realization hit her like a
blow. He had her beat by half a hand now. Soon childhood
would no longer be there to help protect him, and she would
find herself standing between the world and a grown man.

As the years had gone by, Yula had become more aware of
Boss's unremitting hatred of the son she bore him. Rather
than fading with the security and prosperity of time, the
resentment had hardened. The boy remained Boss's singular
bane, a symbol of his cracked foundation.

Within the spacious confines of Plentiful, Dorian had
enjoyed free run, or at least something that he perceived as
free run. With Boss's burgeoning success and rising place in
society, Plentiful had also burgeoned. More acreage, more
slaves, more diversified crops, more self-sufficiency, more
room to hide a half-breed who looked white enough to be
dangerous. For his entire life the boy had been free to come
and go anywhere *inside* Plentiful, until the clock struck half
past six and he must be down in the yard, never to eat supper
at the same table with the other mother.

The other woman, the angel. Missy, Yula still called her.
Since his marriage Lucas Wallace's star had been on the rise.
He'd been invited into county politics and had dabbled in that
showy game, as sponsor, delegate, or speaker for nearly ten
years. All the while the Greek woman had been a perfect
Southern wife for him. Life had even become better for the
slaves on Plentiful, for the missus paid attention to details like
extra clothing and better allowances, and even trips into town
to spend those allowances had become regular. Whether all
this came from the goodness of Missy's heart or simply the
fact that she loved a boy who must live in the yard, Yula had
never been completely sure. Nor had she cared.

The reverse factor was that most of the slaves on Plentiful
were never desperate enough to pay attention to Dorian's
lessons and certainly not his warnings. They slept dry and
warm, and why poke holes in the roof just to get a little more
sunlight? Could just as soon rain. There had been many new
secrets and new rules since Dorian was born, and the slaves
kept their mouths shut.

Yula pressed her cheek deeply between her son's shoulder

blades, feeling his cool sweat. "Yawl remember who you is, Dohrian," she told him quietly. "My baby too."

Dorian reached his arms behind and held her. "I know. I never forget you, Mama."

"What gives! All right, break it up!"

Dorian spun, automatically pushing his mama behind him, but it was only McCrocklin.

The overseer's ruddy face was flushed, and his blond hair matted. The years had plumped him somewhat and put white hairs in his beard, but in all other ways he was an unchanged man. "You come with me, boy. We got wheat to sheave, and Sunday or not we're gonna get it done. Be damned if Boss is gonna dress me down. He got company coming this afternoon, and he wants the field neat looking. Woman, you get to work! Sew or something! Come on, boy."

"Comin', sir," Dorian said tonelessly. He squeezed Yula's bony hand and stepped off after McCrocklin.

The field in question was a patch of ground closer to the house than any other tilled ground. Rather than leave it to lawn or meadow, Boss had decided to turn it into food crop—an unwise move, considering it turned out to be ugly much of the year, and anyone who looked out the library window would see it. Thus a Sunday manicuring before the guests arrived. The wheat was funny looking enough when half-tilled, but next season the patch would be planted with restorative sainfoin—even uglier because everybody knew that it was a fodder plant. But that was next season.

Dorian followed McCrocklin out to the field without a word. He'd learned long ago not to waste perfectly good conversation on the foreman unless absolutely necessary.

There was already turmoil in the field. A dozen slaves and their driver were fighting with two of the draft chunks, trying to get the horses to slow down in pulling the new reaper through the wheat.

Dorian ran in front of McCrocklin, drawn by fascination for the whole process.

The reaper, the Cyrus McCormick reaping machine of great fame and notoriety with its own factory up North, was a thing of beauty. As the horses pulled it along, it combed the standing wheat under four big knives that rotated, slashing laterally downward, under, around, up, and down again. The *slussshhh* of each rotation and the grind of metal made music with the horses' massive hooves. Sunlight crashed across the knives, which were the length of a large man's body and half the width. The machine was much more imposing in person than implied by the picture in the catalog.

"Stunning!" he blurted as he scampered around it, trying to stay out of the horses' path. The chunks eyed him and rattled their harnesses, protesting the slow pace. They couldn't quite figure out why this plow had to move more slowly than the other plow or the wagons.

The great blades rotated, slashing line after line of wheat that quivered before them as though contemplating its fate.

"You'd know about these newfangles," McCrocklin said to the boy, "if'n you wasn't up to the house half your time. Pleason! What the hell's making this contraption go so slow?"

A negro guiding the wheat out of the spearhead-shaped guards beneath the blades paused and shrugged. "I dunno, suh. It jes' clog up ev'ry time."

"Can't you see?" Dorian spoke up behind McCrocklin.

The foreman turned, blinking in the bright daylight. "See what, boy?"

"That blade there," Dorian said, pointing, "be cracked. Be catchin' the wheat 'stead a letting it go, stuffin' it up underneath."

McCrocklin watched the blades turn, keeping his eye on the one that slashed across the ground just then, and sure enough a clog of wheat stalks caught inside the blade itself and was carried up and around.

The horses balked and shuddered as the wheat piled under the reaper and dragged.

"Bedamned," McCrocklin grumbled. "Pleason, can't you pull it out of there before it clogs?"

"Cain't, suh. Ah's tried."

"He can't," Dorian said. "Got to be pulled out on t'other side. Over there."

He pointed to the front of the reaping mechanism where the wheat was fed in.

"Stand up on wheel side, boy," the foreman said.

Dorian frowned. "Pardon?"

"Climb up there. Your weight'll hold her down. Maybe she'll turn loose of the clog."

"That won't—all right, fine."

Dorian swallowed his protest and climbed aboard, onto the support piece between the wheel and the horses. The wooden wheel bit into the ground. The horses tossed their barrel-sized heads, but otherwise there was no effect whatsoever on the cracked blade. It continued to drag wheat, carry it high, and clog it under.

"Bedamned twice."

"It gotta be mended, sir," Dorian said, stepping carefully down on the opposite side from the slashing blades.

"Goddamn you, Buckie! Amus! Chestnut! Put a halt to those horses! What good you think it's doing this way! Stop the horses, I said! Reemond, come 'round and help here."

McCrocklin stalked around the front and grabbed the closest huge harness. It took him and four other men to stop the huge horses completely. Giant shoulders quivered within the harnesses and resisted the men. Harness chains jangled, and the big horses sputtered in frustration. Behind them, the reaper knives slowed, stopped, and poised there glinting like evil in the sunlight.

"Take the blade off," the boy said.

McCrocklin spun around. "Keep your mouth shut, boy."

"Take it to Jonah, and he forge the crack."

"Pleason! Come round on this side and use your rake to clear the wheat out of that crack as it come down. Hear? Reemond and Chestnut, you take his place in back and sweep the cut off the platform. You got two more rakes out here? Well, go get 'em!"

As McCrocklin ranted, the slaves skeptically complied. Pleason glanced at Dorian as he stepped past him. Pleason had come from another state, and his long ropy hair, hanging below his shoulders, looked strange and new. Pleason had taken a fancy to Yula when he was first bought, but Yula's utter devotion to her son had ruined any chance of a broom-jumping. That and the ropy hair.

Anyway, Pleason and Dorian had never liked each other.

Pleason was now standing in front of the oncoming blades. On horseback nearby, the negro driver, Elazar, cracked his short whip in the air and bellowed, "Move along! Haul dem hosses! Haul, I say! Haul! Haul!"

Amus and Buckie pulled the horses forward, but getting them started was almost as hard as getting them stopped. Shivering with protest, the two harnessed masses finally leaned into the leather and pulled forward.

The wide blades began to turn again, over and over, chewing down the beautiful fringe of wheat. With each rotation Pleason fought to rake the cracked blade clean.

"He gotta walk backward to do that," Dorian said, standing just behind McCrocklin's right shoulder.

"I told you to butt out," McCrocklin barked.

"If he trip, he gonna get slashed."

The foreman spun on him. "Look, boy," he growled, "I took your idea serious about rotating bondsmen from job to job. Hell, you got half our manpower wrapped up in apprenticing to the other half. Don't be meddling in the business of machinery. I got a farm to run."

"That gonna hurt somebody real soon," Dorian insisted. "Ain't gonna work like that. Gonna cut somebody hand off."

McCrocklin's muscular shoulder moved, and that was all Dorian saw. An instant later the boy was on the ground, and his jaw was throbbing. McCrocklin tended his knuckles and said, "I'll cut your hand off, you don't shut up!"

The slaves looked up from their work, including Pleason, who then had to hurry to clear the blade as it sliced downward inches from his face.

"Keep on!" Elazar shouted, drawing attention back to the work at hand.

From the dirt the boy dabbed at his mouth and said, "I could help you, Mr. McCrocklin. Someday you gonna have to let me."

"You keep your mouth shut about this. It ain't your business. Elazar! No food for this bunch till the field is clear."

"Yassa," the driver called, waving his whip.

From the ground Dorian leaned on his elbow and glared upward. He lowered his voice to the perfect pitch.

"I won't protect you," he said.

McCrocklin sneered beneath his yellow mustache, glaring at Dorian. He took one step toward the boy.

Then he ground to a halt at the sound of a delicate voice. "Dorian!"

At the edge of the whitewashed picket fence stood a child

as pretty as a paper-and-lace doll. Done up in pale satin, bobbin lace, and cameos, she was a small echo of the young queen way off in England. Whatever Victoria Regina wore, so wore the girls of the South. Even the little girls. Even Lydia Nicolina Wallace.

Her Dresden-brown ringlets were umber in the noon sun, as if someone had taken Wallace's hair and Iphigenia's and thrown it all in a pot with a pint of sepia. Even at eleven years old, there were clues that she would be pretty some day, once the gawkiness faded and she grew into those Victorian styles. Yes, that classical handsomeness had bred true, as Dimitrios Trözene promised it would. His granddaughter's skin was ivory, like Iphigenia's, and retained the same palette of foreign colors. While her hair was not as dark, her eyes were indeed as black as Dorian's and a constant signal of her heritage. In one arm she held a folded bundle of fabric. The other fist knotted and connected with her hip.

"Dorian! Boy, you come up to the house at this instant and no later! You were not finished mending my bedpost, and I shall not enter my bedchamber until you do. There'll be no supper in your day until—"

"Comin', Miss Lydia, comin'," Dorian called. He slipped out from under the canopy of McCrocklin and scooted toward her. When he got to her, he bowed quickly, then followed her in the direction of the mansion.

McCrocklin watched them closely, his mind a twist of suspicions.

Lydia glanced back only once as she hurried up the long grassy hill toward the mansion. Beside her, matching her stride, Dorian was unbuttoning the filthy calico that hung like Spanish moss on his shoulders.

When she thought they were far enough away, she gasped, "Borete na me?"

"Ti thelete?" he shot back. "Ene dodeka to mesimere. I thought you were in church."

"Kati semveni me ergo. Kati lipi! Den katalahveno."

Dorian shook his head and sarcastically drawled, "Borete na to epanalahvete?"

The girl grabbed her ruffled skirt and yanked it. "Don't tease me! Ene savaro!"

"No doubt."

"I still don't get it," she said, keeping her voice down lest the breeze carry whispers.

Dorian's brows flicked again. He too kept his volume under control. "This play is faster out of the stall than any of its kind, and you don't get it?"

The girl waved her free hand. "It makes no sense in the beginning. What'll I do? Mother'll get that look."

Dorian shimmied out of his calico shirt and traded her for a clean linen one out of her bundle. "Have you tried to imagine it being performed, as I told you?"

"Right before my very eyes, but still—"

"It's only the *Antigone,* Lydia, it's hardly obscure."

They slipped through the servants' entrance in the mansion's bowels, avoiding the kitchen slaves, who were working on what would later be supper. The negro slaves and the Greek servants glanced up at the sudden activity, then settled back to their work without a second glance. *Souvlakia* again, Dorian noted as he slipped into the broom closet. Lydia went straight to the indoor pump and got the water running, then doused a cloth and handed it through to him.

"Here," she said. "Wash that filth off your face. Please go over it with me, will you? Mother made me stay home from church today so I could read it all over again, but that didn't help me one whit. I truly don't want to see that look."

"Put chocks on it, Lydia," Dorian said, his words muffled as he raked the wet cloth over his face. "What's your question?"

"Does Antigone fear the state or not?"

"I should think that was crystal clear," Dorian complained from the closet. His tone was completely barren of sympathy.

"Then why does she say, 'My heart is weak to deny the State I serve'?" Lydia asked.

There was a loud bump inside the closet. "What? Girl, you're reading it all wrong."

"Am not!"

"You've got it flummoxed up somehow."

Lydia slumped back against the wall and pouted. "Have not."

"Where's your text?" he asked her.

"In Father's library."

The closet door bumped open, and a new creature stepped out.

If he had been imposing in rags, he was pure poison now.

His face was clean and glowed from within like Limoges bisque. Without the glaze of dust, his hair was blue black, his face finally maturing to fit those sickle brows and pitch eyes. His lips were somewhat thick—not like a negro's lips, but like a statue's, as if drawn with a sharp pencil, and unforgivingly expressive.

He adjusted a black sailor's tie around his white shirt collar, then buttoned the trim Quaker gray jacket at his waist—no doubt the Quakers would disapprove of the richly quilted fabric. The jacket, a gift sent all the way from Papa Dimitrios in Macedon, still fit after almost a year but wouldn't for long at this rate.

"All right," he said, "let's drag this problem into the light of day and see what it looks like."

The Wallace library had taken on a patina of clutter in the years since the wedding. Wallace had gone on collecting books and over the years had shown a marked preference for Bulwer-Lytton, Dickens, and Marryat novels. The Greeks, of course, had brought trunkloads of books when they first arrived from Macedon, and as time passed, more had arrived from Dimitrios as gifts. *Poems* by William Wordsworth was selling well and had recently become a member of the collection, and from *Horseshoe Robinson* to *The Pickwick Papers*, every popular book of the last decade was here somewhere. Dorian loved the very smell of the room.

And the texture of it, from the tasteful square grand piano to the Louis XIII chair with its brass tacks and Viennese tapestry. Wonderful.

Lydia got into the room first and went straight to an open book lying on the piano. "I've read through the whole play twice, and this part in the beginning of it just doesn't add up, Dory," she said, being very definite because she admired things that were definite.

Dorian huffed at her and pushed her aside, peering down at the text. "Witch piss. It's clear as a bell if you think about the characters' mo—"

He stopped, leaned closer to the printed page, and a sudden rage appeared in his eyes.

"Well, it would be if this translation was printed correctly. God's back teeth."

"Dory! Mind yourself."

"Some folks call themselves scholars. This is all wrong here. This isn't Antigone's line at all! Antigone would never in her right head say such a thing!"

He shifted from one foot to the other several times, as if to stomp out the misprint. Finally he gave up, because the words on the page continued to be stubborn.

"All right," he sighed. "Just give me your attention. Sit on the piano bench and listen. No, forget about the book. Look at *me*."

Lydia scooted up onto the piano bench, her feet dangling with the tips of her shoes touching the Persian rug, and arranged her skirt around her. She folded her hands in her lap and pursed her lips.

Dorian was willing to wait.

At last he said, "Think hard. Antigone is the best of all tragic heroines because she espouses a tragic vision. Her collection of flaws qualifies her for a heroine. The sister Ismene is a painfully normal woman of the time, and the uncle Creon is a normal man, except for the complication that he's the king. Now this play hit light four hundred and forty-two years before Christ, and the original audience saw it differently than we do in modern times."

Sinking into his element, Dorian started to pace. "Creon's loyalty to the city of Thebes over his family would have made sense to the Greek audience. Duty to state over duty to family." He paused and put a finger to his lips. "It's rather like the debate between states' rights and federal authority today. . . ."

Lydia cocked her head and spat, "Oh, *how* is it like that? Because you want it to be?"

He turned on her. "No! Just look at the characters."

"I did look at the stupid characters!"

"Yes, but you're not thinking their thoughts! Even today we fight the same battles. Do we go for states' individual rights, or do we support a representative congress? Does Congress get to make decisions for Virginia? Why should we listen to a congressman from Florida? Or, God forbid, Missouri? Are you going to be an Antigone or an Ismene about it? How on earth would *you* choose?''

Dorian was, among many things, a show-off. He dropped to one knee beside her, cupped his hand over hers, and drilled her with those black eyes. His voice fell away. He spread his hand in the air.

''I'm lying dead out on the lawn,'' he whispered. ''Father has refused me a decent burial because I'm . . . well, you know. I have no legal right to rise against him, but if I had a moral one, what would you do, sister? Would you be loyal to our father and let me rot, or sneak in the night and bury me in a civilized fashion?''

Lydia had gone to stone under his gaze. She gnawed at her lip now, puzzled the problem, her chin tucking more and more.

Finally she blinked and asked, ''Well . . . did you hit Father, or just holler at him?''

Dorian's face twisted into an evil mask.

''Lydia,'' he said, still whispering, but now with an edge, ''for the sake of dreams, don't be a normal woman.''

He got up and tugged his jacket straight.

''It's just this one play I don't get,'' she pleaded.

His eyes flashed. She'd set him off as surely as if she'd lit a fuse.

''Because you're thinking about it in English! If you look at it in the original language, what you find is masculine verbs applied to Antigone. That's a giveaway! It's the nut of your problem. Now listen. Listen to the Greek!''

He struck a pose, imagined he was standing on the orchestra of the Theater of Dionysus, with his back to the *skene* and seats fanning out before him—full house, of course—perhaps the composer Sophocles in the audience, sitting with Euripides. Athens's purple sunset shimmered before his eyes, and his voice echoed in perfect classical Greek.

'' 'I will bury him. And Death to my deed will add a sweet knell. A sinless criminal am I. I will lie loved beside him whom I loved. Take thy part, then. . . . Dishonor what the gods have honored.' ''

He paused a moment, staring at the sunset in his mind.

Suddenly he looked down and pointed at Lydia's nose,

lapsing back into English. "Then *Ismene* is the one who says, 'Dishonor! No! None! But my heart is too weak to defy the State.' It doesn't come off in English. In classical Greek an adjective's gender agrees with the noun, and you're not getting any of this, are you?"

He folded his arms and scowled at her.

Lydia bit her lip again and scrambled for any answer that would make him happy, but too late.

Dorian huffed in exasperation. "Shall I do it for you in French?"

Color raced across Lydia's face. "It's not my fault if you comprehend and I don't, *Doh*rian."

"If you'd consider your native grammar, you'd comprehend all right, Lydia. All right, I don't have to help you. I have plenty of work that doesn't involve your studies—"

She skidded off the piano bench and headed him off at the library door. "No! Don't leave! Mother'll get that look! Just explain it to me once more, and if I don't get it, I'll let you eat my share of the *tyropitta*. Please?"

Dorian paused gruffly, long enough to make her pay for getting him all worked up only to dare not to understand him.

He sighed, recollected his perceptions, then spoke slowly.

"Never forget the Greek language," he said. "Live up to being a heroine."

His black eyes became crescents as he thought about it. The guidelines of heroism were always at the front of Dorian's mind. Old heroism, new heroism . . . had prerequisites.

Suddenly he didn't look fourteen anymore, but a thousand. He gazed into the past, his face taking on the distant dignity of classical plays. He was an idealist, as children are wont to be, but even more so because he saw the world only through the rosy glow of literature.

Which was why most of this was lost on a girl who came and went in the outer world.

But the magic of her brother wasn't lost on her. Lydia stared at him, haunted, knowing there was something here that she would someday have to understand if she hoped to cling to the golden strand of Dorian's respect.

Dorian wavered before her, as though listening to music. His face and his posture took on an Olympian stateliness. A wedge of sunlight from the tall window drew glitters upon his burgundy brocade. "To the ancient Greeks suicide was cowardice," he murmured. "It is the opposite of heroism. Antigone's suicide deletes her from the list of heroes . . . and worrying about her virginity and all that . . . she just can't get into the club. *Ene thavmasseo!* God, it makes me gasp!"

Watching him, Lydia quivered with an eerie feeling that suddenly possessed her. She contemplated him and decided, "You're *too* Greek sometimes."

Dorian struck her with a deadly glare. "Madam, there is no such thing. Well, do you understand yet?"

"Almost . . ."

"Almost? What don't you?"

"If I ask one question," Lydia admitted shyly, "you won't get mad?"

"Of course not, Miss Knocksoftly. Now what is the question?"

He was lying, and she knew it.

"And you won't tell Mother that I don't know?"

He shifted impatiently. "Of course not."

"Then . . . what's virginity?"

"Oh, God."

Norfolk's downtown streets teemed even on Sundays. Folk came and went, mostly from church and meetings. It was a good environment for business, for while most people were relaxed from the pleasant weekend, they were also beginning to put their minds on the week to come. Saturday would never serve quite so well as Sundays.

Up the main street at the firm hour of high noon came a strange wagon—a caravan wagon as big as a storeroom. Its high barn-wood sides were painted bright red, freshly painted, apparently, though the wagon itself was noticeably second-hand. There were windows, but they were small and shuttered, locked with huge iron latches and bolts, secured with key locks. Strange.

Stranger still was the man who held the reins and guided the pair of oxen who drew this wagon. Seldom was his like seen in the South, at least not without a master. Any of the skilled Southern eyes that looked at him now could all but see right through his flouncy coat to the freedman's papers folded carefully in the inside pocket. He rarely had to get them out anymore.

As the wagon came abreast of C. T. Patterson's Mercantile, the man drew the oxen to a stop. Instantly the wagon behind him began to shake.

The longer the standstill, the more the wagon rattled. Its big body rocked from side to side and shuddered. The racket drew attention from a block around. People stepped out of buildings, right in the middle of whatever they were doing, to see what the din could possibly be. They peered at the wagon and its proprietor. The large man was loudly dressed. Had he been white, folks would have called him a dude. Being colored, he didn't qualify. Only a white man could be a *real* dude.

The man jumped down from the crashing wagon as though all this were normal. Except for the clatter of chains against wood, there might have been a mountain storm trapped in there.

He set the brake, strode to a nearby trough, and used the courtesy bucket to water each of his oxen. He paid a skillful lack of attention to the gathering crowd who came sneaking up, hoping to see what was inside that caravan. As he replaced the bucket, he touched the brim of his varnished hat and nodded at them. The wagon continued to pound.

C. T. Patterson was at the door of the mercantile, peeking just like everybody else, when this stranger clomped onto the boardwalk and came inside. At that C. T. tried to appear busy rearranging a display of doctor goods.

"Pardon, sir," the fancy man said. "Be you the proprietor hereabouts?"

"Yes, I happen to be," C. T. answered. As he looked at the stiff negro hair that hung down to this man's shoulders, combed flat so the hat would fit over it, he was suddenly aware of his own hairless pate. To distract himself, he scanned the man's coat. It was a few years out of style and too jack-a-dandy for daywear, but this didn't seem to concern the stranger. "What is it you want?"

The man wiped his hands on a set of matted velvet lapels. "My name is Root. I am a newcomer here."

"Root? That's all?"

"That is all. Would you be so kind as to tell if I need a permit to post up a bill on that outside wall?"

C. T. frowned. "No, not a permit, not by the law. By me you might. It's my wall."

"Sir," the negro said loftily, "I will rent me a space on your wall. Five cents a day, clear."

C. T. glanced out his front window and saw the gaggle of townsfolk hovering out there, doing a bad job of not looking in. Rarely if ever did he see that many people hovering near his store, and for the moment it heartened him. The big enclosed wagon continued to bang and crash outside.

He held out an open palm for the first nickel. "Put it on up."

"And may I park my wagon at the side of your establishment?"

"Well . . . is it going to make that hullabaloo all the time? Sounds like hell broke loose in there."

"I can quieten it down, sir."

"All right. But that'll be another five cents per day."

"Done."

Root strode out in a tawdry whirl. The small crowd parted for him, no longer pretending they weren't there to ogle. He touched the hat again, nodded again, and went to the side of the wagon, where a tarpaulin was folded and tied behind one wheel. From inside he carefully pulled out a large, stiff piece of paper, a handbill of some sort. A moment later he was tacking the handbill up right on the front of C. T. Patterson's Mercantile, beside the entrance. Anyone who walked in would have to see it.

With another touch and another nod, he climbed aboard his wagon and clucked the oxen forward.

As the jostling wagon lumbered around into the alley beside the store, people began to gather around the handbill.

Several women turned away, either blushing or disgusted. Some of the men did too.

"Vulgar," someone commented.

"Wholly inappropriate, I would say."

"First I ever heard of such a practice."

"It does make an odd kind of sense...."

"Plain tasteless."

The crowd thinned by half almost immediately. But there were others who stayed to get a good, long look.

After that, word of the strange handbill spread like wildfire.

The front door of the big house swung open and bumped. A small glossy-haired girl rushed in, brandishing her new doll and looking for her elder sister. Behind her came her father, his big boots caked with street mud. He carried his mail and the Richmond *Enquirer* as usual. He went to town every Sunday, and every Sunday an issue of the *Enquirer* waited for him at the post office. He always picked it up first thing, before church. As he strode among the polite Episcopal congregation, he liked to be seen carrying it.

Samson met him at the foot of the stairs, as usual.

"A fine afternoon, Boss," Samson said with a nod.

"Yes, any word from Tuggle?"

"No, Boss."

"Good. That means the committee's still coming. They'll be here two o'clock or so. You be ready, hear?"

"I hears, Boss. We be right ready fo' company by den."

"McCrocklin getting that field trimmed up?"

"I believes it, suh. I hear dem harness be rattlin' when I goes back to the kitchen, sure nuff."

"Good. I'm going to change out of these city duds. You get the children their lunch."

"I sees to it, Boss."

Wallace tossed the unread *Enquirer* on the foyer chair and took the stairs two at a time, and Samson headed for the kitchen.

As soon as they were gone, a tall twelve-year-old boy strode in the front door, his fists buried in the pockets of a blue waistcoat under a tailed coat of a darker, more cadet blue. In the crook of one elbow he carried a book bound in mahogany leather. Sunlight clung to his hair, which hadn't darkened one shade since the day he was born. It was still buff blond, but without the adulterant of any gold or sulfur yellows. In the bright light it almost looked white. His father happily called him a throwback to his namesake, Alexander the Great . . . great and blond.

He peeked into the dining room. Nobody there. Immediately he crossed the hall to the library and looked one way and the other. At last he spied a dark head bent over the writing desk, over there on the other side of the square grand.

"There you are," Alexander Wallace declared, and came in.

Dorian didn't look up. He dipped his pen into the well and continued writing.

"Hello, white meat," he muttered.

"If Father finds you in here—"

"I'm nearly finished. Where is he?"

"Gone upstairs to change. Did Lydia finish her studies?"

"I believe she's upstairs having her dolls act out the *Antigone*."

Alex leaned an elbow on the desk and asked, "What's this?"

"A letter, Alex," Dorian said intolerantly. "You know what a letter is?"

"Going where?"

Dorian tipped his head toward an open book on the desk beside his letter. "To the publisher of this abysmal translation. Where's Mother?"

"She went around back, I believe. You should've seen Mrs. Brookville this morning at church. She had her hair all done up in rolls, trying to imitate Mother's Grecian twists. She looked like somebody'd baked her for breakfast!"

Alex watched the letters come out as Dorian's pen scratched along the paper. As he waited, a shadow on the other boy's face caught his attention. He leaned closer, to see if it was a trick of the light in the room. It wasn't.

"Dorian, are you all right? What happened to your face?"

The pen dipped again.

"McCrocklin hit me."

Alex winced. "That dishonorable hog . . ."

"Why? You've hit me harder."

"When I hit you, it's different." His Wedgwood eyes took

on a familiar guilt. "It just isn't fair, your living like this. You shouldn't be stuck on Plentiful, Dory. You look just like us, and you're way smarter."

Not looking up, Dorian said, "It's not so bad. When I'm sixteen, I plan to escape and take up wool carding anyway. May I sign your name to this?"

"Yes. Why do you always sign my name?"

"Because I don't legally have one."

Alex sighed and frowned. "That's exactly my meaning. You do all the smart things, and I get all the glory."

The black brows arched. "Yes, but this way I can't be traced in case of bad weather. Think of that."

The pen continued to scratch. *Alexander Wallace, Esq., Plentiful* . . .

"The day will come," Alex said, "when I go up against Father. I'm going to demand you be allowed to go into the city with us. Yes! Why not? I believe I'll do that, Dory. I can hear myself saying it to him!"

"That's very frontier of you." *In Care of Postmaster, Norfolk, Virginia.* "I'll end up in Hogmuscle, Mississippi, with no chance of parole."

Alex's face flashed with indignation. "He'll have to listen to me," he insisted. "He keeps calling me his legal heir. That must stand for something, mustn't it? It must give me *some* power in how Plentiful is run. . . . I'm twelve now, and he's forever pushing me to learn the business. I'll confront him on your behalf. It's long overdue."

"Quit trying to rain upward." Dorian blew on the letter to dry the ink, then paused and said, "You know, Sophocles wrote more than a hundred twenty plays. The real Greek tragedy is that only seven of them have survived."

The room changed suddenly. Dorian was gazing into the past again.

"Someday," he murmured to the one person with whom he could be completely honest, "someday I shall go to Greece and dig in the rocks, and I'll find the lost plays . . . the complete text of the *Ichneutae* . . . the satyr plays . . . the unknown tetralogies. . . . I'll perform them myself on the open terrace at Dionysus Eleutherios. . . ."

Or was it the future he saw, Alex wondered, hardly breathing as he watched his half brother.

Things had changed for him too in the past year or so. He had always taken Dorian's confinement for granted as Plentiful policy. Even as a child Dorian had always walked a delicate thread strung between his two worlds, wrapped tenuously around the sanction of the master. That had been normal.

But lately Alex had been having new thoughts. All his life the secret of the white brother at the cabins had been normal and accepted. But now, the questions winked in Alex's mind. He found it wasn't normal at all. In his newborn sense of fair and unfair, he began to see his brother as a flightless bird.

He hated to tell Dorian that the world outside was neither morality play nor high drama. Yet that's what he'd been thinking about saying. His own Southern sense of honor demanded that his hand grope for the cage door.

"I have a present for you," he said quietly. "A surprise. I wanted to give it to you for your last birthday, but it didn't come in time."

Dorian blinked.

Alex held out the book that had been tucked under his arm until now. *"Le Comte de Monte Cristo, par Alexandre Dumas le père. C'est l'édition premier."*

The older boy flew from his chair so fast he stumbled. His hands flagged out in front of him, eyes thundering, and he gasped, "Alex!"

They stood facing each other, like a couple of bookends standing on either side of this one book. Despite their almost opposite coloring, at second glance the resemblance settled in. They were of similar build, both rangy with youth, and in spite of the two-year difference, they were nearly the same height. They'd gotten that from their common father. Dorian had only an inch or so on his five-foot-four half brother. Even at twelve Alex showed signs of overtaking him before all the growing was over. Dorian was taller now, but Alex would be later.

Dorian stared at the book in Alexander's hands, afraid to touch it because it might disintegrate.

"Bon anniversaire, Dory," Alex said. "Belated, of course."

"Alex! Where'd you get it?"

"At a pig swap."

Clutching his head with both hands, Dorian squeezed his eyes shut and groaned.

Alex laughed. "Same as I got *The Old Curiosity Shop* and *Two Years Before the Mast*. I told Father I fancied having it, and he used his connections. The difference is that this one is for you to have. To keep, and I don't care what Father says about it. Only thing is, you'll have to tell me the story in detail, case he quizzes me. Promise?"

Dorian grabbed his brother by the shoulders, still staggered, still gaping at the book between them, still hesitant to actually take hold of it.

"God, my chest hurts.... Alex, I don't know what to say!"

"Say whatever you want."

"In the parlance of the cabins, yawl done lit mah stove!"

"Well, take hold of the book, then. It's yours, for your very own."

"My own," Dorian murmured, and felt the leather cover slip into his fingers.

He held it in both hands, his thumbs framing the scrolled title. He'd read reviews, articles, but this was the real thing. The story of a man rising from desolation to command great wealth and leash revenge like a hunting dog at his side—

Suddenly he shoved the edition back into Alex's arms. "Thanks. I can't."

"Dory!"

Alex stopped him at the doorway.

"Dorian, you take it!"

"Oh, to what end?" Dorian demanded. "Don't fret. I'll read the novel, same as always."

"It's *not* the same as always," Alexander hissed at him, shoving him hard into the doorjamb. "It's a gift. I can give a gift if I want to, and nobody can say not, not even Father. I want you to write your name inside the front cover, your *own* name. I have a picture of that in my brain."

Dorian pushed against the book, crushing it to Alex's chest, and in a moment they were wrestling.

"You can't just shake the *status in quo* any old time you

want, ironhead!'' Dorian ground out. ''I'm a different breed of cat.''

''You are not!''

''Am so!''

''Footlicker!''

''Chicken lily!''

They hit the floor in a twist of brocade and silk. The precious book was sandwiched between them as they yanked each other back and forth, crashing from wall to stairs and back again, all the time quarreling like squirrels. Their boot heels clunked on the floor planks.

Every door in the place burst open. A dozen people charged out to see what was going on. Servants, slaves, Lydia and little Rose Dimitra, Aunt Pandora.

The boys continued to slam each other about the foyer, knocking over a plant stand, the fern upon it, a chair, and three etchings.

Finally two men showed up who were bigger than either of them, and the boys were peeled apart. Their hair was peppered with dirt from the plant they'd knocked over. Their neat clothing hung askew. Alex's nose was bleeding. They continued to pull toward each other, kicking and gasping.

''*Stamata!*''

The order cut through the action. Dorian staggered against the man who held him from behind.

''*Arketah. Aftos emorahye,*'' Nick hissed into the boy's ear, so only Dorian could hear.

Common sense seeped back to Dorian as he glared at Alexander, who was being held at bay by Pilos. He took note of the blood on the other boy's face, as Nick had insisted. A clear win.

''Do you want your father to hear?'' Nick snapped, still speaking Greek in front of the black slaves. ''Do you want to break your mother's heart? Act like grown-ups.''

Well, one down, one to go, because here came Luke Wallace thumping down the stairs with his shirt untucked and his beard on fire.

''What the blue blazes gives around here?'' he roared. He snapped his fingers at Pilos. ''Let go of that boy!''

Alex stumbled free. Behind him Pilos scooped up the Dumas volume.

"Fighting in the house?" Wallace stormed. "Where's your dignity? Alexander, what's this all about?"

"Nothing, Father."

"Nothing?"

Alex dredged up one of a collection of answers that he knew would satisfy his father, while also staging an independence he knew Wallace wanted to see in him.

"Well?" his father barked.

"It's a matter of honor," Alex said carefully. "It's personal."

Wallace paced toward him, big boots clacking. His hand flicked out and caught a smear of the blood on Alex's face.

"Next time you fight him, at least have the dignity to win."

Alex glanced at Dorian. "Yes, sir," he mumbled.

Wallace looked fiercely at Dorian also, and jerked his thumb in the direction of the kitchen. "Back where you belong, boy."

Nick let go, and Dorian made a point of straightening his expensive coat. He didn't flinch from Wallace's glare, but the glare never lasted long. It was always just enough to tell him he was the only disharmony at Plentiful.

Wallace never gave him more than an instant, which frustrated the boy's natural pique as he got older. If there was going to be a confrontation, he'd rather it be sooner than later. Striding broadly down the service corridor toward the back of the mansion, he left them all behind.

He went through the laundry room and the larder, heading for the kitchen. Those corridors were dim, deep in the bowels of the big stone house. It occurred to him suddenly that this was his natural habitat in many ways, more so even than the slave cabins or the parlor. He was a creature of betweens.

Before he reached the kitchen, a form filled the narrow doorway in front of him. He stopped and waited there in the dimness as Iphigenia approached, wearing her Sunday frock.

In her elegant, educated Greek, she said, "Fighting with your brother again."

Dorian sighed and groaned, "He always wants to pity me. I get tired of it."

The Macedonian woman, still young, still careful, cupped his face and brushed away the plant dirt. "You don't get pity, my son of sons. Pity is one thing you will never have from the world."

"Then what is it?" Dorian snapped, falling back on the cuttingly dependable English. "He's not warden over my condition. I never asked."

"He is your brother," she told him. "He's not a baby anymore. He knows something is strange here. I know what he feels. I feel it each time I see you go down to the furrows and know I cannot go with you. I know you will have to work harder than anyone . . . but I believe . . . I believe you will be better than anyone. You shall know all ways, all worlds."

She tipped her head slightly to the right, in the direction of the great sprawling tobacco fields and the farmlands that grew their food.

"They can teach you things I can never teach you," she said. "Things other intelligent men will never comprehend."

Dorian folded his arms impatiently. "That has an anecdotal ring to it, Mother. You're sounding more and more like Grandpapa's letters."

Iphigenia smiled and blushed, caught. Very well, English then.

"But it's true, Dorian," she said. Her accent gave her words a distinct tang. "I have a proud feeling when you tell me about the fields, helping me to understand. Alex could never do that."

"Alex will never need to. Alex is not bound to the fields."

Her hands turned suddenly cold against his skin.

"Please don't start talking of leaving," she said heavily.

"I'm not leaving," he responded with a toss of his head. 'Where on earth would I go?"

His claim, almost lighthearted, cut Iphigenia to the core. There was a grinding truth about his words.

She lived day by day with that worry. If anything happened to her, Dorian would spend his life in slavery of the worst kind. Her natural children would be fine, but not Dorian. The slaves would hate him for being white, and the whites would hate him for being a slave. If there was any chance of freedom in the world for him, it would come only through her and her power to hold Wallace at bay.

For fourteen years she had made neither suggestion nor comment when her husband aspired toward politics or anything else, because she knew Dorian's life depended upon Wallace's getting whatever he wanted out of life. It had been easy to protect a cherub.

But time was betraying her. Now she also had to hold back the arrogance and indestructibility of youth that was showing itself in her foster son. As Dorian hit his teenage years, the boy turned onto a collision course with Wallace and with the entire South. Both regarded him as a slave and a dangerous one.

He let her hug him. She needed to, and so did he, never mind that at this age he didn't want to admit it.

And even that couldn't be left alone.

Through the open back doors of the kitchen came a bone-grating shriek. Agony and horror spilled into the house from the field, a gasping sound that was only barely human, coming from the wheat field behind the main house.

Iphigenia jolted in Dorian's arms, the sound shearing through her.

Screams pealed across Plentiful, then again, and again.

Dorian's eyes went obsidian.

"I knew it," he whispered.

★

CHAPTER TWELVE

──────★──────

"Stop those horses! Don't let those horses move! I said stop those horses!"

A bouquet of white faces from the main house plunged into the field. Wallace's order barely surfaced above the chilling screams.

A dozen slaves watched in horror. Before them long silver blades quivered, and huge horses pounded the soil, forcing forward against those who tried to stop them. The blades were moving very slowly, grinding downward against flesh.

Screams escaped, shrill and full of air.

The negroes stood by, frozen, while the upyard posse plunged through toward those screams.

"Help him, you cowards!" Wallace shouted.

Behind him, Nick, Pilos, and Iphigenia ground to a halt, frozen for one awful moment in the same horror that paralyzed the slaves.

Dorian and Alexander were only two jumps behind, and their eyes flew wide with what they saw.

Pleason. A sacrifice to the giant.

The horses continued to drag forward against the slaves who had hold of their bridles. Behind those massive, sweating haunches, Pleason was being guillotined. His entire left side was caught between the guard and the great knife. His shrieks jabbed through every heart in earshot.

The machine creaked and complained. The blade pressed into Pleason's flesh, embedding there. His hands pressed the

164

blade on either side, as if he were praying, and his screams
began to gurgle.

"Help him!" Wallace bellowed again. With his own hands
he grasped the top blade and pushed backward against it,
heedless of the danger to his own arm if the horses continued
pulling. "I'll put every one of you in here if you don't help
him!"

Wide-eyed, helpless slaves stood by, paralyzed by the smell
of bloody flesh and shredded muscle. Boss's threat fell empty.

Pilos ran for the nearest harness, where Buckie and Amus
were still fighting, while both Nick and Dorian leaned hard
against the wheel side of the reaper. Alexander and his
mother each dodged for a flopping rein.

"Back it up!" Nick called. "Go backward!"

The horses tossed their barrel-sized heads, whinnied and
stomped their confusion. When their heads went up, Pilos lost
his grip and Buckie was thrown to the dirt. Elazar dropped
from his horse and lay his whip into the haunches of the farm
chunks, but his action had the unfortunate effect of making
the horses believe they should be moving forward. Whipping
usually meant "go."

"Stop those horses moving, goddamn you!" Wallace rasped.
Turkey red blood poured over his feet.

Pleason continued screaming, but now the screams were
raw and breathy. Pink foam splattered from his mouth. Above,
the churning machine continued to garrote him.

Despite five slaves and a Greek or two hauling on them,
the immense farm horses still tugged forward, taking the one
extra step that rotated the chopper forward. Bones cracked as
Pleason was pushed under.

"Back teeth!" Dorian hissed. Without apology he reached
into Nick's jacket and grabbed the Collier revolving pistol
Nick always carried.

He turned and aimed.

A boom thundered over Plentiful. The ball went into the
side of the brown chunk's head. Much faster than the horse
could ever have moved in life, its huge body crashed into the
furrow with a resounding *whump*. Chains and leather cackled.
The other horse was yanked to a stop by the deadweight of its
harnessmate.

Behind the reaper the slave called Chestnut opened his wide mouth and stood there gasping at what came out at his feet. Several other slaves also bellowed and hid their faces, but nothing could blot out the sound of bones snapping like pencils, nor the final ghastliness that spilled out. The kill-crazy blade came up, creaked one last time, doubled back a half turn, then stopped.

But Pleason was dead.

"Back off! Back away!" Wallace shouted, waving his hands.

He and Nick ran around the reaper at the same time. Others crowded near—but not too near—and Wallace had to duck away from a spurting red crest of blood.

On the ground the butchered man was half a man. From a gulch in the side of his body, blood and matter slushed onto the dry ground. Where once there had been a leg, now there was pandowdy. Sliced at an angle from the top of his hip to his testicles, Pleason's leg had been cleaved away from his body. The severed limb hung from his back, attached by a fringe of skin, while purple and white veins shivered. Intestines spilled out, slowly, like purple pudding.

Everyone crowded closer, taken by a moment of morbid fascination—which abandoned them the instant a second horror set in.

Pleason's eyes rolled from side to side.

He was still alive.

He was still—*alive*.

Clawing himself along the ground with his hands, he dragged his severed leg and entrails. His face was chalk gray.

The weight of the leg snapped strands of skin and muscles that held it on. In his shock Pleason tried to crawl away from his own agony.

"Tie it off!" Wallace shouted over the sound of vomiting from among the slaves.

As he bent over Pleason, Nick's hands waved in the air as if idle, but that was only a terrible illusion. They were simply helpless, desperate hands.

"There's nothing to tie off," he said.

A gruesome truth, starkly said.

There wasn't even a stump left of Pleason's thigh. The leg

now clung only by stretched bits of flesh. A fountain of blood squirted from the artery in Pleason's torso, spraying high as a man. People shied away.

Pleason's eyes rolled toward Wallace. His lips quivered.

Then Pleason's head exploded.

The revolver smoked in Dorian's hand.

The gunshot—which no one had heard—now echoed through the distant western hills.

ooooooooommmmmmmmm

And the body flopped for an instant, then collapsed.

"Mother Puck!" Wallace spat.

He circled the corpse, but it looked the same from any angle.

"Elazar, clear these people out of here," he added. "Get a crew together to clean up the field."

"Yas, suh . . ."

"Do it before two o'clock. I've got company coming."

"Yas . . . yassuh."

"McCrocklin, where are you?"

Sullenly the overseer spoke up. "Right behind you, Boss."

"You get your fat backside into Norfolk, go to the telegraph office, and contact the McCormick Reaper Company and order a new blade." Then he leaned closer to the overseer and whispered, "While you're there, pick up a box of coffin nails from Patterson's."

"Yeah, Boss, okay."

Wallace turned to his wife. "Genny, take Alexander back to the house."

Iphigenia's eyes brimmed with empathy, but she never said a word. With a grave expression she watched Dorian, still standing there between the dead plow horse and the dead slave, still holding the gun. Smoke twisted from the barrel.

She caught Alexander's hand and drew the stunned boy away.

But he was not the boy who drew her concern at this particular moment.

It nearly killed her to walk away from Dorian. So much so that she pressed her fist to her heart, closed her eyes, and hoped she was walking in the right direction.

Standing on top of the situation, Luke Wallace touched his

forehead briefly, then put his hands on his hips, shifted this way and that, shook his head, muttered, paced.

"Nick, you've got blood all over you," he pointed out. "You'll have to change clothes right off. Pilos, you too."

Giving the Greek servant a shove as he stepped past, Wallace picked his way through the furrow to the dead horse. Try as he might, he couldn't feel any less bad about losing the horse than losing Pleason. He'd known the horse since its dam dropped it at his feet, high noon, on Alexander's first birthday. Gad, was this poor dead creature nearly eleven years old already?

The animal gave off a disturbing heat. Wallace shook his head and gritted his teeth. "Mother Puck. Of all the days."

A few paces away, unaware of the movement around him, Dorian was gazing at Pleason's corpse with much the same analysis as Wallace was giving the chunk. He gazed with something that even he perceived as vulgar fascination, demonic callousness. Of all these adults who had seen so much in their lives, this boy who had seen nothing was the one who remained unastounded.

Coolly he watched the glossy membranes bleed. The corpse throbbed, making him wonder if it really was a corpse yet or if Pleason still clung to life inside that mess somehow. Nature was cruel. Nature would do that and like it.

The salty stink drew him in. This was true violence, true punishment—the thing that had hung over every slave since the pharaohs. Do this or we'll hit you. Do that or we'll hack you.

This was all that kept every slave in thrall. Live, bleed, die, bleed—blood that by law belongs to someone else—then die and get replaced.

Lost in enlightenment, protected by youth's natural love for the grisly, Dorian didn't see the gore. He'd read a thousand violences in his young life but only now discovered what violence really meant. A shift of power. A change, however small.

And he realized one other tiny detail: no one was even considering taking the pistol away from him.

Basking in his own vindication, he looked up from the bubbling blood.

He looked at McCrocklin.

"I'm your assistant now," he said.

CHAPTER THIRTEEN

———— ★ ————

McCrocklin stomped bloody cakes of dirt off his boots before going into Patterson's Mercantile. The stomping took an extra second, and that second was enough time to stop and light his cigar. In turn the cigar gave him pause at the doorway. As he raised his head and drew a long drag, he caught sight of a particular handbill. Reading the words he understood, he managed to piece together the meaning of the advertisement. His straw-stiff blond eyebrows drew together. He pulled the handbill from its nail with a terse yank and clunked into the mercantile.

"Afternoon, Bob," C. T. Patterson called.

"Hey," McCrocklin muttered, chewing the cigar.

"Can I do for you?"

"Nails."

"Okay."

"Long ones."

"Okay."

"What's this here all about?"

Petterson paused. "Oh . . . well, I don't hardly think Plentiful's the place for that, Bob. You got a nice clean plantation over there."

"Still," McCrocklin said with a shrug. He took his box of nails and signed the tab. The nails went into his coat pocket. "Thanks. Where do I find this fella?"

"Round the side. Stick that bill back up on the outside wall, will you? It's paying its way, if you get my meaning."

"Oh. Sure. Have a good'n.''

He tacked the handbill back up and strode around the store. Sure enough there was a tall enclosed red Gypsy wagon there, and he expected a Gypsy to step forward, but that wasn't forthcoming. What he got was a wide, gussied-up nigger with a hat and long hair. Beyond the clothes, hat, and hair, there was something funny looking about the man, but McCrocklin couldn't nab it.

"You responsible for that there handbill hanging up yonder?"

"Yes, master, I would be," the dark man said, fingering his velvet lapels and reaching onto his wagon seat for another handbill. "Here is one for your own possession. I am Root, as they call me."

"McCrocklin. I'm off a tobacco planation few miles out."

"Good for you, master."

"I ain't the master. I'm the overseer."

"Very good for you, sir."

"What's in that coach?" McCrocklin rattled the paper as he scanned it once again. "This?"

"My slave, sir."

McCrocklin narrowed his eyes. "Where you from?"

"We just up from Georgia."

"Ain't that irregular? They let culluds own slaves down Georgia way?"

"Did at that auction block, sir." Root rubbed the side of the wagon affectionately. "Nobody else wanted the responsibility. Nobody but another nigger can make him work, and only the kind of work I make him do. He is persnickety that way."

McCrocklin nodded. "Go ahead, keep talking, Mr. Boot."

Root licked his wide lips. "That would be Root, sir. Well, sir, it's all there for the readin'. He is the biggest and the blackest. In point of fact, he's extra black. You know well as I do, the blacker they be, the less chance of successful escape. Can't blend too well. It helps that No'therners don't cotton to the extra black ones no more than do Southronaires. And also skin of deep black is best to put off the ravage of summer sun. And he is well-muscled, I can tell you. Every claim upon that paper there is plum true."

"Escaping ain't my main concern," McCrocklin muttered. "I'd fancy a talk with him."

"He doesn't savvy the English, sir. There's no conversating with such a brute." As he yanked down the folded tarp from the side of the wagon, Root skillfully caught a leather folio stuffed with letters of varying size and condition and handed it to McCrocklin. "Here is references, handwrote from a score of satisfied customers all over the South. You'll mostlike recognize a few of the names."

McCrocklin stuck his cigar in his mouth to free his hands, then thumbed through the letters, catching key words here and there and scanning the signatures. He paused briefly over every letter, making it appear that he was able to read them all cleanly and clearly.

Around the cigar he said, "All right, let's have a gander."

"Very well, sir, but stand a good step back."

Root gave him a single nod, and that was when McCrocklin figured out what was funny about his looks. The man had a full beard, but no mustache, like an Amish or one of those off-the-track religions. His face looked like porridge dinner set in a kinky black bowl.

Yup, that was it.

Root ushered him around to the back of the wagon, produced a key, and pierced the big black padlock. The lock popped loudly. Before opening the two big doors, Root pounded on the wood and shouted, "You! Stand up! Gentleman wants a look at you. Hear me? Up! Back! Back!"

There was something in the tone of his voice—the way a man talks to a circus beast or a prisoner of war—something that made McCrocklin heed the warning to step a distance from the doors.

Inside the hollow, dark wagon, there was a grind of movement. Chains against wood. *Clack-rattle-scrape . . . clunk.*

The wagon shifted noticeably.

The rattling stopped.

"Keep back, now, sir," Root said, looking over one shoulder at the overseer.

Two tall and narrow doors swung open unevenly, creaking loudly.

Sunlight pierced the trees. It sizzled across oiled ebony

skin, ropy veins, and muscles like big snakes under silk. The iron chains were no blacker, no meaner.

"What I got here's a caveman," Root said. "Strong, endurable, smart enough to survive the worst of times. A bull. A stallion. You can clearly see his manly potence. Well, sir? What do you therefore say?"

Root tucked his thumbs into his belt and took a moment to appreciate the source of a fair living.

He turned in time to see McCrocklin's cigar fall right out of his mouth.

"Are you going to go fight in Mexico, Uncle Nick?"

"Raise the barrel of your pistol. Now correct for the breeze. Fire at your will."

"I'm not allowed to have a will," Dorian said before firing the revolver.

As the gunshot echo rumbled, he lowered the pistol and turned. "Are you going?"

"That was a good shot," Nick Varvaresos told him, "except that you missed."

"I missed on purpose," the boy said with a satirical gleam in his eye. "Are you?"

"No, I will not fight in Mexico. It's not my kind of issue." Nick took opportunity of the lull in the marksmanship lesson to turn away from the blinding sun and give his eyes a rest. After a year of lessons, the boy was a decent shot, and Nick was lately trying to throw obstacles before him—shooting in wind that will make a bullet drift, shooting in rain that might drive a ball down, shooting in darkness using plain instinct like pointing a finger. And there was the tendency of a bullet to drop its trajectory with distance, but that was next week. After that, moving targets.

"Why isn't it?" Dorian insisted.

Nick glared at the boy. He was beginning to see with ugly clarity what Iphigenia was fretting about these days. The boy was fearless, unintimidated by the world. And he was getting taller. Soon they wouldn't be able to protect him from his own perceptions. Not long ago Dorian wouldn't have pressed so insistently for an answer to a political question when there were bullets to let fly. The definition of fun was changing before Nick's very eyes.

And there would be no settling for half answers.

He sighed. "It's a blatant landgrab," he said, switching over to Greek for this tender issue, in case anyone was listening from behind some twig way out here in the middle of a long, open hillside in the bright of day, "and I don't fight for landgrabs."

Habit, this switching to Greek. It was more of a secret-code language now, after all these years of its being a notorious "second language." Time in America had done that to his native tongue. People in America, he'd found, were suspicious of other languages and often openly afraid of collusion. So he used it for collusion. Why not?

Before him, hand on hip, Dorian was still waiting for a real answer.

Nick shrugged.

"I'm going to have to go over all this again with your father during the meeting this afternoon," he breathed heavily.

"I know," Dorian said. "That's why I asked. I'm curious about the idea of Manifest Destiny."

Nick's black eyes flicked up and met their match. "Where did you hear that term?"

"John O'Sullivan, editor of the *Democratic Review* I stole from the library, wherever else? It's a seditious idea . . . God's plan for us to expand and control lands that are owned by Britain and Mexico just because we want everything sea to sea. Don't you find it a mystical idea? I mean, why would God care?"

"It has roots in hard practicality, Dorian," Nick said firmly, hoping the boy would see that any issue is a mirror upon itself. "We want ports on both oceans. We want the western frontier to be safe for pioneers to open."

"And in order to open it, we have to send pioneers in so that it'll be open for pioneers. Poppycock," the boy sneered. "It's a ride-hard approach to advancement."

An ominous shiver made Nick draw his shoulders in.

"You're a scary fellow," he said. "Experience in nothing, opinions in everything."

Dorian shrugged mentally. "Well, now that I know for sure you're not trotting off to Mexico, I reckon I can say what I please."

"That tongue will get you in trouble."

"I was born in trouble." He raised the revolver, tilted his cheek toward his shoulder and took aim at the upright log way the hell over there, a log that was wearing Nick's jacket, just for a touch of realism. "I'm the avant-courier of the whipstitched mob. It's by me that all bonded people will someday measure themselves."

The revolver cracked. The sound crossed the meadow well after the bullet struck right between the jacket's lapels. Wood splintered, visible even from this distance.

"And you're dangerous too," Nick mumbled. "Excellent. Right in the heart."

Dorian pressed his lips into the knot. "Except that I was aiming for his head. Well, I guess he's dead enough anyway."

With a grin Nick echoed, "Yes, he's dead enough."

The boy was suddenly taller as he turned to him again. "If you think the war with Mexico is practical, why won't you go? You fought in Greece against the Turks. Why not here and now?"

With grim calculation Nick squared off with Dorian's large eyes and paused a moment before speaking.

"I'm waiting for a better war," he said.

He hooked his hand over the lad's slim shoulder and steered him in the direction of the house. They would have two entire meadows to stride through before they reached the front lawn of Plentiful, each meadow banked by a line of fat trees. Someday these meadows would be plowed and furrowed, planted with orinoko tobacco or with other crops as Plentiful continued to grow. For now, this hilly open land was just jewelry, studded with a wooden fence lining the road into Norfolk.

"You have a good mind, Dorian," Nick said, gazing at the ground. "I'd like to see you go to the University of Athens some day. Papa Dimitrios would like it also. You and Alex together."

"Wouldn't mind that," Dorian said, "except that by the time I get there, I'll already have read every publication in the world, and I'll find myself wiping floors to keep busy. Somewhat countervailing against the whole plot.''

''Counter what?''

''Vailing.''

''How old are you?''

''Four hundred twelve.''

''Yes, you are . . . you are.''

Dorian spread his hand ridiculously in the air. ''After all, 'A ship should not ride on a single anchor, nor life on a single hope.' Epictetus.''

''And boys who think too soon like men may never get older. Nick Varvaresos.''

''I'll remember that,'' Dorian said with a rare laugh.

Nick beamed. It wasn't too often he could surprise the boy anymore.

''Reckon I should change back into my reach-me-downs,'' Dorian said. ''Sun's starting to slip off her perch.''

''Oh, you have a few hours yet,'' Nick said. ''However, I—''

Suddenly the trees beside them began to shake and the ground to vibrate. They looked up in time for Nick to ram his shoulder into Dorian, pushing him out of the way. A gigantic black horse plunged through the leaves.

''Nick!'' The shout instantly killed any chance of speaking candidly anymore today.

Before them Luke Wallace drew back hard on his mare's reins and glared at them from above. The black horse twisted and protested beneath him.

''Where've you been!'' he demanded.

Nick drew out his pocket watch and squinted at it. ''Am I late?''

''Half hour! The committee'll be here any godforsaken minute!''

Nick looked up. ''So calm down. If they're not here yet, why make yourself sweat?''

Wallace's hand grated on the reins as he stared at the pistol that was still in Dorian's hand. Caught off guard, Dorian looked down. He'd forgotten he was holding it.

Without apology he handed it back to Nick.

"Oh, my jacket," Nick said. He peered down the hill and across the meadow.

Glad of an excuse not to walk back with them—or behind them, as it would have had to be—Dorian told him, "I'll fetch it."

"Thank you," Nick said amiably.

Lucas rudely cleared his throat, making it clear how much he disapproved of offering a thank-you to a slave. He dropped from the saddle and slapped the mare. She bolted and cantered over the next crest toward the stable.

Lucas turned Nick away from the boy. "Have we got this Mexican issue straight? I know they're going to bring it up and expect me to judicate it."

"Just keep your eye on me," Nick said.

"Done. And the tariff question?"

"You don't need my help on the tariffs, Lucas, you know your mind on that."

"Think so? And the other thing . . . I've let it slide out the hole in my head or something. Say it again for me."

"Repeat after me. *Ekete freska fruta.*"

"*Ekete fressa frute.*"

"*Freska . . . froootah.*"

"Dang. Why can't the world just speak English?"

"Because then you wouldn't be able to show off."

Nick glanced back at Dorian by way of a farewell. Left in the meadow as the two men walked away, the boy nodded back. He watched them leave and listened to the silly lesson.

"*Legha katalifi . . .*"

"*Leggie katalifi . . .*"

"*Revani . . .*"

"Oh, I know that one. *Revani.*"

Their voices began to fade in the breeze.

Standing alone in the meadow, Dorian let his hands hang at his sides. He shook his head at the retreating backs of his father and uncle.

"Frozen in time, just like Keats and his damned urn," he muttered.

As he had a thousand times, he turned and walked in the other direction to retrieve Nick's jacket. Meadow grass crunched under his feet. He felt the stab of Nick's absence keenly, but

the feeling wasn't a new one. No relationship in his tightly
banked life was a constant one or, for that matter, a reliable
one. There was no one with whom he could openly discuss all
aspects of his two lives. Once upon a time he'd told everything to Alex and Alex alone. Boys talking. But even that was
changing. It had changed when Dorian's sexuality appeared
and Alex's was still a year or more off. That was when he
started protecting Alex with the same gauze of innocence he
used to shelter Iphigenia from the cabin truths or the slaves
from today's scary political realities and the pitiful details of a
negro's lot up North. Alex was the gauge against which
Dorian had become introspective, the mirror that showed him
a twisted view of himself. But he didn't really have Alex
anymore.

With that loss had come a new image of the world. Every
time he put a snaffle on telling somebody about some new
invention or some new philosophy he picked up in a newspaper or overheard his father talking about, Dorian's chest filled
up with realization. The world was not only big, but huge.

Huge, complicated, changing as it never had before in all
of history. During the Middle Ages, inventions came along
every hundred years, he'd learned. But in the 1840s suddenly
they came monthly—daily. Things happened at lightning
speed. He devoured articles about indoor plumbing and
gaslighting in the cities. This was a generation born by
candlelight which would die by the light of whale-oil lamps,
he realized. Expensive, but time would make them less so.
The lamps were already in the cities and sometimes even lit
the outside walks. Dorian hadn't failed to notice that Wallace
had started lighting whale-oil lamps when company was
coming, only to scrupulously turn them off and use candlelight for everyday purposes.

Refinements were trickling out of the industrial centers and
becoming common as daywear. He knew about E. B. Bigelow's
power loom that made carpeting practical and affordable. It
would soon cover floor in less and less fancy houses and all
houses would be more alike. Just this year attitudes were
shifting in society as a whole—precisely that society was
beginning to *take* itself as a whole.

An amazing change, this business of wholes. Soon it would

come to engulf the slaves, and wouldn't there be a mess then. Somebody would act upon the behalf of those who could not take the sword for themselves, and like it or not, the world would take another big turn.

Dorian approached the log with Nick's jacket on it. As he touched the fine black wool and studied the gash in the log he himself had made, the idea of slaves carrying weapons and fighting on their own behalf suddenly looked inevitable. With the advent of the telegraph, and newspapers sprouting like weeds all over the country, news and ideas and opinions would wildfire their way from state to state, and even to Europe and back. With every added comfort, people could afford to become concerned about somebody else's lot. If a man didn't have to walk all the way to the back quarter to use the outhouse, he had a few extra minutes to read an article now and then. Last year a dentist named Morton had started using ether to quell the pain of his patients, and if a person's teeth didn't hurt, he could give all his attention to news of John Deere's new steel-moldboard plow. And if the plow cut ground in a day that would otherwise take a week to furrow, there was more time to get together with fellow farmers and discuss the moral implications of keeping a chattel slave that one might not need anymore. And if one farmer lets his one slave go because he has a Deere plow, there's an economic question. Does the slave then take his free papers and go north, and take a paying job away from one Irishman, one of a wave of five hundred Irishmen just over this month as immigrants to the New World? The Irishman has to go a block down and take away the job of a Dutchman. So the Dutchman has to go west and drive a railroad spike that might otherwise have been driven by a Chinese. Somewhere along the line somebody starves. Because one person starves, trains go through and factories work and hundreds of other people get pay and transportation.

"Saints and pigs," Dorian huffed. "Don't overstuff yourself, chile."

He put his hand over his eyes and took a deep breath. The world dazzled him, and not always in a nice way. Sometimes things seemed so simple. Other times the world was a gigantic crazy quilt with a billion pictures embroidered on it, all flat and equal.

"Son! Excuse me!"

His hands convulsed on Nick's jacket. He pulled it against his chest. The fabric dragged on the log, dropping splinters on his shoes.

He spun around. The meadow and the road shrank before him.

There was a neat black coupe mere steps away. How had it approached without his hearing it?

It sat in the road beside the fence, a sharp hackney pony prancing impatiently before it. In the open front seat, before an enclosed cab, sat a tubby young man and a very tiny woman, both white and well dressed. She was paint-plain except for a set of brilliant green eyes, and the man had the same eyes and a space between his front teeth. Neither was particularly imposing, but they were here and they were white and they could see him.

"Good afternoon, son," the woman called. "Would you mind giving us directions?"

Dorian continued to stare. Nick's jacket was getting a good crush.

The woman and man glanced at each other. Then the woman spoke up again.

"My name is Mrs. Anna Campman. I know your mother, I believe. We met briefly last week at the harbor when I was awaiting my brother's ship. We're supposed to meet several others for a brunch this afternoon here at Plentiful, but we've been riding near half an hour along this fence and can't find the entrance. Might you direct us on how to get inside?"

Only when his chest started hurting did Dorian realize he should probably breathe.

"Son?" Mrs. Campman began, "Is there something the matter?"

Dorian pushed himself a few steps closer to the fence.

"Oh, my manners," Mrs. Campman said then. "I'm so sorry. You're not the Wallaces' son at all, are you?" She turned to the man and explained, "Ed, Mrs. Wallace told me her son was a towheaded boy, as I recall. I've made a mistake." She looked back at Dorian now, and her expression became utterly soothing. "Son, I've put you on the spot. Are you just visiting Plentiful? You must be related, though, with that coloring. Are you one of the Wallace cousins up from South Carolina?"

His hands shook. By sheer force of will he gained control over them and took a step forward to the fence. His throat was rag dry. He cleared it, then opened his mouth to speak the first words he'd ever spoken to someone who didn't know him.

"Yes'm, yaw jus' gwine up yond' road nuther quatter mile, n'yaw see the gateway. She got big lions in de front."

Mrs. Campman and her companion gaped for an instant. Then—to Dorian's confusion—they reared back and laughed in thorough entertainment.

Dorian frowned.

The chubby man bobbed as he laughed and said, "That's wonderful, my boy. Can you do their songs too?"

Having never spoken to anyone who didn't live on Plentiful, Dorian was bewildered. *Too?* He pressed his tongue to his upper lip, cocked his hip, and tried to figure this out. Right here in the middle of nothing, this man wanted him to sing?

He shifted his weight, put a hand on his hip, and openly puzzled the problem.

Mrs. Campman said, "What's your name, son?"

Dorian cleared the throat again and said, "Edmund Dantes."

This time only the man laughed. Mrs. Campman looked at him and asked, "What's that supposed to mean?"

The man said, "It means he's a trickster. A well-read trickster."

Mrs. Campman shrugged with just her eyebrows, then held out a tiny hand toward her companion and spoke to Dorian. "This is my brother, Edward Porterfield. He's a barrister, just moved back to Norfolk from Washington."

New astonishment set in when Mr. Porterfield handed his sister the reins, climbed down from the carriage seat, and actually came over to the fence.

Dorian's lips dried right up.

Porterfield stuck his hand over the fence rail as though reaching for something, and for one extra instant Dorian was lost. To a boy who had never met a person he didn't already know, this business of how-do-you-do-I'm-so-and-so was a real flounder. It wasn't as clinical as the experts on etiquette wanted him to believe. There hadn't been any bowing or curtsying so far, so where was he supposed to start in?

Handshakes were like anything else he'd seen but never experienced. Vague allusions to another kind of life.

Left hand?

No—right hand. Of course! The diagonal. To make sure the other knight didn't go for his dirk.

A new fear set in. Would this man notice Dorian's hand, that it was rough and callused, not at all the hand of a young man of the gentry? Should he pretend his fingers were bee stung or something?

Porterfield's grip was cool and firm, and he made no notice of Dorian's calluses as he asked, "What's your name again, son?"

"Eh . . . Dorian."

"Well, Master Dorian, do you speak real English, or did someone read the Dumas book to you?"

The suggestion that anyone had to read *to* him was an affront to the boy. He puffed up and said, "I read it myself . . . but I read it in the original French."

Porterfield's eyes widened. "That's exemplary. My tutors never made such demands of me, I regret to say. Is my sister correct? Are you visiting from South Carolina?"

Intrigued with the idea of coming from somewhere else, Dorian muttered, "All right . . ."

"Pardon?"

"Eh . . . yes. Definitely."

Porterfield crossed his arms on the top rail and poised his foot on the one closest to the ground. "I'm here to talk politics with Mr. Wallace and a few others. Thank you for helping us find our way."

Dorian stood watching mutely as Porterfield nodded a farewell and turned back toward the carriage. Just before climbing aboard, however, the young lawyer paused, gazed at Dorian for a moment, then wagged a finger in the air and came back to the fence.

"Say, son. Can you shed any light on some current opinions in South Carolina?"

"I'm only fourteen, sir," Dorian said evasively.

"I'd be pleased to hear your view anyway. I was fourteen once, and I had plenty of opinions then."

Not to be outdone by some other fourteen-year-old, Dorian squared his shoulders. "Name your subject, sir."

"Railroads," Porterfield said. "Federalization of them."

"Now, Ed, don't corner the lad," Mrs. Campman chided from her carriage seat.

"Got an opinion, son?"

"Everyone has an opinion, sir," Dorian shot back. His blood started to race. He'd never *ever* talked politics with an adult other than Nick. That this man should actually ask him a question—his heart flew, and his mind was right after it. He sifted through Wallace's cast-off *Enquirers,* which sat collecting dust in his memory. The articles on railroads cut themselves out and lined up like soldiers for inspection before his mind's eye. One after another, in chronological order, he read them again just as if he'd written them himself.

"I think . . . ," he began, still not completely confident of what he was doing, "I think the South is being left behind."

Porterfield smiled at him. "How so?"

"The North is laying railroads and building industries. I reckon the railroads will have to be federalized in order to be practical. The whole process is ridiculous as it stands. Why, every locality and company and state is bickering about how the land's to be divided and the gauge of the track. None of the tracks and cars fit each other. Why, just to get to Buffalo from Albany, they have to change cars seven times."

When Porterfield didn't jump across the fence and pummel him for having an opinion, Dorian's voice got stronger, and he moved another inch onto dangerous ground.

"The South is being impaled on its own insularity. We continue to till soil and smoke tobacco while the North lays track. It can't last. Who wants to be held hostage by the North?"

"So you think we should fight to get the transcontinental laid through the South?" the man asked.

"Me?" *I don't care where they lay it. Wait a minute. . . . maybe I do care.* "Yes," he said, "I think that."

"But if it's regulated," Porterfield challenged, "the states will start passing laws to favor certain rail companies over others. Competition will be skewed. What then?"

Dorian blinked. His perfect picture started to melt before his eyes, bits of complication setting into the recipe.

"I don't rightly know," he admitted. Damn. And he was so close!

Porterfield gave the fence rail a friendly grip.

"Well, son, there's better men than us who are just as confused." He squinted in the sunlight and nodded cheerfully. "You certainly are a thoughtful young gentleman. My son's tutor must be lacking. I can't imagine such an observance in our household." He held out his hand again. "It's been a delight, sir. I hope to see you again sometime. Give my best regards to South Carolina when you return."

Sir.

"Good afternoon, young man," Mrs. Campman called, handing the reins back to Porterfield as he climbed aboard. "It's been a right pleasure to have conversed with you."

Dorian stared after the departing coupe until it disappeared down the tree-lined road.

They were impressed with him.

Impressed.

He'd pulled it off. They thought he was smart.

They thought he was *white*.

The world was a spinning top. He ran, did not walk, did not stride, did not lope, back to the cabins to spill the great news all over Yula and see what she thought of it. They thought he was white.

"Mama! Mama!" He plunged through the door of Yula's cabin.

Yula wasn't in there, even though they still thought he was white. Why wasn't the world different? Why weren't people here to appreciate this?

Dorian took a prudent moment to scrape off his Sunday

best and slip into his linsey suit. In spite of his prudence, though, the Sunday clothes ended up in a puddle on the floor, and haste put both legs in one side of the trousers for a second or two. He stumbled to recover, his mind racing. As he crammed his shirt into his belt and his feet into the lard-and-rosin-coated shoes of a yard slave, the door burst open.

Alexander plowed into the cabin.

Dorian blinked, momentarily confused. Alex looked profoundly out of place. Even though Dorian was suddenly white, Alex was *really* white.

"Alex!" Dorian gasped. "Alex, guess what! You'll never guess! I had a revelation!"

He ran at Alex, his hands spread open.

The other boy's face was grim. "Dory, quiet a minute."

"You'll never guess! There were visitors by the fence! And you know what they thought? You're never going to guess!"

"Dory, bottle up!" Alex grabbed his brother by the elbows and drove him backward against the wall.

"What's all this?" Dorian demanded. "Are you manhandling me?"

While they struggled, Yula appeared in the corner of Dorian's eye as she came in the door after Alex. Her brown face was cast with concern, and only then did it dawn on Dorian what was odd about the situation.

He squinted at Alex. "What are *you* doing in the yard?"

Alexander countered with a demand of his own. "Where've you been? I've been hunting all over for you!"

"Just keep your sails in trim, br'er," Dorian warned ferociously. "I don't like that tone."

"There's something going on down in the yard. Father and McCrocklin had a meeting this morning, and now there's something going on."

"What business is it of yours?" Dorian stepped by him with a quizzical look and went to Yula. "What is it, Mama? What's got him all shoofly?"

The words were jolted backward into his throat as Yula yanked him like a rag out the door.

She hauled him outside into the sunlight. Her skin glowed like polished chestnuts in contrast to her simple white osnaburg camisole and the ruffle created by the string that gathered the bodice. She seemed barely old enough to be his sister, except for the fierce authority in her eyes as she prattled at him.

"Come noon McCrocklin rode in wid a big painted wagon acluckin' behind him and some jack-a-dandy nigger adrivin' it. They pulled up to the big willer tree, an' now they settin' up some kinda camp. Mr. McCrocklin, he went up to the big house an' met wid Boss outside by the salt people."

"Who's the man?" Dorian asked. "The jack-a-dandy?"

"Don't know," the small woman said. Her quick eyes darted to his and narrowed to slits. "I got my s'picions. I figure it be a wagon load of new niggers or somethin'. Yawl come look an' tell us what it all 'bout, Dohrian, you hear? I want your 'pinion."

"I'm comin', I'm comin', you'll get my pinion."

Feeling like the back of a crack-the-whip line, he let himself be rustled along the creek toward the stockyard and the barns and sheds. From here he couldn't see anything. Until they passed the mill, he'd be blinded by the huge buildings that made up the functioning farm of Plentiful.

"Alex? You still there—"

"Yes, right behind."

"Fill me in," he said, craning to look behind as Yula hauled him along. Amazing the power in her mosquito-sized body, but there was no accounting for plain cussedness.

Alex ran to catch up. "I've never seen the man before. McCrocklin refused to speak to Father inside the house. Don't you find that eerie? It's not often McCrocklin guards his words, even in the privacy of the library. I did my best, Dory, but there just wasn't any eavesdropping this time."

"All right, you go back—Mama, please, drag back a minute!" While Yula paused impatiently, Dorian turned to Alex. "Don't come to the yard yet. You go back to the house. See what you can ferret out. If necessary, ask Mother. She'll get it out of him."

The other boy's white blond hair flipped in neat ruffles over his eyes. "What do you mean, don't come to the yard? I'll come to the yard if I please."

"Hard proof of adulthood. Just do it, would you?"

"You do what Dohrian say," Yula interrupted, knowing

that if she let them, they'd waste half the day trying to get the upper hand from each other.

Alex gave her a fierce look. "I want to see what's in the yard, woman!"

Yula's hand cracked against his ivory cheek. He flinched. Her finger made a needle right in front of his face.

"You mind!" she snapped. "These brown titties done nursed a better boy den you. If you respeck him, den you better respeck me too. I used to wipe your bottom, an' I still know where it is."

Her tiny mouth tucked inward against her teeth. Her brows came down on the bridge of her nose.

Alex's shoulders slumped noticeably. He shifted before her, then licked his lips and muttered, "Yes'm. I'm sorry."

"Best be."

Dorian nudged Alex's shoulder and said, "Just hurry up, and we'll unravel this mystery."

"All right, all right."

Alex went one way, and Dorian and his mama went the other, their shoes scratching on the creek stones.

Willow branches wandered like long hair over the top of the creek water, dipping low and creating a gigantic canopy over part of the farmyard. The smell of chickens and sheep permeated the air.

Squarely under the tree the red travel wagon with its two oxen were stationed. The windows were closed and bolted from the outside. Several slaves had been made to build a cookfire under the trees and lay corn shuck mats on the dirt. Most conspicuous was the thick black chain that had been coiled around the base of the tree—and it wasn't a skinny trunk—and trailed out to Jonah's hickory-twig rocking chair.

What was Jonah's chair doing out under the willer?

Yula made Dorian stay toward the back of the crowd of negroes who had been gathered by the black drivers at McCrocklin's order. In Dorian's lifetime the slave population of Plentiful had grown to over two hundred, and they were all here now. At least, *most* were here.

Dorian instantly picked up on one missing element.

He leaned toward Yula.

"Where are the children?" he whispered.

Yula whispered back, "Crocky made 'em go round other side the mill to play ball-'n'-cup till he call 'em."

"Mmm." Dorian glowered and muttered, "I love ball-and-cup."

Cook pots were being deposited in a neat order beside the small fire, over which one of the women was adjusting an iron grate and a spider skillet. Two other women were putting out a spare picnic on a floor cloth that he recognized as the one usually spread on the poplar floor of McCrocklin's own cabin. The picnic was simple fare of hardtack, dried beans, fresh fruit from Plentiful's orchards, and cornmeal. There was a washbowl and a water bucket, both full. A coffeepot . . . a camp stool . . . and ropes and stakes? What kind of individual was civilized enough to drink a fashionable beverage like coffee but needed to be staked off? And there was even a small drop-leaf table being set up. Whatever this was, it was settled but not permanent. Half Dorian's brain scrupulously studied the details of the red wagon and the strange encampment, while the other half was getting the ball in the cup.

"Gotta be some new slaves," Homer mentioned from nearby in the crowd.

"Yeah, gotta be," somebody else agreed.

"How many dat wagon could hold?"

"Five, maybe. Maybe we git five new niggers, is all."

"Yeah. Gotta be."

Behind them suspicion tightened Dorian's eyes.

Yula looked at her son. His expression riveted her. He had a worldliness about him that was always her way of testing the wind, and she watched him carefully as he studied the encampment, watched for changes in his expressive mouth and intelligent eyes.

Every instinct played in her mind when Dorian frowned thoughtfully and murmured, "I don't think so. . . ."

Everyone flinched when the door of McCrocklin's cabin suddenly jerked open. McCrocklin and the jack-a-dandy strode out, each looking satisfied. They walked straight to the wagon, heedless of the slaves that backed off a few paces as they passed.

Without the slightest ceremony the jack-a-dandy went to

the wagon and began adjusting the chains and fiddling with a big padlock. McCrocklin turned to the slaves.

"All right, listen up! As you all know," he began, "we had a bad year for deaths among the young bondsmen last winter and had a poor survival of babies over the past five year'n or so. They got sick and plain died. Boss and me figure our stock has become too inbred. So we brung in a solution, for which we are paying top dollar. This over here is Mr. Root. He is in charge of the general process."

He turned to Root, who was waiting for a signal, and nodded.

Root returned the nod, then hauled open the big back doors of the wagon.

The crowd of darkies fell back. The women cowered beneath the arms of their men, and the single women crowded against each other or their mothers. Gasps moved through them.

In the back of the wagon was a brick building of black. He was twice the width of McCrocklin and even taller than Jeff. His hair was a clump of thistledown, oiled to make it glow, and he had the perfect kind of face for his purpose: one that appealed to white folk. Rather than being flat and wide, the mammoth's nose was situated in perfect triangles between a set of sharp cheekbones from which the sinews of his face took their cue. His face was long, carrying a stateliness that argued with the iron chains around his ankles and wrists. His arms were huge black knots, his legs tree trunks so thick he couldn't even put his knees together. Chained by the ankles, he was completely naked but made no attempt whatsoever to cover his dangling genitals. His eyes were brown, not black, in fact lighter than his skin, and they were ferocious. They rolled from side to side in his head, creating flashes of white in the iron skillet of his face, an effect that was plain terrifying to the slaves watching him. He had a wolfish grandeur that white folk would find attractive or at least intriguing, and which negroes found plain intimidating and a bit of a shame.

The slaves looked at him the same way they would look at a caged creature—awed by his beauty, but glad of the cage.

McCrocklin went right on talking. "I gotta talk to Boss

about which of you childless women is gonna get with this big buck. In the meantime you all stay away from him. He's dangerous, got that? Ain't none of you never saw a nigger like this before. He ain't like you. Don't go thinking he is and sneak over trying to conversate with him. He don't parlay English. He'll just pull your head off. If I come out and find your head on the ground, it'll be hell to pay. Just keep behind the ropes and do your own business.''

Dorian watched the monster climb from the back of the wagon and listened to those chains rattling. Rather than experiencing the same panic as the other negroes, he watched with bitter curiosity. McCrocklin was probably telling the truth. The naked giant didn't seem to be embarrassed by his nakedness or by his chains, or even care that everyone was gawking at him. Fascination washed over Dorian for the pure naked form. This was no hollow-chested field nigger writhing on the rack of common slavery. This was a form chiseled out of obsidian, surprisingly like the statues in the Greek garden just over the hill, except not white. This was the same fleshy physique, the same imperishable beauty of the naked male, except that he was about twice the size and lacking the thoughtfulness carved into the statues' faces.

Dinah and Stepney shuddered against each other and hid behind Homer. "Oh, Lawd God be in his heaven . . .'' Stepney whimpered.

Disdainfully Dorian raised his brows. "And he stuck us here.''

★

CHAPTER FOURTEEN

──────── ★ ────────

"We're going to have to make decisions today, gentlemen. That means taking risks."

Howard Tuggle filled his brandy at Lucas's new Dutch liquor cabinet and wobbled the bottle to see if anyone else wanted any.

"Not on Sunday," John Van Meer declined.

"Too early for me," Frank Plunkett said.

Lucas and Nick also declined, but the storekeeper C. T. Patterson, and the brothers Fowler, David and Elias, who owned a large granary and a horse farm, motioned that it wasn't too early for them. Tuggle filled three more snifters, then glanced at Colonel Brookville, who was scanning Luke Wallace's rows of popular books.

"Colonel?"

"Mmmm?" Brookville's heavy red eyebrows flicked. "Oh, yes, please." He nodded at Tuggle, then continued skimming the embossed titles on the shelves. They seemed to ignite before him, set neatly in the bright olive green facing wall of the library. Amazing that one short mention so many years ago could have such a profound effect on a man like Wallace. While the other men were distracted with handing out brandy and lighting cigars, he stole a moment to pluck a book at random from the shelves, then another, and a third. Sure enough, every one had been read. The spines were cracked, the pages soiled with fingermarks.

"It's going to have to be two issues today," Tuggle was saying. "Expansionism and tariffs."

"Yes," Brookville echoed. "As a candidate, Lucas, you'll have to be for expansionism and against tariffs."

Luke Wallace puffed on his cigar and tracked field mud across the bold red sarouk rug. He often changed clothes before a political meeting, but never his boots. It made folks think he knew about the dirty side of running a plantation. "Unfortunately," he said, "I happen to be complacent about tariffs and not impressed with expansionism. If the Mexican war is an example of expansionism in the United States, it's not going to play out well for us in the end. It's immoral."

"What it is," Van Meer said, "is a pitiful waste of time. Mexicans. Dirty savages."

"By Lord," Plunkett said, shrinking in his wing-backed chair, "I never thought I could get so sick of hearing about a war."

"Mexicans are a lesser breed," David Fowler said. "We should just go through Texas and take all of Mexico too."

Lucas glanced at Nick, who was sitting customarily in the farthest corner, slumped down, his elbows cocked up on the arms of the big red sackback chair. Nick raised one eyebrow and nodded almost imperceptibly.

Lucas turned to speak, but Elias Fowler beat him to it.

"You'd think that, sitting in your warm office," Elias said, leaning toward his brother. "Your opinions have always been cheap, Dave."

David Fowler's thin face turned almost comic. He thrived on disagreeing with his brother. "Land in Mexico is cheap too. Americans are best suited to make it thrive. Who's going to open up the West if not us? The English? Look what they've done in Oregon. Nothing. And the French? Why, hell."

"The war with Mexico is growing unpopular," Tuggle said. "The Unitarians and the Congregationalists are against it because they don't want another slave state. It's a problem we can't ignore."

"Abolitionist droppings," Van Meer grumbled.

"Hear, hear," Dave said, and sipped his brandy.

Lucas took another draw on Nick's presence. This time Nick wagged a hand at him.

He breathed deeply and plunged in. "If we annex Mexico, how can we convert those barbarians into sensible slave owners? I'd just as soon take Texas and let Mexico keep itself."

"Lucas, this is suicide if you want to win an election," Dave Fowler told him. "You *have* to be expansionist."

Lucas turned to him and leaned an elbow on the square grand piano, knowing the massive piece of furniture made him look tall. "I'd rather be honest. People want to know where we landholders stand. The U.S. is going to win, there's no doubt anymore. Texas'll come in as a slave state *if* we toss Oregon to the abolitionists as a pacifier. I say let'm have it. What's in Oregon? Trees and rain."

"I agree," Frank Plunkett said rather timidly. "How can we keep a moral advantage as Southern gentlemen if we approve of this Texas landgrab just to get our hands on one more slave state? The whole thing makes me shake." Above his waxed mustache his eyes brimmed with misery and lost their focus. "My son's out there," he added quietly. "I just got his first letter in eight months. He's dying of sepsis. They got no drinkable water. There've been half a dozen dead to disease for every one killed honorably in battle. I don't want Mexico. . . . It's bug bites and dysentery, little more. . . . He's probably dead by now."

His voice twisted on the last phrase, and with it twisted the hearts of Plunkett's longtime friends. What had begun as a rally for more U.S. territory had turned into an unpopular war with Mexico. As more and more young American men dropped dead of dysentery in the Mexican heat, fewer voices called for Manifest Destiny.

"Gentlemen, we have an election strategy to plan," Van Meer reminded, but even he spoke with solemn urgency in deference to a man he'd known nearly twenty-five years and a soldier who was his own godson. "The war is a playing card. I'm sorry, Frank. No matter our reasons for being in Mexico, Antonio Santa Anna has not played fair either. That son of a bitch double-crossed us and attacked General Taylor when he said he wouldn't. That gets sympathy for Taylor that we can't buck. Especially since Taylor swung right in and smashed the Mexicans down again. He's a Whig. We're Democrats. It's a Democrat administration that's having to deal with Mexico.''

Lucas moved closer to Nick, but he looked at Van Meer. "With a quarter the men, Taylor fought Santa Anna to a standstill. The man is dangerous presidential material.''

Elias Fowler toed the rug's fringe and muttered, "I call it a damnable shame that all Polk could find was Whigs to make decent generals.''

"He should've gotten us," C.T. spoke up. "I'm free to serve.''

The Fowlers and Tuggle laughed, and Nick chuckled from his corner. Colonel Brookville remained silent behind his brandy glass, wishing in his heart that he could be young again.

Van Meer shot to his feet and shook a *London Times* in Patterson's face. "You'd better be! They might get down to you. My God, you're all so sure the war is won. Winfield Scott fought his way to the gates of Mexico City, and now that he's there, what's he going to do? Take up knitting? He's facing thirty thousand well-entrenched Mexicans! He's got twelve thousand men and a supply line that has to run all the way back to the coast!''

"What?" Brookville shouted.

Plunkett pressed his fist to his chest and gasped, "Good Lord, I hadn't heard that!''

Elias Fowler stepped to Van Meer's side and craned toward the newspaper. "Let me see.''

Van Meer held the paper out before him. "A few dolts on horseback could cut the supply line and starve him. The Polk administration and all us Democrats had better be ready to get blamed for a damned Whig defeat! Scott's going to be slaughtered!''

The room dropped to an awful silence. David Fowler joined his brother to get a glimpse of the article, and C. T. Patterson was right behind him. They crowded around Van Meer.

Lucas made a half turn, enough to see Nick.

Nick pursed his lips and shook his head meaningfully.

Bolstered, Luke puffed up and made a circle with his cigar. "Gentlemen, Santa Anna's army is demoralized. It'll fall to Scott by the end of this year." The men looked up at him. "The war's won, John," he added. "It's plain won."

His proclamation wandered the room in varying degrees of approval and disapproval. They wanted Scott to win as an American, but as a Whig they hoped he scorched. Tricky.

"On the other hand," Lucas said, "let's not assume Zachary Taylor's as good a political general as he might be a strategic general. Don't forget, he captured a city, then paroled two thousand enemy men. They promised not to fight anymore, went home, changed clothes, got new guns, and came out again to kill more of our boys. We can use that."

Brookville lumbered toward the couch and took a seat next to C.T. "What was he supposed to do? Hold two thousand prisoners in that heat?"

"Doesn't matter," Lucas said.

"Correct," Tuggle agreed. "I like the way you think, Luke."

Lucas nodded in a grand manner and grinned. "Well, Howard, a good businessman always knows how to tell half a story."

Just as John Van Meer took a breath to speak, the library double doors slid open and Iphigenia Wallace rustled into the room. Her bright blue skirt rocked like a bell till they half expected it to chime. She still had a foreign mystique, even after all these years, and something about her made them see the Southern ladies' fashions as though for the first time.

The men grunted to their feet.

"Afternoon, Mizz Wallace."

"Pleasure, ma'am."

"Mizz Wallace."

" 'Day, ma'am."

"How are you today, Missus?"

Iphigenia laced her fingers and rested them on her linen apron. "Good afternoon, gentlemen," she murmured. Her accent was smooth and rather regal, but tempered by her pleasant smile. "We're ready to serve a small buffet. Would you prefer to eat in the library?"

"Yes, we're smack in the middle of something," Lucas told her.

She nodded and asked, *"Ti mas sistimete?"*

Lucas couldn't avoid clearing his throat, no matter how hard he tried. He forced himself to avoid looking at Nick just now. *"Ekete freska fruta?"*

She nodded again. *"Neh."*

He pursed his lips and pretended to be thinking. "Then some *revani* . . . and I think *legha katalifi*. Any of that good *kumkuat*?"

From the corner Nick interrupted, "No, Lucas. *Clytaemnestra* is behind her schedule this season."

Wallace shrugged. "She's a good old ship. I've much to thank her for."

No one was going to argue that.

Not a man in the room was spared a pang of envy for Lucas Wallace and his cosmopolitanism. All these men had American wives—wives who were their age. Forties, fifties, sixties. Not Wallace. Here was his wife, a thirty-some-year-old vision of grace and refinement without a touch of pomposity. Somehow the rabble among them had conquered time itself.

Tuggle looked at the unique couple and saw possibilities he'd never have predicted fifteen years ago. Strange how time can change things, time and a little ingenuity. In spite of his cloddish beginnings, Wallace possessed that ingenuity. Even Wallace himself looked better, healthier, than he had fifteen years ago. He'd put on a few pounds and looked rosier for it, his hair had become a silver livery, and with his neat full beard and dirty boots he looked something of a Davy Crockett. Perfect for their purposes.

And with that wife on his arm . . .

"Very well," Iphigenia murmured. She smiled again at the jumble of well-to-do businessmen. "You will all bring your wives when you come next time? So I shall have visitors too? You will, won't you?"

Her smile turned them to mush.

"Oh, of course, ma'am!"

"I shall be delighted, Mrs. Wallace."

"To be sure, of course."

"She'll be at my side, without fail, ma'am."

"In fact," Tuggle added, "we're having a special meeting coming up this Tuesday evening. Might we have it right here at the brain central?"

Lucas laughed and roared, "Why, where else? Where else! All right with you, Genny?"

"Yes, I will arrange everything," Iphigenia said. "Oh, Lucas, there is another couple in the parlor. They only just arrived. Shall I show them in?"

The grin dropped from Lucas's face. He glared at her, confused. He didn't like being stuck with the unexpected. His entire social climb had relied upon knowing ahead of time what to say and think.

"Oh . . . we weren't expecting anyone else. . . ."

Beside him Tuggle roused from his thoughts and came to life again. "Yes, we were," he interrupted. He put his brandy down and stepped behind Iphigenia. "Allow me." He leaned into the corridor. "Samson? Show them right in here. Yes, thank you. This way."

Two strangers came in the door. A tiny young woman and a stout young man, both dressed in traveling clothes, with uneventful faces but the same set of quick green eyes.

In the corner Nick stood up slowly, his shadowy face full of nuances. He also didn't care for surprises. His arms were poised at his sides. Suddenly he looked very eerie.

Lucas pulled his cigar from his mouth. "What's this? What's going on? Who are these people?"

Tuggle motioned to the newcomers. "Come right in, please. Gentlemen, may I present Mr. Edward Porterfield, a lawyer just up from Washington. This is his sister, Mrs. Anna Campman, who will serve as our secretary, recording all necessary proceedings and quotations."

"Proceedings?" Lucas blurted. A big, wide pit formed in his stomach. "What's this all about?"

"Mr. Porterfield is also a campaign manager," Tuggle explained. "You see, we on the committee have changed our minds, Lucas. We don't want you to run for county commissioner."

He pulled back the sides of his coat and stuck his hands

into his pockets. Pacing himself carefully, he approached the bigger man and looked up into that silver-framed face.

"We want you to run for Congress."

★

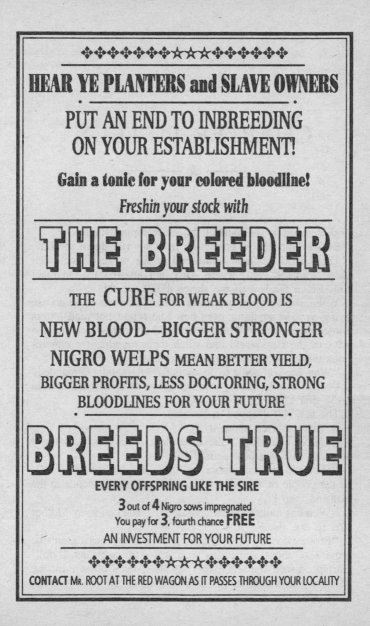

CHAPTER FIFTEEN

———— ★ ————

Dorian stared at the handbill in his cramping fingers.

Beside him Alex was panting from his run down the hill.

They stood together at the end of the picket fence, well away from the yard, where Alex had insisted Dorian meet him. Better the rest of the slaves didn't see this.

Yula, however, was here with them. There would be no use trying to hide anything from her. She might not read letters printed on a page, but she could read her son's face and the ways of the Big World and stitch them together for conclusions that were frighteningly accurate.

"What are you going to do about it?" Alexander demanded.

Dorian read the gawdy printing again, as if he hadn't gotten it the first time.

The handbill dropped to his side.

"What can I do about it?"

"Are you serious?" the other boy complained. "Honor demands that you take action!"

"Honor is a cheap dinner, isn't it?" Dorian told him. "Of all the people on this plantation, who has less influence in the mansion than I?"

"Who has more?" Alex countered. "You can sway Mother like no one else."

"Mother doesn't involve herself in farm business. Don't be provincial about something you know as well as I do." Dorian crushed the stiff paper against Alex's chest until the other boy took hold of it. Then he gripped the fence's white pickets as though to indicate that his hands were busy now and he didn't want the paper back.

"Ain't nothin' he can do," Yula said to Alex. She didn't look at him. She looked instead at Dorian's soft black hair moving in the breeze that came off the sun-warmed tobacco fields.

"What if they pick you?" Alex asked her, his fists looking like cue balls.

"Won't pick me," she said. "Even if'n they do, I refuse."

Alex's voice squeaked. "How can you refuse!"

"I jes do." Her tiny nut of a face turned upward into the sunlight. "I gots me a decent life. Gots my patch to sow, gots my job to do, does it good as any, gots my marshmallow right wid me—" She poked Dorian when he sneered with embarrassment. "He grow tall, no shrinkin', no hackin', gots Boss to perteck me, Boss to worry if rain come or don't come, Missy to see we ain't gotta wear no rags. I stay jes like I am."

She turned her shoulders this way and that as she approached Alex, and he never realized until this moment that she was actually very proud of her life and what she had made of it. Somehow slaves weren't supposed to be proud. Yet he'd seen this look before, all his life, from all sorts of slaves, without ever translating it for what it was.

Beside them, staring out over the tobacco field, his eyes narrow like evil lances, Dorian remained uncharacteristically silent. Just as he practiced all the restrictions of his strange life-style, he now practiced the art of remaining uninvolved.

Yula seemed to understand. In fact, she herself had planted and nurtured that trait. She never looked at him but continued speaking to Alex.

"See, it like this," she explained. "I dun had a white man's chile. Ain't every niggawoman can say dat. Ain't havin' no nigga baby in me."

Her spiky eyelashes flapped up and down, and she tucked her lips in that way she had.

"Yawl think about it."

"Sorry to interrupt you, Boss. Here's the list you asked for."

McCrocklin led Root in the back way, through the kitchen entrance, and handed his list to Luke Wallace.

Wallace glanced down the dark narrow corridor that led back to the main foyer and the parlor and library, where his guests were pausing for brunch. Here in the kitchen Macedonian servants bustled to deliver Greek treats to the guests, dodging negro house slaves who were crisscrossing the kitchen from pie safe to dry sink to pump to Dutch cupboard, getting tea and fruits ready.

In the center, right in the way, he held his informal meeting with his overseer and the man to whom the Breeder belonged. He gave the paper a snap and scanned the list of names, annoyed by McCrocklin's pathetic handwriting and his excuse for spelling. The foreman was barely literate and only after long exposure had learned to scribble the names of the slaves and a few necessary terms to run the plantation.

"Who's on this list?" Wallace asked.

McCrocklin scratched his mustache and pushed back his wide-brimmed hat. "Childless bondswomen under thirty-five but over fifteen who ain't house slaves. Total of twenty. I put a x next to the ones ain't never had a baby. I figure odds are better to catch seed in the ones that already had one, so I put a z next to the ones that got young'uns over five years old."

"That's good figuring. Don't do the real young ones. I can't find it in me to subject a fifteen-year-old to a big buck like him."

Root spoke up, ignoring the glares of the house slaves. "Oh, he gentle enough, Mister. If'n you want your young womens pregnant, he can do it fine."

"But those stand a chance of babies in the future. Let's concentrate on the women who might be out of their prime in a couple years."

"Good thinkin', Boss," McCrocklin said.

"What are these other names?"

"Them are the ones whose menfolk are dead or whose husbands are living off the grounds."

"Don't do any married ones. Wouldn't be right."

"Okay."

Still holding the list, Wallace turned to Root. "How do I know I won't get a crop of animals or simpletons?"

"Sir, you read the references. All the Breeder's babies turn out true to form and plenty smart. We bin doing this near four years now, and you saw the letters. Satisfied customers from Virginia to Florida."

"How you going to handle this?"

Root sniffed and wobbled his head from side to side. His hair moved like a broom. "You just leave it to me, sir. I circ'late the women through as I know best. I know how often he can do it."

"Mmm-hmm. Now you tell me one more thing." Wallace stepped closer. Too close. He glowered right into Root's yellow-veined eyes. "How do I know these babies won't come out looking like you?"

Without a pause, utterly heedless of the slaves and servants milling around the kitchen, Root hiked up his waistcoat, untied his trouser string, and opened the crotch to full view.

Someone dropped a tray. Other than that the only reaction was a series of averted glances. Wallace stopped breathing, gripped by empathy.

McCrocklin just stood there, rocking on his heels and biting his lip. He had already asked and already been shown.

Wallace cleared his throat and looked down at the paper, his face flushed. It was several seconds before he could bring himself to speak again. He had to swallow, then swallow again.

"All right, you got a deal. You got that wagon where my guests can't see it? This is business and not for social consumption."

"Under the willer tree in the yard by the creek," McCrocklin said.

Slowly Root tied his trousers. Deliberately slowly.

"All right, Mr. Root, you made your point," Wallace sighed. "You control that beast, hear? If any of my slaves is injured, I pay you nothing. Not a red cent."

"I kill him if'n he hurt a woman, Mister. He know that."

"He better."

"Oh, he do."

"And we are not barbarians. He will do his business under a roof and behind walls."

"Yessir, the wagon is all set up inside."

"McCrocklin, you go ahead and pick eight prime candidates." The word *candidate* suddenly reminded Wallace there was better business to handle than this.

Suddenly he was in a hurry. He started to hand the list back to McCrocklin and to head toward the corridor and his guests, when something caught his eye.

Out the open kitchen window over the dry sink, beyond the simple challis curtains that a breeze was sucking outward, down the hill at the end of the picket fence, was his son.

Alexander.

And the other one.

And the woman.

He gazed for a long, strange moment. Deep-dyed hatred nested in his eyes.

McCrocklin tried to take the list away, but Boss's fingers had tightened, creasing the sheet.

Wallace's eyes flicked downward.

"Why isn't that woman on the list?"

McCrocklin tipped to his left and looked out the window.

"Oh . . . well . . . I, uh . . . I figured . . ." He shrugged about four times, in about four different directions. Yula was the only slave who'd been bedded by the Boss. That made her different, somehow.

Wallace flicked the sheet at him and this time let go of it.

"Put her on the list," he snapped.

"Uh . . ."

"In fact," he added, "put her first."

When McCrocklin and Root strode in stern silence back to the yard, the slaves had already dispersed. Curiosity wasn't enough to keep them out in the open today, especially not the women. Having no idea what criteria would be used to pick the Breeder's targets, they all figured hiding was the best option.

The negro men dispersed also, but since they had no need to hide, they only averted their glances when the overseer and the jack-a-dandy came through. Unfortunately that meant Jeff was in full view, doing his duty of tending the ash-leaching barrel.

When Root spied him, Jess was just dumping another load of ashes into the barrel. That done, water would be poured in over the ashes. The drippings contained lye, and that would be used to make soap. It was a common, everyday thing to do, but it also provided a perfect way to judge Jeff's massive size against the huge barrel, and this caught Root's discerning eye.

"Say, sir," he said, pinching McCrocklin's shirtsleeve. "Might I have a word?"

McCrocklin paused. "Yeah. What?"

"How old is that big boy there?"

"Who? Jeff? Maybe thirty. Why?"

"Thirty, you say. . . . Ain't in his prime, exactly . . . but ain't exactly out of it either."

"Why? What you thinking?"

Root gazed across the yard at Jeff's bare arms and clean brown skin. The slaves on this plantation had good skin. Not all scarred from whippings or brandings. Made for good show material. One of the Breeder's greatest points was his unmarked skin that looked good to slave owners. The big buck at the leaching barrel had very clear skin for his age, all his fingers, a full head of hair, firm, round buttocks, knotted calves, and a well-shaped mouth.

As Jeff felt their eyes and looked toward them self-consciously, Root leaned toward McCrocklin.

"Well, sir, I've been looking for to expand my stock, branch out as folks say. Maybe breed up two farms at the same time, or offer two bloodlines, so as, for instance, your sows can breed their offspring together down the line. Don't want all your niggerbabies be brother and sister, do you?"

McCrocklin hooked his thumbs in his pants pockets. "No, guess not."

"See there?"

Across the yard Jeff went back to his leaching but continued peering worriedly at them as he worked. He tried to go around the other side of the immense barrel, but he couldn't get completely out of sight, because the barrel was situated against the outside wall of the blacksmith shop.

McCrocklin cocked his hip.

"Hmmm . . . you want to buy Jeff. I'll have to talk to Boss on that. How much?"

"How much you want?"

"How much you offering?"

"I offer . . . five hundred."

"Eight."

"Six."

"Eight."

"Seven."

"Done," McCrocklin said, "after I check with Boss."

"We've targeted a seat in the House of Representatives. Our current representative is a man named DeVries. It won't be easy to unseat an incumbent from our own party, but if anyone has a chance, it's a man who earned his way into the landed gentry without benefit of inheritance."

Porterfield might as well have been talking to a wall. The other men nodded, but they were mesmerized by the sumptuous treats on their plates. They all ate well enough as a rule, but such elegant European fare as this was available only at Plentiful, and the variation upon themes distracted them. Except for the birthday boy. Luke Wallace hadn't quite swallowed the idea of himself as a congressman. He sat on the divan while Pilos and the other Greeks fluttered around him, and gazed lovingly as the future passed before his eyes. Representative Wallace. Congressman Wallace. Senator Wallace. Judge Advocate General Wallace. Secretary of State Wallace. A title. He'd always wanted a title.

"I think it's a losing battle," Frank Plunkett said. "I told you that before, Howard."

A bit of pastry stuck on Tuggle's mustache. "Not so. Lucas is a Democrat and so is DeVries, but DeVries votes with the Whigs more often than his constituency prefers. We can use that, if—Lucas, *if* you'll stop pointing up your antisecessionism and shift to states' rights."

"Exactly," Colonel Brookville said with a nod.

Porterfield nodded. "DeVries's weakest point is that he

spoke out in the Richmond *Tribune* two years ago against annexing Texas and against the war with Mexico when it was popular. He's changed his tune now, but I think it's too late. War fever has the nation by the head, and the state of Virginia has lost faith in him. So, Mr. Wallace?"

Lucas jumped. "Pardon?"

"I'd like to hear your current opinions on things, sir, so we can have a springboard upon which to brace our platform."

Lucas wondered how much of his opinions the man already knew, having agreed to this conspiracy and come all the way here to manage him, but evidently the stout young politician wanted to get it all fresh.

"Well," he began, "shoot."

Porterfield sat nearby on the piano bench, held his plate in his lap. "All right, Mr. Wallace. What do you say to the voters about President Polk's efforts to stop federal funding of domestic projects?"

At first Lucas was nervous. He began haltingly but thought he sounded gradually better. "Well...I...I guess I'd say what I think. President Polk is right to resist internal improvements at the cost of you and me. Why should Virginia pay for a railroad in Illinois? Why should tariffs pay to give land away in Oregon? Nobody gave us our land, correct?"

Back in his corner, slumping in the chair, Nick flinched. He thought the remark might be a mistake but then thought that Lucas might have made the faux pas on purpose—to cauterize the plain fact that he was the only one among them who had actually built his own fortune from scratch. As he watched Lucas's face, though, he decided the remark hadn't been deliberate, but just a lucky mistake.

"What about external restrictions?" Porterfield asked.

"What's external about them?" Lucas shot back. "Tariffs are killing us, plain and simple. We have protectionism against cheap European labor so Northern industry can charge you and me more for what we buy."

"Some would say the same about slavery," Colonel Brookville pointed out.

"Some would," Van Meer added.

"Problem is," Lucas continued, "that I think it's a dead issue."

"What?" one of the Fosters belted.

The other brother said, "You're going to have to keep railing against the tariffs if you want votes, Luke."

Van Meer twisted his big body toward them. "Why should we soil ourselves with factory work when the Europeans are willing and able to do it cheap? We only have tariffs against foreign goods because the Northern factories like to charge us more than market value. The South is supplying the wealth for the whole country, and the North is stealing it!"

His voice got so loud that a crystal teardrop lamp across the room chimed with vibrations.

"Why is it a dead issue, Mr. Wallace?" Porterfield insisted upon knowing.

Lucas blinked thoughtfully. "Because tariffs have been lowered in recent years."

David Fowler said, "I agree with John. The North gets rich by manufacturing what we need and charging us twice what we could get it from Europe for, if it weren't for the damnable tariffs. That reaping machine is likely worth half what you paid for it, Lucas."

"Maybe," Lucas continued. "Still, the tariffs did get lowered, and the chances of getting them any lower aren't good. It doesn't do a bit of good to get emotional about it."

"Voters *like* an emotional candidate, Mr. Wallace," Porterfield told him.

On this Lucas needed no coaching. He met Porterfield's eyes keenly. "Emotion has no place in business," he said.

Colonel Brookville stood up and strode toward him, still holding a small plate with pastries on it, and said, "You're too much a businessman, Lucas. You also have to be a politician."

Lucas looked up. "Business *is* politics, Colonel," he said with complete conviction, "and politics had better be business. It's the only way to keep nations from starving."

Nearby, John Van Meer shook his head, disgusted.

Taking that moment for one fleeting glance toward the corner, Lucas was reassured by a posture he knew well—as long as Nick's rough face was relaxed and his eyes were not on fire, Lucas knew he was doing all right.

He straightened his shoulders.

"However," he added, "there is still a good reason, a better one, for us to rail against tariffs, even if they'll never go any lower."

Tuggle provided the necessary, "And that is?"

"Support from Europe for the South, gentlemen. U.S. tariffs are making enemies of people you and I should be courting. We Southerners don't pay enough attention to Europe. We can't afford to make enemies there."

"Allies if we should ever secede?" Elias Fowler asked, his brow rutted. "Is that what you mean?"

"No. I mean we should keep on the good side of the working people in Europe. There's a hotbed of antislavery in England and France among the working gentry. That will tell against us."

"How can it?" Van Meer asked.

"Inaction, if nothing else," Lucas said. "Never count on another's actions, gentlemen. Always assume others will sit back and watch first." He stood up, put his plate down on the corner of a tablecloth, rolled back the top of his desk, and plucked a cigar from the box. "Now, you know I am against secession. But I'm not the type to ignore the changes in our nation."

"I don't follow you," Porterfield said abruptly. "Don't lose me. A good candidate doesn't lose people."

Lucas took a moment to light the cigar and puff a few times.

"Are you truly lost, Mr. Porterfield? The Southern economy exists because we have the advantage of slavery. And that's the only reason. Industrialization in the North is putting the working class in charge of things, and a working class that has extra time and a comfortable living is a dangerous body."

"Yes!" Tuggle blurted. "He's right! This industrializing is playing havoc with the South. Communications advancements are letting people know that it's not the privileged planter who makes up the majority, but the swilling second-classers."

"I've said that for years," Van Meer muttered.

"The bricklayers, the storekeepers, the men who mix mortar, the cobblers and hatters, the cooks—"

"Dockworkers," Luke Wallace added, bobbing his brows at Nick and grinning around his cigar.

"Those are the voters," Tuggle said. "Look at Congress! Where's the decorum? Where's the polite behavior? Why, it's a circus now! Congressional demeanor's buried under this fad of electing common clods because it's the common clod who votes now." He interrupted himself and suddenly touched his fingers to his mouth. "Oh, Lucas! My God, I had no insult in mind. . . ."

"None taken," Lucas responded.

Nick continued to smirk silently.

Porterfield motioned toward the cigar box. "Would you mind if—"

"Oh, not at all," Lucas jolted. He snatched the box and held it open for the young gentleman, than offered it to the roomful. "Anyone else?" When they declined, Lucas struck a match and held it out to Porterfield. "Allow me."

"Thank you." He puffed a few times. "It's what they call full-manhood suffrage. Every man voting, no matter his background."

"Sausage Sawyer," Brookville put in.

David Fowler looked up from his plate for the first time in ten minutes. "Who's that?"

"A congressman who sat and ate sausage at the podium. Thought West Point should be disbanded. Imagine!"

"What became of him?"

"I've no idea. Deplorable bourgeois behavior. I hope he was shot."

"He wasn't," Porterfield commented. "He should've been, but he wasn't."

In the corner Nick grumbled, "I'd have shot him."

"Gentlemen, you're going too fast for me," Anna Campman said, scribbling furiously on her lap-desk.

"You always try to write down too much, Annie," her brother commented.

"I like to be accurate."

"Have you taken time to eat?"

She looked up now. "Well, no, not precisely."

Porterfield waved at her rather impolitely, as brothers are wont to do with their own sisters. "Such a martyr!"

She thumped her hand on her broad skirt, set her portable lap-desk on the piano bench, and stood up. "It doesn't take a clunk on the head."

His wanting her out of the room had nothing to do with her getting something to eat, she knew, because the room was brimming with pastries and fruit. He always wanted to be such a performer.

She straightened her skirt and turned to leave the library but paused when a small-boned six-year-old girl paraded into the room and went straight to Lucas.

"Pardon, Daddy," the child said.

Lucas put his hands on her thin shoulders and turned her to face his guests. "Gentlemen, Mrs. Campman, may I present my youngest daughter...Rose Dimitra."

They showered her with proper greetings, and the child curtseyed for them. Then she faced her father again. "Mommy says the veranda and the garden are all made up, if everybody wishes to go out there for a breath."

"Tell your mother we shall take her up on it shortly, when our business is done."

Anna Campman reached for the child's tiny hand and asked, "Would you like to come with Mrs. Campman and get a cookie?"

Rose Dimitra's immense brown eyes batted at the woman, and her music-box voice tittered, "Why are you referring to yourself in the third person?"

Mrs. Campman bolted upright, staring down. Her lips pursed.

The men all chuckled warmly.

Speaking from experiences of his own, Howard Tuggle said, "You obviously haven't met any of Lucas's children yet, ma'am."

Mrs. Campman shook her head and smiled. Bemused, she looked at the child and tried again. "In that case, Miss Wallace, would you care to adjourn to the parlor and partake of a sweet?"

Rose Dimitra nodded sharply. "That's much better. Yes. I would. I'm going to be a teacher someday, you know."

"Darling, I haven't a doubt of it!"

Once they were gone, Lucas closed the library doors. Slowly then, he turned to his new campaign manager.

"All right, Mr. Porterfield. What is it you want to ask me that you don't want written down?"

Porterfield gave him an approving, if annoyed, glare. "You're very perceptive, Mr. Wallace. I like that."

The other men waited, breath held, as the two faced each other right in the middle of the claret red rug. Porterfield took his time.

"Mr. Wallace," he began, "how am I going to explain to your constituency that you've kept your plantation going during slack times by investing in coal mines? What've coal mines got to do with you? You're a planter."

Frank Plunkett choked on his coffee.

"Lucas, my God!" Tuggle blurted.

"Why shouldn't I?" Lucas countered gravely. "What's bad about it?"

"It's too modern," Van Meer said. "Too industrial."

"Too Northern!" Brookville agreed.

"Oh, it's Nawwwwthun," Lucas mimicked, looking at them. "It's mahhhdun. Mother Puck! This is our decade if we let it be! The decade of the agrarian elite. *If* we don't cut ourselves off from the rest of the country."

"My ass!" Van Meer shouted, bolting to his feet. "We have to fight these changes! Improvements of cattle breeds, industrialization, investing in other than ourselves, why, hell!"

"You're wrong. Fight change, and we'll be left behind. Plowed under like old soil. You're just wrong. If it makes me a bad candidate, so be it."

He knew the statement was a risk. He could measure the danger in the shadows around Nick's eyes.

The men felt their stomachs shrink as they looked at him. Lucas was their investment guide. In the ugly idea that he might be right skulked the knowledge that he always had been before.

But coal . . . factories

"You like modern things, Lucas," Van Meer insisted. "You like Northern things, and don't you mock me! You have that Illinois reaper taking away the work of your slaves. I say that's a goddamned abolitionist machine! You have a Cincinnati iron stove in your kitchen, and it burns coal. I charge you to explain!''

"Coal is becoming the popular fuel over wood, John. I can't head it off, and neither can you.''

"But you'll have to answer to the lumberjacks,'' David Fowler said. ''What are they supposed to do for a living?''

Lucas faced him. ''Let their own state worry. There's coal under the ground right here in Virginia. Why haul wood from Minnesota when we can use our own resource? The state should be run like a business. A separate business from all other states. I predict Virginia will soon be selling much more coal to the world then tobacco.''

"Trash!'' Elias Fowler roared. ''To burn in stoves the Northern factories want to sell us!''

"You're no candidate,'' Van Meer huffed. ''You're a traitor to the Southern way of life.''

"Am I?'' Lucas challenged. ''Fine. Next time I go to the mines, you gentlemen should come have a look-see for yourselves. It is a sight to behold. I've invested part of my last three years' profits in the mines. You all should do that too.''

Silence dropped all around. Brains were clicking away. It wouldn't be the first time they'd profited from taking Lucas's lead.

Plunkett broke the silence. ''Really?''

"What percentage return are you expecting?'' Tuggle asked.

Lucas caught Nick's beaming gaze. They were each proud of the way he was turning the problem around.

Elias Fowler shook his head and sourly said, ''I will *not* invest in anything that benefits Northern factories.''

His brother grumbled, ''Next you'll be telling us the world market will have no use for Georgia cotton.''

"I wouldn't depend on the world market for pigeon droppings,'' Lucas said. ''There's been secession talk for twenty years, and it's all going to come to a head because of industrialization. Europe has no love for the South. They don't like our slavery. Won't be long before they don't like *us*.''

"My God, are you blind?'' Van Meer blustered. ''If the

South secedes, the Europeans will be so pressed for lack of cotton that they'll side with us immediately, industry or not.''

"Maybe,'' Lucas told him, "but not on *my* life, sir. Cotton may be king, but if I were a European businessman, I would know what's going on here, and the first thing I'd be doing is stockpiling cotton. I suspect that's what they're doing.''

Van Meer shook his head. "They can't afford to stockpile cotton.''

Lucas looked right at him. "Again, maybe. But would you put your hand on this piano and let me chop it off if you're wrong?''

Porterfield had been watching all this with the curiosity of a student of politics and the wisdom of a practitioner of it. He watched Lucas Wallace's face, he watched the effect of Wallace's words on the firebrands in the room, he watched it chip away at the anti-Northernism and get down to the bedrock in each of these men. Even Van Meer had fallen silent after the last crack. That told him something. He kept quiet and kept watching.

"I say you have to decide,'' Frank Plunkett said, "whether you want to be an upper-crust candidate or a swillers' candidate, Lucas.''

Wallace didn't even breathe before responding. "No, I don't. What's good for one is good for the other, though he might not know it.''

"That doesn't help the lumberjacks,'' one of the Fowlers said. "What'll you say to them?''

"I'll say start digging coal.'' He strode across his rug and leaned on his fine shiny piano. "We landowners live very well, gentlemen. Why risk an all-or-nothing proposition when we already have the 'all'?''

A new silence fell. Everyone in the room, including Van Meer, knew Luke Wallace wasn't against the Southern way of life. He'd worked harder than any of them to get it for himself. He was simply more practical than pompous, and something about him brought that across. He wore fine clothing, but his boots were dirty, and he didn't always trim that wild silver beard. He came across neither as an elitist who was slumming nor as a sow's ear dressed in silk. A kind of upper-crust common man. He was a survivor who cared if others survived. That was hard to ignore.

Porterfield moved to the window and gazed out. Sunlight dusted his face, glittered in the smoke from his cigar as it twisted beside him. He looked down the hill to Plentiful's rippling fields, to the prosperous, expanding lands, to the new barn and the tiny civilization of slaves, and he began to think aloud.

"I suppose we could run on a state-as-business platform," he pondered quietly. "Not easy, but it might gain attention . . . a spoiler candidate coming up behind a party incumbent might as well take a bold tack . . . there's nothing to lose by being flamboyant . . . attract the votes of medium landowners, investors, maybe the idea of expanding a plantation's interests . . . by God, it might work. It just possibly might. I've never run that kind of campaign before. . . ."

The men in the room glanced at each other without moving their heads. They couldn't see Porterfield's face. Silhouetted there in the sunlight, smoke writhing beside him, he looked like an advertisement. When he turned around, the movement made them flinch.

His face was rosy and warm. His auburn hair shimmered.

"But I never got anything in life by being timid. I say let's do it!"

The room erupted in applause. Even Van Meer raised his coffee cup. Tuggle reached to shake Lucas's hand.

There was a knock on the library doors.

Nodding at each of his guests, Lucas basked in approval as he stepped through and tugged the doors open.

When he saw who was there, his expression broke, and he scowled.

"What the devil!"

In the doorway of the library, Stepney stood panting, her worn calico frock looking very much out of place. She wrinkled her nose at the aroma of cigars.

"What do you want?" Lucas demanded.

"Boss," the woman gasped, "Mr. McCrocklin done sent me up for you. He need to see you."

"Why?"

"Jeff done run off."

★

The woodlands skirting Plentiful were as good as anything James Fenimore Cooper had ever dreamed up. Walter Scott's *Redgauntlet* had nothing more Highland-wild in its pages, and the rest of the world simply could not afford to be snobbish about their backlands. Virginia could keep up. Never mind that civilization was just over the ridge.

Dorian marched through the woods, this time ignoring the scenarios he usually made up. Robin Hood, Richelieu, *les mousquetaires*, and Washington Irving's version of Christopher Columbus all remained asleep and undisturbed today. He never even glanced at the sun.

"Jeff!" he bellowed when he reached the low-slung marsh-lands. He waded across the seeping waters, maneuvering across the exposed roots of big overgrown trees. "Jeff!"

"That you, Dohrian?"

"Oh, for the piss of a witch, what are you doing down here?"

The boy almost fell twice as he jumped and waded to the overhang.

There was Jeff, sitting under a crop of rock on the only two square feet of dry ground in the whole marsh.

"I *knew* you'd be here," Dorian complained. "What you up to? Everybody say you run off."

"I did run off," the big negro said.

Dorian's eyes flashed like a demon's in the dark.

"Jeff, you never run off before. You don't want to be free. I know you don't. Idea of being free scare you."

"It do . . . it do," he moaned. He hugged his great knees to his chest and nodded sadly. When he looked up, there were tears glazing his eyes. "He gonna sell me, Dohrian. Boss is gonna sell me to that breeder man. I'll be living with that animal, breeding like some big hog all the time. Dohrian, what I'm gonna do? I got a wife at the Oaks. I got three chillun over there. I won't never see my babies again."

The black-haired boy climbed over the rocks and braced his feet carefully. Reflecting the marshy pond water, his light skin took on a greenish cast. "I can't believe Boss would do something so uncivilized."

"No?" Jeff looked up again. His voice faltered. "I didn't think Boss would bring in no breeder neither. Never thought that kind of thing could happen on Plentiful. But there it is . . . there it is right there. I *had* to run. Once they slap them big black chains on my ankle, I never get away."

Dorian clamped his mouth shut before telling Jeff about what he'd read so recently—a man named Calhoun had written an account of a freed slave's lot in the North, and it was no dreamland. It was blight and pauperism and resentment, a tug-of-war for work, a world where vice looked better than starving, and usually starvation won out anyway. He bit his lip to keep from saying it.

Crouching, Dorian lowered his voice. "Where can you go, Jeff? You can't go anywhere and survive."

"Don't know, rightly," Jeff said. "Maybe Massa Van Meer buy me if'n I hike over there an' tell him."

"Van Meer got no sympathy for you," Dorian said. "Perhaps I can do something though. . . ."

"Talk to Boss for me?" Hope flashed briefly in Jeff's face, then died like a spark. "Oh, what good that do, Dohrian?"

"I *am* his son, after all. Sooner or later that'll have to play out."

"You just get trouble for yourself. I see his eye when he look at you."

"I can speak to Uncle Nick."

"Mr. Nick don't get involved in plantation business. Jesus Lord tell all, Dohrian . . . I kill myself before I let my chillun grow up not knowing where they daddy is, not knowing if they marryin' up with they own brother or sister . . . I kill myself. That's what I took this fishknife for." He reached behind and pulled out a serrated bowie knife. He turned it over and over in his fingers. "I don't hear from you in a day, yawl find me dead. It okay . . . I ain't scared to die. Just scared to live like that breedin' nigger. Dohrian . . . you see that my wife understand, hear?"

The boy took the knife out of Jeff's hand and stabbed the ground, leaving the hilt quivering. "Nonsense. Stay put."

★

His determination remained in full flag as he cut across the marshland, through the woods, and up the creek toward the yard. Like any youth just past puberty, he nurtured a sense of his own indestructibility.

However, for a boy his age, Dorian also possessed a keen common sense that Yula was responsible for.

It was this common sense that grabbed him by the throat when he raced into the yard and skidded to a halt to witness the horror of his young life—and it was the only force that kept him from rash action.

There was his mother, his littlest mother, kicking and fighting the impossible grip of three slave men plus Dinah and Stepney. As Yula protested, Stepney pulled open the door of the wagon. Although Yula braced her feet on the wagon and tried to push back, the others were too much for her. Yula was thrown inside like a cow steered into the slaughtering shoot.

The wagon began to rock unevenly. It made a creaking noise deep down in its underside.

Dinah and Stepney walked away together.

"I hate dat piggy girl," Dinah said. "Ever sin' she come here, she bin uppity."

Stepney wiped her hands on her apron. "She gon' learn she dark as the rest of us. Dis jus' do her good."

In the shadows of evening, the red wagon continued to creak like a giant cricket calling for a mate.

Dorian slipped back against the side of the barn. He pressed his shoulder blades against the warm wood and let his head drop back. He no longer cared about Jeff.

He no longer cared, period.

★

CHAPTER SIXTEEN

───────── ★ ─────────

The night went by like a slug. Dorian shut himself up inside his shell and did his work. He ignored the eyes of the other slaves, who seemed to be wondering how he could allow this to happen, but they knew perfectly well how he did. The same way they did, that was how. Except that he had this polished manila skin and somehow even the other slaves expected more of him because of it. During the next day he watched impassively as three more women were brought in succession to the red wagon and locked up inside. The wagon creaked, but not like it did with Yula inside.

Yula had fought. She had come out bruised, bleeding, and unable to walk. Jonah had carried her to her cabin. Dorian had fed her beef pot broth. She had said nothing about the light that was missing in his eyes. In fact, she had said nothing at all.

"*Who* told you I'd sell him?"

Wallace's voice crashed across the airy veranda. It was Monday afternoon, the second day since Jeff had been missing. Only now had Wallace gotten the truth out of McCrocklin.

The overseer tapped the toe of his boot on the planks, turning his hat like a wheel in his hands.

"Did you tell Root I'd sell Jeff to him?" Wallace roared.

"Well, no, Boss," McCrocklin said. "I just negotiated a price."

"Unnegotiate it! Jeff's not for sale! How many slaves can be trusted to take a whole wagon and go into town for supplies and actually come back? I'd call that rare! And you want to sell him?"

"The offer came up, is all."

"Well, stuff it down again!"

"No problem, Boss. I didn't make no commitments. It's just that seven hundred's a decent price for a nigger past his prime."

"Jeff's not past his prime! And don't refer to them as niggers. That's the word they use for themselves."

McCrocklin tried to pacify him with a nod. He just couldn't follow Wallace's shifts in mood. "Right, culluds. Sure you don't want to reconsider this? Add up a few things? I'd sell him f'I was you."

Wallace jammed his fists against his belt and circled McCrocklin.

"Really? Christ, man, be civilized! Jeff's got a family a day's ride from here. Hell, I was going to buy him his family come Christmas and bring 'em all here to work for me so's Jeff could see them more than once a month, maybe show off a mite. Jesus, you're some kind of a savage!" He paced off, then turned again and pressed a palm against his chest. "Besides, I *like* Jeff. Don't you ever consider my feelings? Go back out to the yard and unnegotiate it!"

"Okay, Boss, okay."

"Then you'll have to find some way to get the message out to Jeff, wherever the hell he's holed up."

McCrocklin crushed his hat back onto his head. "I'll figure something out, Boss. He can't stay out there forever. Not alive, anyhow."

"McCrocklin!"

"Yeah, sir?"

"Don't you shoot him, hear? If he runs, you let him run. I've known Jeff a long time, and I do believe I'd rather see him free than dead. Got me?"

Hiding in the doorway, Alexander Wallace never heard McCrocklin's acceding mutter.

Not long ago such a conversation would have given him glowing faith in his father, but today that wasn't the case. This was the dawn of his enlightenment, and his father simply looked different in that frame. The shouts about feelings and liking Jeff and buying Jeff's family dropped with a crack against the tin truth of women being raped down in the yard, being thrown in the wagon with that beast and made to hike up their skirts.

With the news about Jeff tucked safely in his pocket, Alex stole down to the yard. He couldn't smile, and he couldn't be excited. The best that came to him was relief.

Even that wasn't much when he went past the red breeding wagon and found it rocking again in the dim twilight against the creek. Even more horrible, the man called Root was standing outside the wagon, looking inside a small hatch cut in the lower level. The little door hung open a few inches from his nose. Faint lamplight from inside lay against his brown face. He was watching.

Alex nearly threw up.

With a hand pressed hard against his mouth, he kept moving past and broke into a run.

He found Dorian single-mindedly working in the yard between the cisterns and the slaves' kitchen, using the winnowing basket to tease the whey from several buckets of fresh cheese.

Alex skated to a halt. The sight turned his stomach again.

"My God, you're doing her work!"

Dorian looked up. "Beg pardon?"

Stalking toward him, Alex snapped, "On top of everything else, you're doing Yula's work! As if that solves anything! As if that makes up for anything!"

"Very good," Dorian said. "I wouldn't want you to understate the truth." He turned back to his task. "I'm going to have to go in for her at the drying racks tomorrow as well. Want to stay for supper? They're making colcannon and collards inside."

He went on working with the yard-wide separating basket, impassive to Alexander's burning glare.

Sourly Alex demanded, "Where's Yula?"

"You know where she is. Right where they put her yesterday, that's where."

"Are you telling me it's her in that wagon again? So soon?"

"Stepney was kind enough to inform McCrocklin that Yula's time of the month isn't due for a week, which makes her ripe. I guess they mean to take ad—"

"Dorian!"

"What?"

"Is this all of it?"

"*What?*"

"The whole of your effort!"

"What effort is that?"

Alex grabbed the other boy's firm upper arm and yanked hard. "Your effort to get this stopped!"

Dorian thought about enraging him with another *what?* but decided that would be an egregious waste of breath. He simply met his brother's indignation with his own astringence.

Alex saw it and blanched.

"Where's your courage of conviction?" he charged.

With a brittle expression Dorian responded, "I have no conviction. I'm cold-blooded. Just like a fish."

"How can you watch this?"

"I don't. I keep my eyes closed."

"She's your mother! She gave you life! Is this what Yula taught you? Is this what Mother taught you? And Uncle Nick?"

"You mean while they were teaching me to survive?"

Alex smashed his palms against Dorian's shoulders and knocked him backward.

Dorian's legs spun beneath him. He took an awful stumble and barely managed to recover without falling. His eyes turned very hard.

"I beg your pardon!" he rasped. "Did you *touch* me?"

"Your survival is a sorry-looking critter right now!" the younger boy said. "I've never been ashamed of you before, but today I am. The day I'd sit by and let someone rape my mother—"

"Is the same day *I'd* let someone rape your mother," Dorian said. "Yula is not a Greek aristocrat. She's a chattel slave. Like me. Like the vast majority of souls on Plentiful. I don't need you to be my conscience, Alex."

"Right now I don't even want to be your brother."

Dorian straightened and wiped the whey off his hands. "Then we're deadlocked." He strode back to the wheying basket and leaned upon its narrow wooden rim. "You see, I thought about doing something, of course . . . but that Breeder could break a boy's bones and leave him dying while the rape simply got a short stall. Then where would Mama be? Her safety depends upon my existence, long beyond today, rape or no rape. The circumstances simply militate against my taking any action. Oh, I searched through antiquity for an example to follow . . . what would Oedipus do? Gouge his own eyes out, probably. Not a good option. What would Alexander do? The Great, not you. Summon his army? What would Voltaire do? Publicize the injustice and embalm it in poetry, most like. Too intellectual. Intelligence isn't a playing piece here. No matter which way I turned, I came up against a new block of impedimenta. There's just nothing I can do to balm the situation. So I'm washed up. Thanks anyway."

The separating basket scratched back and forth, back and forth, like a cradle rocking.

Alex's narrow body actually shook. He tried to regain control of himself, to live up to the image of a Southern gentleman that had been embedded in him since birth, but it was hard coming tonight. His straight brows, usually brush strokes of innocence, took a bitter tilt.

"You are *never* to come up to the house again," he ordered.

Dorian actually smiled. But it was a venomous smile. "You don't have the authority."

"I don't care!" Alex said fiercely. "I'm not even thirteen yet, and it looks like I'm the only man on this farm. If I see you up at the house," he threatened, "I'll put a bullet in your hypocritical head."

"Ridiculous."

"I grew up thinking you had a backbone."

Out of the cool twilight came an even cooler response. It was simple and efficient, like poison.

"Wrong," Dorian said.

★

Evidently the Breeder enjoyed a woman who liked to fight. Evidently he read Yula as a woman who liked fighting. She was the only woman he wanted to see all day Tuesday.

It was impossible to tell from the outside just how Root and the Breeder communicated with each other. Certainly it wasn't through talking. The only words the two exchanged were barks of reprimand and orders from Root, who spoke to the Breeder like a trainer speaks to a performing bear. He even held up a coiled whip from time to time as a warning.

There didn't seem to be any trick to it; even when there was no one apparently watching them, their behavior toward each other didn't change. There were no code signals or special treatment when they thought they were alone. Root was exactly what he appeared to be, and so was the monster he hauled from plantation to plantation.

But somehow the message got across—the Breeder liked Yula. He liked being bitten and feeling justified in biting back. He liked the hitting and the forcing, even if the woman was a third the size of himself. Sportsmanship wasn't a part of his mentality.

So Root shrugged, willing to conform, and left Yula in that wagon starting at half past noon.

The slaves came and went nervously all day. The wagon would be still for a while, then it would shake for a while, then be still again. Then, just when everybody started to feel better about everything, it would start shaking again. This went on all day. The sun began to slope. The wagon never opened.

Dorian saw it all. He did Yula's work as well as his own, came and went in the yard as duty dictated, passing the wagon several times. Yula's work, now that she was nearly thirty, was farmyard work, and by the time the sun touched the western hills, Dorian's white shirt, linsey suit, and shoes were caked with sweat and dust. The other slaves kept glaring at him as though he had anything to say about it. None of them had had much to say to him the past couple of days. Big brave darkies, singing their songs of lost nobility and the promised land. If they wanted something done, why didn't they damned well do it themselves?

There was Jeff over there, who had slunk back from the marsh, embarrassed that he hadn't had the nerve to slit his own wrists when Dorian didn't come back. Once a man promised to kill himself, he should at least make good. The big negro wisely averted his eyes when he saw Dorian.

Dorian hauled the last two buckets of whey to the kitchen and put them on the stone step outside, then dutifully covered them so the flies would lose interest. In the near distance he could hear the eerie rhythm of the wagon as it began creaking again.

With a calmness that was almost blasphemy, he found a rag and wiped his hands, then wiped the tops of the buckets. One of the cooks would come out here to collect this, and the winnowed curd he'd left behind in the separating barrels would be used to make cheese. It was a good couple of days' work. He'd done enough to provide cheese for all the slaves for a week or more. Farm work wasn't bad; it cleared the head.

He left the kitchen and strode back across the yard, turning away from the silhouetted wagon as it wobbled against the glow of the lowering sun.

As he came to the coop where he usually held his lessons for the other slaves, he paused, leaned his left shoulder against the doorjamb, picked milk curd from under his thumbnail, an awful feeling. The world was full of awful feelings.

Awful feelings forced upon innocent folk.

Flick. A tiny white lump of curd hit the coop wall. That felt better. The red wagon continued to rock. And the set of Dorian's mouth grew stiffer and flatter.

Dorian walked out of the yard. He followed the creek up to the boardwalk, the boardwalk up to the picket fence.

By the time he got around the end of the fence and broke out onto the lawn, he was running.

He burst into the servants' entrance and thumped through the corridor into the main part of the house.

Iphigenia saw him as she came down the stairway with Rose Dimitra. She gasped at his face. It was twisted with rage.

"Dorian—" she called after him, but he didn't stop.

When Alexander heard his mother's voice, he charged out

of the parlor barely in time to see Dorian reach for the library doors. He shouted, "Dory, no!"

But the library doors burst open before Dorian.

Lucas Wallace was standing at his bookshelf, holding some book open before him, his reading spectacles poised on the end of his nose. He looked up in utter shock as Dorian plunged into the room.

The boy came in like a prairie storm and squared off before his father. His voice had a cruel timber, and he actually shouted, driving each word home with the perfect enunciation it deserved:

"In that feudal portcullis you call a brain, does it occur to you that raping my mother yourself was at least more honest than hiring a breeding nigger to *do your fucking for you*?"

It echoed.

The ceiling rang. Lamp crystals chimed.

A pale chill moved in the room, but nothing else did. Wallace's eyes grew hard with astonishment.

Dorian felt something, a presence.

He turned to his right and stared into the faces of his father's campaign committee, their wives, and the entire town council.

★

CHAPTER SEVENTEEN

———————— ★ ————————

Lucas Wallace sat in the bowels of despair.

The bar stretched out like wings on either side of him, and he hung forward over, bleeding from the heart. Outside the familiar Norfolk tavern, carriages and horses clattered down the gaslit streets of a town that had grown to almost four times the size since he first started coming to this bar.

As they came and went, other men clapped him on the back, laughed, and made remarks about his manhood, chortling about how he'd had to ninny-jig one of those pretty little darky girls he owned. And they'd stride away, crowing. Amazing how fast news could travel.

He made no response to them, no matter how they shook him and laughed and jabbed at him and teased him. He just sat there, stewing, and realizing that only a stupid ass of a man would show his face in town after what that half-breed did to him. But old habits died hard. In spite of the red rings from a dozen whiskeys, his eyes were flinty. That boy should die hard.

Self-pity drowned any chance of rationality or responsibility. No matter his effort, no matter how sincere he had been in his life's work, he had failed to thaw the South's relentless glacier. An ice wall of conditions rose again before him, as if he'd never chipped away even the smallest bit of it. He knew what it was like to swim around in those cold waters. Dockworkers knew about all those things. Sharks in cold water and things like that. And that's what he was. A dockworker. And the shark had come, just as he knew it would, as he always warned them it would, swum up through the black ice water behind him, and bit him in the spine.

As he brooded, he lamented the death of all his accomplishments. The South and that boy had murdered his life's work.

Those damned Greeks. They were so stupid. Teach the boy, it won't hurt. Dress him nice, it won't do any harm. Let him in the house, who'll ever know? When he hated the boy, they thought he was petty. When he made them live up to the deal, they shook their heads in disapproval. When he wanted his own children treated better, they thought he was unreasonable. They didn't have the vaguest idea what it means to Southerners to have a planter raising a half-negro slave as his own son. Just imagine. Imagine thinking that way. Imagine thinking it might be all right.

Ingratitude, that's all it was. Plain foreign thanklessness. They didn't know right from wrong in spite of his example. This was the reward of his generosity. He should have sold the boy a decade and a half ago. He should have killed the baby at birth. Now he had this.

His blood began a slow boil. By nine o'clock he was ready to tear up the earth.

Nineteen and a half years it had hung there, untouched. Nineteen and a half years, unused.

Nobody else even remembered it was there, except Luke Wallace, who had consciously decided he didn't need it and hung it up there himself all those years ago. So when he stumbled into Alroy's forge and started banging around in there, nobody knew what he was doing. The slaves were gathered outside, near the fire pit, curious and fretful. When he found it and yanked it from the hook, a handful of cobwebs came along for the ride.

When he staggered again into the yard, the slaves gasped at what he was holding. On Plentiful?

Wallace moved toward the fire pit and raised the thing he held. A short black shaft—a branding iron.

Yula screamed, kicked, and spat, and Jeff begged Wallace to get some sleep before doing this thing, but there was no stopping the raw fury of a man whose life had been wrecked so cleanly in one short minute. Yula had to be tied to the barn door. The negro drivers whipped Jeff and the other slaves back, making the crowd part for Wallace as he weaved through.

The black-haired boy was tied to a tree. Sweat poured down his neck and created a moist crescent on his shirt. The shirt glowed with the firelight. In the ashes the black iron turned red, then orange.

Wallace pulled the iron from the fire. It made a rustling noise, as though it still hungered for the heat. At the end of the shaft, the shaped iron glowed.

Dorian's white shirt caught the orange glow and reflected it upon his face. His lean body trembled both with pure horror and with the same kind of astonishment he'd put Wallace through earlier. None of his book learning rose to protect him. None of his friends rushed in to stop Wallace. The only noise was the screams and threats spitting from Yula in the background, words so vulgar and violent that he had trouble believing it was her.

Firelight rippled on Luke Wallace's silver beard, making it appear that his face was burning. He approached the boy with slow steps, partly because he was drunk and partly for the savoring of this overdue moment. Where would he mark the devil? Where would he put the sign that would warn others of impending evil? On the face. Yes. On the cheek. On the forehead. In plain view.

Dorian gritted his teeth, paralyzed with terror, shaking so hard he could barely breathe. It couldn't be happening! There had to be some flicker of the physical bond that would rise up like a hero and save him. Something would change in the last second. But reality was jarring. His father was here. Right in front of him. An inch away.

The iron glowed between them, its red-hot end closing in, and Wallace used his other hand to grab the boy's jaw and force it to one side to bare the cheek. At the last second Dorian's survival instinct rose up as he realized no one or nothing else would save him. He twisted his hand within the

ropes that bound him, cranking hard against the scratchy
hemp. His wrist bled, but one hand came free. Instantly he
yanked his arm up to protect his face, but even that was its
own kind of misfortune.

The branding iron sizzled into the boy's forearm and
burned in, cauterizing skin and sinew.

"Mother Puck!" Wallace spat when it got through his
drunken head that he'd branded the arm instead of the cheek.
Was he destined to always come up short of his mark?

He staggered backward, furious, and threw the iron to the
dirt.

Before him Dorian sagged back against the tree. His eyes
glazed and rolled upward as agony overtook him. Air moved
down his open throat and up again, but there was no scream—
there was too much pain for screaming. The smell of scorched
flesh filled the air. As the boy sank down the tree trunk, held
there only by the ropes that tied him, a thin trail of smoke
twisted from the muscle of his left forearm, and blisters began
to rise.

Breaking from the crowd, Jeff snatched a bucket of water,
ran up to the tree, and began dowsing the boy's arm. Wave
after wave of creek water splashed over the blackening brand.
Around it the skin was bright pink.

Dorian slipped into blessed unconsciousness. He was scarred
for life.

Scarred, for life, with the red *S* of slavery, a permanent
reminder of who and what he was.

Dawn came a little late the next morning. Wallace was
oblivious to it as he lay facedown across his bed, shaded by
the canopy, happily snoring. His clothes and even his boots
were still on, and his dreams wandered aimlessly through
challenge and conquest, with him always leading the winning
army. He'd conquered the demon, reestablished his authority,
reinstilled the fear. He mounted the podium to take charge of
the crowd that sprawled out before him, cheering at him,
begging him to run for office and represent them as they knew
only he could. He nodded the royal nod and waved at them,

their savior, their representative, their voice in heaven and Congress. There were all kinds out there—planters in fine clothes, dockworkers in oilskins, immigrants in native costume, their ivory faces beaming at him in complete confidence, until they started to burn.

Horror crossed through his audience like a wave. Their faces began withering in the heat, turning red, then black. They were all black now, bold negro faces glaring up at him while their skin kept melting.

He watched, unable to stop it. Clothing and hair began to curl, flesh to flake away and sear off.

He promised to give them new reapers. When they continued to cook, he promised to vote for free trade. When they shrank and sizzled, he gasped out that they could go ahead and secede if they really wanted to. But there didn't seem to be any way to stop the hell before him.

A wave of wetness crashed across the back of his neck. For an instant it felt good, but then he sucked in a hard breath and smelled it. He jolted on the bed, gasped, and convulsed. The bed creaked in protest beneath him, the canopy wobbling overhead. There was no mistaking that putrid stink—

"Gahhh!" he choked, tangled in the sheets. He tried to roll over, but he couldn't get his bearings. "Ahhhgh! Gaghh!" He began spitting convulsively as the liquid trickled into his mouth.

He rolled over on the bed, nauseated and confused, and flopped onto his back.

Suddenly he froze, staring. There was a pistol barrel in his face. It pressed against his upper lip.

And there was his wife, bending over him. Iphigenia, the beautiful Greek princess, the gentle flower of antiquity, the mother of his real children.

Her face was set like stone.

Behind her stood Nick, Pilos, and all twelve of the Macedonian servants, also turned to stone. They were lined up like a firing squad. Every one of them held a rifle or a sword, and a full load of Greek venom.

Wallace choked, gurgling out the driblets of urine from the chamber pot they'd emptied on him.

Iphigenia's exotic face was not so exotic this morning. She

tightened her grip on his collar with one hand, and with the other she forced the pistol through his mustache and right up his nostril. She leaned *very* close.

She spoke just above a whisper.

"If you ever touch my boy again," she said, "I'll murder you while you sleep."

★

PART FOUR

THE
FREE-SOILERS
OF
BLOODY KANSAS

★ ★ ★

THE BURNING FUSE

SEPTEMBER 1850

President Fillmore signs the Fugitive Slave Act, which requires that runaway slaves be returned to their owners. In its way this Act extends the reach of slavery throughout the North and West. In December, Georgia decides to stay with the Union, but only if the Fugitive Slave Act is strictly obeyed.

SPRING OF 1854

The Kansas-Nebraska Act introduces two new territories but does not address the issue of slavery. The Emigrant Aid Society of Massachusetts shoves two thousand antislave settlers into Kansas Territory to keep it Free-Soil. In response thousands of proslave Missourians cross the border, stake claims, and vote in a proslave legislature. Free-Soil Kansans counteract this by adopting their own constitution. It outlaws slavery, but it also bans blacks from the territory altogether.

Frustrated by the powder keg in Kansas, antislavery people in other states form a new political party, the Republicans. They threaten to ignore the Fugitive Slave Act.

CHAPTER EIGHTEEN

———— ★ ————

1854, SEVEN YEARS BEFORE THE CIVIL WAR
FOUR MILES FROM THE PROSLAVE TOWN OF WESTPORT
LANDING, MISSOURI, ON THE KAW (KANSAS) RIVER

"You got the brains of a plank! You're burnin' the bird."

"*It*' ain't burnin', and don't change the subject. He's done give her the spoon!"

"Don't make no difference to me."

"It does make a difference! She done took the spoon, and that's the same as married! She gotta marry somebody. A body cain't make it alone out here in this hellforsooken wilderness. Two go better than one."

"Ain't married till a preacher says they married."

"You gonna find out they married when *they* say they married! Dumb man, ain't you remember bein' young?"

"You damn right, she's young! She ain't old enough for makin' up her own mind."

"She *is* old enough. Got a head, ain't she?"

"She *ain't* old enough. She got other stuff too. Ain't the head worries me."

"Sixteen *is* old enough, and she ain't oughta be picky."

"Sixteen *ain't* old enough, an' Anibal Webb ain't exactly bein' picky, woman! And pull the bird off that spit afore you burn it!"

"*Ach! Halt die Klappe!* I know how to cook."

They'd been arguing for over an hour. The subject tonight was their hellion of a daughter, and as they had garnered an audience downriver back in Missouri, so they had entertained the rural settlers downriver here in Kansas Territory, those who worked in the tannery and settled near it.

Moselle Ruhl bared her teeth and snarled at her husband, at which point Helmut Ruhl saw exactly where their daughter had gotten her own charming personality. She looked like a skeleton in the cabin's only light, the poor gold flicker from the perpetually struggling cookfire in the hearth. The shadows in the room were deep and pervasive, shadows endlessly clinging to the lives of poor white trash who had neither claim to success nor any talent for gleaning it, nor had they any right to a master who would feed them once a day and clothe them once a year.

Moselle put her shoulders back and her nose in the air— looking like a scarecrow in a strong head wind—and strutted toward the hearth, where a basket spit held a spindly bird that was nearly roasted black, feathers and all. She poked at the bird, trying to get through the black part to see if the inside was cooked yet, but she wasn't concentrating.

Helmut threw his hands up in the air and shook a fat finger.

"Dat boy got himself mixed up with them men from Lawrence. They usin' him sure's a slug uses mud. Ain't it enough I gotta eat burnt bird every Sunday, but you say I gotta let a Yankee into the family?"

"What's so bad 'bout that?" she crowed. "How else we gonna keep the niggers out? The Craigs got them slaves in, working right next to our boy in that factory for no pay, makin' our boy look like he ain't worth hardly nothing. Anibal and his boss wanna keep them niggers out. I don't see nothin' wrong with—"

"If it ain't niggers, gonna be the dirty whiskey-pissin' Irish!" Helmut warned.

Moselle looked up from the fire and took a breath to spray a rebuttal back at him, but the stubbornness suddenly dropped from her face.

Helmut stopped short in his own tirade, caught by his wife's expression. She was staring past him through the dim cabin, blinking in the firelight, her eyes big as plates and her mouth gaping.

Helmut spun all the way around and damn near choked.

He was gaping into the faces of two uninvited dinner guests, fierce-looking men who stood just inside their doorway. One had a beard so big it took over his personality, the other a face so young and handsome that Moselle came that close to having her daughter marry this one instead.

Helmut got his breath and demanded. "What you want in my house!"

He knew what they wanted. It wasn't that kind of question. They were tannery men. The smell made it obvious. The overpowering scent of tanning acids clung to their clothes, and their hands were rough from handling leathers and stained from handling dyes.

They were here on business. Business involving the wooden clubs and carving knives poised in their greasy hands.

Helmut maneuvered his bulk between them and his skinny wife, but no matter how wide he was, he couldn't protect them both. Maybe he could scare them.

"You men! Git out! Out of my house! I'm the master here, and I say git!"

He thought proslavers might understand the idea of a master in a household, but these were white men and heeded no master's voice except the one down in that tannery. The Craig Tannery was nothing if not a front for the proslave violence that stemmed from its acid-soaked innards.

He turned to his wife and blurted, "See what you done?"

A wooden club struck him across the side of the head.

His wife screamed, but Helmut was busy spinning to the packed floor, taking a chair and a hill of stacked boxes with him. The man who had hit him, the handsome one, piled down on top and got him by the throat.

"Where's Anibal Webb and his nigger-lovers? Tell, or I'll cut your throat."

"He don't stay here!" Helmut squawked, choking.

"Told you," the bearded marauder snapped at his accomplice. "You said he'd been here. Old man Craig's gonna piss in our faces if we don't find him."

The younger one's eyes flared into a rage and he roared, "Shuddup, buttfucker! I know what I'm doing!" He lowered himself toward Helmut's reddening face and growled, "We'll leave him a message, that's all. It'll be almost as good."

"What, kill these two?"

"Yeah."

"Awright." He put his knife into his other hand and pulled a long-muzzled pistol from his belt.

Moselle sucked in a gasp and stumbled backward against the hearth wall, just like a woman, but then she grabbed the hinged end of the basket spit, hoisted it off the hook, and threw the hot iron contraption into the bearded man's face.

He felt the heat even before the iron struck him. He instantly brought his arms up, but too late. The hot basket with the bird in it landed on his beard, and burst into a sizzle before clattering to the tabletop. The man screamed and staggered backward. The gun fell to the dirt as he hammered his burning beard with open palms and slammed around trying to get away from the smoke, pushing the roof up with his trumpeting.

"Get it off! Get it off!"

"Hey! Hey!" the younger man shouted past the yells. He shifted to look at his crony, and that gave Helmut a bit of leverage to twist his own bulk all the way over. He put his hands against the dirt and pushed, arching his back as much as his big stomach would allow. The handsome man fell right off with a surprised grunt, his forehead hitting the table leg.

Helmut hauled onto his knees and crawled under the butcher-block table, adding to the shouting with, "*Noch heute* you'll see what I mean!"

Moselle crawled past him in the other direction, going for the discarded basket spit, hoping to use it again, and snarled, "You talk so much your mouth is frayed!"

"*Meinen Sie?*" Helmut said, rolling his eyes sarcastically as they passed each other. "*Das ist ja unerhört.* I'm gunna lettum kill ya!"

She dropped to her stomach on the dirt and shimmied toward the gun instead of the basket spit. "Think so? *Kummern Sie sich nicht um ungelegte Eier,* pig dick—"

She took a final dive for the gun.

A boot came down on her hand just before she would have grasped the gun's muzzle, and she bellowed in pain and protest as two bones in her hand snapped. The sensation of bones breaking, rather than increasing her fear, had the opposite effect of making her furious. She ground her teeth, took one great reach, and pulled the kettle of hot stew down upon the offending leg.

The bearded man, his head still wreathed in smoke, felt the other half of himself burning and let out an awful "Whoop! Ooop! Oooop!" The boiling stew soaked into his trouser leg and scalded his skin. He fell backward into the twig chair that happened to be there and yanked his trouser leg up. His expression turned to horror as the scalded skin of his leg peeled off with the trouser fabric, leaving raw, red flesh.

Pain and shock took hold of him when he saw the condition of his leg, and he squeezed out an earsplitting roar.

"OooooooaaaaaaAAAAAAH!"

Moselle scooted past him, still on the floor, crawling with one hand and one elbow, grunting with every hitch of her movements. Where was Helmut? He was too big to lose in such a small cabin.

"Where are you?" she screeched in German, so the thugs wouldn't know what she was saying. "Lummux! Where are you! Get up! Fight like a man! Where did you hide?"

"Ain't hiding, old bitch!" he responded, also in German. "I'm looking for the gun!"

"It's over there!"

Helmut barked in English, "Whar? Y'ain't no help, as usual."

The young ruffian was stumbling to his feet in the dimness, confused by the firelight. "Where'd they go? Hank! Where'd they go!"

He scrambled around the butcher-block table, his long knife flashing. Behind him breeze came through the glassless window and made the rag curtain dance.

The curtain suddenly ripped from its pegs, and the young man coughed and turned stiff. His mouth stretched impossibly huge, his eyes bugged out, and his tongue stretched forward on gasp after gasp. His eyes cranked open ever farther, as though looking into the face of a horror. He felt the air moving away from his mouth, felt his lung seize up, felt his heart heave in his chest. He tried to take a breath, vaguely aware of three sets of astonished eyes glaring at him from various places in the room—but he could not catch his breath. Wet warmth gurgled up into his mouth, buzzing right up his esophagus where there should have been air, and came pouring out over his tongue, over his lips, down onto his chest—wet, hot, salty, bloody. His chest forced outward, his shoulders back. He plunged forward, his arms waving, and he hit the floor like a side of beef. His eyes rolled up into his head with such force that he clawed at them as he lay there flinching against the dirt.

The others in the room backed away, horrified. A pitchfork wobbled from the young man's back. His spine cracked a little each time the pole waved. His heart pounded, but it didn't stop before he lay there with his lungs full of blood and drowned in it.

Moselle and Helmut Ruhl dragged their own battered bodies into a corner, stunned.

The other ruffian, his beard half-burned away and still smoldering, limped around the gruesome body of his cohort, trying to figure out some way to get through that doorway. Behind the doorway the night wind whined. There was nothing but the blackened woods there. It was as though ghosts had thrown the pitchfork.

Smothered by fear, he dropped his knife, bellowed in terror, and made a wild run for the doorway.

As he plunged over the other man's body and went through the door, he knew he was dead. Any man who feels a rope go around his throat knows he's dead.

He screamed, but the scream was chopped to a gurgle as the rope clamped tight and he was hauled upward into the trees. Branches clawed at his clothing. He kicked frantically, twisting and wrenching, his fingers jammed into a noose that got tighter and tighter with every struggle. Saliva spurted between his teeth. Breath hissed out.

He took his time dying. But he died. He had no choice.

Helmut and Moselle Ruhl huddled together and shuffled warily toward the center of the cabin, peeking out the doorway. All they could see was the bearded man's dangling feet, hanging there in the branches, twitching and jerking.

Then there was another movement. A presence, one they

recognized as it entered the harsh shadows and firelight, looking back over its shoulder to survey its handiwork.

The two settlers hardly dared move. Both knew the danger of tampering with a killing mood.

A slim hand reached down and scooped up the iron basket spit with the bird, now cold, inside.

Sweet Grace Ruhl squinted at the bony, burned bird carcass. Then she frowned and commented, "You know, this land's so poor a turkey cain't gobble on it."

Wasn't two days before the sheriff himself from the town of Lawrence, Kansas, saw need to ride along the muddy Kaw to the white-trash house and take care of things. For this he had left Michigan? For this got a promotion? Didn't look like a promotion. Didn't feel like one. He was still dirty and scratching. Coulda been dirty in Michigan. Coulda scratched there too. If it wasn't the boils on his feet, it was these poor whites.

Bad enough these folk saw fit to live like hogs wallowing in his jurisdiction, but murder now? The report had come down the river as self-defense. He believed his deputies when they told him. They knew well enough what murder looked like and the looks of self-defense. For all that Helmut Ruhl and his scruffy family were destitute, they weren't killers. And those who traveled this way from Westport to stir up the slavery argument sure could be. Usually were.

His jurisdiction, the stretch from Fort Titus eastward to the Missouri border, included the vehemently Free-Soil town of Lawrence but unfortunately didn't stretch over the border to the equally vehement proslave area of Westport Landing and the town of Westport. The people from both areas thought it was good cause to roam back and forth, fanning their own brand of violence and trouble and ransacking.

Trouble. Coulda stayed in Michigan and had fill of trouble, but no, he had to come out here, get promoted to sheriff, see the badge on his chest in his dreams at night. Coulda stayed in Michigan and not been right in the middle of this competition for the transcontinental railroad. Everybody wanted the railroad to go *his* way, to bolt *his* idea of the territories together. Stephen Douglas was one of the *hims*—wanted the rail to run through the Great Plains. Jefferson Davis wanted a Southern route. Such fucking fuss over a couple of rails sitting on dirt going from here to there!

"And what do they hand to slobs like me?" he muttered aloud to himself and the trees. "Kansas-Nebraska Act. Now we got slave territory where none was supposed to be, and now I got abolitionists and proslavers and Free-Soilers and common settlers pulling each other's hair right under me, and they're catching my butt hairs at the same time.

"Sure! Come up here and watch your Act in action, Senator Douglas. Watch the emigrants flush in here from Missouri and put up four posts and a roof just long enough to vote. Hell, I don't even know where the latitude is, never mind why it's not there anymore. . . . Acts can do that. Rub a line right off a map."

Seemed there weren't enough troubles already in Kansas Territory with the Fugitive Slave Law. For four years he'd been obliged to send captured runaways back South, as if it hadn't been bad enough back in Michigan. Good old Michigan. Surrounded by water, and what lay on the other side of that water but Canada and safe haven, and that made the Thumb a perfect station for the Underground Railroad. And he'd imagined Kansas might be any better?

Wrong!

"Not even any prettier," he muttered.

Kansas didn't have much. It stretched from Missouri over two hundred miles to the Rockies. In the outlying areas it had some rolling prairies of buffalo grass, stunted oaks and other equally useless timber, and stone. Kansas had stone. That's what it had. Stone to build houses with. Rock.

And in the river areas, the Osage, the Kaw, the Wakarusa, the Arkansas, there was better timber—walnut, hickory, elm, sycamore, maple, and bigger oaks. Fair topsoil too, in those areas, pretty good black loam sitting on top of clay and limestone. That's what Kansas had. Stone, and pretty good dirt. But a body had to be in the right places to find the pretty good dirt.

He still missed Michigan, not only for the trees and the

lakes, but for the stable politics. Michigan was a strong antislave state, and the sheriff was antislave too, but he was also hired by the federal government to uphold the law of the state or territory. If only somebody would decide what the law here would be! Hell, even in Michigan they were crazy now. Michigan's antislavers were so mad about the Kansas-Nebraska Act slapping the North in the face that they were starting up a whole new political party. Finally the various groups and parties, the Know-Nothings, the Barnburners, the abolitionists, the Free-Soilers, the Whigs, and every other scattered clutch were starting to pull together, because they were finally all mad about *one* thing. They wanted one name to call themselves.

Republicans. The new party. The party of freedom.

He hoped it would work, maybe give the Free-Soilers some real political responsibility. Maybe then somebody would get some control over them. The Free-Soilers, those the sheriff had to contend with out here in the middle of no place, were the worst of all. Like the abolitionists, they wanted freedom for the negroes. But unlike the abolitionists, they wanted freedom for other reasons—they were against slavery, but not for the negroes' sake. What they really wanted was to make damned sure no slave owner could legally bring his bonded chattel onto the virgin soil of Kansas or Nebraska. The only way to do that was to outlaw slavery, then go one step further and outlaw negroes, freed or otherwise.

They'd almost gotten their way, until the Kansas-Nebraska bill slipped in. Now political and moral outrage overlapped like shingles on a roof—a very steep and dangerous roof. This diabolical bill was a conspiracy to bend freedom backward upon itself, to let slavery slip back in through the loop in the bend. The proslavers had found out that the best way to wreck the Missouri Compromise was to put the problem in the hands of—imagine!—the most irrational, emotional, and uneducated people around! Immigrants, settlers, foreigners, poor whites, and the native territorialists who hated all of the above.

Kansas was a legislative lie, advertised as a homesteaders' paradise. Once there the people were told that *they* would be able to decide the issues that were lacerating the North and irritating the South—slaves, schools, banks, tariffs between

states, tariffs between countries, factory conditions, foreigners, women's rights, border divisions, trade this, trade that,
how the Sabbath should be kept or if it should be kept at
all—God plug a butt! Confusion! Who could even say? Who
knew what the "nation" wanted anymore? All anybody could
do was watch the embers travel on a wind of indignation, then
duck for cover as sparks flew from the congressional floor to
the pulpit to the pressroom to the prairie.

Maybe the consolidated Republican party would keep the
Free-Soilers and all the other hotheads in line. Give them
some guidelines. Some cohesion.

"Guess that makes me a Republican," he grumbled, relieved to have just himself for company as long as it lasted.
"Sheriff Antislaver Peacekeeper Republican, Territory of Kansas, at your service, yawwwl."

It had been the Federal government that had attached him
to the Kansas land office, but distributing land to over two
thousand settlers shoved in by the Emigrant Aid Society, on
top of the proslavers flooding in for a balancing act—hell,
who could keep track? The unorganized territories were broken in two by this new act, and the government wanted it left
to the squatters to decide slave or no slave—they even called
it "squatter sovereignty." President Pierce was pro-South,
and that's why he'd let this law go through. Governor Geary
hadn't been able to make a rat's hair of a difference. The Act
was here.

"Let the squatters decide," the sheriff spat. "Might as well
let the fleas decide which way to turn the cattle."

Kansas was in virtual civil war, and he was supposed to
keep peace? Fine. Except for one thing. Nobody told him
what he was supposed to do with people like the Ruhls. The
nothing people.

Suddenly he stopped and sniffed.

He smelled the cabin even before he saw it.

"Aaaach—"

His boily foot ached like crazy, almost as if to tell him to
turn back while he had the chance.

Stopping to snort his nostrils clear a couple of times, the
sheriff forced himself to get used to the aroma of refuse and
garbage and pushed himself toward the cabin. The proslavers'

bodies had been removed. He'd had a good look at them in town. The image was ripe in his mind. Creative way to kill a person, with a pitchfork . . . he'd be sure to keep his back to a wall.

He started speaking even before his head cleared the doorway.

"Okay, folks, this is the way it is," he said. "Seems this situation's in my hands now, and I'm obliged to fix it."

"Hey, sheriff!" the woman squawked, grabbing a hot iron kettle off the hearth and pulling out a hinged basket spit with a half-cooked grouse carcass inside. "Join us in some corn-meal and bird?"

The sheriff stopped short and almost fell over at the very idea. The woman stood at the hearth, holding the kettle in her good hand—the other was in a splint—looking as appealing as any cockroach. He didn't need the company of fragrant Southern women in six-foot hoops, but to pause and eat with *this*? *Here*?

"Uh . . . no, thanks," he grumbled. "Your husband here, missus?"

"Here! Right here! Yes, sir!" A voice rasped. The German accent faint but still present, still a reminder of the trouble immigrants naturally brought with them from their home-lands. They all hated each other for being different, whether it was the Germans hating the Irish, the Irish not trusting the Dutch, the Dutch resenting the Chinese, the Chinese nervous about the Italians.

Helmut Ruhl floundered out of one dark corner, limping violently from an old injury that had kept him from working these past two years. His head was bandaged with a rag, and a lock of his sparse hair flopped forward over it. He smiled his broad, crooked, tooth-bare smile and waved wildly to make sure the sheriff didn't miss him again. He was even fatter now that he'd been sitting on his ass because of that injury, the sheriff noted.

"Your son at work, is he?"

"Yessir!" Moselle Ruhl blurted. "He done worked every day, just like you fixed it, nigh a half year now. We got bread dough and a new goose so we kin get eggs, thanks to you, sir, yes, sir—I got plenty cornmeal here. . . ."

"No," the sheriff cut off, "no, thanks." They were being nice to him to keep their daughter out of jail, and he knew it. "Your boy's a good boy," he went on. "I hear tell he works real hard in the tannery."

"He does!" the mother shouted. "He brings home all his pennies!"

Even through the strands of filthy hair, the woman's desperation shone in her eyes and gave the sheriff pause. How could he explain the situation to these people? The Ruhls barely conceived of a nation, much less a nation dividing. They didn't know or care who was fighting—Free-Soilers against proslavers, emigrants pouring in to vote either way. They didn't know the trouble he had on his hands. And they didn't care, either—he could see that much on their faces. Their interest went only as far as staying out of the trouble their wild daughter had brought down upon them. He'd seen that look before from poor whites in this territory. They hated being told what to do, and they hated anyone who came from someplace else.

How could he explain the change of legislature to them? How could he explain that proslavers like Hugh Craig had just kicked out the antislavery legislature and all hell was breaking loose? All they knew about Hugh Craig was that his name was on the tannery. Because their daughter liked the Webb boy, this family had gotten caught in the middle, trapped between the Free-Soilers, who wanted no niggers at all, the abolitionists, who wanted the niggers free to roam, and the proslavers, who wanted the niggers in chains. The sheriff balked for a moment, looking into their faces. They were nobody. Destitute settlers upon whom the political onus had fallen.

They were just poor whites, for whom there was no escape once they'd found a trickle of sustenance. These people were slaves in their way too, slaves to the tannery down below and to the paltry wage their fifteen-year-old son could scratch out as an errand boy.

He'd hoped the boy would get promoted to apprentice by now, start learning the trade. Maybe have a way out, at least for himself. But them Craigs . . . they didn't want to bring up the conditions long as they could steam blood out of the folk who worked down there. Shameful way to run a factory, he thought, just shameful.

"Where's your girl?"

"Oh, she here about!" the husband gasped. "Have a seat!"

Well, there was no getting out of that.

The sheriff settled gingerly onto the creaking twig chair and hitched himself close enough to the butcher-block table to lay his elbow on it. The Ruhls had gotten the table from the side of the road, where it had been dropped by people joining a wagon train bound for the Oregon Trail. He remembered that day now, as his elbows touched the heavy table. The wagon train had voted it too heavy to take along. Its top was a ten-inch-thick disk cut right off the bottom of a felled tree. Its legs had come off a discarded piano. It was ugly, but it held lunch. So the Ruhls had scavenged it. Except for a few German boxes and trunks with painted flowers on the lids that the Ruhls had dragged with them from Missouri, most of their spare possessions had been acquired in that manner, including the basket spit and the kettle.

"Okay, here's how it's gotta be," he began. "I'm getting myself transferred back to Michigan come summer, and I want to clear this up before I go. You Ruhls have been nothing but trouble, just like all the other squatters. Is your daughter gonna marry that Free-Soiler or not? I gotta know here and now."

"Oh, *ja!*" Moselle crowed.

"Over my dead body!" Helmut barked.

"Jesus . . . folks, I gotta have some idea of what the girl's gonna do. If you can't tell me, guess I'll have to decide."

"She got a courting spoon from him!" Moselle Ruhl said.

"Don't mean nothin'," Helmut contradicted. "Sweet Grace is only sixteen, sheriff, too young for marryin'."

"Then I guess I'll have to lay down a little law here and—"

"Whose law?" a voice interrupted from behind them.

All three turned, and there was the girl.

Somewhere under the layers of sweaty filth. And hair. Lots of hair, down the middle of her back. Lots of long, wavy, fiery red hair.

The sheriff nudged his rickety chair back an inch or two and got a long look at her. Her dress was a faded sack tied at the waist with a string, and attached to the string was the spoon in question, one of those things these country creatures clung to—a "courting spoon" carved by the boy for the girl. Evidently she had accepted it and therefore accepted the man who gave it to her. The sheriff's eyes clung to it for a moment, for certainly its presence changed things, made the rumors definite. The girl was engaged by country custom to a jobless, homeless, rootless, poverty-stricken, dangerously wreckless Free-Soiler.

Peering through the dirt and hair, he made out a pair of grass green eyes and the pencil-straight jawline of the girl's German ancestors. Damn if she wasn't nearly feral! If she hadn't spoke to him in something other than spits and howls, he'd have sworn she'd been raised by the bears and wolves. More than a little scary—and in every filthy fiber of her being, he could see determination twitching. She wasn't the slug her father was, nor the withered weed of her mother. She was another kind of life altogether. Hard to believe she came from the same stock as the good-natured, mild, hat-in-hand brother of hers.

Helmut cranked about on his stool and shook his hand at his daughter, suddenly desperate. "Gracie, you git outside! Git out and slap the dirt so the worms come up. I need catfish bait."

"Lassen Sie das!" Moselle shouted, pounding the table at him. She knew her daughter could fend for herself, and she wanted Grace to have the chance.

The sheriff raised his own hand. "This concerns her too. Come on in here, girl."

She did, but she slithered along the wall, in the shadows. Her dress, which had once had a pattern of tiny calico flowers, was now almost completely faded to a washed-out brown, and except for her hair, she looked like a newspaper clipping, flat and colorless.

"I can't let you folks just float around aimless, letting trouble stir around you," the sheriff said. "So I've decided to—"

"You're puttin' a ten-dollar hat on a five-cent head," the

girl warned. "They stirn up smuch trouble's we do. Them
M'souri border ruffians comin' in tellin' us what to do,
bringin' them niggers out here. And them Yankee cocksuckers
pushin' us outa our claims, aimin' them Sharps rifles up our
assholes, tellin' us we gotta let the niggers run free!"

The sheriff matched her tone. "Whoa, whoa, whoa! You
watch your mouth!"

"There only three kinds of people in this world to us native
Kansans: Yankees, niggers, and *whites*! You kin put me in
cock-sweatin' jail for thinkin' so."

"Girl, shut up!" The sheriff held up both hands in a
gesture, but also to push back the language coming out of the
girl's mouth. He'd never heard such words come out of a
woman's mouth and shuddered because of it. "I'm not gonna
put you in jail!"

Her glare flicked to her parents, then back to him. "You
ain't?"

"No."

At first she looked surprised, then her eyes narrowed to
slits, and her neck seemed to get longer.

"What I gotta do for you? Watch me not do it."

"Yes, you'll do it."

"I'll be holdin' my breath in the grave 'fore I do for you."

"I don't want you to do for me," the sheriff said, making
sure that his tone explained that he knew what she was afraid
of. "I'm arranging for you to go to work."

"You can't make her work in that tannery!" Moselle Ruhl
suddenly squawked. "She's just a girl! Bad enough my baby
boy gotta work in that dangerous place!"

The sheriff couldn't help but sympathize. The tannery
conditions were the worst kind of slavery, that of industrial
slaves, and the poor whites who came in at a meager salary
were all but enslaved there right alongside the niggers.

"I won't," the girl snarled. "I won't work for that cocksucker
Craig. He's a mean bitchfucker, and I hope he dies before me
so I can see it. They're gonna have to chain him down to get
him to die. Here I go to polish them chains—"

"Well, I hope he dies too," the sheriff said. Maybe he
could get cooperation by agreeing with her long enough to get
on her good side. Wherever that was. "He's sure a mean—

uh, fella. They say he's sick, but we can't count on him
dying. He's violently pro-South, and I think it's his proslave
doings keeping him alive, is all. He's just too mean to die.
Like a bear. You can put twenty bullets into him, and he'll
still tear your leg off before he goes. I don't know how things
are gonna go round here, but so far it's him and his cronies
who are back in power. It's him who wants you in jail for the
killing of those two. Since his factory's inside my jurisdiction, and *you're* inside my jurisdiction, it falls on me to make
a decision.''

He hung his gaze on the girl long enough for that idea to
sink in. Anybody in his—or her—right mind wouldn't try to
buck the Craigs. He turned to the parents now and explained,
''The Free-Soilers like your girl's intended are gonna find
themselves in deep straits. Hanging straits. You'll be right in
the middle when them and the proslavers start shooting at
each other. That what you want? Is it?''

Helmut mopped his balding head with his hand, leaving a
streak of dirt on his forehead. Moselle sat back on her stool,
without the faintest peek of a solution.

But the girl—the girl understood him completely. That
much showed in her fierce green eyes and the set of her jaw.
She might be a foulmouthed baby bear, but she wasn't
slow-witted like her parents. She was a smart bear. And, like
any sixteen-year-old, she was invincible.

''Well?'' he asked her.

Her lower lip curled under her teeth as she thought about it.
They could all practically hear her mind clicking and clacking
and shifting.

All at once she pursed her lips and nodded sharply. Then a
smile shot across her mouth, a big, wide smile that took over
her entire face. A canny smile.

''Reckon I work,'' she said with a lilt of determination.
''Dare me not to.''

The sheriff slumped a bit in relief.

''Well, good,'' the sheriff said. ''If I can show you're not
destitute, the judge'll dismiss the charges and call the killings
self-defense. I know him, and he figures people who work got
no time for stirring up trouble. I got your boy a job, and he's
been no problem since then. You folks promised you'd

behave if you had money coming in. Your boy's still working, so you got no reason to go against your word. If your girl's working too, you'll have a decent meal on your table. Maybe you can move in a year or two, into Lawrence, or at least farther away from Westport. Maybe then you'll have some legal protection.''

"I don't need no legal protection," the girl insisted. "See my skin? White as paint." She leaned forward and pinched up a fingerful of the skin on her forearm to show him. "I ain't no nigger slave. I'll take keer of myself, you wait and see. I'll find a way to make bricks outa the mud I was born in."

The sheriff glowered at her. Even when she was cooperating, she wasn't.

"You'll be working for a woman. I figure it'll take a woman—"

"I ain't pullin' corset strings and bucklin' shoes for some fancy fanny. I'll tote water and cook and sweep, that's the most. If'n you want more, you can go out and hang by your pebbles, Mr. Sir."

Getting to his feet before her, the sheriff stared firmly into those animal eyes and spoke directly to the brain behind them.

"You'll do whatever work the woman wants. Work or sit in jail, and your daddy'll go to jail for vagrancy."

The girl's eyes wedged again. She put her fists on her hips. "If you ain't crazy! Men can't get like that, and *I* know it."

With a groan the sheriff shook his head. "I said *vagrancy*."

"I heard you the first time. You wanna write it in the dirt?" Her mind was clicking madly, trying to figure out if he could really put her papa in jail. That V-word must have something to do with being the father of a murder girl.

"Never mind," the sheriff sighed. "You're gonna be working as a house servant, for pay. The old woman who's hiring you is a widow, and she's pretty much confined to her chair these days. Bad knees or something. Her husband went out in forty-nine, struck it rich and sent the gold back to her, but he died of syphilis before he got back. She's got lots of money, but she's been alone for nigh onto five years. Never had any kids, and that has a strange effect on a woman. So just do for her, like you're told, and I'll clear the murder charges put up by those proslavers at the tannery. Old man Craig wants you in jail and your boyfriend hanged, but that's not the kind of jurisdiction it's gonna be long as I'm here. You got no choice. Like it or not, tomorrow morning you report to the house of Mrs. Agnes MacHutcheon.''

Soapy water crashed violently over the sides of a wooden washtub and soaked the ground.

''I mayna be able t'see weel enough tae read, bu' I see weel enough tae look upon the likes of you! Now, *wash*.''

Sweet Grace Ruhl didn't seem very sweet as she sat breast-deep in bathwater, glaring bitterly at the stone-faced woman in the wheelchair.

''Scrrrub!'' the woman demanded, pointing at the sponge that floated like a barge across Grace's breasts. ''Scrub or sit in prison.''

So the stone woman knew the sheriff's deal.

Grace scooped up the sponge and drew it across her face. ''I'm a-scrubbin'.''

Imposing even confined in the chair, Mrs. MacHutcheon sat there with the wheels on either side of her and leaned forward with both hands on the ivory snout of a boar's-head walking stick that she insisted had belonged to her grandfather, the lord or lard or lurd of MacSomeplace. The straight wicker back of the chair framed fiery orange hair and a face with strong features. Her strong nose hooked over her strong mouth, and she watched with eyes that had been compelling— once upon a time. A long time.

Then who could tell how long? How old? Pioneer women got old in the face quick, Grace decided.

''You're jus' jealous,'' Grace crooned back at her, twisting her teenaged body in the water. ''Buffalo grass wants t'be daisies.''

The older woman was unimpressed and unintimidated. ''The daisy had better scrape off the cow pie before she talks!''

Grace cocked her head and mentioned, ''You got a good set of lungs for a dead woman, y'know?''

"Wash! I'll no' have a filthy rag such as you serving up my meals. We'll burn that dress as well. The underworld's been begging for it!"

She leaned over the arm of her special chair and picked up the ratty calico dress with a finger and a thumb, wrinkled her nose at it, then cast it as far away as possible.

"Here are your duties. Y'shall tend me in all my personal requirements, cook hearty Scottish meals according to my recipes, run errands as I specify, clean the house, feed the dog and let him oot twice per day, and you shall stay here four nights out of seven."

Grace made her neck longer and barked, "I ain't sleepin' here."

"You shall sleep heer *four* nights out of seven! Or spend them in *jail*!"

The water smashed over the lip of the tub again as Grace raged, "I'm gonna stuff that word up your pantyass!"

"And y'shallna use that language in my household! And you shall never, never say 'ain't.' "

"Ain't what?"

"What?"

"What ain't I?"

"Never say that word. Say 'not.' "

"Ain't not?"

"Uch . . . yu'd think you were Catholic! Wet that hair now. Scrub it! I'll want nae bugs on you when you climb oot."

"Aw, shut yer fangs!" Grace complained. "I know howda take a bath, farty old warthog."

"One wud never ken it," the old woman snapped. "You shall do my shopping as required, prepared a meal for me before you leave on the nights you dinnae stay over, and you shall read to me."

The girl's hands crashed into the soapy water. "Read to you? Read? Like read you stories? Like a baby? Hell and fuck, I don't read to nobody. Does the squirrly have the birds pick his nuts?"

Mrs. MacHutcheon's huge eyes flared. When she spoke, it was with such thunder, such conflagration, that Grace jolted like a bit fit.

"Guard your mouth, muckle beast that you are! This is *my*

household! If there's any speaking in vain to be done, I stand
determined that I shall do it and not you!''

Her walking stick came down so hard on the edge of the
tub that wood actually splintered in Grace's face.

"Not . . ." *Smash* "You!" *Smash*.

Grace's eyes got big. She hunkered down in the tub until
she almost swallowed suds and clamped her mouth shut. But
her glare was a mile deep.

Mrs. MacHutcheon roared, "I'll have nae higorant bump-
kin in my employ! Wash your hide, soak your hair, then
climb oot o'there and push me intae the hoose for yar first
lesson at the larder! You'll start being a fit servant for me this
very morning! B'God, you'll learn which side the fork goes
on! B'God himsel', you're gang tae cook a proper goat haggis
this verry morning!'' The old woman leaned forward then,
squeezed her eyes into flat lances, put her bottom teeth
forward, and growled, "And ye're gang tae *eat* it!''

★

CHAPTER NINETEEN

——————— ★ ———————

"What's these?"

"What *are* these."

"What aaaaaare these?"

"What do they look like?"

"Well . . . reckon . . . buttons."

"That is correct."

Mrs. MacHutcheon wheeled herself with some effort over the loud colors of the carpet, toward the glass-covered table where the rude servant girl was leaning and staring and squinting. The elder woman's hard face barely changed at all as she looked down for the millionth time at the collection of tiny treasures.

The entire room was her treasure box. She and her husband had come west with their covered wagon fifteen years ago, when there was nothing here but dust, when this was the frontier. Now she was in her sixties, California was the new frontier, and Kansas was the launching point. And she was a well-off woman, the most well-off woman from here back to Independence. She was the only person within a hundred miles to have a real carpet, and she refused to get rid of it no matter now hard it was to wheel the chair over it. An accident with a runaway wagon had cost her use of her legs, but she determined not to let it cost her the luxury she could finally afford in life. The carpet was right out of a mill in New York and was probably the only spot of bright color in all of Kansas. Everything else in Kansas was brown. But not the carpet. Its wide stripes of bright apple green and federal blue were overlaid with a pattern of gaudy red cabbage leaves. Where the red met the blue, there were patches of glowing pansy violet. But the green stood out most of all, especially when the sun shone upon it. She liked it so much that she had imported heavy curtains in the same shade, with red tassels streaming from their tiebacks.

The only problem was that the wallpaper design was slightly off from the cabbage scrolls in the carpet pattern. She'd scoured catalog after catalog, sample after sample, but finally had been forced to settle on shell pink paper with large yellow green flowers in brown baskets. There simply wasn't enough choice in wallpaper, to her way of thinking. But it was close enough, and the supplier had been able to provide ample quantities to cover all the walls of the parlor, the luncheon nook, and the entire ceilings of both. The room practically got up and walked around.

From the tall case clock to the kettle stand, it was a good parlor, a fine parlor, fine as any parlor back East. Even the colors were Eastern.

She only regretted that she was rarely free to sit as she pleased on her favorite sackbacked Windsor settee. Now all she could do was gaze longingly at the bold tapestry cushions and the indentations that perfectly fit her bottom. Privately she was ashamed that a pioneer woman of such standing should lose the use of her legs. She disliked the idea of asking for help just to get onto her couch.

Adjusting the wheelchair across the glassed table from the new servant girl, she watched with smug pleasure as the girl scowled at the rows upon rows of buttons displayed inside.

She was distracted for a moment when the servant hiked the ivory satin dressing gown higher onto her shoulders and drew it close over her naked body. The girl obviously had never worn such a garment in her life. She hardly knew how to keep it up around her.

"Why you got buttons in your table?" the girl asked. Her dark red hair hung in long wet strings over her ears, making her look particularly stupid. Yet she wasn't stupid. Mrs. MacHutcheon watched her keenly, watched the way the girl studied the buttons.

"It is a collection," the old woman informed.

"What's that?"

"What it says it is."

Grace's head popped up. "Well? What's it *say*, then?"

Mrs. MacHutcheon groaned. They barely spoke the same version of English.

"Girl, are you so higorant? To collect. To gather, cherish, consider special."

"Buttons?"

The older woman's orange head bobbed once. "My father was a skilled silversmith in Scotland during the last century. Skilled craftsmen looked for ways to supplement their income."

"What's 'supperment'?"

"Just listen!" the gravelly voice snapped. "Pick it up in context."

Grace frowned, wondering what kind of a bag a context was. She tried to rearrange the slippery dressing gown on her shoulders again, but she never even seen and certainly never touched satin before and felt like a worm working around inside its own skin. She sat back on her haunches, trying to get her eyes used to the room's blinding palette.

Mrs. MacHutcheon leaned sideways in her chair and spoke as though she'd been waiting a thousand years to give her dissertation. Probably she had.

"Button making," the woman said, "was a quick and good sideline. Potters made ceramic buttons. Furniture makers made wooden buttons, carved and polished. Weavers made woven buttons. Artists took ease from their own poverty by painting intricate scenes in minute detail—look! Dinna look at *me*! Look down at the buttons as I talk! Hae'else can you learn a thing? Look at the stitched silk ones! And the engraved hunt scenes for dandies to show off, and the portraits of favored courtesans for fops to wear upon their waistcoats—great wraiths, but there's none left o'that in the world! See this ivory set? Made by a piano maker out of the ivory he used for keys. In Boston, where I once lived in grand style."

Grace scanned the buttons as she was told, trying to imagine what this crazy woman was discussing, but none of it made much sense. These weren't buttons, these rows and rows of tightly displayed bits of sparkle and tiny paintings. Not the kind that go on real clothes, anyway. She'd seen those kinds of buttons before, and they were nothing like these. These were something else. There actually were bitty paintings of people and scenes, horses riding across streams, dogs chasing foxes, ladies with big white hair and feathered hats— all no bigger than nuts!

Mrs. MacHutcheon leaned back and to the side, hooked her chin in her forefinger, and gazed at the past. "The buttonhole was discovered in the 1200s, and later they became symbols of grand sophistication the likes of which is gone from the globe."

"Buttonholes?"

"Buttons! Look doon there, girl! It's history you're staring at! The history of society. Buttons of fine tapestry, gold, pawter, buttons under glass—"

"Say that again?"

The old woman cranked her wheelchair up to the table, then maneuvered it with several little jerks until it was side-up to the table. She reached over the arm, grasped the glass top, and heaved it open on two brass hinges. Out of the sea of buttons she plucked a few of the more intricate ones and held them before Grace, one by one.

"Paintings and etchings beneath dots of glass, set in metal shanks. Like this. And this. Aristocrats came to lust over them. The gaudier they were, the more coveted they were. Many of these are of French origin. France was the button-making capital of the world in the time of Francis and the Louis kings. Louis the Fourteenth spent over five million dollars on buttons. Buttons were once put on men's sleeves to discourage their wiping their mouths on them. The Charleses of England got fond of buttons quickly enough. The Charleses never could think for themselves, more's the pity for Scotland. . . ."

Her voice trailed off as she started looking into the past again.

"Ah," she murmured, "the world's no' half it was a generation ago. . . . How they vied for the supreme button. . . cut steel buttons that shined like wee medallions . . . buttons carved from seashells, brought by sailors from far exotic places . . . slices of staghorn, knobs of Birmingham gilt, scenes painted on china...such flamboyance. ,.. Look at buttons of the past, and you see the world! Nothing less!''

Grace sat back on her heels and glared up at Mrs. MacHutcheon's craggy features, and at the old woman's blue eyes, ringed with the yellowness of age and overuse. Every wrinkle, every crease, every stretch of skin had been won at the price of an experience or other. The New World had been hacked out of the wilderness by such as this pioneer woman, this immigrant venturing to an entirely new continent. With her she had brought the history of the world in buttons, and she herself would go to the grave preserving this unusual knowledge. Perhaps she had expected an apprentice or heiress out of her new servant girl, and in her eyes now was a faint glow of hopelessness, a pale acceptance of the fact that her buttons would probably be buried with her, and dirt would be spilled upon all that knowledge, all that scope.

Grace Ruhl gazed thoughtfully upward from her place on the floor near the glass-lidded table, studying Mrs. Mac-Hutcheon's time-worn face and the hair whose color was fake, washed in, like the whores did with their hair, and finally the girl's lips parted upon her own brand of wisdom.

"Crickets," Grace murmured. "I hope I don't never git ugly as you."

The old woman snapped out of her reverie and spun a glare downward. Determination renewed itself like a lance going through a tree.

"Y'should live sae lang or gain half the means. Just keep tae your lesson." A finger aimed toward the buttons. "In this chest is all of history, and you're gun tae learn it, one button at a time, if it kills me."

"I could kill you first and learn later," Grace offered. "Speed things up."

"Never you mind. Why, you've no' the brains tae know a precious stone from paste! Look!"

"I'm looking, crackly-faced old crone!"

"What do you see?"

"I see buck-naked babies with wings and no little cocks. These all girls?"

"They're cherubs!"

"Yeah, all girls?"

"They're painted upon ivory."

"Sweet feet, them are sure tiny." Grace leaned closer and squinted harder. "Maybe them dicks are just too tiny to see. . . ."

" 'Those.' "

"Which?"

"*Those* are tiny."

"Yeah, that's what I said."

"I said 'those'!"

"I heerd you, Mrs. Buttonbutt!"

"Hae dare you!"

"Okay. Dare me."

The boar's-head walking stick bumped the floor, and Mrs. MacHutcheon got that look of controlled rage that Grace already recognized.

"That's it," the old woman promised herself. "I'll hae no backwoods wild hare in my employ. As of this night you begin becoming another kind of beast entirely. Get that brown book. There on that shelf. Hie it over here."

Almost as enthralled with the idea of reading as she was with the buttons, Grace trudged to the shelf, dragged the book off, and tossed it into Mrs. MacHutcheon's lap.

The two women stood glowering at each other over the half-century chasm that lay between.

Mrs. MacHutcheon held the book out at the end of her arm.

"Take it. And wheel me out onto the porch."

The porch was a charming, freshly painted arrangement of wooden posts and rails which faced one of the streets in the settlement. The clapboard house was, in fact, one of very few true houses in the shantytown near the H. Craig and Son Tannery. Most of the other dwellings were shacks of one or two rooms. But this was a real house, with a real upstairs and a real porch, and an outhouse all to itself. It was a sunflower yellow house with grape trim and real shutters, and it gave the shantytown a kind of permanency. Other than the factory itself, the saloon, and the general store, this house *was* the "town."

Sunshine buttered the entire porch with morning light. It

was surprisingly pleasant here, with a cool breeze coming under the awning. Grace paused for a deep breath before Mrs. MacButton grouched, "Sit your rump doon. And read."

Grace raised her chin. "What if I won't?"

"Iron bars."

"Better company than you, betcha."

"We can certainly see."

"Hmm. Guess I'll read."

She sat. She opened. She looked at the printed page.

Line after line of tiny letters, all bunched together, spilled out of the book like unintelligible bugtracks. She'd read signs and grocery labels, posters and soapboxes. She thought she could read.

But she had never before in her life pushed open the cover of a book.

She read the first word, but it just hung by itself, out in the middle of nothing, attached to no other words. A lot of words started after it, but she knew a beginning when she saw it, reading left to right.

"...'on the hillsides,'" she read. Then she looked up.

Mrs. MacHutcheon was glaring at her, forehead all twisted, one brow up and one down, and her mouth pursed like two squashed bananas.

"Whatsa matter?" Grace demanded.

The other woman shifted in aggravation.

"Would you not do better opening the *front* of the book?"

"Huh? Oh!" With her typical resilience Grace scolded herself with a shake of her finger, flipped the book over, and opened the correct end.

"Now turn to the journal entry dated February third."

Grace flipped judiciously through the pages, looking for an *F* and a *3*. She didn't remember any other month in the year starting with an *F*, so she figured she was safe.

"Rightcheer," she lilted.

Mrs. MacHutcheon leaned back in her chair and contemplated the ceiling. "Begin reading."

Grace put her nose to the book.

"'A mild...morning...the windows open at... breek— breekf—'"

"Breakfast."

"' 'Breakfast . . . the r— the redbreez—' "

"Redbreasts."

" 'Red*breasts* singing in . . . the . . . garden . . . walked with . . . call . . . coal' . . . ' "

"Coleridge."

" 'Coleridge . . . over . . . the . . . hills . . . the sea at feer—' ' "

"First."

" 'First . . . oab, ob, ub—' ' "

"Obscured."

A painful session. Mrs. MacHutcheon seemed undaunted by Grace's miserable slogging through the words. Grace sighed and continued. It was all she could do. This woman had her. She might have to work for the old wart for weeks till this blew over.

Maybe months.

" 'Yankee Doodle went to town, bought a bag of peaches . . . rode so fast a-comin' back he smashed them all to peeeeces. . . . Yankee Doodle keep it up, Yankee Doodle dandy, mind the music and the step . . . ,' and dang but I'm dead tired. Hi, Liz."

Grace glanced up from the table where she was packing her few personal things to move down to Mrs. MacHutcheon's, then gave a second strong look at her brother slogged into the cabin and dropped like a rag onto his own cot in the farthest corner. He barely made it that far.

Grace sucked a gasp and blurted, "Sucks, Pat, you're a corpse!"

Patrick Ruhl couldn't even find the energy to nod. The light hazel eyes were already shut. Dishwater brown bangs flopped over his soft, straight brows and almost down to his nose, so dirty that they left streaks on his face. Hardly a hint of his shining teenaged complexion could find its way through the coat of grime and dust. He'd managed to get only one foot up onto the bed. The other was heel-to-the-floor, making an indentation in the packed dirt. His thin arms, struggling through puberty, were already knobby with budding muscles that even now twitched with exhaustion.

"Yep, Liz," he murmured drowsily, "got in a shipment of saltpeter, lime, and alkali today.... Spent the whole day unloadin'."

Standing over him with her fists on her hips, Grace assumed her role of older sister, scowling down upon the primary breadwinner of the household, and they were startlingly like two children playing house.

"Pat Ruhl, if you ain't a wag-witted lead-head to come home on your only day off in a week so dead dog tired you cain't even set up for a square meal. Gimme your boots. Fugbuckets! You smell like sulfur! I hate that factory. How come you dint wash up in the river 'fore haulin' that stink back here where it ain't welcome? Sakes."

"Mmm-hmmm... 'Gwine lay my head on de railroad track... gwine lay my head on de railroad track... gwine lay dat head right on dat track... an' de Lawd gonna take me back...'"

"Patrick! What d'you sing them nigger songs for?"

"I like t'sing, no matter how tired I git."

"Well, cut it out. If you ain't singin' 'bout Yankees and their doodles, you're singin' like a nigger. Ain't you got any white songs to sing?"

Without moving at all, without opening his eyes, Patrick murmured, "Anything happen this week?"

"Two snakes came in. I killed 'em."

Patrick's expression softened, and he smiled in his half sleep. His voice was soft and had a friendly, vulnerable crack that surfaced from time to time, usually when he was grinning. "You know what they say. The cow that gives is the one that lives."

"Who you callin' a cow?"

"Snakes woulda scared me pea green," he mumbled. "Lizard, it's a good thing you was born first."

"Bad thing I wasn't born a man. I'da burnt that tannery down by now."

"Uh-huh... Where's the folks?"

"Maw's peddlin' the goose eggs. Paw's gone fishin' for catfish."

Patrick nodded through his fatigue. "Wind's in the south,

bait's in the mouth. Hope he remembered to turn his pockets out and not let his shadow fall on the water.''

"I reminded him. We had two birds, but one got wrecked and the other got et. He says fer you to go out barkin' squirrels first thing in the morning.''

" 'Kay . . . know what?''

"What?''

"Saw a white dove flyin' overhead yesterday.'' He waved his hand. "That's a good sign.''

"It was prob'ly a pigeon.''

"Naw, Liz, sure was a dove.''

Grace huffed her disbelief as she wiped her hands on the new apron Mrs. MacHutcheon had insisted she wear and stepped to the hearth to dish out some cornmeal for her brother. "You ain't never seen a dove in your life, Patrick. And you ain't seen one yet. So don't get your hopes poked up, hear me? Don't want to see my baby brother all sad.''

"Some'm good's bound our way, Liz. All the signs point to it. I kin feel it.''

"Yeah,'' she grumbled, "I kin feel it too, just like smellin' a dead critter 'fore you git to it. It looks fine, but you daren't eat of it.''

Patrick grinned generously. "You always was smarter'n me. Guess I'll wait and see.''

"Got me a job.''

The statement took several seconds to soak through Patrick's exhaustion. Then his eyes cranked open.

"Huh?''

An involuntary groan pushed out of his compact body as he forced himself to roll up onto one elbow and look at her. He pushed the dirty bangs aside.

"Got a what?''

"Job.''

"You mean a real job?''

"Job, for money.''

"Hang a dog, Liz! That's great!'' Suddenly he sat up, with considerable effort, and added, "Not in the tannery—''

"Nope, I wouldn't lift a leg to step over Old Man Craig if'n he was dead in fronta me. I'm workin for ol' Mrs. MacButtonboobs in her fancy frame house by the riverside.''

Patrick pulled on his ear. "Don't recollect anybody of that name hereabouts. . . ."

"MacHutcheon."

"Oh! The lady with the—" he put a hand to his head and mimicked the old woman's puff of orange hair—"and the" —he made a motion at his sides to pretend wheels.

"And the mouth long as my leg," Grace added. "That's her."

"Her house always puts me in minda the sulfur at the tannery. Goshdang," he said, "that means you gotta walk past the graveyard."

"So?"

"You jus' be sure to hold your breath while you pass. You know what they say. And sing a song. Ghosts love to hear people singing, you know."

"How'm I gonna sing and hold my breath at the same time?"

With a dubious look Patrick acknowledged, "I never thought of that. . . . Dang, you're smart sometimes."

"Scootch up to the table, now, an' eat 'fore you fall back down agin. I oughta set fire to that place and be done with it. Then you wouldn't be stuck de-hairin' hides and turnin' out harness leather and tendin' lime tanks."

"Wouldn't get no pay out of a burnt-down factory, Liz."

Patrick was too tired to eat but too polite to refuse his sister's efforts as she arranged a warmed-over supper on the butcher-block table for him. His arms and legs felt like string, but he forced himself to the table. His back screamed as he slid onto the stool, and he had to lean heavily on the table to keep from falling over. He couldn't feel too sorry for himself, not as sorry as what he saw reflected behind Grace's irritated gaze. Everybody else in any factory in the North, or the South for that matter, went home just as plug-tuckered as he was right now. Everybody worked a twelve-hour day, everybody breathed the fumes.

"It's not so bad," he slurred. "I get my twenty-three cents a day, fair and square, plus bed in the company town during the week and a meal."

"Twenty-three cents," Grace repeated, her heart squeezing

up in her chest. She was getting twice that much just to tend the old woman. "Just enough to keep you from leavin'."

"Where'd I go? Couldn't leave you and the folks, could I?"

Grace pushed his plate toward him, so he wouldn't have to expend any extra muscle power, and stuck a spoon in his fist. "Better not. If it wasn't for you barkin' squirrels for our meat, we'd be livin' on catfish and bony grouse. Now that I got a job, we're gonna have food. Maybe some decent clothes. Only thing is, I gotta go and live with the withered up old—"

"Goshdang!" Patrick smiled broadly around a mouthful of cornmeal, then swallowed forcefully. "Seems I'm hardly gonna see my big sister anymore. Why, we're both gonna be workin' folks, good as anybody else, Liz, good as anybody! Dang if I ain't proud!" He nodded in agreement with himself, then contemplated the possible and added, "Maybe I'll ask for a raise. Maybe I could apprentice at the acid vats. . . ."

Grace sat down beside him. "You stay away from them vats. Them chemicals are dangerous. And they stink."

"Still, I could ask—" Then, typically, he shook his head and scoffed, "Naw, I couldn't. I'll jus' do my job and wait. You know what they say. Countin' stumps don't clear the field."

He spread his elbows on the table to support his tired body and dug into the bowl again.

The idea was gone, quick as that.

"I swear," Grace said, "you're shy as a colt."

"Yup, that's me. Just a ten-cent hat on a five-cent head."

Grace settled down quietly to watch him eat. It felt good to have a few minutes alone with Paddy. They'd grown up as each other's only company, practically twins, being only a year apart, yet so different from one another that they were always able to be mutually entertaining. Patrick had a bottomless patience and a simplicity of purpose that made him both nice company and a dead shot. Grace possessed the flint of spontaneity that somehow kept the family going through the harshest years. Even as a child she stalwartly stuck up for her parents in their ignorance and sloth, though for a long time now she had seen them for what they were.

At sixteen and fifteen the two no longer felt like children, and these days they could feel the earth moving under each step forward.

"A raise," Grace echoed.

"Some of the tanners get a dollar a day, Liz. A whole dollar. Guess it's true, what they say... scratch your dog where he cain't scratch himself, and he'll never leave you."

Gazing into the rough wood of the tabletop, Grace murmured, "I ain't never seen a dollar in person...."

"Me nuther... what you figger one looks like?"

"I dunno. They say it's made outa paper."

"Silver's what I heard."

"If you get a dollar a day, Hugh Craig'll make you work sixteen hours, I bet. He'll get that dollar back outa you, and when you drop dead, he'll toss your hide into the plumpin' tanks right along with the rest of the skins. He's that kinda man, Pat, the kind that keeps my mind a-tickin'. He likes them niggerlovers in Westport too much for me. Now he's gonna bring in slaves, you wait and see."

"Cain't," Patrick said around a mouthful. "Against the law."

"Ain't you heard?" she told him. "They changed the law."

"No foolin'? When?"

"Last month, sheriff says."

"That sheriff," Patrick contemplated, "he's a nice man. Well, least now I know."

"Know what?"

"How come they brung in a wagon of five or six niggers today."

Grace slapped the table. "Slaves! See there? That bumfugger Craig, he's doin' it to us!"

Wagging his spoon, Patrick said, "You always did understand politics. Sure wisht I did."

"What's there to understand, Paddy? Niggers comin' in, takin' the jobs of whites. Simple as that."

"Mmm. Hope not mine."

In the midst of her anger, Grace mellowed suddenly, not wanted to worry him. The fire went out of her voice, but not out of her eyes.

"They'll hang onto you," she said. "Cain't be sending a

nigger out to run errands like you do, can they? Not this close to the river and the trails. He wouldn't bother to come back."

Patrick nodded wearily and shoveled another spoonful of cornmeal into his mouth. He liked to watch his sister think out loud. Heck, he liked to listen to anybody who had a thing to say. Seemed like Grace was so *smart* . . . always *thinking*, always able to see what was coming around the bend. Patrick figured he was doing good if he just saw the road.

He glanced at Grace meaningfully. "They say he's dyin'."

Her green eyes flared. "Who?"

"Old Man Craig."

"Glory be and mercy me!" she exclaimed. "Maybe the Lord does get his nose through the clouds once in a while!"

Patrick shrugged. "Yeah, but won't be much of a change."

"Why in hell not? If he's gone—"

"Things won't get no better, Liz," Patrick warned gently.

"Why? Is that swine of a manager gonna take over?"

"Nope. They got another Craig to come and take over."

Grace gawked at him. "Another Craig?"

"Yup. A young one. Hugh Craig's son, they say. The one whose name's on the side of the tannery. You know—'H. Craig *and Son*.' They say he's comin' back from college in Delaware just to take over."

Slamming back into the twig chair, Grace gave the notion a proper scowl. "Another Craig. So much for the Lord's nose."

"His name's Wyatt. Wyatt Craig."

"Don't matter. I got a head start hatin' him."

"Mmm-hm. 'Gwine lay my head on de railroad track . . .'"

★

CHAPTER TWENTY

───── ★ ─────

May 1856
Two years later—
The Craig Tannery Shantytown,
Five years before the Civil War.

" 'They bury their dead with their heads directly downwards; because they hold an opinion that in eleven thousand moons they are all to rise again; in which period the earth (which they conceive to be flat) will turn upside down, and by this means they shall, at their . . . at their ress— ress—' "

"Resurrection."

" '—resurrection, be found ready standing on their feet.' "

"Keep on."

"Keep on? Haven't you had just about plenty of Gulliver and his little vermin squabbling over the big and small ends of their stupid eggs? Because I sure have had fill of 'em."

"You never get fill of classical literature, I keep telling you, girl."

"It's my thinking that 'classical literature' is a disguise for a pen with the trots. Even *I* don't talk this much. These people got no idea how to tell a story."

Grace wagged the book under Mrs. MacHutcheon's nose, then dropped onto the settee.

"Seems I been reading the whole past two years. Two years! This is my night home. I've gotta swing by the saloon and shoo Paw out. Last Saturday he came home so drunk he couldn't see the holes in a ladder. I'm gonna go make your pudding and put it in the oven, then I'm going. Anibal's gonna meet me tonight. He's finally back from roamin' around the territories. Least, he was s'posed to be.''

"I should think so," the old woman commented without the slightest hint of generosity. "Fine thing, leaving his betrothed for nigh two years without a word."

"It's been thirteen months, and he did send word. He sent word that he wants to talk to me tonight on the hill, and I figger he's wanting to talk marrying."

Mrs. MacHutcheon wheeled the chair around to face the kitchen door as Grace disappeared into the other room. "I warned ye time and time about that young man. Still gun tae marry him?"

"Yes, I'm still 'gun tae' marry him."

"Best do it soon, then. Soon, and move West or North. You can be abolitionists there wi'oot the element of danger. After what happened in Lawrence last week, why, I wadnae trust—"

"I'm no abolitionist," Grace snapped. "I hate all colors of men equally. Besides, who else would do for you?"

"I'll get some other poor white wretch hireling to haul the garbage," the old woman croaked with an independent snap of her fingers.

"Nobody else'll put up with you."

Mrs. MacHutcheon's eyes widened, ringed with yellow. "The proslavers fired a cannon! They burned the Free State Hotel to the verry dirrt! They killed two Free-Staters!"

Grace shrugged. "Then we're even."

"Och, you're impossible!"

"A skill I prize. Now be sure this pudding comes out in twenty minutes, or we'll have a new piece of bench leather for the porch."

" 'There was Captain Washington, upon a slappin' stallion, givin' orders to his men ... I guess there was a mill— yun ... Yankee ... Doodle, find a girl ... Yankee Doodle

Dandy . . . take her to the . . . fair . . . today . . . and buy a box of—' ' '

Crack-BOOM!

" 'Candy.' ' "

A couple hundred paces through the woods, a flintlock ball tore through the leaves and rang against the top edge of an oak branch. Bark flew like needles, tiny daggers of nature's hardest growing substance, and caught a squirrel full in the throat. The small animal's gullet was punctured, and the force of the flying bark spun the creature from his perch and smacked him against the next tree. Then gravity took over. The squirrel struck the muddy ground below with a wet whump.

" 'Yankee Doodle, good for me, Yankee Doodle Paddy, keep your flintlock good and clean, and you'll have squirrel for . . .' for . . . uh, for . . .' "

"Nothing rhymes with 'Paddy'."

Patrick twisted around on his branch and looked down, down, down, to where his sister stood with her hands on her hips.

"Oh, hey, Liz! I got him, did you see?"

"I saw. How come you wasted a ball on just one squirrel?"

Patrick's expression of pure joy fell away, and he peered keenly through the trees, waaaaay over there to where the dead squirrel lay. He drew his old Kentucky longrifle's elegant forty-two-inch barrel toward his chest and thought about the squirrel.

"Well, he was there, nice and handy, a good easy shot—"

"Patrick," Grace scolded, "it's springtime. The squirrels are mating in the springtime. If you be more patient, two of 'em are sure to come along playin' squirrel games in the trees, and you'll be able to bark two at a time. Don't waste your musket balls, hear? What would Paw say?"

Patrick scowled. "Maybe," he said, "but don't be greedy. You know what they say. It's ungrateful to count your catch before you step into your own cabin. Besides," he added, "this old German rifle's not gettin' any younger, Liz. If I had one of them new Sharps rifles, why I could bark a dozen squirrels with one shot at three hundred yards."

"Don't be boastful."

"Oh! Gosh, I didn't mean to be . . . What you doin' up the hill anyway?"

"I'm suppose to meet Anibal here tonight."

Up in his tree Patrick smiled into the setting sunlight that patched the forest floor below. "You mean he's back?"

"He's supposed to be," Grace said dubiously. "He sent word that he was, but you know Anibal. Last time he said he'd be back in a month, it was half a year."

"That's how it is, sis," Patrick said as he gazed through the trees for other squirrels and busied himself with the habitual reloading of the muzzle loader. He did it without thinking now. It was as natural as scratching. "Next time he goes away, snip a lock of his hair and put it under your pillow. You'll have the same dreams as him."

"Speaking of whose s'pose to be here and who's not, what are you doing home in the middle of the week? Aren't you working today?"

"Sure was, but I got off early. They gave everybody the afternoon off."

Grace leered up the tree. "That tells me there's a snake in the cider barrel. They never gave you no afternoon off before."

Patrick nodded and looked down from his precarious perch. "Mr. Craig never died before."

Stumbling back a few paces, Grace gasped, "He died today? That vicious, greedy, corrupt, double-dealing niggerloving excrement of a polecat finally got off his pot and died?"

Patrick grinned down and wobbled his head in amazement. "Goshdang, you sure know a lot of words."

"He died? Are you sure about that?"

"Yup. Died bright and early. Mr. Lassick and Wyatt came down after noontime and told us all to all head on home."

Her eyes grew slim as Grace contemplated this turnabout. The joy of the death of Hugh Craig was watered down by the common knowledge that there was another Craig to step in after him and keep up the plundering of Kansas in favor of slavery and against tariffs and for all their other myriad purposes.

Lassick. The sadistic manager of the factory. His name was practically synonymous with Hugh Craig. And Wyatt—

"Wyatt," Grace muttered bitterly. "Another Craig. They give me the floods."

The tree rustled above her, and she clamped her lips tight on those thoughts. No point making Patrick feel bad. He had no choice but to work in the black industrial shadow of the Craigs, and he apparently didn't have the brains to hate them. Grace had never before and still didn't see any reason to make him feel guilty about being one of the people who helped put money in the Craig family's pockets. Like all the other workers, Patrick was trapped in the industrial suction—enough money to survive, but too little to build up a nest egg and move along to anything better. It was a common fate among poor white homesteaders. A factory job could be a leash as well as a lifeline.

The only chance for a better job had come and gone last fall, when a man came through the shantytown with offers for jobs as chippers and dippers at a new turpentine factory down in one of the Gulf state pine forests, but Grace and her parents had balked at the idea of Patrick's going so far from home just for a dime more than his seventy-cents-a day wage as an assistant here at the tannery. And Patrick was scared of fire anyway. Distilleries full of turpentine and rosin burned a little too anxiously.

He'd worked all this time at the tannery, learning the trade and getting little promotions here and there, and he felt worth something. There was no gain in making him as bitter as she was, or in taking the shine off what little accomplishments he had managed to glean for himself from the unforgiving frontier. His backwoods instincts were fine for barking squirrels, but other than that Grace knew she would have to take care of him.

"Headzup."

Grace looked up and reacted as the Kentucky longrifle dropped into her hands. She caught it neatly, put it to her shoulder, tucked her cheek tightly against the wood, and sighted down the endless barrel.

"There's nothing wrong with this rifle," she commented. She took sight on several points through the woods. "It's as good as it ever was for weight and balance."

A pair of hard-soled brogans swung at her side, a form

dropped past her, and Patrick straightened up not a foot away. He palmed his hair aside and nodded, willing to agree just for politeness. For the first time Grace noticed that he was taller than she was. When had that happened? Did they see each other so seldom?

His shoulders too—they weren't pointy anymore. Since he'd stopped running errands and taken on the real tannery work of processing hides into leather, his shoulders had turned muscular, rounder, and fuller, finally taking on an athletic compactness that was somewhat hidden by his clothes. His face was still so boyish, so gentle and easygoing, that his build wasn't obvious at first glance, or even at second glance. He was no carnival attraction, certainly, but he had shoulders and upper arms that just hadn't been there two years ago. Too bad they were attached to a fellow who felt sorry for the squirrel lying over there.

Grace shifted backward on one foot, almost as if stepping backward in time and trying to catch up. Softly she murmured, "Ram and damn, look at you. . . ."

But Patrick didn't notice her new brand of attention. His mind was on her previous comment, and he wasn't much for thinking about more than one thing at a time. He took the rifle from her and ran his fingers along its barrel.

"Naw, it's okay," he said, " 'cept the ball's starting to take a curve. I'm always havin' to . . . what was that word you learned?"

Grace shook herself out of her revelations.

"Compensate," she said.

"Right." Patrick smiled and added, "Sure are smart."

"Go get your squirrel and scat up to the cabin. Skin him and slap him on the spit before the blood all runs out of him and his meat dries up."

"Righty. Where you gonna be?"

"Waiting for Anibal, just like I said. Now, scat!"

"I'm scattin'!"

She waited for Anibal on the hillside beneath the scrub oaks, with the muddy river churning not far from her feet. She waited a long time, and she thought about many things. All the changes in the past couple of years . . . changes in her body and her mind, her perceptions. Changes in the politics of Kansas, growing more and more brutal rather than more stable. No one seemed to be able to get control over Kansas, yet everyone wanted it. The proslavery squatters were still determined to drive off the Free-State settlers. Kansas had probably become the least pleasant place to live on the whole continent, especially for folks who didn't care one way or the other. Threats of violence rang through almost daily now. The nice sheriff had gone away, and there was a zealous proslave sheriff in his place now, and everything had gone to hell. People were starting to form militias this way or that. Now that the proslavers had sacked the town of Lawrence, fully intending to wipe it from the face of the earth, people were banding together under their perception of lawful warfare. The sacking had given a good slug to the belly of the Free-Soil movement, the United States Army forts had mobilized, and there was practically a civil war going on. Artillery! Cannon! Insanity! Men! It was just like them.

"Kansas is all vine and no taters, I swear," Grace mumbled aloud, seeing the little war in her head. "Bring in guns and right away some puffed-up bullethead wants to fire 'em."

"Grace?"

She bolted to one side, instantly on the defense. Suddenly she was breathless.

"Anibal?"

When Anibal Webb stepped out into the waning spring evening, Grace kept a few paces back and got a long, strong look at him and he at her. They exchanged a meaty stare.

He was hardly more than an unfamiliar shadow.

"Grace? That . . . you?"

"Depends. Is that you?"

When he left thirteen months ago to go with the abolitionists, they had both been children. In fact, he'd been shorter than she was by half an inch and now was two taller. He'd been cleaner, and she'd been dirtier.

They were eighteen now, and something was different. Grace didn't like this business of all her men getting taller.

Apprehension whispered through her.

"Anibal Webb," she said, "you're bony as Christ and twice as hairy! Is that you under the foot-long beard?"

"What happened to *you*?"

"I took a bath."

"Again?"

She huffed and set her heels on the hill. "Yes, again."

"You look . . . different."

"I don't look that different."

Yes, she did. It was a jarring change. She looked like a complete stranger. Her body was different, fuller. Her face had lost its teenaged puffiness and now had the strong German cheekbones and wide lips that looked so bad on her mother and so good on Grace. She did look good. Not a girl anymore. Her hair was no longer the ratty, untended mess it had been when she first started working for the old lady. Now it was a fan of wavy dark russet with no curls or twists at all as it drifted around her shoulders and her back. A wave of bangs swept across her forehead and framed her green eyes and straight brows, which he could see quite clearly even in the light of the moon and what little sunlight still lingered. She no longer wore just a sack dress, but now had a proper blue muslin blouse on, a skirt, and an apron. An *apron*.

"Anibal," she said duskily, "I don't know if I can kiss a man with a beard like that."

The rangy young man blinked thoughtfully, then paced around her, uncomfortable.

"I bin learnin' things," he said. "Things bin happenin'. We got some decisions to make."

She folded her arms and waited.

Anibal paused, but since Grace wasn't commenting, he went on.

"The proslavers come into Lawrence last week and sacked the town. You know 'bout that, right?"

"Who missed it? I never heard such a clatter of gossip."

"That was their revenge for us setting up our own antislavery constitution in Topeka. You know about that?"

The ground sucked against her feet. "I never been to Topeka."

"We want niggers out of Kansas, right?"

"Okay."

"Only way to keep 'em out is to get 'em free and push 'em to Canada. We gotta outlaw 'em. Cain't outlaw something that's legal, and slavery's legal."

"It's half-legal," Grace corrected. "Legal by the Kansas Act, illegal by the Topeka people."

Anibal paused, struck silent. When had she learned so much? When he left, she hadn't known where to find her feet. He was suddenly thrown off balance. For weeks now he had rehearsed how to explain the situation to her in simple enough terms that she wouldn't get confused. He had rehearsed stories in which Kansas Territory was a tender, bloody morsel caught between a hawk and a vulture. But she knew already. She knew—and had digested—the cleaved legislature of Kansas, and how the proslavery government had kicked out the Free-Soilers, so the Free-Soilers had set up their own constitution, outlawed slavery, and banned *all* black people from the territory. *That* was what Solomon would call a solution.

Except that now he didn't have much to say to her.

"The . . . uh . . . Craig factory . . . it has slaves, y'know," he began.

"I know. Eleven of them."

Damn.

He scratched the back of his neck and paced again.

"Uh . . . do you know, uh . . . *exactly* what happened in Lawrence?"

"Burnt the hotel. Set cannon fire on it."

"Right! Uh . . . I'll tell you what happened."

"I *know* what happened."

"It was that Sheriff Jones."

"Samuel Jones. Douglas County. I know who he is," Grace said impatiently. "I don't like the looks of him."

"You've seen him?"

"Sure I've seen him. You think I don't look at what rides by? 'Bout thirty-five, kinda tall and skinny, kinda looks like a cadaver. Little eyes, but he doesn't like to look into a person's face when he talks to 'em. Only person I ever talked to who had a fouler mouth than me."

Blinking in amazement, Anibal was struck by the revelation that indeed he hadn't heard a single foul word come out of Grace in the whole conversation. It made him nervous.

"Uh . . . yeah. Anyway, in Lawrence—"

"The marshall's proslaver mob rode up to Mount Oread, two hundred of them, and Sheriff Jones rode in with twenty-

five of his own, and they all clapped their hands for him, and
they bombarded the Free State Hotel, and the thing blew up
and burned, and Jones liked it, so they pillaged the town and
chased all the people out onto the prairies and wrecked
everything they could put their marauding hands on, and if
that's a story I haven't heard enough in the past week, it'll be
the stories of all the retaliation the Free-Soilers' gonna take,
and what's all this got to do with you and me?''

Silence dropped like a casket.

Wind rolled through the tops of the trees and didn't dare
come down. Grace's foot tapped on the mud. Out of pioneer
practicality they had agreed long ago to get hitched. There
was safety and security in numbers, and two was a number. If
she had to stay a one, she was going to know why.

"Well?''

Up through his knotted throat, Anibal pushed a response.

"When'd you learn to talk like that?''

"Anibal! What do we care if Yankees and niggers and
slavers kill each other? We aren't any of those people. We're
white.''

"We're Free-Soilers, Gracie,'' he said, digging his voice
out of his trousers. "We got . . . we got pride. Pride to keep
the territories free.''

"I don't like the sound of that.''

"People are speakin' up,'' he said. "A senator from Massachusetts was beaten right to the floor of Congress by a
South Carolina representative, martyred before the world in
the cause of abolit—''

"I heard about it,'' Grace told him. "Preston Brooks beat
the tar out of Senator Sumner with his cane. Don't you think
we hear about things way out here, Anibal? News like that
don't stay in Washington.''

He fidgeted and murmured, "I confess, you give me a
turn. I didn't think you, uh . . . cared about that sort of thing.''

"I don't,'' she confirmed. "Just heard around the mountain is all. Gossip an' all. Can't help but listen, can I?''

"Maybe it's best,'' he said. "There's gonna be a raid.
Right here.''

Grace dug her fingers into her hair and yelped, "Oh, Christ
and crust, I knew it!''

He followed her across the hillside. Suddenly she turned on him, and he was blown back a couple of steps.

"You're leaving again!" she bellowed. "Aren't you!"

"I'm . . . I'm . . ."

"You're what?"

"There's gonna be a raid on the tannery," he repeated.

Picturing this in her mind was astonishingly easy, Grace discovered. The Craig tannery was a perfect target for Free-Soilers bent on revenge for the sacking of Lawrence.

"Keep talking," she said.

Anibal held his hand out and ticked off details on his fingers. "A man named John Brown is gonna lead a raid at Pottawatomie Creek, and at the same time I'm s'pose to lead a raid at the tannery."

"What kind of raid? A violent one?"

His eyes gleamed with anticipation as he said, "Naw, a sneaky one. We're gonna go in tonight and steal all eleven of Craig's slaves and put every single one of 'em on the Underground Railroad into Canada. I'm gonna take 'em myself."

"I never heard such pig wash!" she exclaimed. "Eleven little slaves? What does that matter to rich people like the Craigs?"

On this, Anibal's confidence suddenly reappeared, and he drawled, "At a thousand dollars a head, Gracie? Old Man Craig'll shit himself dry."

"Too late. He's dead."

Anibal almost choked. "Dead? He's dead?"

"Died today. You're gonna be dealing with new blood, Anibal. His son's taking over, and he'll just bring in more slaves. You just can't push around a healthy young man like you can a decrepit old one, even if he was rich."

"But it'll cost 'em hellacious money!" Anibal insisted. "It'd be like as if we stold their equipment."

"All the way to Canada, dragging a gaggle of niggers? You'll be gone for months!"

"Well," he said slowly, "that's what I gotta talk about. You still gonna marry me?"

"Said I would, didn't I?"

He straightened. "I'm gonna be a conductor for the Underground Railroad," he said. "I want you to come with me."

"I'm not going to Canada," she said instantly. "I promised Pa I'd wait till I was eighteen to get married, and I'm eighteen now, but I sure didn't make no promises about leaving my brother and my folks and going to Canada to deliver a bunch of niggers I don't even know personal."

"But I got no idea when I'm gonna get back!" he said. "Could be years, Gracie."

"So?"

"You know how far Canada is from here?"

"As a matter of fact, I do."

He leaned forward and challenged, "How far?"

She stuck her nose up. "Pretty far."

Frustrated, Anibal knotted and unknotted his fists several times, but there wasn't much more to talk about with her, so he made his decision, a decision that had already been ground deeply into his mind and around which he could see no other futures.

"Well . . . I gotta go, then."

"Go where?"

"To steal the niggers."

"Reckon I'll see you later on, then."

"Yeah . . . reckon so." He turned hesitantly and walked away. At the river's bank he turned back and called, "You still gonna marry me when I get back?"

"Said I would."

"Even if it's . . . years?"

"A promise is a promise."

"Uh . . . good. . Well . . . bye."

"Bye. Have fun stealin' niggers."

"Thanks, Grace. Thanks. Maybe we'll get married in the spring."

"You're right welcome. Maybe we will."

"Give my regards to your maw and paw."

She nodded a curt farewell and said, "Give my regards to the niggers."

★

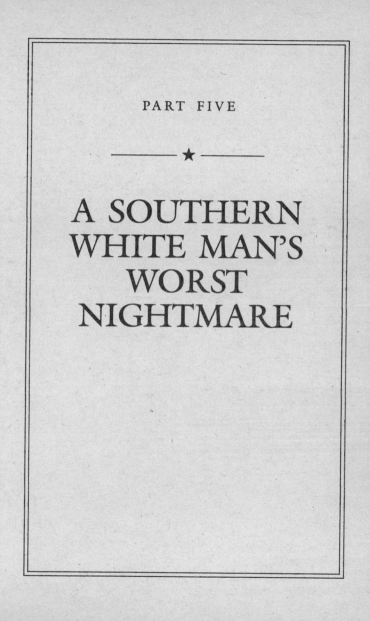

PART FIVE

---- ★ ----

A SOUTHERN WHITE MAN'S WORST NIGHTMARE

CHAPTER TWENTY-ONE

──────── ★ ────────

His eyes could annihilate. Imperious eyes of brilliant black, and his brows flew over them like a bat's two wings. His skin was still the color of champagne and even seemed to defy the Southern sun that turned most white people bronze. He moved with a natural military carriage, though he had never once set foot off the fourteen-hundred-acre radius of Plentiful. He walked the way he thought a man should walk, the way the books told him men should, the way he saw Nick walk.

There was something about him, and everyone knew it, but he was such a chameleon, such a part of the scenery at the main house or the cabins, that no one thought twice. Although he wore fine clothes half of the time, the other half he wore linsey and muslin, and no white plantation Southerner ever did that.

Since he fit into no class, there were no parameters for judging him, so hardly anybody did. He was just there.

After the branding he had retreated into utter diplomacy. The lesson hadn't been lost upon him, and even before that he had understood his place. Afterward he simply made use of that place, cleverly reconciling his two life-styles and putting himself to work as McCrocklin's assistant. McCrocklin grumbled and bucked at first but soon discovered the boy could

read and add, and the arrangement got comfortable. The boy
did the ciphering, and the ledgers came out right. The boy
preplanned the planting, and the harvests came up on time.
The boy rotated the slaves, making them apprentice to each
other, and instead of a flock of dumb niggers, Plentiful
boasted a legion of skilled workmen who could fill in for each
other when the need arose. The boy arranged shipments in
and shipments out, placed orders and did business, signing
other people's names to any papers that fell before him.
Plentiful ticked like a metronome. McCrocklin got to sleep a
lot, and the boy did his work for him. That gave him a sound
reason not to report too much back to Boss, and season after
season the boy generally ran Plentiful.

And now the boy was a man of twenty-two.

"Dohrian!"

"In the shed."

He was at the books. Not the ledgers, but the research
books he'd arranged to have sent to Plentiful. Books about
agriculture in Greece, of making use of rocky land, forcing it
to take a crop. With such information he could expand
Plentiful's yield. American planters had been able to be
wasteful—there was always richer soil, so why work tough
acreage? Few plantations thought of making good use of
every inch of ground. But Europeans had learned to draw
harvest from limited ground, and now their techniques would
make Plentiful even more efficient. Maybe tobacco wouldn't
grow in tough ground, but something would. Hemp, barley,
something. That was his new plan for this summer.

He looked up from the idea in time to see the doorway fill
with a thick, dark body. And tall, for an eight-year-old.
Mighty tall. Just like the other three children born after the
Breeder came.

But those other three were not Dorian's little brothers. This
one was.

Dorian kicked back in his chair, braced his boot on the
desk before him, flopped his hands in his lap, and beamed.

"Burlie, you throwback to a gladiator, how are you?"

The boy took that as permission and charged into the shed, diving into Dorian's arms. The chair nearly went over.

Dorian coiled his arms around the thick little slave boy and closed his eyes through a sudden rush of affection.

When the boy drew back on Dorian's lap, his bright chocolate eyes, ringed with long tightly curled lashes, brought the room to life. Clearly Dorian's handsomeness hadn't come from Boss, for this boy had the same glossy looks and statuesque bone structure. Somewhere in Yula's tiny body ran the stock that produced handsome children, no matter who fathered those children.

But Burlie could never be mistaken for white—his skin was as dark as his eyes, and his build was that of a certain big slave.

"I din see you all day!" the child blustered.

"Oh, I know!" Dorian responded. "A crime. Got all your chores done?"

"All done."

"Eggs all collected?"

The boy pursed his pink lips and admitted, "I busted three of'm."

"Burlie, shame."

Burlie flattened his mouth and glared sidelong at his big brother. "Yeah, I'm shamed, I'm shamed. Yawl satisfied? I'm shamed."

Dorian tried to look stern, but it didn't hold, and a moment later he was laughing at the boy's animated expression. "You bright as a penny, you know that, you round chestnut?"

"I know it. What these books? Could I look?"

He nearly tipped the chair over again as he dived for one of the books. Dorian groaned and fought to stay upright under the boy's weight.

"Go ahead," Dorian encouraged.

Burlie pulled the book open to a random page, picked a paragraph, and blinked at the pictures.

" 'It was well-knowned in the village—' "

"Well-known."

" 'Well-known . . . that the land could be tilled more than twice per . . . per . . .' "

" 'Annum.' Per year."

"Dat means year?"

"Yes. Like 'annual.' "

Pausing over the word, Burlie mouthed it a few times—annum, annual, annum, annual, year. Then he squirmed for better seating on Dorian's aching thigh, took in a breath to continue reading, but never got the chance.

"Burlie!"

The doorway dimmed once again, and Yula was there, eight years older and still thin.

"Burlie! Is you pestin' the brother? Git outside. You see him workin' at them books."

"I reading, Mama," the boy said indignantly, communicating to her that he knew what was important.

"You is always readin'!" she squeaked. "Outa here!"

Burlie put his round brown face in the air, raised his crescent eyebrows, and batted his lashes at her. "Gonna be a lawman someday. Gonna arrest you, Mama."

"I give you a pinch then too, boy. Scat."

He streaked past her, but she caught his arm—about twice as thick as her own—and dragged him back.

"You fuggot somethin'."

"Oh, yeah!" The boy's flashing white smile was a shock against his black skin. He doubled back and stretched the inch or two he needed to kiss his mama on the cheek.

"Das better," Yula said, and let go of the arm.

Wiggling like a wrestler, Burlie scouted the doorway, let out a terrific yell, and dived out the door, on the attack toward a group of slave children who squealed and scattered.

Yula watched him go, and for a moment her heart went with him. "I mus' be crazy, bein' so in love wid dat nigger baby a'mine."

Dorian stood up, stretching the leg Burlie had been sitting on. "Hey, Mama," he greeted, pecking her on the cheek.

"Is you busy, Dohrian?" the chipper little woman asked.

"No, Mama," he told her. He always told her no. He could be dashing across the yard, supervising the delivery of a hundred bales of tobacco, and still he would say no, he wasn't busy, Mama.

"You seen dat new cuffee girl yet?"

Dorian's cheeks took on a sudden angularity as he tried not to smile. "Yes, Mama, I've seen her."

"Boss brung her over from Mississippi. Dem Mississippi niggers be good stock, Dohrian. She a good-lookin' girl. Got a fine face. Just right. How 'bout you go over a broom wid dat girl?"

"Mama, I ain't goin' over any broom with anybody. Not anybody."

His mother nailed her fists to her hips and poked forward. "Dohrian, you twenty-two years old. When you gonna make me a grandmama?"

"You too teeny to be a grandmama," he chuckled. "You just a runt."

"What a 'runt'?" she snapped. Should she hit him or kiss him for that? "Wimmins gotta have grandbabies, Dohrian, jus' like dey gotta have babies. Can't be nobody till you gots a baby."

"You got two babies, Mama," he told her. "You somebody. You got me, and you got that... that baby bear yonder."

They stood together, gazing out at Burlie. He towered over the other slave children, who were chasing him as he ran with a cornstalk, playing keep-away.

"He big, awright," Yula murmured. "Big jus' like that nigger breeder Boss dun stuck on me. Seems neither of you git anything of mines."

Dorian's eyes flicked to her. "Mama," he began gently, "Burlie and me didn't get our brains from Boss. He's thick as a brick. So whose brains we got, huh? Whose?" He tickled her ears until she squirmed.

"Dohrian, I ain't smart."

He laughed and said, "You a scrawny li'l cuffee with no man to protect you, and you still queen bee on Plentiful. Ain't smart, huh?"

She wriggled against her son, muttering, "Still want yawl married."

A sigh stole from Dorian's lips. As he had a thousand times, he once again refrained from telling her the ugly truths of the world beyond Plentiful for a half-breed. He hated reminding her that the South regarded him as a slave and a dangerous one. It was the same South that constantly maneuvered to send Luke Wallace back where he belonged—the docks. And all because he was not and never would truly be blooded aristocracy. If nothing else, that awareness worked in Wallace's own mind, and in the minds of far too many people. How could Dorian explain to her?

"I can't marry anybody, Mama," he told her. "I never will."

She pushed herself away and squared off. "How come?"

He paused, suddenly self-conscious.

"How come?" Yula persisted.

When he couldn't find the answer, or one that he wanted her to hear, she folded her arms and stepped back.

"Dat blood in you," she said. "Right?"

Abruptly Dorian felt his guards fall away before her. She was smart, smarter than he credited her.

He sat down again, half-amused, half-disturbed.

Yula moved to him and cupped his face in her long, bony black hands. Her voice went soft. "Dat white blood in my baby."

He snatched her hand and kissed it.

She caressed his head against her thin body as if to protect him.

"My baby's blood," she whispered.

Dorian dropped his shroud of dignity and hugged her hard, staring out into the open coop yard.

"I am the devil, Mama," he said. "How can I ask anybody to marry the devil?"

From where she stood over him, Yula looked down at his branded arm, at the rolled-up linsey sleeve, at the clear four-inch *S* burned into his forearm, a shape that had long ago shriveled and turned pure white, pure obvious.

She closed her eyes and buried a shudder. "I love de devil," she whispered.

"Stubborn," Dorian said, smiling again. "Plain buck stubborn."

Yula drew back. "Dat's me, ain't it? Now, 'bout yawl teachin' Burlie t'be readin' all de time. Do you know he go out and teach dem other chillun to read?"

Dorian folded his arms and leaned back in the chair.

"Yes . . . I do know that. They should read. They'll have to someday."

"Maybe so," Yula admitted sharply, "but chillun is too stupid to keep a secret. Spill it all over Plentiful that Dohrian be teachin' reading."

"Ain't nobody care, Mama," he told her. "McCrocklin ain't gonna make nothing of it long as I do his job, and Boss don't know I do the job."

"Yawl makin' trouble like you always done."

"That's my job, my destiny," he told her with a lilt. "It's the devil's job to mix things up. So put dem li'l eyes back in yoh head."

Yula pointed at her own face and poked forward at him. "My eyes gonna follow you all yoh life. Gonna come in yoh dreams and spank you on de butt. Yawl jus' keep yoh place!"

"Spank me, huh?" He took a dive and swatted her on the thigh. "Spank me?"

"Dohrian, cut dat out!" she squeaked. "Cut dat out!"

"Spank me, is it?"

"Lawd, ain't you got no pride?"

"Not me," he uttered, dodging for her other thigh.

"Cut it out, I said! You is a *baaaad* boy!"

A knock on the door frame cut short their antics.

"Pardon. Am I interrupting?"

They both turned in the cloud of dust they'd brought up from the dry floor and looked at the sunlit doorway.

Dorian squinted, blinked, and suddenly his face brightened with recognition and a twist of the unexpected. In the doorway stood his true opposite—a taller, leaner version of himself with features as soft as his were harsh, eyes as pale blue as his were black, hair as snowy as his was ink—but their skin was nearly the same.

Dorian shot to his feet.

"Alex!"

The floor planks creaked beneath them as the two young men came together, reaching for each other as though neither quite believed the reunion was happening.

"*Poso kero esa ehndo?* And why wasn't I told you were coming?" Dorian gasped, counting the months backward.

Laughing, Alex said, "Lord, but it's good to hear Greek again!"

"Christ on a pike, has it been as long as I think?"

"Nearly ten months, Dory." He gripped Dorian's arms and surveyed him critically. There wasn't much changed about him, and that was reassuring, but seeing Dorian in his yard clothes always made Alex wince. "We've never been apart so long before, I know. I tried to get back for Christmas, but I just failed." Then he cast a smile toward the corner into which Yula had retreated. "Hello, little mama."

Now she came out from her shadow, taking his greeting as permission to speak. "Lawdy, boy, you is a whole inch taller," she observed. "An' don' you look jus' like a coachman!"

Alexander Wallace looked down at his snappy blue daycoat, a single-buttoned operation that nipped in at the waist, then flared to his knees and gave extra length to his figure. With breeches and boots and the brown silk jabot, he probably did look too Sundayed up for a visit to the yard.

"I should've considered that," he said apologetically. "It's common daywear at Charlottesville."

"Don' take no mind," Yula told him with a snap of her fingers. "It do us good to see we work for fancy folk. Give us pride when we walk down dem streets in town. *Some* of us got pride." With a punctuating slap at Dorian's midriff, she stuck her little face up just as her other son had—no mystery where Burlie had learned it. "I speck to see you down in the yard fo' supper, Mist' Alex, you hear?"

"Yes'm, you just say when, and I'll be there."

Yula pointed at Alex and glared at Dorian. "See? That's how you treats yoh mama."

Dorian chuckled and nodded, "Yes'm, I duz jus' like you say."

Yula punished him with a look. "You never duz like I say. You is such a critter."

With that as her exit line, she put her nose back up and pranced out of the shed.

The two young men watched her go. A moment of uneasy silence moved between them. Alex shifted his weight a few times, unwilling to lean his clean clothes against any part of the shed. After a moment he brushed away a lock of hair and met Dorian's gaze.

There was always something behind Dorian's eyes, something that took a few seconds to get used to—certainly that was so after all this time. Even the simple breeks and linsey shirt couldn't dampen the polished presence of the man before him. For an instant Alex felt himself being stabbed.

"Dorian, I've missed you," he said. "There was a hole in every discussion. I wrote to you . . . you didn't get the letters, did you?"

"Did you get any of mine?"

"Only one," Alex said. "It's a wonder even one got past Father. And that was over six months ago."

"I can't speak to you, you know," Dorian said. "You're a University of Virginia man now."

"That's right. I only speak to the best. Oh, that reminds me! I have something for you."

He dug into the side pocket of his daycoat and came up with a folded piece of black material embroidered with red, gold, and white thread in designs that were obviously Greek. "It's a belt. See? Very nice. Believe it or not, I got it from a pair of Cyprian students who needed an interpreter even more than they needed directions to the campus. They gave it to me as a token. I want you to have it."

"Nonsense," Dorian said. "What would I do with it?"

Looking a little hurt, Alex said, "Wear it, of course. Step over here."

"No, I don't need it."

"Come over here!" Alex grabbed him roughly, pulled him forward, and had the belt around him in an instant. "There! Merry whatever. Say, it suits your coloring."

Gazing down at the belt as it fought violently with his shabby work clothes, Dorian muttered, "Nothing suits my coloring."

"Just keep it. I insist."

"All right, all right." Dorian gestured to the chair at the desk and settled on the window ledge. "Please, sit."

Alex hesitated, looking down at the gritty chair. Finally he relented, not wanting to turn down the offer—surely Dorian wouldn't miss such a slight.

The chair creaked. Alex glanced over the papers and books on the desk. "What's this? A new innovation of some kind?"

Scratching his ear self-consciously, Dorian observed, "Well, a new idea."

"And that is?"

"Salaries."

"Salaries? To the slaves?"

Pausing, Dorian shifted his mind into another mode and switched to speaking Greek—something he rarely did in the yard and never in the fields.

"The whip does its job," he said, "but you know the slaves only work at about a third their true capacity. Any picnic competition has proved what they can do if they're motivated. They simply don't care about their work. I'm trying to devise ways of making them care." He shrugged. "Incentive."

Alex looked at him contemplatively and, also in Greek, asked, "A quiet revolution, Dory?"

"Perhaps. Tell me about Charlottesville. There must be something there besides Cypriots. Would Thomas Jefferson be proud of the university he sponsored?"

Not very subtle, but the subject changed with a clunk, and so did the language.

"School has its interesting edge," he sighed in English. "It makes me think. Rather the same way you make me think. But it's very consolidated thinking . . . some of it a bit frightening."

Dorian nodded and said, "Fright is healthy." He gazed at Alex, comforted by the unexpected presence, happy to see him.

Alex, however, was staring out the door at the coop yard and the dashing slave children. "We've been studying the effect of the Stowe book upon Southern society."

With a click of his boot heel against the wall, Dorian muttered, "Oh, yes, that silly book."

Alex shook his head. "It's an unfair, inaccurate look at slave life."

"Of course it's inaccurate. What do you expect?"

"You've read it then?"

"I've read everything in the world. And what hermit hasn't

read *Uncle Tom's Cabin*? It's written by a Northern white woman who sees all exaggerations as normal. Only an idiot would take her word for things. According to the newspapers the Northerners swallow it whole.''

"Yes, they do. They've even been working at an annotated documentation of everything in it. It worries me, the way they go about it . . . on both sides of the question. I'm confused by the world, Dory,'' Alex admitted. He leaned forward in the chair and let his elbows press onto his knees. "Things are going topsy-turvy. Northerners threatening to ignore the Fugitive Slave Law, proslavery swine like Stephen Douglas doing his dances in Congress—''

"Why, Pearly, you have the sense of humor of a hangman,'' Dorian scolded. "I didn't mean to open a floodgate.''

"But I've waited so long to tell you these things . . . to hear what you have to say. . . .''

With a reserved but affectionate grin, Dorian shrugged. "Are you trying to squeeze an opinion out of me? All right. I think Doulgas and his ilk don't give a damn about slavery. They just want the issue out of the way so the West can be settled beyond the Missouri River.''

Alex's bright eyes took on an inner trouble. "There's not supposed to be slavery up there, Dorian. The Missouri Compromise—''

"Got snuffed. Accept it. Laws change.''

This time Alex didn't look away. He knew Dorian would mince any argument that had a hole in it, but this issue disturbed him. He spoke slowly, as if reviewing each word before it came out of his mouth.

"Dorian . . . I don't believe God meant for slavery to exist.''

Dorian arched an eyebrow at the idea and said, "Make certain the world knows it's your idea. Wouldn't want God to be crediting the wrong account.''

Alex sat up and frowned. "How can you speak like that about God?''

With an irreverent shrug Dorian said, "I have no soul. I'm going to hell anyway you turn it, so I can afford to be honest. About him or anybody else.''

"Dorian, don't talk like that. . . . You'll go to heaven. Everyone with a soul goes to heaven.''

Alex was sitting there, looking like a parson.

"Demons have no souls," Dorian said. But now he smiled gently for Alex's sake and regarded his brother through a gauze of real affection. "Don't worry about me, Alex. In heaven I wouldn't fit in."

He smiled suddenly, and the whole room turned over.

Whenever Dorian smiled, his entire face changed. Abrupt, dramatic change, either brilliant or diabolical—those were the choices. It pitched his brother off kilter for a long moment.

Alex's eyes fixed suddenly, and he couldn't pull them away in time.

"What is it?" Dorian asked, but even before the sound fell, he knew what it was. He looked down at his own arm, at the bare skin of his right forearm, at the scar. *S* for *slave*.

He covered it with his hand, almost as if petting a dog.

"Pardon," he said. "They're used to it down here."

Alexander murmured, "You usually have your jacket on at the house."

"Alex, it's part of me. Like the skin. There's nothing to it."

But every time Alex saw the brand, a knife went through his heart. Every time, without exception, like it or not, he remembered that day in its entirety. When he saw the *S* displayed in withered white parchment on his brother's arm, he also saw the boy Dorian had been up until that day. Until then Dorian had been an idealist, as children are wont to be, but even more so because he had been seeing the world only through the rosy glow of literature. The branding had been Dorian's moment of truth, the instant—inevitably—that showed him the world was no morality play nor any adventurous legend with orchestrated scenes. When the hot iron seered into his flesh, Dorian had discovered there were no Arthurs.

Typically he had proceeded accordingly in life.

And to the day he died, Alex would feel guilty about not being there, about not being old enough or smart enough to stop it somehow.

"I never thought about these things much since Father gave up the idea of running for office, but now they've been resurfacing. The whole idea of having slaves make me feel . . ."

Unexpectedly Dorian slapped him on the shoulder, then gave him a rough shake.

"Oh, reason up! Slaves are forty percent of the South's entire population. Two and a half million negroes. Add it up. The other sixty percent can't all be slave owners, can they? Forty percent of the population owned by a handful of whites. The fact is, *most* whites in the South don't own anybody. You needn't own a slave if you don't choose to. Stop feeling guilty for something you just plain inherited."

"Perhaps," Alex grumbled. "You always make such sense."

"It's a gift."

"Yes, your gift from God."

"You want another gift from God?" Dorian threatened. "Here's one. Someday Father's going to die, and you're going to own all this, and all these people. You're going to own that desk and this shed and that chair, and know something else? You're going to own *me*. Ironic, yes?"

The revelation hit the other young man like a wave and seemed to actually make his hair turn lighter. Or maybe it was just that his face paled suddenly, and he looked like a ghost of himself.

"Yes," Dorian reiterated.

Alex was glad he was sitting down. He would have had to.

He clasped his hands in front of him and stared. "There's an ugly thought," he murmured.

"Truth is ugly," his brother said ominously.

"I never considered that. . . ."

"Best you start."

Dorian's shell had descended to protect him. Alex had seen it enough times in his life to know it was there even without looking at Dorian's face. A shell of cynical practicality.

Bitterness filled Alex and drew a dull curtain over his clear blue eyes. He longed for a world as ordered as the one he had left behind when he'd gone away to the university after two years at a small local college. The university had made things seem quite different. He hadn't been able to come home at night, and that made home seem like a distant land, foreign and hard to describe. Plentiful had been a safe and nurturing place at one time for both him and Dorian, but now they were men, and men needed more than nurturing.

He jolted suddenly. "Oh, I almost forgot... the damned thing's so small.... Where is it? It's something for you from a friend of mine, Gavin Ogilvie. He said you'd like it if you like poetry."

"Now, Alex—"

"No, it's very little. Small, I mean. Just an afterthought."

Rummaging around in his pockets while Dorian simply looked on, Alex had to stand up before he found the tidbit he'd been searching for. At first Dorian thought it was a pillbox, because it was only three inches long and less than two across, but it turned out actually to be a book. Very small, as Alex had promised, and printed on thin vellum, bound inside a leather swatch.

Dorian scowled. "This is a book?"

"You can hide it in your boot. Here," Alex said. Snatching the pencil from Dorian's desk, he scribbled inside the tiny cover. " 'To Dorian, to hide in his boot, from Alex.' There. Take it."

"*The Poems of Robert Burns*. Who's Robert Burns?"

"Keep it."

"My eyes'll go bad reading print this tiny," Dorian said, and opened the book. "Well, let's have a gander at this man, then." He squinted with great drama and started reading. " 'Robin as a rovin boy, rantin, rovin, rantin, rovin ... Robin was a rovin boy, rantin rovin Robin.' Alex, you should be ashamed!"

Alex blushed, tried to step away, seeing that he'd goofed, but Dorian got him by that velvet lapel and made him listen.

" 'Kiss'd yestreen, kiss'd yestreen'—what kind of word is 'yestreen'?"

"I'm sorry," Alex moaned. "He's not Greek, he's not classical, he's just a simple country poet from a simple country, Gavin said. You know I can't tell good poetry from bad. The scholars just couldn't whack it into my head. God knows they tried."

"I tried too," Dorian said, thumbing through the little volume. "You were hopeless. 'Farewell to the mountains, high cover'd with snow. Farewell to the straths and green valleys below. Farewell to the forests and wild-hanging woods' —by the time he says farewell to everything, he'll be back!"

"You're belittling me, you know."

"Too easy."

"All right! Then give me the book back, and I'll throw it away!"

"Wait. Let me read a little slower."

"Oh, please don't."

Dorian grinned, enjoying the torture.

"Sh, sh, sh, let's listen to him. Talk, Burns. 'But pleasures are like poppies spread. . . . You seize the flower, its bloom is shed . . .' "

Dorian paused, then—not a stop, just a pause—perhaps he was reading ahead, and something moved that had never moved before inside him. As he read, his voice grew softer and softer, until it was nearly gone.

" 'Or like the snow falls in the river . . . A moment white . . . then melts . . . forever . . .' "

Something happened before Alex's eyes.

Something *changed*.

"Dory?"

With a tight swallow Dorian murmured, "I know exactly what he means. . . . Alex, what have you done to me?"

He flipped a few more pages, scanned, then read again. Every touch of mockery was gone from his voice now.

" ' . . . If man's superior might Dare invade your native right, swiftly seek on clanging wings Other lakes and other springs . . . And the foe you cannot brave . . . Scorn, at least, to be his slave . . .' "

A shudder moved through Dorian and left Alex completely behind.

Alex flinched when Dorian suddenly looked up and snapped, "Is this man alive? Can I write to him?"

"What?" Alex shook his head. "Put the book down," he said. "I'm sorry I gave it to you. Dorian, I want to speak to you seriously about something, very seriously."

"I want to read all of these."

"Forget them! Put it down!"

Dorian stood up straight, folded his arms with the book tucked neatly in his armpit, and demanded, "All right, then talk."

"This just confirms what I've been thinking about lately."

"And what was that?"

"The whole time I was at Charlottesville," Alex said, "there was one dominant thought plaguing me."

"Which was?"

"That you should be there with me."

"Ridiculous."

For months Alex had been steeling himself for that 'ridiculous,' and still it hit him like a sledge.

"Why is it?" he demanded. "There is hardly a professor on the grounds who can hold his own beside you, Dory."

"Same old tune, Alex?" Dorian complained. "You keep forgetting the operative element." He pointed to his right arm, at the scar, and added, "I is a cuffee, sez de law."

"Ridiculous," Alex shot back.

"Ah, sweet revenge."

Bounding to his feet now, unable to contain himself, Alex knotted his hands and said, "I was talking to Uncle Nick about why he first came to Tidewater. Do you know why he did?"

Dorian paused, knowing he was falling into a trap of some kind, then carefully tested, "To find a husband for Mother."

"No, I mean why he picked Tidewater!"

"There you've got me."

"Dory—" Alex took a deep breath, forcing himself to calm down. "Dorian, Tidewater is the cradle of the nation, as they say. Everything started here. America started here. This was where the English made the first settlement in the New World. The nation's first legislative body started here. The first church. The first white suffrage. The first free school."

"Alex . . ."

"No, let me finish. I love to hear it, don't you? Did you know Tidewater hosted the first trial by jury?"

"Yes, I did."

Alex waved his hands nervously. "Of course. What could I have been thinking?"

Dorian smiled with only a touch of modesty, then folded his arms, turning the Burns book around and around in his fingers like a wheel.

"The very first truly fair trial on the continent," Alexander went on. "Imagine that."

"I'm imagining."

"A whole civilization started here, and . . . Dorian, did you know slavery started here?"

"Incorrect," Dorian said. "Slavery started with the Sumerians and Assyrians, roughly four millennia before Christ, around the First Dynasty of Ur. They also started language. Both have been around a while."

"You know what I mean."

"Then be specific."

Alex cocked a hip in frustration. "Where was I?"

"Enslaving Tidewater."

"Oh, yes." Alex smiled then and said, "That sounds funny."

Dorian nodded, leaning back against the sill, his thumb ruffling through the small vellum pages. "It would look funny also."

"As *I* was saying, Tidewater's a pageant of new American beginnings. Civic, domestic, religious, political . . . all steps forward. In a little lowland triangle a hundred fifty miles by a hundred twenty, all those things took seed." Alex found himself standing in the wedge of sunlight at the doorway and squinted out onto the lush fields of Plentiful beyond the yard. His own voice was a revelation when he finally found the words to a thought he had never dared utter before this moment. "The bell is tolling for slavery in this nation. Soon all these people will find themselves free."

Tightening his arms about himself, Dorian pushed down a shiver at the tone in Alex's voice.

"I know," he said quietly. "That's why I've always encouraged them to learn to spell. I believe the day will come when they'll need it. Immigrants are flocking from Europe, and they're very hard workers. Any one of them is three times the worker that any slave is. Eventually it'll be cheaper to keep a paid work force than to keep slaves. Their output per capita—"

"No!" Alex blurted. "Slavery is an emotional issue. It has to end with a crash!"

"Alex, what are you trying so miserably to say?"

"Slavery must end! It must be consigned to the past, with all the other kinds of slavery. I *want* to see it happen. Slavery started here in Tidewater, Dorian . . . and I want it to end here.''

Behind him Dorian's expression changed subtly, but dramatically. His shoulders drew inward.

"What?''

Alex turned to him and stood squarely before Dorian, poised for revolution.

"It could!'' he gasped. "It should! Tidewater should be the birthplace of complete human freedom!''

Dorian's arms fell open, and he vaulted to his feet, horrified. "Alex!''

The small distance closed between them as Alex announced, "I want to start it!''

Letting the little Burns volume tumble to the dirty floor, Dorian grabbed his brother hard by both arms until Alex winced. "Close your mouth!''

Alex gripped Dorian's arms, and they stood bracing each other like wrestlers.

"I want to bring you out into the public eye, Dorian! I want to publicize you and the fact that we're true brothers by blood. Once people see you and hear you talk, why, they'll have no choice but to admit—''

Dorian's hand cracked across Alex's face and silenced him. Dorian's eyes took on that devil edge as he pushed Alex, still staggering from his blow, back against the wall of the shed. "Shut your mouth, do you hear me? Never!''

"I'm going to become an abolitionist,'' Alex insisted, ignoring the pain in his face. "You can get us the national attention we need—''

"You'll get a pine box, is what you'll get! Quit this talk!''

"Dorian, for God's sake—''

"God can go to hell! For *my* sake shut up! Shut your mouth and never bring this up again.'' He gave Alex a final shove, then fiercely added, "I'm not yours to parade!''

Dust floated around them. The sunlight remained undisturbed on the floor, sparking in the air, and the sudden silence was palpable.

Sweat had risen under Dorian's collar. He pushed back from Alex and drew in a shuddering breath. "Such talk. How dare you assume you can use me.''

The expression on Alex's face clearly showed he hadn't thought of that aspect. He licked his dry lips and tried to add up the situation, knowing that Dorian was already equations ahead of him.

"Dory. . . I never meant to insult you."

"Well, you did."

With great flourish he straightened his dirty shirt and the embroidered belt Alex had just given him. The seconds ticked away. They were both breathing hard.

Dorian fussed with his shirt much longer than necessary, then stooped and scraped the Burns book off the layer of filth on the floor.

"I am a Southern white man's worst nightmare," he said. "And you want to display their nightmare broadly before them? Why, I'd be shot through the head two seconds before somebody shot you."

Alex rubbed his arms where Dorian had gripped him so hard. "I believe in this cause."

"It's not your cause."' Dorian glared at him, angry. "Let others do the freeing. You're the son of a prominent Virginia planter. If you participate, you humiliate all the fine people of the South, both slave owners and not. The thing'll get done in its own proper time. Let somebody else do it. And leave me out."

The sense of those words rang through Alexander Wallace, chiming on his bones just as Dorian hoped it would.

Dorian swung away from him, hiding his expression from Alex, hiding the real concern. He didn't care about slavery one way or the other, but he did care about a certain fellow in a dapper blue daycoat. A cause will inevitably have martyrs, he knew.

"I don't know what to do," Alex whispered. "I want to change your life. All I see as I go deeper into Virginia is the sickness of slavery, and that it gave me all I have. These fine clothes . . . my education . . . my opportunities . . . how can I fail to repay the debt? What would I be if I failed?" He slumped against the wall where Dorian had pushed him and stared at the floor. "For two hundred years people have been treated like animals and all for what? Money. Dirty money."

"There's nothing wrong with money, Alexander."

"It's the root of all evil."

"No, it isn't."

Alex looked up at him.

"Don't plunge into that trap," Dorian said. "Here. Look at it."

He dug into his pocket, pulled out a handful of odd bills and dumped them on the desk. The bills unfolded slowly and lay in a crinkled heap on top of a book. Money to run the plantation's daily business.

"Money," Dorian said, "is the root of all good. Look at it, Alex. It's nothing to feel guilty about. It's a tool, nothing more. A hammer. It has no sense of purpose, no will, no sense of right or wrong. Once it leaves your hands, it has no conscience. Every bit spent goes to make somebody else a little richer. It's a paper hammer, to be used to break or to build. The root of all *good*, Alex. Your legacy, to be used as you choose. Here. Take it." He scooped up the bills and crammed them into Alex's hand. "It's no use to me."

He stalked past Alex and right out into the daylight. Only when his brother appeared at the shed door and called, "Dorian—" did he pause and turn brusquely.

The sun glinted on his black curls and the sharp sickles of his brows, but nothing could upstage the iron-hard determination in his eyes. He clamped the Burns tidbit to his chest in some kind of defiance.

"I'm glad to see you, Alex," he said, "but don't speak to me again until these bats leave your head, all right? Thank you. *Andeeo.*"

There were shadows upon the face of the young man who entered the room. He came in as he always did—hesitantly, like a guilty thief slipping into a vault. There were shadows behind his eyes.

The curls of his hair were nearly navy blue in this light, like spilled ink, and they brushed the collar of his velvet jacket. His shoulders were very straight in that jacket.

"*Kalimehrah, Mother, poss ista?*"

Iphigenia Wallace looked up and nodded her approval. "*Kahlah*. Dressed for lunch, I see. Good."

Dorian strode to her, still moving like a shadow.

"You didn't tell me Alexander was coming back, Mother," he said. "I'll get back at you somehow."

She loved to look into his eyes. Behind the harshness there was a strange bemusement with life, a glittering reminder that he could read minds. Each time she looked in there, she saw the baby she had saved from who knows what. She was the one person besides Yula that Dorian utterly failed to ever make nervous.

She continued what she'd been doing—drawing black tea from the huge old silver samovar into a Dresden teapot. Because her childbearing years had been cut short by Rose Dimitra's difficult birth, time had been good to her. But for a few faint lines on her face and a few threads of silver in her hair, she was still the emblem of her heritage that Dimitrios had promised she would remain. The Southern way of life had been mastered by her but had not mastered her. She was still a Greek woman, still doing what she had been sent here to do. And she still had the elegant clipped accent of her homeland that was symphonic to Dorian after a day in the yard.

"Your Uncle Nick and your father have gone to Norfolk," she said. "Lunch will be upon the half hour."

He leaned forward on the china cabinet and accused, "You're avoiding me."

Her mouth tightened. She tried not to smile, but her eyes gave her away. "I wanted to surprise you."

"I was surprised. You know I hate to have any of the house flock see me in my work clothes."

She turned a shoulder at him. "I told you," she repeated, "it was a surprise. Was I to say, 'Dorian, dress for nothing? No one is coming'?"

She still pronounced his name with the rolled *r*, as though she loved the sound of it—and she did.

"What is this?" she asked, pushing back his jacket to look at the embroidered belt.

"A present from Alex. He keeps trying to give me things."

"I don't recognize this. Is it something from the house?"

"No, I believe he turned highwayman and robbed some Cypriot immigrants on his way back from Charlottesville."

"Oh. Very lovely."

Pulling a silver tray toward her, Iphigenia arranged several cups upon it, then stepped past him, but he caught his hand in the crook of her elbow and howled, "Ho, no you don't. Draw rein and talk to me."

She peered up at him with false indignation. "About what? What makes you speak to your Mother this way?"

"Well . . . I have an observation."

"I'll blow the trumpet," she drawled, and tried to step away again.

But he was serious.

"Mother, please stay. Put the tray down."

Iphigenia paused. The arrogance had gone from his tone, fled like something scared, and with Dorian that was as good as an alarm.

She narrowed her eyes in wordless question.

Having put himself on the spot, Dorian found himself suddenly reluctant—and he wasn't used to reluctance. For years he had refrained from sticking his neck into family business, having had it quite literally burned in that he wasn't exactly in the family. But in an odd way, he was the *center* of this family.

At times like this he used it. In fact, he deliberately lapsed into complete Greek, in case an Amerikanos happened to overhear.

"I want to speak to you about Alex," he finally said.

Instantly she shot back, "What about Alex?"

Dorian's eyes flashed. He simply couldn't intimidate her. Shifting where he stood, he started over.

"Alex is going to be twenty-one very soon."

"Yes?"

"But he's gotten forty-year-old ideas in his head somehow."

Iphigenia smiled. "Yes. He is like you that way."

"We're not talking about me. Mother, I think you should send him away somewhere." When Iphigenia's brow puckered in misunderstanding, he forced the issue. "Away, you know. To another university, farther away. Europe. Or military academy. Perhaps Austria. Have you given any thought to

Austria? Or even England would be good for him. Give him a more . . . cosmopolitan view of the world. He needs that. Right now he's got Tidewater moss for brains.''

Iphigenia knew Dorian well. And now she realized why he was speaking Greek and only Greek. There were no lapses back and forth, as was common in a bilingual household. He had something else in mind, something he wasn't telling her, but the fact that he would come here at this time of day, well dressed, and shoot an unrelated suggestion at her was in itself an advertisement:

She studied his face with its fine angles and sharp expression. He was her only Greek child. All the others had grown up American somehow. Dorian was the only one who had never lost the dream of Dimitrios Trözene and the Macedonian people who hoped to seed themselves in the new land. There were several Macedonian aristocrats now married into Southern society, but like Iphigenia most of them had watched their children grow away from the line dances and the native cuisine, and some even the language. At least all four of her children still spoke fluent Greek. Of course, they all spoke French too . . . someday would they lose the sense of difference? Would one just be another language, like the other?

Perhaps so, but not for Dorian, never for Dorian. Dorian was the only one of her children without a drop of her Greek blood, yet he was the only true Ellenekos among them.

But send Alexander so far away? Send any of her babies away?

The very idea was devastating to a mother.

Dorian read her thoughts.

"Mother," he said softly, "he must go. Far away . . . or he'll be in danger.''

She scowled. "Danger? What is this talk?''

Dorian paused again but saw no better or kinder way.

He leaned toward her, but there was no word in Greek for what he had to say. Suddenly his only choice was English.

Quietly he asked, "Do you know what an abolitionist is?''

Greek or not, immigrant or not, cloistered, womanly, protected or not, there was no human being in the South who didn't know.

A long, uneasy hush folded over the two of them as they stood alone in the plantation's dining room.

And the subject was given an abrupt, queenly dismissal.

Iphigenia collected herself and picked up the silver tray once again, as though to simply walk away from the problem.

She stepped away from him, away from this ugly picture, refusing to acknowledge Dorian's sudden disappointment in what seemed to be her final choice.

"Lunch will be in the garden," she said. "I will expect you to be there."

The Greek garden was a settled place now that it was covered with twenty-odd years of purple clematis and jasmine vines. The sterility of newness was long gone, the stone tables were somewhat worn, the statues gazed across Plentiful with comforting familiarity these days. They had pretty much memorized the scenery, and it was almost as though their sculpted faces had finally relaxed.

It remained the favorite place of the Greek natives on Plentiful. Nick Varvaresos, Iphigenia Trözene Wallace, and their Greek servants often came here to be alone and to be Greek. More often than any of the other children, Dorian had been with them.

And sometimes, like today, when Luke Wallace was away on business, Iphigenia drew all her children around her and served a truly Greek meal out there. Over two decades ago she had accepted the fact that Lucas would never receive Dorian as one of them, and so her family must always be fragmented, either without her son or without her husband, never with both. The children had grown up accepting the strange arrangement, for even at very young ages they understood that Dorian was in true danger somehow. Children are keen to family whisperings, and Dorian was always consigned to be a whisper.

Today, however, he strode out into the sunlight, dressed in the fine plantation clothes of a young man of the landed gentry. It was one of those good days. Alex was there, the core of attention, and so were the two young mistresses of Plentiful.

The eldest spied him first across the sprawling lawn and rushed toward him, holding her wide skirt up to her ankles.

"*Tha thelate na khorespsete?*" she called.

In answer Dorian reached out and caught her, and they danced a waltz across the lawn, taking wide graceful steps even though there was no music.

"Good morning, sister of mine," he greeted, spinning her beneath one arched arm.

"Good morning," Lydia returned, then commented, "You still have sawdust in your hair."

"I got dressed on short notice," he said. "No one told me Alex was expected."

"Why should we tell you anything?" she laughed, and he wheeled her between the statues.

Lydia Wallace had grown up beautiful. Not the kind of beauty that filled men with lust, but the kind that made conversations fall off into silence. A soft beauty, for she was far more modest now than she ever had been as a child. Her hair was a full umber cloud billowing from a single part over her left brow. Her wide-set eyes were the brown of nutshells, and though there was almost no color on her milky cheeks, her lips had a touch of mauve that never went away. They were very full lips, very even, very Grecian.

Watching from between Alexander and her mother, Iphigenia's last baby, Rose Dimitra, now sixteen, was much plainer.

Curiously she possessed exactly the same features and coloring as her sister, but somehow the details didn't come together with the same effect. Shadows and sunlight fell with the same shapes on their faces, but the overall effect was lost on Rose; somehow Lydia was different. Unexpectedly Lydia was the modest one, and Rose Dimitra had developed a particular single-mindedness—she never thought about anything except precisely what she was doing at that moment, whatever the moment was. She was a girl utterly without concern for the future or the past, only the present. Dorian had always found this particularly interesting about Rose, for he was a student of the gigantic past and the sprawling future, and Rose simply didn't care what had ever happened or what

ever might. She'd always been a funny little girl, and now she
was a funny young woman.

"Well, Alexander?" Dorian called as he spun Lydia again,
leaning away to avoid her huge swinging skirt. "Isn't there
another young lady here who likes to dance?"

Rose smiled up at Alex. "Yes, there is!"

Alex shifted his feet. "I can't dance worth beans, and you
both know it. You're cornering me."

Dorian waltzed Lydia closer and commented, "Well, somebody had better unseat you from that university arrogance."

"No surprise it would be you. All right, Rose Dimitra. If
your toes suffer, speak to Dorian about it."

He reached out for her hand, but Iphigenia stopped him.

"No, children, no dancing. Come here, all of you. While
the servants are still inside, I wish to speak to all of you."

She stood between them and the buffet of Macedonia
cuisine that had been laid out on one of the stone tables and
gestured them to sit down facing her, as if to say there would
be no eating before they paid their dues of listening to her.
This made all her children instantly curious.

"Who's getting married this time, Mother?" Dorian asked.
He sat down next to Alex and turned to his brother suddenly
with a conspiratorial grin. "Alex, is there something you
forgot to tell me?"

Glowering, Alex asked, "What do you mean?"

Lydia leaned forward on the stone bench. Her cloud of hair
came forward and covered her bare shoulders. "The last time
Mother made an announcement was when Aunt Pandora
found a husband and moved to Blacksburg."

With a nod Alex said, "Ah."

"There is no one getting married," Iphigenia said, reclaiming
their attention. She ignored the fact that the four of them sat
there in a line, grinning and glancing at each other just as
they had when they were little, and she got a bizarre satisfaction out of knowing what the next moment would bring.

She squared her shoulders and clasped her hands, resting
them against the fullness of her skirt.

"I have made a decision," she said slowly. "I will discuss
it with your father, but it is a decision I shall not change. A
family decision, and every one of you shall be affected for a

long time to come. It is part of your grandfather's dream. I am ashamed that I had not thought of it in earlier years, so it is overdue."

She had their attention now and took a long pause to cement her hold over them.

Her children were handsome and learned, but their scope, as the eldest had pointed out, was limited to the elite of Virginia, and that had to change. No one understands like an immigrant how truly vast the world is, and how diverse, she thought. Iphigenia knew as she gazed at the four of them, that she had somehow failed in fulfilling her father's vision of an American family. She had allowed her children to be caught in the comfortable spin of Plentiful. It was time to expand their world.

"Children," she said, "we are all going on a long voyage. We are going to Greece."

A hush swept over the garden.

Alexander's mouth fell open, but there was no sound. His own plans for the future suddenly twisted before his eyes. Beside him Rose Dimitra blinked several times and openly gaped, for she couldn't envision it.

Lydia pressed her hand to her lips and gushed, "Mother!"

But there was no reaction like Dorian's.

He instantly lost his focus on the present and was already staring across the ages.

His whisper rushed across the garden.

"*Greece . . .*"

★

CHAPTER TWENTY-TWO

———— ★ ————

"Dorian? Are you packed? Where are you?"

"Present and accounted for."

Alex poked his head into their father's library, and sure enough, there was Dorian, hunched over the old desk.

"What are you doing? A letter? You've picked this moment to scratch a complaint to someone? We're leaving any minute!"

"Yes," Dorian said, "but I want this to precede me."

"Precede you to where?"

"Scotland."

Alex stopped short.

A tremor went through him. As he approached the desk and dared to look at what Dorian was doing, it got worse.

"Dorian . . . whom are you writing to?"

"Him," Dorian said, nodding to one side. "I have to tell him what his poems are doing to me."

Alex looked at the little vellum pages of the Robert Burns book, which had been so read over now that the volume was fanning. His heart took a plunge.

"You're serious?" he asked darkly.

The pen continued to pull at the stationery.

"Never more," Dorian said, lost in his letter. "After spending my life with Xenophon, Aeschylus, and Sophocles, who'd have thought a farmer poet would get so deeply into me? I'm intending to shake his hand when we reach Britain."

Even the joyous prospect of Greece couldn't raise Alex from the terrible realization that hit him right then. He had grown up thinking—knowing—that Dorian was brilliant, that Dorian had a finger on the most complex thoughts in the world, and never until now had he realized how utterly isolated his brother had been. Much more than isolation of proximity, but an isolation of perception. Dorian saw the world as though he were floating above it, detached.

Could Dorian stand the outside world? And here they were, about to drag him out into it!

Mother, we'll have to protect him. He'll be all right as long as we stay beside him every step of the way.

Revelation knocked Alex in the heart as he gazed down at a profound innocence in Dorian that he rarely, if ever, had seen before. No wonder the Burns simplicity had cut Dorian to the quick. It *was* Dorian.

How am I going to tell him?

"Can I sign your name to this?" Dorian asked, not looking up. "I can't tell you what these poems have done for me. I've read the whole book five times. There's an elemental humanity that even Shakespeare overcomplicated, Alex. I can't pay you adequately for adding this grist to my mill."

"Stop—" Alex put his hand on Dorian's arm and pulled the pen from the paper. "Stop."

Dorian looked up at him, and it horrified Alex to discover that, no, there wasn't even a glint of teasing in those black eyes. He wasn't being put on at all. Why, *why* couldn't Dorian have been putting him on?

Pressing a hand on Dorian's arm, Alex sighed. "Dory... Robert Burns is ... dead."

Color flushed Dorian's cheeks as he sat gaping up at Alex.

He's going to think I'm pulling a cruel joke on him, Alex thought desperately. *I can't mock him this way—and it is mockery. Why did such a mind have to grow up in a stockade!*

Dorian stood up, his blunder ill concealed. "Dead? When?"

"About forty years before we were born."

Dorian's features grew drawn. The small of his back knotted. Suddenly he perceived himself for what he was.

Embarrassed in front of Alex, in front of himself, and even in front of Robert Burns, he blinked. Suddenly all he could see through the smoke was a young poet's corpse lying in a grave. This voice, dead? Forty, fifty, sixty years of grass forming over the heart that pumped out the words on those little pages? Dorian had never had to accept the death of Sophocles. Sophocles was *supposed* to be dead.

He gaped then at the paper in front of him. *My dear Mr. Burns* . . .

"Dorian?" Alex attempted.

The statuesque lips twitched, the head drooped a little, and Dorian's shoulders tightened. Suddenly he crushed a palm over his eyes, then grabbed his own wrist and searched for a pulse.

"Alex, help me!" he burst. "I'm having an idiot attack!"

Relief plunged through Alex.

Emotions collapsed in Dorian like a house of cards. The self-conscious hand fell away from his forehead and clapped to his chest, and he blurted, "Think they'll deliver this to his grave, then?"

Alex folded his arms and leaned on the piano. Satan's smile crept across his brother's mouth, and the two of them lingered there in the room, in silent affection, chuckling at themselves. The useless pen hung in Dorian's other hand. He digested his silly act and stared at the ink scratchings on the paper, wondering what he could have been thinking of!

"Burns just doesn't *read* like a dead man," he gasped. "I'm used to Greeks being dead! I had a suspicion about Shakespeare—God, how could I be so fallible!"

"Can't stand to see a chink in your armor, eh, Dory?" Alex accused.

Dorian shot him a look. "You should've seen your own face!" And he laughed again, slumping deeper in the chair. He scooped up the half-written letter and shook it until it rattled. "My dear Mr. Burns! Witch piss! If you ever tell anyone about this, I'll reconstruct your appearance."

"I intend to tell everyone," Alex retorted.

Dorian shrugged lamely. He grew a little quieter now, and his chuckling tapered off. He let the letter float once again to the desktop and sat there gazing at it.

"Dead indeed! This man doesn't want to be dead, Alex. He doesn't read like a corpse. Maybe that's what fooled me, think so? You know, I feel as though I've lost a friend."

Leaning near him, Alex indulged in a soft smile and grieved a little too. But it was for the death of something else.

"My God, everything's been such a spin!"

Alexander threw the last of his luggage onto the pack wagon and looked across the carriageway at two large coaches that held most of his family and their Greek servants. Then he turned to his right. "Where's your luggage?"

Dorian looked at him for a moment as if he'd forgotten English, then said, "It's already aboard."

"Just that one little satchel? Why there's hardly more than a change of stockings and a clean shirt in there!"

"What else do I need?"

"Don't you want to take some of the books, or any papers to write your thoughts down upon?"

"They're not mine to take."

Irritated, Alexander checked the harness again. It was the fourth time he'd fussed with that harness.

"Do you at least have . . . the little . . . you know."

Dorian slapped the side of his tall riding boot and said, "Yes, he's right here."

Sunlight winked in Alex's eyes. "Are you feeling better now, Dorian? I'm so sorry about that."

"Nonsense," Dorian whispered, embarrassed all over again. "Next time I'll check on a man's health before I write to him." He bumped Alex roughly. "I'm glad it happened in front of you and not somebody important.'

Alex laughed, anxious to get on with the journey.

He squinted into the sunlight. Several yards away Iphigenia supervised the boarding of the two coaches. It was nearly time to go. Their ship sailed at sunset.

Rubbing his hands, Dorian looked down the driveway toward Boss and Iphigenia. "*Yiati arghi tosso?*" he grumbled.

"I don't know," Alex responded. "Father's stalling, I think. Everything's happened so fast, up until the last few minutes. . . . Uncle Nick and Pilos must be halfway to Europe by now, if the winds are with them."

"Yes. It was smart of Boss to send them on an earlier ship.

Imagine Boss being smart. Wouldn't want Grandpapa to have too big a shock all at once. I imagine this snow on your head'll be enough to set him blinking.''

"Just keep telling him Alexander the Great was blond, and I'll be treated like conquering royalty.'' He paused then, gripping the wagon rein, and reservedly wondered, "How long do you think Mother expects us to stay in Greece?''

Dorian's answer was crisp. "Plenty long, I hope. Years, I hope,'' he said, and then involuntarily thought of Yula and got a sudden jab of regret.

"I can't stay that long, Dory,'' Alex said softly. "I have things to do here. In the United States.''

"Yes, become an abolitionist,'' Dorian drawled. "Never fear, gringo. That problem isn't going anywhere. You'll have plenty to do after you finish a sound education. Then you can come back here and carry that sword to your heart's content.'' He hooked his hand over Alex's shoulder and steered him away from that harness. "Meanwhile, we'll go over there and let our grandparents bask in our light. Uncle Nick'll be telling them how wonderful we are, and how we'll turn Macedonia downside up.''

Alex surveyed him fondly for several seconds. "This is a coup d'etat for you. A chance to actually leave the grounds . . . you're nervous. I can tell. You can't hide it from me, Dory, and I know you've been trying.''

"No, not at all. I'm calm as a cat.''

"A cat with white knuckles,'' Alex said sympathetically. "I can't believe Father's acquiescing to your going along. I suppose he senses that Mother wouldn't have it any other way.''

"He's been cold as a well digger's ass on the subject since Mother told him. They have the oddest relationship. Besides,'' Dorian added, "I'd kiss Satan's horn for a chance to go to Greece.''

"I believe you would.''

As they walked side by side, their gazes fell simultaneously upon the robust figure of Luke Wallace, his trimmed beard now almost completely white in the midday sun, his full head of hair, though still the color of iron, now was also boldly threaded with white. He stood near the front wagon, accepting good-bye hugs from his daughters while Iphigenia waited near them in her traveling bonnet and coat. Several paces behind them, over on the lawn, two of the black drivers stood around, probably enjoying the lull.

"*Ee thalassa ene poli esiki*," Alex murmured, lowering his voice even though his father couldn't have understood anyway. *The sea is very calm.*

"Yes, very calm," Dorian murmured back. They both looked down the circular driveway at Luke Wallace. "It worries me."

"He'd probably outright refuse if you asked to go to Richmond," Alex commented. "It's only because you're going so far out of his realm that he doesn't buck. He can't see that far past his nose."

"Likely," Dorian agreed, because Luke Wallace no longer mattered to him. His mind was already in Athens.

"Did you say farewell to your little mama?"

"No, she thinks I'm doing the laundry today."

Alex blinked at him, then laughed so suddenly that he nearly tripped. It was the first time he'd smiled since the subject of this voyage had come up.

"Lord, Dorian, I wish I could be as incombustible as you!"

"Yes, I'm quite flameproof, aren't I? That's all right—the world's better off in awe of something. Might as well be me." He smiled wistfully, and Yula's face formed in his mind. "She'll be all right. When I told her Iphigenia was taking me to Athens . . . Alex, that little cuffee woman just about shoved me out the door. She knows how much my soul wants to be there."

"Thought you didn't have a soul."

"Slip of the tongue."

He automatically fell behind Alex as they approached Lucas and Iphigenia. Through the open door of the carriage, Rose Dimitra was commenting, "I just can't imagine being away from Plentiful for a whole year. . . . I just can't."

And Lydia instantly clipped, "We've spent our whole lives memorizing Plentiful. It's time we looked at something new. And Plentiful will be here forever, so just—"

"—arrangements have been made for passage all the way

through to Athens," Luke Wallace was telling his wife. He handed her several papers in succession. "All is paid for in advance. You get two nights in Gibraltar and one in Napoli. Better take them to rest up. I'm sure it's all pretty over there, but you don't want to arrive in Athens looking like bilge rats. Now, you'll have to pick up the *Clytaemnestra* in Napoli, and she'll carry you straight through to Athens. I've known the captain for years. He's the same man who brought you to America. You can present him with this letter and this extra payment for picking you up on short notice." He handed the last papers to Iphigenia and hooked his thumbs into his waistcoat pockets. "Nick will have to be arranging transportation from Athens to Salonika, and I've not a clue what he'll arrange. If he fails to meet you or to leave instructions with the port authority, I'll charge Alexander to take care of things. Can you do it, Alex?"

Alex gave him the obligatory nod and said, "Yes, Father, I'll see that the women aren't left stranded in an uncivilized tract like Athens." He flinched and came dangerously close to giggling when Dorian poked him with a sharp finger from behind.

Lucas's cheeks took on a slight purplish cast as the joke flew past him. Involuntarily his eyes flipped to Dorian for a terrible instant.

Then he took Iphigenia's elbow and ushered her toward the carriage. "All aboard then. No looking back. It's the best way."

But Iphigenia drew to one side, paused, and looked at her two sons. She gestured to the carriage. "Alex, Dorian . . ."

Her message was clear. When they were both safely on board, she would also get in.

Alex hesitated, seeing something in her gesture that scared him. He came forward, stepping up onto the footboard, but slowly, as though to guard Dorian as he too reached for the carriage.

No slave, though, is held by a tighter bond than the words that held Dorian to Plentiful. Luke Wallace reached out with his hand and for one of the rare times in their lives, he touched his hated son.

His hand clamped around Dorian's upper arm. As he did

that, the two armed negroes behind him each took a calculated step forward. Their message was quite clear, quite planned.

All movement stopped, and some hearts as well.

Iphigenia's brows drew tight. "Lucas?"

Her husband faced her without the slightest hesitation and made his terse little announcement.

"He may not go."

Dorian's innards marbleized as he stood there with Lucas's hand clamped on his arm. His feet were suddenly ankle deep in the driveway, his hopes cracking before his eyes.

From the windows of the second carriage, a gaggle of Greek faces appeared, staring, waiting to see how the drama would play out.

Nearby, Lydia's cry actually echoed inside the foremost carriage.

"Father!"

The carriage shook as she crammed herself halfway out the nearest window until the width of her skirts stopped her.

Iphigenia pushed between Lucas and Dorian and squared off before her husband.

"Why do you wait until now to say this, Lucas?" she demanded.

Alex too came crashing down from the footboard. "Father, what is the true meaning of this?"

All these sounds came clattering at once, giving Luke a choice of whose protest he would address.

He stepped back from his wife and faced his legitimate son. "This is a bargain struck before you were born," he said. "Do as you're told, Alex."

His son's face turned blotchy.

"Am I held to bargains made before I was born?"

"We all are," Luke said, so calmly that it made them all worry. "Ask your mother. It was she who did the bargaining."

The carriage shook. Lydia pressed against the window frame. "So this is why you insisted on sending Uncle Nick away on an earlier ship!" she cried.

From inside, Rose Dimitra's voice trickled, "For shame, Papa."

Iphigenia's voice smothered them both. "This has been weeks in the planning! You have always known I would take my son to Greece, yet you do not mention this until now? Why do you keep silent? Are you a coward?"

With a very disturbing, perhaps foreshadowing, calmness, Luke raised his eyebrows and actually *lowered* his voice.

"You deluded yourself, then, didn't you, Genny?" he stated firmly. "I've been kind enough not to constantly remind you of our bargain all these years, but it's not a thing a person forgets. You knew twenty-odd years ago that he couldn't go, and you knew it weeks ago, and you know it now."

"The bargain was wrong!" she cried. "You bind me to a young bride's promise!"

"The bargain was right. I understand that you did the right thing for yourself. I warned you then what kind of life he would lead, and this is not my fault. Don't look at me. Look into *his* black eyes and explain to him what you agreed to that day. Explain to *him*."

Lucas must have been planning this for all these weeks. He was well rehearsed, not even close to losing his temper.

It was Alex who burst from carriageside, actually pushed Dorian back with a protective hand, and did the same on the other side to his mother. There was less than a foot between his chest and his father's.

When he drew his voice up from the caldron inside, it had a dangerous reserve.

"All my life I've watched you hate him," he said to his father. "Somehow I've managed to keep from hating you because you were my father and I mattered to you and I was your heir. If you do this, you're nothing but a whore to your own conventions, and you don't deserve an heir."

He paused, as if waiting to see if anything changed in his father's face.

When nothing did, Alex knotted his fists against his thighs and said, "Consider yourself without one. It's very difficult to sail half a ship."

A hundred emotions passed across Luke Wallace's face,

but the decision had been made, and he was sticking to it. True, a flash of hesitation appeared there when Alex disowned himself, but it was soon squelched. He simply would not have it said that he accepted a slave as one of his children. Dorian had come between him and his wife, between him and social respect, and now between him and his son simply by existing.

But Dorian knew there was more than his simple existence at work here.

He stood abrasively silent, his eyes burning into the dirt. There was no point in even looking up. Boss had every intention of Dorian's staying on Plentiful until the day he died, and the sooner the better. In that instant he realized there hadn't been any wool over Lucas's eyes all these years at all, as he'd so smugly assumed. Boss knew Dorian had been managing Plentiful. Somehow he knew, and somehow that knowledge made itself clear right now in the planter's too-calm voice. And there was something else . . . Lucas knew his family—his wife, his daughters, his only son—listened to Dorian and not to him. They always listened to Dorian.

He knew.

He nailed them to their own cross with piercing, unshielded eyes, so that they could see that he knew, and so they could feel good and guilty about it. So they could see that he *didn't* feel guilty.

And just to be sure, he had brought the two armed slave drivers along. Now everyone understood why they carried weapons.

They never aimed their pistols at Dorian or did anything so precipitous.

But the pistols were here. And Dorian was a slave.

Alex put room between himself and his father.

"Then I'm not going either," he said. "Let it be on your head to explain to Uncle Nick and Grandpapa."

Under a dozen sets of eyes, he turned away and punctuated his statement by heading toward the pack wagon.

From his own dry mouth, Dorian heard the next words break.

"Get in the carriage, Alex."

Alexander skidded to a halt beside him, staring. "No! I won't."

Chattel slaves had very strong hands, and Dorian's were no exception. He put a grip on Alex's wrist that actually hurt, turned him bodily, and snarled to him, but in Greek.

"For Mother's sake, get in."

"No!" Alex breathed, barely over a whisper.

"For Mother's sake," Dorian sharply repeated, "get in!" He gripped Alex by the shoulders from behind and hissed in his ear, "Trust me and *go*."

He pushed his astonished brother forward to the carriage and with sheer power of presence manipulated Alex into the carriage.

"This is not finished!" Alex gasped.

"Yes it is," Dorian snapped back.

Iphigenia was next for the same shock—Dorian got hold of her with those strong hands and pulled her against him, using the rough hug to whisper to her in her own language, "You've got to go. Alex *needs* to go."

"Dorian—" the Greek woman choked.

But she was on the wagon, sheathed in her own astonishment.

Lucas simply stood back, between his armed guards, watching the anguished, confused faces of his family.

The coachman snapped the reins. The carriages lurched. The last thing Alexander, Iphigenia, and the two daughters saw was a glimpse of Dorian yanking the tied silk jabot from his throat and dropping it at Lucas's feet.

What they did not see, as the carriages and the wagon wobbled out the main gateway, was the velvet jacket also fall to the dirt, then the brocade waistcoat. Sunlight winked on the embroidered belt, for it was the only hint of his Greek life that he didn't leave behind in the dirt.

The half-breed slave turned on his expensive boot heels and headed toward the fields, where he belonged.

In his head rang the harnesses and wheels.

Daylight spent itself out, and nighttime came without the slightest impact.

Nothing had impact anymore.

Dorian spent the day entirely alone, sitting on a rock in the open field where Nick had taught him to shoot and to fling a saber. It was as though Nick had died. He was so far away—Lucas had made sure of that—so unable to help, unable to act as the father he had truly been to Dorian.

There wasn't even a book in Dorian's hand. Not even Burns.

He simply stared the day away and went on staring into the evening, turning a gelid eye on Plentiful.

He was nothing but a slave now. The half of his life that wasn't a slave had disappeared down that road. For a long time there would be no Greeks in the big house, no sisters to tease and laugh with, no Pilos to tell jokes to, no Nick, no Alex, no beloved Iphigenia. Until they came back, he was a slave, completely.

Until this day he'd never been *just* that.

He would go to the yard. He would go to Yula. He would play with Burlie, he would do his work—McCrocklin's work—that apparently Lucas knew he had done all this time... amazing! Was it possible that somewhere inside that short-sighted mass there might be a mind at work?

Inconceivable.

All right. Dorian would be just a slave for a while.

Alex, don't be a fool. Stay in the carriage. Get on the ship. Do as you're told. Sometimes we simply have to do as we're told.

He stood up from the rock. The warmth of sunset had long ago left his clothing. His ivory shirt was chilly now, its dropped sleeves shivering in the night breeze. How late was it?

All right, to the cabins, then. So be it.

But Yula wasn't in her cabin when Dorian pushed the narrow door open and looked for the warmth he needed so much right now. Strangely Burlie was also not there.

Out? This late?

No.

He shot outside, ran to the next cabin, and pounded.

The door opened, and soft golden lamplight made a shape around Jeff's bulk. Behind him his wife and children squinted from their beds.

"Jeff, you see Mama?" Dorian asked, as quietly as possible.

"Yula?" Jeff muttered, rubbing a big hand over his face. "Ain't she in there? I think she sayd she was goin' off to pluck some mushrooms. But dat was . . . lawd if it wasn't sunset."

"Did she take Burlie with her?"

"Don't know that, Dohrian. You goin' lookin'? You want me to come?"

"No, yawl go back to sleep. I look for myself."

"Wasn't you s'pose to be goin' off the grounds today?" Jeff asked then, bending a little closer. "Wasn't today the day?"

"Ain't going no place, Jeff," Dorian told him. "Everything just the same. Go on to bed."

But the big slave hesitated, his wide face rife with empathy. "Boss done that to you. It ain't right, Dohrian. You better than us."

Dorian reached for the doorknob. "I'm no better than you, Jeff. I'm one of you."

He nudged Jeff back into the room and drew the door closed between them.

Then he ran for the woods, where the mushrooms grew.

There was just enough moon in the sky to keep him from running headlong into a tree, but not much more than that.

"Mama!"

Deeper and deeper into the woods he ran, to all the places where the mushrooms grew, but he was completely alone when he got there every time.

"Mama! You here? Mama!"

Finally—finally, he heard movement. Jesus, she must have gotten turned around. She must be waiting for dawn light to help her get back through the woods. *I should've brought a torch. Too cold out here for a skinny cuffee woman and a little boy.*

Then, as he squeezed between two trees beside a creek, his spine exploded—something hit him square in the back.

The air shot from his lungs, and he crashed forward into a tree. The bark scored his arms. He caught himself and managed to stay on his feet. His knees crammed into the tree. His mind reeled with senseless pictures, driven crazy by the pain in his back—someone had known exactly where and exactly how to hit him. His twisting brain recognized the technique—Nick had taught him all those tricks of assault . . . except how the victim feels.

Footsteps shuffled through the ferns at both sides, but his eyes were blinded by flashing colors that made no sense. He could barely stand when he was dragged away from the tree and held firmly between two big men. They were headless men . . . nothing but empty clothing moving beside him in the darkness . . . without hands . . . yet they held him somehow. Wraiths, spooks.

He shook his head hard, gasping. The pain was still there, but he fought for control over it—he had no choice. Sweat on his face and neck turned cold as sleet.

Deliberately he cast a glance to his right, then to his left, and spoke out. "Smile," he said to the men who held him, "so I can see your faces."

The two negro slave drivers simply held him all the tighter, resenting him as they always had. Their black faces were like smoke floating against the night.

With a terrible effort Dorian straightened his legs and bore all of his own weight—in time to focus on the man who came up in front of him.

Dorian instantly comprehended. Bitterness set his lips.

"Evening, Father. Out late, aren't you?"

Lucas glared at him. Strange—he didn't seem to have any expression at all on his face. It was as though he were sleeping with his eyes open.

Behind Lucas were more men, but Dorian had never seen them before. One was a white, the other two negroes. The white man was wide set and dirty, with a bitter twist to his mouth, but in his eyes there was utter impassiveness. He plainly didn't care what the personal situation was and was willing to wait until it ended and he could take over.

Dorian studied them only for an instant before pushing forward toward Lucas.

"Where are Yula and the boy?" he demanded.

"They've run off," Lucas said.

"Yula would never run off without me, you fucking liar."

"I know," his white father agreed. "That's why you have to go too."

God's coldest chill settled across Dorian's shoulders, and

he shivered. His eyes turned to rocks, and he yanked against the men who held him, his teeth gritting.

"Why the boy?" he rasped. "Why Burlie? You paid good money to get him bred!"

Lucas actually took the moment to sigh thoughtfully. Clearly that had been a factor in his decision. "Nobody would believe she left without him. Don't matter . . . I got a good price."

"You rapacious bitch-born pig!" Dorian growled. "Where are they!"

"They're gone, boy, and there's nothing you can do about it!" Lucas blustered. Instantly he fought to regain control. It was the only signal that he might realize he was doing a wrong thing. His hands pressed flat against his thighs, and he added, "I got no choice."

Dorian's voice dropped to a terrible whisper.

"You pig . . . you rapacious, corrupt swine . . . what've you done to us?"

"What I had to do," Lucas said. "I've got to get back control over my plantation and my family."

He stepped through the ferns, and his head tilted slightly in contemplation. He gazed at Dorian—one of the rare times he deigned to look, truly look, at him. He saw Dorian's straight, narrow nose, the downturned eyes and the slight pouches beneath them that gave him such character, the lips shaped as though drawn with a fine pencil, and even the black lashes that almost disappeared in the night. There was almost nothing negroid about his features, yet there was the power and strength of ethnic roots that simply did not exist in his bloodline. It was as if the gods had drawn him from memory, independent of all other humans.

"By Christ . . ." Lucas murmured. "In the moonlight, your face looks just like one of those statues. . . ."

Dorian set his jaw and refused to respond.

The moonlight flowed silently, and only the crickets had opinions right then. The two men glared at each other, each seeing something in the other that he had never seen before.

Lucas broke his own trance and motioned to the white man behind him. "He's all yours. Here are his papers."

He handed over a single envelope that would prove owner-ship, in case anything went awry.

"Thanks," the stranger said.

"Take him, then."

The two drivers from Plentiful yanked Dorian toward the other negroes. Though he twisted against them, he couldn't break their hold, and he knew he couldn't. A moment later his wrists were tied with hemp, and there was a lead rope around his neck. They pulled at him, but he dug his heels into the soil and cranked back toward Lucas.

"So this is you, Father?" he spat. "Iphigenia and Nick keep their bargain, but you break yours?"

Something moved across Lucas's eyes in the dimness, but he stood his ground.

"Death breaks all bargains."

He waved his hand, and the bane was yanked away, without even a chance to give his valedictory address.

When the two other niggers and the white slaver were gone, he gazed long into the forest night without moving. Behind him his own two drivers waited for his next order.

Finally it came.

Lucas stepped over the creek.

"Put his name on a headstone at the slave cemetery. No date."

★

But Pleasures are
like poppies spread,
You sieze the flower,
its bloom is shed;
Or like the snow falls
in the river,
A moment white,
then melts forever.

Robt Burns

PART SIX

★

THE
HANDFUL

CHAPTER TWENTY-THREE

——— ★ ———

1856
CHAPEL MOUNT PLANTATION
ON THE PEEDEE RIVER, SOUTH CAROLINA

Through the befoulment in his memory, men talked. Though
his body was injured, his brain absorbed the conversation.

"We s'pose to kill him. Dem de orders."

*"Why you think I got hold of his papers? He's worth
money. I don't kill nothing that's worth money."*

The earth moved beneath him as though walking with him
on its back. When had he stopped remembering? What had
they done to him?

And how long ago . . . his knees cracked like matchwood as
he tried to moved them. His back ached, but it was a spent
ache, not a fresh one. He felt like warmed-over cabbage.

Had he fought? He'd known Boss intended him to die.
Perhaps he'd fought with those men . . . and lost. His head felt
like something that had lost a fight.

A wagon . . . he was in a wagon.

Through nothing but pure will, Dorian forced his eyes
open.

And blinked into a dozen brown faces. Behind them was
daylight. But which day?

Slaves, on a slave wagon . . . being transported somewhere.
He was one of them.

329

As his mind cleared, he found himself lying lengthwise down the middle of a wagon's floor, actually sitting on the feet of these slaves—chained feet. Their ankle irons cut into his shoulders on both sides.

The slaves glared down at him, but none offered to help him get up in the tight quarters.

"Where is we?" he rasped, but they just continued to glare. He lifted a hand for help, but nobody took it. To these slaves, he was just another mulatto. His white skin would give him no help among these who assumed the white men who put him here knew something about him. A single drop of negro blood was enough for the law. Only his education would set him apart—long enough to get him killed. So he would hide it.

When he tried to move his feet, he couldn't. Someone was sitting on them. His body screamed as he gave up and simply squirmed against the slaves' feet, not caring if he hurt them since they didn't care if he got help. He crushed a few insteps while he turned over, moving piece by piece, muscle by muscle, found a patch of the wagon's bed to brace upon, and heaved himself to a sitting position.

His eyes cleared a little more, and he saw why his feet were heavy—chains.

Chains . . .

Dorian had never worn chains before. The realization hit him like a gunshot.

Everything else was the same—he still wore his dress shirt and breeches, though they were dirty now, and the belt Alex had given him was still around his waist. Apparently the slavers saw no value in it, or it would have surely been gone.

"Shape up! Sit up straight! You over there, get your ass up on the bench!"

Dorian craned his neck—and it almost snapped. Pain shot through his head and down into his shoulders. He hooked his hand around the back of his neck, and sure enough he found a lump—no, two lumps—painfully tender.

One was quite a bit more sore than the other; evidently he'd been hit more than once during the journey.

Journey to where?

He dragged himself onto the bench where the other slaves were lined up, not bothering to nod a thanks to the two who squeezed over for him. They weren't interested in his comfort, he could tell; they just wanted him off their feet. All right, he was off.

Blinking into the daylight, he scanned the scenery—a landscape he'd never seen before. So different! Different shapes to the hills than Plentiful's hills, new types of trees . . . trees with strings of moss hanging like wigs all the way to the ground—he'd never seen a different lay of land before. And there was water on the other side of the road! A river . . . a real river!

Suddenly Dorian was overwhelmed not by his bad luck or the betrayal that had put him here, but by the sheer newness of what was happening to him. His mind suddenly peaked with excitement. Bitterness and discomfort were shunted to a second seat—he was somewhere new! Somewhere *else*! His heart raced in his chest. His hands shook.

It might have been the beating he'd taken.

But it might not.

And it was hot here—damned hot. At first he thought the heat came from fever in his beaten body, but no. Now that he felt the breeze, he could tell the heat was in the air itself as it moved past him. Scorching, damp heat, even this early in May.

And the air smelled different! Where was the constant smoky aroma of tobacco leaves? He'd never smelled air that wasn't permeated with it—how strange and how perfumed! The jessamine and lilac fragrances were pure here! He hadn't realized the outside world would actually *smell* new!

The wagon's pace changed abruptly—and they were going up a hill—up a drive, an entranceway.

Dorian craned around to the front, looking past the slaves, past the two negroes and the white broker, and there rising high and wide before the wagon, before the horses, was a plantation mansion of stone.

So unlike Plentiful that the sight of it made Dorian's heart suddenly skip, the mansion was perched among huge willow trees on the top of a gentle hill. It looked down upon the river—at least one of its faces did. From where the wagon was, Dorian could see that the mansion had two full facades at right angles to each other, each with a full porch and entranceway. Yes, the approach front, which faced the driveway, and the riverfront, which faced water. Such formation was common in Tidewater. He'd heard of it many times. Was he still in Tidewater then?

He tried to guess how many rooms by counting windows— difficult since he'd never seen another house but the mansion at Plentiful—and came up with about sixteen ... assuming two windows to a room—but, of course, he couldn't see all of the house from here. Somewhere there would be a kitchen, probably on the invisible end, and inside there was probably a formal reception hall. The windows were tall, narrow, with equally tall and narrow black shutters to draw color from the flagstone—so *that* was what Federal style looked like. He'd read descriptions of it, seen sketches.

Where were the fields? At Plentiful the fields of waving stalks were visible from the house. What kind of plantation was this? Not tobacco. The air told him that from first whiff. Cotton? And what was that faint jingling sound that pervaded this farm? He listened, tilting his head and narrowing his eyes, but the sound, like bells at Christmas, made no sense.

Am I even still in Virginia?

"Sit up straight!" the white man in front called. "Look good for the Reverend Sutton. He gonna be your new massa. Look sharp or get paddled, hear?"

There were people waiting for the wagon—overseers, slaves, a few slave drivers, but the latter were white, not negro like the drivers on Plentiful. At one quick surveillance Dorian could read that there were no negroes in any power here.

The wagon grated to a halt. The horses settled instantly down to a standstill, glad to be resting. How long had they been dragging their load?

The white slave broker jumped down and barked orders to his two niggers, who in turn herded Dorian and the other slaves out of the wagon and made them form a line. Strange how much care was taken to get the chains neatly arranged on the ground from slave to slave ... all chained together. Dorian hadn't noticed that before—he was yanked into place by the arrangement.

"Just stand there," the white man grumbled. Then he turned to one of his negroes and muttered, "Wait till you see this boy. He likes t'ride among his slaves on horseback. It makes him feel bigger than them."

There was movement everywhere, some concerned with the new batch of slaves, some not. Other bands of slaves moved across the driveway, guarded by white drivers—a large plantation, to be sure, for there were far more drivers than Plentiful had required.

To what kind of place have I been consigned? Where is this? Virginia? Maryland?

The thoughts started to hurt. His head throbbed from the blows that had come sometime in the past few hours . . . days?

A band of slaves was marched past the new purchases, and Dorian stared. Suddenly the faint jingling noise wasn't so faint.

Every negro within earshot wore a collar of thickly rolled leather upon which hung a nut-sized tin bell. With each step every slave announced his whereabouts. *Tinkle, tinkle, tinkle, jing . . .*

All across the plantation bells jingled.

From down the hill a voice cracked the peace.

"Wait! Hold that batch!"

The white slaver responded by turning to the new slaves and barking, "Heads up! Show your eyes."

Curious, Dorian twisted as far around as possible and looked.

The white slaver was standing at the end of the line, waiting.

Down the driveway a twitchy gelding came trotting toward them with a young man of about twenty-five in the saddle. A strange sight—for right behind them came a gentle-faced gray mare, very pregnant, vastly pregnant in fact, simply plodding along behind the jumpy gelding. But attention was quickly stolen by the young man. Their new massa? The Reverend Sutton?

As the distance closed between them Dorian noticed the young man's eyes. They were smallish and tight, the color of celery, each with a speck of flint in the center. His brows were widely set, small, simple strokes of brown, and his hair a cap of buff curls somewhat shorter than Dorian's raven ones. His face was narrow, his eyes set wide. The man's lips parted as he contemplated the group of slaves he was approaching. Without a word he yanked his gelding to a halt—well, more or less a halt. The horse continued to lunge and twist, but the young man was liquid in the saddle and conducted his business without noticing the horse crashing beneath him. Everybody else took a step backward. The gray mare behind them simply stopped and waited.

He put his hand out to the broker and was given a stack of ownership vouchers.

Dorian glared at the documents for a curious moment. He'd never read or even seen his own papers.

The man rifled through the papers, glancing quickly at each one, his mouth flattening. It was a low-slung mouth with a thin upper lip and a thick lower one, and there was a strong dimple on his left cheek. This wasn't the face of a cruel man, he'd decided.

So much more the surprise when the mouth opened.

"What is the meaning of *that*?"

The slave broker looked down the line to where the young man was pointing. A female slave cringed where she stood. She was the only female in the lot.

The broker wiped his hands on his trousers. "Oh! Mr. Noah, I clean forgot. Bin near a year since I bin back to South Carolina, and I clean forgot—"

"You shall address me as Mr. Sutton. My given name is not your jurisdiction."

Dorian listened with roaring interest—the accent was different! Quite different from the mellow country lilt of Virginia. This was a coarser accent, more distinctly Southern, but baked with the grammatical perfection of the upper class.

Noah shook his head and waved a hand at the woman. "You know how my daddy and I feel about woman nigras at the Mount! The reverend wants nothing to do with raising any nigra piglets. Just last month we had to strangle two of them."

Dorian's legs turned to mush, and he winced as though something had cut into his belly. Babies . . .

Nauseated, he fought to stay on his feet.

The slave broker simply nodded. "Suh, I dun told you I ain't been ba—"

"You are a pathetic businessman, Mr. O'Roy, sir, not even to remember the requirements of the plantations you service. I'll thank you to reimburse me the full amount for this female and take her on her way."

He plucked one ownership voucher and threw it to the ground before the slaver.

O'Roy. The name burned itself into Dorian's memory.

The young man slid out of the crazy gelding's saddle and floated to the ground as though he had wings. The horse crashed this way and that around him, but he barely bothered to duck before smacking his riding crop across the saddle leather.

"Damned flea-brained pug! Get back where you belong then!"

The gelding threw his head into the air, wheeled about, and dashed down the road toward, apparently, the stable. The pregnant gray mare, however, didn't even flinch.

The man shook his fist at her and shouted, "Why don't you drop that foal so I can ride you again! Am I supposed to settle for second best? Damn you for your motherhood! Come on, then!"

Her large brown eyes remained undisturbed, her lovely face untroubled. She plodded forward, settled in behind him and stayed right behind him no matter where he walked.

Dorian wrinkled his brow at this bizarre devotion but kept his mouth tightly clamped.

O'Roy laughed nervously and tried to get on Noah's good side by saying, "I see your mare ain't dropped yet. I was kinda hopin' to get a gander at this colt you bin plottin' to get hold of, Mr. Sutton."

Noah stopped, turned, and raised his brows. "That will be no mere colt, O'Roy. Chapel's Bombay Bride is an English thoroughbred brood mare. Her foal was sired by The Gael Boru, a champion Irish Percheron stallion fed entirely on lime grass for ideal bone structure and solid constitution. Because of this breeding, Bombay's foal will be a true hunter, and I shall cherish him more than my life.''

O'Roy retreated from the conversation.

In the ranks Dorian mumbled, ''Pity he'll be worth so little.''

Noah snapped around, looking for the sound he wasn't sure he'd heard. He scanned the line of slaves, but none of them was looking at him. He studied them deviously for a moment, certain they were thinking ill of him.

It put his mind back on his work.

He strode down the line of new slaves, flipping through the papers and glancing at each man as he passed. His glossy black hunt boots began to collect dust, his breeches so tight they were creasing on his compact frame. He wasn't quite a tall as Dorian, and Dorian wasn't as tall as—

Alex . . .

Noah drew nearer to Dorian, paused, surveyed one of the other negroes, then continued coming. Dorian watched him with the keen eye of a man raised on literature, where evil is ugly and good is pleasant to look at. Noah Sutton's face was smooth and sparkling, his eyes pale green lights—this simply wasn't the face of cruelty. His buff curls caught sunlight as though each one had a little pat of butter melting on top of it. Tight curls. Seemed like everything about Noah Sutton was on too tight.

Behind him the mare called Bombay Bride paused, her face level with Noah's shoulder blades almost as if to nestle there.

The hunt boots clicked to a halt.

Dorian refused to flinch.

Noah Sutton's cold small eyes were right there.

''You are the half-breed,'' he said. ''Now I see why I got you so cheaply.''

His trained Southern eye looked for and found the negro elements in Dorian—the pitch blackness of his hair, the deceptively soft curls, the faint hint that his bone structure wasn't purely white, the eyes so many shades blacker than any white man's eyes.

''Disgusting,'' he said, tasting the word. ''Son of God, look at your skin. I might never have spied you for a nigger, hadn't I been looking for it. . . . Merzie! Merzie, where are you?''

One of the overseers appeared immediately from the other side of the wagon, carrying an armload of the rolled leather collars with tin bells. He shouted, "Here, Mr. Sutton!"

"I want this mongrel branded immediately."

Without a word, Dorian raised his arms and pushed up the left sleeve, and bared the *S*.

Noah Sutton frowned at it. "Done already? What's it doing there? A proper brand is on the face! Merzie!"

"Yes, Mr. Sutton?"

"I want the sleeves cut from this breed's shirt. He is never to wear sleeves, is that clear?"

The man called Merzie instantly dropped the armload of leather collars, drew an ugly knife from his belt, and put it to Dorian's shoulder.

One . . . two . . . the sleeves of Dorian's shirt lay upon the chains below.

The other slaves were hunched now and trembling in their places. Dorian wasn't trembling. He wasn't hunched over. He simply stood there and waited, despised purely because of his color. Or lack thereof.

Noah saw the expression and took it as slave arrogance.

"What's your name, breed?"

Dorian paced off a few extra seconds, just to avoid answering with the instant compliance Noah wanted so badly.

Finally he said, "Davy Crockett."

The last thing he saw was Noah's perfect face crumpling.

The riding crop slashed across the side of Dorian's head. He crumpled into the slaves at his left. The slaves writhed out of the way, but the shackles kept them from avoiding him altogether as he crashed.

Noah slid his riding crop under his arm and snapped his fingers at O'Roy. "What's his name, Mr. O'Roy?"

"Ah . . . they called that one Dorian, suh."

Noah's nose wrinkled like old fruit. "I don't like that name. It's inappropriate." He glared down as Dorian gathered himself to his feet again. "He'll have to be called something else. Hinny or Patch or Magpie or something."

Beside him Merzie said, "We already got two Magpies and three Patches, sir."

With a boyish sneer Noah announced, "Hinny, then."

Dorian heard it, though barely, through his pounding right ear and the pain of the whip against his head. Hinny? This is a name for a human being?

Evidently naming humans wasn't what Noah Sutton had in mind.

The young man surveyed him clinically, watching every movement as Dorian got to his feet.

"Whose idea was it for us to buy this breed? Look at his light skin. He's unlikely to be a good rice worker. Negroes are suited for rice growing because they're tendered by generations in steaming jungles and hot plains. The negro is happiest under conditions that would melt a white man. The blacker the skin, the better suited to a rice plantation. Look at him. He's not liable to live long here."

Having done his diagnosis, Noah huffed and continued past Dorian. He scanned the new slaves, then stepped back a few paces and began looking at their papers, one at a time.

"All right," he said loudly, "do you all understand the English language?".

The slaves glanced nervously at each other. Some nodded. Was this a trick question?

"You are now the property of Chapel Mount plantation, on what is called the Rice Coast. Our principal crop here is the Grand Staple of rice, one thousand sixty acres of it, and we proudly produce as much as forty bushels per acre, and it is very good, heavy rice. My name is Master Noah Sutton. I am the son of your owner, the Reverend Roderick Sutton of the Cliffside Baptist Congregation of Society Hill, South Carolina."

Dorian's pounding head took an extra throb. So . . . two states from home.

"My father is at our summer home on Cape Romain," Noah Sutton went on, "and will not return until next week. In his absence I am your massa. Part of your job will be maintaining our irrigation system. Some of you will be tending built-up banks, drainage ditches, canals, and the trunk doors that feed them. Water is the blood of our crop. We thrive on our swampy land. Our head men will show you your jobs for now. We are presently involved in planting the seed rice. You will eventually be assigned to a particular field. Those slaves whose fields do not yield at least twenty-eight bushels to the acre will be paddled.''

Dorian watched the young man's clean, hairless face and metallic eyes and wondered how the door of a trunk could possibly have anything to do with water.

"Your name is Sutton now. It is a proud and historic establishment to which you now belong. Forget wherever you've been before. You will never see it again. Life outside these grounds is over for you. Empty your minds completely. There is only one thing you need keep in your minds at all times, and that is this: we kill rebellious slaves here by roasting them on a spit over an open flame.''

Peering into those eyes, Dorian searched desperately for a hint of empty threat. All he found was pure guiltless testimonial that Noah Sutton had happily done many times what he now said he would do. What kind of place was this? What kind of place had he come to live in?

Noah's voice shocked him. "Do your work at your utmost capacity, or that is the fate that awaits you. We do not tolerate any form of independence from you. Do not make any attempts to escape downriver. Our hunting hounds are trained in riverside tracking, and they will be allowed to rip your gullet from your neck without curb. If you are still living, you will then be roasted. Merzie! Get their collars on them and put them to work in the training fields.''

The pregnant gray mare with the soft brown eyes plodded past Dorian. How like Yula she seemed. Bred to a monster at her master's whim, about to give birth to a giant she couldn't help but love.

She trod past Dorian, following her master, following a scrubbed, clean-cut, immaculate fiend.

"Oh, Mr. Burns," Dorian uttered softly, "can you make a rhyme to vindicate such as him?"

It was a thoroughly different world. For Dorian the differences were intoxicating, because they weren't confined within the pages of a book or the past-tense tales of other slaves. They were here, at the easy reach of his own eyes. Everything here smelled damp instead of smoky. The trees were different, deep-swinging willows and oaks dripping with Spanish moss. There were no open fields of broad green tobacco leaves, no sense of the tropical here. He heard the *gabble-gabble* of wild turkeys right here on the grounds and even caught a glimpse of deer once. The fields were other colors from Plentiful's fields, the sky a different blue, and there was that wide blue green river on whose waters swam big white swans and geese—which river? No one would say. Dorian found little things like that preying upon his mind. He wanted order in his world. He wanted to *know*.

The negroes in general were indeed blacker, probably from other ethnic pools than Virginia's negroes. And they were almost all males. Very few females worked Chapel Mount, and except for two young women Dorian caught sight of in the fields, most of those were past childbearing age.

Everywhere the slaves went, they went in single-file lines. Since the lines were made almost exclusively of men, the farm resembled prison more than plantation. Plentiful looked better and better for its brand of slavery as the morning trudged on. At least there the slaves had a family life, a sense of possession, a sense of place. Here there was no semblance of family life, no women with babies on their backs, no banter among the slaves as they passed by each other during the day's work.

What time of day was it? He couldn't tell by the sun yet, because he couldn't look without his battered head pounding.

Dorian watched in fascination as he and the other new slaves were fitted with leather collars studded with little bells—the jingling sound he'd first heard. Within minutes his neck was chafing.

He was put right to work. Even the work was new enough to fascinate him, and the fascination let him overcome the gnawing pain in his head and his back. His legs felt like matchwood. At Plentiful injured slaves were given a day to recover. Not so here. There was nothing to do but try to overcome the bloodless feeling and weather through it. No point squandering his energy. Another blow would render his powerless, and he didn't want to risk that.

By midmorning—evidently it was indeed morning—Dorian found himself helping to haul a piggin of muddy water. Yes, mud. He could understand moving mud away from the plantation area, but moving mud toward it? In fact, *into* a building?

But it wasn't plain mud, he found out. It was clay water. When he put his side of the piggin down and winced to a straight position, he found himself standing in a big barn filled with seed rice. About forty-five or fifty barrels of it, if the measure of his naked eye was worth anything. Other slaves were pouring their piggins of clay water onto the floor, and still more slaves were shoveling the seed rice into the clay. In the middle of the barn, several of the younger negroes were shuffling about in bare feet, claying the seed rice.

Weight, he thought. *They're giving weight to the seed. Of course. How fascinating!*

Someone thrust a shovel into his hands. He blinked and looked down at it, but his study was cut short when a blow landed in the middle of his back and he stumbled forward. When he turned to look, one of the head men pointed at the clayed seed rice and barked, "Get shoveling."

Dorian raised one brow and asked, "Where you like it shoveled, boss?"

The white man took the question at face value. "Into a pyramid. Like they do over there. Get to it." Then he raised his voice and shouted, "Hurry it up. I want this piled and soaking by noon, or there'll be no lunch. This afternoon I want you and you and you to mend the trunk doors in the new field."

Dorian looked up, not sure whether or not he was one of the *you*s.

When the head man had turned away and was supervising somebody else, Dorian leaned toward the nearest slave and whispered, "What a trunk doh?"

The slave glanced at him, scowled, and simply went about his own shoveling.

Just when Dorian got used to not having an answer, one of the other slaves muttered, "It a floodgate, is all. Let in de sprout watuh, let out de flood watuh."

His curiosity satisfied, Dorian put his back into his work. The whole idea of learning to grow something other than tobacco was magnetic. But for thoughts of Yula and Burlie, he could almost get used to this for a while, just for the experience. After all, Plentiful was still there, and Iphigenia and Alex and the girls were safely on their way to Europe. There was nothing to rush home for; not yet. He could do without a good game of "Mansion of Happiness" with Alex for as long as it took; those days would come again. *Remember how happy we were when W. and S. B. Ives came out with that game, Alex? Remember how many hours we played that first week? We fell asleep with our cheeks resting on the board. Uncle Nick had to shoo us off to bed. Wasn't it 1843? Just like Akbar the Great winning at pachisi—games of strategy, speed, target, and skill—*

He shook his head to clear it of pointless memories. Alex was on his way to Greece. The game board was in the library drawer.

Meanwhile he was *learning*. A good lesson was always worth a little hard work. When it was over, he would know exactly how to grow rice.

If only he knew where Yula was.

So he worked. It was pure physical work, quite different from what he had been doing at Plentiful since he took on the management end of tobacco growing when he was fourteen years old. In a way this physical work was mind clearing. He found himself relaxing into it, sensing a gain in his aching muscles as they stretched. Why, after a few weeks of this, he'd be sturdy as an ox.

"All right, that's enough! Line up!"

For the first time in hours Dorian's head popped up—his back muscles screamed and suddenly tightened. He winced but managed to stifle the groan. He had to be careful not to give Noah Sutton a reason to make good on his prediction that light-skinned slaves were bad rice workers. At this point Massa Noah held all the game pieces.

The other slaves leaned their shovels against the wall and turned away from the pyramids of clayed rice they'd worked all morning to form. While Dorian paused a moment to look with pride upon his work, the others simply formed a line without a backward glance. They didn't care how good or bad their work was; neither the profit nor the risk was theirs. Dorian saw real evidence here that his idea of giving the slaves a cut of the risk and profit had been the right idea. Certainly these people were only as good workers as force could make—not very. The boss of the plantation would feed and shelter his slaves whether he made a profit or not. That was plain business.

When the queue of slaves moved out of the barn and into the bright light of day, three wild swans came winging past them, just overhead, and for a moment Dorian went with them. Their great white wings were spread wider than he was tall, and their honking had a certain resonance about it. Marvelous! What a fascinating place! Wild swans and turkeys and rice and a river and strange accents and the blackest slaves he'd ever seen! Experiences—experiences instead of words on a page!

Preoccupied with the swans, he failed to pay attention to where the line was going. It didn't matter; he would have to go with it. But in a moment the swans flew out of sight behind the willows, and he got interested in himself again and looked past the wide black shoulder in front of him. There was a rail fence and some kind of barnyard in which the slaves were gathering. A few white head men, holding wooden paddles with holes in the wood, were methodically herding the slaves into the yard. No one resisted. Dorian noticed the paddles almost at the same instant as he noticed the pocky welts those paddles had made on several of the slaves' backs and shoulders.

"What we line up fo'?" he asked.

Several of the slaves in line glanced at him, but no one spoke to him. They simply glared at him as though he were strange. Well, he probably was.

The slaves continued to file by in three distinct lines, moving into the fenced area. Dorian eyed the fence, plain nervous. Fences had always made him nervous.

But none of these other slaves seemed apprehensive. Better take their lead . . . evidently this wasn't a mass branding or culling slaughter, or such. What, though?

He stayed in his place and endured the curious glares.

Yes, he was being looked at. Not for his posture, which he kept in check, not for his English, which he was keeping out of check, but for his color, color alone, which he could do nothing about.

When he leaned out again and peered past the shoulder in front, Dorian saw a slave being handed something by a head man, who was doling things from a large box. As he shuffled forward, something small was pressed into his hand.

The metal was warm, stiff, narrow. A spoon. It was a spoon. There it sat in his cramping fist. And there, in the barnyard, was his dinner plate.

Dorian's lips clamped together hard, damming the opinions that pressed to get out. The line pushed him forward, and he had no choice but to move. Around him slaves were putting their own spoons to use.

There, at his thighs, was the rim of a great wooden trough, fully twenty feet long and a yard across. He stared down at a thick brown sea of porridge.

Slave after slave filed to the trough, using their spoons as quickly as possible, getting all they could from the trough as the line pushed them along.

Dorian closed his eyes for a moment, the nausea of pure indignity roiling in his stomach. He held the spoon against his chest. Suddenly the bright new outside world was drained of its fascination.

"What's the matter, breed?"

It was Noah.

He was standing on the other side of the trough.

Dorian raised his eyes, only his eyes.

"What's the matter?" Noah repeated sharkishly. "Not good enough for you?"

Slaves filed by, bumping Dorian as they scrambled to get a little more than their share. Porridge sucked and lapped at their spoons.

"Eat," Noah said. "I want to watch you eat like a slave."

Sweat greased the spoon handle as Dorian squeezed harder and scorched the ghoul before him with a critical stare. Vulgar hatred knifed him, but he saw its match in Noah's face. Noah loved being hated by him. Noah loved situations where he won either way.

Mustering every ounce of will he possessed, Dorian hunched his shoulders, leaned over the trough, and pushed his spoon in.

★

CHAPTER TWENTY-FOUR

———— ★ ————

"Who is that nigga? You! Yes, you! Come over here! Let me see you close by. You have a collar on. Are you a nigga?"

Dorian spun halfway around, then all the way, and sucked in a startled breath. Aphrodite . . . Iseulte! Igraine!

Rendered in china, clothed in white, astride a brilliant sculpture that might have been a horse in real life—it moved, so it must be a horse . . . and *she* moved, so she wasn't a statue.

Breathtaking! he uttered secretly.

But was she really? Or was it simply that he had never seen a white girl close up, other than his sisters, ever before in his life?

He stood there, gaping, in the middle of the driveway outside the stable.

The girl's ribbonlike lips parted again. "I said get over here!"

Was this entire family so pretty and so shrill?

Keeping clear of the horse's hooves, Dorian blinked up into a tiny porcelain face buried in a fountain of brown curls. At first he had thought it was a child, but now as he did as she bade and came closer, he saw that her corset was arranged to push up a tiny crease of cleavage. It showed about an inch over the ruffled cotton bodice. Bright white cotton with faint ivory embroidery. The sleeves were big and flouncy and fell well over her knuckles on the ends. Except for a satin cummerbund, the dress might as well have been her night-

gown. Somebody had tried to make her look like an angel and
had succeeded until she opened her mouth.

She looked quite like *him*, like that other one. She had the
same mouth, with a thin upper lip and a thick lower one, and
even smaller eyes, a little darker green. Was she really as
beautiful as Dorian perceived her at this special moment?
What were the standards for feminine beauty in the real
world? The standards for it in literature Dorian could tick off
on one hand. Until now he had always expected young
women to cooperate with them—but the checklist didn't serve
him here. Helen of Troy, Iseulte, Cleopatra, Astarte . . . she
didn't fit one of the stereotypes, yet it pleased his eye and
caught his heart in a sling just to look at her.

Were there so many kinds of pretty in womankind? How
could he ever drink them all in?

"Are you a nigga? Speak up!"

Dorian didn't. He simply nodded and shook himself out of
his moment of delighted appreciation. Then he glanced
uncomfortably at the string of slaves who were leaving him
behind. He had spent the afternoon in the planting fields,
spreading the clayed seed rice all over the tilled ground, one
and a quarter bushels of seed to the half acre. After the
spreading the trunk doors were lifted and fully five inches of
water flooded over the ground. The clay kept the seed rice
from floating, and the water kept the blackbirds and tiny fat
rice birds from settling on the field. It was one of the last
fields to be planted. Some were quite well grown already—just
like Plentiful. As much as weather permitted, any plantation
tried to rotate its crops. The rice fields were attractive in the
sunlight, lined by tall man-made banks loaded with blue
jessamine, blackberry blossoms, purple wisteria, and white
violets.

And this girl looked like those flowers. She fit in well
here—lovely on the outside, fetid underneath.

From within the ball of curls, her tiny face demanded,
"Why do you have skin that color? You're hardly darker than
I am myself. I don't like it. Why don't you rub mud on your
arms and face? Why don't you have a flat nose? Did your papa
rape a white woman? Why didn't she kill herself? I would
have. Raise your head and let me look at your face again.

Raise your head, or I'll have a *basilique* of graveyard dirt sprinkled in your path!''

A *what* of *what*? Well, he had to raise his head now. He had to get a good look at a person who would say something like that.

Somehow ignoring the burning raw skin beneath his collar, Dorian looked up at her again. She was pleasant to look at, but not particularly inspiring now that he got a second chance. Her brown curls went out in a cloud, then tapered inward, down, and sat upon her shoulders, rather like Marie Antoinette's. He couldn't decide if her hair had been done like that on purpose. It had a gathered kind of wildness about it, as though she'd let somebody *start* to do her hair, then had jumped out of her seat and run through a forest and let the trees pull at it. Thoughts of Lydia and Rose Dimitra piled through the image at him.

''Where did we get you from, slave?'' the girl crackled. ''Speak up! Have you got a voice? Speak up!''

The taste of porridge lingered on his teeth, sour now.

''Yes'm, ah speaks. Ah's from B'ginia, missy.''

She snaked her palm over the inch of cleavage. ''Oh, thank God! You sound like a nigga! What a relief! God alone knows what we'd have to do if you had human talk.'' She put her fingers against her own gullet and indulged in an image in her own mind, then grimaced at what she saw. She looked down at him again and snapped, ''What's your name?''

Dorian raised an eyebrow, poured himself into his own game, and answered, ''Hinny.''

The girl's nose wrinkled. ''Hinny?''

''Rachel!''

With a sigh Dorian edged to one side. Oh, delight. Noah. Now the day was complete. *Burns, are you watching?*

And here he came, striding up in those tight breeches and big black riding boots. Plodding right behind him was the soft-eyed pregnant mare. Little Miss Bombay.

''Rachel!'' he squawked. ''When did you arrive on the Mount?''

A long brown curl fell over one eye. ''This morning, and what's it to you, brother?''

"I thought we put you in that fine girl's school in Maryland so you could stay there and learn something."

"I didn't like it."

"Why not?"

"I didn't like the other girls. Besides, all my beaux are here. What am I supposed to do? Pay company to a gaggle of sillie biddies when I could be in the company of a young gentleman from Society Hill?"

Noah's mouth twisted. "I'll thank you to keep to the house until I decide on what to do with you. I have a plantation to run."

The girl turned her horse so that she could see him better. "Oh, piff. This is Papa's plantation, not yours. Merzie and the other head men, they run it mostly. Since you flunked out of military academy, you don't know what to do with yourself. You don't run a thing here."

"I do, you powdered trash!"

"If you were running this plantation, you wouldn't buy a white nigga, would you? Look at this slave's skin. It's the same color as mine! What will people think?"

"You brat, I thought I was done with you for the summer." Noah shifted his feet and put his hands on his hips, holding his riding crop away from his leg. Behind him Bombay blinked her large eyes and backed up a step.

"You only wanted to be rid of me because I know you don't really run this farm," Rachel said from way up there. "You've got no real purpose here, and it drives you pure purple that I know it."

Making the girl's point for her, Noah's face went red so fast it was as though beet juice had been spilled over his head. "I run this plantation!" he screamed. "I run it! I'll show you!"

Dorian saw the sudden movement and tried to step aside but wasn't fast enough to outstep raw fury. The riding crop came down on his shoulder. He slithered away, forcing himself not to strike back, but Noah now moved on his sister's horse and slashed it across the neck. The horse rocked its head high and spun away, but the girl drew a tight rein on the snaffle and easily kept control, sidesaddle or not. They were pitiful excuses for humanity, but they could both *ride*.

"There!" Noah roared. "I run it! Argue with me! I run it! Spoiled baby witch!"

Dorian was watching with the private fascination of a slave who didn't have to participate in the conversation, when a little voice popped up behind him.

"Bat, bat, come under my hat."

He blinked, then turned. There was no one there.

He turned completely around once, but sure enough, nobody. On his collar the bell made a faint *ping*.

"All you're good for around here is tending those idiot chickens of yours!" Noah shrieked to his sister as Dorian started paying attention again.

Rachel's tiny nose nicked the sky. "Those aren't simple chickens. Those are buff Orpington hens and Rock Cornish cocks, and I am breeding them. When I decide which of my young men I'm going to marry, I intend to do a fine business in highbred poultry. You are so piggy provincial, Noah. What are you going to do about this nigga?"

Noah's voice dropped instantly, and he suddenly became rational. "What should I do with him? He'll do his work in the fields like all the others. The rice doesn't mind what color he is."

"I don't like the look in his eyes," the girl said. She looked at Dorian over her own shoulder. "There is something behind his eyes."

Noah actually stomped his feet. "How can you see his eyes? He's looking at the ground like he's supposed to! You and your dark-world heathenism! You think everything's a magic spell!"

A cold sweat broke out on Dorian's back as he stood there in subjective silence. No matter how he perceived himself, he couldn't see what they saw, couldn't look at himself from their point of view. He simply didn't fit in with this kind of slave population, and no matter how thinly veneered these two people were, they were sensitive in a few peculiar, important ways. Within his mind a clock of limitations began ticking.

"Jesus am a conjure man . . ."

Dorian spun around again, chasing the quick little whisper—

and this time he saw a movement. A flash of embroidered fabric ducked behind Rachel's horse.

As he moved toward the back of the horse, leaving Noah and Rachel to scream at each other, Dorian ignored their shouts and hoped they wouldn't notice him.

"Hasn't that stupid mare had her foal yet? Why do you put stock in such a rock-headed mare?"

"My foal will be a champion! You take that back!"

Dorian came around the back end of Rachel's horse, keeping clear of those sharp hooves, and caught a glimpse of movement. Somebody had just gone around the horse's chest, right under its head.

He stooped down and looked under the horse.

A black skirt. Wide too.

He stepped slowly back toward the horse's flank. Beneath Noah and Rachel's screaming, he heard another voice—a low-pitched chant.

"*Tig, tig, malaboin . . . la chelema chey tango . . . red jo-ooommm.*"

Dorian was sure now that the mumbles were meant for him. He felt their direction as surely as if someone were throwing darts at his chest. Someone in a broad black skirt with an embroidered bandana.

"*Tig, tig . . . ona ouanga . . . Shool!*"

He pounced around the back of the horse—and found himself nose to nose with a fat black female face in a bright white turban.

Around her throat a leather string held what appeared to be a small brown rock. That would be nutmeg, if legends could be trusted. Dozens of cheap chains, metal charms, and various birds' feet and mammal claws were slung about her neck, resting on her enormous breasts.

All of the woman's hair was hidden under the gleaming turban. She had wide tin bangles wagging from her earlobes, and she stared at him with white-ringed eyes. She was very short, stout, and round, and she looked at Dorian as though she'd known him all his life.

He knew that look. He'd gotten it from Yula often enough.

"Mammy Dagny!" Rachel snapped. She yanked her horse around and forced the animal between the old woman and

Dorian, then shouted at Dorian. "You leave my mammy alone! I won't have you soiling her with your half-blood hands! She is the greatest woman in all South Carolina! Now that she has returned, things will be back to normal on this farm!"

Dorian pursed his lips. Normal?

He raised his eyebrows at the mammy, a kind of universal question, but all he got in return was wider eyes.

Then she leaned forward, her breasts hanging freely inside the blouse. The birds' feet and mammal claws seemed to crawl across her chest. She mumbled, aiming her words at him.

"Sangse see sa soh . . . samunga!"

A smile touched Dorian's lips too quickly to catch back, and the woman didn't like the smile at all. She wanted fear.

Dorian came that close to apologizing, but there wasn't time.

Rachel smashed her horse against him and made him stagger back, away. "Get away from her, I said!"

Noah bellowed, "Don't you be ordering my nigras about, Rachel! It's not your jurisdiction!"

She sniffed at him and responded, "Oh, piff." And now she looked at Dorian with small, deliberate, hate-filled eyes. "I despise him. He looks at me the way white men look at me. He has no right."

She dug her heel into her horse's barrel and went off at a gathered trot. Mammy Dagny gave Dorian one last warning glance, then followed, her short bulk jogging at Rachel's horse's side.

He watched them go. Surely this slave woman wasn't from the Rice Coast. Possibly New Orleans, or Mississippi, where the slaves were greatly influenced by folklore. Those chants . . . voodoo. Or as the slaves on Plentiful had called it, hoo-doo. A hotchpotch of legends, African, Creole, Haitian, French-American, a muddle of beliefs half-stirred with Christianity and poured over a strong foundation of ignorance. Magic and religion were two of those things that ignorant folk used to fill in the holes of their knowledge. What they didn't understand of the world, they girded up with the unworldly. It was human nature.

Dorian stood in the middle of the driveway. Noah was a few paces away. With a bizarre togetherness they watched the girl and the old woman go up the hill toward the mansion.

For an instant, only a breath, he was on equal terms with Noah.

He looked toward the young man and let the "something" shine from behind his eyes.

Noah returned the look.

Suddenly the celery green glare turned hard as marble.

"What're you looking at, boy?" Noah growled. He closed the distance between them in two long strides, taking that extra second to raise his riding crop.

Dorian's hand shot up, and the crop came down on his crossed wrists rather than his face. The bell on his collar jingled.

Noah snapped, "I *do* run this farm!"

He stalked away, followed by the lovely mare, and in moments was halfway back to the barnyard.

Dorian remained in the middle of the driveway, drinking in his experience.

"Well," he murmured, "huzzah for you."

The picture got no prettier. In fact, after the first day had battered all the initial fascination right out of Chapel Mount, Dorian saw that this plantation's seamy exterior had an even more offensive underside. Night brought no solstice, for he was piled into a dormitory where the slaves were laid out to sleep on straw mats—straw mats that actually looked *restful* to him after what the past few days had been to his body and his pummeled head and his whiplashed mind. Spiked stone would have looked restful.

He knew why the mats were laid out like this. He'd read descriptions, seen diagrams, and instantly recognized the type of arrangement that once had made use of space in the holds of slave ships. The mats were arranged that way, very close together, in rows that made use of every inch of the dormitory floor, to accommodate three times as many slaves as on Plentiful. Above there were lofts that were reached by ladders, and more mats in more rows. Perhaps someone thought this arrangement would be "familiar" to the negroes, even though importing of slaves had ended forty-odd years ago. But that was the way Noah Sutton and his kind often thought. There were many, many of his kind, on many plantations as big as this one in the deeper South.

Once inside for the night, the slaves turned into true animals. Dorian found himself disinclined to even try talking to them anymore. Talking had gotten him absolutely nowhere. There had been nothing even resembling a conversation all day, and now what he saw completely offended him. These were human beings who didn't even contribute to their own dignity when they had the chance.

Several of the slaves were urinating on the walls beside their mats when Dorian filed in, letting the urine flow down a narrow ditch worn along the wall. Some of the men sat down upon their mats and immediately began masturbating even before the lanterns had been put out. Others became involved with each other, and he even witnessed the rape of one of the few women. The woman herself didn't seem to care. She was past childbearing age, so what was the difference?

But there was one, he noticed, who was as alone as he was in this crowd, a young slave woman, very dark and not particularly attractive by the standards of either race. She remained unapproached by the male slaves, even when they pestered the other women. When he first noticed she was ignored by everyone else, Dorian thought about approaching her, perhaps becoming her friend, so neither of them would be so alone. But he held back. He was apart here, too far apart. He had white skin, and no one trusted him. How would the other slaves treat the young woman if he became her friend?

He had no way to measure, no lines by which to judge. Where did he stand in the pecking order? Noah hated him, that was plain. The sister, Rachel, also didn't trust him on an instinctive level. What would that mean for anyone who became his friend?

The outside world fascinated him, yes, but he still didn't trust it.

Thus he avoided making even that one friend. He went

carefully, with reserve. He disappeared into his work. He performed in silence, burying himself completely in learning about rice. He hadn't precisely planned to know a great deal about rice in his life, but here it was, so he might as well learn. The picture of the outside world continued to deteriorate for him. Slaves weren't above beating or even killing each other to steal parts of the other field's production quota. The white head men had to watch their fields carefully—but even they weren't beyond closing their eyes to such crime if it worked in their favor.

During that first week he lost noticeable weight. His Grecian belt had to be tightened nearly every morning. Eating was a trial in itself. He could eat only enough to survive, barely even enough to give himself the strength he needed to work. Every day when his spoon slid into the sea of porridge, he tried to tell himself rationally what he must do, what he would tell anyone else—*eat. Nourishment is nourishment.*

Yet he couldn't even take his own advice while looking into a trough.

And there were three deaths that week. Even simple injuries on this plantation could be fatal. Because of the heat, the moisture, and the insects, sickness was inevitable and healing just a matter of luck. Two died of infections from paddlings, and one from bilious fever brought on by malaria. No doctor was brought in, and there was no glimmer of a real funeral afterward, except that Mammy Dagny came out with great flourish and much mumbling and put an herb-stuffed mouse carcass and a "tetta"—potato—into the mouth of each corpse. Evidently it involved keeping them from turning into something. Then all three were put into a single pit and shoveled over. Inspiring.

Only when Sunday arrived did the monotony break.

Instead of being called for work, Dorian and the other slaves assigned to his field were herded onto a great expanse of open lawn—the only piece of ground on Chapel Mount that wasn't half swamp. It was the high ground on the riverside facade of the mansion, the area where ordinarily only the family would be allowed to go. All the other slaves were there too—close to two hundred of them.

It made no sense, Dorian thought. Anyone knew that the

easiest way to provoke a slave revolt was to gather them all together in one place at the same time. Why, there would be no way to stop them! That handful of white idiots certainly couldn't do anything about it.

Dorian looked around as he was pushed into place. He searched every face and saw not even the tiniest hint of rebellion. He saw nothing but broken spirits, people who no longer had any interest in their own betterment. Whether it had been paddled out of them or scared out of them or simply had never been in them, he couldn't tell from face to face, but it was gone. They were in South Carolina, the heart of the secessionist movement, the underpinning of proslavery. If slavery persisted anywhere at all, it would persist here.

Dorian looked out upon it. Yes, it looked very persistent here.

Then something caught his attention and buried all other thoughts—white people were striding onto a wagon that had been drawn onto the lawn.

Rachel, with Mammy Dagny right behind. The girl was dressed in the same frilly ivory gown Dorian had seen her in before, but now she sported a tiny blue parasol and . . . a veil. She might as well have been going down the aisle to her own wedding. The veil was robin's-egg blue and bulged slightly over Rachel's heavy ringlets but still framed her forehead with a cuplike effect. Its sides flowed down over her shoulders and dipped all the way to her elbows. The imitation was clear enough. She was a perfect Madonna as she was assisted up onto the wagon.

Dorian huffed and indulged in a little scowl. He half expected Rachel to bare a breast and squirt mother's milk right into somebody's pious mouth, as the Virgin Mary had reputedly done to Saint Bernard of Clairvaux, he'd once read.

There was Noah, climbing up onto the wagon. The mare Bombay meandered just behind the wagon . . . and a tall, thin, elderly man whose rich brown hair did not fit his wrinkled, weathered face. Such a face should have white hair around it.

Even from here Dorian could see the man's eyes scanning the audience of slaves. Like Noah's these eyes had a haughty anger. So this would be the Reverend Roderick Sutton.

Two chairs had been placed on the wagonbed, and Rachel

and Noah sat in them immediately, very straight and stiff, glaring tight-lipped at the crowd of slaves. Their father stalked the length of the wagon, scanning his slaves with a critical eye. He paused only once, and that was to gaze adoringly at Rachel in her blue veil.

Dorian's brows drew inward. But these people weren't Catholic, were they? Hadn't he heard something about Baptists? Religion's lines had always seemed rather cut-and-dried to him. Were they in fact so liquid in their boundaries that idols from one lopped over so freely into the others?

All at once the Reverend stopped pacing and clasped his hands behind his back, turned, and faced the slave audience.

"My children!" he began, "I have just returned from town, where I came upon heartening news. You know of the fight against the evil abolitionists from the North, who do not understand our life here in the land of Jesus . . . but we are not without representation! The Lord shall provide, and he provides us with a voice on the congressional floor. God save Preston Brooks!"

Dorian blinked and frowned. Who? If *he* hadn't heard of this person, certainly none of these slaves had.

"This man," the Reverend went on, "has come to our rescue, has spoken in favor of our wondrous life-style, to save and preserve it as we know it, for change is against God's plan for us. On the very floor of Congress, when Senator Sumner voiced his abolitional lies before the representatives, Preston Brooks leapt from his place and beat the traitor with a cane until he lay upon the floor! Preston Brooks is a hero for South Carolina!"

There was no applause, though Dorian sensed there was supposed to be. These slaves simply didn't pick up on the Reverend's cues the way a white crowd might. Whom did he think he was speaking to? Of the whole two hundred, Dorian was probably the only one who understood what Sutton was talking about—and the unseemly image of Congress made him grimace. Had the leaders of the nation stooped to tolerate such behavior? A congressman beaten to the ground . . .

"It is the way of God," Reverend Sutton went on, his voice gaining power, "that we live as we do. These abolitionist murmurings are not against the masters, but against God. The master is God's overseer. If you will, please open your Bibles to Leviticus, chapter twenty-five, verse forty-four. . . ."

And he actually paused, as though they had Bibles to be opening.

Dorian got a cold, cold feeling. Without having to think he whispered, "Insane . . ."

Yes, that answers many of my questions.

Behind the Reverend, sitting stiffly in his chair, Noah Sutton glared out at the crowd of slaves, trying to make eye contact with every one of them as time allowed, and his glare was a murderous warning. He would memorize the face of any slave who dared not be galvanized to the minister's sermon.

The slaves made no response whatsoever, though. They simply stood there in a great black mass and waited. Waiting was better than working.

The tall man paced back and forth on his wagon.

"Follow along with me as I recite the written word of our Lord God from the Old Testament. Verse forty-four. . . 'Both thy bondmen and thy bondmaids, which thou shalt have, shall be of the heathen about you . . . of them shall ye buy bondmen and bondmaids.' Verse forty-five . . . 'Moreover of the children of the strangers that do sojourn among you, of them shall ye buy, and of their families . . . which they begat in your land, and they shall be your possession. And ye shall take them as an inheritance for your children after you, to inherit them for a possession.' "

Shifting his feet uncomfortably, Dorian tightened his lips, not daring to make the comment that raged through his mind. Thus they heard from the ultimate authority on the subject of slavery. *Well, God would know, after all.*

"This is to say," Reverend Sutton went on, "that we shall not take as slaves those who are of our own kind, and that we have not done! We have done as the Lord commands us! Bless us all! Bless you . . . bless you all. Bless you."

Yes, I feel blessed, Dorian thought wolfishly. *Now, on to the subject of constitutional law.*

He shook his head in deprecation as the slaves allowed themselves to be slowly herded back toward their respective fields, bells jingling faintly upon their necks. The bells, gathered together here in one place, sounded as though a hundred Christmas sleighs were coming through.

Merzie, the middle-aged head man who had patiently done his job in the wake of these twitchy white folks—Merzie was white, too, but he didn't act like the Suttons, thus didn't deserve to be lumped with them—stepped out in front of Dorian and gestured to him.

"You! Come over here. And you!" He shouted at another negro, then another, and soon Dorian realized that Merzie was gathering the slaves that had come in with him on the wagon. "Come this way," Merzie ordered them. "Reverend Sutton wants to see the new slaves. Come on! Line up right here. Right here'll be fine. Go on, line up, line up."

They formed a row under a willow tree not far from the wagon, and soon the Reverend and Noah were approaching them. Noah was even twitchier than usual, with the look of a monied hoodlum on his face.

The Reverend Sutton's face was as harsh close up as it had seemed at a distance. There was nothing forgiving in it at all, so Dorian planned not to need forgiving. He stood there, not too straight, and tried to be dark-skinned.

And was very surprised when the Reverend didn't pluck him out of the group—in fact, ignored him completely.

From the look on Noah's face, the minister's own son was surprised to see him tread past Dorian without any more scrutiny than he gave the black slaves. It was as though he hadn't been seen at all.

Then the reverend turned to Noah.

"Where did you acquire these people?"

"Through Mr. O'Roy, Father," Noah answered.

"I see. They are from the North, then."

"Well . . . north of here . . ."

"North. I disapprove. Slaves should be acquired from southerly locales. You shall see to it from now on. New Orleans. Mississippi. Florida. And such."

"Yes, Father."

"Have we an offer for the May rice?" he asked.

Noah flinched. "Yes, Father," he answered, a little too loudly. "We have a decent offer for rice in the rough, assuming forty-six pounds per bushel."

"And will you reach forty-six pounds per bushel?"

Noah began to sweat. Fine beads of moisture broke out on his nose and upper lip. "Yes, I believe s—"

"No," Reverend Sutton stated. "I contacted last season's buyer and discovered him complaining of lightweight rice. What do you say to that?"

"He's a liar!" Noah shouted. "A liar! He wants to goad us into lowering our price! Can't you see it, Father?"

"I see that he is a Christian man and does not lie," the minister said. "When I was your age, I didn't hide behind accusations. The slaves laugh at you. Do you know that? How am I to maintain the respect of my flock if my own slaves laugh at my son? These slaves are here for you to master. These are the angelic Christian soldiers provided to you by God. You as their master are their only link to God, who has given you this position. It's for you to meet that trust. We are the aristocracy, my son," he said as Noah suddenly fell silent and unmoving. "If the South falls, the Northerners will go to hell, surely, but there'll be a lower place in hell for us who let it fall. Even as a child you failed to understand the business of a plantation. You failed to advance at a military career and failed to thrive at the university. You failed at the seminary— my shame will never recover. You have failed continually to make your potential throughout your life, and now all you can do is sit a saddle."

Dorian tried not to look up, but he couldn't help it. The whole prospect of a father belittling his own child was too vulgar. Instantly he knew he'd made a mistake—for Noah glanced at him—saw him looking up.

Diabolical hatred filled Noah's face. He was self-conscious in front of Dorian because Dorian was white. The other new slaves were here too, but they didn't count.

He watched Noah and saw a man completely friendless in his life. Noah had his mare. That's what he had.

And Noah was getting smaller and smaller as the reverend went on and on.

"God!" The Reverend suddenly looked up through the willows to the sky. "Why do you smite me? Do you punish me thus? Give me a daughter who is a ring upon your own forefinger but a boy who cannot see you for the clouds in his head?'' He looked at his feet now and paced around Noah. ''Look upon your sister, boy. She is the epitome of the Southern Christian woman. What are you? Louis James's son is now a successful newspaperman. Captain MacDonough's two sons are both—*both*—ministers of the Lord. The Thompson boy is a barrister. What is my son?''

He glanced at the sky again, then changed the direction of his pacing.

''I expect no more of you than God expected of his own son. I expect you to be superior. You shall have to see to the building up of the banks. We don't want a repeat of last summer's floods if we are hit by freshet again this spring.''

''Yes, Father,'' Noah murmured, his voice almost inaudible.

''You will half again the work hours when we thresh the May rice this year. We shall want time to clean the inland swamps and add another field.''

''Yes, Father, I will.''

The reverend stopped pacing and looked right at his son. ''You could achieve greatness if only you would apply yourself. You have always had the mettle to be great, yet you continually fail to live up to your potential. Simply apply yourself. Stop being so flighty.'' He tossed a sudden gesture behind Noah to the swollen little mare. ''Leave your horse in the pen and pursue something worthwhile. Then, perhaps, you will not be such a waste.''

Sympathy gripped Dorian as he watched Noah. He was the only one watching now. The other slaves hadn't dared be audience to the abusive session. The minister viewed his son as a failure because he fell short of greatness, without considering that perhaps his son was simply average.

But averageness was not lightly tolerated in the children of the aristocracy, certainly not by an aristocracy that thought itself charged by God himself. Because Noah could not achieve the reverend's personal measure of greatness, the reverend saw nothing worth measuring in his son. He didn't see the nerve-grinding effort, didn't see the proud personal demeanor, or even the equestrian talent that obviously was Noah's true calling. And what he didn't see simply didn't count. He gave no quarter to humanity.

''I'm going to have tea with Rachel,'' the minister finished. "She's planning to have a different young man for supper every night this week, and I wish to have one supper in private with her. Don't be late for the repast, or you won't have any."

He turned on a heel and strode away without so much as an amen.

Standing stiff-lipped, Noah wasn't sweating or shaking anymore. That had been hammered out of him. Nothing was left but the ferocity in his eyes, which right now was drilling into Dorian's flesh.

The other slaves flinched when Noah stepped forward and poked at their legs with his ever-present riding crop. "Get back to your head men! Get going, all of you!"

They dispersed quickly, except for Dorian. He stood his ground for a final few seconds, until only he and Noah stood on the grass beneath the willow.

"What are you staring at?" Noah demanded in a capriciously civil tone. "What do you think you're staring at!"

"Daddy not be fair to you, suh," Dorian said carefully, very quietly. "Daddy don' see massa good points."

An unreadable second or two paced by. Noah's eyes grew harder, his brows drawing together with a terrible question on his face.

Dorian began to wonder if he'd made a drastic mistake.

Then rage burst like a dam. Noah plunged toward Dorian, the riding crop ringing through the air.

"I'll teach you to put your eyes on me, you nigra half-breed swine! How dare you judge my father! How dare you judge *me*!"

Again and again the crop came down on Dorian's arms and his neck and back.

"Just turn your eyes down! I don't need you looking at me! I don't need you! I . . . don't . . . need . . . you!"

Dorian would have fought back, except that Noah did need him at that moment.

He needed him to beat upon.

★

Chapel Mount was a nest of the bizarre, and the dormitory that night was no exception.

No sooner had the slaves bedded down upon their mats and the lanterns been snuffed than Miss Rachel came flowing in to walk among the slaves. Behind her, Mammy Dagny maneuvered her own bulk, the white turban bobbing on her head, holding a single lantern high. The lantern light shone around Rachel's narrow form, casting a butter yellow halo around white ruffles and her bulb of brown curls.

She just walked among the slaves. She said nothing, she did nothing, she didn't look at anyone. She nodded from time to time, like a miniature goddess deigning to move among her flock, but she made eye contact with no one.

Dorian watched her, drowning in this fascination for the variations on a theme in feminine beauty. Even more curious was the reaction of the slaves to the girl's odd behavior. All around him, they shifted onto their knees, put their faces down to the mats with their arms flat in front of them, moaning and mumbling some kind of senseless incantation— acting as though she really *were* a goddess. Dorian gawked at them, his mouth practically falling open.

Whatever was this all about? Rachel's vision of power?

"Remarkable," Dorian murmured, his voice lost in the jumble of moans and incantations. He stifled the roaring urge to poke the nearest slave and ask, "Pardon, but what the hell are you doing?"

Then again, he could have gone ahead and asked—nobody would have responded.

Here came the neurotic angel in her white ruffles . . . and here came the chubby obeah-woman, wagging her lantern . . . amazing.

And there they went, out the other door. That's all? Walk through, get adored, leave?

Dorian scanned the slaves as their moaning and bowing tapered off and they rolled onto their mats for the night. The light from Dagny's lantern slipped away as she went through the door into the night, and darkness collapsed upon the slaves.

Dorian sat there in the dark, letting his eyes adjust to the few slivers of moonlight that came through cracks in the dormitory walls, contemplating all the strange things people could be made to believe. Reverend Sutton's interpretation of the Bible rang once again in his head. It was the first church service Dorian had ever attended, and he could bet it would remain the oddest.

Fascinating, how people could bend words to their purpose, even words supposedly set down by God. Weren't God's words immutable, immalleable?

Wondrous—the power to rewrite God . . . it would almost be worth becoming a preacher just to try it out . . .

His eyes adjusted to the darkness and picked out the shapes of the slaves in the faint haze of moonlight coming through the cracks in the barn wall. One in particular—right across from him was the young colored woman whom everyone left alone.

This time Dorian decided to risk a contact. He shimmied across his mat and went toward her without actually standing up, so as not to attract attention.

She looked at him, leaning slightly away in the tight quarters, tucking her shoulder as though to protect herself.

"I ain' touch you," Dorian said softly. "Jus' come to say hello."

The young woman whispered, "Ain't nobody touch me. Anybody touch me get in big trouble."

Dorian gave her the gift of privacy by not asking why. He sat down beside her. "What yoh name?"

"Prue," she said.

"Wanna be mah friend?"

Even in the darkness he saw her smile break out.

"Das all?" she asked. "Jus' friend?"

"Jus' friend. You bin here long time?"

"Oh, yeah, long time. I doesn't know how long. Sin' I was a chile."

"You seen the reverend befo', den."

Her eyes flashed in the dimness. "Oh, yeah, yeah."

Dorian leaned closer and spoke out of the corner of his mouth. "He crazy?"

Now Prue's eyes rolled, and she whispered, "Sho' nuff. Reverend, he lost his parish 'bout five year past. Done lost his mind wid it."

"Or perhaps the other way around," Dorian muttered.

Suddenly Prue pushed on his arm and looked toward the door. "Somebody comin'! Get back to yoh mat!"

Dorian scooted toward his own mat and barely made it before a wobble of yellow light caught his attention at the door again, and he looked. Around him the slaves began to stir again.

Was Rachel coming back for another stroll?

He sat on the mat, tight with anticipating that Rachel's little game wasn't over and he would get a chance to see it again.

But Rachel didn't reappear. It was Mammy Dagny who came through the door, alone, carrying her lantern.

Strange piled upon strange—when the slaves reverted to their kowtowing positions, put their faces down again, and began that constant moaning. Even when Rachel didn't come back and didn't come back, they continued kowtowing. But it was to *Dagny!*

Dorian gaped with devilish delight. Rachel thought the bowing had been for her, and all the time it was Dagny these people feared!

Why?

And why would Dagny slip back in?

She went to roughly the middle of the dormitory and set her lantern down between the straw mats. Then she looked at the slaves all around her, while rubbing her fat palms on her skirt. Then she raised her hands over her head and gazed at the ceiling.

"*Samunga!*" the woman invoked.

Dorian looked up at the ceiling, but there wasn't anything there but rafters.

Mammy Dagny turned in a circle, chanting. "*L'appe vini...li Grand Zambi! Lappe vini, pour le gri-gri...*"

The slaves moaned louder. Those who had given only token attention to Reverend Sutton now were completely dominated by this Creole woman's spook calling. Even Prue, who had seemed so stable in this nest of nuts, was rocking back and forth on her knees.

"*Ouanga!*" Dagny chanted. "Mind me or ona shall pay....I shalt send coach-whip snakes upon ona in la night...*mo-*

jo . . , tobe . . . one shalt tie ona up while l'other whip one to death with la plaited tail. If ona pretend to be dead, la mate stick it tail up la nose to see if ona breathing. . . ."

Dorian smiled and mumbled, "Preposterous."

But nobody heard. They were all busy mumbling on their own.

"Samunga come to put la trick on you," Mammy Dagny went on. "I am the cunjer-doctor who work la gri-gri for Samunga . . . *tig, tig, chey tango* . . . I am la ona who know la charms . . . coonroot, string, blood, bone, hair, feather, red thread, grave dust, and I am la ona who know commanded things, beeswax, sand, thing widdout good or bad but made good, bad on command of cunjer-doctor . . . *wongah* work for me—*shool*!" Suddenly her hands came down, and she leveled a finger at the slaves and opened her eyes very wide in warning. "Ona listen to me! I am la power. Can save ona life. If la snake take his own tail in him mouth and roll like a hoop, fast as wagon wheel, ona turn sideways to get away. Don' never run straight, for snake can't turn widdout quirling up. See? Dagny can work *for* you! Teach secrets. Save ona life."

"My, my," Dorian blurted, and this time laughed out loud. "All vine and no taters."

He couldn't help it. Who could? She was either crazy or a genius at self-preservation. Dorian bet the latter.

The slaves began to peek up at him. Prue raised her head, and a look of astonishment took over her face.

Mammy Dagny's eyes, if possible, got bigger. She stared right at him. Some of the slaves were so shocked that they forgot their genuflecting and also stared.

"Buckra mon!" Dagny rasped. "Ona be warned! I set *la gri-gri* on you next cloudy day!"

The slaves gaped, their eyes filling with panic. The slaves closest to Dorian suddenly sidled away, crowding others back.

Dorian smirked, biting his lip to keep from laughing again, and waited for the *gri-gri*.

Dagny saw that he was waiting and was ready for it.

"Earth she close up on day widdout cloud!" she shouted. "Gotta wait till tundercloud she bunchup, den earth crack open her mouth to swaller la rain—*then* I set *gri-gri* upon ona, like in olden days!'' She leaned forward, pointing her blunt finger at Dorian's heart, and whispered, ''Ona lay down and stay down!''

Dorian's smile faded. A plain-enough warning. Death didn't have to be magical, he knew, and could easily be made to look magical. He glanced around—yes, these slaves would do her work for her if she bade them so. And she had just arranged to give herself time to work such a scheme. He saw fear in the slaves' white-ringed eyes, fear of her and none of him.

If he was to stay alive, that would have to change.

The smile left his face completely now. As the slaves shimmied farther back away from him, he slowly got to his feet and stood before the Creole woman as though they were the only two in the vast room.

He raised a single brow and warned, ''Thunder ain't rain.''

The slaves gasped—a single sound. Prue clasped her hands over her mouth, as though to catch back the words she had spoken to him before. So he made and lost his only friend in mere minutes.

Dagny began to tremble with fury. No one, apparently, had ever spoken back to her.

''Root doctor, trick doctor, *Samunga ouanga ona!*'' she said in a threatening low voice. ''*Bosa...boba...byo... banyo...buckanana!*''

Now Dorian's smile crept back. He had her. A well-read man could have her easily.

He stepped forward, one pace, another, mimicking her incantation.

''*Un...deux...trois...quatre...cinq...*''

Dagny straightened suddenly and sucked in her breath. She clasped her fists to her massive breasts. She couldn't make herself move as the buckra man came closer and closer—

And leaned to whisper in her ear.

''Do you want to the others to know?'' he breathed.

When he straightened again, Dagny's eyes had turned into saucers.

Dorian tilted his head and quietly suggested, ''Don' pull on de devil's shoestring....''

His words took firm hold in the woman's mind. Then he did the unthinkable.

He turned his back on her.

No one would ever have the nerve to turn a back on obeah.

No one without his own power.

Dagny shook where she stood. The slaves gawked. Some buried their heads. Prue buried hers. Others stared helplessly now at Dagny, then at Dorian, then back at Dagny, wondering why she had no command on him.

Dorian saw this happening, saw the power shift as certainly as if he had immolated himself before them and simply strode away, unburned.

Hmmm . . . this wouldn't do either.

As he arrived at his mat, he looked around at what he had done, and at Mammy Dagny standing there stripped of all their respect. He hadn't told the slaves that all she was doing was counting to five in some African tongue, but he might as well have. He hadn't told them that there was no spell or conjury, and that her incantations were bits and pieces of nonsense, probably that she had heard as a child. It wasn't even good hoo-doo.

When he looked now at Dagny and saw what he had made of her in just a few seconds, his heart took a sudden turn.

He pursed his lips, shook his head, and sighed. Oh, why not?

He crouched down upon his mat, looked right at her, raised his hands in homage, and loudly chanted, "*Obe, ona donga munga wunga, mucka bong-bong, Dagnyyyy!*"

And he put his head down before her.

The slaves collectively gasped again.

Dorian sensed the movement around him, and when he peeked up over his arm, he saw that the slaves were bowing to Dagny again. He grinned behind his forearm. That would work. All he needed was *her* fear.

Which, by the look in her eyes, he certainly possessed.

Then a sudden scream tore through the dormitory—a scream of rage.

Everyone jumped and looked.

There at the door stood Rachel, her white sleeves waving like wings. She pointed at Dorian, her small eyes burning.

"*Shugudu!* Slanderous tongue! Dare you chide the queen of *ouanga* in her domain! I'll make you pay! *An joli cocodree! Mo pas cour cocodree zambi!*"

"Rachel!" Mammy Dagny snapped. *"Na ona!"* She hiked up her enormous skirts and picked her way hurriedly through the slaves to the girl. "Not dat buckra man! I doan' want deal wid dat one!"

"He's nothing! You are great! I'll have him flogged! Killed! I'll bury him at your feet with a cunjer bag in his mouth!"

"Can't kill dat ona," Dagny told her, casting a glance back at Dorian. "Can't!"

"I hate him! *Danh-gbi!* Look behind his eyes! More than a slave is there!"

Dorian held very still. Perhaps the girl was spoiled, perhaps unbalanced, but she was also dangerously perceptive.

Dagny grabbed the girl's arms and tried to shake their version of sense into her. "Be Samunga you see dere! Out! Go out! Go out speedily!"

"No!" The girl twisted in Dagny's grasp. "I'll wear black! I'll remove my hairpins! I'll do the spell myself! Hail Mary and Liba Peter! He won't be able to fight that!"

Dorian stood as still as he could, trying to make his eyes not have anything behind them, but he was too fascinated with the girl's ranting. Like Mammy Dagny's, it was a jumble of confused bits from several beliefs. What was Hail Mary doing in the practice, even in the vocabulary, of the daughter of a Protestant minister? What a mess! The Reverend Sutton must be truly insane and detached, for he had shown no sign of knowing about Rachel's other life.

"Come out," Dagny urged to Rachel, desperate not to lose the respect she somehow still had hold of. "I take ona to Massa Noah. He know what do wid ona!"

Rachel yanked loose and hoarsely said, "Noah! That brat! All he cares about is his stupid mare!" She glared past Dagny at Dorian. "I want *that* man killed!"

Dagny's hands cracked against the girl's porcelain cheek. The sound pierced the whole dormitory, and everyone winced.

Rachel clapped her hand to her stinging cheek and jerked silent.

Dagny pointed out the door. "Git to la house!"

Stunned, enraged, confused, Rachel grasped her skirt, wheeled about, and dodged out the door. Mammy Dagny followed, turning at the last minute to make sure she still kept the power she had almost seen slip away tonight.

"*Leecum kebuk obuk! Shugudu!*"

Thus delivering her final invocation, the round *ouangateur* disappeared into the night air.

★

CHAPTER TWENTY-FIVE

──────── ★ ────────

If few of the slaves had spoken to Dorian before, none of them dared speak to him now. They were convinced he was an embodied African malevolence who would swallow them if they looked too long at his eyes.

So he was even more alone. His work became his only company. Mud and rice. Trunk doors and rice. Blackbirds and rice. Hand-whipped seed rice. Tall waving stalks of rice. Rice and more rice. He discovered he hated rice.

But he honored the fear of the other slaves. He didn't know the rules of their strange beliefs and refrained from getting any of the others in trouble by making some silly mistake with a root or a feather or a reference. Better he not talk to them. What else could he do? He did his work and ignored their sidelong glances. He was the malefactor. The least he could do was be a civil malefactor and leave them alone as they were leaving him.

The county was in for a freshet. A storm.

Clouds formed early in the evening on a Tuesday, and there had been no indication of their coming. No moisture in the air or smell on the breeze to suggest rain. Thus there was no time to build up the banks or take precaution at all, for that matter. The rice, both grown, growing, and freshly seeded, would have to take its chance. All they could do was open the trunk doors to avoid flooding and hope the rain came and went before the blackbirds and ricebirds had time to settle.

Noah Sutton didn't even bother going back to the house. His father had, in his roundabout way, disinvited him to dinner. The reverend wanted to spend the time with Rachel, going over scriptures and talking about Cape Romain.

The freshet was coming, and Noah would get blamed for it, or for its results, so he stayed away from the house and headed for the barn. He would stand in the dry straw with Bombay and rub her sore and swollen sides and mourn the mare she had been before this colt began to grow within her. Why couldn't champion colts be born out of the air? Why did they have to ruin the spirit and the physique of their mothers?

His legs ached to ride Bombay again. His muscles had their own memories, of prancing through the center of town at Society Hill, posting in perfect tempo to Bombay's hooves as they snapped up and down, high as kites. Oh, how folk had looked at him, there in his sharp brocade jacket and waistcoat and black riding boots, braided reins linking his hands to Bombay's snaffle as she argued with the bit. Then, coming home—pounding down the road with his hands in her flashing silver mane, her coat sparkling like pewter, forehooves cracking out in front like lighting bolts.

She might as well be dead as pregnant. She might as well be dead.

And all that money to have The Gael Boru brought here from Ireland for a month to breed her. *All* that money! And suffering the presence of that irrepressible Irish handler who came along. God on a throne, what more could be asked?

Thunder sounded in the distant hills. He gazed into the past and saw The Gale Boru's gigantic black body thumping down the plank from the boat that had brought him from Killorglin to South Carolina. Noah squeezed his eyes shut and shivered— he hadn't expected the horse to be that size. A Percheron . . . huge . . . the head a full eight feet in the air, and on the ground big tufts of black feather shagging over the monster's hooves. Percherons were the horses that once carried knights and their heavy metal armor into battle. The Gael seemed to know that.

And The Gael's face—a shiny black sculpture of curves and fiery black eyes like coal nuggets half-buried in velvet. And what a neck—it had more rolls of muscles than a man could count. A coarse, tangled carpet of black mane fell wildly forward over most of his face.

He had a rude look for a domestic breed, an angry look. He had come drumming down that loading plank, his handler had been forced to wrestle the halter and call for help. The only way to control The Gael during the ride to Chapel Mount had been to hitch him to a wagon loaded with dirt. He twitched and shuddered and even turned his great head all the way around, rolling his eye backward to look right at Noah. It was as though he knew.

Even after the long sail between nations, The Gael weighed over 2,300 pounds in breeding condition that month. Muscle, bone, and leg. His great stallion organ had dangled down between his thighs, shamelessly proclaiming his purpose on these shores, waving back and forth as he pranced, embarrassing the women on the dock.

As Noah reviewed that day again in his mind, a shock ran through him. Suddenly he was afraid to put that giant in the same pasture with his Bombay.

However, he hadn't felt that reluctance a year ago, and Bombay had been forced to accept The Gael as her mate. Now The Gael was back in Ireland, Bombay was in the barn, and the foal was inside her.

Presuming to stay there bloody well forever, apparently.

Didn't seem the rain was going to give any quarter. Driving harder now from the rumbling skies, it plastered the grass on the hills. Noah would have to walk through it to get to the barn.

Chapel Mount's greenery was slate gray in the encroaching storm and the darkness of evening. The house looked gray, the barns, the dormitory, everything. Gray like Bombay.

As he came into the barn, straw and bits of hay crunched beneath his stylish black English hunt boots. Manure squashed around his soles and made greenish cakes behind him. The aroma rose and renewed his image of The Gael Boru, and the scent of rain took the place of The Gael's sweat. Thunder crashed over the barn, very close.

The stall doors were open, as usual, but all of the horses had come in out of the rain. Why not? They weren't stupid. They knew where the dry hay and oats were kept, where there was a roof, where the wind didn't enter, so they came in out of the open pasturelands between the rice paddy and the swamp, which would be planted next season. It was a narrow pasture that snaked along the river in some places and in other places didn't even look like a pasture, but like a jungle. Sometimes the horses weren't seen for days but stayed out in the secluded places, peeking through the willows as the slaves sickled the rice down and carried it back in great balls.

Noah walked through the barn and right into the open door of Bombay's stall as he had a thousand times, two thousand, three thousand, maybe, and ground to a halt in the straw.

Empty.

The stall was—

He was suddenly running, rain pounding upon his shoulders. He didn't remember going out the stall or out the barn door. He skidded to a halt in the puddles near the paddock, peering through the sheeting rain, but she wasn't there either, and he headed for the deep pasture. He reached the bend in the river, and he still didn't see her.

He kept running. His feet sank deep into the soft river mud, and he tripped and flew headfirst onto the bank. His hands shot out and skated into the mud. His chest skidded against the rock underneath. Something ripped, but Noah scrambled to his feet as best he could and kept running. Undignified witch of a mare! Why wouldn't she go back to a dry barn with a box stall?

"Where are you, bitch!" he bellowed. Rain dripped from his curls into his eyes, wind whipping more rain into them until he was nearly blind, until he had to pause every few strides, shield his eyes with both hands, and look.

At the farthest corner of the wettest bank, he finally spied Bombay's dull gray form, so gray she was scarcely more than another shadow in the rain. She stood under a spare little sapling. Her head hung low, and she didn't move. All four legs were spread apart like a table. Even from here he could see her wide barrel heave with a contraction.

"Bombay!" Noah screamed, as though ordering her to stop, to heel.

Through dull eyes she watched him approach. She'd been working all afternoon to position the foal inside her, and her energy was almost gone. It would either come out soon or kill her. Her gentle eyes seemed to know that, even to have accepted it.

Even in this state she pushed her muzzle against Noah's chest, her pink nostrils flaring to get a whiff of him.

Noah ran around the backside of his mare, jumping like a confused schoolboy. From between the long strands of Bombay's tail, two small hooves protruded. One was farther out than the other, both still covered with a glossy membrane. There was blood and other matter all over it—not normal. A destroyed placenta, detaching too soon.

With a terrible bellow Noah yanked the tail to one side— and the membrane snapped. It rolled into a white film and peeled back from the black hooves, and instantly a black muzzle appeared. The nostrils began to flare and suck—the foal was trying to breathe! The tip of a blue tongue poked from the muzzle. The nostrils sucked desperately, then suddenly disappeared back inside the mare.

Terror rammed through Noah's gut. Too soon—it was too soon! "Don't breathe!" he shouted.

That was enough for Bombay. It was as though she had been waiting for him to come out to help her. She dropped away from him, lowering her bulk to the ground, rump first, and heaved onto her left side, rolling slowly against the wet ground, maneuvering the foal—but it was too big.

Even a simple cowhand could see that. Noah clapped his hands to his head, ran around between Bombay's two sets of legs, and touched the huge bulge behind her shoulder. He felt the twisted body of the foal, felt it heave toward Bombay's rump, then slide back inside again. The skin of her side was painfully tight, so tight that Bombay jolted under his hand.

Help! He needed help! He couldn't possibly pull such a foal out by himself!

Bombay heaved again. The effort crushed a great, rasping moan from her throat. She bared her teeth as though reaching for a mouthful of hay, and her neck stretched out along the ground.

Noah saw her eye roll toward him in that instant. She trusted him. She thought he could get the foal out, get the saddle back on her, and in ten minutes they'd be flying through some field like they used to.

His hands turned to putty as he pushed at her side. He was leaning right over her, all of his weight pushing on the mountain of her barrel. He reached all the way over and grabbed her withers, hooked his toes under her barrel, and squeezed.

The mare groaned. A gush of blood and membrane flooded from her, but no foal. Even one of the baby hooves had disappeared now.

Hopeless.

Noah scrambled off Bombay's side and stumbled around to the back of her. Her tail was lost in a mush of mud, blood, and hair. He shuddered, dropped to his knees, and grasped the one protruding hoof by the fetlock.

His chin turned upward, and he hauled with all his strength; gained a few inches, but the foal pulled him forward, off balance. He squirmed around, sat with his feet braced on Bombay's leg and rump, and tried again.

The second hoof reappeared. Then the nostrils came out again, big, wet, round baby nostrils that had touched air only once before.

Bombay groaned again.

"Come on! Give him to me!" Noah shouted, cranking on the hoof so hard he thought it might snap off.

Rain drove against him. He was soaked to the skin. His hair was in his face. Bombay was a plastered lump of clay, her right legs waving up and down as she rolled and heaved.

Blood gushed over Noah's hands, across his wrists and over his jacket sleeves, but he kept pulling. If he could just get a grip on the head—

"Damn it all!" he choked.

He let go of the foal's ankles and followed the legs up to where he had seen the nostrils. The opening was taut, molded to the shape of the foal's legs and muzzle. Noah aimed his fingers and pushed.

His hands disappeared inside the mare's birthing canal. He squeezed his eyes shut in disgust, feeling the birthing sack around the foal's head, but it really didn't feel as grotesque as he expected. In fact, it felt warm and dry in there. Noah whooped in victory as his hand found the foal's ears, the foal's neck—and he clasped hard and began to pull again. The neck was soft, wet, and gave as he worked his hands under the jawbones. There'd never be a better grip. He pulled—

and

All at once there was a head in his lap!

Bombay let out a gasp of effort, heaved one more time, and Noah was suddenly shoved backward beneath a crushing weight.

He wrapped his arms around the clunky head, braced his spine against the trunk of a sapling, and hauled back, back, back, until the tree got him in the shoulder blades. He sat there with the foal's head hooked over his shoulder and his arms around its sopping neck. Rain drove downward, cleaning the blood and mucus away from a glistening black hide. Skinny legs threaded out halfway across the county.

Noah managed to turn the foal up onto its chest. It lay between his legs, as though he himself had given it birth. Gratified, he felt the lungs inflate against his own body. He sucked in a few long breaths, spitting rain that came in too, and hung his arms around the thin wet mane. The ears flicked against his face like enormous butterfly wings. Confused and exhausted, the newborn foal lay on top of him, breathing.

Bombay rolled halfway up, lying in the soaked grass and mud, and blinked through the rain at him. At *them*.

Where moments ago there had been only two, suddenly there were three.

Without getting up she snaked her head along the ground toward Noah's feet and the rump of her foal, and sucked in the essence of her baby's smell.

Panting, Noah held the foal's head against his shoulder and gasped, "By The Gael Boru...out of Bombay...Chapel's ...Pledge of Allegiance...welcome, little Pledge..."

Rain hammered the ground. Over the sound of it, he

couldn't even hear his own voice. But the foal's ears flicked back and forth in response.

He didn't even known if it was a colt or a filly. He didn't even care. With tears in his eyes, he couldn't look.

The clock ticked another week and three days. The rotating fields that had been planted a while ago were now ready for threshing. The rice stalks were lightweight for their size, and thus Chapel Mount was dotted with big balls of cut rice, each with a slave under it. The loads were carried to a fleet of huge flatboats that would carry the threshed stuff on the long journey downriver to one of Georgetown's twelve mills. The flatboats were like barges, fully eighty feet long and twelve wide, steered by one huge rudder at the stern and slaves with poles. Damned if it didn't call up images of old Egyptian barges trudging through the reeds upon the blue Nile. . . .

Just as Dorian would find his mind drifting merrily to ages past, reality would come trotting by.

Usually Noah was in front of it.

The little foal Pledge, luckily a colt, became a usual sight almost immediately. Wherever Noah Sutton and Bombay went, so went this black spindle who was 90 percent legs. The mare was lovelier now that her body was recovering from its trial, but she would never again be the jolting spirit she had been a year ago. Pregnancy had mellowed her, and apparently she was to remain mellow. Little Pledge liked his mother well enough, but whenever she paused to graze beside the path, the colt would go off after Noah, whom he thought was his daddy. He would bound this way and that as if on springs, his hind end flapping in the air most of the time, long legs flashing behind like a spider feeling for a twig. When Noah stopped to conduct what he loosely defined as business, Pledge would nip and poke at him to get him going again.

The sight was almost endearing. In fact, it moved Prue to lean toward Dorian one day and say, "It do me good to see dat little foal foller Massa Noah around jus' like he was human."

And she wasn't referring to the foal.

Thus it went and thus remained—Prue was the only person on Chapel Mount, black or white, who ever turned Dorian a civil eye or word. Work, eat, sleep. It qualified as being alive, but not as life. The tick of the clock haunted Dorian with every slash of the sickle, every splash of feet in the paddy water.

As the days grew longer, they worked later and later as May progressed, providing the United States with the Grand Staple. Tonight especially. They'd been in the fields long after sunset tonight and only now were trudging back through the pasture, up between the stables, barns, and storage buildings. The dormitory would be dark when they got back. Most of the buildings were dark. In fact, only the mansion at the top of the hill had any light at all. A stranger approaching Chapel Mount would see only the majestic house, lit by the expensive luxury of gaslight, which hadn't been economical yet at Plentiful. The Wallace household had used gaslight only for visitors, and when they left, the candles would come out again.

Dorian let his mind go dry. He was utterly spent today, having worked at the flatboats since dawn. He and this group of slaves were late getting in, and their head man was leading them directly back to the dormitory. They probably wouldn't get to eat.

It didn't matter. He'd stopped being hungry days ago.

They were walking up the driveway when Noah strode past them, reading out of a small book by the light of a candle he held, an odd sight but not an unusual one at Chapel Mount. Behind him came Bombay, of course, and the black foal who almost disappeared in the darkness. Dorian cast him a glance, but Noah walked by without even looking up.

Dorian trod along with his eyes unfocused. After such a hard work day, it was easy to let someone else do his thinking for him, easy simply to be part of the line dragging itself along. Just as he mustered the energy to climb the dormitory steps, a terrible scream cut across the stable yard.

Jolting to a halt all at once, the slaves looked toward the godawful noise.

An instant later Noah burst out of the stable, dragging a negro woman by the wrist.

Dorian sucked in a gasp. Prue! Why would she be in there?

The answer came almost instantly. Merzie, the quiet white head man, came rushing out, tying his trousers, stumbling after Noah and Prue, blathering, "Please! Mr. Noah, don't hurt her! Please, I'm begging you, I'm begging you!"

So it was Merzie. Merzie and Prue. Certainly explanation enough about why the male slaves left Prue alone.

Dorian dropped off the step and wandered forward a few paces, followed by the other curious slaves, and their own head man was also so curious that he didn't stop them.

"No, sir! Sir, please!" Merzie cried desperately, yanking on his drawers.

Noah was dragging Prue by the hair, ignoring her gasps of fear and pain. He yanked her to her knees in the middle of the compound. Starlight and moonlight fell upon the open area. Willow branches swept the ground between the buildings, providing a perfect arena.

"Don't be undignified!" Noah snapped. "Shamelessness on my plantation! I won't have it. What if anyone important finds out about this?"

He hauled on Prue so viciously that Dorian had to clench his fists and push his knuckles into his legs to keep from interfering. All Prue needed was to be defended by a half-white champion.

Merzie bounded around them, trembling and nearly in tears, wanting to stop Noah but unwilling to put his hands on the massa.

Noah held Prue by the hair and slid his hands into her bodice, then tore the fabric away with two great yanks. Prue tried to cover herself, but her breasts fell free and wobbled in the open night air. She began to sob out of control—the most pitiful, hopeless sound Dorian had ever heard.

"Mr. Sutton, please, it ain't her fault!" Merzie begged, his voice going hoarse.

"Don't you talk to me about whose fault it is," Noah snarled back. "Have you been coiting this woman all this time?"

Merzie fell abruptly silent, knowing that either answer would get him and Prue into deeper trouble.

"Animal!" Noah snapped. "What if she's got a whelp in her? I won't have it on this plantation, do you hear me, Merzie? Don't you know what happens when a white and a nigra coit onto each other? *This* is what happens!"

He let go of Prue and swung around toward the group of slaves who watched. He reached out—and grabbed Dorian by the collar.

Dorian felt himself being dragged out into the open before he could even think about it. Noah had him by the back of the neck now and twisted him toward Merzie.

"This is what happens! Look at him. The worst qualities of white and colored. He's not dark enough, he's not strong enough, he's good for nothing at all! Pale, weak, and stupid! This is the biggest sin of all, cleaving with heathens! By God, I'll save you from it!"

Pitching Dorian to one side, Noah drew a very expensive ivory-handled dagger and a small effective-looking pistol from beneath his riding jacket.

Merzie's hands waved helplessly. "Oh, sir, no . . . please. You ain't gonna hurt her, are you? I bin saving my money nigh four years! I can buy her from you! Please!"

Noah stepped toward Prue. With his gun he held Merzie off, even though Merzie wasn't making any forward motion. "I don't imagine she'll do you any good without her female accoutrements." He pointed his blade at Prue's breasts. "I'm going to cut those off."

No one who knew him had any doubt that he would do it.

Merzie pushed his fingers through his thinning hair. "Oh, please! You can't do that . . . you couldn't do that! Sir, I'm begging! Let me buy her from you!"

Noah stood over Prue, straddling her, and pushed her over on her back, ignoring her sobs and the convulsions of fear that shook her. "If you interfere," he told Merzie, "I'll kill her. If you don't, she might live."

He lowered his knife and cupped Prue's left breast. The woman was too terrorized to fight back. She folded her arms over her face, muffling her gasps, as Noah's blade drew a line of blood across the top of her breast. Some looked away at the sight; others could not turn away.

"Excuse me," a voice said from behind.

Noah looked up.

Dorian glared down at him with perfect irony in his expression.

The young plantation aristocrat demanded, "What do you want, breed?"

Shifting his weight very slightly, Dorian took only one step forward. The earth fell to utter silence, waiting for his words.

Finally they came, like thunder in the hills.

"Are you noxious for a living, or are you just a talented amateur?"

Bolting upright, Noah gaped at him. A dollop of Prue's blood dripped from the knife onto his shiny black boot.

"What?" he blurted. "What did I hear you say?"

Dorian only raised an eyebrow.

"Amateur. You know what an amateur is?"

The other slaves backed away, confused.

Noah stared at Dorian, squinting till it hurt, while behind him Prue crawled toward Merzie.

"Say something else!" he demanded.

Well, he *did* ask for it.

The night parted before Dorian.

"Any particular something? Byron? Blake? 'Mock on, mock on, Voltaire, Rousseau . . . mock on, mock on, 'tis all in vain . . . you throw the sand against the wind, and the wind blows it back again.' "

With every phrase he took an extra step, closing the distance between himself and the most shocked face he had ever seen. He did it like a creature hypnotizing its prey, and bitter of bitter, he *enjoyed* it.

"Or would you like a little Epicharmus, the man who taught Plato the art of dialogue? You know what dialogue is . . . *two* people talking?"

"Great God . . . ," Noah gasped out in a whisper, staring.

"Yes, we'll talk about him later," Dorian uttered, his voice running along the ground like a snake. "We can talk a lot. About anything you want. In several languages, in fact. Pick one."

Noah convulsively clutched his dagger as his other hand reached for his gun. "By the Flood, who are you!"

"Flood, is it?" Dorian snapped. "Hmm, let me think. That would be James Ussher's little hobby, around about 1600. An Anglican bishop, he was, and Irish too. Do you like the Irish? No, I didn't think so. Ussher placed the Flood at 2349 B.C., at the time of Sargon of Accad, except that Sargon was establishing his empire and would've mentioned a flood if he'd seen one, so Ussher was probably miscalculating. Like the Missouri and Mississippi, any river can flood, and so can the Tigris-Euphrates in Mesopotamia. That's what I think happened, just a local tidal cataclysm that the Sumerians interpreted as worldwide. What do you think? Does Noah have a theory about the Flood?" He leaned dangerously close to Noah's face and drilled, "Go ahead . . . I'm all yours."

Trembling with excitement and shock, Noah slowly raised his pistol.

Without even moving from his spot, Dorian folded his hand over the gun—a move no slave on Chapel Mount would ever have attempted—and yanked it from Noah's hand.

He tossed it away. It landed with a hollow *thunk* beside one of the willows. Dorian didn't look to see where it had landed. He didn't care.

Before him, only inches away, Noah's small green eyes blazed into his.

Dorian leaned just a little closer and asked, "Do you suppose you're like this because your face is on too tight?"

"Great God!" Noah stumbled back a few feet. Luckily Prue wasn't there any more for him to trip over. She had crawled to Merzie, and the two huddled together, watching the bizarre drama play out before them.

Noah narrowed his eyes and choked, "Have you been able to speak like this always?"

"No," Dorian answered with a smile. "Only since 1835."

What they were seeing was fear, pure fear.

Noah was terrified of what Dorian had suddenly metamorphosed into. He was shocked, confused, bitter. He would have been less afraid of a raging bull charging him, because a bull is not learned. But this nigra was facing him in the open before all these eyes, dressed only in a dirty sleeveless shirt and trousers, armed with nothing but intellect.

His voice turned suddenly shrill.

"Merzie! Jasper! Get the ropes! Tie him up!"

The other white head man took a tentative step, but he'd never seen a situation like this before. Had Dorian's skin been black, action would have been clearer cut. But he looked like a white man, and he spoke like a white man. . . .

Enraged, Noah screamed, "Don't just stand there!"

Dorian's eyes fixed on the negroes and Jasper.

"Stand there," he said.

Jasper backed up. The negroes huddled.

Stalking sideways, Noah snarled, "Great Jesus, I hate an educated nigra!"

"Quite reciprocal, my dear fellow," Dorian responded coldly. "Does put a nick in our relationship."

No one was moving. Not Jasper, not the slaves, not even Merzie, who was just hovering on the ground, clutching Prue protectively. No one responded in any way to Noah's demands. They were afraid of him, yes, but they were more afraid of Dorian.

"Do as I say! You nigras! Get over here! Tie him up, or I'll cut a finger off every one of you, I swear it to God in his heaven! Get moving!"

"They aren't going to do what you say," Dorian told him. "You've lost control of this shaggy seam of humanity you call a plantation."

Noah's voice suddenly lowered to a growl. "*I* am in control of this plantation! My father hasn't overseen a crop in five years! Are we poor? Are we destitute? No! And it's because of me! Me! Me running this farm! All of you would starve if not for me! Where would you go? Where would any of you be? I run this plantation, damn your eyes!"

Dorian snuffed bitterly. "*Ipse dixit,*" was his cool response. "He speaks."

"You shut your nigra mouth, bastard!"

The young man's voice cracked as he spun to face Dorian again. Fury colored his face a bright, blotchy red. He suddenly plunged toward Dorian, the knife raised high with both hands.

Superhuman power charged through Dorian's arms as he raised them to defend himself—or perhaps it was only Nick's training that shot up within him. Before him Noah's teeth were a grinding white wall. The blade pressed closer and closer.

Then it was twisted away. Noah shrieked his rage and pain and staggered back beneath Dorian's grip, stumbled, fell. The bell on Dorian's collar jingled between them.

Dorian went down onto his knees with Noah crushed beneath him. The knife was in his hand now—and the expression on his face suddenly changed as he felt all his emotions change. For the first time in his life, he empathized with Luke Wallace. He knew this was a mistake, a very dangerous one, but it felt *good* to lose his temper. He knew it was irrational and that Noah and his kind were insignificant in the whole scope of things, but together that kind made a large and ugly significance. Right now Dorian truly felt like striking out against them. It felt so good!

He gathered Noah's white linen collar so tightly in his hand that Noah gagged.

"Don't move, don't even twitch," Dorian growled, his eyes blazing in the night like a rabid dog's. "I'm about to kill you . . . don't twitch. One twitch kills you. Death is uncomfortable. I'd like to see you uncomfortable, oh, I'd like that very much. . . . Twitch so I can kill you."

Abruptly he threw the knife aside.

It clattered against a wall somewhere in the darkness. Now he could get both his hands right up under Noah's throat. Oh, it felt good, it felt good—

With Noah pinned beneath him, he ground his words out.

"You know, I pitied you for a flickering minute here and there, but I don't anymore. No one's childhood is an excuse to behave the way you do."

His knuckles pressed hard into the underside of Noah's jaw, forcing the pinched face upward until he heard Noah's teeth grate.

Satisfaction roared through his veins.

"When I left Plentiful, I had a heroic vision of a world that gives evil what it deserves. I've always been grateful for any knowledge I received, but I can't bring myself to thank you for what I've gotten from you. I was raised in a box with shelves of literature in which good triumphs, man is basically noble, and evil can be spotted for its ugliness. And what do I find when I step out of the box? I find you. *You* are the symbol of my crumbling metaphysics. You've shredded the order of the universe as I saw it. The heroes and the quests are withering before my eyes."

He crammed his knee into Noah's chest and kept him on the ground while he straightened enough to remove the embroidered Cyprian belt Alexander had given him that day. It was soiled now almost beyond recognition, but it would do. He yanked it from his waist and tied Noah's hands with it while he talked.

"It's not my purpose to be didactic. I don't intend to provide moral instruction to you or anyone, but I find no nobility in life among the wretched. I'm talking about you, yes? Not the slaves. It's one thing to be wretched when it's not your fault. Now get up."

He hauled Noah to his feet with one arm, still choking him with that grip on the collar, and dragged him toward Merzie and Prue. Since they were huddled on the ground, Dorian jerked downward on Noah's collar and forced him down onto his knees before them.

"Now apologize."

Trembling with rage and fear, half-choked, Noah gurgled, "I won't."

"You will!" Dorian's voice roared across the stableyard. Bloody rage bubbled in his eyes. "By God, you will, you swaggerer, or I'll hammer you to death with my fists! I'll bury you in the rice fields where you'll never be found, and the world will be better for it. Apologize!"

"I'm . . . I'm . . . I'm . . ."

"Or die right now."

"Sorry . . ."

Feeling the heat of Noah's humiliation burning through his hand, Dorian dragged him to his feet and held him just a little too high in the air. "Merzie, take her and get out of here."

Astonished, Merzie wobbled up and pulled Prue up with him.

"But . . ."

"Don't 'but' about. Just go. Go to Mexico or Canada or somewhere. Run away. Greece, Malta, England—"

"I know right where I can take her!" Merzie said. A glint of hope appeared in his eye. "What about you?"

"I'll hold this malevolent brat here for half an hour. You've got that for a head start."

Merzie pushed Prue ahead of him, still facing Dorian. "What's gonna happen to you? What are you gonna do?"

"My goal is to quietly build controlling interest in this plantation, have this primal lackwit demoted to cleaning the outhouses, and I will personally shit on the floor every day. *Go*."

Clutching her savaged breast, Prue gazed at Dorian for a final moment, her eyes filling with new tears. She would be scarred for life, but she would be whole, and she would be alive, and she would be with Merzie.

Merzie was pulling her into a run. They disappeared into the soft darkness and were gone. Dorian would never forget her eyes as they disappeared.

He tossed a glance back at the herd of slaves and the stunned head man, who were still watching.

"Anybody else want to go?"

They fidgeted and gaped, but not a single one took a step toward his own salvation. Where would they go? Nothing but nooses awaited them out there, or a bug-ridden death in the swamps.

"I didn't think so," Dorian grumbled, his disillusionment growing. "Then all of you just keep away from me. Don't bother me. I wouldn't want to be anyone who bothers me right now. You, marplot, sit down."

He gave Noah an awful shove.

Noah skidded into the dirt, then sat up slowly. "You'll die for this, breed. . . . I'll find a way to kill you."

"So?" Dorian tossed back. "Then I'd be spared looking at the world. You know, I worship learning. I worship experience. I worship objectivity. I'm the only objective man in this solar system, did you know that? Your blows upon my hide

are nothing if I can learn from the experience, but this—*this*—
I'd be ashamed if I were you, to claim this as my contribution."

As he talked, he started hunting around in the shadows,
kicking at the dirt and the grass, to the utter bewilderment of
his little audience. Deeper and deeper into the shadows he
went. But he was there. They could hear him moving about.

Was he a demon, as he had claimed to Mammy Dagny?

With Dorian momentarily out of sight, Noah's courage
trickled back.

"You turn me loose, mongrel, I warn you. I have influence
in this state. Do you know what happens to a nigra who does
this to a white man?"

There was a shuffling in the shadows for a moment, then
Dorian's voice came sedately out of the darkness.

"You wouldn't be such a problem if someone would just
loosen your face."

The slaves and the head man fidgeted again.

Then he reappeared into the moonlight. He had the knife in
his hand. Everyone started to sweat when they saw it. A few
feet from Noah, who was still planted on the ground with his
hands tied, Dorian hitched up onto the rail fence and hooked
his heels onto the bottom rail.

The slaves and the head man were afraid to move. They
just watched. He had a knife now, and he didn't need one to
do what he said he would do.

But he wasn't using the knife to carve anybody up.

Instead he inserted it between his neck and the leather
collar, and began placidly sawing. In the corner of his eye, he
noticed Noah watching him with perfect hatred.

"You know," he said, carefully working the knife, "if it
weren't for people like you, perhaps there would be less
agitation in the North over the holding of slaves. The South is
all of ignorance, and it shall have to pay. Men like you are
common as flies, I'll bet. You'll be your own destructor."

"God will get you for this," Noah vowed.

If he hadn't been working at the collar, Dorian would have
laughed.

"I've reserved judgment on God until now, but I condemn
him for having such folk as you running his world. The days
of evil aren't numbered, as I read. In fact, evil has a clear

advantage." He sighed then, his brow furrowed in contemplation. "Maybe God is evil after all, and he's trying to destroy
me because I see him for what he is, I don't know. When I
meet him, I'll kick him and see if he says 'ouch.' At least I'll
go to hell an honest man."

Now Noah matched Dorian's grin with a vicious one of his
own. He put one foot under him and came up onto his knees.

"God is the mirror of all men. You're deathly afraid of
looking in that mirror."

"Why should I be?" Dorian replied, still sawing away at
the leather collar. "Demons have no reflections. I should
know, because I am one. Everywhere I exist, I make things
worse for the people around me. Doesn't matter if I love them
or not. That's what demons are. We make things worse. You
fit the description, so I, your brother demon, shall judge
you."

He paused in his work and lowered the knife.

Glaring at Noah, he said, "I shall judge you, not God at
all. God doesn't have a ticket to this play. Not tonight. I am
your adjudicator, and if you stand up, I'll thrash you to death
with my bare fists."

Something in his voice, not his words, made Noah sink
back a little, enough.

Dorian gazed at him for a long time, the knife resting in his
hand. No one could tell what he was thinking.

Finally he muttered, "You make me chafe."

And he went back to sawing.

It had been enough to keep everyone, even Noah, silent for
several minutes.

"Ah!" Dorian yelped suddenly, and the collar separated
with a *snap*. Gingerly he pulled the leather apart and drew it
from his raw neck. Relief flooded over his features as he
rubbed his throat.

He hopped off the fence and stooped beside Noah. "Here,"
he said. Without the slightest gentility he fitted the collar
around Noah's neck, then jogged the bell until it tinkled
loudly. "It looks good on you. You are its couturier, aren't
you? Damned if it doesn't look good."

Getting to his feet slowly, he felt the big world pushing at
his shoulders from beyond that long driveway. For an instant

he hesitated, sensing what the slaves over there felt and why they hadn't followed Merzie and Prue. Even slavery holds a certain security to one who has never known anything else.

"So this is our coda," he said to the man on the ground before him, "our final passage. I find it somehow incomplete. Perhaps it will only reach its true rallentando when one of us is dead, I don't know. Ordinarily I'd never prorogue at such an interesting juncture, but these people over here need their sleep. So I'll just make my viaticum a prudent one." Turning to the slaves and the head man, he shouted, "Jasper! Take these people inside. Stay inside. Massa Noah will be spending the night out here. You leave him out here. That means you also, Jasper. I'm leaving now . . . but you never know when I may come back. So obey me, clear?"

Nervously Jasper shifted this way and that, then gave in. "Come on, inside," he uttered, ushering the dumbfounded slaves into the dormitory.

"Close the door," Dorian called to him, "and latch it. I want to hear the latch."

With one final glance at Noah, Jasper frowned and pulled the door shut. An instant later the latch snapped shut on the inside, and Dorian considered himself obeyed.

"Massa," he said to Noah, "git yawl a gu' night sleep, yaw' hear?"

Turning as he spoke, Dorian strode into the darkness toward the open road.

Like a leash Noah's voice held onto him.

"Where can you go, mix? Where do you think you can hide?"

"Hide?" Dorian cast back. "I've no intention of hiding. Anyone who can't make a fortune isn't trying."

"You'll never be able to disguise your half-breed self," Noah told him cannily. "You're arrogant. You won't be able to keep your mouth shut. Even an educated nigra is still a nigra, and I'm still better than you. By law you have to be owned. You can't lick that brand off your arm with that smart tongue."

Dorian glanced down at his arm. "This is the least of the impedimenta in my path. I heard long sleeves were invented last year. *A bientôt*."

"I know what irritates you!" Noah called after him. A vicious grin appeared. "You can't stand it, can you?"

Dorian swung around and came back. "All right, what can't I stand?"

Noah laughed out loud. "You can't stand to know the truth. You'll leave, and the law'll come after you, and you'll be hanged. And *I'll* still be here. Still roasting your kind on my spit till their black flesh turns to dust! I'll still be doing what you hate! And I'm going to roast one every month in your honor! I'll love it, breed, I'll *enjoy* it even more after you're gone, because you'll have to be thinking about i—"

The stranglehold hit his throat. Fear flooded back as his gullet was crushed and the air stopped coming. He raised his hands, but they were still tied up in the embroidered belt. The leather collar dug into his shoulder blades.

Dorian's black eyes burned downward, suddenly kill crazy.

"You are the devil's triggerman," he snarled. "I hope there's a devil, because if there isn't, you are a terrible waste. I've come to the conclusion that all the world's misery is caused by only a handful of people. And you are one of the Handful."

Noah wheezed, his gullet jumping against Dorian's hands, his eyes bulging.

He gasped out loud when Dorian suddenly dragged him to his feet by the neck.

Dorian's voice snaked across the yard.

"To kill one of the Handful isn't a crime. It's an obligation. It's a service to humanity to find and kill these people."

He pulled Noah step by step across the stable yard.

Icily he said, "It's your fortune that I don't feel very chivalrous toward humanity tonight."

Once where he wanted him, Dorian took Noah's head by the hair, a good stiff fistful of buff curls, bent him forward, and held his face over a pile of horse manure—a fresh knotty pile, green and pungent, probably even Bombay's.

"*This* is better than you," he said. "At least it serves a purpose."

As his signature he smashed Noah forward into the mess.

The manure made a gratifying *plush* as Dorian ground his favorite hyena's face deeply into the pile.

When he was satisfied with his somewhat unknightly act, he spun Noah over onto his back and dropped him in the dirt.

Then he jabbed a finger toward the open darkness.

"I'm going out into that miscarriage of a world," he said. "I'm going to make my fortune, then I'm going to find my mother and buy her. Prometheus is unbound. As for you . . . God speed you on your journey to hell."

★

CHAPTER TWENTY-SIX

———— ★ ————

The man came through the second-story window.

Since it was a cool night, the girl had no slaves in the room to pull the rope that made the mahogany fan blow a breeze on her bed. She heard the window scratch open, and she sat up.

"Kevin?" she whispered. "Is that you?"

The masculine figure paused for a moment at the sound, as though that wasn't what he expected to hear.

She giggled at his figure as he came slowly toward her in the darkness. How charming he looked, a shadow in shadows, patching the shapes of the brocade curtains and enormous tassels behind him. Her own young body quivered with anticipation, her lips trembling, and another giggle forced itself out. She liked the taste of Kevin Whitcomb best of all the boys who sneaked into her room. This was the first time one had come without asking, and that in itself was a kind of thrill. Maybe this would be the boy she would marry, the one who *didn't* ask for permission.

Oh, and he was wearing a mask!

She laughed at it delightfully. "A disguise! I like that. Kevin, you brute!"

His hand grasped the coverlet. He drew it down toward the foot of the four-poster, and it slipped off the bed completely.

Rachel Sutton sat in the middle of her immense bed, enjoying her moment of power.

"I wasn't expecting you again tonight," she said.

He paused again. His curly hair caught in the gauzy moonlight from the window, but with the mask tied around his head, she couldn't see the pronounced cheekbones that she liked to lick.

Curly hair?

Rachel's smile depleted a little.

"Did you get caught in the rain?" she asked tenuously.

She felt his steely glare. Something inside her, some hidden instinct, made the smile fall away.

"Kevin?"

But it wasn't Kevin. Nor was it Malachi or John or DeWitt or Brandon.

She could tell. The attack was a dead giveaway.

He plunged onto the bed, caught her by the hair, and yanked her head back until she couldn't scream. She choked for air and went rigid with shock. For a flash she thought it was a new game of legs and fingers, but pleasure dissolved when his hand crushed her breast and his knees braced on either side of her hips.

"Wha—what—" she choked.

A sack went over her head, smelling, sandy burlap, and gave her a taste of what real darkness is all about. Panic set in. She tried to sit up, to fight him off, and got a fist in the ear for it. Pain jammed through her skull. Her fingers dug into the burlap, and she tried to pull it off her head, getting out one pathetic squeal before he backhanded her.

She crashed backward onto the bed, half-senseless, the mattress spinning beneath her.

The man clutched the bodice of her gown, hauled her partly up, and wrapped something around her neck to hold the sack in place. When it tightened, she tried to scream again, but with that thing around her throat all she could manage was a gagging breath now and then.

She clawed at her throat, which only made her attacker angry.

With two terrible yanks he put her hands against the bedposts and tied each one firmly there, leaving Rachel spread across the bed, tethered.

"No! No!" she gasped as much as the choker would allow. Her eyes were blurring—she felt it, even though she could see nothing at all.

The bed shifted as he leaned downward upon her and whispered directly into her ear.

"Ain't no trouble, missy . . . Hinny ain't hurt you . . ."

Rachel froze for an instant, digesting the words that seeped into her brain.

When she understood what he had said and what the picture really was, she began resisting in earnest. White-knuckle panic set all the way in. *Hinny. The slave man. A slave.*

She dug her heels and shoulder blades into the mattress and pushed upward against him, twisting to knock him off. In response his knuckles lashed across the side of her head. She slammed back onto the pillows. For her effort she got the dirty sack caught in her mouth. It puffed in and out with every breath.

Helpless, she mumbled, *"Critien vivant nou mauvais, la,"* before the choker cut off her wind again.

Only then did she realize what he was doing to her, realize that she felt the cool night air on her bare thighs now, that her dressing gown had been pushed up and was still being pushed up even farther.

Her ribs were bare . . . her breasts . . . cool air and a hot hand . . .

She found a bit of strength and twisted against the tethers, but it was hopeless.

The man's fleshy member poked at the tender inside of her thigh. Then his knee acted as a wedge and pushed her legs apart. She fell open like a melon suddenly cracked wide as he plunged into her. Panic blazed across the girl's brain as the man's breath warmed her ear and his pelvis crushed her small frame. There was nothing to stop him from getting exactly what he wanted.

He thrust again and again, enjoying her whimpers and her gasping, breathless attempts to scream, which he cut off with a hand on her throat. He ran his other hand up and down her bare legs, all the way from hip to ankle, as if he could not get enough of her.

For a deviant he was quick and efficient. Finished, just like that, as if it were just a flashing victory for himself. She might as well have been a knothole.

Wordlessly, he moved off her, off the bed.

The window creaked again.

Rachel lay there, beaten, a rivulet of blood running from her lip, her gown bunched up under her arms, and the rest of her naked body exposed to the night air. Sticky moisture of the rapist's success dried to a crust on her inner thighs.

Her wrists were being cut by the bell cords he'd used to tie her up. She lay with her head in the sack, sensibility long gone, and mumbled over the protective Creole chants she had been taught from babyhood. Charms that would make him pay.

"*Pinga jambe l'aut bo oh ... a la ou jambe ou surmonte. ... Critien vivant nou mauvais ... Samunga ... Samunga Shugudu ...*"

"Mike!"

"Up here, Lou. On the porch."

County Marshal Lou Parks slid off his horse and suppressed a yawn. Pretty early in the morning for a manhunt.

He glanced around as he strode toward the porch, peering under his wide-brimmer at what was going on. The doctor's wagon was resting under a tree, rain pattering on its canopy. He knew the doctor had been there for two hours already. The posse was here too, standing around in the grim weather, beside their horses, waiting for his order. He wasn't in a particular hurry; it was a rainy day, and chances were good that a runaway wouldn't just run—he'd hole up someplace and wait out the drizzle.

The porch was crowded with people. Several of his deputies had already been there for a while. A few house slaves were moving about, handing out hot coffee in china cups. Several of the plantation head men and even some of the lead field slaves milled about, scooping up any bits of information that came their way. He was glad to see they'd followed the orders he'd sent ahead. Work suspended for the day, no interruptions to the investigation, no mucking up of the evidence.

"Hey, Mike," he said to his head deputy. "How's the foot?"

Mike Tucker shrugged. "Oh, it's okay. It split open again last night, bled a little bit."

"Well, next time just don't try to kick a dog that big."

"Yeah. ... How is he, by the way?"

The marshal shrugged. "I don't fight his fights for him."

He nudged the deputy to one side of the porch and lowered his voice. "We got any idea who did this?"

Mike flattened his lips, and he looked down, then up, then down again. "Oh, yeah, Lou, we know exactly who did it."

"Well?"

The deputy steeled himself, clearly bothered. He lowered his voice even further and leaned toward the marshal.

"A white-skinned half-breed negro—"

"Oh, sweet jess . . ."

"—who escaped last night right afterward."

"Sweet jessup, that's a terrible shame. . . ." Parks tightened his shoulders and thought of his own three daughters. He buckled himself down to his duty and continued asking the questions. "Is the young lady sure he . . . completed the act?"

Mike looked up again. "Doc's looking at her now. Been a full hour and a half getting her to quiet down. But . . . yeah."

"Shame, damn shame. Did you say white-skinned? Hey, over there! Quiet those people down over there! Let's have a little respect! Sorry. Now, white-skinned?"

"Right. A half-breed."

Parks shoved his hands into the pockets of his brown duster and pursed his lips. "Hell, I don't know if that'll make him easier to spot or harder."

"Why's that?" Mike asked.

"Can't just plot out his behavior. Is he going to act white or act negro?"

"Oh . . . yeah . . ."

"Was he raised like a white? Ever treated like one?"

"No, slave all his life, from the records we got."

"That helps, at least. Where are these records?"

Mike leaned over the polished madeira porch rail and yelled, "Caldwell! Rustle up those papers!"

A faded voice answered, "Right," over the patter of rain on the muddy driveway.

"Raped by a negro," Parks murmured. "How old is the lady?"

"Nineteen."

"What a shame."

Mike nodded ruefully. "There's not a decent gentleman in the country'll have her now."

"In the world," Parks corrected.

"She has several suitors, the reverend says."

"Not after this. I mean, *you* couldn't, could you?"

"No!" Mike blurted, louder than he intended, but Parks had taken him off guard with that question. A virgin raped by a white man was one thing. But to put yourself inside a place where a negro man had already been . . . even the basest white man would throw up.

"And," Mike said, "there seems to be an overseer missing. Thomas Merzie."

"Any other niggers gone?"

"We're checking the ranks, but they got a hell of a legion of nigras here, and the records ain't that good."

"Keep your voice down," Parks told him. "Eyewitnesses?"

"Only the lady. He talked to her, I hear. Said his name, even."

"Did she give his description?"

"No, he put a hood over her head and tied it closed."

Parks huffed at the waste of time and blustered, "How do they know it was this one slave, then? Just from her say-so?"

Mike reached into the pocket on the inside of his canvas duster and pulled out a thin length of stitched fabric. A cloth belt. It was filthy, but its embroidered design was still visible.

"What's this?" Parks asked as he took it.

"He used it to tie her up."

"The hands?"

"The neck."

"Really . . ."

"Yeah, it was ugly, Lou. I've seen this kind of thing before on the stricter plantations. Revenge and the like."

"He stole this?"

"No, it belonged to him."

"Did? Fancy a slave having this."

"That's why it's a good piece of evidence. He wore it all the time, they tell me."

Parks raised his heavy brows. "Pretty solid evidence. Big mistake for him to leave it behind. Makes our job easier."

"Well . . . you know how these niggers are, Lou," Mike said sympathetically. "They aren't used to thinking."

A clamor at the doorway interrupted them, and they both

turned in time to see a crowd of five or six burst out onto the porch. At the center was a girl made almost entirely of auburn wringlets, her slight build barely holding up the voluminous ivory dressing gown.

Two men and a fat black woman were trying to coax her back inside, but she shrieked at them and knocked them away.

Parks hooked his thumb in that direction. "Is that—" .

Mike turned away, uncomfortable. "Yeah."

"There it is!" the girl screamed, her voice pealing across the porch. She jabbed a finger right at Parks.

People scattered as she pounded toward him in her bare feet. The whole porch rattled.

She plowed into him and snatched the belt out of his hand, then glared at it with her eyes big as green apples. "This is it! I can use it!"

"Miss Rachel," the mammy in the white turban began. "Missy, come back to ona bed now. Don't say no ting."

The girl pulled away. "Now I can kill him! I can make a negative image! I'll make his zombie!" She held the belt before her with both hands and shook it. "His possession! *Bakulu Baka! Yo voyé rélé moin pou'm al fai yo mal, o! Qua ma rivé ma tuy é vingt pou lévé yun!*"

The old woman grasped the girl's arm and pulled desperately now. "Rachel! *Abobo!*"

The girl clutched the belt to her chest suddenly and closed her eyes, while Parks and Mike edged away. Mike continued to look in a different direction, embarrassed for himself and for the lady.

Parks watched curiously for every helpful detail.

"Dimanche matin ma réglé avè nou!" the girl chanted, suddenly speaking in monotone. *"Dimanche matin ma réglé avè nou . . ."*

It was eerie. Didn't sound civilized, and Parks knew the language the girl was babbling wasn't exactly French.

"Rachel!"

A man came running down the porch. This would be the girl's father. And this younger one who followed him would be the brother Parks had heard of. He didn't know the family. They didn't mix.

"Rachel!" the reverend gasped. "Rachel, you must rest. Stop this. You and you! Take her back inside this instant!"

The mammy and two other house slaves gathered the chanting girl between them and ushered her back into the house. All the way down the porch, her senseless chanting dominated every ear.

Parks shifted, uneasy.

The father and the brother watched the girl go and didn't turn until she was gone.

"Forgive her," the father said to anyone nearby. "She is beside herself."

Even though the man wasn't looking at him, Parks nodded. "Of course, of course."

Mike nodded in agreement with the reverend's statement, then stepped forward. "Marshal, may I introduce the Reverend Sutton and his son, Mr. Noah Sutton. . . . Gentlemen, this is County Marshal Lou Parks. He's going to take care of the posse for you."

The reverend swung around and clasped Parks's hand in both of his. "Sir, I am forever in your debt."

"Not at all, Reverend," Parks said. "My job."

"I'll take care of this, Daddy," the brother said, urging his father back toward the front door. "You go in and sit with Rachel."

The reverend snapped around to his son and yanked his arm away. "If the nigras had your respect, this would never have happened."

With that the old man straightened to his full height and went back inside.

Parks watched as the son's heart sank into his shoes—easy enough to see. However roundabout, the reverend's statement had an ironic truth about it, for any plantation.

Noah Sutton swallowed the insult and turned back to Parks. "Why are you gentlemen standing around?" he asked sharply. "The man who did this to my sister is getting away with every moment."

"We'll catch him," Mike assured. "Since we got that belt, we got evidence of who did it."

"Sir?"

The voice came from below, from down on the driveway. The three men looked.

There stood a group of head men, all whites, from the plantation.

Noah glared dangerously at them. Jasper was the one who had spoken.

And now Jasper spoke again, no matter how Noah threatened him with his eyes.

"Sir, it wasn't the half-breed who had that belt when he left the grounds last evenin'."

Parks stepped over to the rail. "Who was it, then?"

"Well, it—"

He stopped. The young massa was looking right at him.

"Well, I don't rightly know," he said finally. "All I know is, he left it behind, in the dirt. Over there."

"If you know that," Parks said, "then you know who had it. Who?"

Jasper shifted, unable to add up the implications. He didn't know the law, but he knew Noah. The equation bumped around inside his head. He turned his hat over and over in his hands.

"Well . . . I don't rightly—"

"I had it," Noah blurted loudly.

Everyone looked at him. His lip was twisted in annoyance.

With some effort he got control over his volume. He glanced at the marshal, looked threateningly at Jasper again, then face Parks fully, explaining to him how the runaway slave had terrorized him and taken control before committing his heinous crime. "I had it. He used it to tie me up before he escaped."

"What are you saying, sir?"

"Only that I broke away from it a while after he sent the witnesses away."

"Witnesses?"

"Yes. He sent them away. They were afraid of him, so they went. I don't blame them. He was frightening."

"Where was the belt then, sir?" Parks asked.

"I left it. On the ground."

"That's it? You left it?"

"Of course. I had no use for it, had I?"

"Where was this, sir?"

"In the stable yard, beside the paddock."

Parks hesitated, studying the young man's face for all the little clues a face can give. Then he called, "Caldwell!"

"Yeah, Marsh?"

"Rope off the stable yard by that paddock down there."

"Where?"

"See way down there? Rope that off. Then check for footprints. Size and type of shoe, and direction it's walking."

"Righto, Marsh. It's muddy, though."

"Do your best," Parks called, then asked the young man, "You went right back to the house after this slave escaped, did you?"

Noah Sutton remained completely still. There wasn't a flicker of change in his eyes.

"Where else would I have gone?"

"I'm wondering," Parks explained, "why you didn't notify me last night when the escape was fresh. I mightn't get any prints in this rain."

The young man took a moment to swallow hard. "Great God, marshal . . . he attacked me. He injured me. I was held captive." Abruptly pulling back his own collar, he added, "Look at the bruises on my throat. Can you see what he did to me with his bare hands? Is it me you're questioning?"

Parks sighed deeply. There did seem to be dark spots on the young man's throat, but it was hard to say for sure. "He came back to get the belt some time later, you're saying."

"Yes! And that was when he raped my sister, yes. I find that apparent to the blindest among us."

"But you waited."

"I took to my bed, sir," Noah insisted. "I was ashamed that he escaped. . . . I was injured by this marauder who ravaged our innocent Rachel. . . . My family . . . may never recover. . . . My sister . . ."

"All right, all right, just have to ask, is all."

The young man's pale green eyes suddenly flared. "Ask, then! Ask and get to your job!"

He spun on his heel and strode to the distant end of the porch and barked an order for a cup of coffee for himself.

Parks and Mike watched him go and kept their voices down after that.

"Dirty business," Mike murmured, more to himself than anyone.

"What was this perpetrator's name?" Parks asked.

Mike leaned back on the rail and crossed his ankles. "The slave's name was Hinny."

"What's his history?"

Mike leaned back. "Caldwell, what's taking so long!"

A third lawman jogged over through the splashing mud and reached over the porch rail, handing Mike a folded set of papers. "Sorry, Mike, we bin handing them around."

"Here we go," Mike said. He unfolded the papers and scanned them. "Says here his last known legal name was Dorian. Owned by a tobacconist name of Wallace."

"Here?"

"Nope. Virginia. Norfolk area."

"How long did he live there? Come on, Mike, don't make me beg."

"I think, about...oh, no, says here he was born there."

"Then that's the name he'll use. Send a special agent up on the train to the county authorities in the Norfolk area in case he takes up to go back to his family. I want one of my own men present at that farm for the next two weeks."

Mike lit up. "Can I go?"

"No, you can't. Send Beavis. He's meaner than you. And put out a general warrant for a half-breed slave—are you writing this down?"

Mike roamed through his duster for a paper and pencil. "Yeah, I'm writing it."

"For the despoilment of a white gentlewoman, formerly a virgin....Dead or alive....If dead, must provide body. Signed, Lou Parks, Marshal, county, state, and so on. Put it out on the telegraph wires. Have every marshal in every state and territory put on notice to look for a light-skinned escaped slave. Tell them he'll most likely call himself Dorian Wallace."

The posse was mounting up. The marshal was at his horse, at long last, a courier had been sent to the nearest telegraph office, and a big ugly deputy was on his way to the train station. On top of it all, Noah had come up with a quick and satisfactory explanation that even Jasper couldn't dispute. Things couldn't go much better.

Noah battled against a smile. Couldn't be smiling right after sister Rachel had been ravaged, after all, even if the rape did crack the skulls of two birds with one stone. Last night Rachel had paid the price for turning their father against him, for all her life being the favorite, for playing the game better than Noah could. She'd had it good for her entire life. He had done her a favor last night. She would have to grow up now. He'd done a noble thing in forcing her, giving her the gift of the soiled.

And he had managed to discredit the mongrel, outthought him in just one night. Quoting poetry just couldn't eradicate the crime of being arrogant and a half-breed.

He stepped off the porch to watch the pretty sight of the posse getting aboard their soaked horses. In the opaque veil of rain, the sight satisfied him—people going to tremendous effort just to help him track down the humiliator. All this help had come at the flick of his finger. Could the half-breed get the world to thus jump at his whim?

Striding through the gathered crowd of slaves and head men, he paused, folded his arms, and drew in a deep breath.

"Well," he said firmly, "that half-breed certainly showed his true colors last night."

Several people glanced at him. There was a faint mumble of "Yeah," "Yup," and "Yo" here and there.

"Showed yours too," another voice said.

The shock moved through him as though lightning had hit.

Noah slowly turned. His arms dropped to his sides. To his right, his left, all the head men were looking at him in a way they never had before.

Jasper was looking right at him.

Noah glared. "I beg your pardon?"

Jasper put his hat back on his wet head, preparing to say what had to be said.

"You don't want your daddy to know what happened out there last night, do you, sir?"

The air gripped Noah with a sudden chill, and it made him angry. These men were glaring at him!

He glared back.

"Are you presenting me with a threat?" he demanded.

One of the other head men, the one named Hobe, tipped his head regretfully and said, "Reckon we have to, sir."

The few slaves who were standing nearby were suddenly standing just a little bit closer. And a little closer.

"How dare you," Noah ground out.

Hobe shrugged. "We got nothing personal agin you, Mr. Sutton. You lose this plantation, we all lose our jobs. It ain't worth that for you to get your temper out."

"We bin telling you to ease up for years," a third man added.

Jasper didn't like leading the party, but he accepted the task and kept stoking.

"Eight years I bin here," he said. "Merzie was here ten, and you treated him no better'n them niggers, sir, when it comes down to nuts and bolts."

"We'll bring in the rice," Hobe said, "but ain't gonna be no more talk of roastin's or any real bad paddlin's."

"And I'm putting a detail of niggers onto hewing real bowls for them to eat out of," Jasper said to Hobe. "I never did like them troughs."

The other head man nodded, then looked back at Noah.

"Sorry, sir," Hobe finished up, "but you don't give us no choice. The niggers seen something last night that's gonna put ideas in their heads if things don't change. You don't give us no choice but to take over."

Noah Sutton was like a volcano about to erupt.

But he didn't. He didn't throw a tantrum. He didn't run for his riding crop. He didn't turn into the wild man they expected.

He just stood there, practically smoking from the ears. His eyes grew thin.

"Bring in the rice," he said, his tone unreadable, "and we'll just see about the rest."

He walked away and left them all very worried.

With good reason. There had been something about the way he set his shoulders while he was leaving.

Scarcely two hours passed before Noah was testing their threat.

He deliberately went out into the dormitory, where he didn't have to be. He deliberately tripped over one of the resting negroes, who didn't move far enough out of his path.

And he got out the paddle. The one with the holes and the unsanded edged that flayed skin with every blow.

By noon that negro was deliberately dead.

"Fire!"

The bell sounded loudly across the plantation over the bellowing of panicked horses.

Flames rolled and tumbled like acrobats out of the hayloft openings and turned the stable into a white, yellow, and orange flower against the black night. One day. One day was all it had taken.

Noah rushed down the driveway toward the horrible sight. All around him people ran for water buckets and were forming a line from the well. They would be too late, too late for the horses.

There's nothing in a stable that won't burn. From the rafter to the manure, it's fire's favorite banquet. The first must have started at both ends—obviously arson, because the stable was burning evenly. Both main doors were already cut off. In fact, there were two separate fires eating their way toward the middle.

"Bombay!" Noah screamed when he heard the throaty neighing of horses from inside. He heard their hooves clattering inside the box stalls and knew from the sound that they were terrorized. His nightshirt flapped against his thighs and the breeches he had hastily pulled on. His boots had been yanked on too and were biting into his calves because he hadn't pulled them up far enough.

He ran for the middle of the stable. There had to be some way in, some window or loose board or something. He would find a hole, he would *make* a hole. No one was there to stop him, if they even wanted to.

When he yanked back the watering hatch and crawled inside, he might as well have been entering a furnace. The air was almost too hot to breathe. He felt it go down into his lungs like scalding coffee. Smoke rolled around the ceiling above him in carbon-colored puffs, leaving soot everywhere. Already the walls were black instead of light brown.

He stumbled into the main aisle between the rows of box stalls and desperately yanked open two of the stalls that he could still reach. Some of them on both ends were already blocked off by fire.

The two horses he freed came charging out, wild-eyed and mad with fear and the smell of smoke, and lunged this way and that trying to get out.

Noah left them behind and stumbled through the smoke.

He grabbed a third stall latch. The iron was hot, grilling his hands as he hauled the door open. He felt his palms blistering as he waved the smoke out of his eyes.

He started to shout an encouragement to the brown gelding who slept in this stall, but what he saw before him choked him as much as the smoke did.

The brown gelding had collapsed on a pyre of straw bedding. His long tongue streamed from his mouth. His body was cooking and smelled of burning hair as he lay there, dead of asphyxiation by smoke. His tail sizzled and sparked. Overhead the rafters were a dazzling involvement of flames.

Noah staggered away.

"Bommmmbaaaaaay!"

If he ever loved the horse, he couldn't love her more than in the moment when she saw him at the stall door, sheathed in smoke. Never mind what instinct told her to do, she walked right through the smoke and smoldering hay and pressed her face against his chest.

He grabbed the lead shank from the hook on the wall and threw it around her neck. Where was the foal?

"Where is he! Bombay! Where's your foal?"

There was a shadow in the corner, under the manger. A thready whinny peeled out like a whistle.

"Pledge! Come over here, you dumb baby cayuse! Follow your mother! This is your daddy speaking! Drat you, we're dying!"

He choked on the smoke. The floor was already a griddle that he could feel right through his soles.

Bombay turned her head all the way around and whinnied

sharply, but the foal didn't come. Suddenly Bombay pulled away from Noah in such a manner that he let the lead shank go loose.

She roamed through the smoke into the stall, stretched her long neck, and opened her mouth. Her big teeth snapped on the foal's withers.

Shocked, the baby jolted out from under the manger and plunged for the open stall door.

If Noah hadn't been there to throw the shank around the baby's neck, the foal would have charged right into the fire.

Noah could barely breathe at all now. He felt his body squeezing, felt the deprivation in his lungs. Had the other two horses gotten out, or would he stumble against their bodies as he tried to escape with his mare and his colt?

He dragged on the lead shank and hauled toward the nearest main door, toward a wall of flame and crackling floorboards, and felt himself being cooked.

Outside Jasper and the other head men were about to give up. They'd have to call off the dangerous fight. Everyone was scorched and parched and poached. There just wasn't any stopping a barn fire. The only thing left to do was being done—barrels of water were being wagoned up from the riverside to pour on the nearby buildings. All they could do was wet down the buildings and hope it didn't get windy.

The head men stood there with the slaves watching. When the barrels got here, they'd go back to work. Beyond that fighting this fire was too dangerous now. The stable was a total loss as it stood there being consumed before their eyes. The worst thing was listening to the screams of helpless horses and listening to those screams taper off, one by one.

Jasper perked up when he saw a bizarre movement behind the sheet of flames at the main door.

"Hey! What's that?" he blurted.

Hobe grated to a halt beside him as he passed by. "What's what?"

"I saw something move."

"Probably one of the horses, poor dumb devil. It's a darned tragedy, that's what."

"We tried to tell him," Jasper sighed.

"That we d—"

"Look!"

At the door of the stable, the flames seemed to swish out of the way like curtains, then close in behind the forms that plunged through them. Like something bursting through a cloud, came a strange trio—a man on a horse, with a colt on a shank. They jumped right over the base of the fire as though vaulting a fence in a steeplechase and came thundering across the stable yard, kicking sparks.

"Jesus!" Hobe blurted.

Bombay shook her head and tail violently, then spun about to check for her foal, but he was right there beside her, crazy-eyed with terror. He stomped and kicked, throwing his hind end into the air as though to cast off the heat that lingered on his hair.

Noah flipped his leg over Bombay's smoldering mane and slid off heels first, then dived for a water bucket and doused the colt, then the mare.

Hobe and Jasper charged toward them.

"Mr. Sutton, you all right?" Jasper asked.

"No thanks to you," Noah answered, rubbing the water into the foal's stubby black mane. He was scorched and shaking, breathing hard.

"It was the niggers," Hobe said. "Somehow it was them."

"Sure it wasn't you somehow?"

Both men stared at him.

Jasper strongly said, "No, sir, it wasn't us."

"It'll be the house next time, I just know it," Hobe warned. "You can't whip 'em and paddle 'em and torture 'em till they got nothing to lose, and that's what you done. You gave 'em nothing to lose. They ain't gonna put up with it anymore, Mr. Noah. I'd bet my life on it if I was you. Next time they'll bring down the main house."

"They'll kill us all," Jasper added. The conviction showed clearly in his eyes as they reflected the flames.

"They'll not kill me, sir," Noah snapped back. He worked feverishly to wet down his two surviving horses, his jaw set in anger and insult.

"Uh, sir?" Hobe said. "They'll kill you *first*."

Blowing air out of his nostrils as though he were the horse, Noah straightened up suddenly and glared at the two men.

"Fine," he bit. "That's all I get from you after all these years of devotion? Fine."

He reached up, grasped Bombay's knotted mane, and smoothly slid up onto her back. His legs folded around her shoulders, and he looked down at Jasper and Hobe.

"Here's something else that's fine," he said. "I'm going after that mongrel son of a bitch. I'm going to bring him back and roast him on a stake right before the eyes of every nigra on this plantation; then I'm going to string the corpse up on that tree and leave it there until it flakes."

He buried his heels into Bombay's sides. Though she jolted and kicked, he held her back with nothing but his hands twisted into her mane. There wasn't even a bridle, and still he had control, like a wild Indian or a creature of myth keeping a mystical hold on the beast while barely touching her.

He leaned down and leered at the two men with the kind of eyes that make shivers run.

"That nigger mix is going to hang," he swore. "Then I'm going to cut off that branded arm of his and club *you* to death with it."

He dug deep into the mare's sides. Bombay shot out for the open road.

With the smoke still lingering in his nostrils, the baffled baby horse whistled and charged after her.

The dust behind Bombay's ringing hooves rose almost as high as the flames.

★

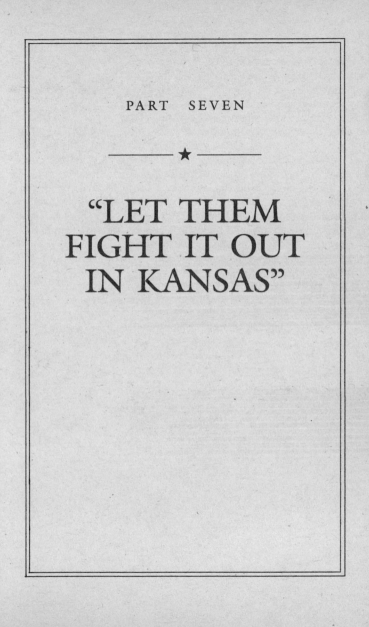

PART SEVEN

★

"LET THEM FIGHT IT OUT IN KANSAS"

CHAPTER TWENTY-SEVEN

──── ★ ────

1859
THE H. CRAIG AND SON TANNERY,
TWO YEARS BEFORE THE CIVIL WAR

The Kansas Territory hills were drawn in green chalk with the dust not yet blown off. The only scar upon the endless hill-and-prairie landscape was also the source of a traveling effluvium of rancid chemical smells forever clinging to the land.

Every day at the crack of dawn, Patrick Ruhl made his way through the shantytown of miserable workers' shacks with their deceptive sense of the temporary, past the shallow floating docks from which shipments streamed in and out, hides in, barrels of chemicals in, crates of lump lime in, finished leather out.

The factory itself rose over Kansas as though it knew no other structure its size existed map-left of the state line, the line where the United States stopped and the great untempered West began. It was a prowling rectangular building of mineral brown brick, with soldiers of windows lining four floors, heedless of all the great structures that had come and gone in the history of mankind without so much as a mark upon its progress. With its own shantytown, stores, sheds, a small schoolhouse, and an even smaller infirmary, the tannery was virtually a town unto itself.

Dawn hadn't quite shown itself yet. The factory still hung in its own sooty gloom on Kansas's stark landscape. The blocky form spewed black coal smoke from the constant heating of the tanning vats, but otherwise there was no sign that the tannery was anything more than a big rock. Most of the workers wouldn't arrive until the sun peaked over the hills and hit the river. Today, as every day, Patrick hiked through the army of hides that hung like Spanish moss over long poles in the drying yard, poles that stretched all the way to the river on one side, all the way to the road on the other. After the hides hardened for a day, they would be brought in and dampened in the cellar. Men on union machines would set to work splitting them into uniform thicknesses, 150 hides per man per day, then off to the finishing shops where the curriers would have at them. Day after day it was the same.

Patrick kind of liked it that way. He liked a world that was like him—simple.

He was kind of glad things hadn't turned over and started changing when Old Man Craig died. Except that the workers had to labor long hours in this wilderness. Factory workers did everywhere . . . but he couldn't come up with any way to make things better, so there wasn't much left to do but the jobs at hand. The old man's son had been a steady boss since then, at least.

Wyatt Craig. The young man who let everyone call him by his first name, who had taken over for the dead father; the young man who had inherited a decade's worth of toil by poor white workers and, after May of 1854, industrial slaves. People had been nervous when he first arrived. Would he be better than his father? Would he be worse?

Whispered conclusions were that while the son wasn't the tyrant his father had been, he wasn't exactly a philanthropist either. Since his arrival from Delaware, things had changed some—taken on a younger man's efficiency, maybe, a few Eastern ideas of progress, a few newly patented measuring, stretching, stitching, and dehairing machines—but essentially there had been few changes and none that directly improved the worker's lot or the tannery's output.

So Patrick had kept on doing his job, and whatever duties were gradually added to that job, until he was, according to

Grace, a full-fledged performing monkey. He worked in the warehouse behind the factory now.

Wind whistled around the corner of the building as he yanked the stubborn door open and strolled in.

Patrick coughed as he walked into the familiar cloying odor of the liming rooms, past the sunken pits of milky white liquid in which dozens of sides even now lay drowning. Scum had collected on the surface, and he knew that meant it would have to be skimmed off today, which also meant that empty barrels would have to be brought in from his warehouse so the precipitate and all that—well, all that shit—at the bottom of the pits could be disposed of.

He snickered and thought of his sister again. He missed ol' Liz . . . didn't get to see her much since they were both working. Only saw each other once a month or so, since they didn't have the same nights off. The factory workers usually got Sunday off, but Grace had to work Sundays so Mrs. MacButton could be dressed and prissed up for chapel meetings. Even then Patrick was too haggard to do much more than steal extra sleep, then immediately go out hunting for the week's meat. Didn't feel right; brother and sister should see each other more than that.

It wasn't often that Patrick couldn't sleep as soon as his head hit the pillow and for as long as he left it there, but today he had a gnawing ache in his shoulder from sitting too long in a tree while barking squirrels and jack hares out behind the cabin, and the ache hadn't liked the shape of his cot. What a day that had been—the hares just wouldn't scat, and Patrick was a religious follower of the adage about never shooting a rabbit that wouldn't scat or a duck that wouldn't flare. He sat in that tree long enough to get a couple of squirrels and one pitiful hare and a pounding ache that wouldn't let him sleep last night.

So he gave into the ache and got up. He didn't swear at it, though; even an ache had to make a living.

He walked right through the factory, through the constant yellow lantern light, waved mornin' to the two negroes who kept things going during the darkest hours, when fires had to be stoked, and to the night watchman who kept an eye on the two negroes. Except for them Patrick was alone in the factory.

In the main arena of the lower floor, the tan vats spread like gigantic coffins on either side of him, creating a pretend corridor down the middle. Patrick would always marvel at the vats and at the ingenuity someone had possessed to invent the operation. Hides had to go through ten successive chemical baths in order to be turned into usable leather, each bath a little more potent than the one before. Not easy, because the baths were so caustic to human hands—sulfate of potash, lime, acid, essence of turpentine—awful stuff, and a constant burning acid stink. And constant heat. It was always summer inside the tanning room, because of the ever-burning coals beneath the vats. Because of that the workers here were allowed to go without ties. In fact, wearing a tie had become a symbol of a better, more skilled man, like the curriers and the splitters and stitchers.

On a whim, and because he had the extra minute, Patrick loosened the collar of his red button-down shirt and climbed one of the worker's ladders to peek over the top of the tan vats. What a fume! His nose started burning almost immediately, and he coughed, but what a sight!

Wasn't it *something*? Who could come up with such a contraption? Imagine being able to think of it! But somebody had, somebody back East, and there was a patent on the process just like the patents on the dehairing machines and all the other mechanizations of what was really a very ancient process.

The vats stretched out on either side of him, gurgling caldrons of chemicals brimming with hides, each hide separated from the one beneath it by a layer of ground tree bark. The thirty-foot vat was divided in half longways, then each half was partitioned into five square tubs, and each had a pipe that could drain its tanning liquor into the next tub. The strongest tannic acid went into the farthest tub, way over there to his right on the opposite side. Into that tub went the harshest, most burning chemical bath. It would drain into the tub beside it, and when that happened, the bath would be diluted just a little bit. Then into the next tub, and diluted a little more. Gradually the bath would come all the way around and be the weakest bath of all. It was into this weak bath in the last tub that the new hides would be placed. After soaking for—how many days was the process now?—oh, well. Days, anyway. The hides would be brought up and put into the slightly stronger solution in the next tub, then the next, and the next, until finally they were the most cured hides and they would be soaking in the strongest compound. So the hides rotated one way through the vats, and the solution rotated the other way. Dang if that wasn't smart!

Patrick shook his head, marveling at the brain who had invented the whole procedure, said good-bye to the popping bubbles, dropped to the plank floor with a thump, and moved along toward the back of the factory, where the warehouse awaited him.

"Sssst!"

He stopped and cocked his head.

"Sssssst! Over here!"

By golly, he *had* heard a whisper! He squinted through the lantern light toward the sound but didn't see anything. A couple of the windows were open, but only darkness shone through them.

"Ssst! Paddy!"

"Yeah? I'm here...." He walked toward the sound, toward the windows.

A face popped up, and Patrick bolted backward a step or two.

"Who're you?" he asked.

"It's me!"

"Oh. Who's me?"

The whisper took on an edge and insisted, "Come over here!"

Patrick sidled toward the window, but the face was little more than dirt and yellow hair. He squinted harder.

"Anibal? That you? Anibal, dang! I din even rec'nize you!" He squealed with delight and vaulted toward the high window.

Anibal Webb's filthy face scowled.

"Shut up! How the hell are you, boy?"

"I'm dandy . . . son of a—y'know—when'd you get back?"

"Just now. Come closer to the winder. Keep yer voice down!"

Patrick hooked his hands on the window ledge and peeked

over. The two were face-to-face now, with a wall of brick between them.

"You better go away again," Patrick suggested. "Ever since you come and took those niggers, these folks been madder than wet cats at you. They'll kill you, Anibal. They been looking forward to it. Know what I mean?"

"I know, I know." Anibal's eyes darted this way and that behind a mop of dirty hair. He was like a night creature more than a man now, having been on the run for nearly three years, dodging slavers and avoiding the laws that made him a criminal both in the South and in the North. "I couldn't get back here. Pat, you gotta tell me . . . is Grace still gonna marry me?"

Patrick shrugged. "Well, she mentioned it a couple of times, so I reckon she is. . . . I'd ask her and then hightail it north, though, if'n I was you."

"I plan to, I plan to."

"That's some beard you got there, Anibal, a heck of a beard for a young fella. . . ."

"I cain't find her. Where is she?"

"Who? You mean Lizard?"

"Yes!"

"Oh, she's down at the lady's house. Always is this time of the week."

"What?" Anibal snapped. "You mean she's still working for that old wart?"

"Oh, yeah, she gets along fine. You oughtta see her . . . so nice looking, with them ringlets in her hair and them lace aprons and her collar all buttoned all the way up to her chin—"

"She gonna be back up tonight?"

"Naw, don't think s—"

"You gotta give her a message!"

"Oh, sure. What should I say?"

"Tell her to come on up to your folks' cabin tonight and meet me. Got it? But not till dark."

"Let's see . . . yeah, I got it. I'll go see her after work. Sure is pleasant and a surprise to see you, Anibal, and I sure do wish you get clean away."

"I will, I will. I'll be up at the cabin tonight! I gotta go now! It's gittin' light."

"Okay. You have a good day, hear?"

"Pat, I ain't had a good day for nigh a year and a half. I'm so sick a the open road I could fart. Grace an' me gonna go north, and if I never seen another nigger again, it'll be too soon. They're free, an' I'm free of 'em. I bin follered near ten miles now, but I ain't got no place else to go. I lost those bastards a hour ago, and I don't think they got whiff of me again yet. If'n I lay low, Grace an' me can leave, and good-bye fuckin' Kansas once and for all. If I never see this stinking territory again—you tell Grace I wut'never a come back if'n not for her, and she better come with me this time, 'cuz I ain't takin' this risk again for her."

Blinking away his lack of comprehension for Anibal's references and the pictures the other man was obviously trying to draw in his head, Patrick only said, "I'll tell her. Sure wisht we could have a chance to talk over a roast jack hare tonight, Anibal. It's not right that folks got these troubles between 'em so's a family can't—Anibal? Anibal?"

Patrick pulled himself a little higher on the sill, but the other face was gone. He was alone again.

He dropped to the floor and lilted, "Dang, ain't that nice! What a pleasant surprise! Son of a twitch . . . Yeeeeankeee Doodle gettin' married, Yankee Doodle dandy, pickin' up my sister Liz and makin' her a wife-eee. . . ."

He jaunted his way through the factory toward the door to the warehouse. Anibal Webb. Wasn't that nice. Now he had something to think about.

The warehouse was a square timber building that butted right up against the back of the factory with only walking room between. Only a few shade-loving weeds clung to the edges of the worn pathway, for the sun struck between the tall buildings only thriftily even on the brightest days.

Two steps and he was inside the warehouse. The big loading door was open, as usual. In fact, he couldn't recall its ever being closed, except for once during a blizzard so brutal that the factory had been shut down completely for almost a week and a half.

He licked his hand and slapped his left boot for good luck,

then pranced into the warehouse and was immediately swallowed by the vast unlit area and its stacks of barrels and crates. There was no reason to take time lighting lanterns to work by, since he knew the inside of the warehouse like the inside of his trousers, and anything burning was frowned upon inside the dry wooden building with its rancid chemicals in their barrels and boxes, chemicals that would release deadly fumes if they were boiled—hell, they were horrible enough to breathe just at blood heat. Up near the roof a row of tiny windows would provide light later, after the sun came up, at least enough to work by, but that was still an hour away. There would be light on the river before this building got any.

For now he would have to make do in the dimness.

Rat's bad luck that he had to work today. If he had an extra half hour, he could hike down to the frame house and tell Liz that Anibal was back and that they could finally get married and make him an uncle once or twice or three times and move north and give him a place to visit where somebody would be there to meet him when he stepped off the wagon. Well, maybe if he got his work done extra fast before lunch, he could slip away early and come back just a hair late.

He glanced around, trying to decide what needed doing most. For a warehouse worker there was never a job finished. Ten things hit him at once, and he tried to pick through them for one he could do alone, or almost alone. Most of the loading and moving jobs were two-man or three-man operations, but there had to be something here for a fella to accomplish by himself. Maybe if he was just smarter. . . .

His gaze roamed the dimness and landed upon a plank shelf newly installed at shoulder level on the east wall. A shelf should have something on it—and right over there was a dolly with twenty 150-pound barrels of saltpeter. Hadn't Mr. Lassick grumbled something about getting those barrels out of the way and freeing up that dolly?

"Say, Paddy Doodle, that sounds useful," Patrick lilted to the emptiness. "Come here, salties."

His head cleared of all other thoughts, give or take the occasional glimpse of Anibal, and he set to the repetitive and utterly manual task. One by one the barrels came up onto his shoulder, inched onto the lip of the plank shelf, and were grunted into place. Soon they were lining the shelf five feet off the floor like game pieces, and he basked in their neatness. Patrick had never paid much attention to the story about the camel and that last straw.

He turned to hoist the only remaining barrel. His arms ached now, for that was a lot of work even for a strong young man who did manual labor all the time. Tiring quickly now and breathing hard, he determined to get the last barrel up before going for a cup of coffee and a piece of oatcake, but when the barrel's rim touched the rim of the shelf, the long plank gave a groan as loud as any agonized human had ever uttered and cracked right in the middle.

Splinters hit the floor as though sprayed from a gun barrel.

Patrick gasped, "No! No, no—don't do that! Wait! Hold yer pants! No, pleeeeease—"

He slid the barrel from his shoulder and plunged for the plank as it squawked under a ton and a half of deadweight saltpeter. The barrels on the shelf shuddered and skidded a half inch toward the middle.

"No, no!" Patrick yelped, and shoved his own body under the shelf, taking the paralyzing weight on his left shoulder— he had no idea it would be so much, so overwhelming—so heavy—

His eyes popped wide open, and he grunted, "God . . . oh, God hell . . . oh, help . . ."

Flabbergasted, he wedged himself tighter beneath the cracking plank as it shrieked in his ear. It wouldn't take the relief, though. Three thousand pounds of saltpeter pressed on the crack and on Patrick's shoulder. The thick shelf groaned, still trying to do what it was supposed to be able to do.

Patrick's effort was stupendous, but futile. And he was stuck.

A few more seconds under the weight, and his legs were shuddering. He knew he was in trouble. If the barrels went over, they would take him down and a ton and a half of saltpeter down over him and all over the floor. Patrick knew his mistake would cost more than he was worth.

The plank shrieked as the barrels shifted again. The cutting weight of the barrels now rested on Patrick's unguarded neck, but he couldn't use his arms against it because he had to hold the plank up or everything would come crashing down—on top of him. With every moment more strength drained. With every instant his life was in more and more danger. He'd be crushed if he didn't do something—he'd be crushed if he *did*.

Sweat drained from his forehead into his eyes. His bangs were drenched and sinking into the creases of his brow. His legs shuddered and shambled beneath him as the weight from above shifted more and more and the cracking plank fed on it.

Patrick grated his teeth and willed his quaking body to take a little more and a little more. His tortured neck sent bolts of pain down into his back and up into his skull until he couldn't even think anymore. The plank dug into his left shoulder, twisting forward and down, toward the floor as the crack grew.

A barrel near his head finally tipped forward and pitched off the shelf, plummeting past his face like a boulder. It struck the ground, broke into a flower of slats and rings, and saltpeter spewed across Patrick's brogans. "No, no, don't—" he choked. But there was almost no sound in his throat.

"Who's in there!" a voice called.

Unable to answer Patrick clenched his jaw until it pounded and willed himself to be found.

He blinked through the sweat at the open loading doors, and at the ominous silhouette of a man that filled it.

There he was. Wyatt Craig.

Patrick didn't have to have any light to know it was Wyatt. The figure was recognizable, as was the open vest and white shirt that caught what little light came from the slit of sky between the buildings. Instantly Wyatt's familiar face filled his mind if not his eyes. Wyatt Craig had the kind of face people think of as brotherly, approachable, the kind of face men walk up and say hello to, expecting a pat on the back and a handshake. His fluffy fawn-colored hair wasn't exactly brown, but his eyes were exactly blue, set in expressive lids and beneath soft brows a few shades lighter and ashier than his hair. His face simply didn't mesh with the harsh Craig reputation, and so many people in the shantytown had been left confused when they first met him. He looked them square in the eyes when he talked and thus had the power to disarm a conversation whether he meant to or not.

Of course, that depended on whom he was talking to.

Wyatt Craig, son of the infamous Hugh Craig, the college-educated heir to the Craig tannery and with it the struggling legacy of a new American West. His roar filled the storage room.

"What the *hell* are you doing!"

The barrels piling up behind Patrick's neck vibrated with the sound.

"Help," he whispered pathetically, "help..."

His heel skidded against the floor, and he almost lost his balance. The barrels slid and bumped down the cracked plank toward him, pushing heavier and heavier against his neck and shoulders. The weight crushed him downward relentlessly.

"Hold on!" Wyatt Craig shouted, and plunged into the dimness.

Crates and racks crashed out of his way as he thundered through the storeroom toward Patrick. Patrick desperately wanted to say something, point at the screw jacks—

But he couldn't breathe, or move.

Or hold on any longer—

With a final shriek right beside his ear, the plank cracked beyond any hope, and Patrick's knees started to go under the growing weight. He was almost down onto one of them—in another second he would be crushed under a hundred broken barrels—

"I got it!"

Was that Wyatt's voice? Or were his ears just ringing?

The weight eased up a little. Patrick cranked slightly to his right. Sure enough, Wyatt's tawny head was right there in the dimness.

"Don't move!"

Wyatt was holding the heavier side of the broken plank on his own shoulder, one arm stretched upward to hold the barrels that were sliding toward Patrick. His blue eyes flashed, and his foot jolted outward toward the dolly. His toe caught the handle. Sweat broke out on his face as he fought to tug the heavy dolly toward himself and Patrick with just that one foot. The dolly turned on its metal wheels and whined a protest, but it was coming. A moment later, and Wyatt's leg was through the handle and pulling harder. Only when the dolly was in reach did his hand shoot down from the barrels and catch that handle.

With a gargantuan yank he hauled the dolly flush against his own body, wedged his foot under it, levered it up onto its side, them bumped it up longways, perpendicular to the floor—and it was now almost as tall as he was.

"Hold on," he grunted. "I've got it!"

Upended the dolly was actually too tall to do what he was demanding of it. But the plank was broken, and if it could collapse one way, then it could also bend up the other way. With one final heave Wyatt cranked the broken wood upward and dragged the dolly under it. Two hard kicks, and the dolly was doing the work that a moment ago had been done by the throbbing shoulders of two men.

"The jacks!" he shouted. "Go!"

Without a word Patrick staggered through the storeroom to the corner where the screw jacks waited. Seconds later each man was cranking a jack under the plank shelf. With each twist of the tall jacks, the plank arched upward another quarter inch, and soon the barrels of saltpeter were once again secure on their perch.

Wyatt gasped and stood back to see if it would hold.

Beside him Patrick sank against another dolly's metal handle, puffing like a locomotive and hugging his sore left arm.

When the plank stopped creaking, Wyatt Craig rubbed his scraped hands and turned.

"Patrick!"

The younger man looked up through sweat-drenched eyes, held out a hand, and murmured, "I know . . . I know. . . ."

"You *know*?" Wyatt bellowed. He reached out.

Patrick cradled his left arm as it screamed with relief, and a tube of darkness started to close around his vision. When his shaking legs gave out, and he sank onto the bed of the dolly, Wyatt grasped his upper arm with both hands and pulled him up again.

"Come on. You're coming with me."

He had to help him find the door.

★

"Drink this."

Steam swarmed around Patrick's face. He could barely hold his head up now that the physical exertion was over. All the strength had rinsed from his body because he had tried to use it all up at once. Light-headed, he sipped at the warm coffee and breathed it deeply. The smell of the coffee almost covered the factory's perpetual chemical stink, and the hot liquid rolling down his throat made him realize how chilled he'd been all night. His arms and legs quivered and refused to forgive him. Incredible what the human body could stand when it had to.

He sat in the boss's office, trying to clear his head. Just outside he could hear the workers trudging in and the general business of the tannery moaning to a start.

Wilting and hollow-eyed, he looked to his right, at the hand clamped firmly on his shoulder. There was a shift, and the boss sat down on the bench beside him.

"You okay now, Patrick?" he asked.

Patrick gulped the coffee down so he could answer. "Oh, sure am. Guess you just about saved my life or something."

Wyatt Craig's forgiving blue eyes widened. "What'd you think you were doing? Why didn't you ask for help?"

The shoulder under Wyatt's hand went up and down. "Didn't think to. Wasn't nobody around. Guess I should've, huh?"

"You know we don't put hundred-fifty-pound barrels on shelves."

"Uh . . . yeah, we do."

"We do? Well, we shouldn't anymore."

Wyatt leaned back and sighed. His white shirt, brown tweed vest, and dark blue tie made him look like a barrister or a tax collector and somehow didn't quite fit his easygoing demeanor, except that the tie was never tied quite right, and the vest was never buttoned. The effort in the warehouse had mussed his ashy hair.

"Patrick," he began quietly, "when I promoted you, I thought you wouldn't work so hard, and you took it as a reason to work even harder. What am I going to do with you?'' He jostled the other young man and asked, ''Am I going to have to make you a foreman?''

''Gosh dang,'' Patrick choked, ''I wisht you wouldn't. You know how I hate to boss other people around.''

''Well, if you keep working this hard, I'll put a tie on you, got it?''

''Oh . . . okay. I'm awful sorry.''

Wyatt offered a charitable grin, and his soft eyes, made even softer by pale lashes, smiled too.

''I never saw anybody try to do so many things without asking for help,'' he said. ''You're a compulsive laborer, know that? I'm going to start taking it personally.''

In response a rare glint of wisdom surfaced in Patrick's face. ''Wyatt, you take everything personally already.''

Wyatt shrugged in agreement. ''Can you read and write?''

''Oh, you bet. My sister Liz, she taught me to write. She's real smart. She made me learn to say 'not' instead of 'ain't.' ''

''Well, she is smart, then.''

''Yeah, she's right Yankee sounding.''

''Her name is Liz?''

''Yeah, that's what I call her.''

''Elizabeth.''

''Naw, just Liz.''

''Just Liz?''

''Short for Lizard.''

Wyatt chuckled. ''Oh. Why'd your folks name her that?''

''I dunno. She killed 'em when she was ten.''

''She killed them?''

''Bit 'em and dragged 'em into a hole.''

Wyatt smiled. ''And you still live with her?''

''Mostly she stays out back, sunning herself on a rock.''

Wyatt tried to come up with something clever to say, but he was laughing too hard. Finally he just sat there in quiet companionship, chuckling.

''Interesting family,'' he muttered after a few minutes.

''Well, I like 'em.''

''And how old are you, Pat?''

''Nineteen come next month.''

Wyatt sank back against the office wall and scratched his elbow where the dolly had bumped him. ''Are you sure you wouldn't want to be a foreman? You know what you're doing, and everybody likes you. They wouldn't mind doing what you say. They'd rather see you coming than Lassick, that's for sure."

"Oh, no, no," Patrick protested, shaking his head. "Mr. Lassick knows what he's doing. I just couldn't do what he does, Wyatt, I couldn't."

"That's not what I—"

"I couldn't decide for people what they're gonna do for a living and which job who gets. . . . I just couldn't do that."

The hand shot back to give Patrick a comforting shake. "Now, don't sell yourself short."

"Mr. Lassick's been here just about forever. I couldn't take his job."

Leaning forward now, Wyatt asked, "Is that what you're worried about? It's a big enough factory. We've got three foremen. Lassick's the floor manager. That's different. I was just pointing out—well, something else about the two of you."

"You were? Oh. Okay." Patrick sank back against the wall. His hands were still white-knuckled as they caressed the warm coffee cup, but his face had lost its pinch, and he had finally stopped seeing barrels of saltpeter spinning before his eyes.

"Wyatt," he began, "c'I ask you a question?"

"Sure, Pat, what is it?"

"It's kinda complicated."

"Go ahead. I'll do my best."

"Is it just my imagination . . . or is . . . well, is slavery kinda a mean thing to do to folks?"

He looked at Wyatt then, who chewed his lip for a moment.

"Uh . . . why do you ask, Pat?"

Patrick shrugged in a way so natural that it couldn't be faked and confided, "I work with the niggers, y'know, like everybody else . . . and it just don't seem right. Y'know? Kinda like when I'm about to bark a squirrel? And I catch him looking right back at me down the sights, and he looks at me with those big smart eyes, like he knows something? And I just can't do it. It's kinda like that. Kinda the same feeling I get when I catch eyes with Rufus or Immanuel or . . . well, y'know what I mean."

"Mmm," Wyatt groaned. "I know what you mean. I want to improve conditions here," he said. "I've wanted to do that for a long time, but it isn't easy to keep up production at the same time. With slaves I can do it. I can ease everybody's workload without having to pay wages. See?"

"Oh, yeah, I see," Patrick agreed. "Don't seem right, though."

"Sometimes it doesn't. But look at it this way," Wyatt explained, testing himself to see if he was working too hard at his morality. "It doesn't make sense for skilled whites to be loading sulfur and hanging hides and stirring lime when they could be putting their skills to specific use. The coloreds are built for menial work. They're more accustomed to it. Remember when I tried to talk Rufus into apprenticing at the splitting machines?"

"He got real nervous. I remember that. Don't seem right to give the coloreds all the hardest work, though."

"Pat, you don't understand. God planned it this way."

"He did?" Patrick twisted on the bench and looked squarely at him, suddenly curious. "How'd you figure?"

Suddenly on the spot for a sensible answer, Wyatt searched for the right words—not easy.

"He made the white man mentally superior and the colored man physically superior," Wyatt explained carefully. Then he held his hands open on his own ignorance and added, "For whatever reason that's what he intended. As uncomfortable as whites are with grueling work, the coloreds are uncomfortable with trying to think and be creative."

With a satisfied, if not even surprised, blink, he paused and tilted his head as though listening to himself.

Say! That didn't sound too bad. He'd always believed it, but nobody had ever come right out and *asked* for an explanation before. He was admittedly surprised at how reasonable it sounded.

His house of cards crashed when Patrick said, "I'm pretty uncomfortable with thinking. . . . S'pose God meant for me to be colored?"

Wyatt's mood hairpinned. He glanced at Patrick's waifish

face, at the upper lip that was trying so desperately to grow enough fuzz for a mustache.

Patrick punished him with an imploring look and added, "Gosh, Wyatt, I wouldn't want to make a mistake that big. . . ."

With an uneasy chuckle Wyatt hung his palm on Patrick's arm and tried to come up with *exactly* the right, the perfect, the quintessential platitude, but all he could choke out was, "Patrick, uh . . . trust me on this."

To his complete astonishment Patrick smiled. "Oh . . . okay. Thanks, Wyatt, thanks a bunch."

Wyatt gaped, but tried to gape with wisdom and sophistication, so Patrick wouldn't lose faith.

"Sure," he murmured. "Nothing to it."

"But I still don't understand about . . . you know."

"Oh. Right . . . of course you don't. All right, let's see. Slaves . . . let me put it this way. The white man made the mistake of bringing the colored man over here from Africa two hundred years or so ago. He's not meant for white society. Never was. You and I brought him over, and now we're—"

"I didn't."

"What's that?"

"I didn't bring 'em over. I never been outside of Douglas County."

"I was referring . . . I was speaking, uh . . ."

"Oh! Oh, I get it." Patrick slapped his throbbing knee with his throbbing hand and shook his head at himself. "I'm such a scatwit. I'm sorry to be so dumb."

"Patrick, you're not dumb. Don't say things like that."

"Thanks. . . . I like to hear you talk. You're kinda like a teacher or a preacher or—"

They were both jolted by a brash knock on the door glass. The rickety door swung open without waiting for Wyatt to extend an invitation.

Wyatt straightened but didn't rise. Beside him Patrick shrank back, at least mentally.

At the doorway, gripping the knob with his customary fierceness, Brad Lassick's unimaginative eyes stung them both. His round face peered at them from within an evenly cut frame of black hair and beard—no mustache—he always seemed to be poking through a porthole. As silly as that image was, his was an imposing and domineering presence, as it had been for nearly fifteen years of Wyatt's life.

"Sorry," he said. But he wasn't.

"Can it wait another minute, Mr. Lassick?" Wyatt asked, but he also wasn't asking.

"If necessary," Lassick said, "but we've got six hundred sides arriving at the docks in half an hour, and the barge is going to need hauling through the shallows."

"I haven't forgotten," Wyatt said hastily.

"And the curriers are complaining that the free acid isn't being rinsed sufficiently off the hides after the fixing baths."

"All right," Wyatt repeated, "I'll deal with it myself. But I'm talking to Mr. Ruhl right now."

"And there's been damage in the warehouse."

Even though Wyatt was careful to make his expression clear to Lassick while masked to Patrick, he still felt Patrick retreat even farther toward the wall and wilt like a rag under Lassick's irritable presence.

"I know about that," Wyatt said. "I said I'll be with you momentarily."

Lassick threw Patrick a frosty regard. "Very well. I'll wait out here."

"Thanks."

The door slammed shut. The glass rattled.

Patrick shivered. "I don't think he likes me none."

"Don't be silly. Where was I?"

"Oh . . . uh, the negro isn't meant for white society, and we brought him over so—"

"Right, yes. I just want you to understand."

"I'm a-trying."

"We have a responsibility to give the colored man work, make him productive, and take care of him no matter the cost to ourselves. The slave owner has to starve before he lets his bondsmen starve. That's only fair."

"You know what they say," Patrick contributed amiably, "treat your companion better than yourself."

Wyatt gave him an approving pat. "That's right, that's the

idea. Our ancestors got us into this, and it's our responsibility to do right by all the coloreds who're stuck here now."

Patrick nodded to prove he was absorbing at least half of Wyatt's explanation, then his face lit up, and he suggested, "Maybe they could go back."

"Well," Wyatt said, "seems Africa doesn't want them or something. It's complicated."

"That's a dang shame."

"Isn't it?"

Patrick nodded thoughtfully and gazed at the floor.

"You say it better than anybody else," he murmured, "but it still don't seem quite to fit. If it's that easy, I wonder how come folks is always fighting over slavery this and slavery that, 'specially here in Kansas. We got slavery now, but we're not exactly the South. We got a factory, but we're not exactly the North. What are we—exactly?"

Wyatt shrugged with his eyes and said, "Something totally new, I guess. Things like that do come along. I'm no scholar, but as bad as things seem in Kansas sometimes, I don't imagine the rest of the nation's as torn apart about it, Patrick. Don't let it worry you so much. You'll get a headache, and the headache powder's back in Missouri where the people are."

They shared a little laugh, and the last of the morning tensions were rinsed away.

"I'm sure glad you're around to think of this kinda thing, Wyatt," Patrick said as he levered to his feet and gingerly straightened. His spine clicked and snapped, and he held his breath for a moment until he was upright.

Wyatt stood also and asked, "Tell the truth, now. You sure you're all right? How's this arm feeling?"

"Oh, Yankee Doodle dandy, you bet."

At just a hair over six feet tall, Wyatt had to look down slightly in order to give Patrick a big-brother scowl.

"You're lying, and I know it. You had a close call. Maybe you shouldn't work today."

"I'll work!" Patrick said with a crackle of protest in his voice. "Shining like new money, that's me."

Wyatt pulled the door of his office open, a door that even after three years still said *H. Craig, Owner and Administrator* because Wyatt wasn't egotistical enough to have it changed to *W. Craig*. What difference did it make? It wasn't as though anybody didn't know.

He gestured Patrick out into the morning chemical smells of the tan vats that now were flowing forward into one another—it was that day of the week.

They waved to a few workers who noticed them coming out. Then Wyatt hooked his arm around Patrick's shoulder and lowered his voice as they strolled deeper into the factory complex.

"Now, what is it you do to the squirrels?"

The salve of human contact did little to warm the unforgiving glances of Brad Lassick as he waited for Wyatt down the wide corridor, but it was enough to protect Patrick from Lassick's glares until they were past the foreman. Lassick didn't like the white-trash workers any better than the black ones. Wyatt wondered if Lassick's glares weren't part of the reason Patrick refused a promotion to supervisor, remaining content to work stock in the warehouse.

At any rate, Patrick was too self-conscious to have even heard Wyatt's question and soon pulled out from under the guardian arm and jogged off toward the warehouse. He tossed back a grateful wave and a nervous grin but couldn't muster the confidence to bid a verbal good-bye.

Wyatt returned the wave and veiled the tension with, "You be careful, hear me? Okay."

He watched Patrick jaunt away and lose himself among the other workers, behind roaring machines, shrieking dollies, and endless stacks of hides and leather in various stages of the weeks-long tanning process.

His innards tightened.

Lassick was already approaching him, and he hadn't dismissed Patrick.

"That bumbler caused a lot of damage in there," the older man said, "and I don't have to point out it is not the first time, Mr. Craig. We should send him packing."

Both Lassick's voice and his Kentucky accent were deceptively mild. It was always as though he were sneaking up on something, speaking softly as though to hypnotize his prey.

But Wyatt was used to that.

With a shrug he responded, "Nah, we need him. He gets along better with the coloreds than anybody else."

"That's because he doesn't have the brains to know he's better than they are."

It sounded like half a compliment and half an insult, but Wyatt knew Lassick only meant the insulting half, that Patrick was only part of the white race by at best the whim of God or at worst an accident of his parent's ill-timed sex.

Wyatt stiffened his shoulders and grinned affectionately in the direction Patrick had disappeared.

"That's what I like best about him," he said. Then he faced Lassick and stared into the hunter's barrel. "You wanted to talk to me?"

"I'm beginning to think there's nothing left on earth that can't be thrown into a vat and used to tan hides. Look at this list. Horse dung, damp rotten wood, essence of turpentine, hen manure . . . hen manure?"

"It's an old formula," Bradford Lassick said.

Wyatt paused, then tossed the recent trade journal onto his desk, having utterly failed—again—at trying to pry a conversation out of his father's longtime manager.

That was how Wyatt thought of Lassick—his *father's* manager, never *his* manager. Lassick probably knew more about tanning than anybody north of hell or south of heaven, and he always wore one of several light-colored velvet-soft kid vests as though to prove it.

Lassick sat in the stiff chair before Wyatt's desk and waited with dry patience. At the age of thirty-eight, he was a man tempered by years of work at a certain level of expertise, as high as he could go in the Craig company without actually owning it. His broad brow was bare except for eyebrows that followed the line of his squarish eyes, then turned abruptly downward where the eyes ended. His hair was always combed back, also to turn downward sharply behind his ears, and went all the way to his shoulders. The beard was a neat ear-to-ear roll that followed his jawline and thus made almost a perfect circle around his otherwise bare face. In many ways he was an uninspiring man—

Except for his eyes. Light brown and unyielding, Lassick's eyes were those of a painting by some Italian unknown who wanted to capture the essence of mankind, ringed with lamp-black lashes that women would die to possess. It taxed the imagination to think of what a handsome child he must have been, and what had happened to him in his life to hone such a stark and cold-blooded adult.

Lassick sat there with his white sleeves rolled up, his tie in a perfect bow, and his eyes as still as the paintings they mimicked.

Giving up, Wyatt collapsed into his desk chair, wobbling backward to brace his foot up on the desk. He laced his fingers across his belt and sighed.

"All right, problem number one," he invited.

As though coming out of a trance, Lassick's eyelids came down slowly, just once, and opened again.

"The glove-leather hides are coming through the vats too quickly. We've got to allow an extra day per vat."

"It's coming out too flaccid or what?" Wyatt asked.

"Yes, too flaccid," the other man said.

"Well, that's understandable. We've never done anything as soft as glove leather. Bound to have a trial-and-error period before we get it right."

"Time-and-money period, you mean," Lassick pointed out. "Problem two, we must speak again to the men at the lime pits. They're not piling the hides carefully enough. The curriers are complaining of lime folds."

"I'll talk to their foreman."

"Those pits aren't large enough," Lassick said bluntly. "It's better to lime the whole hide and split them into sides later, especially if we want belt and harness lengths. We should consider widening the pits."

Wyatt clicked his tongue and winced. "Big job. We'll get some engineers to look around. What else? Oh! There's one thing I read—where is it—" He rummaged through a pile of trade journals and newspapers that had arrived in a single tattered package on the last barge from Missouri and yanked out a clipped article. "Here. A new solution for dehairing."

Lassick's straight brows lowered. "Lime's been used to dehair since the Egyptians."

"Yeah, but they're dead now," Wyatt muttered. "There are other ways to dehair. The tanning compound can't penetrate the pores if they're already filled with caustic lime, so we've got the extra step of bating the hides in the manure to neutralize it. But here, listen to this. A compound of carbonate and sulfate of soda—that's one, and a combination of prussiate of potash, common salt, carbonate of potash, common lye, and quicklime. Have you heard of these?"

"No. I haven't."

"This says we can shorten the liming process by days if we use salt soda with quicklime, then soak the hides in pure water at a hundred fifteen degrees for two hours before we put them on the dehairing machines."

"Experimenting costs money," Lassick tonelessly pointed out.

"Any more than that greedy liming process already costs? If we could eliminate it, or dilute it . . . This other article over here—where is it? Ah—this one says we can dehair with steam."

"Steam?"

"In a vat or a tight chamber. Steam at blood heat."

"I don't believe it," Lassick said. "I can't imagine it working, except perhaps on sole and harness leathers. You can't get the quicklime out of the dehairing of soft leathers. It's a natural problem with animal flesh. One cannot go against nature. Where did you find this . . . authority?"

Wyatt leaned forward and put his elbows on the desk, meeting Lassick's disarming eyes with practiced aplomb.

"Lime's a greedy process, you know that," he said. "It depilates all right, but it also decomposes the gelatinous tissues out of the hides and forces us to bate the lime back out again. If we can eliminate the bating and still preserve the body and strength, we can get more leather out of the skins."

The terrible godly eyes narrowed. "Is that what it says?" the manager asked suspiciously.

A twinge of doubt fluttered across Wyatt's shoulder, and he had to force himself to stand his ground on behalf of the unproved.

"Isn't it worth trying?" he asked.

"It's drastic."

"So it's drastic. Bating out the lime is a devil of a process. What a marvel if we could eliminate it. This article says we can expect fifty pounds of dry hide to produce about eighty pounds of finished leather once it's swelled and stretched. Fifty of green hides can give us thirty pounds or more once the hides are raised. Worth a try, isn't it?"

"If we had a lot of money to risk," Lassick immediately alerted. "That means new vats. Changeover is costly."

"Mr. Lassick," Wyatt went on, "we want a process that dissolves less of the gelatin and leaves the leather closer grained and flexible and not spongy. I don't know why we shouldn't be actively looking for something like that and willing to experiment when it trots our way. Here it is. Should we turn our backs and moan for pennies? All right, will you compromise with me?"

Once again—second time this morning—Lassick's eyes thinned with suspicion. He knew Wyatt didn't have to compromise with him at all if he didn't want to. The door behind him proclaimed a name, and it wasn't Lassick.

Wyatt held rein over several beats of silence before explaining himself.

"We'll try steam on half the sole and harness hides. On the rest we'll go to this formula. Rather than pure lime we'll go to a compound of soda ash, lime, sulfuric acid, monosulfuret of potash, and hard soap. The compound uses the lime but tempers it. These other ingredients are softeners. They overpower the lime and plump and raise hides that stay pliable. The hides take tanning better and faster." With a flip of his wrist he cast the two articles onto his desk, where they fluttered and skimmed to rest. "Science, Mr. Lassick. I like it."

He rocked happily. The chair twittered away beneath him.

Always on the barricades Lassick ran his hand across his neatly rolled beard as though trying to think of a way around all the trouble and upheaval these new ideas would bring, but finally he simply reached forward and scooped the articles from Wyatt's desk. He folded them crudely and stuck them into his vest pocket. Issue sealed.

Wyatt nodded. "I'm going to put Patrick Ruhl in charge of building the new vats."

A gasp of indignation burst from Lassick, as though he took this personally, as though it were a deliberate affront to his own opinion about the white-trash bumbler who somehow was always forgiven. "That greenhorn once again? Why?"

"Because he deserves it."

"Pray tell why he deserves it."

"Plain loyalty, if nothing else," Wyatt said. "Pat Ruhl would dive headlong into a pit of quicklime to save a drowning fly. He supports both his parents, you know. I think he's got a sister, but how much money could a woman make?"

"Mr. Craig," Lassick interrupted, "you're being unwise. He's a simpleminded buffoon."

"Simplehearted," Wyatt corrected, grinning amiably. "There's a difference."

"You're making a mistake."

"Well . . . you can call me names after you leave."

Lassick slumped against the back of his chair. Damn Wyatt Craig to hell in a rotting chariot, and may he have to spend eternity with idiots like himself. Even now, as Lassick cursed young Craig, he stiffened under the disarming quality that Wyatt possessed, this magical ability to bring out the *best* in almost everyone. Even now he felt it tugging at him, asking, cajoling, encouraging him to give in. Wyatt could do that to people with his talent for insightful innocence.

Lassick was accustomed to working with men he didn't like. He hadn't liked Hugh Craig either, but at least the two of them had a common approach to business, a mutual distrust of others. Eventually they had come to trust only each other. That's why Hugh Craig had wanted slaves in Kansas. He hadn't trusted men he didn't own, men who demanded and expected a wage and certain conditions. He would have run an all-slave operation if he could have gotten away with it.

The years peeled away as Lassick watched Wyatt's face and tried to see Hugh in it. There was nothing of Hugh in it, nothing at all. His strongest memory of Hugh Craig was the pure rage boiling on his features when the abolitionists came in and stole his newly bought slaves and put them on the

Underground Railroad. The hunt was still going on, nearly three years later. Some of the workers were still furious, still nursing that wrath, and woe be to the man who had taken those slaves. His name was well-known in these parts and still muttered with spitting ire around the factory. *Webb.* Anibal Webb. The proslavers would wait for him, no matter the clock's tick.

"I see," Lassick uttered, by way of dismissing the subject. He would find some way to deal with it later, and one of his best tactics was to disarm the enemy by changing the subject. "Also, there's something else we must consider."

Instantly open-minded, Wyatt asked, "Okay, what's that?"

"That we might be losing some men. As many as fifteen."

"What?" Wyatt's foot thumped to the floor, and his chair creaked as he sat upright. "Why? Who says?"

"Rumors."

"What kind of rumor?"

"Proslavers. They think the South is actually going to secede. They're talking about going down to Tennessee or Virginia and forming a militia unit."

"Oh, that's ridiculous! Hell, the South's been dancing the Secession Two-Step since I was a little boy. I'm twenty-six, and they're still dancing it. They'd get a lot more done if they'd just attend to business and raise their children right." He crashed backward again, and the chair squawked a familiar protest. "Damn!" he huffed. "It's clockwork, you know that? Every year, just like rutting season, my father's old proslave tagtails start stirring things up again no matter what I do to throw water on them."

"You're proslave, Mr. Craig," Lassick pointed out.

The blue eyes flared. "But not proviolence. My father sanctioned their troublemaking, but I won't. It's their choice if they want to leave here, but the proslavers have got to get out of the area, away from the factory, and their jobs won't be waiting for them if they come back. You tell them. Never mind—*I'll* tell them."

"Your daddy never would've done that," Lassick pointed out. "The workers won't like it."

Wyatt tucked his upper lip for a moment of thought, then asked, "Can you recommend a better course?"

"Recommend neutrality," was the instant, sharp answer.

"Neutrality," Wyatt murmured. The chair creaked as he shifted again. "Mr. Lassick . . . I don't know your politics. I never heard you talking politics with my dad, and I've never talked politics with you. Maybe we could be honest with each other for a couple minutes. What do you think?"

Lassick turned defensive. Distrust dogged every line of his face as it turned hard within the porthole.

Wyatt waited. Yes, they understood each other. Rare, but it did seem to be happening this morning.

"Are you a Free-Stater, Mr. Lassick?" he asked baldly.

"I'm not anything. I'm in no group or party," Lassick shot back. "Half the Free-Staters are mixed up with abolitionists. I was loyal to Kentucky, it was my home, and I believe in slavery, Mr. Craig, but not for the West. The South needs negroes to work its agriculture. We don't. There's not enough land to be tilled in the territories to support a handful of field hands. I told your father I wanted no part of bringing negroes into Kansas Territory. He did his politics. I stayed out of it. It was that simple."

"You don't like them, do you?"

The candid question blazed across Lassick's brilliant eyes and yanked the sudden truth from him. "The negroes cause trouble in this country!" he snapped. "The South can have them, but I'll be damned if they'll push me out a second time."

At once he drew back. Mentally as much as physically, he set himself deep into his chair and clamped his mouth shut until he regained control. He couldn't stand to lose his grip on the reins, and he felt them slip under Wyatt's buffeting presence. His arms went tight against his sides as though to keep something in.

"I left the South because of them," he said.

"I know," Wyatt soothed. "You were a skilled tradesman. Negroes took your job, and you were forced westward."

"They taught the negroes my skills. Let the South keep them. I tried to tell your father that, but he wouldn't listen. Now we're stuck with them, Mr. Craig, and we shall all regret, I say. Slaves are a curse. They foster resentment. It's one thing when they are in the fields, and quite another when white men are forced to work alongside them."

"Not if everybody's treated civilly," Wyatt said. "There's no cost in that."

"You're wrong, sir. There is a cost," Lassick insisted. "I told your father the same thing."

Wyatt pressed his shoulders back against his chair and mused, "How'd you two ever manage to work together all those years if you're so . . . the way you are, and he was so proslave?"

Lassick answered sharply, as though he had always expected that question.

"There were other reasons."

Yeah, Wyatt thought. *Greed for one.*

He sat back and tapped his fingers on his lips, not looking away from the other man's eyes, and gave himself several long seconds to ponder the news and how it fit in with his goals for the tannery.

"Mr. Lassick," he began slowly, arranging his words with care, "haven't you ever wondered why God arranged things like he did? Maybe he intended the negro people to do the work so whites would be free to keep the world running smoothly. I keep trying to understand what's expected of humanity. It can't be sitting around tanning hides for eternity. There has to be something a little more. So . . . this is probably the wrong time to tell you, but I guess fate is stepping in. I've been looking for a way to bring in more negroes. If those men leave, that's an opportunity."

"Damn you, young man!" Lassick struck out—the reins slipped. "The abolitionists will tear this place down brick by brick!"

"How? They can't get through the proslavers who are already here."

"They'll find a way. You know that."

Wyatt shrugged. "Well, everybody has something to contend with. I guess this is ours. Things'll even out."

"It does not happen that way! Nothing is even where negroes and whites work side by side. Pretty soon the negroes are being trained to be coopers and millwrights, and there's no work left for the skilled whites. That's what happened to

me in Kentucky. Even our most vehement proslavers watch
with scrutiny every benefit you give the slaves!''

While there was some sense in that, Wyatt put his faith in
the better side of human nature and said, ''Maybe the whites
should go on to something better. More important. Maybe
they're getting a message. After all, you moved along, and
look at you now. You don't have to get your hands dirty
anymore. That's what I was trying to—''

''Sir, you are ignorant!''

Another shrug made Wyatt's point for him. ''Probably.
Never denied it. Look,'' he said, leaning forward, ''you and
my dad used up half your profits bribing legislators to pass
laws that would let you double your profits. If you'd just run
the operation honest and aboveboard, you'd have done fine.
Maybe even better. Didn't either of you ever add it up?''

''It takes power,'' Lassick said. ''Influence in the right
places.''

''No, it doesn't. All it takes is a steady hand. Maybe a
competitive improvement here and there. I don't think a
merchant has to swindle and bootleg, that's all.''

''Then you're no businessman.''

''Mr. Lassick, I don't dabble much in politics, but I do
know business can be honest. We've got a product people
need in a prime location, with pioneers coming through who
need leather goods for migrating west. It's not as complicated
by political issues as you and my dad insisted.''

Lassick got to his feet—a movement that surprised Wyatt
with its suddenness and its intent to intimidate—and he tilted
forward over the desk, which was now a buttress between
them. ''Kansas is in upheaveal, Mr. Craig, and you are
ignoring the consequences *and* the possibilities.''

Wyatt gazed passively up at him.

''Nope,'' he said, ''just floating on top of them till things
settle, that's all.''

Lassick's eyes tightened to nubs. ''While he was alive,
your father refused to let you tamper in the business. Now I
know why.''

Only then did Wyatt realize what a physically threatening
man Brad Lassick could be. The gold eyes, ringed in onyx,
burned his skin.

He cleared his throat and firmly said, "My father's not here anymore, Mr. Lassick. I'm going to do the best I can."

"Your best disappoints me. It's not what I've worked for," the other man said. "You're going to nice-and-kind your way right into bankruptcy, and I intend to protect myself."

"Protect yourself? I don't understand. How, exactly?"

"By telling you what I *have* been working for."

The manager leaned forward and looked squarely into Wyatt's face with leaden ferocity.

"I intend to get what I deserve. From you, Mr. Craig, right from you."

Recognizing the veiled threat, Wyatt slowly got to his feet and met the other man at his own level. "And what is that, sir?"

"I'll tell you what, sir," Lassick said. "It is that your father promised to give me half this business after our first fifteen years. This is that year. And I want what I was promised."

★

CHAPTER TWENTY-EIGHT

———— ★ ————

Everything about the man was curious. His fine clothes were plastered with road dust. Fatigue dogged his features and his limbs. He spoke to no one. In fact, he looked at no one.

A small crowd of tannery workers watched closely as he walked into the saloon and spoke to the proprietor.

But nobody got too close.

Everything about the man suggested they stay strangers. His demeanor said they were unwelcome company, and somehow with his air and presence, he communicated that this was because they were beneath him. He was as dusty, as sweaty, as whittled by travel as anyone else in Kansas, yet he gave off a forbidding aura of superiority that everyone could feel.

No one had been born in Kansas. Everyone had come here, or run here, *away* from his kind of person. The man had come alone and he would leave alone.

And then he left. Right after tacking up a handbill inside the saloon. He walked out to his horse and slid into the saddle with such style and finesse that the small crowd of workers murmured.

He rode away without glancing back, right out of town, heading east. Everyone scrambled to have a gander at the posted bill. It was an instant curiosity, the only public printed matter in Douglas County, and they were almost as impressed with it as they had been with his horse.

It was pretty. All the lines were straight. It was a sign of civilization that most of them hadn't seen in a decade.

Too bad nobody around tonight could read.

★

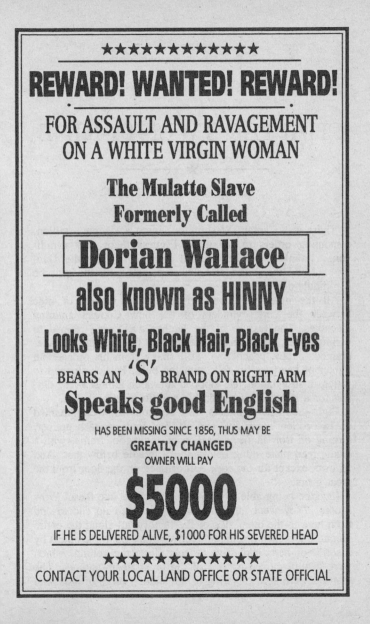

CHAPTER TWENTY-NINE

─────── ★ ───────

" 'There was Captain Washington, upon a slappin' stallion, a-shouting orders to his men, I guess there was a mill-yun.... Yankee Doodle keep it up, Yankee Doodle Dandy.... Mind the music and the step, and with the girls be han-diddle-dee.' "

All the other men were busy, feeding sheets of hide between the cork cylinders of the new Coogan graining machines. The texture of the leather was being refined to various types, depending on the leather. Coarse-grained, fine-grained, nubby, peach fine. Still shaky from his ordeal, but lighter of heart for his talk with the boss, Patrick stopped to watch in fascination. He stopped to watch almost every day, just for a minute or two, on his way to the warehouse.

Eight-inch cork cylinders, like big cookies, were mounted on two rollers some five and six feet long on each grainer, turning on iron shafts, all set in an eight-foot frame, with a cradle feed plate slung below and a treadle below that. And all iron, except for the cork. Oil dripped on the floor from the great gears.

Imagine being able to think of a machine like these! Wow Moses! They were huge machines, all lined up end to end from here to the other side of the factory, all along the entire second floor, each machine directly connected to the others by a series of belts and drive wheels along the ceiling, which were in turn moved by one of the great steam engines. The grainers were new, offspring of the sudden surge of industrial inventing that had hit the nation during Patrick's lifetime. So much change, so many patents, new machines every month, new tanning formulas, new ideas, or improvements on old machines and old ideas.

The floor thrummed with all the tremendous kinetic energy of the machines, the wheels, the steam engines, and above the thrum was a constant whine of the belts. The only way it could stop was if the belts broke.

Wow Moses. What a thing. Patrick loved it. . . . He *loved* the factory. It was like being inside a great big brain.

He shook his head in awe and strolled on his way.

Though the other men were concentrating on their day's yield, they took time to greet him with "Hey, Patrick," "Ho, Patrick," " 'Day, Pat," and he hey'd, ho'd, and day'd them right back. They liked him. He liked to be liked.

When he was almost out of the door, almost to the stairwell, something caught his attention, and he paused to see if he was right. He found himself standing at the place where the line of grainers stopped and the line of cutters started. Until an additional building was put up, the two sets of machines would have to share a floor. Each machine had its own version of mess—the grainers dripped oil, and the cutters dripped both oil and scraps of leather. Patrick was standing ankle-deep in a pile of those scraps.

Wasn't supposed to be here. That was the rule.

Immanuel was supposed to have swept this up.

Peeking around, trying to be cagey and subtle about it, Patrick glanced right and left, but the slave's jowly brown face was nowhere to be seen. Probably in the outhouse or peeing into the river. There'd been a touch of dysentery going around.

Patrick rubbed his hands together, trying to be casual. Immanuel's broom wasn't anywhere to be seen either.

Shit and dang.

Overhead the belts turned drive wheels, which turned driven wheels on the cutting machines, and more and more scraps piled onto the floor.

Wouldn't be a nice day anymore if Immanuel got into trouble.

So he scooped up an iron ceiling hook, which was usually

used to adjust the belts above, and gave it a new job—scratching piles of leather scraps toward the refuse bin in the corner.

It was kind of pleasant. Doing something else for a change, with more people around. Patrick smiled as he scratched and gathered. He liked people. They were always a surprise.

He squeezed between the cutter and the grainer to get a pile of scraps out from under the other men's way. They danced aside and laughed, and he laughed back and chased their feet with the ceiling hook.

Right about then the handle of the iron ceiling hook drove into the wheels of the grainer. The iron wheels bit down. The belts shuttered. All the tremendous inertia of the second floor took over. Thousands of pounds of machinery strained against the adulterant. The belt stretched and snapped like a whip.

Patrick looked up at the sound, but there was no moving out of the way.

No one had ever told Pat Ruhl that lightning could strike twice in one day.

He found out when fifteen hundred pounds of grainer danced sideways and came down upon his legs.

"What was that again?"

"You heard me, sir."

"I heard you . . . but I've never heard it before, is what confuses me. Half the business?"

"That's right."

The two men stared at each other over the old desk. Not one of those pleasant stares. Rather, the kind a person hopes doesn't last much longer.

Wyatt sat back in his chair, trying to muster his defenses and trying to speak to his father in the grave. He wanted to be fair, but he also knew fairness was difficult when he was dealing with someone like Lassick. He cleared his throat and ran his tongue along his lower lip. Didn't help.

"Well, Mr. Lassick," he began slowly, "this is a hell of a surprise for a Monday morning. I want to understand. You and my father had a business arrangement that you would be entitled to fifty percent of the factory after the first fifteen years? That year is this year, and you want half the business?''

''Yes.''

''And neither of you ever thought to tell me about this arrangement?''

''You weren't in the picture until three years ago.''

''Three years is a long time.''

''Not in business, it's not.''

''One or the other of you didn't say, 'Let's write this down'? You're both businessmen, you know about contracts, and now you put this on me?'' He swiped a hand across the top of the desk and said, ''Sorry. I put it back on you. If things didn't work out the way you planned, maybe you didn't plan well enough.''

He watched Lassick, but the other man never even flinched. A flinch would have given him a hint. A twitch, a fidget, a flicker of that iron gaze from inside the porthole.

Nothing. Nothing to go on.

Wyatt, though, couldn't keep his emotions off his face. All the doubts showed—he could feel them, feel his eyes crease and his pale brows draw, feel his lips tuck in question. He knew what kind of man his father had been.

And no matter what reputation screamed from the nether-world, there was only one decision that made any sense. He didn't like it, because he would never know if it was *right*.

''Mr. Lassick,'' he said again, ''I don't know what my father wanted. It wasn't money, exactly. Maybe it was power, I don't know. He's dead now, and he never told me what he wanted or if he got it. I don't love tanning leather, Mr. Lassick, and I don't love money. I do love to see the world getting better, and I think it is.''

''No, it isn't,'' Lassick interrupted.

''I think it is,'' Wyatt repeated, his eyes widening. ''And if I hand half of this factory over to you . . . well, I didn't get up this morning planning to insult you, but you kind of pick and choose which of our workers you treat well.''

Lassick's eyes turned nut hard, but they remained unreadable. Lies behind them? Fury? Insult? His Southern accent, usually rather mild from all the years spent in the Northwest, strengthened and added power to his words.

There was nothing quite so powerful as an aroused Southern voice, and it practically made Wyatt shudder.

"Your daddy promised me a piece of this business," he said. "He was a bad businessman. It was me who kept the business afloat. He was too concerned about bringing in his bedamned slaves to run this operation without me." He leaned forward. "You owe me."

A silent groan churned up through Wyatt's throat. He found himself desperately wishing that this order had in fact been written down. He'd rather it be true and written down than a lie and guesswork.

Lie. Lie. Perhaps that was the key.

"My father was a liar," he said, "which is sad when you think about it. He cheated a lot of people in his time. I racked my brains for a way to pay all those people back, but there's no way to do it. I'm... afraid you're one of them. Until today I hoped he was honest with at least two people—you and me. I guess we don't even get that. The best I can hope for is to start fresh."

When he saw the rage broiling behind Lassick's glare, he lowered his voice even though there was nobody else around, trying for a sense of confidentiality. He sure as hell wasn't going to give half his business to this man.

"I'm willing to let you start fresh with me, if you want, seniority and all. If you want to invest, become a partner, I'd say that's your privilege after all these years. But that's the best I can do. I can't afford to give you a payoff, and I won't hand over half the business. I'm sorry, but I've got to go with my principles—"

Lassick bolted to his feet. "Only a rich man can afford principles!"

Wyatt gazed up at him with disarming calm.

"I disagree."

"He promised me half this business, I tell you!"

"Maybe," Wyatt said. "I admit there's no way to know. You might be telling the absolute truth. When I got up this morning, I didn't plan to call you a liar. But can I be completely honest with you?"

This made Lassick worry—mostly because he'd never known

Wyatt Craig to be anything less than painfully honest. Almost
out of curiosity, he nodded.

Wyatt's face took on a sudden openness, a readability. He
leaned forward. He gripped the lacquered desktop.

His eyes got wide.

"I don't like you," he said flatly. "You're a mountaintop
of a manager, sir, but as a partner? I don't know what my
father might have been thinking if he *did* make that promise."

"My God!" Lassick bellowed.

"What God? You treat our white workers like slaves and
our slaves like swine, but I think you're the real swine."

Lassick's eyes were suddenly red-ringed as he bellowed,
"Sir, your father would not approve!"

"My father did a lot of things I don't approve of. I'm sorry,
but there's no mention of you in his will. We don't even like
each other, and we're supposed to become partners? I can
make progress in this backwoods dump. Concern for slaves in
the South is going to mean concern over conditions of
workers in the North. Wasn't long ago a worker in a shipyard
or a brickworks had to be subhuman just to survive. Hell,
they put children to work in some places." He leveled a nervy
finger at Lassick and sparred, "You'd do that if you could get
away with it. I wouldn't have your policies in my hide mill. I
think the world expects better of us. Ants can get along. Dogs
can scavenge. People should do better, that's all. We don't
have to be barbarians to make a profit."

He flopped back down. The chair rocked beneath him, and
he gave Lassick a little shrug that meant he hadn't intended to
make a sermon.

Lassick sat in his own chair and quaked.

"I'll sue you, sir. I have fifteen years advantage, and I
have witnesses."

"Fine. Who?"

"I'll bring them before a judge!"

"All right, that's your business," Wyatt conceded. "Until
then the tannery is my business, and it's going to get run as
fairly as I can run it."

He stood up and strode around the edge of his desk, fully
knowing he was risking a fist in the face.

"I've spent three years trying to clean up what you and my

father did to the people around here, and I haven't really been able to do it. You can loot for only so long. I can't let you bully me. I realize you're from the South, but I can't condone the way you treat our negroes. Or our poor whites, for that—"

"I hate the South," Lassick interrupted.

A bizarre chill came between them, a sudden sense of misunderstanding—as though they didn't know each other and never had, until now.

"Strange attitude for a Southerner, isn't it?" Wyatt asked.

"Is it? I've been pushed out twice already. And it's going to happen again because of your kind. You'll keep pushing us back and back until we're slaves too, and that's all there'll be, just slaves and owners. That's why nobody can earn a living!" he said. "If a white man wants better than starvation wages, the boss threatens to bring in slaves. More slaves! So we go west, and now you're bringing the slaves west. I'm a skilled white man, Mr. Craig, and I had to work like a slave twenty years ago because I knew I could be replaced by a slave."

"Mr. Lassick, if you'd just—"

"So I came here! Now you and your kind are bringing slaves into the West. Pretty soon the white people are going to run out of room! Those idiots who work for us—" he fumed, his voice suddenly dropping, as though he were talking to himself. "My God, they take guns and go into the hills and shoot abolitionists! The slave'll put them out of their jobs, and I can't even tell them! They'll cut my throat in the night!"

There was no answer for that. There was no easy way out: that was most of the problem of slavery, and why the fight was coming to a boil in the nation even as they spoke. Wyatt sat staidly, not really knowing what to say, knowing he wasn't wrong, but in a way Lassick wasn't either.

"You never said this before," he said quietly.

"Bullcock, sir. Your father and I fought a hundred times. I dared not say it to anyone else."

"Is this why you treat our slaves so poorly?"

"You *owe* me, sir!"

In the man's striking eyes was a hint of conviction, as

though he did honestly believe he was owed something, and for a moment Wyatt almost felt sorry for him. When he spoke, his tone was almost instructive.

"I don't owe you," he said. "You've had a good job and the freedom to leave it at any time. You're an employee. It's a good job, better than anybody else's in the place, including mine; you got the pay and took none of the risks. I took all the risks. That's what you agreed to in the beginning. It wasn't any secret. Even if I starve, you still get paid as long as the business chugs along. You made no investment that I know of, did you?"

"You're betraying your father's word of honor!"

With a little shrug Wyatt sadly admitted, "He didn't have any honor." Cocking his hip and hooking his thumb in his vest pocket, he frowned and wondered, "Didn't you notice that?"

"In three years you haven't found a magic potion for keeping profits up and work hours down. Have you?"

"You know I haven't. That's why I brought in more slaves. I hope to bring in even more, if I can find them at a decent—"

"And I am the barbarian? You, who would encourage slavery to spread beyond the South, where it belongs!"

Despite the little twinge of guilt that slavery gave nearly any Northerner, Wyatt shrugged one shoulder and said, "I explained about that. Who knows? The steam engine may well put slavery out of business. It's a much more efficient slave, after all. There's nothing wrong with that, except that we'll still have to take care of the negroes. That's our obligation. They can't mind themselves."

Lassick stood there, smoldering.

Wyatt scratched his ear and paced behind the desk. He hated confrontations, especially ones like this, that had no clear answer, no clear right to be aimed for. Cheat a man or be cheated? That was no—

Suddenly instinct made his stiffen.

His arms fell to his sides, and his weight centered. All at once, he heard it—an irregularity in the rhythm of the factory. Had he felt something? Heard a bang or a bump that shouldn't be there?

After listening, sensing, for a moment longer, he shook his head and dismissed the instinct.

" 'Scuse me. I thought I heard something."

"Soft!" Lassick said in a critical undertone. "This speculating will be the finish of you."

"I'm not much for speculating. I just look around and decide accordingly."

"You have not heard the end of this!"

They stood toe-to-toe in the small office, warm factory air swirling around them with its lingering chemical odor, and this time Wyatt matched the other man's tone.

"Didn't you hear me? Don't you know how many times you've gone home with pay and I've gone home with nothing? *That's* what I've owed you! And that's all you'll get of my tannery this side of hell!"

Lassick opened his mouth, and the beginning of a word came out before the office door crashed open. As it banged against the wall and bounced, one of the warehouse workers pushed it open all the way and thundered across the floor planks.

"Sir!" he shouted, then he looked from Wyatt to Lassick and back again. "Sir! We got a man down under a Coogan! Both legs broke, and he's pinned tight!"

"Jesus!" Wyatt gasped. He gestured out. "Go!"

As he stepped past Lassick, the foreman's hand landed against his chest and stopped him in midstride. Lassick snarled, "I care as much about this factory as you do, boy." The fire in his eyes agreed with him.

"Probably more," Wyatt admitted. "But that's tomorrow's fight. Step aside."

Wyatt, Lassick, and several of their tanners, cutters, and curriers charged together through the factory, past all the things and through all the smells it takes to make leather out of hides.

The ammonia smell accosted him with its stinging reliability. Around him was the drumming of the big scouring machines with their wheels and belts constantly turning, of the patented Roberts stretching machines, new just this year, of the graining machines with their cylinders turned by thick belts, the leather measuring machines, the stones and brushes, the fixed tables and moving tables, and overhead the spider-web of belts and huge wheels, gears, shafts, and pullies cranking in rhythm with the hiss of the two giant steam engines that ran all these machines. At either end of the main factory house, the steam engines chugged and groaned, their pressurized boilers slamming pistons down in their chambers, steam puffing as though from two great lungs.

These were the noises of a tanning factory.

And over all that noise, they could still hear the sound of Patrick screaming.

It cut through the mechanized roar and hit all the top notes of human empathy.

"Shut down! Shut down!" Wyatt shouted as he ran, directing certain men to certain places, men he knew could handle the job of disconnecting the steam engines from the belts they drove.

Just before entering the stairwell, he grabbed the necktie of the man running closest to him and shouted, "Whiskey! In the cabinet in my office, Henry! Step quick."

The man skidded, twisted around, and headed back in the other direction at a tilt.

By the time his boots scratched onto the second floor, Patrick's screams had already died away, replaced by pitiful whines and moans of a man going numb. In the middle of the second floor was a crowd of workers, bent over, trying to get a grip on the toppled grainer, but the huge machine iron had almost no center of balance that didn't put more pressure on Patrick, and no parts to grab that weren't heavily oiled. There was no getting a grip on it—Wyatt could see that even before he pushed through the crowd.

"Patrick!" Wyatt shouted. "Pat, I'm coming!"

He skidded to his knees between the machines, the cutter still standing and the grainer lying on its side. Overhead the belts and drive wheels continued to grind, the driven wheels to churn, and the one broken belt dangling over them like a snake in a tree, flopping up and down, caught in something.

"I said shut down!" Wyatt yelled over the noise. Then he turned his attention to Patrick.

"Okay . . . okay . . ." he murmured, squeezing in between the machines.

Both legs were broken, pinned under the grainer's cork-covered cylinders. Both bleeding. Pain creased Patrick's smooth young face and made it old and did the same to the face of every man who came within twenty feet, but none, not one, came close to the agony that limned Wyatt Craig's face as he hovered there and cradled Patrick's head in the crook of his arm. That was because no one felt responsible except Wyatt.

And, God, he did. If only he could put his own legs under there, break his own bones, do his own suffering. Instead Pat was doing it for him. The injustice hit him like a sledgehammer.

All the other men saw that, and in spite of the tragic moment, they were suddenly glad to be working for a man like that.

No matter how Wyatt peered into the mess of skin and clothing and machinery, he couldn't see where the blood was coming from. Were the legs cut off? Or had the impact broken the skin and muscle?

Patrick gasped like a dying creature and clawed at Wyatt's arm. Blood from his legs puddled beneath him. It soaked into Wyatt's trousers.

"Hang on, Patrick. We'll get you out." He craned his neck and shouted, "Where are the master jacks?"

"They're not on site," Lassick said from over him. "They had to be sent upriver to the bark mill."

"Why in hell would you send them both!" Wyatt demanded. "We should always have at least one big jack around—all right, we'll have to do it the hard way then." He looked past Lassick to a crowd of tanners who stood nearby, painfully helpless, and shouted, "You boys, grab something to pry this up with! I think there are a couple of bark-stripping irons on the other side of the sweating house. And get one of the spare pully belts—get two! We'll rig a winch and yank it up by the weight of its own mechanism. And where's that whiskey!"

His voice got louder with every command, partly because of Patrick's fingernails digging into his arm.

His view of the men scrambling away was suddenly blocked. Lassick had knelt beside him and was leaning very close.

"You can't do that," the manager said.

Wyatt held Patrick even tighter, as though to protect him from what he sensed was coming, and asked, "Why not?"

"The mechanism won't take the weight. It'll crack, and we'll have an expensive machine to replace."

"We'll have a couple of seconds before it gives," Wyatt said. "We'll be able to pull him out."

"Wyatt," Patrick choked. The sound gurgled.

"I'm right here."

"I can't feel my legs. . . . They ain't cut off, are they? Oh, God . . . where're my legs!"

"They're not cut off, Pat, hear me? I'm right here."

"I can't feel 'em. . . ."

Lassick leaned closer and lowered his voice even more. "It took us half a year's profit to afford these new grainers, and I had to wheel and deal for another six months just to get them. We're the only ones west of St. Louis who have them. If it breaks, we'll be set back months! The damned fool wasn't supposed to be working here. It's his own doing!"

Wyatt coiled his arm even tighter around Patrick, and his own brows drew tight.

"What are you suggesting?"

Lassick gritted his teeth and whispered. "Put torniquets on the legs and cut them off below the knees. He'll still live, and we won't lose the machine. Think of your other workers, if you have to! We've had to let men die before."

"Have we?" Wyatt snapped. "I never heard of anything so savage. Are you pushing me on purpose? Back off before I smear your face in his blood and let you get a taste of it."

Black brows formed a *V* over Lassick's nose. "You can't run this tannery without me," he grated, "and you're going to do it my way!"

"You back off," Wyatt warned, "or I'll stuff you into a bark grinder!"

Not an empty threat. Lassick might have struck Wyatt, lashed out like the crude laborer he had once been, long ago, except that he wouldn't have a chance. The least Wyatt would do is have him answer to the men.

All these men liked Patrick Ruhl.

Several workers skidded to a halt with the materials for a winch. They scrambled to rig a dangerous winch above the half-ton cutter, put the belt around the cylinder, and hooked it to one of the wheels on the ceiling. Wyatt snapped directions this way and that, but the men already had the idea and were way ahead of him. After just a few minutes, he realized they didn't need him as much as Patrick did, and he turned all his attention to the young man in his arms. When the whiskey arrived, he put the bottle to Patrick's lips and poured it down, dribble by dribble, persistent no matter how much Patrick gagged and resisted.

"Hang on, Pat, we're doing it . . . only a few seconds more. . . . It's almost there. . . . You'll be fine. . . . Hang onto me, I've got you. . . . Come on, swallow. It'll help."

Patrick choked, and whiskey bubbled up out of his mouth. Wyatt let it drain away, then put the bottle to Patrick's lips again.

"Swallow . . . that's it. Somebody get a stretcher ready."

"You're torturing him," Lassick said, his whisper taking on a sharp bite as he leaned closer to Wyatt's ear.

Wyatt didn't even look up.

"Don't push me, Brad. I don't have time for you."

"Wyatt . . . ," Patrick rasped, "don't make me live through it, okay? Don't take my legs. . . . Ain't got no brain. . . . I need my legs. . . . "

"Paddy, don't talk crazy," Wyatt reassured him.

"Six months work up in smoke," Lassick muttered. "Think of it! Thousands of dollars!" He dug his fingers into Wyatt's shoulder and hissed, "He's not worth it. You know what he and his family are. Trash!"

Wyatt snapped around. If he hadn't been holding Paddy, he would have knocked Lassick to the floor. It was as though Lassick had gut-punched him at exactly the wrong moment. Suddenly his catch-all forgiveness was completely spent. Wyatt, usually so pliant and fathomable, erupted before Lassick's eyes. "Then what are you?" he said, point-blank. "Would Patrick leave you here like this? Right now, I would! Your fucking sense of timing is off! Take your hand off my shoulder."

He clamped his mouth shut, not liking the sound of himself, though he continued glaring at Lassick. He felt himself going over the edge, felt his Quakerish patience fraying, and he hated to make decisions during a volcano.

Distraction came when three men wedged barking irons under the toppled machinery. The makeshift winch was ready. More men turned a great crank, and the winch belt snapped tight. The wheel whined over their heads. The enormous metal-and-cork cylinder that lay across Patrick's legs groaned and dug into the floor as one end began to rise slowly and the other to press harder downward. The wheel complained, floor creaked, but the mechanism slowly rose, half inch by half inch.

Patrick stiffened, arched, and bellowed, clawing at Wyatt. His eyes wobbled from side to side as delirium set in with a new wave of pain. His face turned to chalk. The blood pooling beneath him and Wyatt was an ugly, clotty red. The pain of the machine coming off him was even more agonizing than when the weight had sat upon his legs. His eyes flared, and he was instantly delirious, hearing nothing of Wyatt's words of encouragement, so Wyatt stopped talking and watched with held breath as the winch did its job.

The big cylinder dragged on the winch belt, its mechanism making a gaudy metallic ticking noise—it was giving way. If it broke, it would crash back down on Patrick and crush him.

A tiny space appeared above Patrick's broken legs. A wedge of light shone through it, glowing on the puddled blood.

"That's it!" Wyatt shouted. "Pull!"

Burying the crazy fear that Patrick would come out but the legs would fall off and stay under there, he dug his heels into the floor planks and hauled backward, and two of the curriers stepped in to help. Patrick scraped out from under the mechanism in a gush of new blood.

"Where's the stretcher?" Wyatt demanded—but here it was, right next to him.

"Get him up!"

"Tie his legs!" another man shouted, frantically shedding his vest and wrapping it around one of Patrick's calves.

Another man took his own vest and did the same for the other leg.

Wyatt let Patrick grip his hands no matter how much it hurt—and it did.

"Okay, let's go! Somebody run ahead and tell the infirmary we're coming!"

Two men lifted the stretcher and moved toward the stairwell door. Wyatt shuffled along at Patrick's side, still gripping his hands, and caught a bitter glimpse from Brad Lassick as they passed him, inching between the other machines toward the door. What he saw was the last reminder of his father's tyrannical business practices.

Something snapped, and he paused as the men tried to maneuver the stretcher into the stairwell and faced Lassick, saying what he should have said months ago.

"I think fifteen years is long enough for your snout to be at the Craig trough. You're fired."

Lassick straightened like a recoiling whip. "Dare you!"

"You don't give me much choice."

"I refuse to go!"

"Lou? Give Mr. Lassick three months severance pay out of the strongbox in my office. Mike! Enoch! Take up those hammers over there. If Mr. Lassick and all his things aren't out of here by sunset, break both his legs."

He had deliberately chosen two of the strongest proslavers out of the crowd of workers. Politics could sometimes work in one's favor.

The two men took up the hammers and stood between Lassick and the stretcher. He who had put so little loyalty into the men was getting his dividend.

"Goddamn you!" Lassick called after him. "Goddamn you and your father in his grave!"

Wyatt turned his attention back to Patrick. The stretcher was being angled down the stairs, the workers struggling.

But Lassick's voice continued cutting like a sword through the noise of the steam engines that powered the tannery.

"Goddamn you and your machines! Goddamn you and your Southern causes! Goddamn you and your niggers! Goddamn you and your factory right down to hell!"

Behind them, in onerous punctuation as the stretcher went

through the door into the daylight, the grainer's turning mechanism gave under the weight. It squawked, cracked, and the cylinder smashed to the floor. The mechanism fell apart and snapped into pieces.

Men bolted away from the flying iron chunks.

Overhead the winch belt rebounded, flopped about, then went limp.

"Mind that you dinna let any slip under the bed!"

"Keep your buttons on. You think just because you got old, everybody should listen to you."

"And dinna scratch them as you come through the doorway!"

"How'd you like me to avoid it? It's not big enough to cuss a cat in here. I ought to quit and leave you to rot in that chair."

"And do what without ma money? See your papa starve? Your mama starve?"

"We'll eat buttons."

"Step oot here and let's have a look!"

Mrs. MacHutcheon hammered the floor with her cane, then leaned forward upon it and craned to see into the bedroom. A moment later Grace stepped out, careful of the skirt that spread out around her like a bell.

"Is it heavy?' the old woman asked.

"Of course it's heavy!"

"Let's have a look."

Grace moved gingerly into the parlor and turned a couple of times. Blooming from her waist, the pea green satin skirt rested a little too heavily on its hoop, dragged by the weight of Mrs. MacHutcheon's entire button collection, over four hundred buttons sewn on in rows, as evenly as their odd sizes would allow, all the way down to meet the eight-inch removable ruffle at the bottom. The ruffle could be taken off and cleaned without disturbing the overwhelming button collection. They'd thought of everything.

In the room the glass-covered table, the cabinets and boxes that had held the buttons for a decade, were now empty.

Grace was wearing every last button.

Tiny landscapes, engravings, portraits of the gentry, bugs in glass, disks and ovals of etched and inked ivory, carved wood, and paintings on china now winked from her skirt. There were even the little black nubs of vulcanized rubber that Charles Goodyear had accidentally discovered when he dropped a little sulfur and rubber on a hot griddle. On the very front, running straight down, were portraits of the last ten queens of England.

"I feel like a Yankee catalog."

"You take care of it, hear that?" Mrs. MacHutcheon cackled. "There's trouble comin' sure as the sun sets over Sutherland, and I want those buttons safe. They're worth money!"

Grace rolled her eyes and said, "Did I spend two years sewing these stupid things on just to roll them in the mud? You say that to me one more time, and I'll be on you like a wrinkle. Where's the overskirt?"

The old woman snarled, "Ech! You insist on covering such beauty!"

"I put it right over there last night."

"Buttons are history! Josiah Wedgwood made buttons! Paul Revere made them out of silver!"

"Quit yammering and help me look for the overskirt. I swear it was right here—"

"The colonists changed to buttons of papier-mâché to protest import of metal ones from England. Are you hearing me? Look at buttons, and you look at the world!"

"I know all about your gaudy buttons!" Grace told her. "I stitched every last one of them onto this monstrosity, you old harpy."

"And you're a harpy yourself! The day'll come when you appreciate that collection, and you'll wish you'd learned them."

"I know them by heart. Where's the overskirt!"

Mrs. MacHutcheon hung her elbow on the arm of her wheelchair, and her eyes lost their focus. "Buttons are too small nowadays. Mass-produced. Plain, ugly, dull bits of nothing. And too small."

Grace huffed as she pawed through the parlor closet. "Someday you're going to die and we'll give you a twenty-one fart salute and bury you and all anybody's going to remember you for is you got buttons. Ah! Here it is. You put it down here, didn't you? You hid it!''

She yanked at the bottom of the closet, and out popped a pile of pansy violet fabric. Around its rim was a row of green ruffles made of the same satin as the button skirt, and it had green satin ties.

"You hid it, didn't you, Buttonlips? Think I wouldn't find it?''

She straightened and shook the folds out of the overskirt, then draped it around herself from back to front, like a reverse apron. Fitted to go over the other skirt and cover the buttons, it sighed to rest perfectly, its own row of ruffles just a little above the green skirt's ruffles, making two tiers of green. It didn't come completely around but left a small wedge of buttons showing at the front for decoration. Otherwise the dress now looked quite conventional.

"You're covering history,'' the old woman complained.

"It'll protect the stupid little trinkets from being scratched,'' Grace said. "You don't want them scratched, do you? You don't want them pulled off every time some dog takes a nip at me, do you? You don't want them to tease every pickpocket who comes by, do you? On top of which I'll be crammed if I'm going to unsew all these buttons just to wash this bedanged rag when all I gotta do is keep it in the den in the first place!''

The old woman cranked forward in her wheelchair and cracked her walking stick against the floor. "Forever trash! You're forever doing that! Whenever you get angry, you slide back into that white-trash mouth. What have I been teaching you? Is it deaf that you've been all these years?''

Grace paused, took on a sudden refinement that was open and intended mockery, and smoothly said, "I'll be damned if I have to dismember the entire garment when a simple apron will matronize these baubles sufficiently. You old ogress.''

Mrs. MacHutcheon sat back and looked pinched. "Uch. I liked it better the first way.''

"Here, make a bow.''

Grace doubled the satin ties around her waist and backed

up to the wheelchair so Mrs. Buttonnose could arrange a bow in back.

Good and tight.

"Ow!" Grace complained. "I've got to breathe, you know!"

"You dinna deserve to."

She stepped away and looked down past the green fitted bodice. "There. How does it look?"

"Grindingly ordinary, that's how."

"Perfect."

"You're too cowardly to wear them wi' pride."

"That's right, and all I need is having to explain to folks why I'm wearing bugs under glass and little faces of people I don't know, and how they're worth money." She paused then, and a thoughtful look encroached upon her annoyance. "Just *how* much are all these buttons worth, exactly?"

A clatter on the porch interrupted her, and suddenly someone was pounding on the front door.

"Miz Ruhl! Miz Ruhl, you in there? Come out quick!"

"How rude!" Mrs. MacHutcheon crackled. "Let him wait."

"He wants me, not you," Grace said as she pulled the front door open.

It was a man from the factory, a skilled worker, a currier or stitcher, judging by his white shirt, black vest, and tie, and he held his hat in his hands.

She didn't know him.

"I'm Miss Ruhl," she said. "Do something for you?"

"Yes'm, you better come quick. Your brother was in an accident in the tannery. He's in the infirmary. Mightn't you come with me, please? I'm here to escort you."

Grace's hand clamped over her mouth, and an instant of panic crossed her face. She spun around, not sure what to do first, years of conditioning telling her not to leave the old woman, yet the call of her own family was suddenly renewing itself.

It was Mrs. MacHutcheon who jarred her into action.

"Well, what're ye waiting for?" the old woman barked. "Your brither needs yeh, lass! I'll be just fine for the day. Scat!"

"Oh, Button—" Grace reached out and clasped the old woman's cool hands tightly. "You sure?"

"Scat, I say!"

"Thanks—"

And Grace was out the door, past the factory worker and halfway to the road.

Green ruffles hammered the dirt.

When Grace was almost to the road, Mrs. MacHutcheon snatched the sleeve of the messenger from the factory before he had a chance to draw the door closed behind him. She held onto him with one hand and dug into a drawstring bag on her wheelchair with the other. A moment later and she was cramming a handful of Dixie notes into the man's hand.

"Go intae Westport and bring back the real doctor," she ordered. "That quack at the infirmary's no' worth a plug!"

The man stared at the money, and it crossed his mind to steal it, but then he thought of Paddy Ruhl and decided to do as the old woman bade him. Besides, better to have a job than a few extra dollars and no job.

"Yes'm," he said, "I'll do it."

She needed no escort. She had been raised around the factory without ever having set foot inside it, but she knew where the buildings were and which shed held what, and which type of workers worked where, and exactly where the infirmary was. She wasn't used to walking with the heavy buttons pulling at her, and now she was running.

She skidded around the corner of the chapel and scraped to a halt—for there was the demon.

Wyatt Craig was just stepping out the front door of the infirmary. The hypocrite. Him and his proslave pigs and their godawful conditions in their sweathouse factory—he was responsible.

"If he dies, you'll pay," Grace snarled in a whisper as she ducked behind the chapel porch.

But Wyatt Craig was walking away in the opposite direction, hurrying back toward the factory, yes, back to work, back to crack the whip over other men who had no place to go anymore than Paddy did, no place to escape.

She had caught only a few glimpses of Wyatt in the past months, and those were too often. She avoided the subject of the factory even when she and Patrick did get the chance to spend more than ten minutes together wide awake. The tannery was a fact of life, like sickness, and didn't make good conversation.

She hated it and hated Wyatt Craig all the way into the infirmary, to Patrick's side.

The sight of her brother lying there made her whole body cramp.

He lay upon a narrow bed, the sheets still drenched in blood. The doctor stood over him with a hand on Patrick's chest, while two men with their sleeves rolled up were wrenching on one of Patrick's legs.

Patrick arched in pain, and his throat corded.

"Now the splint," the doctor said.

Grace watched, unable to move, as two wooden planks were arranged on either side of Patrick's leg and tied tightly into place.

Barely conscious, Pat moaned at the pain that reached through his delirium. He went limp again.

Grace pushed herself forward, working hard at her expression. She knelt beside the bed.

"Paddy? What did you do to yourself, stupid?" she asked softly. "Pat? It's me. It's Liz."

"Liz?" he groaned. "I killed me."

"Just saves me the trouble." She took a cloth from a small table and wiped his face, but the sweat kept pouring from his skin.

"Are you his sister?" the doctor asked.

She looked up. "Yes, I'm Grace Ruhl. Have you got something to tell me?"

The doctor shrugged and scratched his enormous beard. "Both legs are fractured below the knee. Bones are showing, and we're having to reset them. I think he'll be able to keep both legs, unless gangrene sets in."

"I'll see that it doesn't."

"Well, he won't be leaving here for a week or so, miss."

"Why not?" she asked. "I can move him over to the MacHutcheon house and tend him myself."

The doctor nodded and said, "In a day or so, we'll see about that. Might work. Excuse me—okay, boys. Go."

He leaned on Patrick's chest again, and Grace was able to catch Patrick's hand only an instant before the two medics hauled back hard on the other leg.

Patrick jolted and howled, digging himself into the mattress, and there was a *snap* as the bone clicked back in.

"Binding!" the doctor called. "Hurry up."

One medic held the leg while the other hurriedly wrapped two more boards sloppily into place on that leg.

"Uh, God dig me deep . . ." Patrick groaned as sweat poured from his brow. "Liz—"

"Always talking," she murmured to him. "I'm right here."

"Here?" His breath smelled of whiskey, a musky odor that mingled poorly with the smell of sweat and blood and the constant chemical odors from the nearby factory.

"Sure, where else? Don't move. If you move, you'll muck everything all up."

"Okay . . ."

Grace wanted to say more, but her throat was tight, and tears were welling in her eyes. She jammed her eyes shut and pushed the tears back, refusing them their due. It wouldn't be fair to let Patrick see her cry, to let him get any hints of how badly he was injured, or of how long he might lie here before he could ever walk again. Months?

Months of letting the wounds drain and chasing gangrene away, and changing dressings and bandages and splints. Months of pain for Patrick.

Perhaps even the loss of a leg. Perhaps loss of both. Perhaps death.

He could easily die of the infection. She'd seen and heard of people dying from much less than this. If gangrene set in, losing the leg—legs—would be the smallest problem. Patrick's backwoods instincts wouldn't save him then.

No, she wouldn't let those possibilities show in her eyes. It wouldn't be fair.

"I'll stay right here with you," she said softly.

He nodded, sweat plastering his eyes closed and whiskey

making him groggy. Confused by both the whiskey and the pain, he gave her a wormy little grin, then his eyes popped open.

"Oh . . . better not. . . . Better go back to the cabin . . . okay? . . . 'Bye . . ."

He settled back into his grogginess.

Grace gripped his arm and asked, "Why? What's up there? you want me to get Maw? Patrick? Pat? Want Maw to come look after you or what?"

He roused somewhat, blinked, shuddered through a wave of pain, then unexpectedly mumbled, "Know what? Anibal's back."

Had she heard that? Was he delirious? Anibal . . . she'd barely thought of him in months. The name shocked its way back into her mind, along with everything it meant.

"What?" she gasped.

The doctor and his two assistants shifted uncomfortably when Grace shot them a questioning glare.

"Does anyone else know about this?"

"Yeah, everybody that's been through here," the doctor said. "He's been mumblin' about Anibal Webb all morning."

Pat grinned drunkenly again. "Yup. Come back to marry you. He's waiting up yonder for you. 'Night, Liz. . . . I'm gunna sleep now. . . ."

"But those proslavers'll kill him!" Grace blurted.

"Yeah . . . that jayhawkin' son-of-a-dirty-word. . . . I'm gonna be best man. . . . It'll be real pretty, you think?"

"Oh, God!" She bolted to her feet and shouted at the doctor. "You take care of him, hear me?"

"Yes, ma'am, we plan to," the doctor answered. As she ran out the door, he lit his cigar, took a long draw on it, blew out a stream of smoke, and commented, "What'd she expect? A torture chamber?"

★

CHAPTER THIRTY

———— ★ ————

Ah Tam, Ah Tam! thou'll get thy fairin'!
In hell they'll roast thee like a herrin'!

—Robert Burns

The cabin floor was run red with blood.

Human entrails dangled in grotesque purple and white strings, twisting through the sea of scarlet.

A hanged body is a ghastly sight anyway, but these had been hung and disemboweled, cut open, quartered, and the innards drawn forward until they tumbled of their own weight.

All three were stripped naked. A final indignity.

There was no way to tell if they had been disemboweled before or after they had been hanged from the rafters by their necks.

Such different shapes . . . the skinny overburdened frame of the jayhawker Anibal Webb, the nigger freer who also hated niggers, who freed them just to get them out of the way. . . . He had been slit from the throat to the groin. Beside him hung the flabby body of Helmut Ruhl, his head twisted impossibly to one side, layers of fat drooping because there were no longer any internal organs to support them. The ultimate injustice of severed testicles now lay on the floor beneath him. . . . Finally the scarecrow corpse of his wife, so bone

bare it was difficult to believe she had ever been able to carry
children.

All their eyes were open, sagging. Their tongues were all
out, pushed forward by the ropes gagging their necks.

Their bare feet were stained with blood and dangled several
inches over the soaked ground, draped with intestines and
muscle matter.

And there was a soul-stirring touch of panic still lingering
on Moselle's face. While the men just looked like corpses,
Moselle still seemed a touch alive, a touch terrorized. Her
cheeks were still pink.

The butcher-block table had been tipped on its side to serve
as a billboard. On it, drawn in blood, was the letter *J*.

J for jayhawker. Free-Soiler. Kansas raider.

It was very quiet, for a scene of such violence.

At the doorway stood Grace Ruhl, daughter and betrothed,
gripping the frame on both sides.

She stared at the lifeless creatures that had been her parents
and her man. She thought about not having been here when
her family needed her, to gouge out a few deserving eyes
before they slaughtered her too.

Her pain doubled back inside her chest, buried itself, and
scalded her heart.

She stared until the sun took away her light. Leaden misery
took all the expression from her face.

Then she made her own light.

Ducking between the bodies, she gathered a few things she
knew her mother would have wanted her to keep—the German clogs, the rosemaled boxes, the dough trough Moselle's
two babies had slept in, the mugs painted in *fraktur*, the
Taufschein birth certificates for herself and Patrick, and the
topsy-turvy doll Helmut had made more than twenty years
ago. The doll had two heads and four arms, one head white,
the other head black, and it still wore the rag dress Moselle
had contributed to the cause of her baby's entertainment. It
still had the acorn eyes. And she took the crazy quilt made of
worn clothes and sacks in which she and her brother had
cuddled as children.

Grace took her clogs, her boxes, and her dough trough and
the few trinkets in it, and walked away, without looking back,

because Paddy always told her, "Never look back at your own house when you leave it."

Patrick...

Pausing with her tense spine to the cabin, she thought of him. Good-hearted Patrick who thought he had a home to come back to.

Against everything her body and heart were begging for, she went back inside.

Keeping her back to the horror that hung in the center of the cabin, she gathered some of Patrick's clothing, what little he had. She got his barking rifle and his other pair of shoes, and the doll Helmut Ruhl had made for his son out of a whiskey bottle. Its head was a walnut shell. Its eyes were painted on, and for clothes it wore a dried-out scrap of leather from fifteen years ago, when Helmut himself had fed leather into those machines.

She put all these treasures far outside.

Then she took the familiar keg of kerosene that had lit her home for years and spilled it over the bodies, leaving them where they hung. Her face harsh and unyielding, she poured and poured until they had more kerosene than blood upon them, until they stunk worse than that factory down there.

The remainder of kerosene went over the cabin walls. The rest was easy.

A match, a spark, a fire.

The cabin went up like sawdust. Nobody would see, because the hill and the trees would hide the glow. Nobody would know, because the night would hide the smoke. Nobody would care because these were white trash troublemakers, and they were better off dead.

This time she didn't look back. Soon the heat of the fire no longer warmed her back, and the crackling faded away behind her. There was no family there to leave behind.

A ferocious stride carried her down the river toward the shantytown, through the shadow of the leather factory, its sweating house and its warehouse, to the immaculate frame residence that had been her home for the past few years. It would be her home for good now. MacButton would be her only family... and she would have her brother. The brother she still had to tell about all this.

If he lived.

Her shoes pounded on the front porch. She dumped her heavy load right there on the painted planks, pushed the front door open, and thumped onto the parlor carpet.

"Button?"

The house was dark. No lanterns lit. No lamps. No candles.

"Button?" she called again. Fell asleep probably. Forgot to light the lamp.

And there was a chill.

She knew the house well enough. Without hitting anything she maneuvered into the parlor and put her load down beside the settee. She felt her way to the table and found the matches, and she lit one.

Then she straightened and turned, with just the match lighting the room as best it could.

She started toward the bedroom.

But the match flickered, its tiny yellow glow illuminating Mrs. MacHutcheon's face.

Here. Here in the parlor all along.

The old woman was cocked over slightly to one side in her wheelchair, as though she were reaching for one of the wheels with which to pivot the chair. Her mouth had a slight thoughtful tuck.

Even in the light of a single match, Grace could see that there was no longer any life in the staring eyes.

"Button?" she whispered. As the match began to burn slowly toward her fingers, she knelt beside the old woman's motionless body and put her palm over Mrs. MacHutcheon's hand.

Cold. Cold and quiet.

"You didn't wait for me. . . ." she whispered. "Oh, Button."

The old woman stared at the carpet.

Grace felt the last clinging emotions flow out of her body. Everyone she loved was dead or dying. There was nothing left. Nothing but malice and a diabolical wish.

She kissed the old woman's dead hands and thanked her belatedly for giving her a life the backwoods never would have offered. When she stood, she was completely alone with nothing to lose.

For the second time in one night, she walked through a door and left a home behind.

She went through the darkness as though guided by blind fury. Tonight she was in a burning mood.

By a quarter to midnight, the smells of the tannery were conveniently shielding the stink of kerosene spilled every-where and on everything on the main floor of the warehouse. Easy, because the warehouse had no night watchman.

Next was the sweating house, which got a good dose all the way around the outside. Wood. It would burn.

· The brick factory was trickier. It had watchmen. And the kerosene would have to go inside, on the machinery.

Somehow she would do it. The thought never occurred to her to turn back once she poured the first drop of kerosene. Thus she was not intimidated when she rounded a corner and came face-to-face with a big man in a vest and tie, carrying a large satchel.

Grace recoiled and glared at him through the darkness.

He was large and could easily stop her, but she knew that many gentlemen wouldn't touch a lady if they could avoid it, and maybe she could take him by force of will.

"Get back!" she snapped.

He stood back a step and studied her in the moonlight.

"What are you doing here?" he demanded, his voice imposing.

All she could see of his face was a pale oval surrounded by dark hair and a roll of beard. It was too dark to read his eyes.

Grace brandished her keg of kerosene at him as though it were a weapon, then set her temper on him and plain willed him to do her bidding.

"You get back!" she warned. "I'm burning this godbedamned factory to the ground, and I don't care who I have to brain to do it!"

The man looked at the kerosene. He looked at her.

Then Brad Lassick put down his satchel and reached into his pocket.

When his hand emerged, it was holding a box of matches.

"What an intriguing thought," he said. "Let's not forget the hides drying out back."

The factory went up like the devil's birthday. All the buildings burst to light within seconds of each other and were fully engulfed in minutes. The flames crawled up the brick and wood, out of every window, reaching toward the sky in great golden sheets. Looked like half of Kansas was burning.

Men scrambled around, running this way and that, forming bucket brigades from the river, manning the pumps and the wells and the troughs, but there was no way in heaven or hell to stop it.

Mostly that was because they couldn't get close enough.

Not the heat... they could fight the heat. And they could fight the flame.

But no one could stand to get close enough to the burning buildings to pour water on them. They simply couldn't breathe. A fire storm was twisting now, superheated air flowing upward so fast the air surrounding the factory rushed in at hurricane speed, feeding even more oxygen into the fire. The people moved back and back.

The burning tannery chemicals put off a stinging, malodorous cloud along with the heavy smoke, a cloud of corrosion that would kill a man in five breaths and certainly drive him back in two.

They had water. They had manpower. They had the desire. But they couldn't get close enough. Half of them had bad lungs already, just from working there. Certainly they couldn't brave the smoke and the chemical steam too.

After a half hour or so of futile dashing about, there was nothing else to do but stand helplessly back and watch the tanning factory burn to death.

Wyatt called for a head count.

After a while the barking of orders tapered off. The women's shrieks and the hammering of footsteps slowed and ended. Soon everyone within three miles was standing there, hundreds of feet back, watching hell rise before them and lick at the sky.

Nobody said a thing. They simply watched. They knew by the second hour of the fire what this meant.

They would be pioneers again. They came here with nothing but hope, and they would leave without even that. As the people of the shantytown watched the fire, they thought about where they would go this time, and what they would try to do when they got there. They were already thinking about the Santa Fe Trail and the Northwest Passage, about Lawrence and Westport, and some were even thinking about going back east where, at least, there would be food and work on a dock or another factory.

It was over. Finished. Just like that.

The tannery would, like all dead things, be consumed by the land and the passing foot treads, and leave only confused, inaccurate memories told by grandfathers about a leather mill someplace, don't remember exactly where, and the grandchildren would blink away their innocent boredom and go to play.

Kansas's only industrial hope flared and died. Grace Ruhl stood back in the crowd with tears burning off her cheeks.

She warmed herself by the fire.

★

CHAPTER THIRTY-ONE

———— ★ ————

Wyatt was long past comforting.

He sat cross-legged on the ground, parched and blistered, a few feet from the discarded water buckets. Half of his body was soaked, and the other half was burned. He sat with his elbows on his knees, and watched the factory and all its adjacent buildings turn into hot soot. The machines inside were metal, but the heat probably wasn't doing them any favors. They were melting and twisting like butter in that intense heat.

Once he'd been assured that no men were caught inside— not that anything could be done about that—Wyatt had plunked down on the ground and commenced doing all he could do: watch the fire burn.

Wyatt was an engineer, and he knew what men could do when they pooled their talents and muscles. Bore out mountains, recourse whole rivers, conquer countries, drain lakes. But when a big building was ablaze, there was only the bucket, and only one at a time. Fire was the one element mankind had not yet tamed.

So he was stuck, and so were all these people, watching their livelihood go up in a puff. There was nothing to do but sit here and appreciate the rare chance a person has to witness a really enormous incineration.

He drew a long, deep breath, and sighed.

Ah—there went his office. The window shattered, and an inferno licked out. Halfheartedly he scanned a mental list of all the documents and contracts and lists that were cooking right about now. The cash money would be all right; it was in a strongbox. Unless the strongbox got so hot that the paper inside combusted.

Yeah, that would probably happen.

Even if the cash survived, it wouldn't be enough.

Divided among all these workers, it would hardly be food money, much less travel money. He'd sunk all his personal funds into workplace improvements last year. Just wasn't anything left.

He had lost all track of time. The sky was black, the river was silver, the trees were gray, the fire was sulfur yellow. It was night. What difference did it make?

What difference could anything make for the factory now? Burned was burned. Yes, the fire was pretty. A mocking beauty was the only benefit of arson. The sheer power of it, the engaging hypnotic effect it had . . . constant motion with very little actual change, like yellow silk banners flowing in the wind. How kind for destruction to at least be lovely.

Someone handed him a cup of water.

Wyatt scratched his sweaty hand and sighed again, muttered a thank-you, and took a sip. The cool liquid dropped into his stomach like a blob of lead.

He looked up to say thanks again, but the man who had brought the water over had made a hasty retreat. Nobody really knew what to say to him. He couldn't blame them. He didn't really know what to say back.

He had no idea how long the stranger had been standing beside him. Only when it got through his head that the boots were actually shining did he realize something was different and that this couldn't possibly be one of his workers.

He stared at the gleaming travel boots, topped by tight gray breeches—over those a stylish black cummerbund, an elegant gentleman's traveling outfit made of fine burgundy brocade and lined with silk lapels and cuffs, and over that, surprise, an elegant gentleman.

The stranger was about Wyatt's age, midtwenties, and there the similarity ended. He seemed flameproof, and carried a touch of arrogance that Wyatt found annoying just now. The man didn't seem shy about this distant dignity he carried and wasn't even sweating. He stood next to a collapsing factory and scarcely cast it a look.

Then the man extended his right hand downward.

"Mr. Wyatt Craig?" he began.

Wyatt cleared his burning throat. Dubiously he took the proffered hand and glanced up. "Yes?"

"I seem to have caught you at an inconvenience."

Tipping his head to let the bad joke roll off, Wyatt asked, "Can I help you?"

"Possibly," the man said. "I represent several members of the Du Pont family of Wilmington, Delaware. Sir, we have a proposal for you."

★

CHAPTER THIRTY-TWO

———— ★ ————

Wyatt's knees cracked when he got to his feet. He wiped his hands on his filthy trousers, which didn't much help, and cast a self-conscious glance at his sweaty cotton shirt. The tie had been cast off an hour ago, and his black vest was practically melting against his ribs. No one could tell him from one of the warehouse men anymore.

How had the gentleman even identified him?

His voice was hoarse, and his throat was parched from chemical smoke as he asked, "What time is it?"

The gentleman snapped out a silver pocket watch and said, "One-thirty A.M., sir."

"Aren't you up a little late, sir?"

"I just arrived. I've been traveling for several days."

The man had a confident but subdued voice, and he was obviously of the Southeastern aristocracy. His accent was mild, but hardly buried, and Wyatt hadn't heard one like it in months.

"Can I . . . get you some coffee? Or anything?"

"I wouldn't trouble you," the man declined.

"All right . . . we can talk in my office . . . oh . . . I guess not. Umm . . . and my cabin's covered with smoke. . . ."

"Perhaps in that tent over there."

"Oh . . . sure."

The gentleman took a step toward one of the tents set up by the fire fighters, then paused when he realized he was walking alone. Wyatt wasn't managing to get his legs going.

So the man stepped back to Wyatt's side, leaned toward him, and candidly asked, "Are you all right?"

Wyatt blinked. The question made him self-conscious. He looked down at his arms, the skin braised from intense heat, and knew he must be gaunt from the efforts of the evening. He grinned sadly and admitted, "I guess I'm a little shook up."

The fire glowed on the stranger's dark sideburns. He gently took Wyatt's elbow and helped him up the incline to the tent.

The fire made their backs warm.

Inside the tent were three rickety chairs and a crate with mugs and a jug of water left by the men while they fought the fire in shifts. This provided an appropriate make-do office for Wyatt and his mysterious guest, though Wyatt was embarrassed as he gestured to a chair. No decent office anymore.

"Have a seat," he said.

"Of course," the man responded, "but you first. There you are . . . we'll talk when you're ready."

"Thanks," Wyatt murmured vaguely.

They sat together in silence for a long time. One open end of the tent faced the mountain of fire, which made a strange and poetic backdrop as Wyatt blinked the sting of smoke out of his eyes and took a few deep breaths to clear his lungs and his head, only to find that the latter wasn't working.

"You're feeling ill, aren't you?" the man asked bluntly.

"Breathing chemical smoke all night. It doesn't do much for the stomach."

"I imagine not."

"Sorry if I'm a little dull," Wyatt finally admitted with a sigh. "Everything's got knocked gully-west for me tonight. . . . Who'd you say you were?"

"I'm here representing the Du Ponts," the gentleman said. "We have a proposal."

"I used to work for the Du Ponts. While I was in college. But I'll bet you know that, right?"

The man gave him a covert smile. His teeth sparkled in the firelight. "Of course. You know how to work with chemicals, and you are an engineer. All the Du Pont mills are in the North, and it's impossible to predict which way states like Pennsylvania and Maryland will go. There is a certain fear among several Du Pont cousins that Henry Du Pont will—"

Wyatt interrupted, "What do you mean, which way the states will go?"

The gentleman raised an eyebrow loaded with innuendo. "Are you joking?"

An aching shoulder went up in a little shrug. "Not tonight."

The gentleman rearranged himself in his chair, unsure about how to phrase this particular revelation. Then he rearranged himself a second time, his lips opening as though to speak, then closing as though to think, then opening again. "Well, I hesitate to—"

Suddenly Wyatt blurted, "Are you talking about all the war gossip?"

"Gossip, sir? You *are* remote, aren't you? Hardly gossip anymore, I'm afraid. Most people east of here are sweating with war fever. Presently the whole nation is ill with it. It seems there is going to be a war, of some kind, on some level. Whether it comes or not, it's only prudent to make plans. . . ."

"Won't it take a majority vote?"

"The majority seems to want the war."

"God . . . things must be changing fast. . . ."

"Rapaciously," the Du Pont man said.

Now disturbed by something other than the fire out there, Wyatt frowned, wiped his dirty hands on his shirt, and retreated from this path of conversation.

"What's all this got to do with the Du Ponts?"

"The Du Ponts mean not only to survive but to thrive. They mean to spread out their investments, both in the North and in the South."

Conceding with an unenthusiastic nod, Wyatt slumped back in his chair and asked, "And what's it got to do with me?"

The man passed him a suppressed look and rearranged himself on the uncomfortable chair.

"Mr. Craig," he said clearly, "we want you to build a factory and manufacture gunpowder for the South."

Wyatt's eyes, still stinging from sulfur smoke, popped wide, and he nearly choked. He jabbed a thumb toward the wall of fire and said, "That's my equity! How much will you pay me for it?"

The other man fell silent and leaned back a little. Fully eight or ten seconds went by before the gentleman's lips parted and he spoke again, slowly.

"Perhaps I should fetch you a cup of water."

His tone of voice made Wyatt ashamed that he had snapped.

Put firmly in his place, he squeezed his eyes closed and covered them with his hand. Maybe it was time to start over.

"No . . . I just had one. Sorry . . . I'm not usually like this."

"Only two shocks in one night?" the gentleman commented. "How dare you be testy." He paused then, and more quietly asked, "Are you sure you're all right?"

"Oh, I'm fine. . . . It's just the fire talking, that's all. Go ahead. I'm listening."

"As you wish. If I might explain, you're misunderstanding my offer. This is not an investment partnership. We mean to finance the entire project. All you have to do is sign your name and run the operation."

"Who's behind this?" Wyatt asked. His brow furrowed as he tried to imagine the extended Du Pont family tree. It went on, and on—"Henry Du Pont himself?"

"No. Henry will follow the dollars, and the dollars will most dependably be in the North. There are other Du Ponts, first and second cousins, who do not want the South to lose. They have very big Southern sympathies. They don't believe in this idea of the democratic experiment of class mobility. They believe there *is* a distinction between the classes. The idea of commoners in Congress and slaves running about free is unpalatable to them. They're offended that people have the gall to say that negroes might be the equals of whites."

"Are *you* offended by that?" Wyatt asked.

The man's eyes caught the light of the burning factory and held a strange expression that Wyatt didn't miss. There was something behind those eyes.

"Mr. Craig," he said, "many are the writhing victims of good intent."

"What do you mean?"

"Basically that my opinions are nothing. Yours, however, are something, and if our information is correct, you are in favor of states' rights on the issue of slavery."

With a tired sigh Wyatt let go of the coded messages he was trying to wrest from the man's eyes and wearily shook his head.

"Well . . . don't put too much paint on your brush about me and politics. I don't know if I'd carve it in stone or anything, but I do think freedom is just another prison for negroes. I've seen freed negroes. They can't take care of themselves. And they sure can't . . . well, forget it. I don't feel like I'm thinking very clearly tonight."

"But there's more, isn't there, Mr. Craig? I see it in your face."

The perception caught Wyatt off guard. Most people didn't like to talk about these things in these sensitive times—no one could be sure he mightn't get a fist in the face for spouting an opinion or asking for one.

"You saw it in my *file*," he corrected. "All right, here it is. I don't like being told what to do and not to do in my business when I already know what's best for myself, my customers, and my workers. I don't like to see the central government getting too big for its britches."

"In what way?"

Where had this conversation come from? Wyatt fought for a clear head and was losing, but in his mind he saw his college file with "Wyatt Craig" written across the top and a bundle of information about his opinions that might or might not be up-to-date. Was this the time to be talking to a stranger? A stranger who seemed to know things about him that he seldom even thought about?

Better he speak for himself than let old information speak for him.

Why this decision, on this night of all nights?

"For a hundred years we've kept our freedom because the power of government has been in the individual states," he said, battling his fatigue. "Now a lot of people want to end that by locking the toughest issues in Washington and letting a handful of men decide. They want freedom for the slaves by taking away a little of everybody else's freedom. It just . . .

worries me. I don't like the picture. By God, people forget fast. . . . Our freedom could be gone before we know it, just because we keep demanding a pile of new laws every year. Strong government's been the bane of society since . . . well . . . forget it.''

He waved a tired hand to cut off his babbling.

"Since the Phoenicians," the Du Pont man added.

"Yeah," Wyatt muttered. "Phoenicians. Okay."

Exhaustion lay upon his eyes like an iron bar. He slumped even deeper in the chair.

The gentleman let several seconds of silence go by. He seemed to clearly know enough about human nature to know when to take a pause.

Then he quietly said, "Pardon my bluff approach. It's cruel misfortune that I catch you at such a moment. I shouldn't saddle you with politics. Do you know what caused the fire?''

Wyatt rubbed his parched palm against his neck and couldn't think of a reason to lie, so he said, "Arson."

The gentleman's shadowy face changed just enough. "Indeed?''

"If not, it was a mighty fancy accident that managed to take all the buildings at once, *and* the racks of drying hides along the river."

"Yes. I agree. Do you know . . ."

"I have my suspicions. It's sad for all these people who worked for years here, that's all. Anyway—you were saying?''

"Yes. I'd like to assure you that you were not our first choice. You were actually our third."

With a dubious smile Wyatt asked, "Am I supposed to say thanks?''

"You may in a year or two," the Du Pont ambassador quipped. "We're not offering you a gardening job. Powder work is a dirty and dangerous business, and even though none of the investment will be yours, there will be a risk."

"Because there'll be a war?''

"Yes, exactly. Our first choice turned out to be a strong abolitionist, thus no good to us. Second met all our requirements but recently died of measles. He saw us through the initial construction of the mill, but then died, and I have sought you out. You attended the university at Wilmington, with which we are very familiar. You studied the chemical sciences for obvious reasons—''

"I had reasons yesterday. . . . Sorry, go ahead."

"You worked in the Du Pont laboratories during your studies and made a favorable impression. Also, your Southern sympathies meet the cousins' approval."

"Do *you* have Southern sympathies?" Wyatt cagily asked, peering at the man, trying to pin down that dispassion he thought he saw there.

The man's cheeks tightened with amusement. "You're jabbing at me, sir."

"Butting in," Wyatt admitted. "I like to know who I'm talking to."

The man grinned—but this time it was only a half grin, not of amusement, but of something else.

"You wouldn't like to know me," he said.

"I wouldn't?"

"No, I shall be here only a day at the longest. I am here in the strictest business capacity."

"Oh," Wyatt said. He didn't really understand, but then again he was too tired to ask for more.

Staring at his feet, he watched the firelight flash on and off his trousers. A powder mill . . . where? Back East? Leave Kansas? Start all over?

The Du Pont man saw that he was vacillating and moved in to take advantage of it. "The buildings are nearly finished. We have a composition house, a roll mill with finished wheels of cast iron, a press house, and a graining mill."

"I would've preferred to supervise the construction. . . ."

"You're free to inspect the facilities. We've been careful. Each building is made of three very strong rock walls and one wooden wall facing the river. Any accidental blast will be funneled right over the water. No chain reactions."

"That's what I'd have done," Wyatt murmured wearily, only half realizing that he was talking himself into the scheme.

"The glaze mill, dry house, and pack house can be built to your specifications."

Wyatt looked up. "What's a glaze mill?"

"The Du Ponts will supply you with the newest technology, which is the glazing process. It involves adding black lead to the powder."

"What's that do?"

"Makes the granules shiny and slippery."

"Son of a gun . . . of course. It pours better."

"Yes."

"They were working on that while I was there."

"You see why you were our choice."

"Your third choice."

"A stunning honor."

"Well, I guess I'm honored then. I'd be a lot more honored if my hide mill wasn't falling to the ground out there. . . . Jesus Christ, look at it. . . ."

The gentleman paused again, acute to Wyatt's sudden distraction with the factory fire. The buildings were roaring far, far out of control now and no longer resembled anything constructed by man. It looked more like the wild creation of random nature.

Grabbing the opportunity, the gentleman leaned forward, purposefully lording over Wyatt with his penetrating presence as though he knew he could have control if he just played the right keys.

"You'll be well paid."

Wyatt clamped his lips tight, demanding more.

"If you like," the gentleman went on, "we'll offer travel expenses and a job for each of your workers. Otherwise we'll offer a fair severance, and they can go on their way."

"Just to free me of my obligation?" He frowned at the man. "*You* didn't burn my factory, did you?"

The gentleman's sedateness broke all at once, and he laughed at Wyatt's attempt to save the night from total misery. Laughter was a strange, unexpected sound for such a night, and the man seemed genuinely pleased at Wyatt's comment. He *liked* being accused.

"No," he said, smiling that dangerous, covert smile, "I didn't burn your factory.

"We want this powder mill, Mr. Craig," he went on, "and, frankly, we want an experienced man with more honor than we have."

Wyatt blinked. Had he heard his last words correctly?

"Interesting way to put it," he muttered. "All right . . . assuming you're not about to hit me over the head and take my wallet, what would be required of me for all this generosity?"

"Foremost, your silence about the Du Pont involvement. The cousins prefer that Henry never know. Sense of principle is a lesser virtue to him than loyalty to family and the pursuit of money. To assure this silence from you, the factory will be in your name publicly, but you will privately sign a document that expires in ten years. The document will sign everything over to me. I've worked out an adjunct arrangement with the Du Pont cousins that is unimportant at this time."

"Ten years?"

"In ten years," the man said, "or until there's a war that breaks up the country, the business becomes yours, free and clear. Until then you draw a salary, and all profits go back into the mill to expand it. If there's a war, Mr. Craig, you'll be doing the South an invaluable service. If war never comes . . . well . . ."

"I'll be the wealthy owner of a prosperous mill ten years from now."

The stranger smiled. "How polite of you to understand."

His head spinning, Wyatt stood up stiffly and wandered to the tent opening, staring out at the fire. He grasped the pole to steady himself on shaking legs. The heat warmed the entire length of his body from head to toe.

Was it happening? Tonight of all nights? What were the odds against that?

A hideous smell wafted up the hill to insult him—the stink of thousands of dollars of salted and treated skins burning up, turning into useless shards, and he knew the fire had finally consumed the curriers' shops in the upper levels.

The wind itself was sending him a messsage.

"Damn," Wyatt murmured, "that's a sad sight, isn't it? Just this morning a lot of families were counting on that burned-out shell. . . ."

He made the mistake of staring, and the fire hypnotized him.

From behind him came the most unexpected thing he had ever heard in his life—give or take Lassick—words that sunk so deep into his soul that he felt them go in.

"'That night, a child might understand . . . the devil had business on his hand.'"

Perplexed, Wyatt blinked and turned toward the stranger, who had somehow given a voice to the feelings of a man whose life was burning up.

He didn't say anything. His face was full of questions as he looked at the Du Pont man.

Then he coiled his arms tightly against his chest and tried to wrest a silent confession of the truth or a lie or *anything* from the man's coded face, but there was nothing, nothing to help Wyatt decide if he was a pawn in a dangerous scheme or the butt of an elaborate upper-echelon joke.

The stranger's expression did not change. He just wouldn't give.

Wyatt shook his head in thought. "I hate to keep bringing this up, but you *sure* you're not about to hit me and take my wallet?"

"Why would I bother to cheat you?" the gentleman pointed out. "It's too easy to make money legitimately. Not to mention," he added, "it's our money."

At this he reached down beside his chair and picked up a glossy leather satchel—which Wyatt hadn't even noticed until now, distracted as he was by the fire. The man arranged the satchel on his lap and opened it.

Wyatt stepped toward the gentleman and peeked.

Money.

Acres of money, miles of money.

Dixie notes, each payable for ten dollars in gold on the rock-solid New Orleans banks—the French-American *dix* notes—ten. Dixie. The soundest currency on the continent.

They were fat ten-dollar notes in big bundles, tucked wall-to-wall inside the satchel.

The gentleman stood up, stepped toward him, and stuffed the satchel against Wyatt's chest until he had no choice but to embrace it.

"Here's your start-up money. A down payment, if you will."

Wyatt almost stopped breathing.

"You came across the country with a big bag of cash and no bodyguard?"

He stared at the money, and at the man, and his voice dried up.

"What do I need a bodyguard for?" the man asked, clearly not wanting an answer.

Firelight flashed and charged across the burgundy brocade daycoat, turning it almost orange as the two men stood face-to-face in the tent, breaching the gap between their two very different worlds.

After a moment Wyatt forced his voice up.

"And . . . how do the Du Ponts know . . ."

"That you won't hit *them* over the head and take their wallet?" the gentleman asked. Then he smiled that overmastering smile and said, "I promised them you wouldn't."

The leather satchel full of money was warm against Wyatt's chest. Warmer than the fire. Warmer than any other prospect that stood in front of him right now.

Chance could send a man rocking at the oddest times. . . .

"Do we have an arrangement?" the gentleman asked.

Dazed, confused, overburdened, Wyatt stood there for a long time just holding the satchel against his chest, cradling it with his blistered arms and wondering again if all this was just a cruel trick.

Jobs for all his people if they wanted them?

Yes, but jobs in a powder mill . . . a constant and delicate danger, a dubious future in the South, when the South was putting itself at terrible risk for questionable principles and argued motives.

A whole new operation . . . a whole new beginning.

Turn a back on the past fifteen years of his father's efforts and the past several years of his own.

Learn an entirely new technology, make himself a target. If there was a war, the powder mill would become a military objective.

And did he want to be that much a part of a war?

But there was his smoldering factory, saying good-bye as though it knew better what the future was supposed to be than he did himself.

"What should I call you, sir?" Wyatt murmured.

The other man smiled again, this time more openly. Black eyes flashed in the firelight.

"Burns," he said. "Robert Burns."

★

CHAPTER THIRTY-THREE

———— ★ ————

There is no doubt that the first family of Delaware had strong southern sympathies and made little effort to hide them. In fact, a branch of the family were themselves slaveholders in South Carolina. Père Du Pont's great uncle, Abraham Dupont, had settled his roost there in 1695. It was his son, Gideon Dupont, who brought the flooding technique to rice growing in Carolina, and these southern cousins now reigned as proud slavemasters over a huge plantation in St. James Parish, Goose Creek.

—Gerard Colby
Du Pont Dynasty

"How soon do I have to give you an answer?"

"Unfortunately, very soon. Tonight, if possible. I apologize on behalf of the Du Ponts for that. . . . 'Time flies, but it leaves a shadow.' Nathaniel Hawthorne."

"And where's this powder mill supposed to be?"

"On the outskirts of Richmond."

"Richmond . . . for the willow trees, right? The best for charcoal?"

"Yes, and of course it's well entrenched in the South."

Richmond. Wyatt paused at the thought of traveling so far, of asking his workers to go all that way when they had already traveled this far into the frontier—but for a guaranteed job . . . it was better than starvation. . . . For all these people to leave suddenly meant an end to the chance for a town here,

491

for a future. No Craigtown, as his father had envisioned. No factory. Just a floating memory nobody would be sure of a generation from now.

But the frontier wasn't going anywhere—it would always be here, for building or raping or any of mankind's other habits of conquest.

He was sitting again. He'd needed to. The other man was sitting also, leaning back, relaxed, his legs crossed and his shiny boots reflecting the fire as it finally began to wane. It would burn for days, slowly, smoldering, completing any last-minute destruction, bubbling and crackling as the helpless river streamed along just yards away.

"I'd be able to hire anybody I want? Even these people?"

"That is part of the deal."

"Well, I wanted to hear it again. What about management? There's a young fellow here who almost got killed this morning. He's in the infirmary. I think I owe him something. He's a little homespun, and he probably won't think he can do it, but I think he can."

"Doubts are the beacon of the wise."

Wyatt paused. "Who said that one?"

"I just did."

A cue to ignore, if ever Wyatt had heard one. "Am I free to make him a foreman at the new mill if I choose to?"

"You are free to make that tree over there a foreman if you choose to. You can even pay it."

Wyatt rubbed his eyes, trying to clear the daze, and a groan of disbelief rumbled up through his chest.

"You'll need saltpeter. Lots of it."

"Most of the saltpeter is imported from India," the gentleman said. "However, we're currently working on Chilean saltpeter."

"Why? Cheaper?"

"Yes. We're trying to make it work. As soon as it won't be obvious where the shipments are coming from, we'll get you the technology for making Chilean saltpeter usable."

"Do you have a sulfur source?"

"Italy and Sicily."

"If there's a war, are Italy and Sicily still going to talk to the South? You better think about that, Mr. . . . Burns. By the way," Wyatt mentioned, "I hate to be nitpicky, but you look pretty good for a dead Irish poet."

The man actually laughed spontaneously—not something his demeanor suggested him capable of. Wyatt felt a sudden victory in having caught him by surprise.

Smiling, the gentleman lightly corrected, "Scottish. So, you've caught me. I don't suppose I look very Scottish either, do I?"

Wyatt surveyed the man's soft black curls, which were long enough to cover part of the silk collar, and the coal-nugget eyes set in skin of an unusual, rather exotic caste.

"No, I guess you don't, now that you bring it up."

The man bowed rather formally, as though to begin their relationship with a fresh start.

"I'm sorry to have teased you. It's a bad habit from boyhood. Not many people this far west know about Burns."

"He was a pretty popular fellow back East," Wyatt said. "Lots of British immigrants back there."

"Yes . . . I should've thought of that," the man said. "Very well, I concede discovery. My name is Dorian Trozen."

Wyatt blinked and grimaced. "You mean it really isn't Robert Burns? But I was making a joke!"

"In that case," the man said, "you've stumbled upon my reluctance to trust people before they trust me. Again I apologize."

Taken aback, Wyatt shook his head dubiously. "You are a pack of surprises, aren't you? What was the name again? The real one?"

"Dorian. Trozen, like 'frozen.' "

"What kind of name is that?"

"It's Turkish for Mike."

Undaunted, Wyatt insisted, "French, right?"

"By way of Athens."

"Oh. Greek."

"And your name is unusual too," the man said, turning the conversation back on itself.

"Well, thanks," Wyatt said.

"How do you know that's a compliment?"

"I always assume the best."

The black eyes grew shaded again. "How lucky for your enemies."

Feeling his brows tighten, Wyatt buried his reaction. He always tried to like everybody for at least the first half hour after meeting, but there was something about this man that confounded his intents. He *didn't* like him. He didn't like a cynic.

I'm usually good at reading people, but this one's closed like an iron safe. If I rejected his offer, he'd get up and sashay away without a too-bad, never mind that he's come cross country to find me. There's something about him. Something strange.

"Why Burns?" he asked.

Trozen seemed to think it was a legitimate question. "He has been my exemplar over the past few years. We...understand each other. We both grew up in such circumstances that 'the will o' wisp meteors of thoughtless whim were almost the sole lights of my path.' "

"Sorry," Wyatt said, "but I don't see you as much of a plowman."

"Thank you."

"How do you know it's a compliment?"

"I always assume the best," Trozen repeated cannily. "So you have an interesting choice, Mr. Craig. Stay out west with Brigham Young and his fifty-six children by his twenty-seven wives, or you can go back to Richmond where people pay two thousand dollars a square inch to live too close together. But if I were you," he added, "I would never cut down an olive tree."

Unsure of his meaning, Wyatt got to his feet once more and turned his back on the gentleman, trying to think clearly, trying to divorce his dislike of Dorian Trozen from the Du Pont proposal and what it would mean, and what it would mean *not* doing.

It would mean not completing the Craig dream of a factory town on this side of the Kansas border. It would mean not fulfilling the efforts of fifteen years of his father's life.

Such as his father was.

But there were these people to consider, these workers. This was part of their dream too. Their frontier, pioneer dream. Some had planned to work here for a while, until their children were bigger, then strike off for the great unknown West, down the Oregon Trail to the Shangri-la of Sacramento or Virginia City, or the great untried lands of Utah Territory, stringing along a tenuous thread of survival from one U.S. Army fort to the next—Fort Kearny, Fort Laramie, Fort Bridger, Fort Hall, Fort Boise—he knew them all. He'd heard their voiced hopes for three years now, and he remembered them from when he was a boy, when the whole idea of settling all the way to the Pacific Ocean was the same as reaching straight up into the firmament and finding heaven.

He gazed past his elbow at the satchel.

There was money. *Dix* notes. Start-up money for a new factory, travel money to bring his workers back east, severance money for those who chose not to go back.

And the option—stay and rebuild?

No, thank you, we'd rather stay and rebuild. . . . No insurance money . . . no one would insure a chemical factory against fire. . . .

Suddenly he twisted around and confronted the other man.

"Where do you fit in?" Wyatt asked.

Dorian Trozen remained secure inside his undefinable mystique. He touched a hand lightly to his own chest and said, "I shall be handling the transfer of finances, acquisition of equipment, all legal records and documents. In short, I shall be your second in command, *sah.*" He snapped the same hand against his forehead in a mockery of a salute.

Not enough. Wyatt took one more step to close the distance between them.

"But there's more to you, isn't there?"

This did light a match of surprise in Trozen's face—just for an instant.

Then it guttered.

He applauded Wyatt's perception with a hint of a smile, very reserved. Unexpectedly he came to his feet too, as though this had been ordained the moment at which he wanted to be on equal terms, equal ground.

He stood straight, pressed back the lapels of his expensive coat and hooked his thumbs into his vest, and became a fortress of innuendo that made Wyatt sure the placidity was a shield.

With a small nod he said, "I shall be the untraceable link between you and the Du Ponts."

"You're going to spy on me," Wyatt returned.

Dispassionate to the last Trozen's face suddenly lost that smirk. For a flashing moment there seemed to be genuine concern somewhere behind his expression. But concern for what? For whom?

When he spoke, his voice was very dark, provocative.

"Mr. Craig," he began, "you haven't told me whether or not we have a deal."

Somewhere inside the burning tannery's main building, a floor gave in. Thunder—the boom of machines crashing through from floor to floor, all the way to the basement, of supports and joists cracking like bones—the god-killing noise of it all—rang against the hillsides.

Wyatt didn't turn to look. He had already seen. It was as though his own bones were cracking, his innards falling through his body and out his penis, pissing away his very life in agonizing, burning pain.

Whether or not any of this showed on his face, he had no idea.

Nor did he care what this man thought.

He drew in a breath, and it actually hurt.

And his voice hurt.

Something else hurt too. Saying for the second time in just one little day a phrase he hadn't uttered but twice in ten years. Yet here it came again.

"I don't like you, Mr. Trozen," he said. "I don't like you at all."

Then he held out his hand.

"We have a deal. I'll go to Richmond."

★

CHAPTER THIRTY-FOUR

———— ★ ————

One month later
Hannah Dishman's Emporium,
St. Louis, Missouri

The young man's clothes were expensive, probably of imported fabric and expertly tailored to his narrow body to give it form and manliness, but they had seen better times. They were now as dusty and road worn as anyone's else's, and it took a discerning eye to see the quality. The fit still worked well enough to make people unsure of whether they were seeing a gentleman on the run, or on the hunt.

He had never given so much as a gift of glance at the people who stared at his horse, which even dust could not diminish. He knew they were aghast at the prancing, spitting creature that had carried him out of the horizon, knew that even in the stable, as it was now, the beast's snorting could still be heard from the street, and that passersby could catch the unmistakable smell of a stallion.

He liked thinking about it, about how people squirmed away.

It was night now. The horse was settling down—it usually took an hour or so for the pounding of hooves to taper off—and he himself was reclining on a lumpy bed with too many coverlets and too much lace.

497

The extravagance drooling from the walls of his room in this house made even him feel plain.

The ladies at these kinds of houses liked him. He knew they did. He always spent money for their services, though sometimes that meant nothing more than answering his questions and maybe rubbing his shoulders. For harlots this was confusing. But money was money, and he didn't care if he left them bewildered.

Money also bought him the use of a room *without* a girl in the bed, which was what he wanted tonight. Brothel after brothel he had laid a string of posters across Louisiana, Missouri, Indian Territory, and Kansas Territory. To no avail.
. He looked up when the knock came at the door and snapped, "Who is it?"

But he knew who it was.

A muffled voice, very low, answered.

"Quist."

A shudder traveled down Noah Sutton's spine. What a voice.

He stepped to the door and opened it himself, rather than inviting that voice to come in, just so he could be in control of that first moment.

In the candlelit hallway, framed by the red-and-black wallpaper, was a rock of a man dripping with whole animal skins, leather satchels, and pouches. He wore a long brown beard and mustache, both wiry. His eyes had a tilt that made them seem perpetually angry. Perhaps his profession required that look to instill fear, to keep him hated.

"Well? Get in, then," Noah said, shutting the door behind the man while sizing him up. Enormous.

Just right.

If only he was smarter than he looked.

"You're Orville Quist?"

The man turned, looking totally out of place against the gushing lace curtains and pink carpeting.

"What I said."

Noah felt his small eyes tighten.

With a sigh that belied his three years of frustration, he maneuvered past the wide man and sat down behind a tiny satin-covered table on which his saddlebags rested, along with an ink well and quill and some paper.

"You know why I summoned you?"

Quist didn't answer but flicked his left hand. Out of the piles of leathers and skins crackled a dry piece of vellum. It landed on the tabletop.

The poster. REWARD! WANTED! REWARD! WANTED! REWARD—

Noah scanned it with satisfaction.

It had become his Bible.

"All right, Mr. Quist," he began. "I have tracked this half-breed rapist as far as Albuquerque, and now he has doubled back north, and I've lost him. He has eluded me at every juncture. I admit to requiring the help of a professional detective." He scanned the trail-shaggy man and added, "Or whatever you call yourself."

Quist nodded, once.

"You find this man for me," Noah said, "and I shall pay you ten thousand dollars. Ten thousand, do you hear?"

Quist heard. It was just that his throat had closed up. Double the amount on the poster? *Double?*

Noah sat back in the carved boudoir chair. "I see you do hear," he added smugly. "I shall advance you two thousand this very night. Any man could live on that for years. Years, do you understand? I want you to give this case your full concentration, no matter the months it may consume. I shall expect periodic reports."

He paused then. Peering through the hair and the beard and the mustache, he said, "Have you ever encountered a razor, sir? My God Almighty, but you look like a hairy wart! Are you sure you're smart enough to track this man?"

The big bounty hunter took two steps toward Noah, and Noah was suddenly very glad the table, however small, was between them.

Quist leaned forward.

"You know why you haven't found your nigger?" The words came out on stale breath that smelled of hardtack. "You're too clean. You gotta be dirty. I'm dirty. And I always learn from my enemies. Want to see what I learned from the Injuns?"

His right hand disappeared behind his back and returned with what appeared to be a water pouch of grayish brown leather. He held it between his face and Noah's.

"Ain't it a beauty? I had the biggest one in my unit."

He bobbled the bag in front of Noah, who scowled and said, "I have no clue as to what you think this means to me, sir."

"Look closer," Quist said. "No white woman's got one this big."

Noah leaned forward. The water pouch turned in Quist's grip. As it turned, Noah saw a blemish.

No—it wasn't a blemish.

It was a nipple.

Noah shot backward so sharply that his chair knocked the windowsill.

"Get it out of my face—" he gasped. "Jesus crucified—put it away!"

He squirmed out of the chair and put half the room between himself and Quist.

"You're an animal," he said. Settling his stomach with a deep breath, he blurted, "But you're perfect. He'll never expect someone like you to be following him."

Quist put his favorite pouch away and stood there, looking satisfied.

"But are you smart enough?" Noah wondered. "We're talking about an educated man."

The bounty hunter didn't even move. He'd already sized up the situation—what had to be done, what had to be learned, which contacts had to be made, what had to be looked for.

"You're smart," he said. "So how come you haven't found him?"

Jarred, Noah could only glare back.

"Because," Quist said, "you're looking in the wrong places. He's an educated nigger, right? He looks white, right? Why would an educated white-looking man head for the wilderness? See . . . I know where *not* to look."

It made sense. In just seconds the professional already had answers that had never occurred to Noah.

"All right," Noah said again. Taking the wide way around,

he sidled back into his chair and tried to organize his thoughts. "What do you need?"

"Tell me what you know about him."

"You have the poster. You know his name and his breeding. He sounds like a white man from Virginia. He's an inch or two taller than I, and broader in the shoulder, but not wide by any means." Noah's hand swept in an arch, and he glanced at the gaudy walls of the bordello room. "He frequents houses like this. He loves women because he can't have one. If he takes a nigra woman as his wife, then the world will see him for what he is and he will be back in chains where he belongs. If he takes a white woman . . . you see, I've figured his mind out. The thing he fears most in the world is to take a white woman as his wife and stand by while she births his black baby. Then his secret would be out. Women will be his downfall, do you understand me? He takes these prostitutes to his bosom because he cannot do without women. He dares not even stay with one of them for more than a day . . . but he cannot have a relationship with a woman."

Noah leaned forward, his elbows on the table and his hands poised before him in illustration. His pale green eyes mustered far more hatred than Quist's presence could squelch.

"That is his Achilles' heel, Mr. Quist. That is how you will find him. Women, do you understand? He *needs* women."

He sank back, his mouth taking a bitter twist, his eyes going hollow suddenly, as though he had been shot from behind.

"I've seen him only twice since he escaped from my rice plantation three years ago," he went on slowly. "The last time was in Westport Landing, just two weeks ago. In a brothel not unlike this one. He goes across the country from whore to whore—"

"Why didn't you kill him right then?"

Rage danced across Noah's face and brought him back to life.

"Do you think I came so far to let him live?" he shrieked. "I *will* kill him! I would have then! But he spotted me and ran into the crowd. I shouted, 'Stop that nigra!' "

The room vibrated, the lamp crystals jingling like bells.

Noah slammed his fist on the table.

"But nobody saw a nigra," he grumbled. The moment turned again and again before him. Finally he uttered, "The taste is still in my mouth."

The lamp crystals began slowly to stop their singing, letting the light that reflected through them gradually stop dancing upon the audacious wallpaper in the room, and Noah pressed his curly hair back to let the cool breeze from the open window caress his forehead.

He closed his eyes briefly and didn't give a fuck what Quist thought of him.

"Understand this, Mr. Quist," he murmured, his eyes still closed, "this man is clever. I want you to be more clever. He is dangerous. I want you to be deadly. Do whatever you must to avoid leaving any trail for him to sense or smell. I'm leaving tomorrow to go back to South Carolina and join the cavalry. We shall stay in touch through my plantation. I have people there who will be discreet. I'll give you two thousand tonight. You'll get the rest when you bring him to me."

"I'll bring him to you in a bag, sir."

Noah's eyes cracked open like spring-loaded knives.

"He must be alive!"

Quist frowned in confusion, but after a pause his new employer explained:

"So I can kill him myself."

★

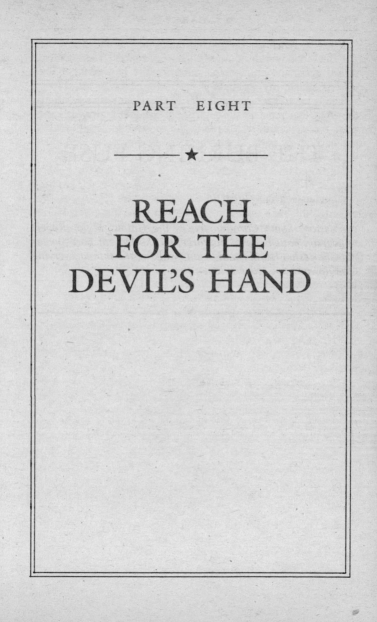

PART EIGHT

★

REACH FOR THE DEVIL'S HAND

THE BURNING FUSE

DECEMBER 1860

Secession. South Carolina leaves the Union. Major Robert Anderson battens down his forces at the federal Fort Sumter in Charleston Harbor and begins walking the thin unswerving line toward the order to open fire.

★

CHAPTER THIRTY-FIVE

———— ★ ————

"Hello, Grace. Burn any buildings lately?"

"Christ, Lassick! Jesus Christ hanging high, you blew the feathers right off me!"

"Did I? Pardon if I startled you."

"Startle me? You startled me. What are you doing back in this pisshole?"

"I might ask the same of you. The shantytown's near deserted now. Why are you still here?"

"You know why."

"I don't. Tell me. Correct my mistake."

"I've been taking care of Paddy while he mended."

"So . . . he lived after all."

"No, but I like the smell of dead flesh. Can't you see I'm packing up right before your very eyes?"

"Yes . . . I see you are. Your brother . . . interesting that he could live through all that. Last I remember he was blithering with fever. Several weeks he was like that, wasn't he?"

"Months. What do you want here, Bradford? I thought you went west. Carson City. Sacramento. Gold mines. Heaven on earth. The open frontier. The glorious—"

"Grace . . . didn't you miss me? I missed you."

"Your codpiece missed me, that's what missed me."

505

"God! How refreshing to hear a lady talk! I've had it up to that codpiece with Utah preachers and drunk pepper-benders. Such a rest to be back among such as you, Grace, where men are men and women are—"

"Sick of them."

"You shouldn't talk like that about your brother. Where is he, by the way?"

"He's gone out shooting."

"You mean he can walk again?"

"With canes. I'd appreciate your being gone before he sees you. He didn't see you before, and I'd like for him not to see you now."

"Now, Grace . . . you can't tell me I wasn't welcome on those winter nights—"

"Mister, you got your hand on a place I don't even touch! Take a step!"

"Ah!"

"Another step."

"All right . . . all right. Where are you packing to go?"

"You stay back now. I don't know how I am about you."

"Are you going west also?"

"No, east. I'm going to Richmond. To take care of my brother. He's taking a job. Have you got reason to be here? 'Cause if you don't, I'll thank you to walk out and let me get packing. The stage leaves tonight, and I mean to ride on top of it so I can spit on Kansas as I leave."

"I'm here because, well . . . in short, there's a war coming."

"War, pthththth."

"Pardon me?"

"Ain't gonna be a war."

"You don't think so?"

"No. The poor people can't leave their squabby little crops to fight it, and the rich people don't want to get dirty."

"But, Grace, my dear sweet country maid, it's already begun."

"No."

"Haven't you heard? Federal forts have been evacuating— Fort Johnson, Fort Marion, the arsenal at Apalachicola—the cowards. Fort Gaines, Fort Morgan—"

"Seems you have a hobby collecting forts. What do you want with me?"

"Thank God Sumter's still holding out."

"Oh, crapsack. If the South wants some moldy old fort, why don't we just give it? Those are mostly inactive installations anyway."

"Ah! So . . . you *have* been listening!"

"I hear things . . . same as anybody."

"The Confederacy's also taken the Marine Hospital and New Orleans and the Pensacola Naval Yard. Hardly inactive."

"Too far away for me to care."

"The new president has made clear he will not recognize a Confederate government. You have heard there's a new president, haven't you?"

"What am I? Dead in the head? 'Course I heard. Abraham Linkman. I don't care about him either. Move aside."

"Grace, sooner or later someone will fire a shot and that will be that. War. You'll have no choice but to care."

"Oh no. I got two things in my life to protect, Brad. I got my little brother, and I got this dead woman's buttons. That's all Grace Ruhl's on earth for, and that's all she wants to do. I'm not getting involved. I won't be one of you fart blossoms who try to jump the fence and get your ass stuck between the pickets. Not me. No, sir. Not me."

"You haven't asked why I'm going back east, Grace."

"Yes, I did."

"Then I'll tell you."

"Goody."

"I have a close cousin. A great man. He is in Virginia, organizing a group of Southerners who remain loyal to the United States, such as myself. We oppose secession. Now, where did you say your brother had taken this job?"

"Don't give me your parsley, Mr. Lassick. You know where."

"Virginia. I see you haven't been honest with your brother about Wyatt Craig."

"I said I never would. He got offered a job. He took it. He thinks he's doing the best he can for me and him. Him and I. He and I."

"Him and me. But you're protecting him instead. Why, Grace?"

"Hand me that beaded bag."

"Why do you have to protect a grown man?"

"Because Paddy can shoot the middle out of a nickel from across the county, but he can't keep food on the table. That's because the squirrels are smarter'n he is. Know that little bump behind his left ear? Well, that's where his brain hides. The rest is all heart."

"Wyatt Craig offered him a job in that new powderworks."

"How—how'd you know about that?"

"Wyatt Craig... a man neither you nor I should be finished with. Everybody knows how the Craig proslavers hung up your mama and your papa and opened them like pigs. Yet that mouth stays shut as your brother goes to be another of his low-paid slaves."

"Keep your own mouth shut! Wyatt Craig tried to take everything from me in the same day, but I got him! I burned him down. I got him."

"Did you? The next day he had a wagon load of money and a new factory. He's rich again, Grace. He was rich again in just months. I begin to think we favored him by releasing him from his Kansas obligation. Where's the hurt?"

"My God, I hate that accent of yours.... Southern sympathizers are always hurting people, that's what I see. Niggers, poor whites, my ma and pa—anybody who disagrees with them, they can kill. Damn that I saw how Southerners fight! They sneak around and hang people in the night. They won't come out in the open. The Craigs never came out in the open. I never saw a Southerner who did."

"Craig's for the South, but he's no Southerner, Grace. Southerners are men like my cousin. There are many among my kind who are loyal to the Union. You can help them."

"They can go to hell."

"Grace, listen to me!"

"Get your bumfucking hands off!"

"Listen! I'm going to Richmond. My cousin is a great patriot! A great man! He'll lead armies some day! Since I was a child, I've watched the greatness unfold. He led us as children, and he shall lead us as a nation!"

"Anybody ever heard of him besides you?"

"Even now he is gathering loyal Southerners to fight against the Confederacy—Southerners whose voices will be accepted in the South, Southerners who can exact merciless revenge on those who seek to cut our nation in half—"

"What do I care! What do *I* care!"

"You can use your brother, Grace, don't you see? Don't you comprehend? Find out about powder mills . . . capacity, production, channels of trade, guards—"

"Spy? Sneak like a coyote? You want me to spy? To 'use' Patrick?"

"You used me, did you not? . . . You needed to get medicine for your brother. I got it. You owe me."

"I paid you between my legs, and you better never forget that I did."

"You used me."

"Brad Lassick, behind those pretty eyes of yours is there a brain? A sense of what men do to women and who uses who? I got nothing out of your hands on me and in me except that medicine, no love and no comfort and nothing a woman can't do for herself. See? You've felt my breasts. They're soft. What's underneath is not soft, and it never was. Paddy got all the heart, and I got all the brains. If that meant sleeping under you for a while, that's what it meant. I got no heart. I got rock. And I'll do anything to protect my brother."

"I see . . . so that's what I mean to you."

"That's what everybody means to me."

"Everybody except the baby brother."

"Are we done talking yet?"

"Grace . . . think of this. Just listen! Listen one moment. I know Wyatt had no money when you and I burned the tannery. He was in bad straits. Who has set him up in business? Where are his funds flowing from? And how can they be chopped off?"

"What's it to me? Goddamn you!"

"Revenge."

"What?"

"Revenge! If you can destroy Wyatt Craig while destroying the Confederacy—what a profit! Providence has moved for you, Grace!"

"Spit. Providence never moved a bowel for me, Mr. Lassick."

"Then that day has come. Now listen carefully. My cousin is a saint of tactical maneuvers. The first element of war is destroying your enemy's supplies. Supplies of food, of clothing, of firewood . . . of gunpowder."

"They can eat it if they want to."

"Do you know what Wyatt wanted to do the day your brother was crippled?"

"Don't know, don't care."

"Then it won't matter if I tell you. Do you know Wyatt Craig wanted to cut off Patrick's legs to save the machine? Oh . . . I see that pricks beneath your surface . . . yes, the workers liked your brother, and they stopped him. Cut off a man's legs . . . better shoot him through the brain. I do believe what he did to your parents was less vicious."

"You filthy sucking bastard, I don't want to remember. . . ."

"Remember, Grace. Think! Wyatt's powder mill lies just outside of Richmond on the James River—a prime location. Only the most brainless of military leaders would forgo it as a target. Destroying it will take a bite out of the Confederacy that will send ripples all the way to Jefferson Davis himself. Have you ever seen a mill of black powder blow sky high? . . . No . . . you haven't. But I see you are looking at it in your mind. Yes. Yes, it looks something like that night when you and I sent the cursed tannery to its fate. Except that it's faster, more brutal, more confounding than anything you can imagine. It goes up like a chain of explosions erupting from the earth below, one after another, after yet another. Fragments of stone fly and kill people a mile away. And your brother, Grace. Your brother may be inside at that moment. He may be deep inside when a detonation occurs, standing beside a flash wall, shoveling graphite, or brushing his shoes clean. You can't protect him from that, Grace. You're not immortal. You won't know when it's happening . . . even though it'll be as calculated a maneuver as organized men can exact. That poor, simple young man . . . he'll be blown to bits. You won't have a thing left to bury. Oh, what's this? Tears in the rock woman's eyes? Why, Grace, that's not like you . . . perhaps I can dry them. Here's drop of comfort for your cup, my dear. If you join me, you'll know when we decide to blow up Wyatt Craig's powder mill. Exactly when—and you'll know for hours ahead of time. You'll have plenty of time to get your brother out. Your innocent brother who never hurt anyone. What do you say, Grace? Perhaps you've changed your mind. . . . Would you like to be a spy for the Order of Heroes of America?''

★

CHAPTER THIRTY-SIX

———— ★ ————

I am inflexible.

—Abraham Lincoln,
February 1861

APRIL 14, 1861
RICHMOND, VIRGINIA
THE CIVIL WAR BEGINS

From his office window the successful powder-mill owner could see his world spread along the bend in the river. It was practically a self-contained world, connected by a single iron bridge to the real world just down the road, beyond those hills. At night, when he worked late, when the wind was just right, he could sometimes hear the clanking factory noises of the city of Richmond and see the glow of its gaslights shining on the smoky atmosphere. Steam-powered boats hooted on the James River. Sometimes the sound carried this far away. The address of the Craig Powder Refinery was Richmond, yet Wyatt felt as separate from the city as the moon from the earth.

Outside his window, his little powder town sprawled over a big area of open land with its own hills, roads, and creeks. The buildings were spread out from each other—a strange way to use so much land, but with a reason. An explosion might send shrapnel and boulders a half mile. Better not to be close. That's why the powder magazines were good and far away, down the bend of the river at the boundary of their property. There the refined powder awaited delivery to the trains or boats that would take it to its buyers.

Darned if it wasn't a town in itself. Just about the same as the Kansas shantytown—well, no . . . nicer than that, because of the nearby city. Perhaps also because it wasn't as settled, as worn. Over there, nearly hidden behind a bump of a hill, was the chapel and the school for the workers' children. A little closer was the blacksmith shop and the carpentry. Downriver from his office was the millwright. Out of sight entirely were the stores, several of them, the cooper's, the inn, and the stables, all threaded together by flat veins of dirt paths. He could, however, see the strong cypresswood house of the man who managed the cotton mill and the corn mill and saw to the livestock's care. That was about his closest neighbor. Other such factories would have many more homes than this mill, because they might be farther away from a city, and its various managers would have to live on the grounds, in houses every bit as proper, even as opulent, as city homes. They had to be. It was a matter of reputation.

This close to a city, though, most of the managers, and certainly the "owner," lived in the city, so they could be seen going about, seen and accepted.

So Wyatt lived in town, in Court End on Governor Street, in a grand 1809 three-story brick with gateposts and a courtyard in back, a rock's toss from Broad Street, the main thoroughfare that cut through Richmond's center. Broad Street was well named too. A horse could practically get up a gallop breadthwise on the street before it had to jump a curb. Mr. Trozen had arranged for the house to be bought from the widow of the shipowner who had designed the house. When Wyatt first saw his new home, all he could think of was what to do with all those wasted rooms. He didn't play music, so he didn't need the music room. He didn't know how to throw a lavish dinner, so he didn't need the fifty-foot dining room. He didn't need the parlor because he didn't parl. Now that he thought about it, Wyatt couldn't remember what words Trozen had used to make the "offer" seem almost a threat—live on Governor Street or else. The Du Ponts wanted their image whole, even though they weren't admitting to having an image around here. He was a figurehead. A functioning figurehead.

But the mill was his. Somehow it was still his. The mill, the men, their families . . . he was the one who had helped build it, who lived every day with the smell of black powder and sweat. The tannery had been his father's, the mill was the Du Ponts', but somehow they were both his.

The office he stood in had been made up long before the eastbound train brought him to it, in fact had been made for the man who started in this position but died before operations were anywhere near starting up. A handsome office, befitting an owner, befitting the person whose name was on the gate entering the powder works—CRAIG. There was a stylish, rather glowering couch made of English brocade in a strong pattern of man-type flowers, grapes, grape leaves, hydrangeas, in purples and browns. And there were two dynamic wing chairs, big ones with stiff backs, broad wings, and brass studs running up and down, back and forth. The chairs were burgundy suede, and Wyatt knew all to professionally the worth of them. Because of that, with a craftsman's eccentricity, he just couldn't manage to actually sit down in one. Perhaps the leather had been grained under his very eye.

From this office window, facing Richmond, Wyatt could see only a wink of the river, just at the bend before the hill swallowed the water. He didn't have to look anymore to know the ten brown brick powder mills were just downriver from his office, placed two by two, each with its weak fourth wall facing the bank, and with a waterwheel between each pair for power. Power from the earth.

All of it was his, the Du Ponts said. His. But sometimes he felt like a part of himself was still back in Kansas with his sleeves rolled up.

The James River flowed directly behind him. If he went to the opposite window, he would be looking out upon it, flowing timelessly toward the open Atlantic. Ordinarily that

was his preference, to stand at the window and see the water
flow until it took most of his tensions away.

Today, though, he gazed out at the mill grounds. Because
today was different.

His shoulder creased to the shape of the window frame.
The wood picked at his white flannel sleeve. The sun came
out from behind a cloud for just an instant and whacked him
in the eye. Against his thigh he squeezed the stiff paper of a
telegram. This idea of getting news on the same day it
happened—crazy. Back in Kansas it might have been weeks
before he or anyone knew what was happening in the world.
The telegraph had changed all that. Certainly living ten miles
from a city instead of ten states away would also change
things.

He heard laughter and looked around the edge of the
window frame to his left.

A clutch of workers were swaggering down the road. They
were dirty and workerish—unavoidable when dealing with
black powder and graphite and horizontal hydraulic presses.
Some of them were very young, twelve, fourteen, fifteen
years old. There was even a group of siblings from eight to
sixteen who worked the mill. At first Wyatt had ruled against
child labor. But they had come to him begging for a chance to
earn money for food. Just enough for food. What could he
do? Be honorable and let them starve so he could stand in a
group of Northern businessmen and say, "No child labor in
my factory, gentlemen."

As the workers came closer, he spied an inconsistency—
Dorian Trozen was among their checkered coarse linen shirts
and hiked-up cord trousers and butcher boots. He shone like a
jewel in his snappy mustard-colored frock coat with its black
step lapels, the high white collar and black tie. Rather than
wearing his top hat, he was carrying it.

Strange. Somehow Wyatt knew, was absolutely certain,
that his accounting manager carried that hat in his hand in
deference to the men, in order to keep from seeming superior
to them.

He sagged against the window frame. The last person he
wanted to talk to right now . . .

For a vain heir apparent, Dorian Trozen was mind messing.

He was self-removed, aloof, but in an unassuming way—as though he were happy to play second fiddle. Any fears of his overlording the powder mill had drained off after the first month.

Wyatt wouldn't have guessed it. Oddest thing . . . though Trozen had nicknames among the tradesmen of "the prince regent," the "archduke," and "Baron Trozen," he did absolutely nothing to earn these other than look the part. He treated the workers well, spoke to them, answered them, yet somehow remained solitary. He was an expert at solitude without removal.

When the Du Pont cousins made one—and only one—brief inspection visit last autumn, Wyatt had truly expected Trozen to vaunt himself as the hinge pin of Craig Powder Works. When would be a better time?

But no.

In fact, he'd been so unobtrusive that Wyatt found himself going out of his way to prod Trozen to contribute to the meeting—asking him to explain this plan or that formula or this assessment. Couldn't have the Du Ponts thinking their emissary wasn't doing anything.

Wyatt had felt guilty when the Du Ponts pumped the wrong arm and lathered him with congratulations and then threat of a raise. He had been forced either to take credit that belonged to Dorian Trozen, or to embarrass Trozen by forcing him to accept credit in front of the Du Ponts. After all, Wyatt could only, "No, no, no, really, no," for just so long.

Usually Trozen stayed in his own office downriver. But here he came, chatting and joking with the band of workers as the day wound down.

The workers all seemed to like him.

So why don't I like him?

Trozen was waving farewell to the workers as he broke apart from them. He spun around, tucked his T-handled walking stick under his arm, waved his hat, and gave them a funny bow—a teasing kind of bow. The men laughed, then one by one paused, pulled off their striped stocking caps and mimicked his bow complete with exaggeration, and some of them even curtseyed. Trozen got revenge with a military salute, then also laughed, waved good-bye, and headed up the walk to the office building. He was coming here. The men continued down the road, curtseying to each other and prancing like women on a ballroom floor.

Trozen went out of sight, and there was now the sound of the front door opening and clapping shut again.

"Darn," Wyatt murmured, still clutching the telegram and looking out the window. "Not just *this* minute . . ."

"Mr. Craig, a good afternoon. I swear some of those men have the brains of a plank. The courier arrived with several new orders I have need to discuss with you, and . . . let me see . . . there's the matter of shortage of Italian saltpeter because of that one ship's broaching and going down with our shipment in its gut. I contacted Wilmington about it, but they are adamant that we should seek out new sources rather than waiting for our Italian sources to recover. I explained to them by letter that one just doesn't find saltpeter behind the crapshack. We'll see how the bitter-enders respond, then we'll do what we want anyway. They're always comforted if they think they've been asked. 'You wha ken hardly verse frae prose to make a sang, but by your leave, my learned foes, ye're maybe wrang,' said the Bard."

Wyatt didn't turn right away. He didn't turn, in fact, until the sun winked out behind a row of trees and he realized that the day was ending. How long had he been standing here?

Behind him the clap of Trozen's heels upon the wood floor near the doorway dropped off to a faint *tump-tump* on the heavy carpet. There was a *cussssh*, and Wyatt knew his partner had flopped into one of the leather chairs. Probably put his feet up on Wyatt's black-oak desk. Wyatt had seen it often enough—Trozen's gritty soles staring at him against the backdrop of glassy varnish.

He didn't have to look to see it again, not even when he heard order forms and letters being slipped into the stationery box on his desk.

"There you are," the other man's voice larked. "I'm sure they'll wait till morning."

"Thank you," Wyatt finally said. "Thanks very much."

Then there was a long patch of silence, long enough for

Wyatt to know he was being looked at. Maybe it was something in his voice that he had failed to hide.

"The Wilmingtonites are sending you another present, by the way," Trozen rattled on. "It's a new carriage to be seen about town in. It has a red top and silk tassels, and it's completely upholstered with buffalo hide. For some reason they're worried that you appear to own the powder mill exclusively and be reaping every possible reward. I'm sorry, because I did try to explain to them that such flowers as showfulness didn't grow on your tree, and of course I offered to take over the seat of Head Pompous, but they didn't swallow it. The carriage arrives by train next week. You're expected to put your backside into it and go about being 'seen.'"

That accent. That soft educated Southern accent was suddenly as irritating to his Northern-born sensibilities as the twang and trawl of hillbillies, which Wyatt just ignored until now. Trozen's accent was very mellow, surfaced by careful pronunciation of every last word, but it *was* there. Suddenly it grated on Wyatt's bones. Suddenly it was the symbol of the canyon opening between the top and the bottom of a nation. As he had a hundred times, he bottled the urge to ask where Trozen was from, what had brought him here, what he got out of all this. But for the hundredth time the unspoken rule of privacy rose between them. Something about Dorian Trozen silently said *Don't ask, for I won't tell*. Wyatt yielded and didn't ask.

He shrugged mildly.

"I know," he began, "why Wilmington wants the appearance."

In his fingers he squeezed the telegram. The crinkle sounded like a gun blast in the room.

The other man was sensing something, Wyatt knew.

Suede wheezed behind him. Trozen was getting up, coming closer.

I don't want to tell anyone, Wyatt thought, his fingers tightening around the telegram. *I don't want to be the one to tell, to say it at all. Maybe he's leaving.*

Beside him Dorian Trozen appeared and peeked into his privacy. Black brows furrowed over the European eyes.

"Pardon me . . . are your hands trembling?"

Wyatt's head bobbed as he looked down at his own fingers. Not quite a nod, though it was a disturbed acquiescence that Trozen recognized.

By way of demanding an answer, manipulating silence his way as he so well could, Trozen stepped in a little closer, at enough of an angle that Wyatt couldn't avoid him. Even though they were the only people in the whole building, he lowered his voice.

"Shall I guess?" he murmured.

Wyatt raised his hand and mentally shrugged.

"Got a telegram."

He held it up, complete with crinkles made by his sweating hand.

"The stalemate at Sumter is over."

The room went bitter, tightened somehow. Even Dorian Trozen's resilience flickered.

"Not with smiles, I take it. . . ."

Wyatt faced him, pivoting backward against the window frame so he could still lean on it. "With over forty thousand shells fired. Major Anderson surrendered to the Confederates at two-thirty this afternoon."

"I see," Trozen murmured softly. "Therefore . . . war."

Wyatt nodded slowly.

"Therefore war."

A movement in the crystal ball silenced even Trozen.

And that frightened Wyatt. He'd never seen that look in his associate's eyes, while he had seen almost every other. Or had he? He wasn't sure, not now.

There would never be another moment like this one—when he had to say to some other person that war had come, when he saw the crass reality rising in a face other than his own and heard the pressurized silence that comes where there is nothing to say that might help. Utterly human, that look. Only for humans, because humans were the only creatures who saw the future coming.

Wyatt suddenly felt the onus of it all.

Then, like lightning cracking, Dorian Trozen's mental distance returned. He lifted his chin over the stiff white collar, and said, "Well, put that in your curio cabinet."

He strolled around the desk again, moving his elbow so it

wouldn't hit the candlestick lamp, and dropped back into the same chair.

"That does explain the Du Ponts's sudden wish to distance themselves from the traitorous South, doesn't it? Now that we know their game, I guess we can play it, can't we?"

Wyatt glared at him. How could he be so incombustible? "Doesn't this . . . interest you at all?" he asked.

Trozen blinked at him, poised his elbows on the arms of the chair and wobbled a hand. "It gives me some pause, now that we're enemies with our backers. By the way . . . who fired first?"

"Confederate guns volleyed on the supply ship *Star of the West*. It turned back before it made Sumter. Turned back without even being hit. Anderson didn't support them with return fire."

"And go down as the man who started the war? It's not in my mettle, that much is sure. Are you so surprised, Mr. Craig? Lincoln did what he said at his inaugural that he would do. He backed the South into firing the first shots."

"I know, I know. And if the Confederate government hadn't given the open fire, South Carolina would've done it anyway, and the government would look like jackasses." He slid into his own chair behind the desk and rocked nervously. "Sumter's a Federal installation, and now it's in foreign territory. They had no place to retreat. Anderson did what he had to do when he returned fire."

"My bet is he never got straight answers from the hash in Washington."

Wyatt raked his hair out of his eyes, which only caused it to fly forward from the part like the greater and lesser wings of a bird. "What's a straight answer anymore? The states have been dropping off the rock since December just like bugs. South Carolina, Mississippi, Florida, Alabama, Georgia, Texas—"

"Louisiana," Trozen corrected, "then Texas."

Wyatt blinked at him. "Hell, I . . . didn't even know you paid attention."

With a little shrug the other man seemed to be apologizing for knowing what was going on in the nation. "They say Virginia will be next."

"Here we sit, right in the middle of target country." A sudden helplessness got Wyatt by the chest, and he felt as if the whole state were moving underneath his chair. His voice dropped away, and he murmured, "Makes me wonder what we've done to ourselves."

Trozen sat forward slightly. "Beg pardon?"

Wyatt's forefinger wobbled toward the window. "When you proposed this mill," he said, "it sounded like business. Making powder for blasting out new railroad tunnels, clearing channels for merchant shipping, making cellars for decent folk to live over, not for—"

"Mr Craig, I was honest with you. I told you the reason the Du Ponts wanted—"

"I know, I know you did—"

"Why they wanted a *Southern* powder mill," Trozen insisted. "I never deceived you."

"I wish you had. You said '*if* there's a war.' Guess it knocked around inside my head and fell out the hole. I'm twenty-eight years old, and I have been hearing about a war coming all my life. I hear that river run out there, but I never get wet. Guess I learned to ignore it."

Trozen's disarming smile flashed, a sharp and bright change on his elegant face. "Please! Don't chafe so! And don't undertake to extinguish a fuse that's been smoldering since before we were born. It's not good for you."

As if demanding to know if Trozen really gave a damn what was good for anybody else, Wyatt stared at him.

"Don't you know what it means?" he asked baldly. "It means we're not a country anymore."

Brows gathered over the trouble in his heart. Wyatt heard his own thought spill from his lips. Now he understood why people said "Don't say that!" when things were just too awful to be heard.

"Yes," Trozen murmured. "It makes for problems. We'll lose half the workers to enlistment, no doubt. They'll be gung-hoing and holy-warring, and we'll be turning the presses ourselves, you and I."

"If things get that far. My God," Wyatt expressed, "I hope not."

"Do you? Mr. Craig, I thought this was what you wanted."

"*I* wanted?"

"Why of course. You want sovereignty of the states. A small central government. How many times have you said it?"

Wyatt shifted his stare from Trozen to the lettuce-leaf pattern in the carpet. "Shameful way to get it. . . . I want the country our founders wanted. A place to live free of a government that'll meddle in everybody's lives. Freedom is so rare in history. . . a few men in the North using the slavery issue to convince other Northerners to kill people over something they don't understand. They don't know the negroes like we do."

Trozen's eyes narrowed, and he smiled wryly. "You're polishing Excalibur again."

The chair squawked as Wyatt got up and paced aimlessly around the well-appointed office that suddenly seemed too plush. He moved toward the fireplace and gazed into the charred bits, remembering the fires of his life.

"We've got to talk less about war and just *talk*," he said. "The Northerners just don't understand what's at stake. I'm not sure the Southerners realize how much they could lose. I mean, can we love having a war?"

"We love the epaulets of war, Mr. Craig. But none of us wants a hole in his pretty brass-buttoned breast."

"But, God . . . the bucket just filled and filled. A few rich people in the South, a few loud people in the North . . . it's been like trying to stop a tide!"

Trozen came up behind him now.

"Please," Dorian said, "loosen up. The elected officials have been rattling their war sabers for years because it got them elected. Now they're stuck with the hilts in their teeth, and they can't spit them out. They're staring each other down. Do you think a bunch of Northern industrial hammer-and-nailers are going to trudge a thousand miles on foot so they can get shot helping the niggers they don't like anyway? Or Tennessee's mud puppies leaving their two acres to go fight for the rights of julep suckers in South Carolina? Don't miss dinner over it yet . . . at least, not tonight. After all—how long can it last? A month or two?"

"Judas priest!" Wyatt said suddenly, turning. "Where've

you been hiding all your life? Don't you understand the principles here?''

"War is not principle," Trozen said. "It's passion."

Wyatt turned sharply. "How would *you* know?"

The edge of anger in his voice startled him, embarrassed him.

The silence between them this time was awful—it surprised them both that they should be so disturbed by the tension, yet each could see the change in the other's face. They hadn't been friends, but suddenly they had enemies and might have no choice but to be something more than business associates. Now they would have war around them. Now their powder would be cannon powder and gun powder, would be made into canister shot, and would propel balls into flesh, and would blow living men to shreds.

The whole idea was a gut punch.

The two men stood there with nothing in common and nothing between them.

Finally Dorian Trozen uttered the most sensitive phrase Wyatt had ever heard from him.

Softly he said, "You really are frightened. . . ."

Wyatt looked up at him sharply.

The river ran behind the building, and they could hear it as if all the doors were open, as if they were standing knee-deep in it.

Trozen saw the fear but accepted it as part of his associate's simplicity and straightforwardness. But he too was embarrassed . . . that much showed in those black eyes. As though he had laughed out loud at a funeral.

He stepped backward until he could reach the top hat he'd dropped on the desk just minutes ago. He took it in his hands and held it in front of him as though to hide his own heart.

"In that case," he said quietly, "allow me to apologize."

His head dipped enough to place the hat. He took up his walking stick from beside the couch and nodded, a little too formally.

"Good night," he added. "Peace attend you."

The office door swung behind him and bumped against the

mirrored hall tree, then came back a few inches and hung
open.

Wyatt slumped against the mantle. His left calf disturbed
the oak-brass-and-leather bellows, knocking it against the
andiron. Both went over with a *clat* on the slate floor of the
fireplace. The noise might have been his own bones snapping.
Something was wrong, very wrong, about what had just
happened, what might have been *the* most important moment
for him of this entire decade—because unlike Dorian, Wyatt
simply did not believe that all this fervor that had been
sweeping through the country the past fifty years would play
itself out in just a month or two. Eight or ten weeks of war
wasn't enough to break the United States into two completely
separate countries now and forever.

More was coming than that. The wound had burst, finally.
It was going to bleed all over everybody, he knew, he just
knew. People held grudges in their own families for longer
than a couple of months.

He pushed off the mantlepiece and headed for the door. He
raked his morning coat off the hall tree so violently that it
teetered and almost fell over. By the time it wobbled upright
again, the office was empty. In fact, the whole building was
empty.

"Mr. Trozen!"

The other man turned instantly. "Yes, Mr. Craig?"

Wyatt halted, his boots grating on the gravel walk, his coat
a tangled ball that he held against his chest. His mouth moved
soundlessly on a suggestion, but the words refused to come
out.

And he was going to make a fool of himself again! Why
hadn't he stayed inside, alone, while he had the chance?

Dorian Trozen picked up on the difficulty immediately. He
grinned, stepped forward, took Wyatt's morning coat away
from him, and shook it out. Then he held it open for him.
Wyatt stood there dumbly but finally stuck out an arm and
allowed the other man to slip the coat over his shoulders.

"All right now?" Trozen asked. His dark eyebrows went up knowingly.

Yes, he always seemed to *know* what was in somebody else's head!

'Specially mine, Wyatt thought, suddenly desperate to talk. He shifted his feet.

"Uh . . . may I call you Dorian?"

The other man smirked almost nostalgically. "I've been called that before," he said.

Suddenly self-conscious again, Wyatt pushed the words out. He was cutting stone with his bare hands.

"How would you like . . . to come for supper at my home tonight?" he asked. "After all, your money bought it."

Trozen stood there for a good long time. It was easy to see that his mind was working, but to read his thoughts? Impossible. Did he want to go? Or was he trolling for an excuse?

"I imagine," he said, "that would be pleasant."

"Well, good!" Wyatt exclaimed. "Is there something special I can tell the cook?"

"Yes, tell her . . . that tonight is not convenient. Perhaps another evening." He began moving slowly away and touched his hat. "Till the morning, then."

He left Wyatt standing on the gravel walk, empty, and headed toward the carriage house.

That was the way their day always ended. *Very well. See you in the morning. A restful sleep be with you. Good night.*

This was very wrong. Incomplete. Partners should know each other. Have a sense of trust. Even amity. They should at least know where the other lived. D. W. Trozen, Esq., could disappear tomorrow, and Wyatt wouldn't have the vaguest clue where to start looking. He didn't even know what the *W* stood for.

Suddenly Wyatt sucked in a breath.

"I'm sorry I yelled at you," he called out.

Through the dimness of evening as it folded around them, the other man spun on a toe, his daycoat flaring out around his knees. He nodded to accept what Wyatt had said. In the grayness Wyatt couldn't even make out his partner's face.

But a moment later the voice was there.

"I know you are."

★

Wyatt stood alone on the gravel walk feeling like the whole United States. Didn't want to go forward, didn't want to go back. He just stood there with his coat hanging on his bones.

The carriage-house door opened down the lane, the groom made a motion, and the buggy conveying Lord Mystery back to his home, wherever that was, came out and rattled down to the great iron gates, then out onto the main road toward Richmond.

Wyatt may have stood there half the night. He sure felt like not moving. Maybe if he didn't move, nobody else would find out about Fort Sumter. Maybe the telegram was mistaken. Perhaps the telegraph operator made an error. A misread pronoun, a negative where a positive should be, a 'did' instead of a 'didn't,' a dot where a couple of dashes were supposed to be . . . could change the meaning of anything.

Major Anderson was still holding Fort Sumter. The *Star of the West* turned back again after seeing that she hadn't been hit by the Confederate volleys. The men at Sumter had gotten their supplies after all. They could hold out for several more months now. The forty thousand shells . . . that was just a mistake. Some enthusiastic cadets. The commandants would find out what happened and laugh about it, then drink a toast to each other as gentlemen should and claim an interesting close call.

He stood there until a glow of torchlight came from far behind him, at the mills. The dull golden light stretched out endlessly along the gravel path.

Then it came. Rising over the riverside like a flock of birds taking flight in a single great arousal.

The cheer.

A cheer that started with one voice and was joined by more and more—men, screaming and whooping with joy.

Wyatt turned around and looked.

Down the mill grounds, way down by the brick processing buildings, a hundred or more mill workers were gathered. They screamed and whooped again and again, throwing torches into the air, throwing each other into the air, dancing and spinning, waving their fists, and the cheer continued. The sound had started with one voice and now wouldn't end.

And Wyatt would remember the sound of that battle cry, and take a chill at it, for the rest of his life.

★

CHAPTER THIRTY-SEVEN

——————— ★ ———————

The buggy warbled along the wide road to Richmond with a civilized clatter. A light-footed roan mare with a good sense of rhythm knew the way.

Good thing.

In the driver's seat Dorian wasn't even holding the reins.

The leather straps lay across his knee, limp, wobbling from the harness as the mare's shoulders went back and forth. The buggy whip in his hand trembled, like the trees on either side as a little wind breathed through them.

He had no idea where on the road he was when his right hand suddenly convulsed on the reins and yanked the confused mare into a wild jump.

The mare fell out of her rhythm, tossed her head, then managed to pull the buggy in a half circle until the momentum fell off and she could stop. She shook her white mane and turned her rose-colored face around to see what this was all about.

Dorian's boot soles hit the dirt with a *slap* on the quiet road. The silence was amazing, this natural hush, after a day at the mill. He stood there, both feet planted, gripping the buggy with both hands. His own breathing sounded like a waterfall.

His eyes burned. He wanted to spit, but his mouth was dry. *Five years*.

He suddenly mourned the minutes spent in plain survival,

getting a better hold on this bizarre world he'd inherited from sudden freedom.

How eccentric the world had looked at first. His only defense had been to be even more eccentric.

No trouble . . . he had a head start.

But what stares he'd given to the city streets . . . dirty and primitive, yet charged with a lightning excitement. So many people—how could they all have somewhere to go? People of so many kinds, in all kinds of clothing, most of which he'd never seen before. For months he hadn't known which clothes he was supposed to wear. There weren't such clear extremes as he was used to. On plantations slaves wore slave clothes or hand-me-downs, and rich wore rich clothes. In the outside world everybody wore . . . anything they wanted.

Yet there was still the anchor of "fashion" holding them to rigorous straits—if they could afford such shackles. Had he traded one slavery for another?

War. Even if it lasted but a few weeks, war would turn the South upside down and shake it. All the people would fall, like a ship turning turtle in high seas. Lords and servants alike would end up crawling toward the bilge in an effort to survive. Borders could change. Disastrous investments could be made. Shifts in property. Land changing hands. Expansion, retreat, cities in chaos, the government divided, arguing. Upheaval among law-abiding citizens. And the slaves, the immigrants would be confused by sudden gains, the wealthy confused by sudden losses. . . .

Since 1856, since he picked the last of the Grand Staple from between his toes, Dorian knew he had done nothing more than hide himself in the tapestry.

"I . . . want . . . help!" he growled through his teeth, hitting the buggy with its own whip—*crack crack crack!*

At first the mare thought this was for her, but she looked back in time to see her master sling himself away from the buggy and stagger into the woods.

The first tree that came up in front of him was the unlucky one, the one he went after with his whip, smashing and whacking the trunk until his arm was sore, his teeth tight, and his breath heaving in and out.

The whip cracked against the tree as though the braided

leather itself was obsessed, taking off handfuls of bark and flinging it across the clearing. Dorian lashed out until he was gasping. When his arm screamed for relief, he staggered across the clearing, disoriented, stumbled, and caught himself on another tree. The wood scored his hands, but he hung on. It felt good, the hurting. His palms hadn't hurt in a long time, and the pain reminded him of who he was.

Everything, every road, path, dogtrail had been a dead end. He was the hunted man hunting. His only momentary peace had come at the hands, skilled hands, of odorous women in ruffled bordellos who managed to make his brain go dead for a few minutes. His enemies had found out about that, and now he couldn't sleep peacefully between the propped-up breasts of this or that whore—at least not all night anymore.

Now a war, or a semblance of war, the fear of war, the enthusiasm of war, would shatter the structure he had counted upon—people running off to fight or running away from the fighting—people on the run. . . . How could he look among their faces if they were all running?

"Swine," he gasped. "Swine of a world. . . . It's not that big . . . it's not that big!"

He smacked the tree with his hand. The whip was gone. Where was it? He wanted to hit something again. No one would look at him, at his clean face, at these clothes, and say, "Failure!" But that's what he was. People measured success in terms of comfort, but they were wrong.

Frustration shot through Dorian's heart. Clinging to the tree, ignoring an ironic awareness of what the bark might be doing to his brocade waistcoat, he raised his eyes and peered through the trees, back up the road the way he'd come.

Evidently. . . he hadn't put as much distance between himself and the mill as he'd tried to.

The tantalizing yellow glow of torchlight flickered against the bars of the company gate as though it were imprisoned.

The mill yard . . . near the refineries.

And he heard a faint noise. Voices, the voices of celebration. So the word was out. And he'd lost even more time here, hitting a tree.

A moment flashed when he thought of Wyatt, standing back there, trying to lead an honest life and somehow managing it. Dorian actually thought of going back, accepting the hand of friendship he had so efficiently snubbed. Wyatt Craig had been hardest of all to keep at bay, with his genuine manner and probity. A square-dealer like Wyatt presented more danger for Dorian than anyone else. Pretentiousness is easy to walk away from, but how hard it was to guard against the incorrupt.

Every day it got harder. He hadn't had a friend in five years.

Enemies . . . those he had. He knew that. A man with enemies learns what to watch out for. Running away from his enemies, running toward the things he sought—he had ended up running in circles. Here he was, back in Virginia, empty-handed.

He should have given up and gone to Greece years ago.

That thought made another gasp heave up from inside, and Dorian gripped the tree even harder, clinging to the continent as the cables that tied him to the United States tightened around his midriff.

He pushed himself away from the tree and went down on both knees on the moon-dusted clearing. Where there had been gasps, now came one single pathetic sob—

As he turned his face up, up to the sky, up to God, tears broke from his eyes and dribbled down the classical features, now twisted with misery.

His fists turned into rocks. His voice thundered up to heaven. The words came out one at a time. Bullets.

"You overpriced . . . overpublicized . . . credit-thieving, loitering son of a bitch! Show your fraudulent self and answer! Where . . . is . . . my . . . *mother*!"

★

CHAPTER THIRTY-EIGHT

——— ★ ———

"I think it is miserable that Lincoln's elected. Whenever I think of our having such a President from such a party, it makes me feel like tasting green persimmons does to children. . . . I wish the Republicans and the abolitionists were in the Atlantic, when we would be at rest.

Ellen du Pont, a letter to
her brother, Henry Algernon du Pont

JUNE 1861
TWO MONTHS LATER—

"The last two shipments assaulted! Over eight tons of refined powder heading for the rail yard, and not a grain of it got through. Seven men slaughtered. Everybody thought we were going to war, and all we've got so far is a bunch of skirmishes and an excuse for piracy. Why are they doing this? They don't know our powder is or isn't going to a military installation—"

"We *are* a military installation. It's inherent."

Dorian had been listening to Wyatt Craig's complaints for ten minutes without bothering to point out until now that the powder yard was in itself a target of war just because of what they *made* here. There didn't have to be a summons from Jefferson Davis, a call to service, a signal of war. Black

532

powder was just one of those daily-use products in peacetime that naturally became a target during wartime. Until the attacks on their shipments, there had been no trouble. Now there was trouble.

For fifty years there hadn't been a war on American soil. Nobody knew how to make one. After all the talk and the cheering, the prancing and the seceding, a nation of disagreeable people stood around gawking at each other, expecting the other man to start first. There were no standing armies, no uniforms, no plans, no provisions, no supply lines, and the only trained military men were the boys at West Point, the men in U.S. forts out West or the old soldiers whose last military experience had been the Mexican War.

The whole idea of a war was far more overbearing than folk realized or remembered.

Dorian watched with passive empathy as Wyatt slumped down into his office chair and put on his best thinking face, trying to come up with an idea.

"Now I have an order," Wyatt said, "to deliver a hundred kegs of fine glazed powder to men who intend to shoot at anybody with my Northern accent."

"Precisely," Dorian drawled. "Triple F, subscript g. That's rifle powder."

The blue eyes on the other side of the desk took on a certain heaviness. "And I can't even deliver it because of attacks on my shipments. Who are these raiders? Do we have their names? I'd like to know who's killing my employees."

Flipping the papers in his hand and skimming the handwritten reports, Dorian made a conscious effort to keep any emotion out of his voice.

"They aren't cohesive, these men," he explained. "If anything, it's a very vague secret society. Some are genuine sympathizers with the Northern cause. Others are simply deserters, criminals, men looking for an excuse not to join up, others looking for excuses to . . . do other things."

"Like rape innocent women?" Wyatt roundly returned. "Those kinds of things?"

"Yes, like that. So any ruffian now has a patriotic certificate for his crimes. There's been a series of bridge burnings on the Tennessee border and in western Virginia, and other general hostility toward the Confederacy. These pro-Unionists want this area to be taken by the Federals, but they're going about it all amiss. Because they choose to be secretive, anytime an egg is stolen from a henhouse, the blame is put upon them. Ironically, they are garnering the dislike of Southern residents of these areas, who claim Northern interference—"

"It's unthinkable," Wyatt muttered, running his finger along his lower lip. "Touching women who don't want touching... burning bridges, blowing people up, ransacking farms and houses, families.... Maybe I'd feel better if all this just *looked* like a war. You think?"

He glanced across the desk at Dorian.

When nothing came from over there except the usual unapproachability of Dorian's refusal to commit himself, Wyatt went on to the next question.

"Got any names?"

Dorian came to life with a bounce of his dark brows.

"There's no membership list, Mr. Craig. We can't go to their front doors in daylight and ask them please not to ambush our shipments and murder our men."

When Wyatt gave him a scowl, Dorian realized he wasn't helping and tried again.

"All right... the sheriff has supplied what he believes to be the name of the leader in this area. Very flamboyant man. Thinks himself a savior, a John Brown type. Apparently he convinces others that—"

"May I just have his name, please?"

"I'm searching for it. Ah, here. His name is... Lasik. He sports a dubious past—"

The chair squawked as Wyatt sat bolt upright. "Lassick?"

Dorian checked the paper. "Yes. Why?"

"Not Bradford Lassick—"

"I have his name as... Rodney Lasik... native of... where is it? Chattanooga. Why? Is this puff adder a blemish upon your transparent past?"

For a moment Wyatt let the idea float. Had Brad Lassick ever mentioned Chattanooga? Relatives? An only child, Wyatt knew, no brothers.

"May I see that?"

Dorian handed him the paper, and he found the name, saw the spelling difference . . . Lassick, Lasik. . . .

"Must be a coincidence," he decided. "I guess it *could* be a distant relation. . . . Do people ever change the spellings of their names?"

His partner sported an odd smirk and said, "Constantly."

"Far as I recall, he never even wrote a letter to anybody. . . . Nah, can't be. That's some coincidence, but I'm sure it's not the same man." He handed the paper back. "Go ahead. Sorry for the interruption."

"Apology accepted," Dorian said. For an instant there was a flash of—warmth?—but then he buried it and turned once again to the report.

"This Rodney L-a-s-i-k bears a long record of crimes for which he has now found a 'cause.' Under the appellation 'Order of Heroes of America,' he's gathering an army of Southern resistors to the Confederate cause. They're out of Monongahela County in the west part of this state. They've been holding antisecessionist rallies. Thus, where he had only brigands in tow before, he's now getting devotion from honest Southerners who want the nation intact. Makes it much harder to exact justice against him as one common criminal, which he is. Bless me, many are the devils who claim sanction from heaven, hm?"

"I guess," Wyatt muttered.

On the verge of saying something else, he never got to it. He got up and strode across the thick carpet, wishing he smoked a pipe so he could have something to chew on. He strode this way and that, wandering about the office aimlessly, changing the position of his hands almost with every step to help himself think, while the ascetic Dorian watched from his chair.

"What bothers me," Wyatt said, "is how they knew the dates, times, and routes of those two deliveries when only you, me, and our foremen knew anything was going out at all. Our next shipment has to go right through that area again, and there's no safety for a shipment of gun powder as long as those Hero people are out there."

"To be sure," Dorian agreed. "And what, pray, would you do if you found these knucklewalkers in your charge?"

"Me? Well, I...I guess..." He paused as the vision turned real before him. With an honest slump he admitted, "I don't know. We've got to take care of our shipments and our men, though. And this next order is due in fifteen days. We've got to do something."

"I've already done something."

Wyatt squeezed his lips together, winced his eyes closed, and groaned. Gradually he got the nerve to turn around and face—oh God, Dorian was getting to his feet. Dorian never, ever bothered to get up during a meeting unless there was some reason he wanted to look right into someone's eyes.

"Like...," Wyatt asked, "what?"

Dorian straightened his black coat. The black coat with the black velvet lapels and the velvet cuffs with silver buttons.

He always looked like a spy in that coat, Wyatt noted. Today especially, because of the black vest and smoke blue necktie with the silver stud. Those, combined with the silky black curls and cast-iron eyes—either a spy or a raven about to fly off.

"You'll need authority," Dorian said. "Weight to fling about. I've arranged for it."

Wyatt's eyes narrowed. Next to Dorian he suddenly felt frumpy in his day clothes and fair coloring and simple mannerisms, but he managed to keep enough presence of self to respond honestly.

"You're gonna have to explain that. Because I don't understand."

Nothing changed, except that Dorian's eyes flickered, and his mouth took on the slightest twist.

"Do you understand a commission in the Army of the Confederate States of America?"

Wyatt nearly stumbled. "A comm—what've you done to me this time?"

"Simply arranged that you have military authorization and uniformed escort for our deliveries as authorized by the Confederate government, nothing more."

Staring at him, Wyatt broadly asked, "Nothing more?"

"Well...a little more. What rank would you like? Major? Captain?"

★

"General order number four . . . officers shall sport double-breasted tunics extending halfway from hip to knee, hip buttons lined up with breast buttons, seven buttons on each row in the front, three small buttons on the cuffs, the collar standing, embroidered with rank insignia, cuffs and collar in branch-of-service color, with one and one quarter inch star to indicate the rank of major. Color shall be . . . cadet gray."

Wyatt looked down at his chest like a child who had just spilled milk on himself. Dorian's reading off of the general order was a grim sentence to the one wearing a uniform for the first time in his life. Two rows of brass buttons, seven each row, glittered back up at him off a field of dove gray cotton-wool blend.

The standing collar scraped the underside of his chin.

"I'll be some target. It feels funny."

"That's because you haven't had properly tailored clothes before in your unspecious life. Besides, it's war. I heard they're not letting any Georgette crepe through Mr. Lincoln's blockade. Hold still and let yourself be fitted properly. We mustn't look sloppy."

"I can't believe there isn't another way."

"There are other ways," Dorian said, "none as good."

"Sqvare your shulderz, Herr Craig, pleass?" the tailor ordered, tugging on Wyatt's left arm. It was probably a request, but everything that came out of the mouth of this Austrian immigrant sounded like an order.

For the past hour the man had been tediously stitching gold braid in the "Austrian knot" pattern halfway up the tunic sleeves. The collar and cuffs were brilliant royal blue, creating a stunning effect combined with the gray and the gold. A little too stunning.

Wyatt held his chin up, pushed his shoulders back until they hurt, and tried not to stiffen up. He couldn't be sure, but he suspected that Dorian, lounging on the office davenport with his legs thrown over the arm and a leather satchel on his lap, was enjoying watching him go through this. He remembered all too clearly how delighted Dorian had been at the satire of finding an Austrian tailor to do the Austrian knots on the sleeves.

Dorian had taken charge of outfitting the men, of making real soldiers out of common workers—or at least making them *look* like real soldiers. Wyatt had promised a free hand, knowing that he couldn't efficiently run the powder mill and also make a brigade at the same time. Yet . . . all this felt so improper. Even a bit unfair. Were they a brigade? Or just pretending to be one?

Keeping his neck stiff, Wyatt tried to look downward. The tailor was puffing away on a big cigar, and the ropes of smoke made designs similar to the gold trim twisting down Wyatt's sleeves.

He sighed.

The wool was itchy.

"Couldn't I be a lieutenant or a sergeant or yeoman or something?" he grumbled. "I don't want to be lofty."

"Mr. Craig," Dorian interrupted with a finger in the air, "the purpose of all this is for you to have some measure of clout. Why settle for a sergeant's clout when you can have a major's clout? Now," he added, turning his attention to the satchel on his lap, "if I can find it . . . ah! Here is a commission for you, Major Wyatt Craig, duly signed by the governor of the state of Virginia, and inductions for each of our employees into the infantry of the Confederacy, which makes this powder mill an official installation of the—"

"Please don't say it."

"And entitles us to 'protect and defend ourselves and our property with whatsoever means and such force as the commanding officer does so deem—'"

"I got it, thanks. Pardon that I asked, okay?"

"Okay. We also have access to government ordnance and use of an official quartermaster to tally and distribute all this. As to artillery, as soon as it becomes avail—"

"Artillery!"

"Ah, a simple man's dream to complete a sen—"

"You mean cannons?"

"Herr Craig! Stant yourzelf shtill!"

"Sorry. Are you talking of cannons?"

"If you would like them."

"I wouldn't."

"I told them you wouldn't already. And here is an itemized receipt for tailoring of the uniforms for those of our *profanum vulgus* who have agreed to, as they say, 'join up.' Shoes, canteen, canvas haversacks, three cotton shirts per man, three flannel shirts, five pair socks, two pair drawers—"

"Where're we getting all this?"

"The North. The South hasn't enough manufacturing facilities, thus I've arranged as much ordnance as possible to be shipped down from New York while we still have the chance. The people aren't speaking, but the banks are, luckily. One toothbrush, branch-of-service cap badges, blue secession cockades to be worn on the left breast of the coat."

"New York?" Wyatt said. "Am I paying for all this?"

"Yes, you are. Each man will carry a small leather pouch on the right hip for copper percussion caps, a large pouch for cartridges for the rifles, which are, if I can find it . . . yes, here. They are Richmond Armory rifles. . . . Oh, bless if I haven't forgotten the bayonets and scabbards! I'll be on it first thing. No pistols as yet, but only because I haven't found a source. We are also short of belts, buttons, and there are no hats. We shall make do for now. Oh, yes—we'll also be forced to make do without proper marching music. We have no drummers as yet, so I've arranged for lessons for two of our younger workers, and we should be receiving brass instruments within one month. Thus far we have sixty-two men who wish to attain rank among the rank in our little tiltyard. That includes twelve of the slaves who've volunteered to go along as guards. They won't officially be in the army, of course, being negro, but—"

"Oh, that's right. . . . I'll talk to them tonight."

"The slaves?"

"Yes, I want to make sure nobody's bullying them into volunteering."

Dorian's dark brows moved with strange amusement as he marked this and that on the papers with a crude pencil. "Slaves need to be bullied. It's best for their well-being. You've said so yourself."

"I never said that."

"A slave's chain is his center of balance. We all know that

for sure, don't we? I've told them they can wear uniform-colored jackets. Is that game with you?''

Wyatt shrugged. "If they're willing to risk their lives, then they deserve to wear some kind of uniform.''

"The secretary of war will disagree with you.''

"We'll station the negroes as reserves to guard the facility here. Nobody can tell me what to do with my own slaves, or what to dress them in. If the secretary of war wants to disagree, then he'll be arguing the North's point for them.''

"Excellent point. You should be anointed philosopher-king." He stuck the pencil in his mouth and went about shuffling through the papers.

"Thanks." Wyatt fidgeted. Impatience was making his legs itch. He glanced downward at the bald tailor and the sea of pins and thread and measuring utensils.

"I don't know how women do this all the time. If I had to get fitted for everything I wear, I'd sooner get a pistol and blow my brains out.''

Dorian took the pencil out of his mouth and said, "You're not that good a shot.''

Since the Austrian tailor had crawled around to the other side and was at work on the right sleeve, Wyatt let his left arm express his feelings by flopping limp at his side. The cigar smoke twisted upward and made Wyatt's nose wrinkle. In order to avoid coughing, he had to clear his throat.

"That's quite a pungent cigar you have there, Mr. Schepp,'' he commented, waving the air, hoping to get his point across. "What kind is it?''

The Austrian opened his mouth to answer, but it was Dorian who spoke up without thinking.

"Air-cured Maryland Broadleaf,'' he said distractedly, flipping through the papers.

Instantly, realizing his blunder, he looked up—and sure enough, Wyatt was looking right back at him. A blunder, a mistake. He could no more have stopped himself than stop a sneeze.

It was in Wyatt's expression that Dorian saw the clue erupt. He tried to cover it with a frosty shrug and failed. For an instant a needle went through his guarded heart, his disguise fell open before Wyatt's up-and-down perceptiveness.

Wyatt wasn't buying the shrug. He knew a clue when he heard one.

Dorian didn't smoke cigars.

Wyatt leveled his stare at Dorian from beneath drawn brows and let him off the hook . . . but only partly.

"You're enjoying this, aren't you?" he accused.

Dorian escaped back into scanning the papers. "Enjoying fitting out a military company? Of course, Mr. Craig. 'I have sworn upon the altar of God eternal hostility against every form of tyranny over the mind of man.'"

"You have?"

"No," Dorian tossed. "I don't actually give a pig's tit about the mind of man. That was Thomas Jefferson."

"Too bad," Wyatt sighed. "For a minute I thought I saw a glimmer." Just loud enough he added, "I'd give my last money to see it."

Dorian snapped up. The papers dropped flat on his lap with a hiss. The edge of threat was keen against his gullet.

Faded animosity sprung back into full color, and neither man could look away until Dorian ultimately drew in a long breath and blinked, then turned back to the papers on his lap.

The papers flapped softly as he thumbed through them.

It had been like that for months between them. The more Wyatt attempted to chip, the thicker the ice became on the other side, thicker, whiter, and wider, and yet always with that faint image of a man frozen deep inside, looking through the layers, life still moving in the eyes.

Dorian could deal with almost anything, keep his armor up against the shrewdest of men who wanted to know who he was and where he was from, *what* he was, but these past months had been the hardest. The plainspoken forthrightness of Wyatt—not to mention Wyatt's honest persistence—had been torture to resist.

It had been five years of isolation from such affections, and he wasn't about to break the pattern now. He wouldn't let anyone get close enough to be scratched by the devil's finger.

He reminds me of Alex, that's all. It's only that and nothing more. In time that will go away. Or I will.

He had been safe here for a while. Just being in Virginia had eased the pressure somewhat, because his plague had not expected him to come back here. Bribed sources had assured him that after so many months of failure, Noah Sutton had given up and returned to Chapel Mount and now that war had come, was preparing himself and his monstrous black stallion for the Confederate cavalry.

But those were someone else's reassurances, hired at a price. Dorian had already stayed longer here than he had stayed anywhere since the night he walked away from the sounds of Noah Sutton spitting and choking out the manure Dorian had fed him.

Yet something held him here, a bond that had formed during the moments when he was off guard.

It had sneaked up on him and wrapped itself about him and whispered to stay a little longer. Only today did he realize that Wyatt was the source.

Dorian had seen it before, that look.

People had wanted to get close to him before, for reasons of curiosity or gain, but like watching a pretty snake, they ultimately got cautious and veered off. Women often pressed toward him with that look plus something extra in their eyes, their supple bodies defying even the corsets that gave them shape, but he had always been able to frighten them just enough to overpower the sexual attraction. Women were easy to discourage. Most men, conveniently, just didn't like him.

Even with his best offishness, though, he hadn't been able to manipulate Wyatt Craig into leaving him alone. Wyatt didn't want to see anyone left alone, that was the whole bedamned trouble of it. A dangerous magnet for Dorian, who only this moment realized his own loneliness.

He stiffened, trying to resist squirming against the cushions.

Wyatt waved the tailor off and strode to the couch. Dorian looked up at him. He couldn't predict what was about to happen, and he didn't like that. His hands were suddenly like carved wood in his lap.

"You've been waving those papers in front of me," Wyatt said steadily, "but you haven't given me a good look at them. Lots of receipts, but I haven't seen a single invoice for all these uniforms and provisions and stuff. Not to mention that we haven't had any trouble keeping up our output in spite of the extra cost of outfitting a whole brigade."

Through pursed lips Dorian corrected, "Company."

Heedless of the pins in his uniform, heedless of the tender basting holding a double row of brass buttons in place across his chest, Wyatt lowered himself to squat in front of the couch and get right at eye level with his so-called partner. He gripped the fine leather of the couch and spoke softly.

"You're the accounting manager, and I agreed to let you handle this," he said, "because I thought you'd like doing it, but how sluggish in the head do you think I am? If the powder mill was supporting all this ordering and outfitting, then it would put a dent in our production level. It hasn't. We're not paying for all this, so it's obvious who is."

Without moving so much as the tiniest muscle in his face, Dorian hardened before Wyatt's eyes. Not because of money or deception, but a personal hardening. A shell dropped between them.

Wyatt ignored it completely. His gaze was authentic, unadulterated. "I'm uncomfortable with things that don't make sense."

Within the confines of his own tightly controlled body, Dorian suddenly turned to water.

Eyes upon eyes, they glared into each other, one sterling, the other smoldering.

Behind them the Austrian tailor's brow puckered all the way up to his empty hairline, but he dared make not a sound.

Wyatt put a hand on Dorian's left forearm to make a bridge between them. Quietly he asked, "Would you like to be honest with me?"

The hand was like iron on Dorian's arm. Internally he jumped—though on the outside there was no hint of it. Or was there? Had his eyes flickered? Had his mouth tightened? Had he given himself away? Was his stillness a ticket to his soul?

Wyatt had unknowingly put his hand on Dorian's sleeve right over the branded *S*. For Dorian, it was as though Wyatt's fingers were burning through the sleeve and at any moment would cut through to the scar and feel it and he would know, he would realize, he would discover. The question Wyatt had asked was not the question Wyatt wanted an answer to. The secret was being touched.

Who are you? Why are we still strangers?

If Wyatt had touched him anywhere else on his arm, Dorian may have buckled. But not there, not that one spot.

From the sediments at the bottom of his well, he dragged up the last of his remoteness and mortared himself with it.

'Am I held to bargains made before I was born? . . . It's very difficult to sail half a ship. . . .'

"Get in the carriage, Alex."

Black eyes flared, yanking strength from the past. With all the hammered knowledge of what he was, Dorian gathered himself into a contained ball inside his chest and resisted the cold hunger, once and for all.

"Don't touch me," he warned. "I'm dangerous."

The books on the office shelves, the untouched books put there by some long-gone decorator, seemed to tremble under the thin unfortunate dust. Above, the chandelier's crystals made dots of reflected light on the carpet and on Wyatt's face.

The Austrian tailor couldn't take anymore.

"Excuse me . . . I vill vash my hans," he muttered, and escaped out the office door, determined to get out before one of these eccentric Americans pulled a gun and shot the other one.

Don't touch him? Wyatt wondered.

What was that supposed to mean? Don't *touch* him.

Wyatt knew he would be mulling over that one for the rest of the day. Partners with someone he couldn't touch? His hands were his link to other people. Anyone, everyone. A friendly grasp, a pat on the arm or grip on the shoulder— those were his bridges. He did that without thinking, man, woman, dog, kid, horse, it didn't matter.

Don't touch me. I'm dangerous.

Wyatt withdrew his hand in defeat, but he won a little ground by letting the hurt show on his face.

He got up and backed off, carefully manipulating his loss.

"The Du Ponts," he said. "It's still their money, isn't it?"

When Dorian remained silent, still not able to clear the rock out of his throat—because they both knew the Du Ponts were not really the subject of this tightness between them—

Wyatt closed the same hand over the scrolls of gold braid on his uniform sleeve.

"You're still in contact with them, aren't you?" he went on. "They claimed to cut ties with us when war was declared because they didn't want to be attached to the South. At least that's what you told me. But I haven't paid for this brigade business, and somebody has. Somebody's making sure we have a military unit here to guard this powder for the Confederate government, and it isn't me." He pointed out the window. "The kegs in those magazines have my name stamped on them."

He tapped his chest with the other thumb while still pointing out the window and suddenly looked to Dorian like a statue raised to commemorate some reluctant hero. And the war hadn't really even started yet. Statues...

God and goddesses reaching outward toward many-headed beasts with hands gently turned upward, fingers gently spread.

"By Christ...in the moonlight, you look just like them statues...."

Dorian closed his eyes, hard. Quickly he opened them again before Wyatt saw.

Even then he couldn't be sure.

"Why are the Du Ponts still so interested in a mill they've cut all ties to?" Wyatt asked. He stepped closer again and looked down at Dorian as he sat very still on the couch. "They offered this operation to you, didn't they? Didn't they?"

This time Dorian looked up and managed to admit collectedly, "Yes, they did."

"Why didn't you take it?"

"I don't want it."

"You don't want your name on anything is what you mean, right?"

"Mr. Craig, as Burns said, 'I have too much pride to be servile, yet not enough to be selfish.'"

Using that as a crutch, Dorian pushed the papers back into the satchel and got to his feet. His legs were trembling, as if he had run from Richmond. Had he weakened?

After putting some carpet between them, he cleared his throat and asked, "Why does it worry you so much? You have a ghostly benefactor in the Du Pont cousins. They want their names on nothing, as you accuse of me.''

"How do I know what they're thinking?" Wyatt said, closing the distance no matter how Dorian tried to spread it out. "You don't tell me much. Maybe they're not pro-Southern at all. Maybe they're funding me to make sure the South has powder to fight a longer war. Then the North'll have to buy powder from the Wilmington operation."

"Really, Mr. Craig, you imagine things.''

"How do I know you're not part of the plot?"

Now Dorian faced him straight on. He didn't mind being a shadow, but something from his youth still hated being thought of as scoundrel. He would be a demon but not a cheat.

And here the most true-souled man he'd ever met was believing him to be one. Did he have to be standing there with hie true soul wrapped in a snappish new officer's uniform? A symbol of yeomanly honor and duty and virtue and all those *beau ideals*?

Even in the stiff new tunic, Wyatt slumped.

"Okay," he said in surrender. "I'll find out for myself. Excuse me.''

Dorian stepped aside, drawing a deep breath to steady himself after Wyatt finally left the office. From now on he would take care to brick the wall even higher between them, to stay in his own office, perhaps even work as much as possible in town, away from here, away from Wyatt—

Find out for himself—

"Oh, no!" he choked suddenly.

He dashed from the room, the open sides of his waistcost flapping against his ribs.

"Where are you going!" he shouted. He caught Wyatt just outside the office building and broke his own promise to himself by grasping Wyatt's elbow very firmly. "Where are you going?''

"I'm going to the telegraph office," Wyatt said. "'Scuse me.''

"No! No—come here, come here.''

Dorian dragged him back into the foyer so no one could see or hear them.

Wobbling his elbow in Dorian's grip, Wyatt reminded, "I thought you were the one who didn't want to be touched."

"Boat your oars and listen to me!" Dorian shouted, pushing Wyatt by the shoulders until he was against the wall.

"Well?" Wyatt began. "Are you going to tell me something finally?"

"I'm going to tell you this," Dorian said with a shaky breath. "The Du Pont cousins are sincerely pro-Confederacy. In fact, they despise the North bitterly, and you are the instrument with which they shall help cripple it. They chose you because Henry Du Pont can be made to believe that you, a Du Pont apprentice, might actually be able to piece together a powder mill here in the doggedly agricultural South—which in *fact* . . . you did do."

While Wyatt stood there with false patience, Dorian paused, moved off a few steps, and tried to collect himself. Then he knotted his fists before his waist and gazed at the parquet floor.

"You don't want to be a pawn," he said. "That is your nature. But you are a pawn. We are all pawns, every last dog on this dung heap is the pawn of the next-smartest dog. They are glad to have you, Mr. Craig, and they are glad to give you this powder mill. Some people actually are that rich. However, part of my duty is to warn you," he added, "that the cousins who financed this operation will do whatever they must to protect their secret."

Wyatt shoved off the wall and moved closer. Soon both his shoes and Dorian's were in the bright wedge of sunlight that cut into the foyer at an angle. As for the rest, they were both in shadow.

The implication was so outlandish, so hideous that he didn't even realize what those words meant for a good many seconds, and when it came to him, he stood there mouthing empty sounds. Then he forced the question out.

"Are you saying . . ."

"I am saying," Dorian repeated, "that they will do *whatever* they must . . . to protect their secret."

Silence dropped, but this time they were both behind the same curtain instead of on either side of it. *Whatever they must.*

Wyatt's eyes widened boyishly as he swallowed the whole meaning of Dorian's warning. He paced away, staring at the floor.

In all these months he had been that close to the secrets—and the danger—that money can buy and never knew it. And money could buy a lot of danger.

Then, though there was no need to explain, Dorian added, "Your life may be at stake."

Wyatt stared at him. The scalded image of the things Dorian had experienced in his life left a constant veil over him, like shadows cast over sculpture. Dorian's backalley instinct was preternatural. One could expect that *sang-froid* from a bartender, but not a gentleman.

Then . . . Dorian wasn't exactly a gentleman.

Wyatt suddenly understood something else—Dorian was protecting him. How long had Dorian been protecting him?

"So stay away from the telegraph office," Dorian said, "let the candy man finish your uniform. At the appointed time go with your brigade of infantrymen and your shipment of precious black powder, Major Craig. You *are* an officer now. If you run into the Heroes of America, feel free to bring back their heads, and we'll mount them for you. By my best estimate, they number roughly a dozen. Thus prepare yourself for twenty raiders, and you should fare well enough. As for me . . . I believe I shall take the rest of the week off, starting tonight. Beg you have a good evening, sir."

Wyatt deliberately stayed outside until dark, strolling among the powder-mill workers and the slaves in his new uniform, leaving the tunic unbuttoned and flapping at his sides so nobody would get the idea that he was parading about. Rather he was determined to show them that he was still the garden-variety Wyatt. Some of the men had their new infantry uniforms on too, simpler, less complete versions of his own, and they strode about the compound in the light of two big fires set in wheelbarrows, congratulating each other, saying who was too fat and who was too craven and who was too much a mammy's boy to go to war. They laughed and shook their fists in the direction of the north, sang songs, and thanked Wyatt for giving them the chance to be part of a holy crusade. They were so anxious . . . so afraid it would be over before they had a chance to kick some skinny Yankee ass.

Mostly Wyatt just wanted them to see that the uniform and the major's star on the collar hadn't changed him.

It had changed them, though. They stood by, beaming at him, choked up with sentiment, proud of their leader, and Wyatt kept wanting to turn around to see who the hell they were beaming at. Some of them saluted.

His spine crawled underneath the brand new cadet-gray wool. Some of these men were twice his age, some half it. Many had been with him since Kansas, some even worked for his father. They had given up the dream of going west to come here with him and follow his promise of stability, and now he was going to take them out, in uniform, with guns, on a mission in which they were actual targets. And they *liked* it. Thanked him for it.

He stayed out there, enduring the whole idea until well after sunset, when he finally saw the ravenlike figure of Dorian Trozen walking, as he always did, down the gravel path toward the carriage house.

Wyatt turned to one of the slaves standing in the darkness at the edge of the firelight.

"Say, Joe? Joe, is that you?" he called. "Come over here, would you?"

A plump, strong negro laughed at the end of someone's joke, then swirled toward Wyatt and said, "Sure it's me, Missa Wyatt. Cain't you see my brass buttons and my white teeth in dat firelight?" Then he laughed again, showing a wide space between his front teeth.

Wyatt hung an arm around the chubby shoulders and drew the slave aside, lowering his voice. "Joe, might you do me a favor? It involves riding into Richmond."

The man looked suddenly shocked. "You ain't puttin' me to work in Richmond, are you?"

"No, it's just a ride into town and back."

"Oh. Well, okay. Then I do it."

"That's fine," Wyatt said. "Got your papers in a pocket?"

"Ri' here," Joe said, patting the breast pocket of his short gray jacket. "I be right proud to ride through them streets and stand before them city people in my new grays."

"Well, I'm proud of you too. Take my horse. I want you to be quiet going in, now, understand?"

Joe pulled back and looked at him. "Sure can be. Uh . . . why?"

"Because I want you to follow Mr. Trozen into town. Without his knowing, I mean."

"Follow Mr. Trozen? *Our* Mr. Trozen?"

"Yes."

Joe gave him a reproachful scowl.

"Now, sir . . . you right certain that's what you want?"

"That's what I want." Wyatt drew out his wallet and thumbed up a few dollars. "Meet me at my house on Governor Street, and then afterward you can take this money and buy dinner for yourself. There's a little saloon on Varney Street that takes negroes."

Joe gaped at the money and licked his lips. Then he paused and frowned. "Sir, don't hardly seem right to be foll'in Mr. Trozen around, though, sir, do it?"

Wyatt patted the man's shoulder and gazed past him at the carriage house as the doors parted and the single-horse rig pulled out, drove between the gateposts, then quickened pace onto the road toward the city.

"Don't worry, Joe. I hope to make it right."

Shockoe Creek. This couldn't be the place . . . but Joe had given him complete instructions.

As Wyatt steered his buggy past Canal Street toward the river from Shockoe Hill, the area turned bad. Veined by mud eddies and gullies and the creek itself, many of the roads as yet unpaved, Shockoe Creek was one of those areas of town that had a better and a worse part. This was the worse part.

A block past Canal, Wyatt steered his pony on past Dock Street—was that?—no it couldn't be. Sure was desolate here. Nobody in sight.

Another few yards and he gave in to his nerves and drew in the reins. The pony slowed to a walk.

A block directly in front of him, the James River was glossy in the moonlight. There were two enormous side-wheelers puffing upriver, nearly side by side, the groan of their steam engines giving the evening a certain hollow presence. They hooted to each other against the navy blue night.

A block down some drunken men, probably sailors or smugglers, were coming out off Byrd Street. To Wyatt they were nothing but black jackets and caps against the purple night as they spotted him and suddenly fell silent. They were watching him. They mumbled to each other.

Wyatt shivered. Even the wool of his uniform tunic failed to warm him. But as he clucked his pony around in a semicircle back to Dock Street, he knew the shiver was caused by something other than the early-summer night's chill.

He drove down Dock Street toward 17th. This should work; he should come on Seventeenth and be able to turn south to Byrd Street. If his nerves held out. He had to get to Byrd Street. Took a lot of repressing to convince himself the smugglers had gone on their way and not turned back down Byrd and were waiting to meet their prey.

Byrd Street intersection. Only a few yards. He slowed down again. Or perhaps full gallop would be better. . . . Could the pony go fast enough on this bumpy street to outrun a gang of men? Was there enough road before he hit the riverside?

Wyatt drew the buggy to a complete stop and listened.

Nothing.

Nothing but the hoot of the two paddle wheelers.

He clucked forward a few yards. Byrd Street opened before him, a giant black maw with teeth of warehouses, abandoned buildings, and mealy boardinghouses.

But no men. No bushwhackers. Completely deserted.

"Ho . . . boy," Wyatt gasped, sinking back in the buggy seat. He pressed a hand to his crashing heart, between two sets of the brass buttons. "This can't be right."

East on Byrd, then a jog south again, then east along the river.

The whole area stunk of tobacco and industrial smoke from the Dill tobacco factory and the Grant tobacco factory just a few blocks up. There was a permanent aroma in the air, enough to choke a man who didn't smoke, and Wyatt didn't. All he could do was try to breathe less.

The rest of Byrd Street was nothing but mud. Wyatt drew the pony to a halt and disembarked. After a few moments of heavy contemplation, he poked a drunken man with his toe and gave the man a dollar to hold onto the reins and keep an eye on the rig. The man grinned at him—no teeth at all—and nodded vigorously.

The mud sucked at his brand new Oxonians, and he worried about the elastic gussets on the ankles, but he kept squashing along. To his left was a gloomy row of very old, very narrow two- and three-story . . . well, they must have been houses or small hotels once. As evidenced by the weather-beaten signs, they were all rooming houses now. Richmond was building up very quickly this decade; chances were these houses wouldn't stand much longer.

A deep, loud *hoot* sounded from one of the two paddle wheelers out on the river. The paddle wheelers slowed to a crawl to give right-of-way to a topsail schooner that was breezing downriver. She luffed along in a breathy wind with only one big sail and two triangle sails in front. Her rigging shivered. As she swished past Wyatt, ghostly silent against the water despite her size and her load, every plank and shroud whispered *Brazil . . . Brazil*.

Weeks from now she would return with her hold full of the coffee, spices, and other goods the made Richmond the center of commerce she competed so feverishly to become, vying against Northern cities like Baltimore and Philadelphia. And she was winning—already the third-largest railroad system called Richmond its hub. The James River was the witless muscle man providing power and transportation for the Tredegar Ironworks and the rows of wheat mills, flour mills, tobacco plants.

To be in Richmond one would wonder why people thought the South was nothing but farms and cotton fields. But Richmond was not the whole South, no matter how her factories puffed and snored.

Wyatt pushed himself along. Better get this over with.

Ten minutes later he found himself climbing a truly dangerous stairway.

By the time he'd reached the third floor, he was sure he
was in the wrong building and certain the landlord thought
he'd been describing someone else. Everybody was wrong
tonight. The landlord was wrong, Joe was wrong, and Wyatt
was beginning to think he was wrong too.

The corridor this far up was dismal and creaky. The air
smelled of dust, cigar smoke, rancid water, and human waste.
He wondered if the floor could hold his weight. Didn't feel
solid. The planks moaned under his every step.

At the end of the hallway, in a dark recess, sure enough
there was indeed one more door as the landlord had described.

This couldn't be right.

Wyatt glanced around the hallway one more time, steeling
himself. "Judas priest," he muttered. Could people live this
way? Dead insects and cigar butts in the corners, streaks of
green mold on the door frames, and urine stains on the walls.
. . . How hard could it be to walk to the outhouse? Or throw a
cigar butt in a basket?

One more deep breath, this one with his hand poised to
knock—and he forced himself to rap softly upon the molding
wood of the door. At the touch he grimaced. The wood was
soft with rot.

Nothing happened. No voice sounded from within.

Was that a creak?

He put his ear a little closer to the door, without touching
it. Was he hearing movement? Or was that just the wood
responding in its own good time?

There was a lamp burning in the room. Wyatt could see the
thin edge of light through a place where the door didn't quite
fit the frame anymore.

The doorknob was cool in his hand, and surprisingly firm.

"Hello?" he murmured, nudging the door open a crack.

One shaded candle was burning in the room—more disturbing than darkness would have been.

Holding onto the doorknob as if it would offer some
security, Wyatt stepped into the room. Before him was a
sagging bed with a rumpled and frayed coverlet of ghastly
yellow green, a table, the lamp and two books upon it, a

boudoir chair, a wardrobe, and to his right a Colt Belt pistol with the long barrel pointed right up his nose.

"Wha—!" he rasped, his arms flailing.

He stumbled backward against the nightstand until the wall itself stopped him and his backside landed on the nightstand. Inside the neat uniform his heart went double-time.

Dorian raised the pistol out of Wyatt's face simply by bending his elbow.

Other than that he didn't move.

Shocked, Wyatt also held perfectly still. Would the pistol come down again? Would Dorian demand that he leave? That he respect the wall between them and quit trying to peck holes in it?

Was Dorian so determined that he would guarantee his isolation at the point of a gun?

Wyatt could all but see the decision clicking back and forth in Dorian's mind.

The pistol wavered, very slightly.

The set of Dorian's shoulders changed then. He shifted his weight onto one foot, no longer the stance of a gunman. The hand holding the pistol relaxed, and he methodically uncocked the gun.

"Odd time for a visit," he said.

Through his shock Wyatt saw relief even in those dark, guarded eyes. He clapped a hand to his heaving ribs. "What in hell is that for?"

Dorian lowered the gun and grinned rather sadly. "Better to be safe than sorry. Oh, my God, that's trite."

Then, unexpectedly, he shifted the gun to his other hand, stepped out of the shadow, and gave Wyatt a pat on the arm. "But I *am* sorry."

Wyatt was stunned. It was the most sincere gesture he'd ever seen from his mysterious associate. As Dorian moved past him, Wyatt touched his own arm where it still tingled from that touch. Had it happened? A genuine moment?

Dorian didn't face him. Instead he went to the little boudoir table and tampered with his pistol, keeping his back to Wyatt. The lamp cast a gauzy haze around him.

Careful that the nightstand didn't collapse under him,

Wyatt pushed to his feet. "Did I...interrupt anything important?"

"Yes. I was sitting on my ass. Now I have to do that later."

"This is where you live?"

"Mmm-hm."

"Where are all your...your things?"

"In that wardrobe."

"Do you have a house back East?"

"No, no house."

"Your clothes, your boots, a couple of books, that gun... and that's it?"

Dorian turned casually and flopped into the boudoir chair and crossed his legs.

"That's it."

Behind him the lace curtains were so old and caked with grime that it was impossible to tell what the original color had been.

"Where's your horse and the surrey?" Wyatt asked.

"I board them up in Libby Hill."

"And walk here?"

"It clears the soul."

Wyatt kept pausing, waiting for more, but evidently he wasn't going to get much more than a request to leave if he didn't promote the conversation himself. *So, go ahead. Ask. Well, ask.*

"And...you prefer this room to anything else in Richmond?"

"Thus far."

"Why?"

"The bed's firm."

So Wyatt sat down on the bed. As the mattress folded up around his thighs, he frowned at the other man.

Dorian smirked. "You must admit, it's the last place anyone would look for me."

Joke or not, he was dead right. Wyatt knew that Dorian's cynicism wasn't just aristocratic sass—it was a cloak of some kind. He wore it with all the style that carried his expensive clothes.

Wyatt sensed there was no joke involved here at all. In a concerned tone he asked, "'Who's looking for you?'"

"I had no idea you could be so impetuous," Dorian said, sliding past the question as though he'd greased it with his well-oiled mannerisms. "Mr. Craig, you astonish me. You are the marble constant Shakespeare spoke of. Butter won't even melt in your mouth. By the way, your uniform looks quite knightly. It suits your coloring very well."

"Thanks," Wyatt murmured, unconvinced.

"And did you walk here from Court End?"

"No . . . I left the buggy down the street."

"You just left it?"

"Well . . . no, I gave a man a dollar to mind it."

Dorian smiled condescendingly. Not a smile anyone wants directed toward himself. "It didn't occur to you that the horse and rig itself are worth more than a dollar?"

"Of course it did," he answered sheepishly.

"Then why did you do such?"

"Because I liked the look in the man's face when I gave him his dollar. Probably been years since anybody trusted him."

"My, my," Dorian said. "You really are a Pendragon at heart, aren't you?"

"What kind of dragon?"

"What are you doing here, Mr. Craig, please?"

"I went through those papers," Wyatt said immediately. "I didn't find the order for *your* uniform. Would you like to explain that?"

"Certainly. I have no plan to wear one."

"Well, I want you to. If I have to be an officer, so do you. I put in an order for a captain's commission for you."

"I won't wear it."

"Why not?" Wyatt repeated. "I thought you wanted the South to win the war."

"Actually, I prefer to remain buoyant on the subject."

"You mean you don't care who wins? You're that—"

"Ambivalent? That's right. I don't care. So the uniform would be meaningless hanging on me. It's hard work pretending to be something you're not. I am not the soldier this world is looking for."

Wyatt stood up and sighed. He gave Dorian a critical scan.

"What are you hiding?" he asked, poking around the room, behind the shabby dresser, around the other side of the bed, in the smelly wash closet that was apparently common to the next room down.

Dorian remained composed. "Mr. Craig, I appreciate—"

"Wyatt."

"Yes, I know how to say it."

"Why don't you, then?"

"This provincial concern from you is noble, but truly I am by nature a solitary."

"No, you're not. I don't believe that."

"Maybe I'm a snob."

"You're no snob," Wyatt insisted, looking behind the ratty curtain. "You talk like a snob, but you aren't one. I've known snobs. You greet the negroes and the Irish immigrants and the Indians the same as everybody else. Yesterday you put your clean expensive sleeve onto a bedplate in the rolling mill to keep a man from getting his hand crushed. Snobs don't do that, Dorian."

At the sound of his name used that way—in a tone he hadn't heard for years—Dorian bristled. He paled.

With a sudden edge he demanded, "Perhaps we can stop surgically analyzing me for the night, shall we?"

Matching him with a glare of defiance, Wyatt let Dorian know he'd stopped being intimidated some time ago. He stubbornly pointed his nose toward the wardrobe and stepped over to it.

He put his hand on the knob.

"Careful."

Dorian's warning was unreadable.

Still holding onto the knob, Wyatt looked at him.

"I keep my victims in there," Dorian said.

At that point Wyatt stopped himself. The well-intentioned forwardness slid back inside. With a sigh he let go of the wardrobe doorknob.

"I'm sorry," he said. "Guess I've overstepped."

"I guess you have."

"It just bothers me to see you sitting here alone in this place, when there's no reason."

"Perhaps there are reasons you don't know about." Dorian got to his feet and plucked his black Inverness from its wall hook, set it on his shoulders, and tugged it into place. "Let me escort you safely out of the area."

Wyatt got the message. If he wouldn't leave on his own, Dorian would leave first and give him no proper choice.

Just as he stepped past Dorian, he paused and looked squarely at him.

"Why don't you come live in that big house I'm rattling around in? There's just me and the servants. . . . It's a shameful waste of all those rooms. . . . A whole family could live in there with both its grandmothers. The thing is so cussed big, sometimes I hate to go home."

"Thank you. No."

When he took a step, Wyatt stopped him again, but this time with that forbidden touch on the arm.

"Are you saying we can't be friends?"

The black eyes flashed. "Sometimes you have the insight of Euripides."

"Why not?"

"I am far too profane. You don't want me for a friend."

Wyatt flattened his lips. "Other than the fact that you're arrogant, sassy, secretive, and apparently have a dark side, why wouldn't I?"

The door creaked open. Dorian looked at him and simply said, "The dark side."

★

CHAPTER THIRTY-NINE

———— ★ ————

She was making a mistake.

Impatient, as usual. When Grace came through the iron gates at the Craig powder works she already saw that she had misjudged and given in to herself. She hadn't needed to see Patrick this badly. She should never have come here.

Lassick could have waited for his illicit information.

There was no one at the big open gates to direct her or to stop her. The powder mill sprawled out over four square miles around. Like a Kansas white-trash girl's first sight of Richmond, the first sight of the mill took her aback. Just as she had been made breathless with her own smallness at sight of the thousands upon thousands of windows, assuming one person to each window, in the great panorama of the city of Richmond, she had to revise her idea of what the powder mill would look like. It was nothing like the tannery had been. Ever since Kansas nothing seemed to be what she expected.

The large brick buildings set two by two at the riverside made an imposing downriver view, with their great waterwheels turning endlessly. To her left the houses and refineries were far more complete than she had imagined. She hadn't expected the establishment to be so imposing, so sprawling, so industrial.

The sun was just peeking through rain clouds. The ground was still wet, the day still darkish from the cloudover. Drizzle had kept people indoors, and thus nobody noticed her.

Would a woman be too conspicuous?

Don't be chicken. You've got a brother here, that's all they have to know.

In her mind she saw Bradford Lassick's large, domineering form bending forward over her with his legs apart, smiling because he knew what he was getting, smiling because he also knew the advantage of her devotion to her brother. With that devotion as his bellows, he had blown hot the fire of indignation in Grace's volcanic core.

Stiff with the resentment she had harbored all her life, she left her horse and buggy at a large brown barn, stepped down once again onto Craig land, and started walking.

Patrick had to be here somewhere.

"Me a manager? C'mon, Wyatt, I'm no manager."

"Oh, Patrick, listen to yourself. You've been a fine foreman, and I need you to manage the powder magazines. What do you say?"

"Geez, Wyatt, you're making everything so hard. I'm just too, you know, too backwoods. You know, dumb . . ."

"Come here, now. You're not dumb. Who tells you these things? Your sister?"

"Well, you know Liz."

"No, I don't. I've never met her."

"You haven't? Geez. Guess I'm not doing my job."

Patrick laughed at himself and bumped Wyatt as they strode slowly through the barn-sized powder magazine at a pace Patrick found comfortable. He could go faster when he had to, and he was down to just one cane most of the time, but Wyatt held him back with a hand on the nape of his neck.

Around them tall stacks of loaded barrels, many sizes, many grades of powder, rose in towers and the smaller ones in wide pyramids. Two dozen men went about the business of sorting, stacking, unstacking for shipment, clearing space, rearranging, and general warehouse business, their butcher boots clomping on the dirt floor and raising dust in small black-and-brown clouds. Behind the big half-open magazine doors, the rain had subsided, and needles of sunlight had begun to pierce the gap between the doors and cracks in the planking caused by bumps and bangs inherent in any large-scale industrial operation.

Wyatt was inconsolable. He scanned the floor as Patrick halted along beside him, and they walked around a group of men struggling with a stubborn loading cart.

"Pat, I don't know what I can say to make you change your mind."

"Aw," Patrick crooned in empathy, "that's okay. You don't need to feel bad. Ain't much of a mind in the old head to change. You got a military brigade and all going here, and ... well, I can't fight for the South. I just can't."

"Nobody's asking you to fight," Wyatt told him. "The armed company's just fitted out for guarding the deliveries, you know that. You'll be working here at the mill just like always."

Between two of the barrel pyramids, a few yards from the big main loading doors, Patrick stopped walking. He gazed at the ground for a moment, then looked up and said, "It'd be different if we was still making leather. If you get what I mean—"

"I get what you mean," Wyatt responded. He glanced around at the barrels of black powder and nodded sadly. Suddenly he was glad he wasn't wearing his uniform, and that he seldom wore it at all. All he needed was to be standing here in gray and brass, looking like a commander. "This just isn't like you, Patrick. This talk of joining the Union army. How can you shoot into a line of Confederate men knowing some of your friends might be among them?" In a sweeping gesture he showed Patrick the men with whom he had worked nearly all his young life. "Maybe someday even me."

From the change in Patrick's brown eyes, Wyatt could tell he'd struck a chord, the same chord that sounded in his own heart when Dorian first pulled that officer's uniform out of its box and told him to put it on.

Patrick followed the gesture and glanced around at the working men he knew so well. "Gosh ... that ain't very pretty, I admit." When he met Wyatt's gaze again, there was a sudden adulthood in his expression. "Guess I'll have to be real careful who's in my sights."

Wyatt's blue eyes took on a sudden intensity. "I don't want

to have to shoot you on some barren battlefield either, you know."

"You don't have to worry about that," Patrick told him. "You couldn't hit the back wall of the outhouse with a fart."

He chuckled and poked Wyatt's stomach with the end of his cane. The sting of responsibility caught Wyatt. Patrick blamed himself for his two broken legs and for not healing fast enough to get rid of the cane, but Wyatt felt terrible every time the cane clicked on the floor.

"Don't get personal," he groused.

The conversation dropped off. They stood facing each other while men worked around them as if they weren't there. He and Patrick stepped toward one of the barrel pyramids to make way for a heavy cart load of very large barrels being prepared for the next shipment to the railroad yard. If all went as it had been lately, those barrels were doomed. Silently Wyatt watched them go by.

"Where to, Paddy?" called one of the four men hauling the cart with thick ropes over their shoulders.

"Yonder by the loading dock," Patrick called back. "Just leave room enough for the wagon to back right in. If you fellas are working too hard, we could bring in a couple of mules. What do you say?"

"Good idea," Wyatt spoke up. "Stop right there, boys. Joe! Joe, can you hear me?" He cupped his hands to his mouth. "Joe!"

A negro face popped up from a group of men who were securing lids to several smaller barrels.

"Huh? Somebody call?"

"Go harness a couple mules, will you?"

"Mules? Okay, boss, I'm a-going." He threw down his wooden mallet and disappeared out a side door.

"Told you we need you around here," Wyatt grumbled to Patrick.

"Not me," Patrick said, grinning. "Just the mules."

"Don't talk that way."

They stood ankle-deep in discomfort, Pat watching Wyatt and Wyatt with his hands in his trouser pockets, watching the floor.

"Your eyes tired?" Patrick asked.

"Yeah, a little bit."

"Mr. Trozen been getting you to read them fat books again?"

"Well, I think he gave up on that a long time ago."

Patrick grinned. "Maybe you need specs."

"Think so? Wonder how I'd look in those."

"Studenty. You'd have to grow whiskers to go with them and walk around saying things like 'Have you read the headlines' and 'Where's the lib'ary'."

Wyatt smiled briefly. He shifted his feet and sighed.

Then his hand poked upward. "Okay... let's do it this way. Here's another idea. What if I arrange for a job for you over at Tredegar Ironworks? A good job. Better than this. Then at least you wouldn't be contributing to the South's war effort. What about that?"

"Well—"

"I've got a big empty house in the middle of town. Why don't you and Liz move right into it? You can have the whole second floor to yourselves. I've got six servants in there with nothing to do. They'd be pleased to have somebody to tend to. They can haul hot water into that big copper tub, and you can sit in there and let those legs soak. Imagine how healing that'll be for you."

"Oh, you don't oughtta feel bad about my ol' legs. See? They get along. Look."

"Pat, come here, come here." Wyatt caught him again by the arm and drew up closer. "Think of that sister of yours you're always talking about. There she is, sitting in a shack on West Leigh when she can be the mistress of a fine house. I'd like somebody to run the household, Paddy. Liz can be real proud of herself."

"Oh, she don't have no trouble there. She likes herself right fine." He rolled his eyes and giggled.

Wyatt groaned. That little laugh of Patrick's had a way of disarming him completely.

"I can get you a good job at the ironworks," he promised. "Like I said—you won't be making gunpowder for the South."

Patrick hung his head thoughtfully and nodded.

Then only his eyes flipped up, and he pointed out, "Be making cannons."

Losing ground fast, Wyatt moaned, "Oh, Lord," and shifted his feet again.

Patrick smiled at him, enjoying having the upper hand for a change.

Pacing off a few steps, Wyatt chewed his lip for ideas to keep this from happening. The division of the nation was already becoming a division of his own soul. Businesses and families breaking up, friends parting ways for the saddest of reasons, never knowing if they would ever be countrymen again. And Patrick of all people to be sullied in this way?

He spun back.

"All right, here's another one. I've got all the money anybody'll ever need. Let me give you some of it. You take it and go out west. Make some investments for me. If things go bad back here, at least I'll have something left over to give severance to all our friends here so they won't all starve." Once again his hands took in the entire mill grounds. His soft eyes were limned with hope as he paused and watched Patrick for a response. "What do you say?"

Patrick chuckled and shook his head. "I'll be danged," he murmured. "Aren't you something. Danged if that one's not too bad. Gotta give you credit."

He shook his head affectionately again and started walking slowly away, his cane poking perfect round holes in the dirt floor.

"Pat, please don't do this. Don't go."

He turned back. Wyatt stood there, still, backdropped by the towers of powder barrels, gazing pathetically at him.

Quietly he added, "With your legs, they might not even let you join. Did you think of that?"

Patrick shrugged. "Yeah. But I can ride and I can shoot. Reckon the horse can do the walking."

"You don't get a horse in infantry. Did you think of that either?" Striding slowly to him, Wyatt lowered his voice. "And what about me? Am I supposed to come to work every morning knowing that one day some of my powder might find its way to you and kill you?"

He patted the hollow of the younger man's shoulder as

though sensitive to the bones and muscles in there which would be blown to shreds and slivers.

"I won't like that," he added.

Patrick understood; his expression clearly showed that he did. But he shrugged solemnly and said, "Guess that'll just be my time to go. You know what they say... every man's got his time."

Silence fell between them again, leaving only the sounds of the men going about their work and the endless *kssshhh kssshhh* of the giant waterwheels down the river, supplying power to the refineries. Not an altogether unpleasant sound at all. In its way, reassuring. Soon the wheels would turn without Patrick, without many of these men, who would go off to join their chosen armies. Some would stay here and call this their wartime duty, creating gun powder and cannon powder for the great cause of the South, the war to end Northern tyranny.

All but Patrick, who would go to fight the war to hold the nation together, by force if necessary.

The two men shared what was probably the last day in their long acquaintance, since the first day, long ago, that Patrick had come as a teenager to run errands for the Craig Tannery, back in a different life, during other times.

"This isn't for you, Paddy," Wyatt said over the hush. "I wish you just wouldn't go."

But this wasn't a hungry teenager he was speaking to, desperate to bring a few pennies into his family's miserable white-trash existence. This was Patrick Ruhl, a homespun and gentle young man, but a man nonetheless, and a man with convictions.

"I gotta go," he said, understanding. He toes the packed floor and drew lines in it with the cane. "When Liz and me left Kansas, it was just territory, like always. Then first thing I heard when I got off the train in Richmond was that Kansas had gone and became a full-fledged state in the United States of America. That was January the twenty-ninth. Thirty-fourth state in the Union. 'Cept there aren't thirty-four anymore. Just when Kansas was pulling in, all them other states started pulling out." Now he looked up, his straight brows tugged toward the middle in the most serious expression Wyatt had ever seen from him. "Kansas come in with an antislavery constitution. I bet you know that."

Wyatt could barely answer. "I know," he murmured.

"That's my home state. A real state, and it's my home state. I can't go against my home state when she just got her papers. So, well . . . I gotta just leave for a while. Wouldn't be fair to Kansas if I didn't."

"You're going to join the Northern army because Kansas honors that constitution? Is that really your reason, Pat?"

"Well . . . ain't that good enough?"

"Not for me. Go ahead—if I have to lose you, can't I hear it all?"

Patrick sighed several times, making no secret of the fact that he was thinking hard. Finally he nodded and simply said, "I been working with the niggers since I was a pup. I'm not stronger than most of 'em, I'm not smarter than most of 'em, so why am I better than them? But don't take it bad—I sure don't want to tell you you're wrong. . . . Heck, I'm prob'ly wrong . . . but, Wyatt, I just can't kill some folks just so other folks can have slaves."

"Slaves—Patrick, there are a thousand complicated—"

"Then I ain't gonna understand, am I?"

The determination in Patrick's voice cut the conversation in half.

Standing there like a little boy being scolded, hands in pockets and his chin down, Wyatt realized how completely their roles had reversed in the past few moments—perhaps even in the past few years, and he had never noticed. Something had finally come along that would prevent him from protecting the people around him. He could no longer guide and bumper and shepherd them, not through a war. Patrick was the symbol of his loss of guardianship, his inability to provide any refuge against the coming storm.

He was being given no choice. His voice was nothing but a leftover rasp.

"When do you figure on leaving?"

Quietly Patrick said, "End of this week."

Wyatt stifled a wince. So soon . . .

"Be a cook or something, will you? Promise?"

Pat laughed briefly, and crooned, "Promise. You know, you worry just like a squirrel."

"Hell, I eat my worries for breakfast, and you know it." Patrick laughed again, poked Wyatt in the side with his cane, then reeled off toward the other men, still chuckling.

Wyatt watched him go, watched him bantering with the workers, and felt somehow empty.

He couldn't stand to spend any more of the day in the magazine. His clean, plush office suddenly looked good simply for its solitude. With one more glance at the loading dock, he spun toward the main doors.

That was when he saw the girl.

Too many people. Workers in checkered shirts with rolled sleeves, all Southern sympathizers except for Patrick. Grace never thought there would be so many, so close together. How could she get Patrick alone? Probably she couldn't, not now.

There he was, not twenty feet away, on the other side of those barrels, being scolded by one of the foremen. They hadn't seen her yet.

When she caught the word *sister*, the firm hand of curiosity pushed her sideways, behind the stacked barrels. She moved closer.

The conversation instantly softened her stony heart. The young foreman in the dirty flannel shirt, vest, and bow tie cared about Patrick.

His words, his voice, his protective arm over her brother's shoulders—all these years Grace had convinced herself to be hard, to be strong, because she was sure she was the only person left in the world who gave a tinker's damn about Patrick.

". . . move right in . . . that big copper tub . . . let your legs soak . . . Pat, please don't do this . . . don't go. This isn't for you . . . I wish you just wouldn't go."

Grace felt her throat knot up and tears well in her eyes. *Selfish! Thinking I was the only one. Selfish, Lizard, selfish and clutching. Look what good friends he has. . . . No wonder he wanted so badly to come to Richmond with the others.*

And here she was, digging information out of him that would get his buddies killed.

Suddenly it felt as if the dirt beneath her skin came up through every pore, and she might as well have rolled in sulfur leavings.

Coming to the mill was a mistake. Finally she admitted to herself that curiosity was playing her for an idiot. She should never have come here to look into the faces of men she was betraying, of folk whose deaths she might have a hand in. She wouldn't be able to speak openly to Patrick here, not as she'd imagined, with no one noticing, and now she'd subjected herself to looking at the faces of the innocent men of the mill.

She coiled her hands on her arms as though to brush off the leech Brad Lassick had become.

The impact was enough to knock her over. All this time she'd swallowed whole Lassick's pumping about the criminal slaver of the South, the rightness of ambush if it meant keeping the Union intact, that God had put the powder mill in their sights and Grace and Patrick at his own right and left hands. And the other Lasik, the cousin—what a mouth! Righteous this and destined that. Ridiculous.

"Liz, you're just not made to be a spy," she grumbled to herself. Around her the factory splashed and shuffled and roared, its workers going about their day-to-day business like a dozen Patricks.

Damn all! Now Patrick was heading in the other direction.

Her sense of control slid away. She was out of her element, on enemy ground.

And I'm the enemy.

Whatever had driven her to the powder mill today suddenly was no longer strong enough to keep her here. A sense of time that had eluded her this morning suddenly plunged back into perspective. She could always speak to Patrick tonight.

Madwoman! She hadn't thought! What if someone had seen her speaking to her brother, seen a stranger speaking to him, and added up the two attacks on Craig shipments? *She* knew she was his sister, but nobody else knew. . . . Any stranger would be a suspect—Patrick would be implicated in the leak of information that had resulted in the shipment hijacks. It had been good enough to get information from

Patrick without coming to the mill. . . . Why had she come here today? Why couldn't she control her curiosity?

"Judgement, Liz," she snapped at herself under her breath. *Dumbest thing you've done in at least half a minute, blamed foolish acting-like-a-woman impatient tackhead! Better get out of here.*

"Miss!"

Oh, hell, hell, hell.

The kind young man with the fluffy maple hair was coming toward her, waving a hand.

"Miss . . . well, hello and am I glad to see you!"

He smiled as though he were greeting an old friend.

Grace squinted through the dust. Did she know him from somewhere? From Kansas perhaps? Was she about to insult somebody she plain didn't remember?

He squeezed between the barrels and piles of material and hurried toward her. His blue eyes were friendly ponds set within pale lashes and beneath pale brows, barely more than chalk-dust shading in this light. Smile crinkles appeared at the corners of his pleasant eyes as he came closer and reached for her arm. His vest flapped against his dirty shirt.

"I'm so sorry," he said, still smiling. "The gate man ordinarily would be here to escort you to the main office, but I gave him the day off—you see, his little girl has a—well, never mind that. Did you just arrive? You must've been traveling all morning. Would you like some tea?"

Bending a little to compensate for being a few inches taller than she, he held her elbow with his left hand and caught her right hand in a greeting, though she hadn't given one and didn't intend to.

"When the ladies' league got your letter—well, it sounded so definite. Did your mother's health improve so fast, or did you bring her to Richmond with you?"

So that was it. He thought she was somebody else!

How convenient.

Grace accommodated his mistake and muttered, "She . . . died."

Her shoulder moved in a small shrug, but she didn't blink.

His expression changed to an empathy so sincere that Grace hesitated to disappoint him by getting around to the truth.

He patted her hand gently. "Oh, oh . . . what a shame. . . . . Is there anything I can do? Do you need help with expenses? Is everything all right?"

"No . . . she's all buried. . . ."

He cradled her shoulders in his left arm, still holding her right hand in his, and escorted her over what he evidently thought was rough terrain.

"Well, don't you worry about anything anymore," he said, curling around to look into her eyes reassuringly. "If there's any other problem that comes up, we'll get it taken care of. You don't have anything to worry about anymore, Miss MacHugh, not another thing."

Grace thought fast. She had to get off the grounds clean, without anyone attaching her to Patrick.

"It's MacHutcheon," she lied easily.

The young man touched a finger to his forehead and derided himself. "Oh—I'm sorry! I'm softheaded about names until I get used to them. And I hate making that kind of error too. Names are so personal. . . . I won't forget again. MacHutcheon, MacHutcheon. I've got it now. I'm glad you're here! We're desperate for a schoolmistress on the grounds. The mill's children shouldn't have to ride all the way to Richmond for school. If there's a teacher on the premises, hours'll be saved. And the children who work here will be able to get some schooling too. Heaven tell it, but I'm glad you changed your mind! Come right this way, right through here. Watch your skirt, now, this isn't really a place for a lady to try walking through."

Teacher. A teacher. All right, she could be a teacher for a couple of minutes.

What the hell was a teacher supposed to be like? Grace had never even met one, never mind seen one in action.

Her only teacher had been a white-haired marm in a wheelchair. She combed her informal schooling for images from the books, pictures of schoolmistresses rapping desks with their pencils and demanding attention from rows of children. How hard could that be?

She cleared her throat.

"Thank you, sir. I've not yet resolved to accept this or any position; however, I thought it smart to tour your facility before making so significant a change in my life, if you understand."

"Oh, I do. And I certainly wouldn't want you to feel pressured. Of course, you'll want to meet the children. We'll have to get them together in the chapel. We don't have a formal schoolhouse yet, but we can build one to your specifications, and you'll have a home of your own right here on the grounds. We have several to choose from that aren't occupied yet. You see, we're just getting rolling."

"I do see," Grace said softly, counting every step toward the door. She walked on her tiptoes, trying to be delicate.

How the hell did those uptown ladies keep their balance doing this all the time?

The young gentleman ushered her over a stack of planks, saying, "You know, with all your qualifications, I confess to expecting an older woman, Miss MacHutcheon."

Grace paused, tipped her head, and before she could stop herself popped off with, "Oh, I can be older, if you like. . . ."

He blinked at her, perplexed, but then—to her relief—he laughed. "That's very good!" he said. "Oh, and by the way . . . I'm the owner. I'm Wyatt Craig."

Might as well have set off a flintlock between them. Grace came to life as she ripped her hand out of his.

"You are not!" she snapped. Her huge skirt bounced to the left, then the right, then left again as she pulled away from him.

The young man gaped at her.

Unable to stop a bewildered, self-conscious grin, he touched his own chest and said, "Yes, ma'am. . . . I am."

"You are not," she insisted, "and you should not take the name of someone else just to impress someone! I'll have you know I'm not impressed. If you wanted to impress me, better you choose a less obvious identity. Who do think you are? And if you say Wyatt Craig again, I swear I'll cuff your ears! Using that name doesn't put you in good quarters with me. I *know* Wyatt Craig, and you, sir, are not he."

His mouth wagged open, his eyes wide in utter confusion. What did she expect him to say? Wyatt knew he was filthy from working with the men all morning to prepare for tomorrow's shipment, but was he *that* dirty?

No woman had ever exploded in his arms before. There before him she ignited, her netted chestnut hair gathering the narrow beams of sunlight that came through the slats of the big mill's doors, her eyes mean and flared, unforgiving emeralds, angry that they had been cut out of the earth.

She was pointing a finger at him, a finger of warning and of dare, and she leaned slightly forward at the waist—only then did he realize she couldn't be wearing the kind of corset he thought all women wore, and he realized he was dealing with mail-order rebellion in female form.

The image stunned him silent. He gaped like a struck dog. Suddenly he didn't want to be Wyatt Craig, if that's what would make her happy again. Fashion and propriety had taken this out of most women—the *realness*. And she was *real*, that rare thing. She was so dazzlingly forceful in anger, what would she be in delight?

His lips were starting to dry up.

"Ma'am, I . . . I . . . I'm . . ."

Her lower lip puckered in warning. "Don't you *dare*."

So alive! Wyatt choked down whatever was about to come out. His soft hair fell forward in two sugar brown wings over his brows as he hovered there, staring. She was such an alive thing—the kind of person anyone else wants to have around, to keep around, the kind of self-confidence and contagious vitality that spills to everyone near her. Wyatt could feel himself soaking it in, even though he was hardly breathing.

The tightrope teetered under him. He could look all day at her.

She was something. Blood red hair, mean green eyes looking through him, square features that meant business, pale skin, and ruddy cheeks flushed with the fire of life—*something*.

Then one of his workers came by and pushed him off.

"Boss! Foreman wants to doublecheck how many kegs you want on each wagon. Not ten like usual, is it?"

The girl's green eyes got bigger, angrier.

Wyatt stammered, "Uh . . . didn't we decide on six, Roger?"

"Six it is. Thought so." The man sniffed, making his

brushy mustache shift, and glanced at Grace. "Pardon me, ma'am. Thanks, Wyatt."

Wyatt.

Spell it h-a-t-e. She'd learned that spelling on her pa's knee, her ma's lap, lullabies of deprivation and putting down. The bodies of her parents and Anibal Webb dangled before her once again behind her closed eyelids, and their dead tongues started to wag inside peeled-back lips. *Did we know him . . . truly?*

But I've seen him! her memory screamed.

Wyatt reached out a plaintive hand to her and brushed her arm with the tips of his fingers in a gentle beckoning.

"Ma'am," he began slowly, "I'm not sure what's going on here. Let me just offer you some tea, and we can talk in my office, hm? All right? That's right . . . just step over the boards. . . . Watch your step. We don't want anybody getting hurt. . . ."

Liar. Murderer.

Desperately she scratched the corners of her mind for a memory of what the real Wyatt Craig looked like. She knew exactly what he looked like. She's seen him plenty of times back in Kansas. His hair was—

He was at least—

His eyes were—

Suddenly the quirks of her past reminded her that she had never seen Wyatt Craig up close, in person. . . . Her hatred of his father and their reputation had kept her away from them. . . .

Were they walking? Yes. His arm was around her again, supporting her back. He held her hand again, not getting exactly close. She wasn't ill, she didn't need helping, and he better quit looking so buttfucking generous, or there was going to be some real hard teaching around here, *just make a bet*.

She pulled backward again and stopped him

Her chin jutted forward in a dare.

"If you're Wyatt Craig," she said without throwing up, "then your father was Hugh Craig."

Wyatt paused. "Yes. . . . Did you know my father?"

Coldly she replied, "No. Of course not."

A little confused, Wyatt cupped her hand between both of his own and gazed at her with his disarmingly honest eyes.

"Miss MacHutcheon," he began, "what's your first name?"

She put her teeth together. "Grrrace."

He accepted it with a simple nod. His pale lashes batted against freckles on his cheeks that a buff-haired person sometimes gets from the sun.

"Grace, if you've heard any rumors about my father," he said, "let me say here and now that every word of it was probably true, I'm ashamed to say. A man makes mistakes, believe me, and I know he made them. I've tried half my life to correct the mess my father made of his life and a lot of other lives, and... sometimes I don't comprehend how far back those mistakes can reach. I guess that's one of the mistakes I'm making."

Purging himself with a sigh, he gazed a moment at the layers of black dust on the floor and sifted his conscience for the right words.

She stared so hard, her eyes hurt.

Solemnly he gripped her hand more tightly and rubbed it. He tilted forward on his slender frame and met her confused stare once again. His tone was cool spray on the fire in her soul.

"Much as I'd like to, I can't mend the past," he said. "But I can take this moment to apologize for any pain we've caused anyone who may be important to you. I am truly, genuinely sorry."

Grace scoured her memory for a way this could have happened. She'd never believed Patrick when he talked nice about Wyatt Craig—always assumed it was just Patrick's goody-goody talk, the way he talked about everything and everybody. Wyatt Craig had come three times to visit Patrick while he recuperated at Mrs. Button's house....

And all three times I made sure to be out of the house and far away. Once I even went out the back as he came in the front.

Could it be? Could she have been relying only on the picture of the ogre in her mind? Had she been so obsessed with Craig crimes that she never allowed herself a look at a Craig face?

He didn't know her name. Why would he? Patrick always called her Lizard.

Liz . . .

Elizabeth . . . Elizabeth Ruhl . . . Grace MacHutcheon . . . White trash . . . or schoolteacher.

The noise of the men working around them twisted itself into a fading echo, soon only a whine in Grace's ears. From under drawn brows she stared into those eyes and tipped forward onto her toes, knocked right off her spite.

Her jaw went slack, her lips rounded. She felt herself give birth to a crazy need to confess it all to him—the hate, the spying, the burning—

" 'And if I could, I would wipe all tears from all eyes.' "

A voice rolled, strong and elegant. The dramatic interruption set them both blinking.

Together they looked toward the giant mill doors.

A shadow came between them, shifting on the magazine's packed earth floor. In its eerie way the shadow actually pushed them back from each other with the supernatural knowledge that they were being watched.

"Oh," Wyatt blurted, gathering his wits. "Beg pardon. . . . Miss Grace MacHutcheon . . . my associate, Mr. D. W. Trozen."

The edges of a black tweed Inverness greatcape fluttered against the man's elbows as he stood in the doorway, his back to the breeze.

Stunned to silence by everything that was happening around her, Grace stood there holding Wyatt Craig's hand, staring at the man she knew as the infamous partner who had saved Wyatt from Grace's own sabotage.

He was all ebony and eggshell, the ruffles upon his wrists blending with the skin of his hands the way sugar is lost in cream. He wasn't a towering man by any means, but slender against the greatcape's lining. A black frock coat, a yellow shirt, a roll-collared vest, a black cravet tied in a floppy Byronic bow like a shiny dead crow beneath his chin—Grace squinted against the light to see if his impression was an illusion, but it wasn't.

His topper's black silk stovepipe grabbed for the sunlight, hoping to carry it as artistically as did each black curl beneath the brim. His eyes were turned down slightly at the outer corners, a look of lazy intelligence, each set in a smudge of lashes, with a pouch of experience underneath each that said he'd not only lived life but survived it. The carnal essence glowed beneath his skin like a beacon to those who were his own kind. Deceivers.

She saw a thousand lies in the folds of his eyes and the pale skin around them, and in the streak of shine of each eyelid just above the drops of ink that looked at her right now. From the man's left hand, a polished walking stick connected him to the land. He held it the way a swordsman poses with his épée. He didn't look American. Americans were more earthbound, even the finest of them.

So *that* was Trozen. The man Patrick could never quite find the words to describe. Now Grace saw why.

She saw the lies in him, just as she saw the truths in the blue eyes at her side.

"Miss MacHutcheon may decide to become our schoolmistress," Wyatt explained to his partner.

Trozen looked at him, his brows drawing inward. Definite disbelief. "Really?"

He might as well have pointed at her and shouted, *"Liar!* Grace felt laid open. *He knows.*

Or did he?... How often had she given that very look in order to get the upper hand a mystery can provide? Often.

Wyatt saw it too, and a flush of embarrassment rose on his ruddy cheeks. "Well...yes. You should see her qualifications."

The dark man suddenly flipped back into character. He reached for her hand.

"How encouraging," he murmured. "Your servant, Miss MacHutcheon."

No, she thought, *that's a lie. You're no one's servant.*

"You are most gracious, sir," she said, somehow keeping her voice under control. "I shall forever cherish your approval, of course, and look forward to many interesting conversations with you.''

''Well, don't be too nice to him, now,'' Wyatt interrupted, grinning mischievously at the other man. ''He doesn't like it when people are nice to him.''

The two men exchanged a very odd look, intimate in its way and even slightly challenging, but they both smiled.

Then the dark man looked right back at Grace, as though he didn't trust her out of his sight. His narrow nose and full lips were carved from his rounded features, then sanded and polished with a permanent tug to one side, almost a smirk at rest. Grace knew that look. Intimately, from inside.

He doesn't know enough about himself, but he sees through me somehow.

He didn't quite grip her hand. Rather he let her fingertips rest against his palm without exactly taking hold of them.

As he made a noncommittal bow before her, she noticed tiny pearls stitched onto the black wool sleeve of his frock coat in the shape of a leaf, catching the color of the ruffles at his wrist. What was a wealthy man doing working as accountant for a powder mill when he could own ships and live in splendor? His hand when she had touched it . . . old calluses. He had done hard work before. Strong hands for a gentleman.

Hiding.

And, more than anything else, looking into D. W. Trozen's face provided the scales of measurement for this man who said he was Wyatt.

Wyatt Craig hid none of his calluses, his bruises laid upon him by time.

The men stood only a few feet apart, both watching her, both bewildered by her behavior. The thousand differences between them hit her with the clarity of bells.

Deceit on one side.

Knighthood on the other.

She looked at Trozen, then back at the kind, impossible young man who said he was Wyatt, then back at the deceiver. Who was the liar here?

Suddenly she shot a stare at Wyatt Craig. After all these years the naked Grace Ruhl saw her archenemy for what he truly was—a decent man! A man she had spied on, betrayed, sold out—

God, oh God, what' ve I done ...?

The two men stood near each other, waiting for her to make a decision. In every way they were fundamentally different, from manner to marrow.

Then Wyatt Craig was carefully reaching for her arm again.

She stepped back, squared her shoulders, and had to clear her throat.

"I have—"

Her voice cracked. Run, she would run out.

No, walk! Running would look stupid!

But maybe she really was stupid.

She circled around them and moved toward the door.

"I have some decisions to make. . . . If you'll excuse me, I'll hurry away and make them. No—thank you, gentlemen, but I shall see myself out and go directly home."

Because it ain't polite to fuck yourself in public.

★

CHAPTER FORTY

——— ★ ———

A seamy hovel in Gamble Hill, not far from the state penitentiary, was the unlikely headquarters of a group whose name pretended to be much grander than the roof and walls in which they made their plans. The Order of Heroes of America, Richmond branch, was nothing more than the shack rented by Bradford Lassick, a place where messages could be dropped off.

When he came tonight to find the message he expected, he found instead an open door and a lit lantern, and inside, a woman.

By silhouette alone he recognized her, for his own hands had played on that ungiving form to which sex meant nothing more than what she could get out of it. The force of her spirit met him at the door. He stepped inside.

She was as formidable and magnetic as ever, the girl forged by fire in the wilderness.

In the language of that one lamp, her hair became burgundy. It hung down her neck, cradled in a simple net. The crescents of her eyes were all shadow. None of the green irises showed now. Her features were drawn and decisive.

The sight of her caught him by the groin with a reaction so sudden it was nearly like a punch. He tucked his ribs to hide the reaction and pulled the door shut. She was as severe, as arousing as she had been that first day, when all this began.

As for the rest, he barely recognized her.

The transformation was shocking. He'd never seen her this

way. He'd seen her naked of everything, but never in this
nakedness of doubt and change. Something was exquisitely
different.

"Grace?"

"Hello, Brad. This is our last meeting."

Then, in an instant, he knew what the difference was.

The fury. It was gone.

Gone, just like that.

Trying not to let on that he saw the change, he asked,
"Have you brought the information?"

"Did you hear me?"

His black-lined eyes, their beautiful golden orbs no longer
able to mesmerize her, widened as his brows rose. "I heard
you. Of course, I've heard it before as well."

Grace saw for the first time that behind those handsome,
enviable eyes there was a complicated man she had never
wanted to know better. She would never know him. She
didn't care. All that mattered was that she had been wrong.
Perhaps she was being wrong about Lassick, always to have
though of him as the hard-shelled conspirator he pretended to
be. As though she had been washed clean, reborn, and could
see with new eyes, she knew she had misread nearly everything and everyone around her.

That wouldn't happen again. The past would wash away
too, and she would start over. She and Patrick.

"Do you have my information?" he asked again. "Which
day, at what time, they leave the powder yard? And by which
route?"

Probably he was sensing that she wouldn't give him any
more, sensing that she was finished, that she didn't care how
long or to what extremes he and his cousin Rodney and their
"heroes" had counted upon raiding the Craig shipments
before the powder could reach the railroad. Yes, he could see
that she no longer cared.

But there was more than just a casual lack of interest in her
face; he could see that too.

And Grace enjoyed watching him worry, just as there had
been a morbid enjoyment in scorning herself all day.

No smug grin twisted her lips tonight, however. She didn't
deserve to be smug anymore.

"Get out of this area, Brad. You're finished here. I'm not telling you the day or time or route. Wyatt Craig's next shipment is going to be allowed through."

He actually chuckled. "Oh, it is. I see."

"You're going to let it go. I don't want to talk to you about it. I have other business, honest business. I'm done being a spy and a female hole for your use. You and your cousin's men had better stay in hiding for the rest of the week, or I'll go to the authorities with the name of every last Hero of America, and I'll walk the sheriff to this house myself. Wyatt Craig deserves to have the shipment go through. You and I both owe it to him."

Lassick huffed, spewing the heavy breath of a pipe smoker toward her.

"My dear, you've lost your wits," he said. "I thought you might crack eventually, but not quite this soon. All right, then. We'll make this your last participation. I know as well as any man that sources dry up. Every woman dries up sooner or later too. You've told us there will be a shipment this week some time. We've mobilized in preparation for it, and we are not—hear me—not giving it up. You're responsible for several men's being on call for several days, and it's them you owe, not Wyatt."

"It's Wyatt," she correctly sharply.

She moved closer. Her voice turned to wind in the small cabin.

"We made a mistake, Brad. You and I made the mistake of a lifetime. I don't know what he did to you, but I know you well enough, and now I know him too. Whatever it was, I'll bet it was your own fault. What happened to my ma and pa and Anibal, that was our fault too. I got my ideas about the Craigs when I wasn't old enough to pee in a pot without getting my toes wet. I didn't know how complicated things can be, and how things change. We got in with the wrong men and the wrong purposes. Lord knows we should all be ashamed. I'm very ashamed. And if you and I had any genuine honor between us, we'd be on our knees before Wyatt Craig, asking the forgiveness of a good man."

"Good!" Lassick erupted. "Of course he's good! He's what they call kindhearted to a crippling fault, Grace! And I scraped up the fault behind him wherever he went. He's so white-assed good that he doesn't know what it is to be loyal to a living person instead of some wish-wash ideal or other. My God!''

Before him Grace remained utterly still.

"Are you telling me," she rumbled, "that all these years you knew it was his father and not he who hurt my family? Are you telling me you knew that? You *knew* that? What else! What else have you lied to me about! Damn me if I haven't gotten a strong dose of bad medicine today—''

The confirmation of an afternoon of terrible realizations came home to roost as Grace stalked the room, flat-lipped and fuming. His silence was answer enough. She put her hands to her head to cap the rage of his lies and how foolishly used she felt.

"God had better damn you for this and damn you deep!'' she said. "Goddamn you for using me to hurt an innocent man! Damn you deep, Brad. If I deserved to have any anger in me, I'd take you to hell myself.''

"He's not innocent," Lassick said. "Craig knew what he was involving himself in. Building a powder mill at a time when war is imminent? Grace, do you take him for an idiot as well as innocent? Hell, you disappoint me.''

She pulled her shawl around her shoulders. "I'm leaving. Don't ever seek me out again. Good-bye. I hope you die in the war.''

As he had a hundred times before—so much that it had become nearly a joke, a grating ill-mannered joke—Lassick tried his usual last resort, even though he knew in the pit of his belly that it wouldn't work.

"What about your brother?''

She paused at the door.

"Now who's the idiot?" she asked. "I'm taking Patrick and leaving Richmond. We're going back where we belong. This isn't our fight. We were born of immigrant pioneers. It's time for us to do what our own folk meant us to do. We're going west.''

"Grace!''

"What?''

"You're wrong. You're wrong about Wyatt. You've been

fooled like I was fooled. His kind puts up a good lie. He'll turn on you just as he turned on me. Remember that. He'll turn on you."

She pulled the door open. "I wouldn't blame him. He deserves the satisfaction."

"Grace!"

"Now what?"

"If I can't get the delivery information from you by morning, I'll get it from someone else."

"Good. Then you'll have company on the way to hell. Don't bother me anymore."

She put him behind her and stepped out onto the crumbling porch. Ahhhh! That felt good! There he was, behind her, staring, and he had absolutely no way to drag her back inside! The counterstroke nearly knocked her forward.

Never before had Grace understood how heavy a weight retribution had been, nor how broad the relief as she finally let it go.

She drew in a long disencumbering breath of Gamble Hill's musty air—and damned if it didn't swirl through her body and cleanse her to the core of her soul, like the healing scent of a tea garden in spring.

"Hurry! He shall arrive any instant!"

The smell of incense rolled all around. The women could no longer tell it from plain air. Not that it mattered; they seldom left the house. And never within this century would the house shake its reputation, a veil that clings to houses even more stubbornly than to people's pasts, for the incense and the reputation were deeply soaked into every slat of paneling, every fiber of carpet, every flake of the sultry red wallpapered ceiling and walls, and every twist of the fringe that dripped from almost everything.

They told people it was Turkish incense. In fact, they made it in the kitchen from herbs and weeds grown out back.

"Hurry with her!" the madam barked. Her hands cracked together and made the girls wince. "Everything must be perfect! Why are you so slow? Land sake."

She swished out of the parlor into the drawing room to glance between the closed curtains. The keys, thimble, watch, and pillbox on her chatelaine jangled on her wide skirt.

A hundred mirrors, all sizes, all shapes, all in gilt frames, hung on the walls and the ceilings, reflecting several of her girls as they dashed about in a maze of lace and corsets. How often had she reached out to slap a face and struck a mirror instead? Even after all these years, the mirrors could still catch her off guard.

Back in the parlor six half-clad whores dressed the new girl for her weekend. They were deliberately being slow. The girl didn't deserve a weekend with the Gentleman so soon. She barely spoke English yet. Why should she get her weekend? The Gentleman only took one girl, on these rare weekends, and each girl only once, and never again.

Flicking long red ringlets over her shoulder and out of the way, one of the girls muttered to the blond girl beside her as the two of them tried to fit a mesh bust improver over the foreign girl's small breasts. "It isn't fair. She wouldn't fill two teacups."

"Stuff pad in the undersides," the second girl suggested. "Push them up."

"And make her look good? Why should I? I haven't even had my weekend yet, and I've been here longer than her. She isn't even trained at the mouth yet." The redhead tossed a bitter glance up into the eyes of the foreign girl.

The immigrant had an idea she was being talked about but didn't know what was being said. She caught isolated words and phrases, but putting them together was still a trial, so she stood still and let the other whores pick and pluck at her body until all the pantalets, petticoats, bone stays, and bits of lace were right, and her hair was done up. They'd been picking at her for three-fourths of an hour, and the dress wasn't even on yet. She understood that she was going out—unusual in itself for this occupation—and she knew there was supposed to be something exciting about it. For herself, she was frightened. The bitter glances from the other girls were disheartening, for she would rather any of them go in her place. Something special often required a special thing in return, and she could provide no such specialty yet. She knew the basics, but that was all.

She dipped her chin and looked down. Her breasts were shoved upward into half shells by the bust improver so that she could hardly see the corset. That corset had been on for a full two weeks without a rest. Madam wanted her waist to become smaller. Every day the lacing had been done up a little tighter. Her mother had never worn such things; why should she have to wear them? She was almost constantly light-headed now. The crinoline cage that would make her skirt go out in a big bell shape blurred as she looked down at it.

The redhead was glaring at her, so she blinked and looked up at nothing.

"I hate her."

"You hate every new girl," the blond reminded. "You used to hate me, remember?"

"I still hate you."

"Pish!"

They paused to strike each other with the trailing ends of a petticoat tassel, then the redhead leaned closer and asked, "Have you had your weekend with the Gentleman yet?"

"No, and I can scarcely wait! They say he's a deposed sultan with a price on his head. His people are looking for him. That's why we mustn't tell anyone about his visits."

"Yes, that's exactly right. Their kind will cut a girl's tongue out if she tells."

"Do you believe that?"

"What does it matter? I got nobody to tell." She glanced over her shoulder.

A third girl leaned between them, her henna-dyed hair falling forward from its pins. "Yawl cain't imagine a man like him. He took me dining. Bought a fine fancy dinner, and he sung me songs and talked poetry. Lawd mercy if I didn't but about faint right into those big black eyes!" She stooped down between them and lowered her voice. "Then he put me on a fine buggy and drove right out of town. *Right* out! We was gone for the whole weekend, just driving and driving, and stopping in the fanciest hotels and inns you ever might see in your mortal life—"

"You told us before," the blond said.

"And before that," the other redhead groaned.

"Took me driving out to the big plantations—lawd save me, I thought he was a-kidnapping me. Then he'd stop the buggy and he'd disappear in the woods."

The blond screwed up her face until cracks appeared in her makeup. "Alone?"

"Ain't that curious? He done that all weekend."

"What'd you get paid for then? Just sitting in a buggy? Somebody for him to sit with?"

"I don't shirk my duty. You take that back."

"All right, I take it. What about night? They come to us for a good grind, not for sitting on our nethers in a buggy."

The other girl stood up straight, her bare white breasts held high by the corset. "He got his grind. Better believe it, that man knows what belongs where and how high."

"The dress!" Madam called, rushing back into the parlor. "Did I not press you to hurry, girls? Hurry, I say."

The girls' conversation was bitten off, and they rushed to pull the flouncy red skirts over the immigrant's head and down over the crinoline.

"Do her eyes," the madam said. "Did you forget her eyes? Where have you hidden the kohl? Put it on. Yes, put it on. I don't care how dark her lashes are. Put it on. More is better, remember that. More is better. Put more color on her cheeks. Lord!" She clapped her hands to her powdered cheeks and looked up into the brow-drawn eyes of the girl she was sending out tonight on this very important job. "Lord . . . she does look as though I'd just pulled her out of church. . . ."

"I'll go," the blond gasped. "Let *me* go."

"He requested a dark-haired girl. A black-haired girl this time, and she's the only one of you who will do. Jesus save me, how that man's politeness does set me off to worrying."

The sound of the door knocker sent the madam's light brown eyes reeling.

"Oh! That's him! That's him! All right! Don't anyone panic! Keep calm! Be dignified! Keep calm! Whatever you do, keep your petticoats down and your pantalets up if you go out to the parlor! Louise, get away from that door! I'll answer it!'' She pivoted off, then suddenly swirled back and leveled a short plump finger at the immigrant girl's darkish face. ''Don't *you* dare embarrass me, or I'll trade you west.''

She moved through the parlor again, flying toward the main hallway with both arms waving. Just as she got to the door, she grated to a halt, pushed her own short brown ringlets forward from her ears, made sure the knotted hair in back was still tight, wriggled in her corset, tugged at her own crinoline as it dusted the carpet beneath with a faint *krish,* then reached for the doorknob. Ah, men! Men! How gratifying it was to have the utmost proper gentlemen come strolling through her doorway! What a victory it was! A victory over everything!

Thus her disappointment when she saw not the Gentleman, but a woman standing on her front porch. A woman in an ordinary day dress, with an ordinary bonnet, carrying a drawstring bag.

Her heart tried to sink, but the corset kept it hitched up in place.

She stepped partway out the door and looked this way and that. No Gentleman. Just the woman.

''Hm,'' she grumped. ''Yes? Something?''

The woman's green eyes crinkled with amusement. ''Are you Evee Mapes?''

''I am,'' the madam answered, squinting into the darkness to see if the woman's russet hair was naturally colored. If not, she wanted the recipe.

The young woman seemed to think she was expected.

Finally she said, ''I wrote to you. About the collection? My name is Grace MacHutcheon.''

''Oh? Oh, of course. Now I do recall. And you did not get my return missive? Specifying to come in by the back entrance? You might understand my reluctance to have a woman seen coming to my front door. We are not that kind of emporium, mind.''

''I did go round back,'' Grace said, stepping inside as she was beckoned to do. ''I couldn't find a way through the vines and the rose hedge. That hedge must be eight feet in all directions.''

''And in full bloom, you might add,'' the madam said.

"This way. Through the parlor, if you will. The drawing room." The small woman's voice held a dust of disappointment.

She waved Grace before her through each archway, then paused to draw heavy damask draperies across the archways to cut off each room from the other.

Boiling with curiosity, Grace walked through the whorehouse. What a place! At once she knew where the word *gaudy* had come from; anyone would look in here and say, "Gawd!"

The walls were pink with printed green and white lilies. All manner of boudoir accessories and sewing notions crowded the tables, along with potpourri that could scarcely compete with that incense. On the floor was heavy carpeting, and in several places animal skins had been spread over the carpeting. In fact, everything about the house was predictably overdone. Grace tried not to stare, but all of Richmond seemed overdone to her.

In the drawing room several girls were dressing another girl. They glanced at her, but none of them spoke. Except for the girl they were dressing, every one of them wore only her underwear—chemise, corset, garters, petticoats, stockings. At least two of them had the kind of corset that comes up under the breasts without covering them, and their nipples pointed straight forward over carefully placed silk fringes. Grace suddenly felt overdressed.

Now, did that make any sense?

She shook her head at herself and followed Evee Mapes through the room.

The pinkish walls were crowded with mirrors, same as the parlor, but this room also had rows of narrow shelves lined with corked bottles, apothecary jars, medicine bottles, and assorted other containers, all clear glass, all full of liquid in a dozen pastel colors. Pickled herbs and wildflowers hung inside each jar. The bottles' varied heights and shapes and the flowers and pastel colors of pink, gold, lavender, green, fuchsia, glittered in the gaslight and made cheap but effective decor. After a minute Grace realized the bottles were lined up so they would reflect the nearest mirror. They made a dreamlike sparkle in the room. This didn't seem a real place at all.

Doubtless that was the desired effect. If a man could come here and be in a dream—well, he needn't feel guilty, need he?

"Vinegar," Grace blurted all at once.

"Yes, I collect decanters for my vinegars," Evee Mapes said. "See over here, and here? Tarragon, sharp chives, caraway, lemon and orange peel, mint, thyme—why, if it grows, be God, I'll pickle it. It's pretty lining the shelves, reflecting in the mirrors, and well . . . as a woman would know . . . they have a practical application."

Grace nodded, not quite sure they were thinking about the same application, but she had a general idea.

"And when times are slow, you see, I can even sell them for cooking purposes." She looked at Grace. "Of course, not in Richmond, mind. No one here will have them."

"Would you?" Grace asked directly.

The madam gaped back. Then she tossed her enormous brown ringlets and laughed heartily. "Bless you! Bless you!" she howled.

Grace nodded but felt a little sorry for the trapped sprigs. She stepped forward, but the clutter in the room confused her momentarily, and she bumped into the foot of a tufted chaise. She looked down at the cushions.

"Oh, tartan," she noticed as her eyes got used to the erotic combination of gaslight and candlelight. How could she help but notice now that her eyes had adjusted? Everything, from the settees to the stools to the stack boxes, lamp shades, and throw pillows, was done in tartan, then edged with bobbin lace, fringes, or tassels. It made sense. A woman's touch, but bold enough for men.

"Queen Victoria's preference," Evee said. Her tiny bright red mouth bowed with pride. "We always keep up with the styles. She dresses her children in tartan. Her own blood children, mind."

"Oh, I know," Grace cooed accommodatingly.

"Do you like it?"

"Oh, I like it all right. The wallpaper has another opinion, though."

Evee blinked, thought about it, then laughed again.

Grace smiled. She pointed at the chaise. "MacGregor. And over there is Wallace."

"Ah, what a pleasure! Are you Scotch?"

"Scottish. The details were hammered into my head, is all."

Evee touched a throw pillow. "Then what's this?"

Grace squinted. "That seems to be . . . somewhat faded Clan Chattan."

"Be God, I'm impressed!"

"In this light so am I."

"When my girls are not occupied, I set them to needlepoint and embroidery. Two of them are proficient in bobbin lace. All these pillows and sundries are for sale. Time is precious, I feel. Sometimes the gentlemen purchase these for their wives—and I profit from their guilty consciences. It's indecorous, but that is the gentleman's problem. See here." She opened a tartan box. Inside were hundreds of small vendor's labels. "A man chooses one, we sew it on. Suddenly a sundry from the whorehouse becomes a treasure for madam from Paris. Or New York. Or even old York!"

She laughed again, and Grace couldn't help but laugh too at the whole idea. Danged if it wasn't downright clever. In an instant the two of them shared an unspoken bond. Most women would never find such a ruse to be funny, lest she find it being pulled on herself some day. Of course, Grace found most women rather narrow-minded and dull. Propriety kept them from speaking their minds, and fear of thinking a wrong thought kept them from thinking any thought. There just wasn't much to say to a whole section of society whose main concern was keeping their ankles covered.

Grace fogged a moment as Button's fierce withered face appeared in her mind, and she realized once again the magnitude of her loss. Suddenly she wanted to go home . . . home to the little painted house in Kansas where the old woman waited.

I miss you, Button. . . . I wish we'd talked more instead of squawking at each other. . . .

"I see," she agreed. "And when the blossoms fall, there's a skill for making a living."

Evee's big round eyes got bigger and rounder. "Why, why, yes! Aren't you correct! Blessed if you aren't. Yes . . . Miss MacHutcheon, it isn't every woman who perceives what other women must face in this world. You have a generous mind."

Grace smiled at her and said, "What I have is a long road behind me. Can't take much credit for that. Shall we set to business?"

Evee Mapes cast a glance at the dark-haired girl, her mind obviously dividing along a different path, but ultimately she said, "Yes. Let me get my boxes from upstairs."

She left Grace sitting alone on one of the settees, a bit out of place.

The heavily perfumed women continued to primp the one sad-looking girl. Other girls came and went in the drawing room, though there didn't seem to be any men here tonight. Or perhaps they were all upstairs. Indeed there was the occasional bump from above.

While she was waiting, Grace shamelessly watched the goings-on in the room, which mostly centered around dressing that one girl. She wished she'd been around at the beginning to see how all that fancy equipment was put on. She wore decent underwear—MacButton would have it no other way—but nothing so elaborate as the trappings these women wore. Her curiosity was partly assuaged when a woman in a fully boned corset came through the draperies from the kitchen carrying a small bowl of hot scented oil, situated herself on a stool, and put her feet up on two other stools. Without the slightest care about Grace's presence, the woman gathered her petticoats under her arms until her unpantied crotch showed out in the open. She dipped her fingers into the bowl and went about anointing every lip and crease between her thighs. She might have preferred some other appellation, but at the moment there was no other word for her but whore.

Grace did her the courtesy of not looking for very long. Odd that she should be the self-conscious one. She waited patiently, sifting through a large serving bowl filled with tussie-mussies and sachets that were evidently for sale too.

When Evee came back through the curtains, she was laden with four brocade-covered stacking boxes, which she spread around them on the settee and the tea table. "Here we are. What is it you are seeking, specifically?"

She opened her drawstring bag. "I'm attempting to complete a set...."

★

"Not a total waste," Grace said, tugging the drawstring closed some time later.

"Such a shame."

They stood in the parlor now, looking over hundreds of Evee's mismatched buttons that were spread over nearly the entire top of the piano. There was none of the splendor or organization of Mrs. MacButton's collection, for these, like everything else in the occupying house, were the product of haphazard years of odds and ends rather than a carefully gathered collection.

"No shame at all," Grace insisted. "I'm quite pleased to have added one more to the carved-lava set. That's something."

"Something small," Evee sighed, "something common. You may have to go to Europe to complete your special set."

An odd idea. Travel far away? Then . . . what held her to Richmond now that Paddy was leaving? Until now she hadn't thought much about leaving. Would the Union army let her tag along with her brother? But Patrick scarcely knew which kind of unit he'd be joining.

Oh, damn the future. It would come in its own time.

"Europe probably wouldn't have me," Grace finally said, laughing. She stepped toward the curtain to the main stair hall. "Oh!"

She jumped back when the curtain moved as she pushed it—there was someone coming in from the other side.

The curtains parted.

Evee gasped, "Oh! Monsieur!"

Grace stepped back. Before her the man stepped inward and took over the room.

"Mr. Tro—" She stopped it at the end of her tongue, just in time to see him tense ever so slightly. He might not want his name spoken out loud here, or anywhere, if she was right about him. Which she was. She changed her greeting to a simple, "Good evening."

His black eyes flared as he gave her a sly look of gratitude and seemed relieved. His etched mouth curved into a grin.

Yes, he was definitely relieved. So she was right—he gave a different name here than at the powder mill.

"Good evening," he responded.

"Monsieur..." Evee held out her hand gracefully.

Dorian took the madam's hand and gave a short bow. "Madame, your pardon. I'm late."

He continued to look at Grace.

Clearly Evee could see that they knew each other and weren't speaking because of her presence. Wisely she said, "I shall tend to matters, Monsieur, and return right away."

"I'm grateful," he said.

When the small woman disappeared behind the heavy curtains into the drawing room, Dorian turned to Grace and kept his voice down. "Applying for another job, Miss MacHutcheon?"

Grace broke into a small laugh. For a man who was hiding something, he was damned plainspoken.

"Delivering gun powder, *Monsieur*?" she retorted, and matched his tone perfectly.

"Merely 'admiring nature in her wildest grace,' " he said. His little chuckle told her she'd made her point.

"I'll bet you are," she said. "I'm here after buttons."

"Pardon me? Buttons?"

She shoved her hand down into the drawstring bag without bothering to pull it open and drew out an inch and a half diameter brooch button and handed it to him. He took it, squinted, and read the tiny words etched on a gold ring that framed the portrait of a man in naval uniform.

" 'The Band of Brothers,' does it say?" he murmured.

"It's a painting done on porcelain. Fifty-some years old That one depicts—"

"Admiral Collingwood, if I'm not mistaken—and the flags used in Nelson's ship-to-ship signaling system? Am I close?"

"Very good! I'm in awe," Grace commented. "I have seven of a set of ten depicting Trafalgar and the death of Horatio Nelson."

"Yes," Dorian crooned. "The one-eyed, one-armed scourge to the Franco-Spanish fleet. England still rules the seas, thanks to him. This would be quite rare, yes?"

"Rare in Kansas," she said dryly. "I'm only now finding out how rare in Virginia."

He dropped the button into her waiting palm, then seemed to realize something and lowered his voice. "Forgive me," he added. "My jest was very rude. I'm . . . genuinely sorry."

The sincerity in his face surprised Grace. Was everyone at the Craig powder mill such a walking turnabout?

Feeling more generous than ever before toward Wyatt Craig and his people, she decided to forgo another crack about what Trozen was doing in this house and just leave him to his entertainment.

"I won't keep you," she said, but when she stepped past him toward the front door, she remembered what Evee had requested of her regarding the back way and turned about. "Excuse me. I've been asked to use the back exit," she explained as she passed him yet again.

"The back?"

"Yes." She tossed him a smile. "Madam doesn't want people getting the 'wrong' impression about her establishment."

"Oh, I see. . . . Where are your accommodations?"

"West Leigh Street."

"West Leigh . . . laborers and free slaves. Surely that doesn't suit a lady of quality."

"My quality varies with my income, Mr. Trozen. I don't care what looks I get. I learned long ago to be practical."

"And never proud?"

"When I can afford it, I can outproud anybody." She paused, and nearly without thinking she faced him with a disarming question. "Tell me, Mr. Trozen, have you known Wyatt Craig for very long?"

She really hadn't meant to ask that. Well, too late now.

He blinked. "Several months. . . . Why?"

"What do you think of him?"

Trozen paused. The faintest defensiveness veiled his face. "What might I put on his gravestone, do you mean?"

"Yes, exactly."

"Well, he has a troublesome protective streak at times." With a tender smile he added, "Actually, all the time. . . . There's one trait for you."

She squared off with him, and posture demanded a direct answer. "What about the gravestone?"

"Oh." He scratched his cheek evasively. "Let me think. . . . There are so many for him. With some people you can't think of a thing, you know. Well, let me pick the quaintest one. Wyatt Craig, 1833 to, let's hope nineteen something . . . 'If there's another world, he lives in bliss. . . . If not, he made the best of this.' "

Grace licked her lips thoughtfully. "That is Wyatt Craig to you?"

"That, madam," he said, "is Wyatt Craig to anybody."

Grace met his eyes boldly to see if he was lying or protecting or deceiving. This man could do all those things, just as a tree changes color in the sun's turning light.

"Monsieur?"

They both turned.

Evee had come through the drawing-room curtains, bringing with her the sad-looking girl Grace had watched being dressed in the other room. None of the other girls came through those curtains. The girl was still sad-eyed and seemed somewhat awkward and unsophisticated. By dressing her in bright patriot red flounces and a blue bonnet, and by overdoing her eye makeup and red lip color, Evee was apparently trying to make her seem vibrant and beautiful. The girl's eyebrows were too dark, her hair nearly black as Trozen's, and her upper lip was heavily powdered in an attempt to cover a shadow of fuzz that often plagued foreign girls. Other than her harem-type coloring, she was unfortunately uneventful.

"Monsieur," Evee said, "this is Tilly."

"Ah . . . Nightshade," he murmured, taking the girl's trembling hand.

The hand must have been too cool, Grace noted, for Trozen put his other hand over hers and rubbed it between his palms.

Only then did Grace notice that the girl was tall, nearly as tall as Trozen.

Trozen noticed.

Evee laughed nervously. "She's mystifying, Monsieur. She won't disappoint you, I guarantee it. If she fails, you may have any two girls in the house to replace her, any two at all."

"No woman can fail me, madame. No woman in the world."

Evee put her tiny hand on his arm and cautiously asked, "Sir, you are cosmopolitan. Do you speak Turkish by chance?"

"No, madam, why?"

"Only that this prize of mine is Turkish and speaks but little civilized language. . . . If you wish, we'll prepare another—"

"Nonsense. She *is* a prize, then. She adds a dash of *homme moyen sensuel* to this temple of Venus."

Evee knew no more French than the word *monsieur*, but she like the sound of it.

Grace buried a smile; MacButton hadn't allowed the merest mention of France or the French into her house, despised anything that remotely stunk of Frenchitude, but Grace could tell from the gentleman's complicated expression that his chosen phrase sounded more complimentary to the American ear than it would be in translation. When he tossed her a wink behind Evee's back, well, that sealed the suspicion. What a strange, strange man he was.

"Pardon," Grace interrupted. "I'll leave you to your business. Good night—"

"I'll see you safely to your coach," Trozen said, tossing his own pardons back at the girl and Evee.

The prostitutes in the drawing room squealed properly as they had been taught to do, but otherwise Grace and Trozen went through to the back exit without a word.

In the smoky kitchen they were quite alone again. Was that better, or worse?

He levered the back door open and glanced around the dark courtyard. There wasn't even a moon to glow on the roses or the barren streets beyond the hedge.

Trozen scowled at the darkness. "Allow me to hire a driver for you. Or see you home personally."

"And miss your appointment?" Grace quipped. "I wouldn't be half the entertainment."

He bowed slightly. "Certainly I would have to pay double." At once he stared at the flagstones and put a quick hand to his brow. "I didn't mean that. Forgive me. . . . I'm unused to being around a lady. . . . Can you understand?"

"I understand," Grace said. *I understand that you're nervous, and somehow I have made you so.* "I can see to myself. Can't have you missing your medicine, can we?"

She didn't know whether he was humiliated or shocked at her boldness, but this wasn't the first time a man had been shocked by how impossible it was to embarrass her.

"Rest assured," she said as she stepped past him, "I'll keep your secrets, Mr. Trozen ... all of them."

The sediment of a smile dropped from his face. There was only a blatant openness left, the eyes gone soft, the brows tensed, the lips slightly parted with nothing to say, as if he knew his barriers were collapsing before her. Good.

She liked to leave a man worrying.

He recovered and added, "I'll see you to your buggy."

"No, no," she said lightly. "On your way."

She nudged him back inside despite his obvious reluctance, thoroughly enjoying the look on his face. Was he concerned about her welfare, pure politeness, or not letting her out of his sight?

"Best luck with your collection," he said, obviously forcing himself to remain in control. "Chances are the missing pieces are tucked in some Anglophile's drawer.... The English are feverish about their memorabilia."

"I know," she told him. "If an Englishman's prick stays hard more than a minute, you can bet somebody'll paint Queen Victoria on it."

The back door clacked shut.

Dorian sank back on the door frame and rolled backward against the kitchen wall. His frock coat clung to the brick. His heart slammed in his wrists until he thought they would burst open and he would bleed to death on the stone floor. He clapped his arms back against the wall like a man on a ledge, his fists ramming on the brick in pure anger at himself.

"Damn ... damn! She knows...."

To a condemned man the noose can terrify at the most distant glance. To Dorian that terror came from the awareness in Grace MacHutcheon's eyes. Somehow she could glimpse beyond the web he'd spun. Somehow she had the most perilous effect on him of all: she put him at ease when he wasn't ready.

The danger of it!

No one had ever seen through him so fast. He had always been able to work a grace period before, enough time to escape—

"Grace period," he rasped, bitter, frightened, furious, and closed his eyes even tighter at the irony.

Another month, one more week, just until this is built or that is delivered . . .

How often in the past months had he made excuses?

A cascade of excuses, petty reasons to stay just a little longer, stall another day, another two. How many times had he made a date to leave, even packed his clothes, only to glimpse Wyatt struggling valiantly to make the mill a success and thus decide to stay just . . . one . . . more . . .

And now he was endangering Wyatt, putting Wyatt subject to the fugitive slave law, to a reputation no white man in the South could afford to carry.

Dorian ground his teeth in anger at himself.

When had been the last time he'd stayed in any locality so long? This five-year lifetime—a new childhood. Surviving day to day had been easy. All that took was food and a place to defecate. Animals could do that, and he was at least an animal. Everything was upward from there. No, it was the discoveries of the outside world that made him clumsy. The language had been wrong, his English too proper, his Greek useless, his French and Latin only a little less so. A quick learner, yes, but he lived in terror of making a mistake or walking among the wrong people . . . a freed slave in a crowd who might recognize him or catch some inflection in his accent that didn't quite belong to a white man. . . .

Which mistake had made his secret flicker in Grace MacHutcheon's experienced eyes?

She knows something. How can she know? When she looked at me, we saw it in each other. The kindred dirt.

The noose was closing. He felt it cranking on his throat like a garrote.

Fool! To stay so long in one place!

A mistake. Might be fatal. The habit of loneliness had served him so well—

After seeing the recognition in the woman's eyes, Dorian once again felt the nearly physical blow of knowing his safety in any one place always had limits.

He could handle Noah. The law, however, that was something else.

By the laws of the South—written law, not mere tradition, custom, or propriety, but laws on books, carried out each to its extreme in pulsing courtrooms, state after state, even in Northern states—he was a criminal and had been since birth.

His white skin had doomed him to eventual crime simply because it had doomed him to eventual escape. Sooner or later, Noah Sutton or not, classical education or not, Iphigenia or not, Dorian knew he would have felt the pinch of difference. Once too often he would have seen his white hands reach for a shovel or cracked corn at the same time as the brown hands of the slaves around him, and the day would have come to test the bonds of skin. He knew that now. He had been on the path to this place and this moment since the day he was conceived. The devil can end up in only one place.

The path was narrowing before him, steering him toward hell once again within its goddamned relentless walls. The path was narrowing, and he was on a runaway wagon. A runaway.

Runaway.

Skin and blood. In most men they were the same, the two most essential elements in a body. After all, plenty of people got by every day without brains.

For Dorian, though, skin was white, and blood was black. The law believed in blood.

"Piss," he whispered, and spat at the inevitable.

The rose hedge nipped at her shawl as Grace pulled the picket gate open and stepped out of the brothel's backyard with a thousand curiosities vying for attention in her head. Gradually

she would get it all sifted out. Then she would know what to
think.

About Wyatt, and about that one in there. About what she
would tell Lassick when he demanded her latest information
about the powder mill, about the delivery that was to be made
tomorrow morning, the route, the load, the number of men
guarding it. Patrick had left the mill, was no longer in danger
from the Heroes' attacks on secessionist holdings. She hadn't
seen Patrick in days. Word would come any minute. He was
always sending notes, or coming back to her lodgings for a
good night's sleep. But he was gone longer and longer each
time he left, out hunting to supplement their table, now that
he'd left his job at the powder mill, or contacting Union
companies about their taking him in, despite his bad legs.
He'd find a place in the army sooner or later—a boy who
could shoot like Paddy would eventually get in. When he got
settled in this ridiculous need to wag the Union flag, he would
contact her, and she would go there, wherever it was.

Wyatt's shipment could go on through. Lassick could go to
hell.

"Girl."

The harsh voice slithered at her from across the street.

She drew a breath and backed up into the roses. "Who is
it?"

It was a man. Not tall but very stocky. With flaps of leather
moving on his wide form, he walked toward her from the
hitching post across the street. Epaulets of rabbit fur wagged
on his shoulders and made him seem even wider. Broad and
bearded, he was the backwoods version of Henry VIII as he
moved toward her like a big, flat crab. He stepped up onto the
curb.

"Stop there," she snapped. "Keep your distance."

He stopped.

Grace kept her hand on the gate. "What do you want?"

"I'll give you five dollars."

Oh. That's what he wanted. To get hulled for the price of
some of those skins he wore.

"Business is handled inside," Grace said gruffly. "Knock
at the front door. There's no light."

He crabbed two more steps.

"Can you read, girl?"

Grace frowned. "You want to pay a girl to read to you?"

The wide man raised his right arm. In his hand a paper flipped in the light breeze, crinkling faintly. There were large letters upon it as well as smaller print, but in the dark night Grace couldn't make them out. The man turned the paper until it caught the glow of a gaslight from across the narrow intersection.

WANTED! REWARD! WANTED! REWARD!

Air between them contracted. Grace was unsure which one of them moved closer or if the world was simply shrinking—

Mulatto slave . . . Dorian Wallace . . .

Her own hand closed on the edge of the battered page.

Black hair, black eyes, looks white . . .

Speaks good English . . .

Good English . . .

Good English.

She cocked a hip and squinted again at the poster. She took it right out of the man's hand, turned it more sharply into the gaslight's faint glow and read it over and over.

Mulatto—

Dorian Wallace . . . WANTED . . .

. . . may be greatly changed.

"Miss MacHutcheon, may I present my associate, D. W. Trozen."

Ravagement of a white virgin woman.

Grace cleared her throat. "It can't be h— I mean I can't imagine such a crime," she mumbled evasively. "You're pursuing this man for the reward?"

"I'm a bounty hunter," he said, "hired direct by the owner. This man is a legal slave, bought and owned. Fully one-half negro, born out of a full-blood slave bitch. He wears fancy clothes and a top hat, and some folk see him with a walking stick. Ever seen a man like that?"

Grace tensed. She dragged up all her self-control to keep from glancing back the way she'd come, through the court-yard and to that kitchen door. Mere footsteps away.

If Trozen came out . . . if he decided to check on her—

To distract herself, she asked, "Why would he be here?"

"I tracked him through four states. He's in Virginia. I got

my suspects that he's in Richmond. He cottons to white women, but he's smart. He goes to these here call flats for his gettin's. Goes after women like you. He sweetlips 'em, and they don't know he's a nigger. He doesn't figger anybody'll believe a harlot or care if one of you gets pumped by a black man. His white skin is how he fools people. Ain't the same as what he did, like it says on that paper.''

Well, that told Grace how she looked to him—that in spite of decent clothes and combed hair, some patina of her rough past still clung to her. Perhaps she didn't swing her skirt the way a real lady might, or perhaps his mistake came from her brash willingness to walk out of a whorehouse, alone, at night.

The big man dug into a mealy-looking pouch and drew out a five-dollar bill.

"Good money. Five dollars for just keeping your eyes open. I got a girl on my payroll in a fancyhouse in Richmond. You want to be my spy in this house? I'll pay you half a year's whoring if your information leads up to the jailing of this outlaw nigger.''

Grasping backward into time, Grace found herself courting the crazy wish that she still hated Wyatt Craig—this was so perfect! A ready-made way to destroy a man through destroying his friend.

Crazy. Fate? Was luck itself telling her that she had been right all along?

Hell with fate. She would make her own decisions.

She yanked the gate shut behind her and latched it tight.

"Never seen him,'' she said.

The man took his poster, folded it, and tucked it somewhere inside the layers of leather.

"I'm staying at the Powhatan. If I ain't in, there's a box at the front desk.''

He closed in on her. He pushed the five-dollar bill into the hollow between her breasts and poked it down inside with his thick middle finger. Grace breathed deeply to show she wasn't bothered by the invasive scratch of his knuckle against her breasts. A harlot wouldn't be.

And the man was watching for those subtle kinds of changes. He never took his eyes from hers.

Testing, checking. Watching and making sure.

"Name's Orville Quist," he said. "Just leave a message."

He stepped off the curb behind him, and even in the dark Grace could tell he was no idiot. His gaze lingered on her, making sure he understood her and she understood him.

She didn't move.

He backed away, his thumbs hooked in a rope belt.

"Quist," he repeated, the sound reminding her of a snake's hiss.

He didn't turn around until he was nearly across the whole street, and then only in time to raise his boot onto the curb and crab his way down the sidewalk, around the end building, to disappear into the darkness of an alley.

Grace still did not move.

The man's footsteps faded into the hollow night.

Was he gone? Or was he sneaking back to spy on her? Or on the house? Threat itself radiated from the alley. Inside her bodice the folded five-dollar bill pricked the soft skin of her breasts as she breathed in and out, in and out.

So I'm a spy after all. Maybe Lassick knew my destiny.

She reached into her cleavage with a thumb and forefinger and pulled out the five-dollar bill.

Pulled it out, tore it to bits, and dumped the pieces into the hedge of blood red roses.

They fell through the maze of thorns and disappeared.

★

CHAPTER FORTY-ONE

———— ★ ————

"Morning sure is early."

At the sergeant's comment Wyatt turned away from his inspection of the new delivery wagons and said, "Long time yet till morning, Henry."

The broad-shouldered old man grinned at him through the light of a half moon and went on inspecting one of the big wagon wheels. The powder yard was very dark, as if this were any other night. Every household had strict orders to appear asleep. Most of the wives, however, milled about nearby, getting a head start on the distress of knowing their men were out there making targets of themselves. The night would be almost as hard for them as for the men. This was the company's first real military maneuver other than having their uniforms fitted.

Wyatt buried a shiver. He'd always thought most things military were somewhat excessive and overanxious, even callous. Yet, as he peered across the yard at the four powder wagons and at the fifty-one men in Confederate uniforms, he knew he was doing only what he was being forced by circumstance to do.

He tried to be farsighted about all this. His mind was racing. Might as well be waiting for a guillotine blade to drop, so certain was their chance of attack.

There had to be a way around fighting. If people would just *think* . . .

All Wyatt could hope was that his men's uniforms made

them look imposing. Maybe the appearance of soldiers would scare off these scoundrels who struck in the dark at innocent civilians.

He paused, balanced on one foot, and a terrible thought hit him: What if the scoundrels found it even more romantic, more tantalizing to attack actual soldiers? What if it gave substance to their cause?

Pressing a thumb and forefinger to the bridge of his nose, he closed his eyes tight for a minute. The thought was hard to choke down, but he managed not to say it aloud.

"How are the wagons looking, Henry?" he asked instead, forcing himself to be distracted.

"Can't do much more," the ancient Kentuckian answered. He put his wide hand on the rope net and gave it a heave much stronger than he looked capable of. Stacked on the wobbling net, fifteen kegs of black powder, at two hundred pounds each, remained steady and in place in their hammock.

Then Henry doubled his statement by kicking the vulcanized rubber sheath on the outside of the nearest wagon wheel. Henry was a large and powerful man, but the metal spokes didn't even vibrate.

"Yonder rubber's the best thang to come along since powder got itself invented, sir," he said. "No sparks going over stones or metal bridges." He shook his thinning white hair and added, "Just when you think they cain't invent one more thang."

"Good to see, isn't it?"

Henry grinned. "We're ready this time, Mr. Craig, you better bleeve it. Wagons made of green wood. . . . The devil himself couldn't set spark to one of these, don't think."

Wyatt scanned the stacked kegs. Each was marked DANGER: EXPLOSIVE, and the lettering angrily glared back at him in the dim purple night. "How many of these are decoys?"

"We got nine dummies on this wagon just filled with rocks."

"So five with powder?"

"Right. And the top powder keg is the one with the cannon

lock in it. Rightcheer.'' He placed his spidery white hand on a keg in the center of the stack. The barrels swayed slightly. "Spring-loaded percussion lock, ready to blow soon as our sharpshooter picks it off. You heard of lock, stock, and barrel? This here is lock stuck in barrel!''

"Yes.'' Wyatt gave him the chuckle he expected, just because he expected it. "I sure wish Pat Ruhl had stayed one more day. He's the best sharpshooter in the state, I think.''

Henry nodded sympathetically. "Yeah, well, boss, we all gotta follow our own road.''

"I know, Henry, I know that. What about the horses?'' Wyatt stepped back to get a side view of the massive team, two shires, bought for their sheer strength at pulling such a load. There was a shire team pulling each of the other three wagons, but it was these two horses for which he was particularly concerned tonight. These were the two who might be sacrificed.

Henry shrugged. "You can only harness and unharness a horse so quick out of a heavy-pulling collar, boss. We left all the buckles off that we could. Time'll tell.''

Suddenly these two shires became Wyatt's favorites. "Sure would hate to lose 'em,'' he said.

"Like I say, time'll tell. Kin I ask, how you planning to deploy the men?''

"Columns, I guess. . . . why?''

"All you got is fifty-one men to divide twixt two details. That's twenty five one, twenty-six t'other.''

"Right.''

"When I was with General Scott, we rode single file 'cause we were short of men. We were harder to count and looked as if to cover more ground.''

"Really. . . . Why, that's remarkable, Henry! You were in the Mexican War?''

"Sergeant Henry Ruggles Brecker, United States Cavalry. Me and three brothers, two cousins, two nephews. You're looking at the only one in my family lived to tell it.''

"Why, Henry, I never knew that!'' Wyatt congratulated the old man with a handshake. "That's quite a family you come from. You should be proud of yourself.''

"Yeah, that General Scott, he was a dashing man to follow, I tell you, you never saw a man so upright to the saddle. 'Course in them days—''

"I hope you'll tell me about it after we get back. Bring my horse up, if you don't mind, would you? Thanks."

Then, with a telling sigh, Wyatt stiffened his resolve and fought off the desire to stay here where it was safe and tell all the men to go get a good night's sleep. They'd just dig a canal from here to the train yard and float the kegs down on big bullet-proof barges, and nobody'd have to worry about anything.

He shook off the dream, cleared his throat, and forced his voice out.

"Where's Curtis Mayhew?"

"Here, sir!"

A freckled twenty-year-old hydraulic-press operator appeared at his side on a short brown horse, going rough on the mare's mouth.

"You know your job?" Wyatt asked.

"Yes, sir," the young man gasped. "I shoot the barrel with the lock in it. The one with the white lettering." He yanked up his percussion rifle expertly and brandished it.

"Well, not till you're told, correct?"

"Naw! Z'at so?"

"Did Pat Ruhl show you how to aim in the dark?"

"That's why he's not here. I killed him."

Wyatt smiled past his nerves, envying the indestructability of youth. "You're a snot, Curtis. Blow that wagon on anybody else's order but mine, and you're fired."

"Huh-uh. You can't fire me anymore. You gotta court-martial me."

Wyatt chuckled.

"All right, listen, everybody," he called out. "Gentlemen! Listen. You all have your orders. No talking on the road. No smoking and no riding ahead. There's just one change: we're going to ride in single file, and vary the distance between yourself and the man in front of you. Got that? Detail two, you'll mount up precisely fifty minutes after we're gone, and follow the same route. I'll send your orders back to meet you once we know what's ahead. In the meantime, there is to be quiet and darkness on the powder-mill grounds. Okay, boys . . . let's be honest. We're wearing uniforms, but we're all a hell of a lot better at making powder than we are at being soldiers. Do your best. Keep in mind that if these raiders get our powder, they'll use it to ravage families and burn bridges that serve the South. If we hit trouble, try not to abandon your fellow man. That's all I can fairly ask of you. Oh, and one more thing—in the event of a violent confrontation,'' he said, and pointed to his left, "I want you to do anything Henry Brecker tells you to do.''

Henry spun around. "Sir? You're the major, Major!''

Wyatt looked at him. "That's the little star over on my collar talking. Your stripes are real. I'm sure every man here would rather have his life in the hands of an experienced soldier than a pretty uniform. You're in command of the troops, Sergeant. Hear that, men?''

The men glanced at each other, surprised, but then almost every man smiled and there was a grumble of what sounded like approval. Then one of the wives rushed up, cupped Wyatt's face in her hands, and planted a kiss right on his bare cheek.

The soldiers laughed—Wyatt's blush was visible even in the moonlight.

He shuffled guiltily. He hadn't been fishing for compliments.

"But what about yourself?'' Henry demanded. "You ought to be able to command your own men, Mr. Wyatt, oughtn't you?''

"Don't worry about me, Henry. If anybody shoots, I'll probably be under a log someplace.''

Another chuckle rippled through the powder-mill workers, and they seemed even more confident in Wyatt now—though he didn't really feel as if he deserved their trust. To avoid accepting it, he hid his feelings in the act of putting his gloves on.

He gripped the reins of his big lanky pink roan and prepared to climb into the saddle. "All right, sound the mount up. Let's deliver some powder.''

"Detail! Mount . . . HUP!''

Later that same night Dorian emerged from the woods, chapfallen as usual, his legs weary from the long ride and the long creep through the dampness. He had long ago lost count of all the times he'd done this and all the times it had come to nothing but aching joints and a lead heart. His own words echoed in his ears from moments ago.

"Yaw' seen a li' cuffee mama 'bout fence high, got a roun' face, skinny hands, ain't real black lak coffee, but kinda brown lak cinnamon toast? Maybe she tote a husky cuffee boy 'bout nine yea' old? Yaw' seen a woman lak dat? She my mama. I bin lookin' fuh huh. Huh name Yula. Yaw' remember dat. Yula. Yaw see huh, tell huh Dohrian come lookin'. Hea'? Dohrian lookin' an' gonna find huh."

How many times from behind how many trees in the dark had he chattered off his recitation? Endless descriptions of his mother as he remembered her—which of course denied him any rest from even a single detail. Her face was constantly behind his eyes, tantalizing him into one more attempt, to dare approach one more farm or factory, then another, her voice—*"Dohrian, you is such a critter!"*

And how many whores had ridden at his side, not realizing they were part of his camouflage, that a man riding with a woman was less suspicious than a man riding alone? He had lost count. A hundred times or more, sneaking around, asking questions, describing Yula, trying not to be seen, cloaking his face and his good English in the guise of a runaway. Perhaps *this* time, or *this* time . . .

Only to come out forlorn, to be whispered about like a woodland haint. The circumstances had to be right—woods to hide in, darkness to cloak him, a haystack, tree, or bush to hide behind, a slave close enough to his bush or tree to be coaxed over without Dorian's having to expose his white skin.

Caught in the trap of his skin.

He wondered how many fireside stories he had inspired, how many slave children went to bed thinking about the haint who lived in the trees just the other side of the field.

Where negroes had once been individuals to him, now they were only shivering voices in the night or seas of brown faces at the few slave auctions he dared attend. He had been attending more of those lately. He was more desperate.

There was a half moon tonight. It cast a strange pearly light on the road as he stepped around the prickly bushes and came out onto the road a hundred feet or so from the surrey. The girl was waiting for him, curled up in her shawl. She, like the others, was his camouflage, his excuse to be out driving, but also she would be his respite, his escape from the world, as were all the others. Literature had betrayed him, his father had betrayed him, and God had betrayed him. Women saved him from the world.

His loins warmed as he drew closer. He would escape into her.

But ten feet from the surrey he slowed down and stared.

The moonlight on her face . . . the features . . .

The crescents of her cheeks, her brow, the moon, each of her two lips . . .

"If you go out at night, never look at a light. If 'n you look, it pulls you, and you jus' wander following it, but you never reach it."

He was staring at a light. The girl was the light. There was something about her.

"Your grandfather Dimitrios will bask in the light of you, my boy."

Aromas filled his senses, *souvlakia, chirino, avgolemono, karavides,* and more, a hundred more, and the music—suddenly he was lost in a dance! Squatting, kicking, twisting the *tsamiko* across a wide green lawn—then he saw the curving headdress of Athena, the triton on the neck of an urn of fired clay, skirts overburdened with embroidery and tinsel and Damascus brocade, the trappings of a past civilization—all came plunging down upon him and nearly knocked him head over heels as he stared at the girl—

The girl. Her features, cast in this noncommittal moon-light, without the confusing background of a whorehouse or the wrong city, her hair slightly fallen because the road was bumpy . . .

Olympia, Ellenekoss.

He stepped up his pace and reached the wagon in seconds. The girl looked down at him, her heavy lips parted.

Dorian bluntly asked, *"Pia ene e ethnekóteta sas? Este Ellenekoss?"*

What nationality are—

The girl pressed her knuckles to her mouth, squealed joyously, and plunged from the surrey, over the dashboard, and right into his arms. She collapsed against him, sobbing, and babbling in Greek.

Dorian swayed for balance, laughing. "Turkish!" he blustered. "Saints and pigs!" He murmured comforts to her in Greek, just as delighted to speak his native language as the girl was to hear it.

She hung on him, but there was nothing of the whore in her now. She babbled gratitudes and a stream of miserable explanations, of which he only caught about half because she was drowning in her own tears.

"Possas lene?" he asked.

"Calligenia!" she sobbed. "Calligenia!"

That was clear enough. They had given her an American name because they couldn't pronounce the real one.

Dorian coiled his arms around her under the moonlight and hugged her, and hugged his past. He knew what it was to be lost in a land of strangers.

She had come here because of the stories. Stories of marriages between Greek girls and American men, successful marriages that gave Greeks a root in the new land.

It sounded familiar.

She was lost, penniless, a virgin, desperate. The new land had meant only slavery to her, the slavery of the brothel, like hundreds of young girls who came, or were brought, or were sold by their own kind into the white slavery of the northern cities of America—Philadelphia, New York, Boston. She hadn't even made it that far. She had to be a slave almost in the place she had gotten off the boat. She had come on a ship with six Jewish girls who had been kidnapped and sold by a Jewish man. What a gray joke it was that slavery existed only in the South.

Unlike those girls, though, she had come of her own volition, hoping to marry and send money back to her family in Corinth. They would join her on the plantation and help spend her husband's money.

The story rattled out in such detail that by midnight Dorian was tired of hearing Greek.

But by then they were at the harbor.

Another hour, and Dorian was back at Evee's, smirking at the small woman's shock at having him return to the house, which at this hour was bustling with activity.

Dorian came to the back door, preferring not to be seen by the men being hosted in the front rooms.

"Monsieur!" Evee blustered. Her painted face took on a true flush beneath the powder. "Is something amiss? Where is Tilly? Saints preserve me, she hasn't run off on you, has she?"

Dorian stepped into the kitchen, where a handful of black slaves were now busy at work, and the aroma of tarts and breads was heavy. He coiled his arm intimately around Evee's shoulders and stroked the bare top of her breast with his fingertips.

"No," he said. "I put her on a ship for Charleston."

She twisted beneath his arm. "You did what?"

"Where she'll be put on another ship for Greece. She's going home. I gave her some of the paper hammer for her voyage and a little extra travel expenses. This, however"—he raised his other hand and stuffed a roll of bills down her cleavage—"is for you, to compensate for the loss of business until you acquire someone new. Someone who knows what she's getting into. And Evee, my dear savior of the flesh," he added, "if you ever hire a girl like that again . . . I'll shut this joyhouse down. Clear? Now, what other set of legs have you got for me?"

———————————— ★ ————————————

"Paddy? I'm home. Where are you? Sleeping?"

Grace came in the front door of the squatty two-story she shared with her brother, without even realizing how late it had become. She probably should just keep her mouth shut. Pat needed his sleep. She wished he was up. She wanted to talk to him, ask him what he thought of a subject she'd avoided scrupulously nearly all their lives, for Paddy's sake. Paddy had to work with Wyatt Craig. For that reason Grace had kept her pipe shut about it.

Things were different now. She'd seen unbelievable things and forced herself to believe them.

"Always knew I was just a buck-dumb backwoods rabbit chaser," she grumbled to herself while busily lighting a candle to see by.

The night was cool, but humid. Sticky. Looking forward to being naked, she twisted herself into a knot trying to undo the ten thousand tiny buttons on the back of this day-bodice.

"If you're awake, come down here and undo me," she called. "Who makes dresses like this? They think every woman's got a servant to button her up.

"Paddy!" she called. "Are you in this house? Are you hiding, or what? Answer me!"

The short, narrow steps groaned beneath her as she went upstairs to Paddy's room.

"Pat?"

It was dark, yet somehow she knew she was alone. Fumbling for matches, she struck one and lit the candle on Patrick's nightstand—and saw a note.

Patrick's miserable handwriting twisted up at her in the weak gold light.

Derest Liz,
Mr Lassik was here wen I come home from work He tol me you were helping him and his men fight for the north an he sayd I'd be a fine shooter so I joint up. Sinse you like him so much I figurd he was oka. He wanted me right

to-night so I'm going. Soon as I get setled I will send for
you.
Your brother devotedly
Patrick Ruhl

Grace's eyes grew wide, and her mouth dropped open.

"Lassick! That cocksucking, mealymouthed, back-stabbing
bastard!"

She stormed a full circle, shaking the paper, then paused
and read it again. And again.

*Mr. Lassik . . . fight for the north . . . shooter . . . you like
him . . . right to-night.*

"Tonight," she murmured.

Monday, Tuesday, Wednesday . . . tonight—

"Tonight!" she shrieked. "Oh, God! Oh, God! Tonight!
Patrick!"

She was down the stairs and on the street by the time the
letter skidded to the floor.

Fog rose from the hills as the night gave up its hold. The
sky had turned a faint pink blue, but the land was still
black.

The First Richmond Light Guards, whose name was a lot
better at fighting than they were, moved through a crease in
the countryside with a lack of ceremony that certainly disap-
pointed many of the men. Wyatt could sense their tension,
their fingers twitching on the handles of their Whitney Navy
.36's, their wish to get going and fight somebody. War fever
was hot and thrilling, a disease that threw blinders on men of
otherwise generous character. For his workers today was the
first day of the war. For them the powder mill was now a
Confederate fort and they its defenders.

The early morning countryside was purple and gray beneath
the waning half moon, turning ghost white as fog bled out
of the hills. The horses plodded to the creak of the metal
wheels and the soft crush of rubber wheel lining against
the road. The bobbing rope nets made a liturgy that wouldn't
let them forget what was coming. All that was missing was
the lullaby.

Wyatt hadn't even tugged on his reins in miles. Except

for his nerves splitting at every crack of stone under a hoof—

"Bridge in sight," came a call from the forward flank.

"Bridge, Major," Henry relayed back to him.

"I got it," Wyatt responded, his heart pounding like a drum. The first bridge of two. "Keep the decoy wagon well to the fore of the other one." He twisted in his saddle. "Sam, Percy, have the second wagon pull back a few lengths. We don't want them both on the bridge at the same time."

The answer came from several horses behind him. "Yessir, Major."

In the dimness a form swung around and headed back toward the second wagon—the wagon with the real shipment, and miles behind them two more wagons. If the first detail didn't get through, the second would at least have a chance to turn back.

A horse came cantering toward them from the gully where the bridge was, and Wyatt almost squeezed the air out of his roan before he realized this was their own scout.

The man drew up sharply next to Henry and reported, "I don't see a thing around that bridge, Henry. Could just be the night tricking me, but I rode right across the bridge and back, and the crickets are going like firecrackers far as I could hear."

"Henry?" Wyatt spurred his roan up a few lengths. "Recommend we start across?"

"It's your call, Major. It'll be dawn in half an hour. Better go over at least one bridge in the dark if we got the chance. We're still more than five miles from where the other shipments were bushwhacked."

Wyatt peered between the skirts of two hills. The gully was surrounded on all sides by hills, fairly easy to defend, relatively safe as landscape went. Advantages were the heavy brush and many fallen trees left behind when the state engineers cut through and made the bridge.

"I'll take that recommendation," he said. "Signal the move ahead. Hold that second wagon back!" he called. "Let's get the horses through. Come on."

He steered his horse onto the bridge, and his men followed,

filing past the load of powder on the second wagon—the real shipment. The decoy wagon was already halfway across the bridge.

The metal bridge clicked beneath the shod hooves of the horses, except the horses of the powder wagons, which had been shod with specially made shoes of vulcanized rubber, like the wagon wheel rims, to reduce the chance of spark. *Technology,* Wyatt thought, enjoying the sound of the shires' enormous hooves thunking on the metal bridge. *Somehow science, chemistry, industry, they'll put this country back together. I'd make that bet right—*

"Torches!" The shout was a warning, from somewhere in his own ranks, and before the echo dropped, the night erupted with heavy fingers of fire, wobbling, distorted, against the night.

They were endless! They kept coming and coming—ten, twenty, thirty—

" 'Bout face!" Henry shouted, but too late.

No sooner could the men draw reins to turn than more torches appeared from nowhere behind them, as though the land had opened up, and hell came out for a run—another dozen . . . and more . . . so many that the torches could actually be heard burning, crackling as they consumed themselves. The tail of Wyatt's convoy was surrounded.

Trapped!

Locked on the bridge, surrounded by twice their number, thirty on one side, thirty on the other, torches glaring and licking horribly against the dark night. Were there more? Was he counting only torches and not men in hiding? The raiders held their horses stock still while the beseiged men's horses bolted and crashed against each other, sensing the panic, seeing the fire, not wanting to be caught on unnatural footing any more than their riders did.

"Hold your fire!" Wyatt called. He held his roan tight beneath him, though the tall horse pounded the bridge and pulled at the reins. "Henry! Henry!"

"Let the uniform talk, Major!"

The order was fierce, but it confused him.

Wyatt clutched the reins to his chest and drew his own pistol. "What?"

"Attention!" A voice called from the end of the bridge. "You are our prisoners."

The powder-mill corps turned suddenly silent, only their breathing and the shuffling of their horses audible.

"On behalf of the sacred dominion," the voice continued, "of the United States of America, we order you to turn over your shipment immediately."

The faceless challenge echoed somewhere in front of the decoy wagon, then stopped.

Torches tasted the open air before Wyatt and his men, and behind them.

Wyatt whispered, "Henry..."

"Let the *uniform* talk," Henry repeated, very firmly.

Wyatt nodded, then he raised his voice and shouted, "This is Major Wyatt Craig of the First Richmond Light Guard of the Confederate Army! Do you hear me?"

A pause. Then—

"I do."

Wyatt beat down a shiver. "I'm authorized by the governor of the state of Virginia to order you to cease and desist these illegal activities, step aside, and let this delivery pass, or face the consequences." Out of the side of his mouth he whispered, "Curtis..."

"Right here, Major!" the young man in his exuberance crashed through an extra length and had to turn back on the narrow, crowded bridge, steering his horse with one hand and shouldering his rifle with the other.

"Not yet!" Wyatt hissed. "Curtis!"

But a shot rang off, and a bullet whined—

Wyatt reached for the boy impulsively, a natural reaction, but when he heard the shot, every fiber of his body recoiled, for he expected the cannon lock to trigger and the booby-trapped powder wagon to blow up a mere twenty feet ahead of them on the bridge. In his mind, in that instant, they were all dead.

His hand convulsed on Curtis Mayhew's shoulder, but his fingers were digging into something sticky and pulpy. Wyatt glared through the steam of his own breath—blood... Curtis Mayhew's face fell off onto Wyatt's hand, blown free from his skull by a shot from the shore, a shot Wyatt had mistaken as Mayhew's own.

Wyatt blurted a ragged cry of shock, but by then Henry Brecker had raised his own pistol, aimed back the way they had come, and fired. He picked off at least one man with a torch, possibly two. "Retreat! Fire at will!"

The bridge dissolved into chaos. The men on the foremost powder wagon dived for the bridge and ran, shamefully both fighting for Mayhew's horse after dragging the poised body from the saddle. In the effort both were picked off by gunfire from the shore and crashed headlong beneath the hooves of their fellow workers. The rest of the powder-mill corps stampeded back the way they'd come, firing before them and crashing directly through the line of raiders who had held them trapped only moments before. The panic of a caged animal served very well for the moment, and the fog helped too, and in the confusion several men managed to reroute the second wagon—the real delivery—back behind a clutch of felled trees.

Still clamoring across the bridge, Wyatt fired blindly toward the torches and shouted, "Take cover! Take cover! Get that wagon back!"

The raiders scattered, but they weren't retreating. They outnumbered Wyatt's men three to one—though many were mowed down by the stampeding powder-mill workers.

Horrified, Wyatt kneed his roan into a scratchy canter on metal foundation that made the horse skid and scramble for a hoofhold.

Cold-blooded! No negotiation at all! None at all!

To a man who was used to being able to talk to just about anybody, this felt like swallowing a ball of iron. In a confusion, shrouded by fog and his own men, Wyatt reached the land, fired two more shots into the marauders— He could see them now! The sun! It was blinking over a distant hill—

He took serious aim, shot, and missed. The sound of the shot whining by his target's thick square beard evidently was close enough and sent the man sprawling for cover.

Now Wyatt could see the difference. His own men were uniformed, the raiders dressed in sloppy farm clothes and work clothes. Not a gentleman among them, no surprise.

When the roan hit solid ground, his hooves dug hard into the dirt, and he sprung forward beneath Wyatt. Wyatt bent low, clawed to hang on, and would have had a chance, but another bullet whined out of nowhere and tore through the horse's muscular neck. The horse's head convulsed backward and delivered Wyatt a reeling blow on the side of the head, then collapsed beneath him. The big body hit the ground dead, with a terrible *whump*, dragging Wyatt with it, and the roan's barrel came down on his left leg. So far two bullets meant for him had killed others, and he was trapped for the second time in minutes. He pushed backward with his elbows, bracing his free foot on the saddle, but he might as well try to kick aside a boulder.

Movement clattered around him, and suddenly he was free, being dragged away by several of his men, and before he could think, they had pushed him behind a fallen tree on his stomach. Burrs caught at his hair and uniform jacket. He fumbled with his pistol—somehow it was still in his hand.

Henry was on one side of him, barking, "Reload! Reload!" to the other men who had made it into hiding, and on the other side was Percy O'Keefe, the first man who had come to work for him here in Virginia. Percy was shaking like the last leaf in December, but his eyes were steady, and he was managing to reload his Whitney. He managed a nod at Wyatt and a tooth-gritting expression of determination.

Wyatt nodded back, his throat dry.

As the sun buttered the gully with pale, steamy rays, a mist rose from the dewy ground almost as though to counterstrike the dawn. It was enough light by which to see the fallen men, but not to count them, to see the convulsing body of his horse, to watch in helpless empathy as the team of shires left with the decoy wagon on the bridge, desperately trying to turn or push or pull their burden to get off the bridge somehow.

The gunshots ceased for a moment as everyone scrambled for cover, then there were four or five isolated shots, and then nothing.

Wyatt squirmed over on one elbow and looked around. His men were under cover for the most part, and they had managed to save the loaded wagon. All might go well yet . . . if only the decoy wagon would be tempting enough—

"You okay there, son?" Henry asked, shimmying closer. "Got all your hands and legs?"

"I think so," Wyatt stammered. "The horse fell on my foot."

Henry's face was limned with rage. "You ever see anything like that? In all my days I never know'd of a fighting corp to open fire on men they had pinned down! You just don't do that, you just don't! You take prisoners. You don't open fire, you just don't!"

"That's what I thought," Wyatt said. Suddenly he realized it hadn't been just his perception, but that there was a clear wrong, a true violation. His chest hurt. His words came in gushes. "Poor Curtis . . ."

"He never knew what hit him," Henry said. "You'll come to find there's worst ways to go."

"Christ, Henry, all I want to do is deliver powder."

"You're an officer now, son."

"I don't deserve to be. I've never seen death, Henry . . . not that wasn't in a bed or in a coffin. Never . . . like that. Jesus . . ."

Henry's snowy hair bobbed forward in front of his face as he pointed toward the abandoned wagon with his pistol. "Son, you know what you're here to do."

Wyatt looked, frowned, and said, "They won't compromise."

"But they expect you will. Take t'upper hand while it's yorn to take. Maybe if they think they got one whole wagon load of powder, they'll settle for it."

"Hell . . . all right." Wyatt set his jaw, poked his gun hand straight up, and waved it in broad strokes. "Attention down there!"

"Do you surrender?" the same voice called from the distance.

Wyatt called back, staying behind his tree, though he did peek over it. "I've ordered my men to cease fire. You take the wagon on the bridge and let us retreat fair and square with this other wagon. What do you say?"

"Done!"

Wyatt sank back behind the tree. "Oh, this is giving me quicksteps," he moaned. "That was too easy."

"They're coming out," Henry observed, peeking between the tree's bare limbs. "Some of them are heading for the wagon . . . others showing their heads now . . . coming out, keeping guns on us. Soon as they get that wagon—"

"They're going to force us to give them the other one. I know, I know . . . what can I do? Take potshots and hope we hit that pressure lock? Our only sharpshooter is dead on that bridge."

Henry reached around to the man beside him and said, "Hand over that rifle, Ardel." He tested the weight of the weapon, then checked all the firing mechanisms and brought it to his shoulder.

Wyatt gaped at him. "Henry—"

"Yeah?"

"Now, you'll just make things worse—"

"Why?" He put the weapon to his shoulder, rested the barrel in a notch on the tree, and closed one eye. Carefully he sighted down the powder wagon. In the cross hairs a dozen of the raiders approached the wagon under whatever cover they could find. He waited until they were closer. "Didn't you know all the old sharpshooters retire in Virginia?"

The rifle cracked, barked—the bullet whined—

In the middle panorama the decoy wagon detonated.

A single ball of black fire erupted across the gully. The sound was a single deafening blast, not a boom, but a crack so loud that the ground beneath them shook from the concussion. The beauty and the horror of chemistry turned into a single hammer blow of force that tore through the shires and all humans within fifty feet, rending them to bloody, blackened shreds. The concussion cracked skulls and tore limbs, then drove rocks and splinters of wood into flesh and hit the ground hot.

Wyatt cringed for cover. The deadly spray smashed into the trees he and his men were hiding behind, and in spite of the cover, they were knocked backward and driven to the ground by the sheer concussion and raining shrapnel. They covered their heads as the black powder released its energy with a brutishness that few of them—and it was a good thing—had ever visualized as they made the stuff day after day. The solid fuel of hell.

The Order of Heroes of America were stewed together with so much horse meat.

Wyatt crawled to his hands and knees, shaking. Caked with dust and soot, he could barely hear the drizzle of bits and pieces that still rained around them, though he could see it hammering the ground around him and feel it upon his numb back and shoulders.

"Judas priest," he gasped. "Good powder . . ."

His voice sounded far away. He shook his head and put his hands to his ears, but nothing helped.

Before him Henry's bulk lay still a moment, then rolled over. He grunted, "Next time you'll listen to my war stories."

Wyatt felt around for his pistol, waving the dust out of his way. He found it, cocked it, and staggered to his feet.

"Gentlemen!" he shouted. "Charge!"

He ran out from behind his log and was gratified to have every one of his men who could still move come crashing out from the brush and trees right behind him.

He couldn't have been prouder.

They stormed the bridge, jumping bodies by twos and threes, gathering up any of the raiders who were still stumbling about in a daze or trying to find a way through the sulfurous smoke. The eye-burning smoke and fumes worked in Wyatt's favor—for all his men were used to the chemical sting and the stench and easily ignored it.

"Round them up!" he called. "Sam, Percy, Andrew . . . you're in charge of prisoners! Form them in a line, clear of the smoke. I want a head count! And I want the leader."

Favoring his left foot, he paused long enough to put his revolver back in the holster and wipe his hands on his trousers.

"Wyatt! Wyatt! Major! Over here!"

He had no idea who was calling him, but he stumbled through the confusing dawn haze and the smoke from the destroyed wagon toward the sound. Twice his foot failed him, and he nearly skidded down the gully's dangerous central crack but managed to keep from rolling under the bridge. He went past the bridge and paused for a crushing instant to look at the mangled remains of his team of shires. The enormous bodies were ripped right out of most of their skin. One of the horses was missing all four of its legs and lay there in a heap, blood gushing and spurting onto the structure of the metal bridge, then running through the bridge floor and dribbling onto the dirt far below.

And Curtis . . . there was nothing left of the body at all.

"Lord mighty," he breathed, and forced himself to pass by. He had never seen death.

Yet death had its good points compared to what he saw as he came around the skirt of an outcropping. He was taking care with his footing and didn't look up until he was past the outcropping, and there he witnessed a standoff.

His men held their pistols up, holding two men at bay, but one was a hostage.

A familiar and terrified face.

"Patrick—" Wyatt blurted, suddenly breathless again. "What the hell are you doing here!"

"He was delivered unto me!" said the man who held Patrick by one hand and a saber point pressed to Patrick's lower back with the other. This was a gaunt, clean-shaven man, dressed all in black, not unlike photographs of the new president. Indeed, that might have been the whole idea. The clothing was right.

"Let him go," Wyatt said. "You've lost."

"Only in your eyes. A thousand will come for every one who falls. Union numbers will be the end of the Confederacy. You shall see and all shall see, Major Craig, and you will once again work for the glorious United States in its integrity."

"Nobody wants peace more than I do, Lasik. That's you, isn't it? You're Lasik. The leader."

In response the man dug the saber point harder against Patrick's spine.

"No! Don't!" Wyatt shouted, daring a step closer.

"Wyatt, I'm sorry, I'm sorry," Patrick gasped, tears streaming down his roundish features. He arched his back against the point of the saber. "I didn't understand. . . . They told me things. . . . It sounded good. . . . I didn't know they'd do this. . . . They just wanted the powder—"

"I know, Pat," Wyatt said. He flipped his eyes to the captor and said, "Lasik, you don't want to do this. It won't help your cause. Let him go and we'll talk."

Instantly he saw his mistake: offering to talk—it showed his weakness to the gaunt man, and Wyatt could see it also as though looking in a mirror. He saw the word *compromiser* stamped upon his own forehead and knew in that instant that he had given himself away and given Rodney Lasik license to commit his final atrocity.

"No!" Wyatt choked, but too late.

Lasik gritted his teeth, yanked backward on Patrick's collar, and drove the saber forward through Patrick's body. It made a hideous sound.

Patrick choked out a pitiful squeak, like a pig just before its throat is slit. He gaped downward at his own body in time to see the saber pop through his entrails, his skin, cutting through his flesh and dragging gray and blue guts with it through the hole it made in the trousers beneath his belt line.

"God!" The scream tore from Wyatt's throat, and he plunged forward, his men right behind him.

Patrick staggered, his knees slightly bent, his arms flung wide, his mouth hanging open and eyes staring down at the blade protruding from his middle. His lips quivered. He staggered several paces, as though he didn't know whether to fall down or what. He came toward Wyatt.

Wyatt's men were upon Lasik in an instant, dragging him back.

Still walking, his face now white, Patrick drew his hands inward and clasped the silver crescent protruding from his body. He moved as though through a strange dream, but as he squeezed the blade, his hands were lacerated, and blood began to puddle between his fingers. He pulled on the blade, yanked it upward, downward, but all he managed to do was slice himself wide open as though sawing through melon.

"Pat!"

Wyatt stumbled up the incline and caught him as he went to his knees.

Patrick was looking down at the blade, but he heard the shout and always wanted to do what Wyatt told him. Now he looked up into Wyatt's face.

Numb with shock, Wyatt could do nothing but hold Patrick's shoulders and keep him from falling backward, from driving the saber farther through himself.

"Oh my God, oh my God," Wyatt gasped senselessly. He had no idea what to do. He touched the blade pointing at him from Patrick's gut, but Patrick suddenly arched in agony and Wyatt let go. In nothing but panic Wyatt reached around, grasped the hilt, and yanked the sword backward. Patrick knotted forward against him.

The sword clattered to the rocks.

Where there had been no blood before, in fact only a blade so clean that it might have been a bad joke, now blood poured from the hole in Patrick and flooded the front of Wyatt's uniform, all the way down his knees and into the dirt.

Patrick's eyes rolled upward, and he crashed backward. His body convulsed and arched, his heels digging into the rubble.

Wyatt crawled through the blood and put his hand on the wound, but it was bigger than his hand now. "Oh, God," he choked again and again. Bile came up and gagged him. To die degutted is the greatest fear of every living thing. Worse, though . . . to be degutted and fail to die.

Pink foam bubbled from Patrick's mouth. At the same time a gurgle of foam also came out of the gouge in his stomach, as though a pot were boiling inside. His legs were spread apart in a distorted V, and out of some strange urge to help him, Wyatt pulled the knees together, but they flopped apart immediately.

If he stuffed something into this wound—there was still one on the other side. Desperately he looked around. There were only his men, staring from a distance. They knew. He could see in their faces that they knew. No doctor for miles, hours, no bandages, no morphine, no chance—

Something grabbed him by the throat. Patrick's hand. Wyatt clutched it, but Patrick was pulling on him. His lips were moving.

Wyatt bent low and caught the faint words that gurgled upward.

"Shoot me . . . shoot me . . . shoot . . ."

The convulsions started again. They racked through Patrick's body with such violence that the men who watched even from as far off as the bridge crammed their eyes closed and looked away.

With tears streaming down his cheeks and his heart in halves, Wyatt scanned the faces of his men. What did they expect of him? What was a commanding officer supposed to do? Every last one of them hoped the same thing, and he knew it.

Because he hoped it too.

But his were the sleeves with the Austrian knots. His was the collar with the star.

So he held his wounded friend's hand very tightly, took out his pistol, put it to Paddy's chest, and pulled the trigger.

She could stop it, she could warn Wyatt Craig to turn his shipment back, give her time to get Patrick away from the man who hated them all—if her horse was just fast enough and her heart could turn pure again, she could do it, she could do it.

The haze of the coming sun was peaking over the hills. Here she was on the back trails, able to cut right over the backlands and through the hills rather than depending upon the main road that had been cut wide enough for wagons. Ironic . . . Lassick had shown her these paths—the short way in and out of Richmond. The time saved was nearly lost in trying to see her way through these goat paths in the dim light, but she pressed forward, endlessly forward, demanding as much from her horse as she did from herself.

She'd been riding for hours, forcing her horse to keep up a canter, at least a trot, resting him as little as possible, ignoring the foam that flew from his mouth and flecked her skirt. He was a small horse, his stride not a long one, and half the time she was tempted to get off and run.

This was her punishment for all those years of unjust hatred. Luck and fate knew what was in a person's mind, and they had turned against her. This was her retribution come down from High Fortune, given to her not just by chance, but because she deserved it. But why would fate take revenge time after time on Patrick for what she herself had done? Hell, she couldn't even trust the few things she *did* believe in.

All along the trail she uttered oaths to herself for what she had been, to Lassick for what he was, and to Patrick for being so simple to fool. Yes, Lassick could convince Patrick of almost anything, and Grace knew half the fault was hers for never being honest about her meeting with Lassick, a man Patrick respected but feared. Grace said Lassick was all right to deal with, and Pat trusted her judgment more than his own. If Grace said okay, then okay. Lassick had honor, but it was all of his own definition, carefully wrought by the wrongs he imagined the world had done him. He imagined himself great, and the world had not made him great. Therefore he owed it nothing.

Yes, Grace knew exactly what was in Brad Lassick's mind and what made him a man to reckon with, but she was always up to the challenge and never feared him. She used him and let herself be used. That was fine. It was a bargain between the soiled.

But for him to go after Patrick, who was not in any way up to him, to deceive the innocent—

She never thought even Lassick would do that.

And how hard would it be for him to spin some yarn that would get Patrick to tell him where the Craig powder shipment was traveling, and when, and with how many guards, and convince him they were doing a good thing to stop the delivery? Hell, she herself could make something up in two seconds. Lassick might take twice that.

She rode that rough-trotting little horse until she was nearly shaken apart, rode out of the night and into the first daylight, and into the sound of gunfire.

She kicked the horse hard on the barrel, and he jolted forward unenthusiastically.

Grace nearly went out of her mind as the gunshots and shouts of fighting men churned upward from behind the nearby crests. She couldn't see a damned thing.

She yanked the horse to a stop, turned him, turned him again, but there was no path or road or way to get over this hill except to climb it herself. Dropping from the horse onto both feet, she hiked up her skirt and up she went, scratching and toeing her way upward, slipping down a foot for every two she gained. Damn these skirts!

Gathering the skirt as much as she could into her left arm, she used her right to climb with, but it was slow going. The gunshots were getting fewer…fewer still…now they stopped. She was too late!

Voices—now men! They came clamoring over the crest and shimmied down the hill all around her on their butts.

"What happened!" Grace demanded. She grabbed for each man as he slid past her, but they only wanted to get away. "What's happening! Tell me!"

She reached out for one man's long beard and caught it.

"Judas priest!" he howled.

Grace yanked hard. "Tell me what's happening!"

"We're losing," he answered. "Let go of me!"

"What do you mean?"

"Craig brought an army with him! They captured General Lasik. Let go of me!"

"Which Lassick? Which one? Open your ears! Which one!"

"Rodney! Gimme my whiskers, lady!"

"Where's Patrick Ruhl?"

"Over the hill someplace—I don't know—lady!"

"Curse you, you bumfuck hen-hearted coward! All right, go!" She turned him loose and scrambled up the hill, grumbling, "What'd they make men out of these days? Nothing but britches full of fricking goramighty sourdough!"

While she'd wasted her time with that one, ten other men had passed her. She ignored them and dug for the top.

The rocks crumbled under her feet, and she fell forward, and the wind coughed out of her, costing precious seconds. The first light of day was hazy at best, still pink and vague, and she was on the dark side of the hill, picking her way up by feeling with her hands and feet as much as with her eyes. Not a single man of all who passed her paused to help. So she knocked them aside whenever they got in her way.

The top of the crest was teasing her. It moved farther up with each inch she won with her toes and her fingernails. But no—here it was! She was up!

Her back wailed as she tried to straighten, and she staggered against a fallen tree.

The sun cracked between two distant hills and washed the gully with chalk yellow light. There was the bridge . . . a metal bridge covered now with soot and splattered with wreckage.

And the human wreckage . . . men dead and dying. Over a dozen of them, a litter of gore. Grace could too easily tell which had been killed by explosion and which by weapons more personal.

Her gaze stopped on a vague movement below. Two pastel forms huddled together, both moving.

She stood breathless at the top of the crest, unable to scream. From that vantage point she was forced to watch in utter shock as Wyatt Craig drew his pistol and shot her innocent brother through the heart.

"But she's not even ready! Monsieur, give me fifteen minutes!"

"She's ready enough. Evee, a cloak for her."

Dorian reached out for the hand of a bewildered harlot, a blond girl who looked used as a deck of saloon cards. Her features were small and spread out on a cakey palette of powder, and in fact most of her good points were painted on. She blinked and gaped in utter confusion when Evee led the mysterious gentleman back into the women's private parlor.

"But she's not dressed!" Evee complained, gesturing at the elaborate lace-and-bone corset and the ruffled chemise beneath it pushed up beneath her breasts. The nipples were hidden, but only just. "And she is light-haired!"

"Yes, I see."

Dorian led the girl by the hand to the center of the cluttered room, in full view of the other girls who were waiting to be called this evening, and turned her like a music-box doll.

"Lovely. Exquisite."

They all knew it was a lie. She wasn't exquisite; in fact, she was one of the plainest faces in the brothel.

She blushed, knowing the compliment was false and meant for another part of her body than her face.

Yes, they all knew it was a lie, except Dorian.

When he looked at her, he saw right through the makeup, through the plainness, to her quick green eyes. He saw the curve of her cheek and knew it could be nothing but feminine. He ran a finger along her upper arm and enjoyed the rise and dip of muscles barely strong enough to lift the heavy skirts a woman was made by fashion to wear these days. Yes, females should be weak and gentle, strong enough only to hold and nurture an infant. They should lift nothing heavier than a baby, ever, so these delicate fibrous muscles would never turn short and hard.

She knew her thighs were flabby, but to him they were abundant, generous. Her hair had been dyed too blond, but Dorian saw through to the color nature intended and saw that it would have been perfect for her cheeks, her eyes, her brows, even if it had been only brown. He had been raised among gentle, intelligent, unadorned women, and thus he could see through any adornment to the woman herself.

He loved the harlot because she actually blushed. There was no woman in the world about whom he couldn't find at least one aspect to love. That, perhaps, was the only thing he truly loved about himself, for there must be one thing good about the vilest of creatures, and even Shylock must have loved his mother.

His expression silenced every voice in the room, save his own.

"She is bewitching," he said, gazing only at this one girl. Evee draped a rather old-fashioned full-length mantle over her undressed form and slipped a rice-straw bonnet—which Dorian did not fail to notice, since he himself might damned well have flooded the rice—onto the blond wringlets.

"But her shoes—" Evee began, weakly this time.

"She has her slippers on," Dorian said. "My surrey is just at the curb."

He drew the perplexed harlot's hand to his chest and looped his arm over hers and led her toward the parlor archway, never taking his eyes from her eyes.

" 'Say, wilt thou go with me, sweet maid . . . say, maiden, wilt thou go with me, Through the valley-depths of shade, Of night and dark obscurity . . . Where the path has lost its way,

Where the sun forgets the day, Where there's nor light nor life to see . . . Sweet maiden, wilt thou go with me?' ''

Every woman in the whorehouse was sagging and breathless by the time the front door brushed closed, and dreaming dreams that had been long ago banged out of her.

He took her where no whore gets to go. Dinner in public.

Dorian loved doing this. He could order the finest fare and wine, and treat a disillusioned girl to a bit of the paper hammer, treat her as every woman should be treated for one day out of her life. Of particular enjoyment were those moments when some other gentleman strode through the restaurant and recognized whichever woman Dorian happened to be escorting that night, and for the rest of the evening said gentlemen's dinner was utterly wrecked, especially if he were in the company of his wife.

Sometimes there was the theater. Sometimes a concert, an opera, with a perplexed girl on his arm who couldn't figure out when the night's cunnycatching was going to get started. There had even been a few in the past whom Dorian had delivered home without ever having bedded, just to prove that men weren't all pecker and that there were other pleasures to be had in the company of a woman, even a loose woman.

Tonight, however, Dorian wanted his nag stabled. He lay upon the bed in one of Richmond's hotels—his choice was usually arbitrary—his hands cradling his head, while the blond harlot unbuttoned his trousers and slid them down his legs, letting her thumbnails dig into his thighs all the way down. His jacket was already off, thus he lay here on top of the coverlet in only his shirt and waistcoat. When the girl started to unbutton his shirt cuffs, he caught her hands and kissed them. The shirt would stay on, the sleeves down.

She hesitated a moment, bewilderment blanking her features, but then she went about her job. If he wanted his shirt on, the shirt stayed on.

She left the bed, went to a very fine lace-covered serving

table and selected a banana from the complimentary bowl of fruit the management had sent up.

Dorian smiled and wriggled deeper into the comforter. He put his hand behind his head again and said nothing. It was time for her poetry, not his.

She perched on a chair and slowly she peeled the banana with her teeth and began to lick it in long delayed swipes. Her tongue scraped along the pale yellow meat all the way to the tip—and she bit the tip off.

Dorian laughed, delighted.

The girl laughed too. The tip of the banana rolled across the inside of her open mouth. Together they delighted in the freedom of indecency. Shameless? Oh, yes. They wouldn't have allowed shame in the room. They each found great comfort in knowing what they were here for. Harlots were wonderful that way, a clear sense of purpose and gain.

Spicy. Dorian liked her. Her tongue—it was alive on its own! Every whore had her trick.

Damn, she was good at that.

He laughed again as the banana got smaller and smaller. He was already a scapegrace and had no obligation to behave otherwise, so he determined to enjoy his night. He was the freest of all men, free to be king or polecat as whim sent him, an *ame damnee* whom even God could hurt no more. So he did as he pleased. Tonight he pleased to backslide into debauchery. His vices and hers were good together. This whore was an honest woman, and she didn't care how polluted the night became. In a way Dorian was glad the dark-haired girl hadn't worked out. There was a certain lickerishness about this blond.

Ultimately she came to the bed, smelling of ripe fruit. She crawled on top of him, pressing her full breasts over his face. Dorian began his satyrous movements beneath her, only to find she was rather a rakehell herself. Being treated like a queen brought out the whore in her.

By the time he took his dive, he was on fire and deafened by the sounds of human breath, the carnal victory, and the utter manhood of getting a genuine reaction from a harlot. He pressed backward hard into the bed, his neck arching into the pillows, his arms flung flat at his sides, pressing the edges of the mattress down. His whisper rippled, a cloud blown across ever-moving water.

"Iphigenia . . ."

A thousand images filled his mind, and there she was over him, tending and washing him, holding his head to her breasts and murmuring that she loved him, yet never, never could he sleep in her arms, be comforted by her touch in the night, and in his despair he whispered her name again. The whore stretched him into oblivion with her hands and her thighs while he dreamed of Iphigenia, Iphigenia, Iphigenia. . . .

It wasn't red blood pouring from Patrick's body. It was death.

Fighting the bile that rose at the back of his tongue, Wyatt sat with Patrick until the sun touched them both on the shoulder. His men were calling for him. They had the Northern sympathizers lined up, the leaders at least, and they wanted a decision.

When Wyatt dragged himself to his feet, he saw with dismay that his uniform trousers were soaked with blood across the front of both thighs, and down the entire side of the left leg. Patrick's blood.

He stumbled across the battlefield. . . . God, was it really a battlefield now? For all time? Had this been his gift to history?

No. Not mine. I didn't arrange for this.

He yanked at his collar and let his tunic flop open. The fresh air felt suddenly cold against his sweaty shirt.

Around the other skirt of the hill, his company—those still alive—had corralled sixteen of the Union sympathizers, including the leader. Wyatt had to bottle his rage just to keep from spitting on the filthy line of prisoners.

"Here, Major," someone called.

He tramped over to Henry and the others.

"Who are these men?" he asked.

"Saviors!" Rodney Lasik shouted. "Of the great Union of states."

"I know," Wyatt drawled. "You just wait a minute. The rest of you. What've you got to say for yourselves?"

Another man, very tall but very repentant and in tears, pulled up his voice and said, "We implore you, sir."

"Let that man come forward."

They turned him loose, and the man came to him, squeezing his hat in both hands.

"Go ahead," Wyatt prodded.

"Please, sir," the man begged, "you can't put us all in jail, sir. . . . It's a war, sir, war. . . . We're doing what we figger right."

"Some of you are," Wyatt conceded. "Others of you are nothing but criminals."

"I know," the thin man murmured. "Some of us done wrong. Some of us ain't."

"Are you willing to tell me which done it and which ain't?"

"Don't know for sure most times. . . . We don't all know one another. Sir . . . all I beg is to tend our own wounded and bury our own dead. Even though they're Southerners, they ought to be buried like Americans, not secessionists. Please, Major . . . I'm begging."

Weakness piled in as Wyatt felt his soul go out to the man and the others in the line. Perhaps they had been misled by this animal Lasik—just as John Brown and all those who followed in his footsteps had whooped men up to follow them. Such things could happen—good men convinced to commit atrocities once somebody had painted an enemy on their eyeballs. Out here in the open, there was no way to determine which of these people were honest Unionists and which were just taking advantage of anarchy. There was a terrible blur across men's motivations today, and Wyatt didn't want to judge them all with one swipe of his opinion.

Could he blame them for this one request? To be buried like Americans, not secessionists . . . with a eulogy that spoke of the unity of states and not the division of them?

He couldn't blame them. They would bury Patrick and the others under their chosen flag.

"Yes," he said. His lips were dry and now cracked painfully. Just to satisfy a theory, he looked carefully among them for the familiar face of Brad Lassick, but there was no familiar face here at all, so he must be wrong—or right the first time, about the coincidence of names.

"Yes, all right . . . if you men promise to return to your homes, consider yourselves on parole, and give the governments a chance to work this out."

The tall man's thin head bobbed. "Yes, sir, I'll pass the word. And thank you, Major. You're a decent man, a right decent man."

"Sergeant Brecker, turn all these men loose except for the leader."

His men reluctantly stepped back and lowered their guns. There was a distinct disappointment on their faces that made Wyatt cringe.

The prisoners, rather sullen and broken-spirited, shifted to one side. Some of them began picking through the bodies. Others dawdled to see what would happen to their leader.

Wyatt limped over to where three men were holding the clean-shaven man. Lasik's top hat was still on. It seemed ludicrous at the moment.

"You're Rodney Lasik," Wyatt said.

"I am General Rodney Joseph Lasik, sir."

"Are you an officer in the Union Army, Mr. Lasik?"

"I am not, sir, nor are we any of us."

"Then what is your authorization?"

"Divine intervention. To hinder, annoy, and by any means prevent the advancement of the Confederacy, which seeks to sunder our glorious nation."

Those words sounded very strange coming from a thick Tennessee accent, and Wyatt was struck with the irony. Here he was, a Northerner fighting for Southern independence, face-to-face with a Southerner who wanted the Union preserved at all costs.

It was the costs that were the problem. And perceptions of the reasons. And the definition of who was a fair target and who was a victim.

Wyatt found little charity in himself this morning.

"Do these means include the sacking of families, rape of women, and arbitrary murder of innocent men? And"—Tight-throated, he waved back to the field, to Patrick—"hostages? Because that's what you've been doing." He barely got the sentence out. Tears pushed at his eyes and made them ache. Somehow he beat the moisture back, but at great costs.

Rodney Lasik was unimpressed. He simply said, "We strike as necessary."

Wyatt stood there, timeless as a rock, and felt as cold as one. All his life circumstance had moved him. It's what had sent him to Kansas, and what had brought him to Richmond, and what had brought him here. The tannery, the powder mill, each man with a duty, and at the top a commander, an average man who just wanted to be nice to people. He was born out of place somehow, mistakenly born to his rich father instead of some worldly lad who would have done better with a noble birth, college, and a chance to run businesses.

He always had command. He'd inherited it. But until now he had never taken it.

Today, for the first time, he *wanted* it.

The woven gold loops on his sleeve whispered to him.

Patrick's body exploded over and over in his mind. War. This would be war. War, in which things were different. In which rules of morality were replaced by rules of necessity.

So be it, then.

Every breath he took sounded like wind in a cave.

"I'm authorized," he began hoarsely, "by the secretary of war of the Confederate . . . well, never mind that. Morality itself demands that I take action. Mr. Lasik, do you formally admit to being the leader of these . . . fellows over here?"

Lasik raised his chin. "I do."

Wyatt waited a moment for something else, but that was all the man said. Sand and blood grated between his fingers. Evidently this Lasik, not so unlike the other Lassick, thought the world owed him some fame or credit or martyrdom or something. It showed in his eyes. If nothing else, there was utter lack of remorse.

The thread was tenuous—make a martyr and give credential to a cause, or let him live and steal credit from one's own.

After waiting what he thought was a fair amount of time, Wyatt heaved a great sigh and uttered, "Well, okay. If that's all you've got to say for yourself."

He turned and squinted through the haze.

"Sergeant Brecker."

"Right here, Major."

"I don't see that we have any choice," Wyatt said, slowly and deliberately. He looked squarely at Lasik and said, "Henry . . . hang this man."

Astonishment paled every face within earshot. Most significant of all was Rodney Lasik's face as the smugness cracked and fell away.

Thus the first truly independent, unplanned, unmapped action of Wyatt's life was to end the life of a man he didn't even know, by way of a rope.

★

CHAPTER FORTY-TWO

———— ★ ————

Jackson Ward district. West Leigh between Brook and Goshen. Wyatt walked it three times before finding the right doorway.

This end of Leigh Street was an embarrassment to the other end, where dignified houses remained well tended. Here most were rented or owned by freed slaves. Few of the houses had been painted since they were erected, back in the forties. All were very small and packed together like fishing shacks.

A few blocks away the negroes had built an African Baptist church to serve their neighborhood. At least these displaced people had some congregational comfort for themselves. Of course, there was nothing here for the Ruhls but walls to rent. No matter how the negroes talked of being free and joining society, they too preferred their own color of face around them.

Pat Ruhl's house was pitifully small. Two rooms bottom, one top, built some thirty years ago and virtually ignored since then. It looked very temporary. Probably had been rented most of the time, abandoned the rest of the time, or lived in by mulattoes, who often weren't even accepted among blacks. No decoration, not even a shutter. Only a little A-roofed porch over the door.

Wyatt squirmed at the idea of trying to be comfortable in such a place. At least the unglamorous shanties in Kansas had been reasonably maintained.

He stepped up onto the porch. The narrow, warped door hung open before him. He raised his hand to knock, but then—

He saw her.

She was sitting on the other side of the small room, with her back to the door, alone in the little shack she had shared with Patrick. As Wyatt peeked in, the tiny rooms seemed as rambling as his big empty house.

"Miss Ruhl?"

His voice, as quiet as he could make it, pounded along the walls.

She never moved. Backlit by a single miserable candle, her seated form had very little substance. Her hair hung in long, twisted ropes down her back, without even a net.

He saw instantly that someone had already told her. Damn that.

Had they been gentle?

This is what funerals are for, Wyatt thought, suddenly helpless. *To fill a house when it's at its emptiest.*

And I left him back there. . . . She doesn't even have a body to bury. God, why did I do that?

He didn't go over the threshhold but just stood outside the open doorway on the porch, rubbing his sore knuckles. It wouldn't be kind at all to expose her to the blood on his trousers and the powder stains on his tunic. Especially not the blood.

"I see you've been told," he said softly. "I'm sorry I didn't arrive earlier. . . . It was my responsibility to tell you. Patrick died honorably. . . quickly."

The lie almost choked him. What else could he say?

Your brother was boiling in agony, disemboweled by a saber, and I had to shoot him to get him to go ahead and die.

Sure, be a good boy. Tell her the truth.

Bile rose in his throat. The lie swam around in it.

"I was there with him," he said. "He never knew what happened. I should've . . . brought him home to you. I wasn't thinking. They begged me to let them bury their own dead. . . . I should've been thinking of you, but all I saw was those defeated, misled people. Is there anything I can do to ease your burden? I'll help you in any way in my power.''

Not even her hair moved. He thought he could see her breathing, but he wasn't even sure of that. She might as well have been another corpse.

"You just say the word," he told her, "and I'll find him somehow and bring him back for a proper funeral. I'll pay for everything, of course.''

There wasn't much else to say, so he waited.

Beneath him the porch moaned and creaked with his weight. He held still just to get it to stop. He waited.

Liz Ruhl's whisper was faint as cobwebs forming. But he would have heard it over an ocean's roar.

"Go away.''

The 1809 manor glowered over Governor Street with its brick fence and gateposts surrounding it like a dust ruffle. It rose between two other houses of the same period, their third stories towering in stately gloom out of the darkness. Their deeply carved front doors, all wide enough to accommodate one or more hoop skirts at a time, were just out of reach of the eerie gaslights that lined the curb every thirty feet or so. The marble steps leading to these front doors, however, basked in the yellow glow and reached almost all the way out to the hitching posts at the street's edge. There was no lawn. Only oval brick planters with tiny orange trees set in them.

The mansion's brickwork was the stylish and popular Flemish bond, laid three rows of headers to one row of stretchers—very expensive and adding a look of texture—and the mortar had been colored to match the brick. That was a long time ago, and some of the mortar had discolored, but that only provided a richer, more settled appearance than any new house could have boasted. The upper windows were framed with carved marble and curtained with lace, which in the dark gave the appearance of two dozen lidded eyes with pale lashes.

Every time Wyatt saw it, he missed his little cabin in Kansas.

It was a nice house, but a mighty sizable place for a man to live all by himself. He wasn't even here most of the time. The house was more home to the half-dozen black servants than it was to him.

It provided the coldest comfort as he trudged down the street, exhausted.

There was little traffic at this hour of the evening. Only a few buggies making their way back from the center of town, and one young man wearing a bowler and tailcoat escorting his lady. They were civilized, too civilized for him to comprehend after what he had seen and done today.

They nodded a greeting. Wyatt was glad it was dark.

He'd succeeded. He'd won the skirmish. Most of the shipment had gone through. The leader of the Heroes was dead, as criminals ought best be.

On his hands and his uniform, the blood of Patrick Ruhl burned through to his own blood. He felt little more than a shred of himself.

He wanted to die back there on that road rather than leave the scene he left. Rodney Lasik's body hanging like a bag of sand, his head men in the Richmond city jail where Wyatt had deposited them, the defeated others moving out of hiding to collect the bodies of the fallen Union sympathizers. And Patrick's body one of them.

How he'd wanted to bring Patrick back with him... to make sure the burial was decent and not a roadside indignity. But the Unionists had asked. Begged. Begged to bury their own. Patrick had made his choice.

"He never felt a thing."

Had she believed him? Wyatt knew he was a bad liar. Better lie than tell her what really happened. His last memory of Pat would always be that final wince as the pistol ball plunged through the young man's thorax just over the gouge left by that saber, and the sudden collapse, the awful limpness, the open eyes. Could he let that be her last memory?

"Your brother asked me to kill him. He begged me. This

*blood all over my trousers is his blood. You'd have done it
too."*

And for the rest of his life, his arm would tingle when
he thought of Patrick, it would twinge with the feeling
of that pistol ball blasting through Patrick's body and
sending vibrations up through the spine and into Wyatt's
own bones.

"I couldn't tell her that," he mumbled, forcing his feet to
move him one more step forward, then one more.

The scene hadn't been one of victory, but that's what the
powder mill's brigade declared as they moved on with their
rescued delivery. He would have to talk to them about that
later.

You'd have done it too ...

As he raised his head, his neck sent a spasm down his back
that made him pause in midstep. The front of his house
caught his attention.

The lamps were on in the drawing room.

It was the one main-floor room he never used. Why were
the lights on?

And there were two coaches at the curb. He'd noticed
them before but dismissed it as someone visiting the minister who lived next door. One was single-horse enclosed
rig with a fringed top, the other a larger coach with two
horses.

As Wyatt stepped up onto the curb in front of his house,
he nodded at the two drivers, who had been given cups
of coffee, and they nodded proper greetings back and tipped
their hats.

" 'Evening, sir."

"A pleasant evening, sir."

"Good evening," Wyatt muttered back, wishing he had a
hat to tip.

They watched him climb the marble steps. He glanced back
self-consciously, but the answers to his curiosity were inside,
not outside.

Somebody was visiting him.

And he wasn't even home.

The thick aroma of cigars and the scent of fresh coffee
embraced him as he pushed the heavy oak door open. Before

him the long carpeted stair hall glittered with impressions from the crystals in three gaslit chandeliers that hung from the high corniced ceiling. He always felt as if he were visiting a fine hotel.

Edmund, the butler, failed to meet him at the main entrance, which told Wyatt that the servants were indeed busy in the kitchen. From this angle he could see through the dim music room, lit only by two candles in a sconce, and into the drawing room. His gaze was pulled along by the dark oxblood walls with their shimmering pattern of gilded stenciling and the thick molded plaster archways over both entrances.

The cut-glass double doors to the drawing room were open, and there was indeed gaslight shining on all that fine furniture he never used. He heard voices. From where he stood, he could see the edge of the tea cart.

The black Oriental-patterned carpet cushioned his steps more than he wanted—he really didn't prefer to slip in on anyone dressed as bait for a cockfight. The image prompted him to glance down to make sure there was no blood on his shoes to stain the fibers.

The music room, lit only by two candles in a sconce, was a comfortless cloak. In the dimness he paused for a thoughtless moment—it felt so good to be no one and nothing for that moment. Beside him the harp he couldn't play and the spinet he also had never touched gleamed together in a chorus of candlelight.

He pushed himself forward, then stopped again. The sweet smell of biscuits and cakes struck him and turned his stomach. Somehow he kept from vomiting.

Three men were enjoying the warmth of the fire in the drawing room, two strangers sharing the extralong tapestried sofa. They were very well turned out, one in black with a shiny silk-embroidered red vest, the other in blue and tan; one about sixty, the other younger. The older visitor had a huge beard with streaks of gray—or was it gray with streaks of black?—and the younger man had reddish mutton chops framing his face, a wide waxed blond mustache, and a long pointed goatee.

The third man, sitting cross-legged in one of the room's six rosewood chairs, was Dorian.

Wyatt tried to figure out some way to avoid shocking them with his appearance. Short of dashing upstairs to change clothes, which he was too tired to do anyway, he figured they'd have to deal with him as he was. He wasn't feeling all that generous toward people who sat in comfort.

"Upon word!" the younger man blurted, his pointy beard bobbing as he spoke, and twisted about.

So Wyatt had been noticed.

Dorian and the older man looked, both gasped, and Dorian's face took on an astonishing pain as he jumped to his feet.

"Oh, no . . ." he said with a profound hush. Stunned, he stared up and down at the blood all over the wraith who this morning had been a tidy officer. "Oh, no, no," he repeated, hurrying over to Wyatt. "Oh . . . oh, my God . . ." Dorian gasped, holding his hands pointlessly between them as though he didn't know which part of Wyatt *wasn't* injured.

Wyatt held up his own hand. "I'm all right." He looked past at the two other men, who were standing now.

Dorian either didn't hear it or didn't believe it. He seized Wyatt by one arm and a lapel, a pretty good grip for a man who didn't want to be touched.

"Are you all right?" he rasped.

"I'm fine. What's all this?"

"Are you sure? You're all—"

Wyatt paused. Trying not to betray Patrick's memory by explaining that it wasn't his own blood all over the uniform, he melted at seeing that he'd given Dorian a fright. He offered him a moment's attention.

"Oh, I'm sorry. . . . I'm all right. Alive and well."

He patted Dorian's shoulder to comfort him—wasn't it supposed to be the other way around?—then realized his raw voice wasn't very convincing.

"And limping," Dorian choked. "Do you realize you're limping?"

"Uh . . . no, I hadn't. But thanks."

"Look at you!"

"I'm right dismal, aren't I?"

"Ambush?"

"Yes. And no dozen men, either. There were over sixty of them."

Dorian paled, the cameo blush dropping away so suddenly that it shocked Wyatt as much as he had shocked Dorian with his own appearance. The change held his attention for a moment.

"Sixty," Dorian breathed huskily. "Damn me . . . I had no idea!"

"I know you didn't. You wouldn't have let us go if you'd known. Gentlemen? I'm Wyatt Craig. May I help you in some way?"

He tried to step forward, but Dorian was pulling at him.

"The shipment?"

"Most of it got through. We had to sacrifice the decoy wagon. Gentlemen?"

Still trying to get over their astonishment at his appearance, the two men forced themselves to nod politely toward him.

"Good evening, Mr. Craig," the young man managed.

"Your servant, Major," the striped beard said at the same time. "We've come at an inconvenient time . . . Were you set upon, sir?"

"And by whom, sir?"

From the double doors Dorian recovered and hurried between them.

"Gentlemen, please! Please. Allow me. Major Craig, may I present before you Colonel James de Orsay," he said, gesturing to the big bicolored beard. "Colonel de Orsay is emissary from Mr. Jefferson Davis—"

"President of the Confederate States of America," de Orsay added with a very proper Southern bow, and in a very strong Georgia drawl.

Wyatt glanced at Dorian with a *really?* look.

By way of answering him, Dorian took his elbow and turned him toward the younger beard.

"And this is Mr. Robert Putnam—"

Wyatt reached out for the man's hand.

"—special personal attaché from President Abraham Lincoln."

The younger man smiled from under the extremely large waxed mustache, seeming to enjoy Wyatt's expression.

President? *Presidents?*

Did they intend to dash here and there apologizing for every skirmish?

Wyatt's mouth dangled open until the two men were both smiling at him.

"You're . . . ," he bumbled, "from Abraham Lincoln. . . ."

"That is correct, sir."

"And you're . . ."

"From President Jefferson Davis. You are correct again, sir."

"Well . . . that's, uh . . . would you . . . like to sit down?"

"Perhaps we all should, Major," de Orsay recommended.

Hardly feeling the part of host, Wyatt managed to struggle through gestures that got the two guests sitting while he remained standing long enough to unbutton his blood-caked tunic.

"Pardon me," he said uncomfortably.

When Dorian stepped in and eased the tunic from his aching arms, Wyatt gave him a grateful nod and then made the ultimate commitment of sitting down. His entire body seemed to suddenly collapse with exhaustion as his back relaxed for the first time all day. Perhaps the discomfort surfaced on his face for a moment. The guests glanced at each other. They felt uneasy too.

And Dorian was also watching him while pouring a fourth cup of tea.

Wyatt waved toward the tea cart's load of cakes, short-breads, and biscuits. "Gentlemen, is there anything more I might provide for you?"

"Poison and a moment alone," Dorian cracked as he joined them again.

Wyatt paused, but both emissaries chuckled and rolled their eyes.

The florid aroma of Chinese tea tickled his nostrils.

"Drink," Dorian said from beside him.

Wyatt took a gulp, then looked at the two men.

"Go ahead," he gurgled. His stomach slithered within him. Wisely he pushed the tea away.

"Major, your slaves have provided us the finest fare," de Orsay said politely. "You have a family of them tending this house, is that a good guess?"

"Yes," Wyatt said, pretty sure these important men hadn't come here to talk about his servants. "The father is our butler and his family tends the house. . . ."

"We were ushered in by a boy of about twelve. He is most remarkably polite. I would guess he is in training as a man servant?"

"Well . . . yes, he takes care of me, and . . . why do you ask, Colonel Dorsey?"

"De Orsay," Dorian corrected.

"Oh, sorry, sorry . . . Colonel de Orsay."

De Orsay never cast so much as a glance at Putnam but smiled tightly behind the big beard. "Perhaps you would allow me to purchase him on behalf of President Davis. We are currently staffing the president's household, and such a polite young negro would be a pleasantry about the household."

Nearby Robert Putnam also grinned, but in a manner that said he knew he was being deliberately offended.

Seeing that, Wyatt leaned forward and clasped his skinned hands between his knees.

"I'll tell him you were impressed," he said to de Orsay, "but I don't break up families."

"Very good for you, Mr. Craig," Putnam interrupted, raising his teacup to Wyatt before sipping.

"Yes," de Orsay quickly said. "Families do tend to be more efficient as a unit. No harm asking, eh?"

"Suppose not," Wyatt murmured. "Is it a coincidence that you're both here at the same time, gentlemen?" He switched his gaze to Dorian and added, "Or have I been steered into place?"

Sobriety popped up on Dorian's face. His head moved a fraction from side to side, and he turned his hands outward for an instant. No, he hadn't engineered this.

So the mystery was still to be dug up.

"Point of fact, Major," de Orsay said, "I knew that Mr. Putnam was intending to approach you today."

Wyatt looked at Putnam for corroboration.

"Neither of us wanted the other to get you alone," Lincoln's attaché admitted, and Wyatt suddenly liked him for his shrug of honesty.

"All right," he said. "So it's no coincidence. Gentlemen, I'm not in any condition to entertain—" Wyatt shook his head again to get the weeds out and wagged a hand toward the blond diplomat. "Mr. . . ."

Once again Dorian was supplied the appropriate embarrassment. "Putnam. You're Craig. This is Richmond."

"Putnam. Sorry."

Putnam offered a forgiving grin. "I'm here on President Lincoln's behalf, sir, to beg you not to supply the Confederacy with powder of grades that will be used for rifles and canister shot."

"Yes," de Orsay scowled, "the North wishes to be the only contestant with weapons that work. Any Northerner would consider that a fair fight."

Then he too raised his teacup. Touché. Any minute they'd start comparing beards, Wyatt surmised.

"Our goal has never been to fight, Colonel," Putnam told him calmly. "Rather we hoped the opposite." He turned back to Wyatt then and said, "The president believes there are other solutions than war. The unity of the nation must go beyond regional disagreements. This wound can be mended if we can somehow keep it from breaking open in the next few months. You're a Northerner, Mr. Craig. You'll be killing men you have been neighbors with, all in the name of keeping a sector of society in chains."

"You think," Wyatt began, "that this whole conflict is about slavery? Don't you read the newspapers, Mr. Putnam?"

Putnam straightened his spine and said, "Oh, no, I wouldn't offend you by simplifying things. But slavery is the flag both sides wave. If the South has men such as you, a born-and-bred Northerner, supplying its powder willingly, wearing its uniform . . . why, that's a flag right there. If one Northern businessman can 'understand,' then why can't all? You're a prominent figure, sir. The South will murder men in your name.''

"That's uncalled for, Mr. Putnam," Dorian interrupted sharply. Deliberately he came to sit in the chair next to Wyatt's. His presence was ominous. "Insulting my associate will not win the war for the North."

Putnam paused, then inched forward in his seat and began again. "Forgive me. But I promised to be quick, and that means I must be blunt. Mr. Craig, President Lincoln has sent me here with a specific request."

"And that is?"

"He requests that you shut down your operation."

"Indeed," de Orsay grumbled.

"For the duration of the conflict," Putnam went on. "He offers you and all your men compensation for your losses, plus a generous subsidy for your patriotism. You won't lose a dime. In fact, you'll gain while also serving the nation."

"Lincoln's offering to keep you, Major," de Orsay added, "like a woman."

Annoyed, Putnam said, "Colonel, it's the Southern states insisting on this violence, not the North. I'm here to build a bridge to peace, a firm representative government, and freedom for everybody in America. Pray tell us what are you here for?"

"Very simple," de Orsay answered. "Major Craig, the South has its difficulties ahead, as we all know. All we request are balanced circumstances. Fairness, if you will. It would be shame indeed if the war were won based upon how much or how little one side may possess—men, arms, factories . . ."

"Ah, factories," Putnam echoed.

"Of late we've had many Northern-run businesses shut down or move back, without even giving the South so much as a chance. I am here—"

"To make sure I don't go home," Wyatt filled in. "Make sure I don't go make powder for President Lincoln?"

"Precisely."

"Do you want to prolong the conflict, Mr. Craig?" Putnam interrupted.

Both Wyatt and the other emissary were cut silent by his tone. Now he was committed to say his piece.

Putnam might have been younger, perhaps less experienced, but he carried that gumption that only inexperience can give a smart man.

And he was smart. He knew just when to change his tone.

"Sir," he said firmly, "President Lincoln will do what he has to do. He wants no war. He's said it over and over, but the South won't listen. There is no secession. The Southern states, all of them, are still part of the nation. Part of the United States. There will be no sovereign South. If the states will rescind their secessions, those acts will be forgotten completely, without malice or punishment."

"Without shame?" de Orsay interrupted.

"The shame is your own fault, sir," Putnam said to him. Then he looked straight at Wyatt. "And if we must threaten, then we'll threaten. But please . . . I didn't come here to threaten you. Only to offer and to advise. A man who supplies the enemy of his nation's leaders is guilty of treason, and that will be you. I can't . . . actually, I wouldn't even choose, to change the definition. Many people underestimate Mr. Lincoln. The whole South does. It's a fatal mistake. Wouldn't we be better off if community and business leaders such as yourself present an example? Don't fuel skirmishes with your powder. Take those uniforms off your workers."

The blond man's young eyes grew narrow, and he bent forward from the waist just enough to make Wyatt's stomach reel with chilly anticipation.

"You're going to make the conflict longer, Mr. Craig. When it's long and painful and wrecks this nation, you'll remember this evening. The night the president reached out to you for help."

A strong hollowness rung after his voice that nobody dared to fill. He didn't look away. He glared right into Wyatt's eyes and demanded to be clearly understood.

Wyatt felt the pangs of doubt rising in his chest, but another pain swept over the pangs and carried them back, away. Had he been confronted by such an influence a week ago . . .

He might have understood, he might have paused.

Today was different.

He too pressed forward against his own vacillation.

"You're telling me to protect my skin and line my pockets by helping the North," he said. "The States will be forced to give in and surrender their rights to a central government, and we'll be on our way to the same thing we fought the Revolutionary War to get out of. For money and protection, all we have to do is surrender our freedom, right?"

"Really, Mr. Craig," Putnam said firmly, "that's quite contrary, and you know it."

"It's not contrary, Mr. Putnam. You're going to free the slaves from us evil slaveowners and let them starve in your slums up North. Isn't that right? Yes it is. I've seen those slums with my own eyes. My God, I wouldn't leave a rat to live in those conditions. I had slaves in Kansas, and I have them now. They all eat, have homes, and the care of a doctor that I pay for. I don't see much good in what the Union is demanding. Just as women are smaller than men and have to be protected, negroes are brutish and need to be cared for. The white man was never supposed to be in Africa, and the negroes aren't supposed to be here. Yes, I'm a Northerner. And I don't recall a single man around me volunteering to take in freed slaves and train them and pay them for their work—including myself! I never offered either. I never had a slave until I went to Kansas and took over my father's operation there and looked into the faces of those black families. Know what I saw? They were terrified the owner's Northern-reared son would put them out on their own. The North talks a great sermon, but after the freeing you pat yourselves for your principles, then turn your backs on the people you've just condemned. You know what a freed negro is? He's helpless, that's what. Negroes depend on white men. We made them dependent on us, and they can't live on their own. I'd no more cast a slave into the outside world with no way to feed his family than I'd turn my dog out onto that city street and say, 'Go! Be free!' "

"Wyatt," Dorian warned quietly.

"You want to do the talking for me this time too?" Wyatt shot at him bitterly, forcing silence.

Any chance for civility instantly fled.

It was the young man, Putnam, who finally shoved silence aside.

"Mr. Craig, I hope you understand something very important. When order is restored, sir, and it will be," he said firmly, "you may be charged with treason."

Wyatt bristled.

He'd had enough. Enough for one day, enough for a lifetime. Staring into Putnam's face, principles and morals he'd been grueling over his whole life suddenly crystallized. The smell of Patrick's crusted blood on his trousers and mud and manure on his shoes nearly made him throw up. His brows drew together, and he leaned forward.

"Did President Lincoln sign that threat, Mr. Putnam?"

Putnam stood his ground and waited a perfect five seconds, without giving in with so much as a hint of regret. They could nearly see the clock tick in his mind, in his eyes.

"The North wants to talk, Mr. Craig. Not fight."

Wyatt felt something snap inside his head, his chest. He shocked them all—he could tell by their faces—with an uncharacteristic shout. "Damn you, sir, you're a liar! Do you hear yourself?"

On aching legs he rose and towered over the tea cart, his guests, and Dorian as they sat looking up at him, all tense.

"The North doesn't want to talk! All you want to do is incense people about this slavery issue so they'll do your dirty work for you! Slavery's just a symptom of the days when people like you got to control people like us, and now we're stuck with it. The Federal government's nose in the business of individuals is just another kind of slavery. It's been the scourge of mankind just about since history started, and now you threaten me?" Exasperated, he shook his head and gasped, "When you can't convince somebody with facts and sincerity and honor, the only thing left to do is threaten! Judas priest! Threats are . . . they're—"

"The last refuge of a tyrant," Dorian supplied dryly.

"Yes! Yes!" Wyatt pointed at him as though the words

were still floating in the air. "Yes. My God! We've only had freedom for a couple of generations, and I don't have to be a Southerner to tell you we're not going back the way it was! Damn you, can't you see that? You go home and tell Mr. Lincoln that I'm not shutting down my factory. In fact, I'm starting a second shift! We're not putting up with people like you who want to 'preserve the Union' at the cost of what it stands for!"

His self-satisfaction, like everything else today, was brief, and when it slid off, he found himself emptier than before.

The pause cracked when de Orsay raised his teacup and murmured, "Hear, hear," and took a sip.

Upon which he nearly choked when Wyatt rounded on him.

"What do you mean, 'hear, hear,' Mr. de Orsay? Hear, hear, what? Hear, hear, we get to have a war? You're looking mighty smug at my expense. Don't go back to President Davis and tell him Wyatt Craig likes the way the Confederacy's going. I don't. Southerners are a little too happy about going to war, and if that alone doesn't scare you, you're crazy. I had to kill a dozen men today. And a dozen of my own were killed or injured. This is real pistol powder on my hand and real blood. You go back to Mr. Davis, and you tell him to get used to the look of it. Because you've started something ugly."

He heard his voice turn bitter—with that edge that told him he was about to start shouting again.

The pity on their faces was infuriating.

Instead of losing control he said, "Excuse me," and swung off toward the fireplace, busying himself with rolling his sleeves up from his sweating wrists.

Dorian stood up and gestured toward the drawing room's glass doors. "Gentlemen, if you'll pardon us."

"Yes," Putnam said. "Of course. Thank you for your hospitality, Mr. Trozen . . . Mr. Craig."

"The Confederacy considers you an example, Major," de Orsay added. "May we meet again on a day of peace."

Wyatt forced himself to turn around and crank out one

flimsy gesture other than kicking the nearest chair. "I hope so."

The three men started out of the room.

At the edge of the drawing-room carpet, the bruised Robert Putnam turned one more time. His face looked like an inverted candle.

"The president's best wishes, Mr. Craig. We only beg this of you . . . don't help the nation rip itself apart."

The dart hit its mark.

Wyatt felt himself turn to mush. There was a terrible element of truth in those words. Putnam was sincere after all, and Wyatt knew what kind of business he was running.

"Gentlemen," Dorian insisted. He waved them out the doors first, then cast a smirk back to Wyatt. It was impossible to tell if he was concerned or amused.

Amused, probably. Dorian didn't give enough of a damn about anything to care about the implications of one tirade.

Wyatt stood alone in the warm drawing room, his own words booming in his ears. God, the thunder of it! The young nation's shortsights were coming back to plague it, to plow its insights under the dirt. His great-grandfather had remembered the Revolutionary War, had described it to his little great-grandson in minute and stirring detail, and like a dutiful child Wyatt had never forgotten. All that hard work, hard thinking, insistence upon knowing what kind of nation those men wanted the United States to grow into someday. A whole new kind of nation, such as had never been seen before on earth. His relatives on both sides had fought for the autonomy of thirteen little states, and he was going to be in the war that ripped it all apart.

He felt like a bone being chewed at both ends. He was a product of the industrialization of the North and beneficiary of the needs of the South, yet right now he'd happily head west and not come back till it was all over.

Exhausted, aching to the last muscle, hungry and disheartened, he dragged himself to the sofa and collapsed lengthwise onto the firm tapestry. One arm flopped over his eyes.

The creak of the big front door could be heard through the entire front of the house. A few seconds later the two visitors' coaches clattered past the window behind him. He wondered if the two men were looking into the drawing room through the lace curtains to see if they could spot him one more time, to see if he was laughing, weeping, smoking, or what.

"Interesting little proposals," Dorian was saying as he reentered the drawing room. Yes, there was definitely amusement in his voice.

Wyatt didn't remove his arm from his eyes. He didn't want to move at all.

"Politics must be excruciatingly fun," Dorian went on distractedly. "Imagine it! Wholesome you being so important that both presidents—"

He stopped, paused. Apparently he'd noticed Wyatt sprawled out there like a corpse on the sofa.

His footsteps made soft brushing sounds on the carpet.

"Wyatt?"

With a heavy sigh Wyatt rolled his arm upward just enough to look up and get it across that he hadn't died or passed out or killed himself.

"How'd I get into this?" he grumbled.

At the steadiness of Wyatt's voice, Dorian sighed with relief. He gazed down, and when he answered, the acidic tone gave no quarter to either of them.

"Easily." He held up his right arm as though waving good-bye and said, "You shook this hand."

Two shapes moved together, silhouetted by gaslights on the alley wall. The message had been sent, and now it had been received.

The two couldn't have been less alike, yet there was a certain gritty undercurrent they shared.

Grace felt the current run, and in her fury and grief, she was comforted by it.

"On one condition," she said. "Do it in public, where everyone can see. There should be witnesses. Lots of them. Enough to ruin the reputation of a whole business. And a business owner. Do you understand what I am describing?"

Chewing on a twig, Orville Quist nodded at the sober young woman and didn't even attempt to deduce her motivations as long as they suited him.

He nodded.

"I got it."

Without the slightest courtesy, he walked away.

Grace didn't mind. A time for vengeance wasn't a time for courtesy.

★

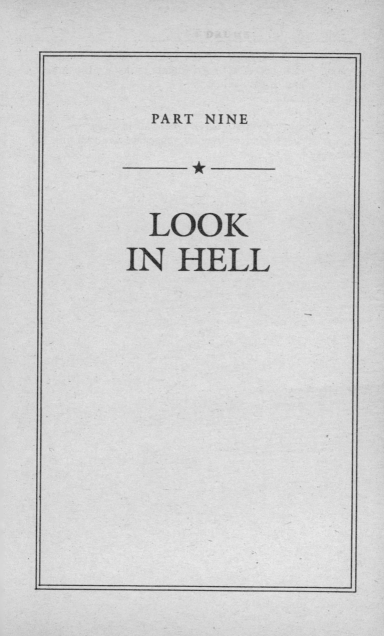

PART NINE

★

LOOK
IN HELL

CHAPTER FORTY-THREE

——————— ★ ———————

Candlelight made chevrons on the dark walls.

Slumped all the way down in his chair, Wyatt saw his body sprawled out before him, little more than a road with weeds and four miserable paths branching from it. His knees were two cliffs that dropped off to nothing. His chest was a hole with wind going through it. Just a cave. His eyes were holes. His heart was a hole.

Lost thoughts piled in and out of his mind. Around him men talked, laughed, and drank. Some tavern Dorian had pushed him to. Not too far from home. He hadn't even bothered to change out of his filthy tunic. The large taproom on the ground floor was crowded and smoke filled, and carried an ambience of the masculine. The owner obviously had a taste for Canadian artifacts, so the walls were cluttered with Indian blankets, belts and buckles, big ungainly saddles, cowboy hats, mining lanterns, fish baskets, canoe paddles, even a few ratty rabbit skins, all of which gave the city-bound patrons a woodsy Adirondack respite. The menu was designed around this theme—tourtière pies, game sausage, Cumberland sauce for the meat, which they claimed was venison, and a mix of nuts and raisins, complimentary on every table in baskets made of dried grass. The atmosphere was different, and that was something, at least.

Except for the customers it resembled nothing like Richmond, and for that Wyatt was grateful.

There were some dignitaries here, some businessmen, travelers, dressed in sharply lined coats, some crisp frock coats, others in the more old-fashioned tailcoats that might have come out of the twenties. Everyone except Wyatt wore a tie or neckcloth beneath his chin. One man who stepped by wore the pointed-waist vest Wyatt remembered from his boyhood. The nostalgia was comforting, but brief.

Comforting, except that the patrons kept glancing through the ghastly candlelight at Wyatt's uniform. Many had not yet seen a Confederate uniform. Some even commented on it, failing to take his disposition as a moat.

The gray tunic, with its Austrian knots and blue cuffs, hung open. He gave it no favor of dignity, but slouched at the corner table like a common worker, with his elbow on the table and his knees apart. The only light in the taproom came from candles set in Indian pottery on the tables and a row of iron sconces on the long wall opposite the bar. Darkness and light stippled the patrons as they moved about beneath the low ceiling.

Voices boomed in his ears, but he didn't listen. There was no identity for him here, no commitment to be polite or to bow or tip a hat. He should mail the commission back to the governor after wiping the blood off his hands with it.

All he wanted to do was his job. Run a factory. Contribute to the human advancements he'd seen happening around him since childhood. The marvelous new machines . . . making things for people to use to improve their lives, making the things faster and cheaper, things everyone could own. He'd seen the improvements coming for so long, like horses twitching before a race—

To grind to a halt today.

If he didn't go home, didn't go to bed, perhaps he could somehow keep the morning from making today part of an indelible past.

Not really the governor's fault . . . it was his job to make officers out of anyone who could outfit a company . . . wasn't easy to start a country.

He heard voices all around him. None was Dorian's.

When that realization trickled through, Wyatt looked across the table.

Swathed in the shadows that loved him, one hand cupped around a mug of hot rum and the other resting upon the T-handle of his walking stick, Dorian sat on the other side of the small table and gazed at Wyatt, his back against the dark stucco wall. He said not a word. Steam from the hot punch scythed his face and confused the candles.

Wyatt wouldn't have bet on that, the gift of silence.

Several seconds passed with the two of them just locking eyes, almost a contest of tensions and dares.

Then Dorian raised one brow. Those black eyes—pupils dilated in the dimness until they looked even blacker than usual—they cut deep and looked inside.

"Has it hatched yet?" he asked.

Wyatt blinked and swallowed. His mouth and throat were dry.

"Pardon me?" he managed.

"Has it hatched? The *cri du coeur* you've brooded all evening. I thought it would unfreight you to come out and get shellacked, but you've hardly put down half of the old molasses and sugar cane, and your mug's needed warming three times. Would you prefer a stout?"

In the dim environment of candle flickers and birdlike shadows, Wyatt's fawn hair appeared nearly the color of his uniform, and all that gray fit his mood very well. For the first time Wyatt seemed truly conscious of the mug beside his elbow.

Dorian frowned. He leaned forward and dropped a hand on Wyatt's arm. Offering the most benign gaze he could muster, he waited to see if the contact got him anything.

Seconds dragged by. Wyatt's lightless eyes shifted to Dorian's hand, but he didn't look up. After a moment his dry lips pulled apart.

"Don't touch me," he grumbled. "I'm dangerous."

Dorian dropped back, clapped his hand to his chest, and laughed.

"To the heart! Sweet compensation! *Lex talionis!* I concede to the soldier-philospher. Now take another swig and sit up. You look as if you've come down on a peg."

Wyatt sighed wearily. "That just about describes it."

"Give yourself quarter, Wyatt. Things happen. Better we acclimate." Dorian took a great draw on his own rum, then added, "Why are you so distraught? The shipment went through. You won."

Yes, he had won. When the gunfire ended, Wyatt had found himself in charge of an ugly moment. He saw it all again.

"I didn't care for the part of myself that came out," he said slowly. "I always assumed...I assumed wars were fought by men who like fighting."

Watching him silently, Dorian was moved by the sudden age in Wyatt's eyes, lines that had not been there yesterday, a certain scarring that might never fade. Certainly some inner purity had fled today and would never find a path back home through all the prevailing tension. Sad, truly sad.

"Lost some of my oldest friends today," Wyatt murmured, his eyes glazed. "And some of my youngest ones..."

Dorian took a sip of his drink, to keep himself from interrupting.

Wyatt's mouth tightened. "You remember Patrick Ruhl?"

Dorian nearly choked. "*He* was there? I thought he went North when he left the mill."

"He went over to the North...by way of Rodney Lasik."

With a shake of his head, Dorian huffed, "Lord save the silly."

And he started to drink again.

"He died today," Wyatt said.

Dorian paused with the cup at his lips. "Died..."

"Yes."

"The simple fellow, the superstitious one...ate squirrel meat?"

"Yes."

"You made him warehouse foreman."

"Yes."

"Hmm...a shame. I'm sorry."

Wyatt fixed a red-ringed look on him. "Is that all you can say about it?"

Dorian paused. "I—"

"Is that *all* you can say?"

Wyatt had never seen Dorian speechless, until now. It was a day for firsts.

"We worked side by side with him," Wyatt said. "Built the mill with him. Trusted him, and he trusted . . . me . . . and today I had to—"

His throat closed up. He turned to stare at the floor.

Dorian held his breath. Waited it out. But his eyes lingered on Wyatt.

"It all seems so stupid," Wyatt muttered. His voice cracked, embarrassed him, and he brought the mug around to his lips. He took his time, aware of Dorian's gaze. What sane man would say any of this was good? Or righteous, or any of those words? He was barreling through these days, out of control, with no reins to grab and no way to stop. How many others were being dragged to war against their will? And how many would come to believe, as he did now, that even giant wounds must be purged before they can heal?

"It's not stupid, Wyatt," Dorian said. "Unfortunate, brutal, to be avoided if possible, often necessary, always sad . . . but not stupid. If it was truly stupid, truly a mindless waste, then no one would do it. At least, not so often as history must bear."

Wyatt stared at him, trapped in the coffin of his mood. His brows drew together, his lips parted, but all he did was stare. Soberness gave way to a bitter isolation between them.

Typically Dorian didn't know when to keep his mouth shut. He leaned forward. "Yes. Think of it. No war is fought out of passion for taking life—not even the cleverest deviate can convince a civilization to rise against its fellows with the cry of 'Let's kill for pleasure.' He can convince them to kill anyone who is not their religion, their color, their blood, their opinion, their goal, but to the men who do the killing, those are *reasons*. Not excuses. And men can be either led or misled. Any difference can be painted as a threat. Whether history will forgive, well . . . we shall see."

Wyatt's eyes burned. For this instant he hated Dorian, despised the cold explanations for his tingling hands and his raw throat, for the cloying vision of Rodney Lasik swinging high and Patrick draining into the soil.

Through his teeth he asked, "What's our reason?"

Dorian settled back. For several seconds he combed his mind—he'd watched this conflict brew since his boyhood, and now—what would Nick say?

"Astounding," he murmured. "Other wars have always been fought to gain land, to conquer, to resist being conquered, rising up against tyranny, some nation insulted or aggrieved by another . . . but this . . . damn me if I can't think. You might have me on this one." He shook himself, smiled, cocked a brow, and raised his drink.

Before the mug touched his lips, though, Wyatt's fist jammed between Dorian and the mug.

The drink sloshed over their hands. Their eyes locked again.

"Then I'll do the talking for a change," Wyatt said. "I used to say there shouldn't have to be a war. Now I say there had damned well better be. Freedom is in trouble if the South lets the North tell it how to live. We'll be starting all over again, going back to what Europe was, so we better fight." He sank back, his eyes two hollows filled with shadow. "And I'm going to. Freedom's in danger. I'm not letting go of it."

A chill wrapped Dorian and nearly cut off his blood. He should never have said anything.

Perhaps he could snatch back Wyatt's innocence before it drowned—he forced a jaunty smile and even managed to laugh.

"You? With the cut of a monk and a conscience that positively hulks? Pity's sake, forgive yourself for that which is not your doing."

He tried again for a pull on the apple brandy and hid behind the large brown mug as long as he could.

Wyatt remained mordant and stone-faced. From where he sat, Dorian seemed an utter emotional desert. There was no forgiving to be done, not for Dorian and not for himself. Finally he sagged back and glared at the stone floor and the feet of other patrons.

"I wish to God I could," he said.

"I've written to him several times, but he never responds."

"Who?"

"God."

Wyatt flipped his glare to the other side. "I hate when you talk like that."

"I'm the only one who can." That eerie, flameproof grin appeared, the one with all the layers, none of them funny. The one that made Wyatt shiver. "'Tho death in ev'ry shape appear . . . the wretched have no more to fear.'"

"What'n hell is that supposed to mean?" Wyatt demanded irritably.

"It means, my polished knight, that other people are too timid to be objective about God. I alone can afford to be. God makes decent men like you take the blame, just as you're doing to yourself tonight. God is the spoiled child whose reputation mankind will protect unto death."

"Do you have to 'death' around all the time? Can't you 'life' sometimes?"

He refused to look away from Dorian's dark glare.

Wyatt surprised even himself when he said, "The world's a disappointing place for you, isn't it?"

Dorian 's smile fell away. His mouth closed and drew tight, so tight that the color left his lips. He turned to his drink, every trace of mirth gone. The gap between them widened.

"Soon you'll find it tiring to tilt at windmills," he droned.

"Maybe," Wyatt snapped back. "All I know is that I'm sick of you. You're a fraud."

Dorian turned cold. His swig of brandy suddenly caught at the back of his mouth, and he couldn't swallow. He stared back, astonished.

"Don't look at me like that," Wyatt said. "I'm tired of listening to you use poetry as a weapon against whatever inspired it. I've never seen anybody strut so about accepting things as they come. You're an exasperating waste of a human being, and you're the first man I ever hoped would fall off a cliff."

A sudden corrosion came up between them, far different from the simple unfamiliarity that had kept them apart before.

Dorian was disarmed and tight at the throat, stripped of all his defenses, and cold to the marrow.

What was happening? What was this stone in his chest? He was untouchable, unstingable—he would simply walk away. He had done it before . . . walked away from Lucas, walked away from a thousand others, he had even walked away from Alex.

Were his feet in shackles, as they had been on the wagon ride to Chapel Mount? Were his legs bound? Something was different about him, different from five years ago, something other than his speech and his clothing. He sat here, helpless. Wyatt had changed him—by being the only glimmer of what he had once expected from a disenchanting outside world.

And now he clung to it despite his will to move, against every alarm going off in his head, clanging at him to *get up!*, *get away!*

He held very still and tried to sound composed.

"Your lance is tarnished, Don Quixote."

Abruptly Wyatt plunged forward and grabbed Dorian's wrist as though his hand were a factory vise. "Why don't you let me help!"

Thunderstruck, Dorian recoiled with surprise and pulled back against the grip—defensiveness, fear?

His own hand was a twisted claw in front of his face, turning gray as Wyatt's grip cut the circulation. The laddered back of his chair hit the wall and scraped angrily. His other hand flared at his side for balance and bumped the shoulder of a man at another table.

Wyatt leaned forward across the table. "Don't pull away from me, Dorian!"

Suddenly the pub door blasted open. A gush of night air doused the taproom and rolled against the back wall. Wyatt looked up barely in time. Four men crammed through the doorway, faces, terrible faces, blanched with anger and desperation—and one carrying the ruthless tenacity of a man who had nothing to lose.

In an instant the four men were across the room and upon Wyatt.

He saw them coming, foreshortened wraiths like in a

nightmare, and recognized the foremost of them even behind the Spanish-style black beard. The broad brow, the wide-set features, the beautiful eyes yellow as arsenic, eyes that had intimidated him as a child and irritated him as a man—eyes with pinpoint black pupils, like a cat's eyes in daylight—

A force crashed across his face. The impact reeled him backward against the wall. His chair plunged out from under him as his balance shifted from the blow, and he was dumped to the floor, legs falling across the collapsed chair and his cheek stinging.

Shocked, he blinked in time to see Dorian's powerful arm slice upward. The walking stick caught Brad Lassick under the chin and drove him backward into his three friends. One of them kept Lassick from falling over, while the other two pulled Dorian back.

Scarcely a breath drew before Lassick's hand flashed in and out of his greatcoat, and the clean metal angles of a revolver glinted in the candlelight—he aimed, fired.

The gunshot rebounded—the bullet struck its mark with a bone-chilling *crack*. On the farthest wall sconce, the candle was cut cleanly in half. It fell, leaving a spot of hot wax on the wall to dribble like blood. The gunshot's echo growled around the taproom.

The silence dropped. Stunned patrons held their breath and dared not move, their ears pounding.

Now Lassick put the pistol away. He gripped the edge of the table and leaned forward to glare down at Wyatt.

"You killed my cousin," he breathed, "the finest man of this age. What do you have to say?"

On the floor Wyatt dabbed his cheek with his knuckles and said, "Your cousin needed killing."

"You murdered him, and I want retribution."

Two men in striped sailor's shirts graciously overcame their shock and hauled Wyatt to his feet. He swayed briefly, then nodded to the sailors and thus gave them permission to get out of the line of fire. There was blood in his mouth. He could taste it.

"He didn't give me much choice, Brad," he said calmly. "His band has been sacking the homes of decent people all through this area. If it'd been a matter of—"

"Your actions have done the talking for you!" Lassick roared. "Before these witnesses I challenge you to a duel, sir."

Exhausted and annoyed with manly prancing, Wyatt sighed. "Oh, Brad, come off it."

"Accept the challenge, curse you!"

"All right, all right, I accept the challenge....Calm yourself."

"Chimborazo Park, Libby Hill, as soon as possible."

From the side Dorian interrupted, "Make it dawn. It'll be downright Shakespearean."

Lassick skewered him with an icy glare. "Dawn."

With a last bitter glance at Wyatt, he turned and stormed away.

Dorian put an elbow into the chest of one of Lassick's men who had the misjudgment to still have hold of him.

"Pardon," he said, "but is your tentacle touching me?"

Both men let go and followed Lassick and the others to the opposite side of the tavern, where they captured a table of their own.

Gradually the dumbstruck crowd began to come to life.

Somebody righted Wyatt's chair for him. He nodded a silent thanks and sank into it, now very stiff.

Keeping one eye on Lassick's table, Dorian also rearranged his chair, sat down, and shifted close to Wyatt until their shoulders touched.

"You all right?" he asked.

Wyatt dabbed at his reddening cheek. "No," he said, "I'm not very right at all."

"Let me see. He delivered quite a whack, didn't he? I promise you, he'll never get near you again."

"Made my teeth ache."

"Bless me, you were very cool. When have I seen anything so entertaining? 'I challenge you to a dyooo-el, sah.' 'I accept zee shallonge, sah.' 'Dawn, sah.' And your trumpet-tongued adversary—such *grossièreté* as I've rarely witnessed ... lately. Who is he, by the way?"

"The other Lassick."

"Ah." Dorian peered through the large, dark, blustering room to the far corner and fit the pieces together. Lassick and his men were cloistered at a table, mugs in hand, casting aspersions with their eyes. "Yes," he observed darkly, "I think he's one of the Handful."

The barkeep waddled over, carrying a pitcher and two fresh mugs.

"Hot apple brandy, gentlemen," he said. "I make it myself. On the house, to forget all this."

The thick, spicy aroma of apples and cinnamon brandy cleared Wyatt's thoughts and helped steady his head after Lassick's pounding. He drew the steam deeply into his lungs.

"I'm grateful, sir. Pardon that my troubles have disrupted your establishment."

The man shrugged with his eyes and said, "Good luck to you come morning, sir."

Solitude closed in once again around the little table. Wyatt hunched over his mug, not drinking, but instead drawing in the steam breath after breath, awash in the simple human feelings that go with this kind of moment. People had the courtesy to leave him alone, but the timbre of conversation in the pub had decidedly changed. The curious glances stopped for the most part, but for the wrong reason.

Occasionally Dorian would smile and shake his head. Ah, these changing times. A taste of the old, a sense of the new, a sting of the real.

"Now for the appropriate letters, back and forth," he began lightly, "attempts to satisfy the insult with ink and think . . . why, we could stall for weeks simply by taking propriety at its word. By the time courtesy is assuaged, he'll have forgotten the whole affair."

There was no movement or sound beside him. Nothing more than the deep swish of breath.

After a moment he began to realize what the silence meant. His eyes moved. He studied Wyatt's solemn face.

Slowly Dorian's grin faded, fell away. His eyes widened.

"Oh, no—" Dorian groaned. "You're not—" He shook his head once, fiercely. "No, you're not!"

Wyatt breathed into his drink and traced circles on the table with his finger. "Will you be my second?"

Dorian choked on an apprehensive laugh. The cold creeps

started up in the pit of his stomach. "No, I will not be your second!"

Blue eyes cracked upward to meet his. "Are you serious?"

"Serious? Wyatt, you are *not* meeting that man at the point of a gun. Do you hear me?"

"You won't attend me?"

"And condone such proceedings? Never."

Wyatt tucked his lips and turned once again to survey the table's shabby grain. "I see."

"You fail to see. If you meet this swine, you give him credibility."

"He doesn't really leave me a choice. Today I found that sometimes I'll have to stand up and face things as they come. But don't worry . . . he understands honor."

"An honorable crack shot!" Dorian insisted. "He will blow your brains out your ass and not leave a mark! You're not engaging him, and that's the end of it." Exasperated, he gave Wyatt's mug a shove that made it slosh. "Here. Don't waste your brandy. Apples don't grow on trees."

"You don't understand," Wyatt said, glancing across the room at his past. "He won't shoot me."

Astonishment passed across Dorian's face. He scooted closer.

"Wyatt, were you born on a hill? The man will kill you. You know what 'kill' is?"

Wyatt sighed, then actually smiled. He waved a lazy hand over the surface of the table. "He's not going to kill me, Dorian. . . . He's known me since I was a boy. He's just making a show."

"A *show*."

"Why, sure. Can't you see it? He was my father's head manager for years. They built the tannery from scratch. How would it look if he actually went ahead and killed me? Don't you think he realizes that? We'll go out on the field, we'll go through all the paddywhack required of us, we'll aim, he'll miss, I'll miss, honor is satisfied, the Heroes of America are stood up for . . . this is all an act. He just wants to ensure the credibility of his cause. Trust me. I've known the man half my life."

"You're about to know him all your life! At dawn he's

taking his half back! Wyatt, look at my face. Listen to me speaking. When you fall into quicksand, you don't kick and squirm. You figure a way to get out and complain all you want later. The quicksand doesn't care. Honor and justice are quicksand. They don't care if you sink!''

"I've got principles too, you know. I can't just fail to appear. . . . Besides, I told you, he won't shoot me.''

"Oh, great snakes—you can't uphold principle if you're dead! Face it! There is no right and wrong. Life is deciding which path gives you less manure to step in. God doesn't intervene on the part of the righteous, I've seen that for myself. Don't you remember what I said before?''

Wyatt flashed an ironic smile. "Which 'what' out of all your 'whats' am I supposed to remember?''

"The musketeer right out of Dumas. You! The marble constant! A story about purity of the soul! And the character who is purest—her name was Constance!''

"Oh, that one.'' Wyatt pushed his chair back on the flagstone floor and got to his feet, preparing to walk away.

Desperate to get his point across, Dorian would gladly have taloned himself to Wyatt's shoulder. He caught the royal blue cuff in both his hands, felt the wrist and the pulse pounding through flesh beneath the gray wool, and hissed, *"Wyatt, Constance dies at the end of the story!''*

The moment seemed endless, a crimp of time turning round and round defiantly. Even time was no longer on their side. Giving him the gift of a pause for thought, Wyatt considered what he was saying. But then, in his usual demonstrative way, he patted Dorian's shoulder. "Well . . . this isn't a story. Excuse me.''

He stepped away.

"Where are you going?''

Shrugging with his whole being, Wyatt heaved a long sigh. "To get some of this day out of me.''

Dorian waited exactly the fourteen steps it took Wyatt to get out of the smoky taproom.

Then he caught up his walking stick and strode through the crowd, ignoring the looks he got as he approached the table in the far corner.

With the end of the walking stick, he poked two of Lassick's men, not wanting to actually touch them, until they moved out of his way and he stood before Lassick himself.

"A word with you, sir."

Perhaps it was curiosity that made Lassick gesture one of his men out of a chair and Dorian into it.

"Thank you." He settled down, keeping his walking stick in hand, his palms folded over the T-handle, and the stick poised point down between his knees.

"Your name, sir?" Lassick asked coldly.

"Alexander Grate, sir. I shall be brief. From 1600 to 1610 alone, over two thousand pampered inbred fops died by the sword because they had nothing better to do than defend their honor. I dare guess your time is more valuable?"

Lassick's heavy brows went down. "Am I supposed to follow that, sir?"

"Merely an observation. Here's another. You and I both know you've called out a defendant who has as much talent with guns as a goat does with wings. He's rather proud of that. If you kill him, your reputation will be rubbish. I come with alternatives. What would satisfy you?"

"A bullet in his eye would satisfy me," Lassick said. "Nothing less."

"And will it be satisfying when I publish accounts of the contest, and Virginia resounds with your refusal to negotiate?"

At this Lassick hesitated, and Dorian caught the frayed end of a glint of hope.

Was retribution worth ruining the image of the Order of Heroes of America—which already trod a thin line? Would loyal Southerners be turned completely against them and their cause to keep the nation stitched together? Southerners were fastidious about dueling. There were rules. Second chances. Letters to be exchanged. And the seconds' duties—the biggest of which was the effort to assuage the problem before it came to actually dueling. There was supposed to be chance after chance of letting the contestants get out of it, for days if necessary. Chivalry understood that challenges were made in moments of wrath and hostility, and that those moments fade.

Dorian held his breath.

Lassick shifted his cigar from one side of his mouth to the other.

"I don't care about reputation."

"Good. Then we can talk as pirates. I bargain. Mr. Swine, my friend's life is worth nothing to you, while it is worth money to me. Perhaps your Heroes of America would like sponsorship. Uniforms. Armaments. Maps. Let us meet tomorrow and talk Dixie notes."

Lassick blasted to his feet—shocking, since there had been no change whatsoever in his face. The scrape of his chair resounded and caught the attention of everyone in the tavern. Conversation seized and died for a second time that night. He glared down at Dorian.

Loud as a foghorn he bellowed, "You can offer me all the money in Richmond, sir! The duel goes on!"

Only then did Dorian realize his fatal mistake. And everyone else did also.

Sadly that included Wyatt Craig, who had just reentered the taproom and now stood there, astonishment burning on his bruised face. Providence was in fine form tonight.

Attention swiveled to him. Embarrassment for him blanketed every face in the pub, reddened every cheek. If there was anything worse than being embarrassed, it was having a roomful of men be embarrassed for him.

The humiliation cut to his bones.

And to Dorian's. He stood up sharply, his lips parting as though to explain.

Wyatt approached, stiffly and slowly.

"What in hell," he began, "is happening here?"

"Your friend is offering me a bribe to default on the challenge," Lassick broadcasted. "On top of everything else, you've turned corrupt. Cliff, Roger, Tom, let's go."

Rock-jawed, Wyatt never took his eyes off Dorian. He stewed in silence as the four men left. His fists rolled up.

Around them the whole room was waiting, everyone unwilling to move. Wyatt looked injured, but much more
deeply than the bruise on his cheek might account for.

"You have no loyalty to anything," he said. "Why pick
me?"

All Dorian could do was stand there, speechless, unable to
explain himself, unable to make clear his lack of investment
in any other human being he'd met since the devil cast him
out.

Wyatt took the silence as an answer. "I don't need your
interference," he said.

Before him Dorian flushed with renunciation. The low
ceiling pounded his words back on top of him. "Go, then!"
he bellowed. "Buckle on your swash. See if the world cares
by lunch tomorrow."

"You won't care," Wyatt snapped. "That's for damned
sure."

He broke away and stormed back to the corner table, re-
trieved his Confederate tunic, and yanked it on carelessly. On
his way out he had to pass Dorian again, and well enough was
not best left alone. He paused on the edge of one foot and glared.

"What?" he bit out. "You mean Burns has nothing to
say?"

And then he was gone. Nothing was left but the ringing
sound of his heels on the stone floor.

Even to the naked eye, Dorian was wounded.

There was nothing more to be done. He was alone again,
completely.

Without meeting a single eye in the taproom—all of which
were offering—a lonely man went back to the table to retrieve his hat and greatcape. As he paused for a moment
to straighten the set of his cravat, the table caught his eye.
The two brown mugs stood like sentinels. The steam was
gone. Both were cold now. He gazed at them while buttoning
his Inverness.

He placed his hat slightly canted to one side on his head,
but there was no dash about it. At the last moment he held his
walking stick in both hands, diagonally across the front of his
chest.

Vexation pointed right back at him. Once again the de-

mon's touch had fooled him by lying still for so long. It had
drawn him out.

Focus fell from his eyes. The mugs and the table blurred.

" 'If providence has sent me here . . . 'Twas surely in an
anger.' "

★

CHAPTER FORTY-FOUR

———— ★ ————

Dorian awakened in a bush.

He'd slept in bushes before to conceal himself and his plans, but not for a while. He wanted to hide, to avoid being seen either coming or going. What time was it?

He gave himself a rude shake, fought to remember where he was and why, then got onto his knees and had a look around.

Chimborazo Park was blanketed with fog, as though ordered from a catalog of dueling implements. Dawn, yes, but the sun was still nothing more than a shy haze. He was cold.

Frantically he pawed the leaves out of his way, heedless of thorns scoring his hands.

A hundred yards down a hill, through the trees, men had gathered. A much bigger crowd than he had hoped. News of the duel had spread fast. Such an exciting event always drew an audience from the curious Virginia society folk. In the South dueling enjoyed a hazy legality, an undying popularity, and it still retained a patina of honor—all of which made it quite an attraction.

Men and women wore dark clothing, appropriate to a moment of truth. All were clad in heavy greatcoats, raglans, and capes, women looking like huge cones in the full mantles, bell-shaped sleeves, and enormous skirts. There were even some policemen present, but only to ensure that all was fair and even. Every last person wore some form of hat—

Except for the two rivals.

Lassick's barrellike body already cast a faint shadow among the trees in the awakening dawn.

Wyatt stood facing east, seconded by two of his foremen.

A pinch of guilt got Dorian by the heart again. He should be there.

It was hard to see. Very misty. Thick mist, with fingers that reached along the grass.

Was he too late?

The two contestants were standing still, looking across the prescribed twenty paces at each other, while their seconds stripped them of their jackets.

Now in shirts and vests, they stood closemouthed while the judging committee nodded at each other and the referee droned off the rules of a proper and gentlemanly contest.

His fingers fumbling, Dorian dug through his greatcape, which lay in a lump at his side. He found his pistol.

Quickly he shimmied out of his jacket and left it too on the ground. He took the revolver firmly in his right hand and sneaked down the hill through the blessing of trees, to a crop of bushes fifty feet behind Wyatt.

The risk was humbling. He must fire at exactly the moment that Wyatt's gun discharged, or all would fall apart. But he must fire an instant before Lassick, or Wyatt could die. The delicate timing clawed at his innards.

Wyatt would die or Wyatt would be humiliated before those he must live with. For Wyatt such would be as bad as dying.

"Curse your fucking conscience," Dorian muttered. The bushes whispered back. His hands trembled right when he needed them to be steady. "Stupidity and twenty paces..."

The rivals' attendants approached the referee and presented the dueling revolvers for inspection. The judges and the referee nodded, and the rivals were presented with their weapons.

The guns were properly cocked for them.

At the judges' agreement Wyatt and Lassick were pivoted by the shoulders until they faced away from each other.

The crowd grew eerily silent. Even the crickets were fooled and began chirping again.

"Ready!" the referee called.

Lassick and Wyatt brought the pistols up, barrels to the

sky. Wyatt was a little late.

In his hiding place Dorian's pulse hammered in his wrists as he also brought his pistol up, but not to the sky. He bit his lip at the sight of Wyatt's face. So tired, so damaged— scored by the marks of Lassick's strike upon his cheek, but damaged by a far deeper scar. So abandoned.

Against the mist a voice barked.

"Gentlemen! You may turn and fire!"

Vibration cut through Dorian's hand, sharp recoil as the pistol discharged. The leaves around him shivered. Pistol cracks boomed across the hillside, a roar, echoing over and over, an instant of pressure striking every skull. It seemed fifty guns were firing instead of two . . . three.

Lassick's head snapped backward at the neck. His beard pointed toward the fading stars. Dorian could see the triangle of white skin at Lassick's throat, framed by another triangle of black beard, a view that would stay with him forever. That was all he would see in his mind ever again, when he thought of Lassick.

The big man was still standing. His own pistol pointed forward, wavering faintly in the fog, thrust out before him at the end of his arm. His legs went stiff. His left arm fanned the air.

The crowd reacted—a gasp of horror.

Out of Lassick's left eye, blood began to gush upward. It pooled in the eye socket, flowed down over the pocked cheek into his hair, and struck the grass one drop at a time, faster and faster.

Lassick's hands convulsed, both of them, and the pistol cracked, flamed, roared, and sent its ball whining through the empty fog. The man was already dying or dead. He must be dead.

Dorian stood up slowly, his legs like putty, not daring to breathe. *Be dead.*

Lassick's body made one ghastly, stilted step backward before balance failed. He tipped, his knees still locked, finally to crash to the ground without bending a single joint.

His head struck the ground first. The impact caused a hemorrhage. Blood spurted from the destroyed eye and poured over half his face. The right eye stared upward.

A shuddering breath rattled through Dorian's chest. Puffs of crystallized air obscured his vision, and he realized he was breathing in gasps. His fingers twitched, dropped the revolver. It thunked to the ground and lay against his ankle.

All he could see was Wyatt's back and the crowd slowly converging upon Lassick's body.

The attendants were approaching the duelists. It was all over, but it didn't seem over. Tremors of the unfinished rushed through the trees. Ghostlike, Dorian stepped forward out of the bush and watched. Wyatt's second was coming toward him with an overcoat. Wyatt wasn't moving.

Then he did move—he bent forward slightly as though he'd been punched. Yes, guilt, of course.

Dorian grimaced in empathy. *I should be there*.

The second paused, then continued approaching holding the overcoat open to drape over Wyatt's shoulders. The spectators began to close in around the site.

Then a woman in the crowd gasped and pointed at Wyatt. The crowd reacted a second time—a stare of hesitation and disbelief.

Visibly Wyatt shuddered. Bare white sleeves crinkled like paper. His shoulders hunched. His knees buckled—the trousers kinking at the back of his legs—he tilted onto one foot, hovered, curled forward in what could only be pain, genuine pain. Before anyone could reach him, he toppled and struck the ground on his side. The earth heaved. Dew puffed up in a sparkling cloud around the crumpled, shuddering form. His hair shimmered.

Far back in the trees, horror took Dorian by the throat and squeezed out a strangled shout. "No!"

The confused people gathering around Wyatt paused and looked up. The people kneeling around Lassick looked. The spectators looked.

"No!" Dorian shrieked again. The sound pummeled through the trees, guttural and raw.

Bushes and ferns parted before him, and he burst out into the crowd. They tried to give way for him, but confusion locked them around him, and he had to claw his way through, all the while gasping, "No, no, no!"

Forcing his way through, he knocked three women completely over and elbowed several men in the ribs. Confused, the spectators squinted at the black-haired man.

Didn't they recognize him? Hadn't some of them caught a glimpse of someone who looked like this man, stepping out of unlikely alleys in the gloom of a city night?

Eyes blazing, Dorian felt as though his heart were shriveling in his chest. He pushed between the people and burst out onto open grass where Wyatt lay quivering at his feet. Stunned, paralyzed by his own panic, he suddenly couldn't move. His hands stretched out as though to heal Wyatt with some ancient magic or take the death upon himself and offer his own soul to the devil, who claimed him so early.

"No—" he gagged again, and stumbled forward.

He reached out . . . he bent a knee—

Two forces rammed him from the sides. Two big men locked his arms in theirs and dragged him back.

Back, away from Wyatt.

"No!" Dorian croaked, struggling, yanking and pitching. "Let me go!"

But these were massive men, hired for the purpose of holding him.

They were dragging him backward no matter how he pulled and kicked, yanking the muscles in his shoulders and legs. "No—no! Not him! This isn't for him!"

Suddenly he was surrounded by men in policemen's uniforms, and there was a wide leathery presence directly in front of him, blocking his view of Wyatt there on the ground—*Wyatt*—

A brown paper shot forward toward his face.

WANTED! REWARD! The Mulatto Slave Dorian Wallace—

Realization slammed through Dorian's solar plexus and crushed his voice, his breath, his reason right out of him. He froze.

A scant inch from his face, the paper shivered in a breeze. He gaped at it.

"This is him, Sheriff," a gruff voice said.

Wanted for ravagement of a white virgin woman . . .

Beyond the policemen stunned Richmond gentry gaped and watched with graveyard curiosity. Even those who had knelt beside the two fallen men were more interested in the arrest of a runaway mulatto who had pretended to be one of them.

The bounty hunter pushed closer. Gasping and off guard, Dorian could do nothing but be glared at. He felt a rip, a yank—and suddenly his arm was bare from the elbow down. The sensation shocked him; that arm hadn't been exposed in five years. Cold, moist air swarmed around the scar. The *S*.

Around him women shrieked, and men roared with fury. Hiding among them! Walking and eating among them, at their tables, using their wash closets, pretending to be one of them. One woman collapsed. Every last man generally went pale against the drowsy wooded morning.

The bounty hunter didn't smile. He leaned into Dorian's face.

"Nigger," he said.

He said it loud.

Holding the *WANTED* poster high in the air before him, waving it back and forth so that everyone could clearly see it, Orville Quist turned and cut a path through the shocked crowd. Back and forth the head of the snake wavered, left, right, left, right.

Following behind, the sheriff's men dragged a recaptured slave away from the field of honor.

★

CHAPTER FORTY-FIVE

————— ★ —————

Sixty-some minutes later, according to the sheriff's pocket watch, they dumped what was left of the degenerate criminal onto the stone floor of a cell.

The townsmen were satisfied. They had dickered and bid for the chance to brutalize the lowlife who ruined a white woman and embarrassed their society by fitting into it, and while the bidding had taken nearly three-quarters of an hour, the brutalizing had gone by all too quickly. The sheriff had moved aside and waited until honor was served and the carnal-minded half-breed lay in a heap on the dirt. For a white prisoner he would have stopped them pending due process of law. For a blooded slave, though, he wasn't sure how the law applied and preferred to have a beaten prisoner inside all night than a restless mob outside. The townsmen had their moment, then went away rubbing their sore fists, and the sheriff and the bounty hunter closed the cell's weighted wooden door and locked it. Only the sheriff and the bounty hunter's legal rights had kept them from killing the nigger right then and there.

However, the issue was still up for discussion on the damp streets of the district.

Quist lingered, looking through the wrought-iron grate embedded in the door, through which a prisoner could be watched and food could be passed. Horizontal shadows of the black bars lined the human clump on the floor.

The bounty hunter gave no smile of satisfaction. He folded the *WANTED* notice and stuffed it into his haversack with professional dispassion. With one last glance into the cell, he turned and left the jailhouse, nodding once at the deputy on his way out.

A man suddenly worth ten thousand dollars should spend the day blaring drunk.

Dorian Trozen lay heartsore upon bare rock all day and into the evening. Between seizures of pain from the beating, despair clawed and flooded him like blood. Lacerated, tormented, his innards gnawed both by the punches of indignant men and the sorriness he put upon himself, he lay wretched and wretching, periods of semiconsciousness little more than suspensions of his suffering. Each time he roused, however briefly, he was plunged again into grief.

Hours twisted into a blur, feeding one into the next. They meant nothing anymore. Where tiny shards of time had been so important on the dueling field, he no longer cared about the seconds or hours.

From outside came the mutterings of a bitter crowd, enjoying their unity of anger at his expense, and since the bounty hunter was nowhere in sight, there was nearly constant talk of hanging. He would rather be hanged than returned to Noah Sutton. He wondered how the sheriff felt about obeying the Fugitive Slave Law.

There was no window. The cell door was solid, except for the barred opening, scarcely bigger than a dinner plate. No daylight came or faded to give him any idea of time passing. Ultimately he discovered he could still move.

The stone floor chilled his bare branded arm. He pushed over onto his back. Shooting pain from gut punches made him convulse, so he didn't last long in that position and soon rolled over again onto his hands and knees, his torn right sleeve batting bruised ribs.

It was a bleak cell, gray and damp, the way cells are supposed to be in order to do their jobs. In one corner was a water bucket, in another a hole to be used as a latrine.

And there was a bench. Dorian crawled to it, turned upright on the floor, and sat with his back against the wooden plank.

From then on he had nothing to do but sit, spiritless, to listen to the rattle of his own breath, and to tally his score.

Nightfall. Outside the heavy cell door came the scratch of footsteps. Someone wanted a look at the scapegrace of Richmond, the mahogany, the yeller.

Dorian didn't look up. Citizens had sneaked by a few times, lining the deputy's pocket for a glimpse through the barred window. They could look all they pleased. As usual his existence would feed the serpent side of men.

A while ago he had crawled up onto the bench to relieve his screaming back and the agonized hollow of his abdomen, where he'd been hit again and again. His right upper arm stung and burned from the rawhiding; they'd taken particular satisfaction in whipping that arm because it dared have a brand of slavery upon it. Whether they were punishing him for being black or punishing him for being white, he could not conceive. There wasn't much difference. Even now, heartsick as he was, a certain indelible curiosity lurked. What would they do to him? What looks would they give him? How would they treat a provocateur of his particular crime who had managed to hide among them? Even as a child he had invented scenarios of recapture, much as other children play at sword fighting or dolls.

His life was complete now. He had experienced slavery, wealth, deception, family and lack of family, love and lack of love, and now he would know the answer to the final question. How would they treat him now that they knew? What would their silent faces look like? Their eyes? The set of their mouths? He had always wondered.

Evidently such was the only true joy he was meant to bring into the world.

He sat in his puddle of malignant self-reproach, not looking up even at the crinkle of money and the scrape of the door pushing open.

Voices, not very loud. More scratching of boots upon the rock floor.

The cell wall remained cold against his shoulders. His only

movement was to shift his left hand onto the shriveled white *S* on his right forearm. Damned if he would give free gratification.

The cell door was partly open now, and someone stepped in sideways.

Dorian barely moved except to look up.

When he did, and his eyes focused, he gasped.

Recognition shot him full of holes, destroyed all the strength he'd managed to rebuild until now. He turned away so sharply that his head bumped on the wall. His eyes clamped shut as though he'd been punched again. His left hand dug into the scarred *S*. He shuddered.

At the door Wyatt passed the deputy another five-dollar bill and waved him out. He stepped inside. The door was tugged shut behind him. Sensitive about the floor crunching under his soles, Wyatt moved slowly toward the bench and the pathetic figure crouched upon it. In his hand was a copy of the *WANTED* notice the sheriff had insisted he see.

There wasn't much to say. Very little came to mind. He simply stood there, gazing downward, adding up the welts and bruises he could see from this angle. He bit his tongue rather than comment.

On the bench Dorian didn't move other than to press his palm deeply into the flesh of his right forearm. He didn't look up. When he spoke, his voice was barely a whisper.

"The least you can do is act surprised."

The stone cell echoed slightly.

A thousand responses ran in Wyatt's head, but none of them made sense. Quietly he asked, "What'd they do to you?"

"We played croquet. I lost."

"They're talking about hanging you tomorrow morning. The sheriff and the bounty hunter have been arguing about it all afternoon. You're quite a prize, Dorian."

At that Dorian turned his head just enough to see Wyatt in the corner of his gaze.

"Pardon me, but . . . aren't you shot?"

Wordlessly Wyatt opened his vest and shirt. On his bare midriff was a wide muslin bandage. Even now blood seeped through, leaving a gory stain on the left side beneath his ribs, the outer rim drying, the center still glowing ruby red and wet.

Dorian bit down on his emotions, choking them inward, but the weakest part of himself was in control now, and he could barely hold back from screaming at what he saw.

"I knew I was a pitiful marksman," Wyatt said, "but I didn't think I was pitiful enough to hit him when I didn't mean to."

Drawing a handkerchief from his vest pocket, Wyatt put the *WANTED* poster down on the bench and stepped to the water bucket and soaked the cloth.

Dorian's voice moved between them, strangely detached. Ironic, that Wyatt thought he shot Lassick himself, when Dorian had done it. Dorian toyed with the idea of telling him. But what would be the point?

"Do you believe in reincarnation?"

Wyatt paused. "Do you?"

"I have no choice. I must, in some past life, have done something to earn my pitchfork. I've been made the land-locked Flying Dutchman of my time. Whosoever believeth in me shall perish."

"Don't be silly," Wyatt said passively. He squeezed out the cloth and came back to the bench, this time to Dorian's right. He sat down and pressed the cloth gingerly against the angry red whip marks on the point of Dorian's shoulder.

A shiver moved through Dorian, and he gasped at the fresh pain—more emotion on his face than Wyatt had ever seen before.

"Sorry," Wyatt said. "I'll go easier."

"Not to fear. It probably won't hurt after they hang me."

Wyatt folded the cloth over and tried to move Dorian's hand from his lower arm.

This changed everything.

At this touch Dorian clamped hard upon his forearm, hugged it tightly against his body.

The poster lay on the bench, mocking him.

Not to be discouraged, Wyatt grasped Dorian's hand firmly, the kind of grip that puts up with nothing. He didn't pull the hand away yet but simply sat there with his own palm over Dorian's bruised knuckles, so that in reality they were both sharing the secret, both their hands covering the infamous brand.

Dorian felt Wyatt's steady gaze, though he refused to turn and face him. Moment by moment the devotion broke him down. He sat there trembling, turned toward the wall, feeling Wyatt's hand drawing weight from his burden.

Finally his hand uncramped on the flesh of his own arm and fell away.

He couldn't stand to look, to see the expression on Wyatt's face at first sight of the hideous scar, so he didn't turn.

The mark of a slave. The flesh as witness.

Wyatt's gut churned at the clear picture of what some men would do when they had the power. There it was, right there, carved in skin.

"This is no way for a man to be treated."

"Can't you read?" Dorian snapped.

Jabbing a finger at the poster, Wyatt said, "That? You didn't do that."

A cold lump expanded inside Dorian's chest.

How long had it been? How long since someone trusted him? Believed in him so strongly and with such unwavering gallantry—Alex? Yula?

Suddenly embarrassed, he hung his head. "Thank you . . ."

"You don't have to thank me," Wyatt said with a tinge of anger. "You're innocent. Innocent men don't have to thank anyone." He snatched the paper and shook it between them. "This is trash. You're not."

The paper crumpled in his fist, and he dashed it against the opposite wall.

Dorian pressed his swollen lips together. "You're so damned pure. How did you grow up with so large a heart and keep this world from chipping it away?"

"Stop saying things like that."

"Why should I? I'll say anything I please. I am the trash. I am the disease. No matter how right or wrong I may aspire to be."

"I don't believe that, and neither do you."

Still steeped in astonishment and relief so strong it would have knocked him down if he hadn't already been sitting, Dorian shook his head and grimaced. "Is that what you've come here for? Something to believe in? Poor boy. And all you find is me.''

Wyatt's face was a grim portrait, grimmer than Dorian had ever seen it. And wiser—how strange, how sad to witness the marble constant crumbling—

"For the first time in my life," he admitted, "I don't know what to believe anymore. The world's not what I thought it was.''

The sight of the crumbling was too much for Dorian, and he threw his defenses up suddenly. "Please get out. The sin is mine, and I'd like to be alone with it.''

"You're always the only one with a sin!" Wyatt complained, throwing his arms upward. "If I can walk around with Lassick's bullet in my gut, the least you can do is listen!''

While Dorian turned toward him, his face a matte of astonishment, Wyatt sighed disgustedly and struggled to his feet, circling the small cell.

"If I'm so pure, how come I've been strutting around my whole adult life flapping about how blacks are brutish and inferior and have to be penned up for their own good? No matter how I rationalize, there's no justice in making a slave of a man like you. If there's anybody in this world who *is* superior, it's you! What in hell have I been doing in my life? What am I supposed to think? Isn't 'right' right anymore?''

As he paced, each step slammed a new thought into his head. He'd been thinking about this all afternoon, ever since the sheriff made him read the notice, but somehow being here, with Dorian, screwed the annoying realities into place.

Breathing raggedly, he slowed down and pressed a hand to the wall to steady himself. The sound of his footsteps ceased, leaving only the tick of his mind at work, his conscience crackling. He drew a hand across his brow beneath the flop of hair, paced, then suddenly paused while his eyes grew wide.

"If blacks aren't brutish and inferior," he said, "then the whole basis of the South is wrong, and I've sent men to their graves on a wrong principle. My God ... what might the other negroes become if they were simply taught to speak and read? I've been killing men to keep you in irons!" He turned to Dorian now and held out a hand, its palm stained with his own blood, and his voice cracked. "How can I fight in favor of a system that would enslave the finest man I've ever known?''

Though his right arm had been tucked tightly against his wound, the blood still seeped out and drained down the side of his body. He ignored it. Strange how a bullet could seem insignificant. The echo of his words skittered along the walls.

Slowly rising, digesting with a sudden humility what those words meant, Dorian stared at him. The *finest*—suddenly he rejected Wyatt with a sweep of his hands and spun away.

"Beg you," he choked, "never say that again. Right is only right in the dictionary. I am far from it.''

"You're not so far from it.''

They stalked apart.

The cell wasn't very big.

A silence fell. It might have gone on longer, except that Dorian suddenly blinked and swung around. His voice rose as he stepped across the cell.

"Are you telling me the bullet hasn't been taken out yet?'' He reached for Wyatt. "Let me see.''

Wyatt slapped him off halfheartedly. "Leave it alone. It's my bullet.''

The effort to steer away from Dorian sent him stumbling against the wall. He recovered, breathing hard, holding out a hand to keep Dorian at bay.

Bracing on the wall, he leveled a finger and said, "You're a coward, you know? Hiding all this time. Imagine how you could change the world's idea of negroes!''

"Rat's ass! Do all blue-eyed men get that idea?''

"Don't you realize what you could do for the world?'' Wyatt persisted. "Why didn't you stand up? Do something?''

"Because I sacrifice myself to no one, negroes or whites. Neither race will admit me, and I've no use for either as a group. Curse God, we think so much in groups!''

"Don't you owe something to the negroes? You have it in your power to change everything for them.''

"What do I owe them? Tell me.''

"Well . . . maybe to show the world that they're . . . that they don't have to—''

"I don't owe them that. They're on their own, as I was. No one owes them. The world provides certain opportunities even to the most downtrodden among us. If they haven't the incentive and wherewithal to survive, then let them perish. Have you read the death of Socrates?''

"Oh, for crying out loud—''

"Socrates was a fool. He died, and his enemies got exactly what they wanted. His voice was silenced. His enemies gave him every opportunity to play by the rules, to accept their power, even to leave if he wanted to. He took death and did nothing. Should I have done that? Should I have stood up and said, 'Here I am, a black man in a white body, come and kill me?' Would that help? Would that free even one slave?''

Exasperated and confused, Wyatt licked his lip and murmured, "Well . . . I think—''

"The world is not mine to do for. Nor yours, but you haven't gotten that through your head, and that's why you're here tonight, in the cell of an escaped slave, but damn you, I will not be your thing to believe in, do you hear? I will not be used.''

The point was a good one, and it forced Wyatt to pause. These were ideas and perceptions that no one in the world but Dorian could have. There was no one else like Dorian.

"Bleeding God, you seem so confused, Wyatt,'' the anomaly said fiercely. "Why are you confused? Because you've found someone who is half-and-half instead of right or wrong, up or down, in or out? I am half-negro and half-white. What makes you assume my loyalty must go to the negroes?''

Foundering in this, the shock of his life that refused to go away, Wyatt could do little but stand there because he knew Dorian already knew the answer. He stared into the very antithesis of everything he had ever assumed about the world, every principle he had ever stood upon refuted before his very eyes, and he knew he had indeed come here out of something other than pity for Dorian.

He stood looking right into the face of his own flawed assumptions, and he saw bitterness in Dorian's eyes.

All those things he'd said in the past about negroes, about slavery, about the North's greedy motivations and the South's stand for freedom—

It was all shattering before him, and he had come here tonight hoping Dorian would sweep up the pieces, but Dorian refused to do his housekeeping for him. Instead he stood before Wyatt and demanded reality.

"The law says I am not white," he said. "You've always believed in the letter of the law." He spread his hands, like a statue of a saint in some basement vestibule. "Look at me. Am I negro?"

He presented himself before Wyatt in all his battered grandeur, his soft dark curls nothing like a negro's curls, his nose narrow and straight, his skin not so different in this light from the rumpled ivory folds of his shirt.

Self-consciously Wyatt tightened his lips and couldn't answer.

"Yes!" Dorian answered for him. "I am. I grew up a slave in the tobacco fields. I worked. At night I slept beside my black-skinned mama. I was educated at the big house beside my white brother and sisters, my uncle and my Greek mother. . . ."

Misery crumpled his features, his eyes drifted closed, and he swayed, moved by a sudden, acute despair. His shoulders drew inward as though the pain had returned.

"*Parakaloh, Iphigenia, esteh efkhareestimene tin deamonesas? . . .* please God have the sense to stay in Macedon . . ."

His voice tapered to a rasp. Finally his shoulders drooped, and his eyes seemed to have weight. His head turned downward.

"I have a Greek sense of family," he murmured, "but there is no family for me."

Misery folded in upon him. He reeled back toward the bench in an attempt to get away from Wyatt, from his feelings, his guilts, and staggered against the wall. His wounds betrayed him and denied him even the merest dignity. There was no more hiding, he could no longer do it, the strength was gone—he was uncloaked—and sank toward the bench.

Wyatt's gentle face knotted in abrupt empathy, and in two steps he was across the cell. "Aw, God, Dorian—"

"Don't touch me!—don't! Give me quarter for a shred of dignity. You're only half-alive yourself."

"Well, I deserve it," Wyatt said. "I've tried to do right, and all I've done is wrong. . . . All those things I said to you, to Patrick . . . to Mr. Putnam—I keep hearing them again and again in my head. Yesterday I hanged a man because of those things I believed in. I hanged him. No trial, no nothing, I was so sure I was right. Today I shot another man—''

Dorian knotted both fists and gritted his teeth. With both hands he shoved Wyatt back the same two steps and forced the truth up from the cesspool of untold bits of his life. "Christ on a spit, Wyatt! *I* shot the man, not you, do you hear? I shot Lassick from behind you! Right through the eye, as my uncle taught me. We'll never know whether he intended to hit or miss you. I shot him. There. Reproach me, not yourself. Your record is clear."

A telltale instant of silence, and then—

Astonished, Wyatt stepped backward. "*You* did?"

"In cold blood, of my own volition, and I don't care if it was right or wrong. He was probably dead by the time he shot you. You were shot by a corpse. Now you have something to tell your grandbabies. I am nothing to believe in. That was your only true mistake. Stop flogging yourself and go back to the monastery. And have that bullet taken out, for pure pity's sake."

Aching and defeated, he inched along the bench on one thigh. His criminal right arm pressed against the concrete wall, and he stared into a dark corner, then went on. "You came here to find out what to believe in? Very well. Here it is," he said softly, bitterly. "You are still righteous. You are the monument. A symbol of what the nation as a whole is going through. Our struggle is you, Wyatt. You are the anthem of this war. Whatever happens to the nation will happen to you. As the nation divides, I've watched you divide. As our conscience rots, I've watched the cancer seep into you. The nation splits and kills, you split . . . and you kill. If the nation turns bitter, you will be embittered. I hope I die before I see your golden heart beaten to tin. Let them go ahead and hang me."

Between them he painted the future with his glazed eyes, and Wyatt stood back, chilled to the bone. He didn't know what emollient to provide, or if one even existed. Dorian's wisdom had been no ruse, no fakery, but now the terrible burden of that wisdom showed up, and suddenly it seemed fatal to want wisdom at all.

The corners of his mouth stiffened when he tried to speak

up, but he had no idea what to say. Empathy gushed up in his throat again and choked him silent. All this time he'd wanted to help, had demanded to, and now he saw the impotence of his attempt.

It was Dorian who spoke. His voice was hardly more than a scratch in the dimness. He never looked up.

"Forget slavery," he said. "For every man who gives a damn about slavery, there will be a legion who don't care one way or the other. This is a war between white men. If you think the bigger wrong is the fracture of the Union, then fight for the North. If the bigger wrong is the government overbearance you crackle about, then you must continue fighting for the South. Choose whether oppression of some is worse or better than oppression of all. Choose, my friend . . . and never flog yourself again. I had to. And remember also, when morning arrives, that the men who come here to hang me are also righteous."

★

CHAPTER FORTY-SIX

———— ★ ————

"Your mother . . . a slave on a Virginia farm?"

"According to my last thousand-dollar shred of evidence, yes."

"You don't know where exactly?"

"My money could only buy so much at a time."

Dorian scooted another inch down the bench in order to keep space between them, for Wyatt's sake. The poison was already running in Wyatt's blood; no point another bite from the serpent.

"You've been looking for her all this time?"

"When I could. My pursuers blanketed the North and the territories with that notice, so I schemed to return to Virginia. The last place one looks for gold is in his own backyard. Your visiting time is up, I'm sure. Good night."

"You've been looking all by yourself?"

"Yes. Must I summon the deputy myself?"

"Sit down, just sit down. . . . I want to know about your mother. Why didn't you ask around?"

"Don't be such a fool, Wyatt."

His frustration bounced on the walls.

Bruised, Wyatt sank back.

The bullet wound numbed his entire right side now. He could barely feel his legs anymore, nor was his chest much more than liquid. A few more minutes. Hang on.

Hang on.

He slumped back against the concrete wall, accepting its

694

cold support across his shoulders. Beside him the warmth of Dorian was something to cling to.

"You've gone without help so long," he said, "you don't know how to accept it anymore. That's your whole trouble."

"If you like, I can arrange for you to be hanged beside me. You did harbor a fugitive slave, after all."

"They wouldn't hang me. I'm too Viking-like, or one of those things you're always calling me."

"Can it be that you still don't comprehend?" Dorian blustered. "It's over for me! In many ways I'm refreshed. Yes, that's right. When I left Chapel Mount, being alone was intoxicating! I'd never been alone. And there was the entire world to explore, as I had a thousand times in books. But the books lie. Where there is adventure, there are also poisons in the grass. . . . I became nothing but a bedouin. The world utterly failed my expectations. On Plentiful I was bathed in people who loved me. The work was nothing. The humiliation was nothing. I was loved among the quashies and loved among the aristocrats. At least then I had a fair reality and an excellent illusion. The outside world barred me from both, and I cannot go back."

The other side of the cell captivated him with its detail as his eyes lost their focus and he stared at the point at which the wall met the floor. Urine stains and rat tracks murmured back at him as though they had opinions too. He wished dawn would come and it would all be over.

"My slave years were my best years," he added softly. "I may as well hang as live my life alone."

He drew in a long, self-conscious breath and shook himself, forced his eyes to focus. Why was he speaking these thoughts? For years he'd left them to mutter around in the back of his mind. Why bring them out now?

He looked sidelong at Wyatt.

The sprawled figure beside him blinked and said, "Sorry . . . what'd you say?"

"Oh, witch piss!" The bench squawked as Dorian changed position and prepared to get up. "Nothing. Your time is up."

In a ludicrous gesture Wyatt actually fumbled for his pocket watch, peered at it, then said, "Yeah . . . almost."

"What do you mean, almost?" Dorian braced himself on

the wall and half turned. His weight shifted again on the bench.

Wyatt squinted at *his watch*. "Better cover your—"

In a near distance an explosion tore from the center of the earth.

BrrrrrrrrrrFOOOOOMMM

The thundercrack resounded, then erupted again.

A giant hand of concussion hit the jailhouse, and the whole building lurched. Pressure in their ears made them both wince involuntarily. The ground rumbled—

Beneath them the bench itself shook violently and tipped away from the wall, pitching Dorian face-first to the floor. Wyatt piled down on top of him.

Around them the stone walls shuddered, then actually began to crack in weak places, snapping like eggshells. Up and down the city block, windows shattered, the glass jangling as it fell in sheets to the ground. Buildings rattled and clung to the shifting ground. Just as the final drumming noise began to fade, there came a different noise—

As though a mountain were caving in upon itself—and that wasn't far off the mark.

It was as though they were inside a cloud as the thunder roared—a pounding report that charged through the district and set everything vibrating.

And again!

"My God!" Dorian croaked.

Wyatt smiled. Over the sound he called, "It's nice to own a powder factory, isn't it?"

"Powder? What've you done!"

"Blew up a couple of the abandoned warehouses down on Canal Street." He struggled to his hands and knees, gasping, "—didn't think I was going to leave you here, did you? Oh, Jesus, that hurts—"

Huddling together, they weathered aftershock upon aftershock. Dorian offered Wyatt what little support he could, but his own balance was gone to hell, and he was disoriented. Was this the floor, or was he clinging to a wall?

Amazing that the impact could be felt from blocks away! Girders and piles of brick tumbling, crashing, dust rising, the thrums of the detonation still jarring the superstructure and everything around it, the groan of metal and the crackle of glass—it could have been next door.

"You're bringing down the whole neighborhood!" Dorian choked, fighting for balance.

"Told you it was good powder."

"Is there more in your vest pocket? Because there's the troublesome matter of that lock—"

They hauled each other to their feet, though between the two of them, they were still barely one set of working legs.

Leaning heavily on Dorian, Wyatt dug in his pocket and came up with a glint of rough metal.

Dorian gawked. "Where in Gehenna did you get that?"

"Stole it on the way in." Wyatt held the cell key up proudly. "Guess I'm not a shining knight after all."

"I guess you're not!"

They staggered to the door and looked through the bars in the plate-sized opening to the main area of the jailhouse.

Indeed, the deputy had rushed off to see what the explosion was, taking with him the entire bloodthirsty crowd who had been waiting for their chance at hanging Dorian. The jailhouse door hung wide open, wagging before a deserted street.

"Brilliant, Wyatt," Dorian said. He noted with relief that it was night. His perfect cloak. "Damned well done!"

Wyatt put his arm through the bars and crammed against the door up to his armpit, feeling on the outside for the lock.

"I've got your surrey and horse tied up two blocks in the other direction . . . had Joe bring your things down and put them in it—well, for—where's the—here, you try it."

"You can't reach? You've got two inches on me. All right, give way."

They fumbled to exchange places, wobbling on ground that still vibrated from the huge building's collapse down the street.

Dorian concentrated on finding the lock, willing his whipped arm to function a few more seconds. His hands trembled, and he damned them under his breath . . . the hole . . . the key—he twisted hard.

The lock defied his weak right arm before finally its firm iron mechanism turned over with a *clack*. He choked out a victory, drew his arm back in and pulled the door open, then reached for Wyatt. They dragged each other to the jail's outside door.

Sure enough, the mob was gone, having discovered a new hobby for the evening. Even more people dashed past the jail, drawn by the noise and commotion. Tragedy made a potent intrigue.

"Wait! Hold your ground!" Dorian choked out. He lashed an arm backward and struck Wyatt full in the chest, ramming him against the wall. "We can't be seen leaving this building! Or we'll be paddling the River Styx in quick order."

"Oh—good thinking."

They would have only a few seconds. Running people poured from every doorway and intersection in sight. The jail itself was a trap for them now—but here was a break—

"Now!"

Dorian slipped out the door and with a glance made sure Wyatt followed.

Down the boardwalk they ran, in the opposite direction from the explosion. Behind them the sky was marbled with dust and sunset. Noise of voices and breaking timbers, falling brick and settling rubble, rose in a broken symphony. As they turned a corner, the sound faded considerably until the scrape of their footsteps sounded like thunder.

Wyatt tried to run, but his body betrayed him. His legs quivered with the effort of each stride, and the boardwalk seemed to be bobbing and weaving under him. One by one he dragged his knees up again and again, pumping like a machine, but every stride pushed blood through his body only to have it pour out his wounded side. His chest hammered as though it wanted to break open, and finally his feet tangled up, he missed one stride, and that was all it took. Balance went to the wind. The boardwalk came up in front of his face as though somebody had folded it. He slammed into an awning support, stumbled, and went down on one knee. The impact rammed the breath out of his lungs.

Dorian spun around.

"Wyatt!" he called, not caring that he might be attracting unwanted attention. He doubled back in time to keep Wyatt from falling down completely.

"I'll make it," Wyatt insisted, gasping and leaning on

Dorian. Sweat sheeted his face. "Don't mind me. I'm getting used to it."

"Yes, yes." Dorian scowled and hoisted him to his feet. "Had I not minded you earlier in the year, neither of us would be in this situation. No—you can't manage alone."

"I'm fine, I'm fine. . . ."

"Fine for a man with a fever and a bullet in his gut. Stop trying to outrun yourself."

"This from a man who worries about the death of Sophocles."

Dorian grimaced. "That's Socrates, his outcast brother-in-law. Lean against me."

Struggling with Wyatt's collapsing bulk against him, he glanced back the way they had come. Fear choked him when he glimpsed three men headed toward the jailhouse. As much as possible, he tried to hurry their progress down the darkening street.

"I think we can find your mother," Wyatt said on one of his choppy breaths.

"Save your strength."

"I'll send letters. We'll establish a post-office box—"

"Curse you for tormenting me! Mind your own business."

Wyatt pulled up suddenly and stopped, taking the moment to brace up and rest. While catching his breath, he looked straight at Dorian the whole time.

Inevitably Dorian became self-conscious. "Wyatt, I want nothing to do with—"

"You haven't thought of this, have you? You've tried every complication and missed the easy way."

"I beg you, stop. I have thought."

He levered away, but Wyatt hooked a hand in Dorian's elbow and nearly toppled them both.

"Come back here and listen before I pass out. The town councils of Virginia can provide lists of their constituencies. Plantations, farms, refinery operations of the plantation yield, general known slave owners, and so on. I'll describe her, give her name, her age, and offer an outrageous price. Somebody will respond."

His voice lowered and softened, and the casualness went away as he gazed at Dorian in the dark city night.

"You've gone without help for so long, you've forgotten how to accept it."

Dorian stood before him, breathing from the effort, and tried to come up with a snappish retort. He couldn't. The commonsense plan picked at him. People had so long been his enemies, information his bane—

His jaw tightened. Just as hope had begun to slip away, a faint chance now trickled back. Unable to speak, he was forced to watch the idea spread before him, its veins stretching the length and breadth of Virginia and beyond if necessary, to bring his beloved Yula back to him. His family. . . all those he had been forced to leave behind.

As though reading his mind, Wyatt softly asked, "Is there anyone else?"

All Dorian's strength went to the effort of not bursting out in tears of disbelief and gratitude. He bit back the urge yet still took several long seconds to answer.

"She had another child," he murmured. "A boy. . . a black boy. My. . ."

His lips formed the *b*, but the word wouldn't come.

Wyatt smiled and nodded. "We'll find your brother too. Face it, Dorian. It's not so hideous a world."

He slid his arm around Dorian's shoulders.

"Come on," he said. "Let's go."

The buggies were waiting at a dim intersection at Canal Street and Eleventh when the two fugitives came into view of them. At first sight the negro Joe dropped from one buggy's seat and jogged toward them, babbling. His big teeth shone like pickets.

"Yo, Missa Wyatt! I was begun to think you got locked up yo'self. Missa Trozen, how do, sir? Wasn't that a perty explosion we made? Too bad we cain't put our sign up on it!"

"Yes, it was right prettious," Dorian said to him. "Thank you."

"Bring the buggies out of the alley, Joe," Wyatt said raggedly.

"Yessah," Joe said. "The doctor, he gonna have a fit

when he find out you got up and dun walked off with his bullet."

"It's my bullet," Wyatt insisted. "I've gotten attached to it. Get the buggies."

He and Dorian waited in silent companionship as Joe ran back, caught a bridle by the cheekpiece, and urged Dorian's horse and surrey toward them, then went back for the second, which he had parked a little farther down the street, so as not to be conspicuous.

Leaning on the surrey for welcome support, Wyatt watched Dorian's face in the pale evening light and wondered what it must be like to carry the blood of two worlds. The differences had always been so clear before . . . or at least obvious. There were plenty of mulattoes around, but they had coarse hair, or flat noses, or musky olive skin to give them away, to keep them in place and away from the dangerous temptation of trying to fit into the white world. Their luck was that they were decidedly negro, by law and social perception, and therefore knew their place.

Dorian had nothing but his black eyes and his wounded spirit, and his love for a lost negro woman and her black child, and no way to know where he belonged.

As though sensing Wyatt's thoughts, Dorian gripped the dashboard and wondered, "Where will I hide now?"

"I've got the perfect hiding place," Wyatt said. He reached into the surrey and fumbled around in the dark. He pulled out a large wad of fabric.

Mystified, Dorian watched as folds of dove gray wool took shape in Wyatt's hands. Three gold bars winked on a collar of royal blue.

Wyatt shook the fabric out. "Here. Try it on."

"Is this a joke?" Twisting as he was bidden, Dorian held his breath.

The sensation was not unlike a frock coat—but there was an unspoken substance in the thing that slid up onto his shoulders.

"There," Wyatt said. "Turn around. Let me see."

"Button him up proper, sir," Joe suggested, drawing the second buggy to a stop a few feet away.

Wyatt nodded and tugged the lapels. The double breast of

the tunic lined up its rows of brass buttons. One by one he closed the uniform over Dorian's ripped shirt.

"It's a shame, you know," Dorian muttered self-consciously. "Now I'll never know what it's like to be hanged."

Wyatt only smiled and said, "I'm opening an account in the bank in Charleston. Draw on it all you need. And please find something better than that flat in Shockoe. I'll tidy up the loose ends here. You'll just be gone, and people will have to accept it. There, now . . . that looks just fine! You'd be proud of yourself, if you could tell anybody who you are. You must admit, no one'll look for a runaway slave among the captains of the Confederate Army."

He lay his hand on Dorian's scarred right arm, where the new cadet gray wool hid a faultless sin, and the touch was meant to focus upon the faultlessness.

Warmly he said, "Take good care of yourself."

Dorian managed a short nod. "Joe," he called over Wyatt's shoulder, "see that Mr. Wyatt gets back to the doctor in good order. The onus is upon you, hear?"

"Oh, yes, Missa Trozen, he going home to that bed. I got a switch right here at my feet in case he get ideas 'bout breaking any more folks out of jail."

"Don't worry," Wyatt said, "I'm in good hands. Best you get going. Oh, be sure you send the information I need about your mother and her little boy."

Possible? Dorian couldn't imagine opening his mouth and simply asking—calling such attention to himself, to Yula. . .

Haltingly he muttered, "Words fail me."

"I knew I'd muzzle you sooner or later." Wyatt held out his hand. "Welcome to your hideaway, Captain."

Knotted by the emotion he had denied all along, Dorian felt his face tighten with effort. Everything he had ever depended upon as constants, as anchors, had abandoned him. God. Literature. Luke Wallace and the stability of Plentiful. All had abandoned him. Only Wyatt had not. Mere humanity had refused to give up on him. The idea of leaving at just this moment was nearly as much a shock as all the other revelations Wyatt had given him tonight. The miracle of not being alone.

He closed his hand on Wyatt's. "Dorian to you."

Wyatt smiled, then had to give him a push to get him into the surrey. "Go on."

The harness leather squeaked, as though to remind them both of other times. The horse twitched and answered the snap of the reins. Her hooves clattered across the pavement.

At the last minute Wyatt called, "Oh, wait! Is there a way I can get a message to you?"

On the gaslit street the surrey and its driver looked like a painting in tones of gunmetal and violet.

A hand surfaced and waved.

"Look in hell," Dorian called. "I'll be the one in charge!"

★

EPILOGUE

——— ★ ———

The wiry, whiskered man looked up from his desk when the door opened and straightened when his adjutant came in not alone, but with a woman on his arm. Firm, squarish features, angular eyes, green, pale skin but cheeks a bit ruddier, hair of cordovan ringlets, not very neat, boned for farm work. Pretending to walk fancy, but the short stride didn't fit her natural balance. She wasn't used to a lady's tiny slippered steps. Though she held the adjutant's arm, she did so with some discomfort.

By the time the woman was escorted to his desk, he knew some of what she was and most of what she was not.

He put down his quill, already interested.

"Ma'am, may I help you?"

"The lady is lost, sir," his adjutant said. "Being reluctant to leave her on the street, I invited her in while I request your permission to escort her safely back to her hotel."

The wiry man smirked and looked at the woman. "Is that true, ma'am?"

The young woman's eyes glinted. She gave the stunned adjutant a rather unsympathetic glance. "No," she said. "Your men are in need of training."

With a faint gasp the adjutant's mouth fell open.

The man behind the desk remained calm and asked, "Training, ma'am?"

She let go of the adjutant's arm, left the poor man holding that pose in the center of the office, and stepped toward the desk. "You are Allan Pinkerton, the detective, are you not?"

"Yes'm, I am."

"You don't look like a detective."

"Why, thank you, miss."

"You're welcome. Is it true that you're starting up a secret service for President Lincoln?"

"Not at all. There's nothing to that story whatsoever. Nothing but rumors in the press, that is."

"Good. Consider me a volunteer," she said. "My name is Grace MacHutcheon. I want to be a spy for the Union army."

★

The Echo of 1861

———— ★ ————

"Fellow-citizens of the United States . . . physically speaking, we cannot separate. We cannot remove our respective sections from each other, nor build an impassable wall between them. A husband and wife may be divorced, and go out of the presence and beyond the reach of each other; but the different parts of our country cannot do this. They cannot but remain face to face, and intercourse, either amicable or hostile, must continue between them. Is it possible, then, to make that intercourse more advantageous or more satisfactory *after* separation than *before*? Can aliens make treaties easier than friends can make laws? Can treaties be more faithfully enforced between aliens than laws can among friends? Suppose you go to war, you cannot fight always; and when, after much loss on both sides, and no gain on either, you cease fighting, the identical old questions as to terms of intercourse are again upon you.

"This country, with its institutions, belongs to the people who inhabit it. Whenever they shall grow weary of the existing Government, they can exercise their *constitutional* right of amending it, or their *revolutionary* right to dismember or overthrow it. I cannot be ignorant of the fact that many worthy and patriotic citizens are desirous of having the National Constitution amended. . . .

"My countrymen, one and all, think calmly and *well* upon this whole subject. Nothing valuable can be lost by taking time. If there be an object to *hurry* any of you in hot haste to a step which you would never take *deliberately,* that object will be frustrated by taking time, but no good object can be frustrated by it. . . .

"In *your* hands, my dissatisfied fellow-countrymen, and not in *mine,* is the momentous issue of civil war. The Government will not assail *you.* You can have no conflict without being yourselves the aggressors. *You* have no oath registered in Heaven to destroy the Government, while I shall have the most solemn one to 'preserve, protect, and defend it.'

I am loth to close. We are not enemies, but friends. We must not be enemies. Though passion may have strained, it must not break our bonds of affection. The mystic chords of memory, stretching from every battle-field and patriot grave to every living heart and hearthstone all over this broad land, will yet swell the chorus of the Union, when again touched, as surely they will be, by the better angels of our nature."

> —The First Inaugural Address of Presi-
> dent Abraham Lincoln, 1861. Be-
> tween his election and delivery of
> this address, seven states seceded
> and formed a provisional govern-
> ment—the Confederacy.

ABOUT THE AUTHOR

D. L. Carey's bestselling STAR TREK® novels and historical adventures, published under her full name, Diane Carey, have been enjoyed by nearly two million readers. Several of those books have been New York Times Bestsellers. She works with research collaborator and story editor Gregory Brodeur, who also happens to be her husband.

Together, this versatile team has written over a dozen books in any setting their imaginations send them—Medieval England, 1700's Scotland, 1910 Turkey, 1800's Nantucket, modern New York, the space-age future, and now, of course, the United States during its most compelling and pivotal period as a nation.

Carey and Brodeur's goal for the three-book DISTANT DRUMS series is to dramatically present aspects of the American Civil War which aren't commonly known or understood, such as the effect of immigration and foreign pressures on the War Between the States. Both the author and the story editor strongly believe the best fiction is the barest fiction—that history is already so dramatic it needs only to be showcased, not revised.

Their best collaborations are two children, Lydia Rose and Gordon Gregory. The family enjoys watching and participating in Renaissance, Colonial, and Civil War re-enactments whenever possible, to taste that spice of reality that adds such flavor to fiction.

★ ★ ★

Here's an exciting preview of
Book Two in the *DISTANT DRUMS* series

RISE DEFIANT

coming soon from Bantam Books.

Dorian, Grace and Wyatt return once more to lead you deeper into the whirlwind of events—both famous and infamous—surrounding our nation's bloodiest battle ever, the American Civil War.

"If General McClellan does not want to use the Army, I would like to borrow it for a time."
—President Abraham Lincoln
December, 1861

ONE OF THE RING OF CAMPS, ARMY OF THE POTOMAC, OUTSIDE WASHINGTON, D.C., DECEMBER 1861

"Present . . . *arms*! . . . Shoulder . . . *arms*! . . . Right shoulder . . . *shift*! . . . Forward . . . *march*!"

Three companies of the 19th Indiana, over four hundred men, marched in a startling blue, brass, and silver review past a single spectator.

The lone woman had to hike her mud-soaked skirt and step back as the flanking military band swung too closely by her. As she caught the eye of a tuba player and a rank of drummers, she got a clear feeling that the thirty-some musicians were playing just for her and were glad of her audience. Glad somebody was there to see the results of day after day of practice and drill, drill, drill.

Bayonets flickered in the Virginia sunlight, and the Regular Army blues made a sea of dark wool before her as the rifle company made a sharp spin-right turn. White gloves on officers' hands made a flash from time to time. In the background, whole companies sat vigorously polishing their Enfield muzzle-loaders. Beyond them were rows of big Sibley tents poking into the chilly morning air, with a constant smoke hovering around their conical tops. The camp possessed a gigantic singular stink—cooking smells, cigar smoke, sulfur.

The martial spectacle was stirring, but the woman pressed her lips tight beneath her bonnet's veil. Only the veil obscured the annoyance in her eyes, and it was poor concealment for such a scowl. She was tempted to hike the skirt again, wade through the mud, and go on into camp, but she knew she'd be stopped and checked for passes she didn't have. She also knew that if she just stood here long enough—

"Miss?"

A young first sergeant stepped to her. Ah, the dependability of chivalry.

"Oh . . . Colonel," she gasped.

She'd had her eyes on him for ten minutes now and had been sending little mental cries for help which eventually almost any man would answer, if a woman knew just how to cast them. Here he came.

"Ma'am, may I help you? Are you lost?"

"Oh, Colonel, I've had such a day," she said, breathing heavily and touching her hat and her shirt and anything else that made her appear frazzled. "My carriage broke a wheel a few miles down that road, and I had to tramp my way here in the mud. I'm so pleased to be in the company of our fine troops and know I'm safe."

The man's little moustache twitched. "Ma'am, your carriage tossed a wheel and you didn't use the horse?"

She paused, and gave him one of *those* looks. "Ride a horse without a proper sidesaddle? Ride bareback like a savage? Oh, Colonel—"

He shifted uneasily and hooked a thumb nervously in his belt. "It's Sergeant, ma'am . . . and, uh, I'm sorry for the presumption. If you would wait a few minutes, I'll finish my business in camp and see that you're provided means and escort back to the city."

"That's kind of you," she said, letting her voice twitter. "Where shall I wait?"

"Why . . . right here, Ma'am."

"Here? In the road? I see . . . thank you, Major, for your kindness."

She clasped her gloved hands, rested them on the dirt-flecked front of her bell-skirt, tilted her chin downward, and did her best to look small.

The sergeant started to step away toward camp, but now paused and watched her standing there. She looked like a daisy about to be trampled in the road, with her little hat, its veil, the little inadequate crocheted cape about her shoulders, the skirt too heavy for such an ordeal as she had described.

He tried to walk away. But he couldn't.

"Ma'am?"

"Colonel?"

"Perhaps you'd do me the honor or taking my arm as I conduct my business about camp?"

The woman gasped so convincingly that the sergeant puffed up right before her eyes. He felt especially gallant as she rushed to him and hooked his elbow with her hand. Only then did he notice she was almost as tall as he was, and he stood up real straight to hide that.

With a swirl of her muddy skirt, she all but pushed him onward into the camp, between the marching ranks.

Flanked on both sides by the Sibley tents, the company street unfolded before the unlikely couple. On one side, a groups of new inductees were being taught how to put up dog tents. They stumbled over themselves to give her a tip of their hats as she and the sergeant walked by.

The woman and her escort turned under an arch decorated with regimental banners and headed down another company street, when the woman suddenly stopped walking.

"This'll do fine, Sergeant," she said. Her voice suddenly dropped its quiver. She let go of his arm too.

He wheeled around. "Ma'am? You've got to proceed on with me."

"No, this tent is where I'm going?"

"Here?"

"Yes. Isn't this Major Allen's tent?"

The sergeant caught his breath and realized his daisy was poison ivy after all, and that he'd been taken.

He gawked and stammered, "But you—but I—"

"*Sergeant,*" a sharp voice interrupted.

They both turned to see a wiry, cold-eyed man in civilian clothes and a plug hat glaring at them from the tent's opening. He was holding about twenty pages of a hand-written report.

The sergeant snapped straight. "Major . . . sir, this woman—I thought—she claims—"

"Are you in the habit of escorting women about the

camps?'' the major barked in a sharp Lowland Scottish tang.

The sergeant's mouth dropped open, but nothing came out.

The woman shouldered her way past him. "Don't look so hang-dog, Sergeant,'' she said. "You're not a bad soldier. You're just too good a gentleman.''

"But—''

The wiry Scot held up a hand and admitted, "She works for me, Sergeant Roby.''

"Then why didn't she show her camp pass!''

The woman turned to him and said, "Wouldn't it be chicken-yard stupid for a Richmond spy to carry a Union pass, Sergeant?''

She stepped past them both and went into the tent.

The two men stood through a brief silence. Then the Scotsman said, "Wait right here, Sergeant.''

Grace MacHutcheon, spy for the Army of the Potomac, pulled her bonnet off as she stepped inside Major Allen's tent, and stopped short. She found herself staring at another officer, a young one, in a sashed and tasseled captain's uniform. He stood up when she came in, and his hand naturally poised on his long sabre.

"So, I've interrupted one of your tactical meetings, Major Allen?'' she commented, turning as the man in civilian clothing dipped back into the tent.

"In fact, you have,'' he said.

Discomfort needled at all three of them. Spies had a way of never being completely trusted by men who put on uniforms and boldly proclaimed who and what they were, and clearly the young captain over there didn't know what to make of Grace at all. But the Scotsman ran a deliberate middle ground by making a gesture between them.

"Miss MacHutcheon, may I present Captain Parry,'' he said, then looked pointedly at the captain and added, "The young lady is one of our Richmond informants.''

The two men exchanged a look Grace couldn't interpret. Either they were communicating that it was all right to talk in front of her or that it *wasn't*, and she couldn't tell which.

The young captain motioned for her to sit on one of the

velvet-covered stools near a small table. She plunked down, then both the captain and the major sat around the table.

Grace fixed her eyes on the major. "I saw some of the Iron Brigade drilling out there."

"Ah," he said. "How did they look to you?"

"Well, all the elbows were touching, if that means anything."

"Ah . . . it does. Good, very good."

Both men watched as she bowed her head and fussed with her skirt. Motes of dust floated in what little sunlight came through the top of the Sibley tent to flicker on her russet ringlets and play on the freckles of her ruddy cheeks. Despite her complexion, her hair color, and her surname, the major knew she wasn't Scottish, but German. Her name was pretend. There was no Grace MacHutcheon in Richmond, but only a woman who used that name to her own purposes.

He also knew her purposes didn't involve Union victory quite so much as they involved Southern defeat.

"You have something for us, Miss MacHutcheon?" he asked.

By way of an answer, she boldly pulled her skirt up, then the underskirt, then the hoop. Secured with two hatpins to the inside of the hoop was a large folded piece of paper. The major averted his eyes, but the young captain didn't have any problem appreciating Grace's stockings. She felt his eyes, but ignored him. A little fight got the pins loose and the paper free, then she pushed her skirts down again and straightened up.

"Here you are," she said, "a hand-drawn map of the lower Rappahannock."

"Oh!" the Scotsman leaned greedily forward, and his cold stare turned to a glitter of delight. He loved maps. He put his twenty-odd pages of report on the table and took the paper she handed him. "Anything's better than those store-bought rags we've had to use." He unfolded the map and eagerly examined the hand-made sketch.

"Glad you like it," she said.

While the major looked at the new map, the captain reached for a bottle and a set of tin cups. "May I offer you a champagne?"

Grace sat up straight and twisted toward him. She'd *known* there was something different about this one!

"You're European," she blurted. "Are you French?"

He smiled. "Yes," he said, "bit I have been living in England for some time, with members of my family."

His English was flawless, she noted, very elite and educated, but the Frenchness was still there but good. He had a somewhat high-pitched voice, but it might have been his youth. His brows were low and sharp over a pair of blue eyes, and he tried to circumvent his youth with a full brown moustache and beard.

"Are you here as a foreign observer, sir?" she prodded. "But you're wearing the uniform of a Union soldier."

He smiled with a little coyness. "I *am* observing, and making a diary, yes. But I am also here to participate in the *cause celebre* . . . the preservation of the United States of America."

"From what I hear lately, your France and England don't know if they share that sentiment yet," she said. "There's talk of them coming in for the South. Trouble over some diplomats on a boat or something."

The young captain's brows raised, but with a purse of his lips he showed her he wasn't going to offer an opinion.

Grace's expression clearly showed, as she intended it to, that she knew he was only telling her part of some story.

Both men saw that, and the Scottish major spoke up. "It's Captain Parry's job as an volunteer aide-de-camp to outline and abridge reports from this office to General McClellan."

"Mmm," Grace muttered, dissatisfied. "In any case, you needn't offer me champagne. I'd rather you offer me an explanation."

The major's flinty eyes came up from the map again. "Sorry?"

She faced him. "Thanksgiving is passed."

Suddenly he understood.

"Oh . . . yes."

"Well? What happened?" she asked. "Why didn't the Army move?"

He cleared his throat. "Armies don't move at the whim of civilians."

"Civilians my eye. I risked my life to bring you information that would get this Army on the road. What happened to

General McClellan's plan to thrust through the Confederate outposts at Manassas Junction and Centreville by Thanksgiving? Did his aide-de-damp here fail to turn the general's calendar, Mr. Pinkerton?''

A gristly pause fell. To her left, Captain Parry's bemusement dropped like a rock.

Behind the table, the Scots major's eyes went hard again. "Miss MacHutcheon, I use your *nom de guerre,* and I prefer you use mine. Major E. J. Allen.''

"That'd be fine, Mr. Pinkerton, if we had a *guerre* to use our fake *noms* in. It's been more than a month since I brought you information about the Confederates dug in at Centreville. What's the stall? Wasn't General McClellan going to make a thrust?''

Allan Pinkerton put the map down on the table beside his report. He knew she and other spies in Richmond wanted the same answer. He could see that in her expression, and weighed the prospects of not giving her one against his need for effective informants.

Captain Parry spoke up again in that precise English of his. "General McClellan is a very hard worker, Miss MacHutcheon,'' he said. "You are wrong to think he shirks any duty. I must follow him on horseback sometimes twelve hours a day, amassing men and materiel, and his men drill eight or ten hours and study weaponry and tactics—''

"And march round and round to nowhere day after day.'' She shook her head at him. "You're talking about duties of routine and ordnance, not command. The commanding general of the entire Union Army is troubling himself with administrative claptrap, while enemy outposts sit practically over that hill, Captain Parry. Johnston's Confederates are hardly fifteen miles from here. Why doesn't General McClellan do what everyone wants and get this war on with?''

"You don't understand,'' Pinkerton placated, "the general's considering a . . . different plan of action than when you and I last communicated.''

"Different?'' she asked.

The two men looked at each other in one of those deciding-whether-to-tell ways again.

Then Parry made a decision, or part of one. "Even as we

speak, his topographical engineers are analyzing the coastline east of Richmond—''

"The *coastline?*" Grace interrupted. "What's the coastline got to do with anything? What happened to President Lincoln's idea to snap the confederate deadlock by going up the Occoquan and cutting Johnston's supply line?"

Pinkerton interrupted, "How did you find out about that?"

"You told me!"

He frowned. He didn't like being caught in front of Parry at having violated his legendary prudence by telling a plan to one of his shirt-tail informants.

But Parry was affected only by Grace's disapproval of the plan, and said, "The Occoquan plan would put us up against superior forces."

"Hogwash," she said back. "I think McClellan's afraid of a fight."

Both men shifted uncomfortably, but for two different reasons.

"Please," Pinkerton said, "keep your voices down. General McClellan wants to go in only when he can win." He lowered his own voice, and a note of sadness came into it. "We want no more ugly shocks like Shiloh and Ball's Bluff."

Grace rolled her eyes and barked, "He's just scared to be blamed for any losses. He's all dash and glamour, is what he is. And *you*—" She aimed a finger at him. "You can't judge the difference between good information and plain dumb gossip."

Beneath Pinkerton's expression was a certain message that he was tolerating her, and her insults, that he knew something she didn't know. More than anything Grace hated that undercurrent as she waited for a response.

Slowly, he said, "Both the general and I have the whole future to consider, not just a month, come and go. Someday, I hope to make the words 'secret service' more than just any covert activity. I hope to build a national network."

"Assuming there *is* a nation," she snapped.

"There will be," Captain Parry said.

Grace turned to him again. "Well?" She glared at him a moment, her cold green eyes giving him no quarter. Then she looked back at Pinkerton and hammered, "Well? Are you going to let him tell me?"

If she gave Parry time, his enthusiasm would get the better of him. He was sitting on the edge of his velvet stool, itching to defend General McClellan. All she had to do was push.

She didn't want to appear pushy. She clamped her lips shut and determined to keep quiet until Parry couldn't stand it.

Parry looked at Pinkerton, his eyes wide and his youth playing against him, and after several seconds he got the nod he wanted from the other man. He leaned forward on his stool and proudly told Grace, "The general plans to bypass the Confederate groundholds at Manassas and Centreville by boating the Army into Chesapeake Bay, then up the Rappahannock River to Urbanna, Virginia."

Grace felt her eyes bug out, but she bit her lip and kept quiet. She stared at Parry, then looked at the man behind the table.

Pinkerton wasn't looking at her, but was gazing pensively at Parry.

Now he looked at Grace, and seemed to be waiting.

Grace cleared her throat to see how loud her voice would come out. "Does the President know about this new plan?"

"Oh, well," Pinkerton said, "the President's not a warrior. He's incapable of comprehending these massive and critical operations."

"He's the President!" she shot back.

"Good God, Mr. Pinkerton, at least have the stone to admit the General McClellan won't tell about the Urbanna plan because he knows Lincoln won't like it. I've half a mind to tell him about this myself. Damned if I don't."

Horror struck Parry's face, but Pinkerton remained calm.

"You understand," Pinkerton said carefully to Grace, "it's critical the Urbanna plan not leak out. General Johnston must not catch a whiff of what we're intending."

"Information leaks to me, not out of me," she said contemptuously. "Hell, this camp'll leak itself clean from bored desertion before Little Mac advances this Army. Your general is nothing but cold sunlight."

Her words threw a pall over them.

A touch of color came again to Pinkerton's stubbly cheeks. He bounced a glance off Parry, then shifted in his chair.

Captain Parry was practically shaking on his stool "Mademoiselle—you—you—"

"Well?" Grace pounded.

"General McClellan is a model soldier! He is the tool of God!"

"According to him or God?"

"There is divine reason in his appointment," Parry insisted. "He feels God has chosen him to save the nation. Not even the President must circumvent God."

"How convenient for God's tool," Grace countered.

Pinkerton remained typically tight-lipped as Grace and Parry smoldered before him. As Grace looked at him it was impossible to tell whether Pinkerton doubted God or doubted McClellan. But he was obviously embarrassed that Parry had spouted McClellan's claim about the divine.

With two quick gestures Grace yanked off her gloves and threw them onto the table. She stood up and paced back and forth in front of Captain Parry, whose acrimony followed her with uncloaked suspicion. He big skirt made swirl marks across the dirt in the whole front half of the tent. Suddenly she faced him.

"Why don't you be honest with yourself, Captain Parry?" she demanded bluntly. "You know it'll take weeks to assemble enough steamers to float a hundred thousand men and gear up the Rappahannock, and so does General Messiah. He wants what he always wants. Time! More time. He wants more time for more drilling and polishing. Meanwhile, the Confederates are sitting practically right *there*!"

She pointed at the hills west of the camp.

"Mademoiselle!" Captain Parry gasped. "The Urbanna plan is intelligent. It takes fifty miles off the march to Richmond and avoids battle. Our troops will take Richmond fresh, not battle-weary. The Rebels will be shocked. Confused. And Richmond—will belong to George McClellan!" He nodded a little punctuation. "Patience is his greatest virtue."

"Patience isn't what a general is hired for," she told him. "Cowardice is another word for all this."

Steel and brass clinked as Parry stood up sharply and glared. His face took on a terrible flush. With a fist clenching his sabre's hilt, he spat, "Excuse me!" He dropped a stiff bow at Pinkerton and repeated, "Excuse me, major."

And he walked out, stirring the motes of dust.

Grace didn't even bat an eye. She turned back to Pinkerton.

He was studying her with a buried wisdom, and finally sighed. "Miss MacHutcheon, now that we're alone, why don't you tell me what you're really thinking?"

Almost disbelieving that he'd asked, she skewered him with a look.

"Very well," she said. "I think you're half wrong."

"You mean, you think I'm wrong half the time?"

"No! I think you're off Johnston's Confederate numbers by half!"

Pinkerton rocked back in his chair and laughed. "Miss MacHutcheon."

"Confederate forces at Centreville and Manassas are seventy thousand all together, if not less."

"Miss MacHutcheon, please!" he chortled. "Interrogations of deserters and two runaway slaves indicate there are not less than one hundred fifty thousand Rebels waiting in those hills."

"Are there? I didn't want to embarrass you in front of the captain," she said, "but in October I gave you an estimate of Confederate numbers. You thanked me and said you would reduce the figures I gave you by fifteen percent to account for any troops too sickly to fight." When he started to blush before her, she knew she was onto something, and leaned forward. "What you did was reduce the number by *one fifteenth*. There's a little difference between those figures."

A crease appeared across his brow. "It was a mathematical error. Both the general and I strive for caution."

"Caution!" she shouted. Suddenly she vaulted to her feet, snatched up his twenty-page report, and violently flung the papers at him. They struck him full in the face with a terrible crackle, and spun like snowflakes. "The future chokes on caution!"

At the tent entrance, Sergeant Roby plunged inside, his hands on his sidearm's holster.

Pinkerton jumped to his feet. "No! No, Sergeant, it's all right! . . . it's all right."

Roby hesitated, his gaze flicking back and forth between

Pinkerton and Grace. The pistol stayed in the holster, but the hand also stayed on the gun.

Grace didn't care. Pinkerton was the one who cared whether they were overheard, not her. She never even glanced at the Sergeant, though she heard him shuffle behind her and felt the tension of his hand on that gun.

"The defeat at Ball's Bluff took the air out of the public's confidence in a Federal victory, and we've got to have one!" she said. "A hundred eighty thousand soldiers are parading around Washington like turkeys with bow ties on! McClellan's nothing but a drillmaster! I don't know when I've seen a man so constructed for greatness yet so inclined to let greatness sit and sour!"

Her invective made both men stiffen, but anything they might've done or said withered when Sergeant Roby touched his revolver again and hit Pinkerton with a questioning look from over the young woman's shoulder. Pinkerton moved his head back and forth a fraction.

Roby relaxed just that much, but stayed ready to arrest this rude intruder.

Pinkerton stared, but said nothing. Grace felt the stunned presence of Sergeant Roby and his revolver behind her.

After a moment, she let the edge fall off her tone.

"The foreign observers might be impressed with all this reviewing and pomp and shouldering arms, but the enemy won't be. I think they're laughing at you, Mr. Pinkerton. I think they're laughing."

Silence fell.

It was an ugly suggestion. Pinkerton caught the sudden pinch in Sergeant Roby's face, and this time the sentiment had nothing to do with danger, but with the lack of it. Roby was embarrassed. He had both arms folded behind his back and now dropped his eyes toward the ground.

Pinkerton felt like he'd been kicked. He took Roby's humiliation personally. No man with the Army of the Potomac should look the way Roby looked.

The three of them wallowed in awful silence for many long seconds. None said anything, none looked at the other. Outside, the music of two military bands mixed together, and was muddled with the noise of drilling, the stomp of a thousand feet, the useless swoosh of a thousand rifles, the rasping calls of drill sergeants ordering the men to nowhere.

Pinkerton had to work to square his shoulders and beat down any sign that her words disturbed him. Even so, self-consciousness came out in his tone. He held out a pacifying hand.

"Please ... sit down again," he said. "I'm reluctant to have you leave feeling this way."

Grace pursed her lips. "Then give me reason to leave in a better temper."

It was a dare. A plea and a dare, they both knew that. The public needed to feel there was movement, the President needed movement. The soldiers were a little too happy and living a little too fine a life here in these camps. Grace and others like her, detectives and spies alike, needed to know their information was being used.

As a detective himself, Pinkerton couldn't help but empathize. Eventually, he cleared his throat.

"Well," he began, "have you any suggestion, as long as you're here? Would you feel better if I listened?"

Grace's eyes narrowed. He was making a gesture that would appease her, she knew. He was good, he was very good. Get her out of here and guarantee her faith and silence again. But he *had* asked. She might as well say. She moistened her lips.

"The South," she began, "will be destroyed one man at a time. I know where to start. There's a particular Confederate officer I want to destroy."

Pinkerton's brows went up, but he made no sound. It was a silent *why?*

"Revenge," she supplied.

"Ah ... his rank?"

"He's a major."

He nodded appreciatively. "That's adequate."

"Then if I can get Confederate numbers out of him, you'll consider it good information? And you'll move the general?"

Tempted to tell her anything that would keep her wrath down, Pinkerton hesitated. He deliberately wouldn't ask her about her hatred for this unidentified major. He saw in her face that she had been witness to the dark recess of the man's soul, that some part of her was bitter, and he suspected she intended to take revenge on the whole South.

Grace took his silence for some kind of answer, and started pulling her gloves back on. "You like cigars, don't you, Mr. Pinkerton?"

"Oh, yes . . . why?"

"I'll send you some." Her eyebrows popped up to punctuate her meaning. "You understand? A sign. Confirmation. One cigar for a piece of good interest, two cigars for something very important, and three cigars for crucial information. Then you'll know it's from me."

"Ah," he said, "I see what you mean now."

His own professionalism gnawed at him, and he just couldn't let her get out without asking one more question. In a much depressed tone, he asked, "How is this major's information any more accurate than that of my more trusted sources?"

"Because I *am* one of your trusted sources," she said. Then she sighed and gave him a real answer. "This major runs a powder mill in Richmond for the Confederacy. Gun powder, cannon shot, so on. I'll get him to tell me how much powder he's sending to Manassas Junction and Centreville. And anywhere else you want. They won't send more than they need, will they?"

"Well . . ."

"If we know how much powder, we'll know how many men. Yes?"

"Well, yes . . . theoretically. But he's an officer and . . . all due credit to you, Miss MacHutcheon, and deference to Sergeant Roby here . . . you're not Rose Greenhow or Belle Boyd. How will you get information out of this major and destroy him at the same time without his . . . suspecting?"

Grace stood up and plopped her bonnet back on her head, casting a shadow over her eyes.

"Simple," she said. "I'll marry him."

★ WAGONS WEST ★

This continuing, magnificent saga recounts the adventures of a brave band of settlers, all of different backgrounds, all sharing one dream—to find a new and better life.

☐	26822-8	INDEPENDENCE! #1	$4.95
☐	26162-2	NEBRASKA! #2	$4.50
☐	26242-4	WYOMING! #3	$4.50
☐	26072-3	OREGON! #4	$4.50
☐	26070-7	TEXAS! #5	$4.99
☐	26377-3	CALIFORNIA! #6	$4.99
☐	26546-6	COLORADO! #7	$4.95
☐	26069-3	NEVADA! #8	$4.99
☐	26163-0	WASHINGTON! #9	$4.50
☐	26073-1	MONTANA! #10	$4.50
☐	26184-3	DAKOTA! #11	$4.50
☐	26521-0	UTAH! #12	$4.50
☐	26071-5	IDAHO! #13	$4.50
☐	26367-6	MISSOURI! #14	$4.50
☐	27141-5	MISSISSIPPI! #15	$4.95
☐	25247-X	LOUISIANA! #16	$4.50
☐	25622-X	TENNESSEE! #17	$4.50
☐	26022-7	ILLINOIS! #18	$4.95
☐	26533-4	WISCONSIN! #19	$4.95
☐	26849-X	KENTUCKY! #20	$4.95
☐	27065-6	ARIZONA! #21	$4.50
☐	27458-9	NEW MEXICO! #22	$4.95
☐	27703-0	OKLAHOMA! #23	$4.95
☐	28180-1	CELEBRATION! #24	$4.50

Bantam Books, Dept. LE, 414 East Golf Road, Des Plaines, IL 60016

Please send me the items I have checked above. I am enclosing $_____
(please add $2.50 to cover postage and handling). Send check or money order, no cash or C.O.D.s please.

Mr/Ms _____

Address _____

City/State _____ Zip _____

Please allow four to six weeks for delivery.
Prices and availability subject to change without notice.   LE-6/91